Willa Cather

COLLECTED STORIES

Willa Cather was born near Winchester, Virginia, in 1873. When she was ten years old, her family moved to the prairies of Nebraska, later the setting for a number of her novels. At the age of twenty-one, she graduated from the University of Nebraska and spent the next few years doing newspaper work and teaching high school in Pittsburgh. In 1903 her first book, *April Twilights,* a collection of poems, was published, and two years later *The Troll Garden,* a collection of stories, appeared in print. After the publication of her first novel, *Alexander's Bridge,* in 1912, Cather devoted herself fulltime to writing, and, over the years, completed eleven more novels (including *O Pioneers!, My Ántonia, The Professor's House,* and *Death Comes for the Archbishop*), four collections of short stories, and two volumes of essays. Cather won the Pulitzer Prize for *One of Ours* in 1923. She died in 1947.

COLLECTED STORIES

ALSO BY WILLA CATHER

WILLA CATHER

Collected Stories

Vintage Classics

VINTAGE BOOKS
A DIVISION OF RANDOM HOUSE, INC., NEW YORK

A Vintage Classics Original, December 1992

Library of Congress Cataloging-in-Publication Data
Cather, Willa, 1873–1947.
[Short stories]
Collected stories / Willa Cather.
p.   cm.—(Vintage classics)
ISBN 0-679-73648-4 (pbk.)
I. Title.   II. Series.
PS3505.A87A6   1992
813'.52—dc20   92-50061
CIP

The stories in this work were originally published in the following collections:
*The Troll Garden, Youth and the Bright Medusa, Obscure Destinies,
The Old Beauty and Others,* and *Five Stories.*
"Tom Outland's Story" was previously published as
Book Two of *The Professor's House.*

Manufactured in the United States of America

3579B864

CONTENTS

This collection brings together all of Willa Cather's short fiction published in book form in her lifetime, along with two volumes of stories that were compiled after her death and published with the approval of the literary executor of her estate.

The Troll Garden (1905) was Willa Cather's first book of prose and consisted of seven short stories. Four of these stories—"The Sculptor's Funeral," "A Death in the Desert," "A Wagner Matinée," and "Paul's Case"—were later revised and rearranged (the revised versions appear in this volume) and were included in *Youth and the Bright Medusa* (1920) with four others that Cather had written between 1916 and 1920. The three stories of her next collection, *Obscure Destinies* (1932), were written between 1924 and the time of the book's publication.

Willa Cather completed three additional stories, which were published for the first time in *The Old Beauty and Others* (1948) in the year following her death. A final collection, *Five Stories,* published by Vintage Books in 1956, brought together short fiction spanning Cather's career. It consisted of three previously published stories ("Neighbour Rosicky," "The Best Years," and the revised "Paul's Case"); "The Enchanted Bluff," an early work, previously uncollected; "Tom Outland's Story," which forms Book II of *The Professor's House;* and George N. Kate's article on Willa Cather's unfinished Avignon story.

The Troll Garden

A Fairy Palace, with a fairy garden; . . . . .
inside the trolls dwell, ... working at
their magic forges, making and making always
things rare and strange.

—Charles Kingsley

"We must not look at Goblin men,
We must not buy their fruits;
Who knows upon what soil they fed
Their hungry thirsty roots?"
—GOBLIN MARKET

Flavia and Her Artists

As the train neared Tarrytown, Imogen Willard began to wonder why she had consented to be one of Flavia's house party at all. She had not felt enthusiastic about it since leaving the city, and was experiencing a prolonged ebb of purpose, a current of chilling indecision, under which she vainly sought for the motive which had induced her to accept Flavia's invitation.

Perhaps it was a vague curiosity to see Flavia's husband, who had been the magician of her childhood and the hero of innumerable Arabian fairy tales. Perhaps it was a desire to see M. Roux, whom Flavia had announced as the especial attraction of the occasion. Perhaps it was a wish to study that remarkable woman in her own setting.

Imogen admitted a mild curiosity concerning Flavia. She was in the habit of taking people rather seriously, but somehow found it impossible to take Flavia so, because of the very vehemence and insistence with which Flavia demanded it. Submerged in her studies, Imogen had, of late years, seen very little of Flavia; but Flavia, in her hurried visits to New York, between her excursions from studio to studio—her luncheons with this lady who had to play at a matinée, and her dinners with that singer who had an evening concert—had seen enough of her friend's handsome daughter to conceive for her an inclination of such violence and assurance as only Flavia could afford. The fact that Imogen had shown rather marked capacity in certain esoteric lines of scholarship, and had decided to specialize in a well-sounding branch of philology at the Ecole des Chartes, had fairly placed her in that category of "interesting people" whom Flavia considered her natural affinities, and lawful prey.

When Imogen stepped upon the station platform she was immediately appropriated by her hostess, whose commanding figure and assurance of attire she had recognized from a distance. She was hurried into a high tilbury and Flavia, taking the driver's cushion beside her, gathered up the reins with an experienced hand.

"My dear girl," she remarked, as she turned the horses up the street, "I was afraid the train might be late. M. Roux insisted upon coming up by boat and did not arrive until after seven."

"To think of M. Roux's being in this part of the world at all, and subject to the vicissitudes of river boats! Why in the world did he come over?" queried Imogen with lively interest. "He is the sort of man who must dissolve and become a shadow outside of Paris."

"Oh, we have a houseful of the most interesting people," said Flavia, professionally. "We have actually managed to get Ivan Schemetzkin. He was ill in California at the close of his concert tour, you know, and he is recuperating with us, after his wearing journey from the coast. Then there is Jules Martel, the painter; Signor Donati, the tenor; Professor Schotte, who has dug up Assyria, you know; Restzhoff, the Russian chemist; Alcée Buisson, the philologist; Frank Wellington, the novelist; and Will Maidenwood, the editor of *Woman*. Then there is my second cousin, Jemima Broadwood, who made such a hit in Pinero's comedy last winter, and Frau Lichtenfeld. *Have* you read her?"

Imogen confessed her utter ignorance of Frau Lichtenfeld, and Flavia went on.

"Well, she is a most remarkable person; one of those advanced German women, a militant iconoclast, and this drive will not be long enough to permit of my telling you her history. Such a story! Her novels were the talk of all Germany when I was there last, and several of them have been suppressed—an honour in Germany, I understand. 'At Whose Door' has been translated. I am so unfortunate as not to read German."

"I'm all excitement at the prospect of meeting Miss Broadwood," said Imogen. "I've seen her in nearly everything she does. Her stage personality is delightful. She always reminds me of a nice, clean, pink-and-white boy who has just had his cold bath, and come down all aglow for a run before breakfast."

"Yes, but isn't it unfortunate that she will limit herself to those minor comedy parts that are so little appreciated in this country? One ought to be satisfied with nothing less than the best, ought one?" The peculiar, breathy tone in which Flavia always uttered that word "best," the most worn in her vocabulary, always jarred on Imogen and always made her obdurate.

"I don't at all agree with you," she said reservedly. "I thought every one admitted that the most remarkable thing about Miss Broadwood is her admirable sense of fitness, which is rare enough in her profession."

Flavia could not endure being contradicted; she always seemed to regard it in the light of a defeat, and usually coloured unbecomingly. Now she changed the subject.

"Look, my dear," she cried, "there is Frau Lichtenfeld now, coming to meet us. Doesn't she look as if she had just escaped out of Walhalla? She is actually over six feet."

Imogen saw a woman of immense stature, in a very short skirt and a broad, flapping sun hat, striding down the hillside at a long, swinging gait. The refugee from Walhalla approached, panting. Her heavy, Teutonic features were scarlet from the rigour of her exercise, and her hair, under her flapping sun hat, was tightly befrizzled about her brow. She fixed her sharp little eyes upon Imogen and extended both her hands.

"So this is the little friend?" she cried, in a rolling baritone.

Imogen was quite as tall as her hostess; but everything, she reflected, is comparative. After the introduction Flavia apologized.

"I wish I could ask you to drive up with us, Frau Lichtenfeld."

"Ah, no!" cried the giantess, drooping her head in humorous caricature of a time-honoured pose of the heroines of sentimental romances. "It has never been my fate to be fitted into corners. I have never known the sweet privileges of the tiny."

Laughing, Flavia started the ponies, and the colossal woman, standing in the middle of the dusty road, took off her wide hat and waved them a farewell which, in scope of gesture, recalled the salute of a plumed cavalier.

When they arrived at the house, Imogen looked about her with keen curiosity, for this was veritably the work of Flavia's hands, the materialization of hopes long deferred. They passed directly into a large, square hall with a gallery on three sides, studio fashion. This opened at one end into a Dutch breakfast-room, beyond which was the large dining-room. At the other end of the hall was the music-room. There was a smoking-room, which one entered through the library behind the staircase. On the second floor there was the same general arrangement; a square hall, and, opening from it, the guest chambers, or, as Miss Broadwood termed them, the "cages."

When Imogen went to her room, the guests had begun to return from their various afternoon excursions. Boys were gliding through the halls with ice-water, covered trays, and flowers, colliding with maids and valets who carried shoes and other articles of wearing apparel. Yet, all this was done in response to inaudible bells, on felt soles, and in hushed voices, so that there was very little confusion about it.

Flavia had at last builded her house and hewn out her seven pillars; there could be no doubt, now, that the asylum for talent, the sanatorium of the arts, so long projected, was an accomplished fact. Her ambition had long ago outgrown the dimensions of her house on Prairie Avenue; besides, she had bitterly complained that in Chicago traditions were against her. Her project had been delayed by Arthur's doggedly standing out for the Michigan woods, but Flavia knew well enough that certain of the *aves rares*—"the best"—could not be lured so far away from the seaport, so she declared herself for the historic Hudson and knew no retreat. The establishing of a New York office had at length overthrown Arthur's last valid objection to quitting the lake country for three months of the year; and Arthur could be wearied into anything, as those who knew him knew.

Flavia's house was the mirror of her exultation; it was a temple to the gods of Victory, a sort of triumphal arch. In her earlier days she had swallowed experiences that would have unmanned one of less torrential enthusiasm or blind pertinacity. But, of late years, her determination had told; she saw less and less of those mysterious persons with mysterious obstacles in their path and mysterious grievances against the world, who had once frequented her house on Prairie Avenue. In the stead of this multitude of the unarrived, she had now the few, the select, "the best." Of all that band of indigent retainers who had once fed at her board like the suitors in the halls of Penelope, only Alcée Buisson still retained his right of entrée. He alone had remembered that ambition hath a knapsack at his back, wherein he puts alms to oblivion, and he alone had been considerate enough to do what Flavia had expected of him, and give his name a current value in the world. Then, as Miss Broadwood put it, "he was her first real one,"—and Flavia, like Mahomet, could remember her first believer.

The "House of Song," as Miss Broadwood had called it, was the outcome of Flavia's more exalted strategies. A woman who made less a point of sympathizing with their delicate organisms, might have sought to plunge these phosphorescent pieces into the tepid bath of domestic life; but Flavia's discernment was deeper. This must be a refuge where the shrinking soul, the sensitive brain, should be unconstrained; where the caprice of fancy should outweigh the civil code, if necessary. She considered that this much Arthur owed her; for she, in her turn, had made concessions. Flavia, had, indeed, quite an equipment of epigrams to the effect that our century creates the iron genii which evolve its fairy tales: but the fact that her husband's name was annually painted upon some ten thousand threshing machines, in reality contributed very little to her happiness.

Arthur Hamilton was born, and had spent his boyhood in the West Indies, and physically he had never lost the brand of the tropics. His father, after inventing the machine which bore his name, had returned to the States to patent and manufacture it. After leaving college, Arthur had spent five years ranching in the West and travelling abroad. Upon his father's death he had returned to Chicago and, to the astonishment of all his friends, had taken up the business,—without any demonstration of enthusiasm, but with quiet perseverance, marked ability, and amazing industry. Why or how a self-sufficient, rather ascetic man of thirty, indifferent in manner, wholly negative in all other personal relations, should have doggedly wooed and finally married Flavia Malcolm, was a problem that had vexed older heads than Imogen's.

While Imogen was dressing she heard a knock at her door, and a young woman entered whom she at once recognized as Jemima Broadwood—"Jimmy" Broadwood, she was called by people in her own profession. While there was something unmistakably professional in her frank *savoir-faire,* "Jimmy's" was one of those faces to which the rouge never seems to stick. Her eyes were keen and grey as a windy April sky, and so far from having been seared by calcium lights, you might have fancied they had never looked on anything less bucolic than growing fields and country fairs. She wore her thick, brown hair short and parted at the side; and, rather than hinting at freakishness, this seemed admirably in keeping with her fresh, boyish countenance. She extended to Imogen a large, well-shaped hand which it was a pleasure to clasp.

"Ah! you are Miss Willard, and I see I need not introduce myself. Flavia said you were kind enough to express a wish to meet me, and I preferred to meet you alone. Do you mind if I smoke?"

"Why, certainly not," said Imogen, somewhat disconcerted and looking hurriedly about for matches.

"There, be calm, I'm always prepared," said Miss Broadwood, checking Imogen's flurry with a soothing gesture, and producing an oddly-fashioned silver match-case from some mysterious recess in her dinner-gown. She sat down in a deep chair, crossed her patent-leather Oxfords, and lit her cigarette. "This match-box," she went on meditatively, "once belonged to a Prussian officer. He shot himself in his bath-tub, and I bought it at the sale of his effects."

Imogen had not yet found any suitable reply to make to this rather irrelevant confidence, when Miss Broadwood turned to her cordially: "I'm awfully glad you've come, Miss Willard, though I've not quite decided why you did it. I wanted very much to meet you. Flavia gave me your thesis to read."

"Why, how funny!" ejaculated Imogen.

"On the contrary," remarked Miss Broadwood. "I thought it decidedly lacked humour."

"I meant," stammered Imogen, beginning to feel very much like Alice in Wonderland, "I meant that I thought it rather strange Mrs. Hamilton should fancy you would be interested."

Miss Broadwood laughed heartily. "Now, don't let my rudeness frighten you. Really, I found it very interesting, and no end impressive. You see, most people in my profession are good for absolutely nothing else, and, therefore, they have a deep and abiding conviction that in some other line they might have shone. Strange to say, scholarship is the object of our envious and particular admiration. Anything in type impresses us greatly; that's why so many of us marry authors or newspaper men and lead miserable lives." Miss Broadwood saw that she had rather disconcerted Imogen, and blithely tacked in another direction. "You see," she went on, tossing aside her half-consumed cigarette, "some years ago Flavia would not have deemed me worthy to open the pages of your thesis—nor to be one of her house party of the chosen, for that matter. I've Pinero to thank for both pleasures. It all depends on the class of business I'm playing whether I'm in favour or not. Flavia is my second cousin, you know, so I can say whatever disagreeable things I choose with perfect good grace. I'm quite desperate for some one to laugh with, so I'm going to fasten myself upon you—for, of course, one can't expect any of these gypsy-dago people to see anything funny. I don't intend you shall lose the humour of the situation. What do you think of Flavia's infirmary for the arts, anyway?"

"Well, it's rather too soon for me to have any opinion at all," said Imogen, as she again turned to her dressing. "So far, you are the only one of the artists I've met."

"One of them?" echoed Miss Broadwood. "One of the *artists*? My offence may be rank, my dear, but I really don't deserve that. Come, now, whatever badges of my tribe I may bear upon me, just let me divest you of any notion that I take myself seriously."

Imogen turned from the mirror in blank astonishment, and sat down on the arm of a chair, facing her visitor. "I can't fathom you at all, Miss Broadwood," she said frankly. "Why shouldn't you take yourself seriously? What's the use of beating about the bush? Surely you know that you are one of the few players on this side of the water who have at all the spirit of natural or ingenuous comedy?"

"Thank you, my dear. Now we are quite even about the thesis, aren't we? Oh! did you mean it? Well, you *are* a clever girl. But you see it doesn't do to permit oneself to look at it in that light. If we do, we always go to pieces, and waste our substance a-starring as the unhappy daughter of the Capulets. But there, I hear Flavia coming to take you down; and just remember I'm not one of them; the artists, I mean."

Flavia conducted Imogen and Miss Broadwood downstairs. As they reached the lower hall they heard voices from the music-room, and dim figures were lurking in the shadows under the gallery, but their hostess led straight to the smoking-room. The June evening was chilly, and a fire had been lighted in the fireplace. Through the deepening dusk the firelight flickered upon the pipes and curious weapons on the wall, and threw an orange glow over the Turkish hangings. One side of the smoking-room was entirely of glass, separating it from the conservatory, which was flooded with white light from the electric bulbs. There was about the darkened room some suggestion of certain chambers in the Arabian Nights, opening on a court of palms. Perhaps it was partially this memory-evoking suggestion that caused Imogen to start so violently when she saw dimly, in a blur of shadow, the figure of a man, who sat smoking in a low, deep chair before the fire. He was long, and thin, and brown. His long, nerveless hands drooped from the arms of his chair. A brown moustache shaded his mouth, and his eyes were sleepy and apathetic. When Imogen entered, he rose indolently and gave her his hand, his manner barely courteous.

"I am glad you arrived promptly, Miss Willard," he said with an indifferent drawl. "Flavia was afraid you might be late. You had a pleasant ride up, I hope?"

"Oh, very, thank you, Mr. Hamilton," she replied, feeling that he did not particularly care whether she replied at all.

Flavia explained that she had not yet had time to dress for dinner, as she had been attending to Mr. Will Maidenwood, who had become faint after hurting his finger in an obdurate window, and immediately excused herself. As she left, Hamilton turned to Miss Broadwood with a rather spiritless smile.

"Well, Jimmy," he remarked, "I brought up a piano box full of fireworks for the boys. How do you suppose we'll manage to keep them until the Fourth?"

"We can't, unless we steel ourselves to deny there are any on the premises," said Miss Broadwood, seating herself on a low stool by Hamilton's chair, and leaning back against the mantel. "Have you seen Helen, and has she told you the tragedy of the tooth?"

"She met me at the station, with her tooth wrapped up in tissue paper. I had tea with her an hour ago. Better sit down, Miss Willard;" he rose and pushed a chair toward Imogen, who was standing peering into the conservatory. "We are scheduled to dine at seven, but they seldom get around before eight."

By this time Imogen had made out that here the plural pronoun, third person, always referred to the artists. As Hamilton's manner did not spur one to cordial intercourse, and as his attention seemed directed to Miss Broadwood, in so far as it could be said to be directed to any one, she sat down facing the conservatory and watched him, unable to decide in how far he was identical with the man who had first met Flavia Malcolm in her mother's house, twelve years ago. Did he at all remember having known her as a little girl, and why did his indifference hurt her so, after all these years? Had some remnant of her childish affection for him gone on living, somewhere down in the sealed caves of her consciousness, and had she really expected to find it possible to be fond of him again? Suddenly she saw a light in the man's sleepy eyes, an unmistakable expression of interest and pleasure that fairly startled her. She turned quickly in the direction of his glance, and saw Flavia, just entering, dressed for dinner and lit by the effulgence of her most radiant manner. Most people considered Flavia handsome, and there was no gainsaying that she carried her five-and-thirty years splendidly. Her figure had never grown matronly, and her face was of the sort that does not show wear. Its blond tints were as fresh and enduring as enamel,—and quite as hard. Its usual expression was one of tense, often strained, animation, which compressed her lips nervously. A perfect scream of animation, Miss Broadwood had called it—created and maintained by sheer, indomitable force of will. Flavia's appearance on any scene whatever made a ripple, caused a certain agitation and recognition, and, among impressionable people, a certain uneasiness. For all her sparkling assurance of manner, Flavia was certainly always ill at ease, and even more certainly anxious. She seemed not convinced of the established order of material things, seemed always to conceal her feeling that walls might crumble, chasms open, or the fabric of her life fly to the winds in irretrievable entanglement. At least this was the impression Imogen got from that note in Flavia which was so manifestly false.

Hamilton's keen, quick, satisfied glance at his wife had recalled to Imogen all her inventory of speculations about them. She looked at him with compassionate surprise. As a child she had never permitted herself to believe that Hamilton cared at all for the woman who had taken him away from her; and since she had begun to think about them again, it had never occurred to her that any one could become attached to Flavia in that deeply personal and exclusive sense. It seemed quite as irrational as trying to possess oneself of Broadway at noon.

When they went out to dinner, Imogen realized the completeness of Flavia's triumph. They were people of one name, mostly, like kings; people whose names stirred the imagination like a romance or a melody. With the notable exception of M. Roux, Imogen had seen most of them before, either in concert halls or lecture rooms; but they looked noticeably older and dimmer than she remembered them.

Opposite her sat Schemetzkin, the Russian pianist, a short, corpulent man, with an apoplectic face and purpleish skin, his thick, iron-grey hair tossed back from his forehead. Next the German giantess sat the Italian tenor—the tiniest of men—pale, with soft, light hair, much in disorder, very red lips and fingers yellowed by cigarettes. Frau Lichtenfeld shone in a gown of emerald green, fitting so closely as to enhance her natural floridness. However, to do the good lady justice, let her attire be never so modest, it gave an effect of barbaric splendour. At her left sat Herr Schotte, the Assyriologist, whose features were effectually concealed by the convergence of his hair and beard, and whose glasses were continually falling into his plate. This gentleman had removed more tons of earth in the course of his explorations than had any of his confrères, and his vigorous attack upon his food seemed to suggest the strenuous nature of his accustomed toil. His eyes were small and deeply set, and his forehead bulged fiercely above his eyes in a bony ridge. His heavy brows completed the leonine suggestion of his face. Even to Imogen, who knew something of his work and greatly respected it, he was entirely too reminiscent of the stone age to be altogether an agreeable dinner companion. He seemed, indeed, to have absorbed something of the savagery of those early types of life which he continually studied.

Frank Wellington, the young Kansas man who had been two years out of Harvard and had published three historical novels, sat next to Mr. Will Maidenwood, who was still pale from his recent sufferings, and carried his hand bandaged. They took little part in the general conversation, but, like the lion and the unicorn, were always at it; discussing, every time they met, whether there were or were not passages in Mr. Wellington's works which should be eliminated, out of consideration for the Young Person. Wellington had fallen into the hands of a great American syndicate which most effectually befriended struggling authors whose struggles were in the right direction, and which had guaranteed to make him famous before he was thirty. Feeling the security of his position, he stoutly defended those passages which jarred upon the sensitive nerves of the young editor of *Woman*. Maidenwood, in the smoothest of voices, urged the necessity of the author's recognizing certain restrictions at the outset, and Miss Broadwood, who joined the argument quite without invitation or encouragement, seconded him with pointed and malicious remarks which caused the young editor manifest discomfort. Restzhoff, the chemist, demanded the attention of the entire company for his exposition of his devices for manufacturing ice-cream from vegetable oils, and for administering drugs in bonbons.

Flavia, always noticeably restless at dinner, was somewhat apathetic toward the advocate of peptonized chocolate, and was plainly concerned about the sudden departure of M. Roux, who had announced that it would be necessary for him to leave to-morrow. M. Emile Roux, who sat at Flavia's right, was a man in middle life and quite bald, clearly without personal vanity, though his publishers preferred to circulate only those of his portraits taken in his ambrosial youth. Imogen was considerably shocked at his unlikeness to the slender, black-stocked Rolla he had looked at twenty. He had declined into the florid, settled heaviness of indifference and approaching age. There was, however, a certain look of durability and solidity about him; the look of a man who has earned the right to be fat and bald, and even silent at dinner if he chooses.

Throughout the discussion between Wellington and Will Maidenwood, though they invited his participation, he remained silent, betraying no sign either of interest or contempt. Since his arrival he had directed most of his conversation to Hamilton, who had never read one of his twelve great novels. This perplexed and troubled Flavia. On the night of his arrival, Jules Martel had enthusiastically declared, "There are schools and schools, manners and manners; but Roux is Roux, and Paris sets its watches by his clock." Flavia had already repeated this remark to Imogen. It haunted her, and each time she quoted it she was impressed anew.

Flavia shifted the conversation uneasily, evidently exasperated and excited by her repeated failures to draw the novelist out. "Monsieur Roux," she began abruptly, with her most animated smile, "I remember so well a statement I read some years ago in your 'Mes Etudes des Femmes,' to the effect that you have never met a really intellectual woman. May I ask, without being impertinent, whether that assertion still represents your experience?"

"I meant, madam," said the novelist conservatively, "intellectual in a sense very special, as we say of men in whom the purely intellectual functions seem almost independent."

"And you still think a woman so constituted a mythical personage?" persisted Flavia, nodding her head encouragingly.

"*Une Méduse,* madam, who, if she were discovered, would transmute us all into stone," said the novelist, bowing gravely. "If she existed at all," he added deliberately, "it was my business to find her, and she has cost me many a vain pilgrimage. Like Rudel of Tripoli, I have crossed seas and penetrated deserts to seek her out. I have, indeed, encountered women of learning whose industry I have been compelled to respect; many who have possessed beauty and charm and perplexing cleverness; a few with remarkable information, and a sort of fatal facility."

"And Mrs. Browning, George Eliot, and your own Mme. Dudevant?" queried Flavia with that fervid enthusiasm with which she could, on occasion, utter things simply incomprehensible for their banality—at her feats of this sort Miss Broadwood was wont to sit breathless with admiration.

"Madam, while the intellect was undeniably present in the performances of those women, it was only the stick of the rocket. Although this woman has eluded me, I have studied her conditions and perturbations as astronomers conjecture the orbits of planets they have never seen. If she exists, she is probably neither an artist nor a woman with a mission, but an obscure personage, with imperative intellectual needs, who absorbs rather than produces."

Flavia, still nodding nervously, fixed a strained glance of interrogation upon M. Roux. "Then you think she would be a woman whose first necessity would be to know, whose instincts would be satisfied with only the best, who could draw from others; appreciative, merely?"

The novelist lifted his dull eyes to his interlocutress with an un-translatable smile, and a slight inclination of his shoulders. "Exactly so; you are really remarkable, madame," he added, in a tone of cold astonishment.

After dinner the guests took their coffee in the music-room, where Schemetzkin sat down at the piano to drum rag-time, and give his celebrated imitation of the boarding-school girl's execution of Chopin. He flatly refused to play anything more serious, and would practise only in the morning, when he had the music-room to himself. Hamilton and M. Roux repaired to the smoking-room to discuss the necessity of extending the tax on manufactured articles in France,— one of those conversations which particularly exasperated Flavia.

After Schemetzkin had grimaced and tortured the keyboard with malicious vulgarities for half an hour, Signor Donati, to put an end to his torture, consented to sing, and Flavia and Imogen went to fetch Arthur to play his accompaniments. Hamilton rose with an annoyed look, and placed his cigarette on the mantel. "Why yes, Flavia, I'll accompany him, provided he sings something with a melody, Italian arias or ballads, and provided the recital is not interminable."

"You will join us, M. Roux?"

"Thank you, but I have some letters to write," replied the novelist bowing.

As Flavia had remarked to Imogen, "Arthur really played accompaniments remarkably well." To hear him recalled vividly the days of her childhood, when he always used to spend his business vacations at her mother's home in Maine. He had possessed for her that almost hypnotic influence which young men sometimes exert upon little girls. It was a sort of phantom love affair, subjective and fanciful, a precocity of instinct, like that tender and maternal concern which some little girls feel for their dolls. Yet this childish infatuation is capable of all the depressions and exaltations of love itself; it has its bitter jealousies, cruel disappointments, its exacting caprices.

Summer after summer she had awaited his coming and wept at his departure, indifferent to the gayer young men who had called her their sweetheart, and laughed at everything she said. Although Hamilton never said so, she had been always quite sure that he was fond of her. When he pulled her up the river to hunt for fairy knolls shut about by low, hanging willows, he was often silent for an hour at a time, yet she never felt that he was bored or was neglecting her. He would lie in the sand smoking, his eyes half closed, watching her play and she was always conscious that she was entertaining him. Sometimes he would take a copy of "Alice in Wonderland" in his pocket, and no one could read it as he could, laughing at her with his dark eyes, when anything amused him. No one else could laugh so, with just their eyes, and without moving a muscle of their face. Though he usually smiled at passages that seemed not at all funny to the child, she always laughed gleefully, because he was so seldom moved to mirth that any such demonstration delighted her and she took the credit of it entirely to herself. Her own inclination had been for serious stories, with sad endings, like the Little Mermaid, which he had once told her in an unguarded moment when she had a cold, and was put to bed early on her birthday night and cried because she could not have her party. But he highly disapproved of this preference, and had called it a morbid taste, and always shook his finger at her when she asked for the story. When she had been particularly good, or particularly neglected by other people, then he would sometimes melt and tell her the story, and never laugh at her if she enjoyed the "sad ending" even to tears. When Flavia had taken him away and he came no more, she wept inconsolably for the space of two weeks, and refused to learn her lessons. Then she found the story of the Little Mermaid herself, and forgot him.

Imogen had discovered at dinner that he could still smile at one secretly, out of his eyes, and that he had the old manner of outwardly seeming bored, but letting you know that he was not. She was intensely curious about his exact state of feeling toward his wife, and more curious still to catch a sense of his final adjustment to the conditions of life in general. This, she could not help feeling, she might get again—if she could have him alone for an hour, in some place where there was a little river and a sandy cover bordered by drooping willows, and a blue sky seen through white sycamore boughs.

That evening, before retiring, Flavia entered her husband's room, where he sat in his smoking-jacket, in one of his favourite low chairs.

"I suppose it's a grave responsibility to bring an ardent, serious young thing like Imogen here among all these fascinating personages," she remarked reflectively. "But, after all, one can never tell. These grave, silent girls have their own charm, even for facile people."

"O, so that is your plan?" queried her husband dryly. "I was wondering why you got her up here. She doesn't seem to mix well with the faciles. At least, so it struck me."

Flavia paid no heed to this jeering remark, but repeated, "No, after all, it may not be a bad thing."

"Then do consign her to that shaken reed, the tenor," said her husband yawning. "I remember she used to have a taste for the pathetic."

"And then," remarked Flavia coquettishly, "after all, I owe her mother a return in kind. She was not afraid to trifle with destiny."

But Hamilton was asleep in his chair.

Next morning Imogen found only Miss Broadwood in the breakfast-room.

"Good-morning, my dear girl, whatever are you doing up so early? They never breakfast before eleven. Most of them take their coffee in their room. Take this place by me."

Miss Broadwood looked particularly fresh and encouraging in her blue serge walking-skirt, her open jacket displaying an expanse of stiff, white, shirt bosom, dotted with some almost imperceptible figure and a dark blue-and-white neck-tie, neatly knotted under her wide, rolling collar. She wore a white rosebud in the lapel of her coat, and decidedly she seemed more than ever like a nice, clean boy on his holiday. Imogen was just hoping that they would breakfast alone when Miss Broadwood exclaimed, "Ah, there comes Arthur with the children. That's the reward of early rising in this house; you never get to see the youngsters at any other time."

Hamilton entered, followed by two dark, handsome little boys. The girl, who was very tiny, blonde like her mother, and exceedingly frail, he carried in his arms. The boys came up and said good-morning with an ease and cheerfulness uncommon, even in well-bred children, but the little girl hid her face on her father's shoulder.

"She's a shy little lady," he explained, as he put her gently down in her chair. "I'm afraid she's like her father; she can't seem to get used to meeting people. And you, Miss Willard, did you dream of the white rabbit or the little mermaid?"

"O, I dreamed of them all! All the personages of that buried civilization," cried Imogen, delighted that his estranged manner of the night before had entirely vanished, and feeling that, somehow, the old confidential relations had been restored during the night.

"Come, William," said Miss Broadwood, turning to the younger of the two boys, "and what did you dream about?"

"We dreamed," said William gravely—he was the more assertive of the two and always spoke for both—"we dreamed that there were fireworks hidden in the basement of the carriage-house; lots and lots of fireworks."

His elder brother looked up at him with apprehensive astonishment, while Miss Broadwood hastily put her napkin to her lips, and Hamilton dropped his eyes. "If little boys dream things, they are so apt not to come true," he reflected sadly. This shook even the redoubtable William, and he glanced nervously at his brother. "But do things vanish just because they have been dreamed?" he objected.

"Generally that is the very best reason for their vanishing," said Arthur gravely.

"But, father, people can't help what they dream," remonstrated Edward gently.

"Oh, come! You're making these children talk like a Maeterlinck dialogue," laughed Miss Broadwood.

Flavia presently entered, a book in her hand, and bade them all good-morning. "Come, little people, which story shall it be this morning?" she asked winningly. Greatly excited, the children followed her into the garden. "She does then, sometimes," murmured Imogen as they left the breakfast-room.

"Oh, yes, to be sure," said Miss Broadwood cheerfully. "She reads a story to them every morning in the most picturesque part of the garden. The mother of the Gracchi, you know. She does so long, she says, for the time when they will be intellectual companions for her. What do you say to a walk over the hills?"

As they left the house they met Frau Lichtenfeld and the bushy Herr Schotte—the professor cut an astonishing figure in golf stockings—returning from a walk and engaged in an animated conversation on the tendencies of German fiction.

"Aren't they the most attractive little children," exclaimed Imogen as they wound down the road toward the river.

"Yes, and you must not fail to tell Flavia that you think so. She will look at you in a sort of startled way and say, 'Yes, aren't they?' and maybe she will go off and hunt them up and have tea with them, to fully appreciate them. She is awfully afraid of missing anything good, is Flavia. The way those youngsters manage to conceal their guilty presence in the House of Song is a wonder."

"But don't any of the artist-folk fancy children?" asked Imogen.

"Yes, they just fancy them and no more. The chemist remarked the other day that children are like certain salts which need not be actualized because the formulæ are quite sufficient for practical purposes. I don't see how even Flavia can endure to have that man about."

"I have always been rather curious to know what Arthur thinks of it all," remarked Imogen cautiously.

"Thinks of it!" ejaculated Miss Broadwood. "Why, my dear, what would any man think of having his house turned into an hotel, habited by freaks who discharge his servants, borrow his money, and insult his neighbours? This place is shunned like a lazaretto!"

"Well, then, why does he—why does he—" persisted Imogen.

"Bah!" interrupted Miss Broadwood impatiently, "why did he in the first place? That's the question."

"Marry her, you mean?" said Imogen colouring.

"Exactly so," said Miss Broadwood sharply, as she snapped the lid of her match-box.

"I suppose that is a question rather beyond us, and certainly one which we cannot discuss," said Imogen. "But his toleration on this one point puzzles me, quite apart from other complications."

"Toleration? Why this point, as you call it, simply is Flavia. Who could conceive of her without it? I don't know where it's all going to end, I'm sure, and I'm equally sure that, if it were not for Arthur, I shouldn't care," declared Miss Broadwood, drawing her shoulders together.

"But will it end at all, now?"

"Such an absurd state of things can't go on indefinitely. A man isn't going to see his wife make a guy of herself forever, is he? Chaos has already begun in the servants' quarters. There are six different languages spoken there now. You see, it's on an entirely false basis. Flavia hasn't the slightest notion of what these people are really like, their good and their bad alike escape her. They, on the other hand, can't imagine what she is driving at. Now, Arthur is worse off than either faction; he is not in the fairy story in that he sees these people exactly as they are, *but* he is utterly unable to see Flavia as they see her. There you have the situation. Why can't he see her as we do? My dear, that has kept me awake o' nights. This man who has thought so much and lived so much, who is naturally a critic, really takes Flavia at very nearly her own estimate. But now I am entering upon a wilderness. From a brief acquaintance with her, you can know nothing of the icy fastnesses of Flavia's self-esteem. It's like St. Peter's; you can't realize its magnitude at once. You have to grow into a sense of it by living under its shadow. It has perplexed even Emile Roux, that merciless dissector of egoism. She has puzzled him the more because he saw at a glance what some of them do not perceive at once, and what will be mercifully concealed from Arthur until the trump sounds; namely, that all Flavia's artists have done or ever will do means exactly as much to her as a symphony means to an oyster; that there is no bridge by which the significance of any work of art could be conveyed to her."

"Then, in the name of goodness, why does she bother?" gasped Imogen. "She is pretty, wealthy, well-established; why should she bother?"

"That's what M. Roux has kept asking himself. I can't pretend to analyse it. She reads papers on the Literary Landmarks of Paris, and the Loves of the Poets, and that sort of thing to clubs out in Chicago. To Flavia it is more necessary to be called clever than to breathe. I would give a good deal to know that glum Frenchman's diagnosis.

He has been watching her out of those fishy eyes of his as a biologist watches a hemisphereless frog."

For several days after M. Roux's departure, Flavia gave an embarrassing share of her attention to Imogen. Embarrassing, because Imogen had the feeling of being energetically and futilely explored, she knew not for what. She felt herself under the globe of an air pump, expected to yield up something. When she confined the conversation to matters of general interest, Flavia conveyed to her with some pique that her one endeavour in life had been to fit herself to converse with her friends upon those things which vitally interested them. "One has no right to accept their best from people unless one gives, isn't it so? I want to be able to give—!" she declared vaguely. Yet whenever Imogen strove to pay her tithes, and plunged bravely into her plans for study next winter, Flavia grew absent-minded and interrupted her by amazing generalizations or by such embarrassing questions as, "And these grim studies really have charm for you; you are quite buried in them; they make other things seem light and ephemeral?"

"I rather feel as though I had got in here under false pretences," Imogen confided to Miss Broadwood, "I'm sure I don't know what it is that she wants of me."

"Ah," chuckled Jemima, "you are not equal to these heart to heart talks with Flavia. You utterly fail to communicate to her the atmosphere of that untroubled joy in which you dwell. You must remember that she gets no feeling out of things herself, and she demands that you impart yours to her by some process of psychic transmission. I once met a blind girl, blind from birth, who could discuss the peculiarities of the Barbizon school with just Flavia's glibness and enthusiasm. Ordinarily Flavia knows how to get what she wants from people, and her memory is wonderful. One evening I heard her giving Frau Lichtenfeld some random impressions about Hedda Gabler which she extracted from me five years ago; giving them with an impassioned conviction of which I was never guilty. But I have known other people who could appropriate your stories and opinions; Flavia is infinitely more subtle than that; she can soak up the very thrash and drift of your day dreams, and take the very thrills off your back as it were."

After some days of unsuccessful effort, Flavia withdrew herself, and Imogen found Hamilton ready to catch her when she was tossed a-field. He seemed only to have been awaiting this crisis, and at once their old intimacy re-established itself as a thing inevitable and beautifully prepared for. She convinced herself that she had not been mistaken in him, despite all the doubts that had come up in later years, and this renewal of faith set more than one question thumping in her brain. "How did he, how can he?" she kept repeating with a tinge of her childish resentment, "what right had he to waste anything so fine?"

When Imogen and Arthur were returning from a walk before luncheon one morning about a week after M. Roux's departure, they noticed an absorbed group before one of the hall windows. Herr Schotte and Restzhoff sat on the window seat with a newspaper between them, while Wellington, Schemetzkin and Will Maidenwood looked over their shoulders. They seemed intensely interested, Herr Schotte occasionally pounding his knees with his fists in ebullitions of barbaric glee. When Imogen entered the hall, however, the men were all sauntering toward the breakfast-room and the paper was lying innocently on the divan. During luncheon the personnel of that window group were unwontedly animated and agreeable,—all save Schemetzkin, whose stare was blanker than ever, as though Roux's mantle of insulting indifference had fallen upon him, in addition to his own oblivious self absorption. Will Maidenwood seemed embarrassed and annoyed; the chemist employed himself with making polite speeches to Hamilton.—Flavia did not come down to lunch—and there was a malicious gleam under Herr Schotte's eyebrows. Frank Wellington announced nervously that an imperative letter from his protecting syndicate summoned him to the city.

After luncheon the men went to the golf links, and Imogen, at the first opportunity, possessed herself of the newspaper which had been left on the divan. One of the first things that caught her eye was an article headed "Roux on Tuft Hunters; The Advanced American Woman As He Sees Her; Aggressive, Superficial and Insincere." The entire interview was nothing more or less than a satiric characterization of Flavia, a-quiver with irritation and vitriolic malice. No one could mistake it; it was done with all his deftness of portraiture. Imogen had not finished the article when she heard a footstep, and clutching the paper she started precipitately toward the stairway as Arthur entered. He put out his hand, looking critically at her distressed face.

"Wait a moment, Miss Willard," he said peremptorily, "I want to see whether we can find what it was that so interested our friends this morning. Give me the paper, please."

Imogen grew quite white as he opened the journal. She reached forward and crumpled it with her hands. "Please don't, please don't," she pleaded, "it's something I don't want you to see. Oh! why will you? It's just something low and despicable that you can't notice."

Arthur had gently loosed her hands and he pointed her to a chair. He lit a cigar and read the article through without comment. When he had finished it, he walked to the fireplace, struck a match, and tossed the flaming journal between the brass andirons.

"You are right," he remarked as he came back, dusting his hands with his handkerchief. "It's quite impossible to comment. There are extremes of blackguardism for which we have no name. The only thing necessary is to see that Flavia gets no wind of this. This seems to be my cue to act; poor girl."

Imogen looked at him tearfully; she could only murmur, "Oh, why did you read it!"

Hamilton laughed spiritlessly. "Come, don't you worry about it. You always took other people's troubles too seriously. When you were little and all the world was gay and everybody happy, you must needs get the Little Mermaid's troubles to grieve over. Come with me into the music-room. You remember the musical setting I once made you for the Lay of the Jabberwock? I was trying it over the other night, long after you were in bed, and I decided it was quite as fine as the Erl-King music. How I wish I could give you some of the cake that Alice ate and make you a little girl again. Then, when you had got through the glass door into the little garden, you could call to me, perhaps, and tell me all the fine things that were going on there. What a pity it is that you ever grew up!" he added, laughing, and Imogen, too, was thinking just that.

At dinner that evening, Flavia, with fatal persistence, insisted upon turning the conversation to M. Roux. She had been reading one of his novels and had remembered anew that Paris set its watches by his clock. Imogen surmised that she was tortured by a feeling that she had not sufficiently appreciated him while she had had him. When she first mentioned his name, she was answered only by the pall of silence that fell over the company. Then everyone began to talk at once, as though to correct a false position. They spoke of him with a fervid, defiant admiration, with the sort of hot praise that covers a double purpose. Imogen fancied she could see that they felt a kind of relief at what the man had done, even those who despised him for doing it; that they felt a spiteful heat against Flavia, as though she had tricked them, and a certain contempt for themselves that they had been beguiled. She was reminded of the fury of the crowd in the fairy tale, when once the child had called out that the king was in his night-clothes. Surely these people knew no more about Flavia than they had known before, but the mere fact that the thing had been said, altered the situation. Flavia, meanwhile, sat chattering amiably, pathetically unconscious of her nakedness.

Hamilton lounged, fingering the stem of his wine glass, gazing down the table at one face after another and studying the various degrees of self-consciousness they exhibited. Imogen's eyes followed his, fearfully. When a lull came in the spasmodic flow of conversation, Arthur, leaning back in his chair, remarked deliberately, "As for M. Roux, his very profession places him in that class of men whom society has never been able to accept unconditionally because it has never been able to assume that they have any ordered notion of taste. He and his ilk remain, with the mountebanks and snake charmers, people indispensable to our civilization, but wholly unreclaimed by it; people whom we receive, but whose invitations we do not accept."

Fortunately for Flavia, this mine was not exploded until just before the coffee was brought. Her laughter was pitiful to hear; it echoed through the silent room as in a vault, while she made some tremulously light remark about her husband's drollery, grim as a jest from the dying. No one responded and she sat nodding her head like a mechanical toy and smiling her white, set smile through her teeth, until Alcée Buisson and Frau Lichtenfeld came to her support.

After dinner the guests retired immediately to their rooms, and

Imogen went upstairs on tiptoe, feeling the echo of breakage and the dust of crumbling in the air. She wondered whether Flavia's habitual note of uneasiness were not, in a manner, prophetic, and a sort of unconscious premonition, after all. She sat down to write a letter, but she found herself so nervous, her head so hot and her hands so cold, that she soon abandoned the effort. Just as she was about to seek Miss Broadwood, Flavia entered and embraced her hysterically.

"My dearest girl," she began, "was there ever such an unfortunate and incomprehensible speech made before? Of course it is scarcely necessary to explain to you poor Arthur's lack of tact, and that he meant nothing. But they! Can they be expected to understand? He will feel wretchedly about it when he realizes what he has done, but in the meantime? And M. Roux, of all men! When we were so fortunate as to get him, and he made himself so unreservedly agreeable, and I fancied that, in his way, Arthur quite admired him. My dear, you have no idea what that speech has done. Schemetzkin and Herr Schotte have already sent me word that they must leave us to-morrow. Such a thing from a host!" Flavia paused, choked by tears of vexation and despair.

Imogen was thoroughly disconcerted; this was the first time she had ever seen Flavia betray any personal emotion which was indubitably genuine. She replied with what consolation she could. "Need they take it personally at all? It was a mere observation upon a class of people—"

"Which he knows nothing whatever about, and with whom he has no sympathy," interrupted Flavia. "Ah, my dear, you could not be *expected* to understand. You can't realize, knowing Arthur as you do, his entire lack of any æsthetic sense whatever. He is absolutely *nil,* stone deaf and stark blind, on that side. He doesn't mean to be brutal, it is just the brutality of utter ignorance. They always feel it—they are so sensitive to unsympathetic influences, you know; they know it the moment they come into the house. I have spent my life apologizing for him and struggling to conceal it; but in spite of me, he wounds them; his very attitude, even in silence, offends them. Heavens! do I not know, is it not perpetually and forever wounding me? But there has never been anything so dreadful as this, never! If I could conceive of any possible motive, even!"

"But, surely, Mrs. Hamilton, it was, after all, a mere expression of opinion, such as we are any of us likely to venture upon any subject whatever. It was neither more personal nor more extravagant than many of M. Roux's remarks."

"But, Imogen, certainly M. Roux has the right. It is a part of his art, and that is altogether another matter. Oh, this is not the only instance!" continued Flavia passionately, "I've always had this narrow, bigoted prejudice to contend with. It has always held me back. But this——!"

"I think you mistake his attitude," replied Imogen, feeling a flush that made her ears tingle, "that is, I fancy he is more appreciative than he seems. A man can't be very demonstrative about those things—not if he is a real man. I should not think you would care much about saving the feelings of people who are too narrow to admit of any other point of view than their own." She stopped, finding herself in the impossible position of attempting to explain Hamilton to his wife; a task which, if once begun, would necessitate an entire course of enlightenment which she doubted Flavia's ability to receive, and which she could offer only with very poor grace.

"That's just where it stings most," here Flavia began pacing the floor, "it is just because they have all shown such tolerance, and have treated Arthur with such unfailing consideration, that I can find no reasonable pretext for his rancour. How can he fail to see the value of such friendships on the children's account, if for nothing else! What an advantage for them to grow up among such associations! Even though he cares nothing about these things himself he might realize that. Is there nothing I could say by way of explanation? To them, I mean? If some one were to explain to them how unfortunately limited he is in these things——"

"I'm afraid I cannot advise you," said Imogen decidedly, "but that, at least, seems to be impossible."

Flavia took her hand and glanced at her affectionately, nodding nervously. "Of course, dear girl, I can't ask you to be quite frank with me. Poor child, you are trembling and your hands are icy. Poor Arthur! But you must not judge him by this altogether; think how much he misses in life. What a cruel shock you've had. I'll send you some sherry. Good-night, my dear."

When Flavia shut the door, Imogen burst into a fit of nervous weeping.

Next morning she awoke after a troubled and restless night. At eight o'clock Miss Broadwood entered in a red and white striped bath-robe.

"Up, up, and see the great doom's image!" she cried, her eyes sparkling with excitement. "The hall is full of trunks, they are packing. What bolt has fallen? It's you, *ma chérie,* you've brought Ulysses home again and the slaughter has begun!" She blew a cloud of smoke triumphantly from her lips and threw herself into a chair beside the bed.

Imogen, rising on her elbow, plunged excitedly into the story of the Roux interview, which Miss Broadwood heard with the keenest interest, frequently interrupting her by exclamations of delight. When Imogen reached the dramatic scene which terminated in the destruction of the newspaper, Miss Broadwood rose and took a turn about the room, violently switching the tasselled cords of her bath-robe.

"Stop a moment," she cried, "you mean to tell me that he had such a heaven-sent means to bring her to her senses and didn't use it, that he held such a weapon and threw it away?"

"Use it?" cried Imogen unsteadily, "of course he didn't! He bared his back to the tormentor, signed himself over to punishment in that speech he made at dinner, which every one understands but Flavia. She was here for an hour last night and disregarded every limit of taste in her maledictions."

"My dear!" cried Miss Broadwood, catching her hand in inordinate delight at the situation, "do you see what he has done? There'll be no end to it. Why he has sacrificed himself to spare the very vanity that devours him, put rancours in the vessels of his peace, and his eternal jewel given to the common enemy of man, to make them kings, the seed of Banquo kings! He is magnificent!"

"Isn't he always that?" cried Imogen hotly. "He's like a pillar of sanity and law in this house of shams and swollen vanities, where people stalk about with a sort of mad-house dignity, each one fancying himself a king or a pope. If you could have heard that woman talk of him! Why she thinks him stupid, bigoted, blinded by middle-class prejudices. She talked about his having no æsthetic sense, and insisted that her artists had always shown him tolerance. I don't know why it should get on my nerves so, I'm sure, but her stupidity and assurance are enough to drive one to the brink of collapse."

"Yes, as opposed to his singular fineness, they are calculated to do just that," said Miss Broadwood gravely, wisely ignoring Imogen's tears. "But what has been is nothing to what will be. Just wait until Flavia's black swans have flown! You ought not to try to stick it out; that would only make it harder for every one. Suppose you let me telephone your mother to wire you to come home by the evening train?"

"Anything, rather than have her come at me like that again. It puts me in a perfectly impossible position, and he *is* so fine!"

"Of course it does," said Miss Broadwood sympathetically, "and there is no good to be got from facing it. I will stay, because such things interest me, and Frau Lichtenfeld will stay because she has no money to get away, and Buisson will stay because he feels somewhat responsible. These complications are interesting enough to cold-blooded folk like myself who have an eye for the dramatic element, but they are distracting and demoralizing to young people with any serious purpose in life."

Miss Broadwood's counsel was all the more generous seeing that, for her, the most interesting element of this dénouement would be eliminated by Imogen's departure. "If she goes now, she'll get over it," soliloquized Miss Broadwood, "if she stays she'll be wrung for him, and the hurt may go deep enough to last. I haven't the heart to see her spoiling things for herself." She telephoned Mrs. Willard, and helped Imogen to pack. She even took it upon herself to break the news of Imogen's going to Arthur, who remarked, as he rolled a cigarette in his nerveless fingers:

"Right enough, too. What should she do here with old cynics like you and me, Jimmy? Seeing that she is brim full of dates and formulæ and other positivisms, and is so girt about with illusions that she still casts a shadow in the sun. You've been very tender of her, haven't you? I've watched you. And to think it may all be gone when we see her next. 'The common fate of all things rare,' you know. What a good fellow you are, anyway, Jimmy," he added, putting his hands affectionately on her shoulders.

Arthur went with them to the station. Flavia was so prostrated by the concerted action of her guests that she was able to see Imogen only for a moment in her darkened sleeping chamber, where she kissed her hysterically, without lifting her head, bandaged in aromatic vinegar. On the way to the station both Arthur and Imogen threw the burden of keeping up appearances entirely upon Miss Broadwood, who blithely rose to the occasion. When Hamilton carried Imogen's bag into the car, Miss Broadwood detained her for a moment, whispering as she gave her a large, warm handclasp, "I'll come to see you when I get back to town; and, in the meantime, if you meet any of our artists, tell them you have left Caius Marius among the ruins of Carthage."

The Garden Lodge

When Caroline Noble's friends learned that Raymond d'Esquerré was to spend a month at her place on the Sound before he sailed to fill his engagement for the London opera season, they considered it another striking instance of the perversity of things. That the month was May, and the most mild and florescent of all the blue-and-white Mays the middle coast had known in years, but added to their sense of wrong. D'Esquerré, they learned, was ensconced in the lodge in the apple orchard, just beyond Caroline's glorious garden, and report went that at almost any hour the sound of the tenor's voice and of Caroline's crashing accompaniment could be heard floating through the open windows, out among the snowy apple boughs. The Sound, steel-blue and dotted with white sails, was splendidly seen from the windows of the lodge. The garden to the left and the orchard to the right had never been so riotous with spring, and had burst into impassioned bloom, as if to accommodate Caroline, though she was certainly the last woman to whom the witchery of Freya could be attributed; the last woman, as her friends affirmed, to at all adequately appreciate and make the most of such a setting for the great tenor.

Of course, they admitted, Caroline was musical—well, she ought to be!—but in that as in everything she was paramountly cool-headed, slow of impulse, and disgustingly practical; in that, as in everything else, she had herself so provokingly well in hand. Of course it would be she, always mistress of herself in any situation, she who would never be lifted one inch from the ground by it, and who would go on superintending her gardeners and workmen as usual, it would be she who got him. Perhaps some of them suspected that this was exactly why she did get him, and it but nettled them the more.

Caroline's coolness, her capableness, her general success, especially exasperated people because they felt that, for the most part, she had made herself what she was, that she had cold-bloodedly set about complying with the demands of life and making her position comfortable and masterful. That was why, every one said, she had married

Howard Noble. Women who did not get through life so well as Caroline, who could not make such good terms either with fortune or their husbands, who did not find their health so unfailingly good, or hold their looks so well, or manage their children so easily, or give such distinction to all they did, were fond of stamping Caroline as a materialist and called her hard.

The impression of cold calculation, of having a definite policy, which Caroline gave, was far from a false one; but there was this to be said for her, that there were extenuating circumstances which her friends could not know.

If Caroline held determinedly to the middle course, if she was apt to regard with distrust everything which inclined toward extravagance, it was not because she was unacquainted with other standards than her own, or had never seen another side of life. She had grown up in Brooklyn, in a shabby little house under the vacillating administration of her father, a music teacher who usually neglected his duties to write orchestral compositions for which the world seemed to have no especial need. His spirit was warped by bitter vindictiveness and puerile self-commiseration, and he spent his days in scorn of the labour that brought him bread and in pitiful devotion to the labour that brought him only disappointment, writing interminable scores which demanded of the orchestra everything under heaven except melody.

It was not a cheerful home for a girl to grow up in. The mother, who idolized her husband as the music lord of the future, was left to a life-long battle with broom and dust-pan, to never ending conciliatory overtures to the butcher and grocer, to the making of her own gowns and of Caroline's, and to the delicate task of mollifying Auguste's neglected pupils.

The son, Heinrich, a painter, Caroline's only brother, had inherited all his father's vindictive sensitiveness without his capacity for slavish application. His little studio on the third floor had been much frequented by young men as unsuccessful as himself, who met there to give themselves over to contemptuous derision of this or that artist whose industry and stupidity had won him recognition. Heinrich, when he worked at all, did newspaper sketches at twenty-five dollars a week. He was too indolent and vacillating to set himself seriously to his art, too irascible and poignantly self-conscious to make a living, too much addicted to lying late in bed, to the incontinent reading of poetry and to the use of chloral, to be anything very positive except painful. At twenty-six, he shot himself in a frenzy, and the whole wretched affair had effectually shattered his mother's health and brought on the decline of which she died. Caroline had been fond of him, but she felt a certain relief when he no longer wandered about the little house, commenting ironically upon its shabbiness, a Turkish cap on his head and a cigarette hanging from between his long, tremulous fingers.

After her mother's death Caroline assumed the management of that bankrupt establishment. The funeral expenses were unpaid, and Auguste's pupils had been frightened away by the shock of successive disasters and the general atmosphere of wretchedness that pervaded the house. Auguste himself was writing a symphonic poem, Icarus, dedicated to the memory of his son. Caroline was barely twenty when she was called upon to face this tangle of difficulties, but she reviewed the situation candidly. The house had served its time at the shrine of idealism; vague, distressing, unsatisfied yearnings had brought it low enough. Her mother, thirty years before, had eloped and left Germany with her music teacher, to give herself over to life-long, drudging bondage at the kitchen range. Ever since Caroline could remember, the law in the house had been a sort of mystic worship of things distant, intangible and unattainable. The family had lived in successive ebullitions of generous enthusiasm, in talk of masters and masterpieces, only to come down to the cold facts in the case; to boiled mutton and to the necessity of turning the dining-room carpet. All these emotional pyrotechnics had ended in petty jealousies, in neglected duties and in cowardly fear of the little grocer on the corner.

From her childhood she had hated it, that humiliating and uncertain existence, with its glib tongue and empty pockets, its poetic ideals and sordid realities, its indolence and poverty tricked out in paper roses. Even as a little girl, when vague dreams beset her, when she wanted to lie late in bed and commune with visions, or to leap and sing because the sooty little trees along the street were putting out their first pale leaves in the sunshine, she would clench her hands and go to help her mother sponge the spots from her father's waistcoat or press Heinrich's trousers. Her mother never permitted the slightest question concerning anything Auguste or Heinrich saw fit to do, but from the time Caroline could reason at all she could not help thinking that many things went wrong at home. She knew, for example, that her father's pupils ought not to be kept waiting half an hour while he discussed Schopenhauer with some bearded socialist over a dish of herrings and a spotted table cloth. She knew that Heinrich ought not to give a dinner on Heine's birthday, when the laundress had not been paid for a month and when he frequently had to ask his mother for car fare. Certainly Caroline had served her apprenticeship to idealism and to all the embarrassing inconsistencies which it sometimes entails, and she decided to deny herself this diffuse, ineffectual answer to the sharp questions of life.

When she came into the control of herself and the house, she refused to proceed any further with her musical education. Her father, who had intended to make a concert pianist of her, set this down as another item in his long list of disappointments and his grievances against the world. She was young and pretty, and she had worn turned gowns and soiled gloves and improvised hats all her life. She wanted the luxury of being like other people, of being honest from her hat to her boots, of having nothing to hide, not even in the matter of stockings, and she was willing to work for it. She rented a little studio away from that house of misfortune, and began to give lessons. She managed well and was the sort of girl people liked to help. The bills were paid and Auguste went on composing, growing indignant only when she refused to insist that her pupils should study his compositions for the piano. She began to get engagements in New York to play accompaniments at song recitals. She dressed well, made herself agreeable, and gave herself a chance. She never permitted herself to look further than a step ahead, and set herself with all the strength of her will to see things as they are and meet them squarely in the broad day. There were two things she feared even more than poverty; the part of one that sets up an idol and the part of one that bows down and worships it.

When Caroline was twenty-four she married Howard Noble, then a widower of forty, who had been for ten years a power in Wall

Street. Then, for the first time, she had paused to take breath. It took a substantialness as unquestionable as his; his money, his position, his energy, the big vigour of his robust person, to satisfy her that she was entirely safe. Then she relaxed a little, feeling that there was a barrier to be counted upon between her and that world of visions and quagmires and failure.

Caroline had been married for six years when Raymond d'Esquerré came to stay with them. He came chiefly because Caroline was what she was; because he, too, felt occasionally the need of getting out of Klingsor's garden, or dropping down somewhere for a time near a quiet nature, a cool head, a strong hand. The hours he had spent in the garden lodge were hours of such concentrated study as, in his fevered life, he seldom got in anywhere. She had, as he told Noble, a fine appreciation of the seriousness of work.

One evening two weeks after d'Esquerré had sailed, Caroline was in the library giving her husband an account of the work she had laid out for the gardeners. She superintended the care of the grounds herself. Her garden, indeed, had become quite a part of her; a sort of beautiful adjunct, like gowns or jewels. It was a famous spot, and Noble was very proud of it.

"What do you think, Caroline, of having the garden lodge torn down and putting a new summer house there at the end of the arbour; a big rustic affair where you could have tea served in mid-summer?" he asked.

"The lodge?" repeated Caroline looking at him quickly. "Why, that seems almost a shame, doesn't it, after d'Esquerré has used it?"

Noble put down his book with a smile of amusement.

"Are you going to be sentimental about it? Why, I'd sacrifice the whole place to see that come to pass. But I don't believe you could do it for an hour together."

"I don't believe so, either," said his wife, smiling.

Noble took up his book again and Caroline went into the music-room to practise. She was not ready to have the lodge torn down. She had gone there for a quiet hour every day during the two weeks since d'Esquerré had left them. It was the sheerest sentiment she had ever permitted herself. She was ashamed of it, but she was childishly unwilling to let it go.

Caroline went to bed soon after her husband, but she was not able to sleep. The night was close and warm, presaging storm. The wind had fallen and the water slept, fixed and motionless as the sand. She rose and thrust her feet into slippers and putting a dressing-gown over her shoulders opened the door of her husband's room; he was sleeping soundly. She went into the hall and down the stairs; then, leaving the house through a side door, stepped into the vine covered arbour that led to the garden lodge. The scent of the June roses was heavy in the still air, and the stones that paved the path felt pleasantly cool through the thin soles of her slippers. Heat-lightning flashed continuously from the bank of clouds that had gathered over the sea, but the shore was flooded with moonlight and, beyond, the rim of the Sound lay smooth and shining. Caroline had the key of the lodge, and the door creaked as she opened it. She stepped into the long, low room radiant with the moonlight which streamed through the bow window and lay in a silvery pool along the waxed floor. Even that part of the room which lay in the shadow was vaguely illuminated; the piano, the tall candlesticks, the picture frames and white casts standing out as clearly in the half-light as did the sycamores and black poplars of the garden against the still, expectant night sky. Caroline sat down to think it all over. She had come here to do just that every day of the two weeks since d'Esquerré's departure, but far from ever having reached a conclusion, she had succeeded only in losing her way in a maze of memories—sometimes bewilderingly confused, sometimes too acutely distinct—where there was neither path, nor clue, nor any hope of finality. She had, she realized, defeated a life-long regimen; completely confounded herself by falling unaware and incontinently into that luxury of revery which, even as a little girl, she had so determinedly denied herself; she had been developing with alarming celerity that part of one which sets up an idol and that part of one which bows down and worships it.

It was a mistake, she felt, ever to have asked d'Esquerré to come at all. She had an angry feeling that she had done it rather in self-defiance, to rid herself finally of that instinctive fear of him which had always troubled and perplexed her. She knew that she had reckoned with herself before he came; but she had been equal to so much that she had never really doubted she would be equal to this. She had come to believe, indeed, almost arrogantly in her own malleability and endurance; she had done so much with herself that she had come to think that there was nothing which she could not do; like swimmers, overbold, who reckon upon their strength and their power to hoard it, forgetting the ever changing moods of their adversary, the sea.

And d'Esquerré was a man to reckon with. Caroline did not deceive herself now upon that score. She admitted it humbly enough, and since she had said good-bye to him she had not been free for a moment from the sense of his formidable power. It formed the undercurrent of her consciousness; whatever she might be doing or thinking, it went on, involuntarily, like her breathing; sometimes welling up until suddenly she found herself suffocating. There was a moment of this to-night, and Caroline rose and stood shuddering, looking about her in the blue duskiness of the silent room. She had not been here at night before, and the spirit of the place seemed more troubled and insistent than ever it had been in the quiet of the afternoons. Caroline brushed her hair back from her damp forehead and went over to the bow window. After raising it she sat down upon the low seat. Leaning her head against the sill, and loosening her night-gown at the throat, she half closed her eyes and looked off into the troubled night, watching the play of the sheet-lightning upon the massing clouds between the pointed tops of the poplars.

Yes, she knew, she knew well enough, of what absurdities this spell was woven; she mocked, even while she winced. His power she knew, lay not so much in anything that he actually had—though he had so much—or in anything that he actually was; but in what he suggested, in what he seemed picturesque enough to have or be— and that was just anything that one chose to believe or to desire. His appeal was all the more persuasive and alluring that it was to the imagination alone, that it was as indefinite and impersonal as those cults of idealism which so have their way with women. What he had was that, in his mere personality, he quickened and in a measure gratified that something without which—to women—life is no better than sawdust, and to the desire for which most of their mistakes and tragedies and astonishingly poor bargains are due.

D'Esquerré had become the centre of a movement, and the Metropolitan had become the temple of a cult. When he could be induced to cross the Atlantic, the opera season in New York was successful; when he could not, the management lost money; so much every one knew. It was understood, too, that his superb art had disproportionately little to do with his peculiar position. Women swayed the balance this way or that; the opera, the orchestra, even his own glorious art, achieved at such a cost, were but the accessories of himself; like the scenery and costumes and even the soprano, they all went to produce atmosphere, were the mere mechanics of the beautiful illusion.

Caroline understood all this; to-night was not the first time that she had put it to herself so. She had seen the same feeling in other people; watched for it in her friends, studied it in the house night after night when he sang, candidly putting herself among a thousand others.

D'Esquerré's arrival in the early winter was the signal for a feminine hegira toward New York. On the nights when he sang, women flocked to the Metropolitan from mansions and hotels, from typewriter desks, school-rooms, shops and fitting-rooms. They were of all conditions and complexions. Women of the world who accepted him knowingly, as they sometimes took champagne for its agreeable effect; sisters of charity and overworked shop-girls, who received him devoutly; withered women who had taken doctorate degrees and who worshipped furtively through prism spectacles; business women and women of affairs, the Amazons who dwelt afar from men in the stony fastnesses of apartment houses. They all entered into the same romance; dreamed, in terms as various as the hues of phantasy, the same dream; drew the same quick breath when he stepped upon the stage, and, at his exit, felt the same dull pain of shouldering the pack again.

There were the maimed, even; those who came on crutches, who were pitted by smallpox or grotesquely painted by cruel birth stains. These, too, entered with him into enchantment. Stout matrons became slender girls again; worn spinsters felt their cheeks flush with the tenderness of their lost youth. Young and old, however hideous, however fair, they yielded up their heat—whether quick or latent—sat hungering for the mystic bread wherewith he fed them at this eucharist of sentiment.

Sometimes when the house was crowded from the orchestra to the last row of the gallery, when the air was charged with this ecstasy of fancy, he himself was the victim of the burning reflection of his power. They acted upon him in turn; he felt their fervent and despairing appeal to him; it stirred him as the spring drives the sap up into an old tree; he, too, burst into bloom. For the moment he, too, believed again, desired again, he knew not what, but something.

But it was not in these exalted moments that Caroline had learned to fear him most. It was in the quiet, tired reserve, the dullness, even, that kept him company between these outbursts that she found that exhausting drain upon her sympathies which was the very pith and substance of their alliance. It was the tacit admission of disappointment under all this glamour of success—the helplessness of the enchanter to at all enchant himself—that awoke in her an illogical, womanish desire to in some way compensate, to make it up to him.

She had observed drastically herself that it was her eighteenth year he awoke in her—those hard years she had spent in turning gowns and placating tradesmen, and which she had never had time to live. After all, she reflected, it was better to allow one's self a little youth; to dance a little at the carnival and to live these things when they are natural and lovely, not to have them coming back on one and demanding arrears when they are humiliating and impossible. She went over to-night all the catalogue of her self-deprivations; recalled how, in the light of her father's example, she had even refused to humour her innocent taste for improvising at the piano; how, when she began to teach, after her mother's death, she had struck out one little indulgence after another, reducing her life to a relentless routine, unvarying as clockwork. It seemed to her that ever since d'Esquerré first came into the house she had been haunted by an imploring little girlish ghost that followed her about, wringing its hands and entreating for an hour of life.

The storm had held off unconscionably long; the air within the lodge was stifling, and without the garden waited, breathless. Everything seemed pervaded by a poignant distress; the hush of feverish, intolerable expectation. The still earth, the heavy flowers, even the growing darkness, breathed the exhaustion of protracted waiting. Caroline felt that she ought to go; that it was wrong to stay; that the hour and the place were as treacherous as her own reflections. She rose and began to pace the floor, stepping softly, as though in fear of awakening someone, her figure, in its thin drapery, diaphanously vague and white. Still unable to shake off the obsession of the intense stillness, she sat down at the piano and began to turn over the first act of the *Walküre,* the last of his rôles they had practised together; playing listlessly and absently at first, but with gradually increasing seriousness. Perhaps it was the still heat of the summer night, perhaps it was the heavy odours from the garden that came in through the open windows; but as she played there grew and grew the feeling that he was there, beside her, standing in his accustomed place. In the duett at the end of the first act she heard him clearly: *"Thou art the Spring for which I sighed in Winter's cold embraces."* Once as he sang it, he had put his arm about her, his one hand under her heart, while with the other he took her right from the keyboard, holding her as he always held *Sieglinde* when he drew her toward the window. She had been wonderfully the mistress of herself at the time; neither repellant nor acquiescent. She remembered that she had rather exulted, then, in her self-control—which he had seemed to take for granted, though there was perhaps the whisper of a question from the hand under her heart. *"Thou art the Spring for which I sighed in Winter's cold embraces."* Caroline lifted her hands quickly from the keyboard, and she bowed her head in them, sobbing.

The storm broke and the rain beat in, spattering her night-dress until she rose and lowered the windows. She dropped upon the couch and began fighting over again the battles of other days, while the ghosts of the slain rose as from a sowing of dragon's teeth. The shadows of things, always so scorned and flouted, bore down upon her merciless and triumphant. It was not enough; this happy, useful, well-ordered life was not enough. It did not satisfy, it was not even real. No, the other things, the shadows—they were the realities. Her father, poor Heinrich, even her mother, who had been able to sustain her poor romance and keep her little illusions amid the tasks of a scullion, were nearer happiness than she. Her sure foundation was but made ground, after all, and the people in Klingsor's garden were more fortunate, however barren the sands from which they conjured their paradise.

The lodge was still and silent; her fit of weeping over, Caroline made no sound, and within the room, as without in the garden, was the blackness of storm. Only now and then a flash of lightning showed a woman's slender figure rigid on the couch, her face buried in her hands.

Toward morning, when the occasional rumbling of thunder was heard no more and the beat of the rain drops upon the orchard leaves was steadier, she fell asleep and did not waken until the first red streaks of dawn shone through the twisted boughs of the apple trees. There was a moment between world and world, when, neither asleep nor awake, she felt her dream grow thin, melting away from her, felt the warmth under her heart growing cold. Something seemed to slip from the clinging hold of her arms, and she groaned protestingly through her parted lips, following it a little way with fluttering hands. Then her eyes opened wide and she sprang up and sat holding dizzily to the cushions of the couch, staring down at her bare, cold feet, at her labouring breast, rising and falling under her open night-dress.

The dream was gone, but the feverish reality of it still pervaded her and she held it as the vibrating string holds a tone. In the last hour the shadows had had their way with Caroline. They had shown her the nothingness of time and space, of system and discipline, of closed doors and broad waters. Shuddering, she thought of the Arabian fairy tale in which the Genii brought the princess of China to the sleeping prince of Damascus, and carried her through the air back to her palace at dawn. Caroline closed her eyes and dropped her elbows weakly upon her knees, her shoulders sinking together. The horror was that it had not come from without, but from within. The dream was no blind chance; it was the expression of something she had kept so close a prisoner that she had never seen it herself; it was the wail from the donjon deeps when the watch slept. Only as the outcome of such a night of sorcery could the thing have been loosed to straighten its limbs and measure itself with her; so heavy were the chains upon it, so many a fathom deep it was crushed down into darkness. The fact that d'Esquerré happened to be on the other side of the world meant nothing; had he been here, beside her, it could scarcely have hurt her self-respect so much. As it was, she was without even the extenuation of an outer impulse, and she could scarcely have despised herself more had she come to him here in the night three weeks ago and thrown herself down upon the stone slab at the door there.

Caroline rose unsteadily and crept guiltily from the lodge and along the path under the arbour, terrified lest the servants should be stirring, trembling with the chill air, while the wet shrubbery, brushing against her, drenched her night-dress until it clung about her limbs.

At breakfast her husband looked across the table at her with concern. "It seems to me that you are looking rather fagged, Caroline. It was a beastly night to sleep. Why don't you go up to the mountains until this hot weather is over? By the way, were you in earnest about letting the lodge stand?"

Caroline laughed quietly. "No, I find I was not very serious. I haven't sentiment enough to forego a summer-house. Will you tell Baker to come to-morrow to talk it over with me? If we are to have a house party, I should like to put him to work on it at once."

Noble gave her a glance, half humorous, half vexed. "Do you know I am rather disappointed?" he said. "I had almost hoped that, just for once, you know, you would be a little bit foolish."

"Not now that I've slept over it," replied Caroline, and they both rose from the table, laughing.

The Marriage of Phædra

The sequence of events was such that MacMaster did not make his pilgrimage to Hugh Treffinger's studio until three years after that painter's death. MacMaster was himself a painter, an American of the Gallicized type, who spent his winters in New York, his summers in Paris, and no inconsiderable amount of time on the broad waters between. He had often contemplated stopping in London on one of his return trips in the late autumn, but he had always deferred leaving Paris until the prick of necessity drove him home by the quickest and shortest route.

Treffinger was a comparatively young man at the time of his death, and there had seemed no occasion for haste until haste was of no avail. Then, possibly, though there had been some correspondence between them, MacMaster felt certain qualms about meeting in the flesh a man who in the flesh was so diversely reported. His intercourse with Treffinger's work had been so deep and satisfying, so apart from other appreciations, that he rather dreaded a critical juncture of any sort. He had always felt himself singularly inadept in personal relations, and in this case he had avoided the issue until it was no longer to be feared or hoped for. There still remained, however, Treffinger's great unfinished picture, the *Marriage of Phædra,* which had never left his studio, and of which MacMaster's friends had now and again brought report that it was the painter's most characteristic production.

The young man arrived in London in the evening, and the next morning went out to Kensington to find Treffinger's studio. It lay in one of the perplexing by-streets off Holland Road, and the number he found on a door set in a high garden wall, the top of which was covered with broken green glass and over which a budding lilac-bush nodded. Treffinger's plate was still there, and a card requesting visitors to ring for the attendant. In response to MacMaster's ring, the door was opened by a cleanly built little man, clad in a shooting jacket and trousers that had been made for an ampler figure. He had a fresh complexion, eyes of that common uncertain shade of grey, and was closely shaven except for the incipient mutton-chops on his ruddy cheeks. He bore himself in a manner strikingly capable, and there was a sort of trimness and alertness about him, despite the too-generous shoulders of his coat. In one hand he held a bulldog pipe, and in the other a copy of *Sporting Life*. While MacMaster was explaining the purpose of his call, he noticed that the man surveyed him critically, though not impertinently. He was admitted into a little tank of a lodge made of white-washed stone, the back door and windows opening upon a garden. A visitor's book and a pile of catalogues lay on a deal table, together with a bottle of ink and some rusty pens. The wall was ornamented with photographs and coloured prints of racing favourites.

"The studio is h'only open to the public on Saturdays and Sundays," explained the man—he referred to himself as "Jymes"—"but of course we make exceptions in the case of pynters. Lydy Elling Treffinger 'erself is on the Continent, but Sir 'Ugh's orders was that pynters was to 'ave the run of the place." He selected a key from his pocket and threw open the door into the studio which, like the lodge, was built against the wall of the garden.

MacMaster entered a long, narrow room, built of smoothed planks, painted a light green; cold and damp even on that fine May morning. The room was utterly bare of furniture—unless a step-ladder, a model throne, and a rack laden with large leather portfolios could be accounted such—and was windowless, without other openings than the door and the skylight, under which hung the unfinished picture itself. MacMaster had never seen so many of Treffinger's paintings together. He knew the painter had married a woman with money and had been able to keep such of his pictures as he wished. These, with all of his replicas and studies, he had left as a sort of common legacy to the younger men of the school he had originated.

As soon as he was left alone, MacMaster sat down on the edge of the model throne before the unfinished picture. Here indeed was what he had come for; it rather paralysed his receptivity for the moment, but gradually the thing found its way to him.

At one o'clock he was standing before the collection of studies done for *Boccaccio's Garden* when he heard a voice at his elbow.

"Pardon, sir, but I was just about to lock up and go to lunch. Are you lookin' for the figure study of Boccaccio 'imself?" James queried respectfully, "Lydy Elling Treffinger give it to Mr. Rossiter to take down to Oxford for some lectures he's been a-giving there."

"Did he never paint out his studies, then?" asked MacMaster with perplexity. "Here are two completed ones for this picture. Why did he keep them?"

"I don't know as I could say as to that, sir," replied James, smiling indulgently, "but that was 'is way. That is to say, 'e pynted out very frequent, but 'e always made two studies to stand; one in water colours and one in oils, before 'e went at the final picture,—to say nothink of all the pose studies 'e made in pencil before he begun on the composition proper at all. He was that particular. You see 'e wasn't so keen for the final effect as for the proper pyntin' of 'is pictures. 'E used to say they ought to be well made, the same as any other h'article of trade. I can lay my 'and on the pose studies for you, sir." He rummaged in one of the portfolios and produced half a dozen drawings. "These three," he continued, "was discarded: these two was the pose he finally accepted; this one without alteration, as it were.

"That's in Paris, as I remember," James continued reflectively. "It went with the *Saint Cecilia* into the Baron H——'s collection. Could you tell me, sir, 'as 'e it still? I don't like to lose account of them, but some 'as changed 'ands since Sir 'Ugh's death."

"H——'s collection is still intact, I believe," replied MacMaster. "You were with Treffinger long?"

"From my boyhood, sir," replied James with gravity. "I was a stable boy when 'e took me."

"You were his man, then?"

"That's it, sir. Nobody else ever done anything around the studio. I always mixed 'is colours and 'e taught me to do a share of the varnishin'; 'e said as 'ow there wasn't a 'ouse in England as could do it proper. You aynt looked at the *Marriage* yet, sir?" he asked abruptly, glancing doubtfully at MacMaster, and indicating with his thumb the picture under the north light.

"Not very closely. I prefer to begin with something simpler; that's rather appalling, at first glance," replied MacMaster.

"Well may you say that, sir," said James warmly. "That one regular killed Sir 'Ugh; it regular broke 'im up, and nothink will ever convince me as 'ow it didn't bring on 'is second stroke."

When MacMaster walked back to High Street to take his bus, his mind was divided between two exultant convictions. He felt that he had not only found Treffinger's greatest picture, but that, in James, he had discovered a kind of cryptic index to the painter's personality—a clue which, if tactfully followed, might lead to much.

Several days after his first visit to the studio, MacMaster wrote to Lady Mary Percy, telling her that he would be in London for some time and asking her if he might call. Lady Mary was an only sister of Lady Ellen Treffinger, the painter's widow, and MacMaster had known her during one winter he spent at Nice. He had known her, indeed, very well, and Lady Mary, who was astonishingly frank and communicative upon all subjects, had been no less so upon the matter of her sister's unfortunate marriage.

In her reply to his note, Lady Mary named an afternoon when she would be alone. She was as good as her word, and when MacMaster arrived he found the drawing-room empty. Lady Mary entered shortly after he was announced. She was a tall woman, thin and stiffly jointed; and her body stood out under the folds of her gown with the rigour of cast-iron. This rather metallic suggestion was further carried out in her heavily knuckled hands, her stiff grey hair and long, bold-featured face, which was saved from freakishness only by her alert eyes.

"Really," said Lady Mary, taking a seat beside him and giving him a sort of military inspection through her nose-glasses, "Really, I had begun to fear that I had lost you altogether. It's four years since I saw you at Nice, isn't it? I was in Paris last winter, but I heard nothing from you."

"I was in New York then."

"It occurred to me that you might be. And why are you in London?"

"Can you ask?" replied MacMaster gallantly.

Lady Mary smiled ironically. "But for what else, incidentally?"

"Well, incidentally, I came to see Treffinger's studio and his unfinished picture. Since I've been here, I've decided to stay the summer. I'm even thinking of attempting to do a biography of him."

"So that is what brought you to London?"

"Not exactly. I had really no intention of anything so serious when I came. It's his last picture, I fancy, that has rather thrust it upon me. The notion has settled down on me like a thing destined."

"You'll not be offended if I question the clemency of such a destiny," remarked Lady Mary dryly. "Isn't there rather a surplus of books on that subject already?"

"Such as they are. Oh, I've read them all," here MacMaster faced Lady Mary triumphantly. "He has quite escaped your amiable critics," he added, smiling.

"I know well enough what you think, and I dare say we are not much on art," said Lady Mary with tolerant good humour. "We leave that to peoples who have no physique. Treffinger made a stir for a time, but it seems that we are not capable of a sustained appreciation of such extraordinary methods. In the end we go back to the pictures we find agreeable and unperplexing. He was regarded as an experiment, I fancy; and now it seems that he was rather an unsuccessful one. If you've come to us in a missionary spirit, we'll tolerate you politely, but we'll laugh in our sleeve, I warn you."

"That really doesn't daunt me, Lady Mary," declared MacMaster blandly. "As I told you, I'm a man with a mission."

Lady Mary laughed her hoarse baritone laugh. "Bravo! and you've come to me for inspiration for your panegyric?"

MacMaster smiled with some embarrassment. "Not altogether for that purpose. But I want to consult you, Lady Mary, about the advisability of troubling Lady Ellen Treffinger in the matter. It seems scarcely legitimate to go on without asking her to give some sort of grace to my proceedings, yet I feared the whole subject might be painful to her. I shall rely wholly upon your discretion."

"I think she would prefer to be consulted," replied Lady Mary judicially. "I can't understand how she endures to have the wretched affair continually raked up, but she does. She seems to feel a sort of moral responsibility. Ellen has always been singularly conscientious about this matter, in so far as her light goes,—which rather puzzles me, as hers is not exactly a magnanimous nature. She is certainly trying to do what she believes to be the right thing. I shall write to her, and you can see her when she returns from Italy."

"I want very much to meet her. She is, I hope, quite recovered in every way," queried MacMaster, hesitatingly.

"No, I can't say that she is. She has remained in much the same condition she sank to before his death. He trampled over pretty much whatever there was in her, I fancy. Women don't recover from wounds of that sort; at least, not women of Ellen's grain. They go on bleeding inwardly."

"You, at any rate have not grown more reconciled," MacMaster ventured.

"Oh, I give him his dues. He was a colourist, I grant you; but that is a vague and unsatisfactory quality to marry to; Lady Ellen Treffinger found it so."

"But, my dear Lady Mary," expostulated MacMaster, "and just repress me if I'm becoming too personal—but it must, in the first place, have been a marriage of choice on her part as well as on his."

Lady Mary poised her glasses on her large forefinger and assumed an attitude suggestive of the clinical lecture room as she replied. "Ellen, my dear boy, is an essentially romantic person. She is quiet about it, but she runs deep. I never knew how deep until I came against her on the issue of that marriage. She was always discontented as a girl; she found things dull and prosaic, and the ardour of his courtship was agreeable to her. He met her during her first season in town. She is handsome, and there were plenty of other men, but I grant you your scowling brigand was the most picturesque of the lot. In his courtship, as in everything else, he was theatrical to the point of being ridiculous, but Ellen's sense of humour is not her strongest quality. He had the charm of celebrity, the air of a man who could storm his way through anything to get what he wanted. That sort of vehemence is particularly effective with women like Ellen, who can be warmed only by reflected heat, and she couldn't at all stand out against it. He convinced her of his necessity; and that done, all's done."

"I can't help thinking that, even on such a basis, the marriage should have turned out better," MacMaster remarked reflectively.

"The marriage," Lady Mary continued with a shrug, "was made on the basis of a mutual misunderstanding. Ellen, in the nature of the case, believed that she was doing something quite out of the ordinary in accepting him, and expected concessions which, apparently, it never occurred to him to make. After his marriage he relapsed into his old habits of incessant work, broken by violent and often brutal relaxations. He insulted her friends and foisted his own upon her—many of them well calculated to arouse aversion in any well-bred girl. He had Ghillini constantly at the house—a homeless vagabond, whose conversation was impossible. I don't say, mind you, that he had not grievances on his side. He had probably over-rated the girl's possibilities, and he let her see that he was disappointed in her. Only a large and generous nature could have borne with him, and Ellen's is not that. She could not at all understand that odious strain of plebeian pride which plumes itself upon not having risen above its sources."

As MacMaster drove back to his hotel, he reflected that Lady Mary Percy had probably had good cause for dissatisfaction with her brother-in-law. Treffinger was, indeed, the last man who should have married into the Percy family. The son of a small tobacconist, he had grown up a sign painter's apprentice; idle, lawless, and practically letterless until he had drifted into the night classes of the Albert League, where Ghillini sometimes lectured. From the moment he came under the eye and influence of that erratic Italian, then a political exile, his life had swerved sharply from its old channel. This man had been at once incentive and guide, friend and master, to his pupil. He had taken the raw clay out of the London streets and moulded it anew. Seemingly he had divined at once where the boy's possibilities lay, and had thrown aside every canon of orthodox instruction in the training of him. Under him Treffinger acquired his superficial, yet facile, knowledge of the classics; had steeped himself in the monkish Latin and mediæval romances which later gave his work so naive and remote a quality. That was the beginning of the wattle fences, the cobble pave, the brown roof beams, the cunningly wrought fabrics that gave to his pictures such a richness of decorative effect.

As he had told Lady Mary Percy, MacMaster had found the imperative inspiration of his purpose in Treffinger's unfinished picture, the *Marriage of Phædra*. He had always believed that the key to Treffinger's individuality lay in his singular education; in the *Roman de la Rose,* in Boccaccio, and Amadis, those works which had literally transcribed themselves upon the blank soul of the London street boy, and through which he had been born into the world of spiritual things. Treffinger had been a man who lived after his imagination; and his mind, his ideals and, as MacMaster believed, even his personal ethics, had to the last been coloured by the trend of his early training. There was in him alike the freshness and spontaneity, the frank brutality and the religious mysticism which lay well back of the fifteenth century. In the *Marriage of Phædra* MacMaster found the ultimate expression of this spirit, the final word as to Treffinger's point of view.

As in all Treffinger's classical subjects, the conception was wholly mediæval. This Phædra, just turning from her husband and maidens to greet her husband's son, giving him her first fearsome glance from under her half lifted veil, was no daughter of Minos. The daughter of *heathenesse* and the early church she was; doomed to torturing visions and scourgings, and the wrangling of soul and flesh. The venerable Theseus might have been victorious Charlemagne, and Phædra's maidens belonged rather in the train of Blanche of Castile than at the Cretan court. In the earlier studies Hippolytus had been done with a more pagan suggestion, but in each successive drawing the glorious figure had been deflowered of something of its serene unconsciousness; until, in the canvas under the skylight, he appeared a very Christian knight. This male figure, and the face of Phædra, painted with such magical preservation of tone under the heavy shadow of the veil, were plainly Treffinger's highest achievements of craftsmanship. By what labour he had reached the seemingly inevitable composition of the picture—with its twenty figures, its plenitude of light and air, its restful distances seen through white porticoes—countless studies bore witness.

From James's attitude toward the picture, MacMaster could well conjecture what the painter's had been. This picture was always uppermost in James's mind; its custodianship formed, in his eyes, his occupation. He was manifestly apprehensive when visitors—not many came now-a-days—lingered near it. "It was the *Marriage* as killed 'im," he would often say, "and for the matter 'o that, it did like to 'ave been the death of all of us."

By the end of his second week in London, MacMaster had begun the notes for his study of Hugh Treffinger and his work. When his researches led him occasionally to visit the studios of Treffinger's friends and erstwhile disciples, he found their Treffinger manner fading as the ring of Treffinger's personality died out in them. One by one they were stealing back into the fold of national British art; the hand that had wound them up was still. MacMaster despaired of them and confined himself more and more exclusively to the studio, to such of Treffinger's letters as were available—they were for the most part singularly negative and colourless—and to his interrogation of Treffinger's man.

He could not himself have traced the successive steps by which he was gradually admitted into James's confidence. Certainly most of his adroit strategies to that end failed humiliatingly, and whatever it was that built up an understanding between them, must have been instinctive and intuitive on both sides. When at last James became anecdotal, personal, there was that in every word he let fall which put breath and blood into MacMaster's book. James had so long been steeped in that penetrating personality that he fairly exuded it. Many of his phrases, mannerisms and opinions were impressions that he had taken on like wet plaster in his daily contact with Treffinger. Inwardly he was lined with cast off epithelia, as outwardly he was clad in the painter's discarded coats. If the painter's letters were formal and perfunctory, if his expressions to his friends had been extravagant, contradictory and often apparently insincere—still, MacMaster felt himself not entirely without authentic sources. It was James who possessed Treffinger's legend; it was with James that he had laid aside his pose. Only in his studio, alone, and face to face with his work, as it seemed, had the man invariably been himself. James had known him in the one attitude in which he was entirely honest; their relation had fallen well within the painter's only indubitable integrity. James's report of Treffinger was distorted by no hallucination of artistic insight, coloured by no interpretation of his own. He merely held what he had heard and seen; his mind was a sort of camera obscura. His very limitations made him the more literal and minutely accurate.

One morning when MacMaster was seated before the *Marriage of Phædra,* James entered on his usual round of dusting.

"I've 'eard from Lydy Elling by the post, sir," he remarked, "an' she's give h'orders to 'ave the 'ouse put in readiness. I doubt she'll be 'ere by Thursday or Friday next."

"She spends most of her time abroad?" queried MacMaster; on the subject of Lady Treffinger James consistently maintained a very delicate reserve.

"Well, you could 'ardly say she does that, sir. She finds the 'ouse a bit dull, I daresay, so durin' the season she stops mostly with Lydy Mary Percy, at Grosvenor Square. Lydy Mary's a h'only sister." After a few moments he continued, speaking in jerks governed by the rigour of his dusting: "Honly this morning I come upon this scarf-pin," exhibiting a very striking instance of that article, "an' I recalled as 'ow Sir 'Ugh give it me when 'e was a-courting of Lydy Elling. Blowed if I ever see a man go in for a 'oman like 'im! 'E was that gone, sir. 'E never went in on anythink so 'ard before nor since, till 'e went in on the *Marriage* there—though 'e mostly went in on things pretty keen, 'ad the measles when 'e was thirty, strong as cholera, an' come close to dyin' of 'em. 'E wasn't strong for Lydy Elling's set; they was a bit too stiff for 'im. A free an' easy gentleman, 'e was; 'e liked 'is dinner with a few friends an' them jolly, but 'e wasn't much on what you might call big affairs. But once 'e went in for Lydy Elling, 'e broke 'imself to new paces. He give away 'is rings an' pins, an' the tylor's man an' the 'abberdasher's man was at 'is rooms continual. 'E got 'imself put up for a club in Piccadilly; 'e starved 'imself thin, an worrited 'imself white, an' ironed 'imself out, an' drawed 'imself tight as a bow string. It was a good job 'e come a winner, or I don't know w'at'd 'a been to pay."

The next week, in consequence of an invitation from Lady Ellen Treffinger, MacMaster went one afternoon to take tea with her. He was shown into the garden that lay between the residence and the studio, where the tea-table was set under a gnarled pear tree. Lady Ellen rose as he approached—he was astonished to note how tall she was—and greeted him graciously, saying that she already knew him through her sister. MacMaster felt a certain satisfaction in her; in her reassuring poise and repose, in the charming modulations of her voice and the indolent reserve of her full, almond eyes. He was even delighted to find her face so inscrutable, though it chilled his own warmth and made the open frankness he had wished to permit himself impossible. It was a long face, narrow at the chin, very delicately featured, yet steeled by an impassive mask of self-control. It was behind just such finely cut, close-sealed faces, MacMaster reflected, that nature sometimes hid astonishing secrets. But in spite of this suggestion of hardness, he felt that the unerring taste that Treffinger had always shown in larger matters had not deserted him when he came to the choosing of a wife, and he admitted that he could not himself have selected a woman who looked more as Treffinger's wife should look.

While he was explaining the purpose of his frequent visits to the studio, she heard him with courteous interest. "I have read, I think, everything that has been published on Sir Hugh Treffinger's work, and it seems to me that there is much left to be said," he concluded.

"I believe they are rather inadequate," she remarked vaguely. She hesitated a moment, absently fingering the ribbons of her gown, then continued, without raising her eyes; "I hope you will not think me too exacting if I ask to see the proofs of such chapters of your work as have to do with Sir Hugh's personal life. I have always asked that privilege."

MacMaster hastily assured her as to this, adding, "I mean to touch on only such facts in his personal life as have to do directly with his work—such as his monkish education under Ghillini."

"I see your meaning, I think," said Lady Ellen, looking at him with wide, uncomprehending eyes.

When MacMaster stopped at the studio on leaving the house, he stood for some time before Treffinger's one portrait of himself; that brigand of a picture, with its full throat and square head; the short upper lip blackened by the close-clipped moustache, the wiry hair tossed down over the forehead, the strong white teeth set hard on a short pipe stem. He could well understand what manifold tortures the mere grain of the man's strong red and brown flesh might have inflicted upon a woman like Lady Ellen. He could conjecture, too, Treffinger's impotent revolt against that very repose which had so dazzled him when it first defied his daring; and how once possessed of it, his first instinct had been to crush it, since he could not melt it.

Toward the close of the season, Lady Ellen Treffinger left town. MacMaster's work was progressing rapidly, and he and James wore away the days in their peculiar relation, which by this time had much of friendliness. Excepting for the regular visits of a Jewish picture dealer, there were few intrusions upon their solitude. Occasionally, a party of Americans rang at the little door in the garden wall, but usually they departed speedily for the Moorish hall and tinkling fountain of the great show studio of London, not far away.

This Jew, an Austrian by birth, who had a large business in Melbourne, Australia, was a man of considerable discrimination, and at once selected the *Marriage of Phædra* as the object of his especial interest. When, upon his first visit, Lichtenstein had declared the picture one of the things done for time, MacMaster had rather warmed toward him and had talked to him very freely. Later, however, the man's repulsive personality and innate vulgarity so wore upon him that, the more genuine the Jew's appreciation, the more he resented it and the more base he somehow felt it to be. It annoyed him to see Lichtenstein walking up and down before the picture, shaking his head and blinking his watery eyes over his nose-glasses, ejaculating: "Dot is a chem, a chem! It is wordt to gome den dousant miles for such a bainting, eh? To make Eurobe abbreciate such a work of ardt it is necessary to take it away while she is napping. She has never abbreciated until she has lost, but," knowingly, "she will buy back."

James had, from the first, felt such a distrust of the man that he would never leave him alone in the studio for a moment. When Lichtenstein insisted upon having Lady Ellen Treffinger's address, James rose to the point of insolence. "It ay'nt no use to give it, noway. Lydy Treffinger never had nothink to do with dealers." MacMaster quietly repented his rash confidences, fearing that he might indirectly cause Lady Ellen annoyance from this merciless speculator, and he recalled with chagrin that Lichtenstein had extorted from him, little by little, pretty much the entire plan of his book, and especially the place in it which the *Marriage of Phædra* was to occupy.

By this time the first chapters of MacMaster's book were in the hands of his publisher, and his visits to the studio were necessarily less frequent. The greater part of his time was now employed with the engravers who were to reproduce such of Treffinger's pictures as he intended to use as illustrations.

He returned to his hotel late one evening after a long and vexing day at the engravers, to find James in his room, seated on his steamer trunk by the window, with the outline of a great square draped in sheets resting against his knee.

"Why, James, what's up?" he cried in astonishment, glancing enquiringly at the sheeted object.

"Aynt you seen the pypers, sir?" jerked out the man.

"No, now I think of it, I haven't even looked at a paper. I've been at the engravers' plant all day. I haven't seen anything."

James drew a copy of the *Times* from his pocket and handed it to him, pointing with a tragic finger to a paragraph in the social column. It was merely the announcement of Lady Ellen Treffinger's engagement to Captain Alexander Gresham.

"Well, what of it, my man? That surely is her privilege."

James took the paper, turned to another page, and silently pointed to a paragraph in the art notes which stated that Lady Treffinger had presented to the X— gallery the entire collection of paintings and sketches now in her late husband's studio, with the exception of his unfinished picture, the *Marriage of Phædra,* which she had sold for a large sum to an Australian dealer who had come to London purposely to secure some of Treffinger's paintings.

MacMaster pursed up his lips and sat down, his overcoat still on. "Well, James, this is something of a—something of a jolt, eh? It never occurred to me she'd really do it."

"Lord, you don't know 'er, sir," said James bitterly, still staring at the floor in an attitude of abandoned dejection.

MacMaster started up in a flash of enlightenment, "What on earth have you got there, James? It's not—surely it's not—"

"Yes, it is, sir," broke in the man excitedly. "It's the *Marriage* itself. It aynt a-going to H'australia, no'ow!"

"But man, what are you going to do with it? It's Lichtenstein's property now, as it seems."

"It aynt, sir, that it aynt. No, by Gawd it aynt!" shouted James, breaking into a choking fury. He controlled himself with an effort and added supplicatingly: "Oh, sir, you aynt a-going to see it go to H'australia, w'ere they send convic's?" He unpinned and flung aside the sheets as though to let *Phædra* plead for herself.

MacMaster sat down again and looked sadly at the doomed masterpiece. The notion of James having carried it across London that night rather appealed to his fancy. There was certainly a flavour about such a high-handed proceeding. "However did you get it here?' he queried.

"I got a four-wheeler and come over direct, sir. Good job I 'appened to 'ave the chaynge about me."

"You came up High Street, up Piccadilly, through the Haymarket and Trafalgar Square, and into the Strand?" queried MacMaster with a relish.

"Yes, sir. Of course, sir," assented James with surprise.

MacMaster laughed delightedly. "It was a beautiful idea, James, but I'm afraid we can't carry it any further."

"I was thinkin' as 'ow it would be a rare chance to get you to take the *Marriage* over to Paris for a year or two, sir, until the thing blows over?" suggested James blandly.

"I'm afraid that's out of the question, James. I haven't the right stuff in me for a pirate, or even a vulgar smuggler, I'm afraid." MacMaster found it surprisingly difficult to say this, and he busied himself with the lamp as he said it. He heard James's hand fall heavily on the trunk top, and he discovered that he very much disliked sinking in the man's estimation.

"Well, sir," remarked James in a more formal tone, after a protracted silence; "then there's nothink for it but as 'ow I'll 'ave to make way with it myself."

"And how about your character, James? The evidence would be heavy against you, and even if Lady Treffinger didn't prosecute, you'd be done for."

"Blow my character!—your pardon, sir," cried James, starting to his feet. "W'at do I want of a character? I'll chuck the 'ole thing, and damned lively, too. The shop's to be sold out, an' my place is gone any'ow. I'm a-going to enlist, or try the gold-fields. I've lived too long with h'artists; I'd never give satisfaction in livery now. You know 'ow it is yourself, sir; there aynt no life like it, no'ow."

For a moment MacMaster was almost equal to abetting James in his theft. He reflected that pictures had been white-washed, or hidden in the crypts of churches, or under the floors of palaces from meaner motives, and to save them from a fate less ignominious. But presently, with a sigh, he shook his head.

"No, James, it won't do at all. It has been tried over and over again, ever since the world has been a-going and pictures a-making. It was tried in Florence and in Venice, but the pictures were always carried away in the end. You see the difficulty is that, although Treffinger told you what was not to be done with the picture, he did not say definitely what was to be done with it. Do you think Lady Treffinger really understands that he did not want it to be sold?"

"Well, sir, it was like this, sir," said James resuming his seat on the trunk and again resting the picture against his knee. "My memory is as clear as glass about it. After Sir 'Ugh got up from 'is first stroke, 'e took a fresh start at the *Marriage*. Before that 'e 'ad been working at it only at night for awhile back; the *Legend* was the big picture then, an' was under the north light w'ere 'e worked of a morning. But one day 'e bid me take the *Legend* down an' put the *Marriage* in its place, an' 'e says, dashin' on 'is jacket, 'Jymes, this is a start for the finish, this time.'

"From that on 'e worked at the night picture in the mornin'——a thing contrary to 'is custom. The *Marriage* went wrong, and wrong—— an' Sir 'Ugh a-gettin' seedier an' seedier every day. 'E tried models an' models, an' smudged an' pynted out on account of 'er face goin' wrong in the shadow. Sometimes 'e layed it on the colours, an' swore at me an' things general. He got that discouraged about 'imself that on 'is low days 'e used to say to me: 'Jymes, remember one thing; if anythink 'appens to me, the *Marriage* is not to go out of 'ere unfinished. It's worth the lot of 'em, my boy, an' it's not a-going to go shabby for lack of pains.' 'E said things to that effect repeated.

"He was workin' at the picture the last day, before 'e went to 'is club. 'E kept the carriage waitin' near an hour while 'e put on a stroke an' then drawed back to look at it, an' then put on another, careful like. After 'e 'ad 'is gloves on, 'e come back an' took away the brushes I was startin' to clean, an' put in another touch or two. 'It's a-comin' Jymes,' 'e says, 'by gad if it aynt.' An' with that 'e goes out. It was cruel sudden, w'at come after.

"That night I was lookin' to 'is clothes at the 'ouse when they brought 'im 'ome. He was conscious, but w'en I ran down-stairs for to 'elp lift 'im up, I knowed 'e was a finished man. After we got 'im into bed, 'e kept looking restless at me and then at Lydy Elling and a-jerkin' of 'is 'and. Finally 'e quite raised it an' shot 'is thumb out towards the wall. 'He wants water; ring Jymes,' says Lydy Elling, placid. But I knowed 'e was pointin' to the shop.

" 'Lydy Treffinger,' says I, bold, 'he's pointin' to the studio. He means about the *Marriage;* 'e told me to-day as 'ow 'e never wanted it sold unfinished. Is that it, Sir 'Ugh?'

"He smiled an' nodded slight an' closed 'is eyes. 'Thank you, Jymes,' says Lydy Elling, placid. Then 'e opened 'is eyes an' looked long and 'ard at Lydy Elling.

" 'Of course I'll try to do as you'd wish about the pictures, 'Ugh, if that's w'at's troublin' you,' she says quiet. With that 'e closed 'is eyes and 'e never opened 'em. He died unconscious at four that mornin'.

"You see, sir, Lydy Elling was always cruel 'ard on the *Marriage*. From the first it went wrong, an' Sir 'Ugh was out of temper pretty constant. She came into the studio one day and looked at the picture an' asked 'im why 'e didn't throw it up an' quit a-worritin' 'imself. He answered sharp, an' with that she said as 'ow she didn't see w'at there was to make such a row about, no'ow. She spoke 'er mind about that picture, free; an' Sir 'Ugh swore 'ot an' let a 'andful of brushes fly at 'is study, an' Lydy Elling picked up 'er skirts careful an' chill, an' drifted out of the studio with 'er eyes calm and 'er chin 'igh. If there was one thing Lydy Elling 'ad no comprehension of, it was the usefulness of swearin'. So the *Marriage* was a sore thing between 'em. She is uncommon calm, but uncommon bitter, is Lydy Elling. She's never come a-near the studio since that day she went out 'oldin' up of 'er skirts. W'en 'er friends goes over she excuses 'erself along o' the strain. Strain—Gawd!" James ground his wrath short in his teeth.

"I'll tell you what I'll do, James, and it's our only hope. I'll see Lady Ellen to-morrow. The *Times* says she returned today. You take the picture back to its place, and I'll do what I can for it. If anything is done to save it, it must be done through Lady Ellen Treffinger herself; that much is clear. I can't think that she fully understands the situation. If she did, you know, she really couldn't have any motive——" He stopped suddenly. Somehow, in the dusky lamplight her small, close-sealed face came ominously back to him. He rubbed his forehead and knitted his brows thoughtfully. After a moment he shook his head and went on: "I am positive that nothing can be gained by high-handed methods, James. Captain Gresham is one of the most popular men in London, and his friends would tear up Treffinger's bones if he were annoyed by any scandal of our making— and this scheme you propose would inevitably result in scandal. Lady Ellen has, of course, every legal right to sell the picture. Treffinger made considerable inroads upon her estate, and, as she is about to marry a man without income, she doubtless feels that she has a right to replenish her patrimony."

He found James amenable, though doggedly sceptical. He went down into the street, called a carriage, and saw James and his burden into it. Standing in the doorway, he watched the carriage roll away through the drizzling mist, weave in and out among the wet, black vehicles and darting cab lights, until it was swallowed up in the glare and confusion of the Strand. "It is rather a fine touch of irony," he reflected, "that he, who is so out of it, should be the one to really care. Poor Treffinger," he murmured as, with a rather spiritless smile, he turned back into his hotel. "Poor Treffinger; *sic transit gloria.*"

The next afternoon MacMaster kept his promise. When he arrived at Lady Mary Percy's house he saw preparations for a function of some sort, but he went resolutely up the steps, telling the footman that his business was urgent. Lady Ellen came down alone, excusing her sister. She was dressed for receiving, and MacMaster had never seen her so beautiful. The colour in her cheeks sent a softening glow over her small delicately cut features.

MacMaster apologized for his intrusion and came unflinchingly to the object of his call. He had come, he said, not only to offer her his warmest congratulations, but to express his regret that a great work of art was to leave England.

Lady Treffinger looked at him in wide-eyed astonishment. Surely, she said, she had been careful to select the best of the pictures for the X— gallery, in accordance with Sir Hugh Treffinger's wishes.

"And did he—pardon me, Lady Treffinger, but in mercy set my mind at rest—did he or did he not express any definite wish concerning this one picture, which to me seems worth all the others, unfinished as it is?"

Lady Treffinger paled perceptibly, but it was not the pallor of confusion. When she spoke there was a sharp tremor in her smooth voice, the edge of a resentment that tore her like pain. "I think his man has some such impression, but I believe it to be utterly unfounded. I cannot find that he ever expressed any wish concerning the disposition of the picture to any of his friends. Unfortunately, Sir Hugh was not always discreet in his remarks to his servants."

"Captain Gresham, Lady Ellingham and Miss Ellingham," announced a servant, appearing at the door.

There was a murmur in the hall, and MacMaster greeted the smiling Captain and his aunt as he bowed himself out.

To all intents and purposes the *Marriage of Phædra* was already entombed in a vague continent in the Pacific, somewhere on the other side of the world.

Youth and the Bright Medusa

Coming, Aphrodite!

I

Don Hedger had lived for four years on the top floor of an old house on the south side of Washington Square, and nobody had ever disturbed him. He occupied one big room with no outside exposure except on the north, where he had built in a many-paned studio window that looked upon a court and upon the roofs and walls of other buildings. His room was very cheerless, since he never got a ray of direct sunlight; the south corners were always in shadow. In one of the corners was a clothes closet, built against the partition, in another a wide divan, serving as a seat by day and a bed by night. In the front corner, the one farther from the window, was a sink, and a table with two gas burners where he sometimes cooked his food. There, too, in the perpetual dusk, was the dog's bed, and often a bone or two for his comfort.

The dog was a Boston bull terrier, and Hedger explained his surly disposition by the fact that he had been bred to the point where it told on his nerves. His name was Caesar III, and he had taken prizes at very exclusive dog shows. When he and his master went out to prowl about University Place or to promenade along West Street, Caesar III was invariably fresh and shining. His pink skin showed through his mottled coat, which glistened as if it had just been rubbed with olive oil, and he wore a brass-studded collar, bought at the smartest saddler's. Hedger, as often as not, was hunched up in an old striped blanket coat, with a shapeless felt hat pulled over his bushy hair, wearing black shoes that had become grey, or brown ones that had become black, and he never put on gloves unless the day was biting cold.

Early in May, Hedger learned that he was to have a new neighbour in the rear apartment—two rooms, one large and one small, that faced the west. His studio was shut off from the larger of these rooms by double doors, which, though they were fairly tight, left him a good deal at the mercy of the occupant. The rooms had been leased, long before he came there, by a trained nurse who considered herself knowing in old furniture. She went to auction sales and bought up mahogany and dirty brass and stored it away here, where she meant to live when she retired from nursing. Meanwhile, she sub-let her rooms, with their precious furniture, to young people who came to New York to "write" or to "paint"—who proposed to live by the sweat of the brow rather than of the hand, and who desired artistic surroundings. When Hedger first moved in, these rooms were oc- cupied by a young man who tried to write plays,—and who kept on trying until a week ago, when the nurse had put him out for unpaid rent.

A few days after the playwright left, Hedger heard an ominous murmur of voices through the bolted double doors: the lady-like intonation of the nurse—doubtless exhibiting her treasures—and another voice, also a woman's, but very different; young, fresh, un- guarded, confident. All the same, it would be very annoying to have a woman in there. The only bath-room on the floor was at the top of the stairs in the front hall, and he would always be running into her as he came or went from his bath. He would have to be more careful to see that Caesar didn't leave bones about the hall, too; and she might object when he cooked steak and onions on his gas burner.

As soon as the talking ceased and the women left, he forgot them. He was absorbed in a study of paradise fish at the Aquarium, staring out at people through the glass and green water of their tank. It was a highly gratifying idea; the incommunicability of one stratum of animal life with another,—though Hedger pretended it was only an experiment in unusual lighting. When he heard trunks knocking against the sides of the narrow hall, then he realized that she was moving in at once. Toward noon, groans and deep gasps and the creaking of ropes, made him aware that a piano was arriving. After the tramp of the movers died away down the stairs, somebody touched off a few scales and chords on the instrument, and then there was peace. Presently he heard her lock her door and go down the hall humming something; going out to lunch, probably. He stuck his brushes in a can of turpentine and put on his hat, not stopping to wash his hands. Caesar was smelling along the crack under the bolted doors; his bony tail stuck out hard as a hickory withe, and the hair was standing up about his elegant collar.

Hedger encouraged him. "Come along, Caesar. You'll soon get used to a new smell."

In the hall stood an enormous trunk, behind the ladder that led to the roof, just opposite Hedger's door. The dog flew at it with a growl of hurt amazement. They went down three flights of stairs and out into the brilliant May afternoon.

Behind the Square, Hedger and his dog descended into a basement oyster house where there were no tablecloths on the tables and no handles on the coffee cups, and the floor was covered with sawdust, and Caesar was always welcome,—not that he needed any such precautionary flooring. All the carpets of Persia would have been safe for him. Hedger ordered steak and onions absentmindedly, not realizing why he had an apprehension that this dish might be less readily at hand hereafter. While he ate, Caesar sat beside his chair, gravely disturbing the sawdust with his tail.

After lunch Hedger strolled about the Square for the dog's health and watched the stages pull out;—that was almost the very last summer of the old horse stages on Fifth Avenue. The fountain had but lately begun operations for the season and was throwing up a mist of rainbow water which now and then blew south and sprayed a bunch of Italian babies that were being supported on the outer rim by older, very little older, brothers and sisters. Plump robins were hopping about on the soil; the grass was newly cut and blindingly green. Looking up the Avenue through the Arch, one could see the young poplars with their bright, sticky leaves, and the Brevoort glistening in its spring coat of paint, and shining horses and carriages,— occasionally an automobile, mis-shapen and sullen, like an ugly threat in a stream of things that were bright and beautiful and alive.

While Caesar and his master were standing by the fountain, a girl approached them, crossing the Square. Hedger noticed her because she wore a lavender cloth suit and carried in her arms a big bunch of fresh lilacs. He saw that she was young and handsome,—beautiful, in fact, with a splendid figure and good action. She, too, paused by the fountain and looked back through the Arch up the Avenue. She smiled rather patronizingly as she looked, and at the same time seemed delighted. Her slowly curving upper lip and half-closed eyes seemed to say: "You're gay, you're exciting, you are quite the right sort of thing; but you're none too fine for me!"

In the moment she tarried, Caesar stealthily approached her and sniffed at the hem of her lavender skirt, then, when she went south like an arrow, he ran back to his master and lifted a face full of emotion and alarm, his lower lip twitching under his sharp white teeth and his hazel eyes pointed with a very definite discovery. He stood thus, motionless, while Hedger watched the lavender girl go up the steps and through the door of the house in which he lived.

"You're right, my boy, it's she! She might be worse looking, you know."

When they mounted to the studio, the new lodger's door, at the back of the wall, was a little ajar, and Hedger caught the warm perfume of lilacs just brought in out of the sun. He was used to the musty smell of the old hall carpet. (The nurse-lessee had once knocked at this studio door and complained that Caesar must be somewhat responsible for the particular flavour of that mustiness, and Hedger had never spoken to her since.) He was used to the old smell, and he preferred it to that of the lilacs, and so did his companion, whose nose was so much more discriminating. Hedger shut his door vehemently, and fell to work.

Most young men who dwell in obscure studios in New York have had a beginning, come out of something, have somewhere a home town, a family, a paternal roof. But Don Hedger had no such background. He was a foundling, and had grown up in a school for homeless boys, where book-learning was a negligible part of the curriculum. When he was sixteen, a Catholic priest took him to Greensburg, Pennsylvania, to keep house for him. The priest did something to fill in the large gaps in the boy's education,—taught him to like "Don Quixote" and "The Golden Legend," and encouraged him to mess with paints and crayons in his room up under the slope of the mansard. When Don wanted to go to New York to study at the Art League, the priest got him a night job as packer in one of the big department stores. Since then, Hedger had taken care of himself; that was his only responsibility. He was singularly unencumbered; had no family duties, no social ties, no obligations toward any one but his landlord.

Since he travelled light, he had travelled rather far. He had got over a good deal of the earth's surface, in spite of the fact that he never in his life had more than three hundred dollars ahead at any one time, and he had already outlived a succession of convictions and revelations about his art.

Though he was not but twenty-six years old, he had twice been on the verge of becoming a marketable product; once through some studies of New York streets he did for a magazine, and once through a collection of pastels he brought home from New Mexico, which Remington, then at the height of his popularity, happened to see, and generously tried to push. But on both occasions Hedger decided that this was something he didn't wish to carry further,—simply the old thing over again and got nowhere—so he took enquiring dealers experiments in a "later manner," that made them put him out of the shop. When he ran short of money, he could always get any amount of commercial work; he was an expert draughtsman and worked with lightning speed. The rest of his time he spent in groping his way from one kind of painting into another, or travelling about without luggage, like a tramp, and he was chiefly occupied with getting rid of ideas he had once thought very fine.

Hedger's circumstances, since he had moved to Washington Square, were affluent compared to anything he had ever known before. He was now able to pay advance rent and turn the key on his studio when he went away for four months at a stretch. It didn't occur to him to wish to be richer than this. To be sure, he did without a great many things other people think necessary, but he didn't miss them, because he had never had them. He belonged to no clubs, visited no houses, had no studio friends, and he ate his dinner alone in some decent little restaurant, even on Christmas and New Year's. For days together he talked to nobody but his dog and the janitress and the lame oysterman.

After he shut the door and settled down to his paradise fish on that first Tuesday in May, Hedger forgot all about his new neighbour. When the light failed, he took Caesar out for a walk. On the way home he did his marketing on West Houston Street, with a one-eyed Italian woman who always cheated him. After he had cooked his beans and scallopini, and drunk half a bottle of Chianti, he put his dishes in the sink and went up on the roof to smoke. He was the only person in the house who ever went to the roof, and he had a secret understanding with the janitress about it. He was to have "the privilege of the roof," as she said, if he opened the heavy trapdoor on sunny days to air out the upper hall, and was watchful to close it when rain threatened. Mrs. Foley was fat and dirty and hated to climb stairs,—besides, the roof was reached by a perpendicular iron ladder, definitely inaccessible to a woman of her bulk, and the iron door at the top of it was too heavy for any but Hedger's strong arm to lift. Hedger was not above medium height, but he practised with weights and dumb-bells, and in the shoulders he was as strong as a gorilla.

So Hedger had the roof to himself. He and Caesar often slept up there on hot nights, rolled in blankets he had brought home from Arizona. He mounted with Caesar under his left arm. The dog had never learned to climb a perpendicular ladder, and never did he feel so much his master's greatness and his own dependence upon him, as when he crept under his arm for this perilous ascent. Up there was even gravel to scratch in, and a dog could do whatever he liked, so long as he did not bark. It was a kind of heaven, which no one was strong enough to reach but his great, paint-smelling master.

On this blue May night there was a slender, girlish looking young moon in the west, playing with a whole company of silver stars. Now and then one of them darted away from the group and shot off into the gauzy blue with a soft little trail of light, like laughter. Hedger and his dog were delighted when a star did this. They were quite lost in watching the glittering game, when they were suddenly diverted by a sound,—not from the stars, though it was music. It was not the Prologue to Pagliacci, which rose ever and anon on hot evenings from an Italian tenement on Thompson Street, with the gasps of the corpulent baritone who got behind it; nor was it the hurdy-gurdy man, who often played at the corner in the balmy twilight. No, this was a woman's voice, singing the tempestuous, over-lapping phrases of Signor Puccini, then comparatively new in the world, but already so popular that even Hedger recognized his unmistakable gusts of breath. He looked about over the roofs; all was blue and still, with the well-built chimneys that were never used now standing up dark and mournful. He moved softly toward the yellow quadrangle where the gas from the hall shone up through the half-lifted trapdoor. Oh yes! It came up through the hole like a strong draught, a big, beautiful voice, and it sounded rather like a professional's. A piano had arrived in the morning, Hedger remembered. This might be a very great nuisance. It would be pleasant enough to listen to, if you could turn it on and off as you wished; but you couldn't. Caesar, with the gas light shining on his collar and his ugly but sensitive face, panted and looked up for information. Hedger put down a reassuring hand.

"I don't know. We can't tell yet. It may not be so bad."

He stayed on the roof until all was still below, and finally descended, with quite a new feeling about his neighbour. Her voice, like her figure, inspired respect—if one did not choose to call it admiration. Her door was shut, the transom was dark; nothing remained of her but the obtrusive trunk, unrightfully taking up room in the narrow hall.

II

For two days Hedger didn't see her. He was painting eight hours a day just then, and only went out to hunt for food. He noticed that she practised scales and exercises for about an hour in the morning; then she locked her door, went humming down the hall, and left him in peace. He heard her getting her coffee ready at about the same time he got his. Earlier still, she passed his room on her way to her bath. In the evening she sometimes sang, but on the whole she didn't bother him. When he was working well he did not notice anything much. The morning paper lay before his door until he reached out for his milk bottle, then he kicked the sheet inside and it lay on the floor until evening. Sometimes he read it and sometimes he did not. He forgot there was anything of importance going on in the world outside of his third floor studio. Nobody had ever taught him that he ought to be interested in other people; in the Pittsburgh steel strike, in the Fresh Air Fund, in the scandal about the Babies' Hospital. A grey wolf, living in a Wyoming canyon, would hardly have been less concerned about these things than was Don Hedger.

One morning he was coming out of the bath-room at the front

end of the hall, having just given Caesar his bath and rubbed him into a glow with a heavy towel. Before the door, lying in wait for him, as it were, stood a tall figure in a flowing blue silk dressing gown that fell away from her marble arms. In her hands she carried various accessories of the bath.

"I wish," she said distinctly, standing in his way, "I wish you wouldn't wash your dog in the tub. I never heard of such a thing! I've found his hair in the tub, and I've smelled a doggy smell, and now I've caught you at it. It's an outrage!"

Hedger was badly frightened. She was so tall and positive, and was fairly blazing with beauty and anger. He stood blinking, holding on to his sponge and dog-soap, feeling that he ought to bow very low to her. But what he actually said was:

"Nobody has ever objected before. I always wash the tub,—and, anyhow, he's cleaner than most people."

"Cleaner than me?" her eyebrows went up, her white arms and neck and her fragrant person seemed to scream at him like a band of outraged nymphs. Something flashed through his mind about a man who was turned into a dog, or was pursued by dogs, because he unwittingly intruded upon the bath of beauty.

"No, I didn't mean that," he muttered, turning scarlet under the bluish stubble of his muscular jaws. "But I know he's cleaner than I am."

"That I don't doubt!" Her voice sounded like a soft shivering of crystal, and with a smile of pity she drew the folds of her voluminous blue robe close about her and allowed the wretched man to pass. Even Caesar was frightened; he darted like a streak down the hall, through the door and to his own bed in the corner among the bones.

Hedger stood still in the doorway, listening to indignant sniffs and coughs and a great swishing of water about the sides of the tub. He had washed it; but as he had washed it with Caesar's sponge, it was quite possible that a few bristles remained; the dog was shedding now. The playwright had never objected, nor had the jovial illustrator who occupied the front apartment,—but he, as he admitted, "was usually pye-eyed, when he wasn't in Buffalo." He went home to Buffalo sometimes to rest his nerves.

It had never occurred to Hedger that any one would mind using the tub after Caesar;—but then, he had never seen a beautiful girl caparisoned for the bath before. As soon as he beheld her standing there, he realized the unfitness of it. For that matter, she ought not to step into a tub that any other mortal had bathed in; the illustrator was sloppy and left cigarette ends on the moulding.

All morning as he worked he was gnawed by a spiteful desire to get back at her. It rankled that he had been so vanquished by her disdain. When he heard her locking her door to go out for lunch, he stepped quickly into the hall in his messy painting coat, and addressed her.

"I don't wish to be exigent, Miss,"—he had certain grand words that he used upon occasion—"but if this is your trunk, it's rather in the way here."

"Oh, very well!" she exclaimed carelessly, dropping her keys into her handbag. "I'll have it moved when I can get a man to do it," and she went down the hall with her free, roving stride.

Her name, Hedger discovered from her letters, which the postman left on the table in the lower hall, was Eden Bower.

III

In the closet that was built against the partition separating his room from Miss Bower's, Hedger kept all his wearing apparel, some of it on hooks and hangers, some of it on the floor. When he opened his closet door now-a-days, little dust-coloured insects flew out on downy wing, and he suspected that a brood of moths were hatching in his winter overcoat. Mrs. Foley, the janitress, told him to bring down all his heavy clothes and she would give them a beating and hang them in the court. The closet was in such disorder that he shunned the encounter, but one hot afternoon he set himself to the task. First he threw out a pile of forgotten laundry and tied it up in a sheet. The bundle stood as high as his middle when he had knotted the corners. Then he got his shoes and overshoes together. When he took his overcoat from its place against the partition, a long ray of yellow light shot across the dark enclosure,—a knot hole, evidently, in the high wainscoting of the west room. He had never noticed it before, and without realizing what he was doing, he stooped and squinted through it.

Yonder, in a pool of sunlight, stood his new neighbour, wholly unclad, doing exercises of some sort before a long gilt mirror. Hedger did not happen to think how unpardonable it was of him to watch her. Nudity was not improper to any one who had worked so much from the figure, and he continued to look, simply because he had never seen a woman's body so beautiful as this one,—positively glorious in action. As she swung her arms and changed from one pivot of motion to another, muscular energy seemed to flow through her from her toes to her finger-tips. The soft flush of exercise and the gold of afternoon sun played over her flesh together, enveloped her in a luminous mist which, as she turned and twisted, made now an arm, now a shoulder, now a thigh, dissolve in pure light and instantly recover its outline with the next gesture. Hedger's fingers curved as if he were holding a crayon; mentally he was doing the whole figure in a single running line, and the charcoal seemed to explode in his hand at the point where the energy of each gesture was discharged into the whirling disc of light, from a foot or shoulder, from the up-thrust chin or the lifted breasts.

He could not have told whether he watched her for six minutes or sixteen. When her gymnastics were over, she paused to catch up a lock of hair that had come down, and examined with solicitude a little reddish mole that grew under her left arm-pit. Then, with her hand on her hip, she walked unconcernedly across the room and disappeared through the door into her bedchamber.

Disappeared—Don Hedger was crouching on his knees, staring at the golden shower which poured in through the west windows, at the lake of gold sleeping on the faded Turkish carpet. The spot was enchanted; a vision out of Alexandria, out of the remote pagan past, had bathed itself there in Helianthine fire.

When he crawled out of his closet, he stood blinking at the grey sheet stuffed with laundry, not knowing what had happened to him. He felt a little sick as he contemplated the bundle. Everything here was different; he hated the disorder of the place, the grey prison light, his old shoes and himself and all his slovenly habits. The black calico curtains that ran on wires over his big window were white with dust. There were three greasy frying pans in the sink, and the sink itself—He felt desperate. He couldn't stand this another minute. He took up an armful of winter clothes and ran down four flights into the basement.

"Mrs. Foley," he began, "I want my room cleaned this afternoon, thoroughly cleaned. Can you get a woman for me right away?"

"Is it company you're having?" the fat, dirty janitress enquired. Mrs. Foley was the widow of a useful Tammany man, and she owned real estate in Flatbush. She was huge and soft as a feather bed. Her face and arms were permanently coated with dust, grained like wood where the sweat had trickled.

"Yes, company. That's it."

"Well, this is a queer time of the day to be asking for a cleaning woman. It's likely I can get you old Lizzie, if she's not too drunk. I'll send Willy round to see."

Willy, the son of fourteen, roused from the stupor and stain of his fifth box of cigarettes by the gleam of a quarter, went out. In five minutes he returned with old Lizzie—she smelling strong of spirits and wearing several jackets which she had put on one over the other, and a number of skirts, long and short, which made her resemble an animated dish-clout. She had, of course, to borrow her equipment from Mrs. Foley, and toiled up the long flights, dragging mop and pail and broom. She told Hedger to be of good cheer, for he had got the right woman for the job, and showed him a great leather strap she wore about her wrist to prevent dislocation of tendons. She swished about the place, scattering dust and splashing soapsuds, while he watched her in nervous despair. He stood over Lizzie and made her scour the sink, directing her roughly, then paid her and got rid of her. Shutting the door on his failure, he hurried off with his dog to lose himself among the stevedores and dock labourers on West Street.

A strange chapter began for Don Hedger. Day after day, at that hour in the afternoon, the hour before his neighbour dressed for dinner, he crouched down in his closet to watch her go through her mysterious exercises. It did not occur to him that his conduct was detestable; there was nothing shy or retreating about this unclad girl,—a bold body, studying itself quite coolly and evidently well pleased with itself, doing all this for a purpose. Hedger scarcely regarded his action as conduct at all; it was something that had happened to him. More than once he went out and tried to stay away for the whole afternoon, but at about five o'clock he was sure to find himself among his old shoes in the dark. The pull of that aperture was stronger than his will,—and he had always considered his will the strongest thing about him. When she threw herself upon the divan and lay resting, he still stared, holding his breath. His nerves were so on edge that a sudden noise made him start and brought out the sweat on his forehead. The dog would come and tug at his sleeve, knowing that something was wrong with his master. If he attempted a mournful whine, those strong hands closed about his throat.

When Hedger came slinking out of his closet, he sat down on the edge of the couch, sat for hours without moving. He was not painting at all now. This thing, whatever it was, drank him up as ideas had sometimes done, and he sank into a stupor of idleness as deep and dark as the stupor of work. He could not understand it; he was no boy, he had worked from models for years, and a woman's body was no mystery to him. Yet now he did nothing but sit and think about one. He slept very little, and with the first light of morning he awoke as completely possessed by this woman as if he had been with her all the night before. The unconscious operations of life went on in him only to perpetuate this excitement. His brain held but one image now—vibrated, burned with it. It was a heathenish feeling; without friendliness, almost without tenderness.

Women had come and gone in Hedger's life. Not having had a mother to begin with, his relations with them, whether amorous or friendly, had been casual. He got on well with janitresses and wash-women, with Indians and with the peasant women of foreign countries. He had friends among the silk-skirt factory girls who came to eat their lunch in Washington Square, and he sometimes took a model for a day in the country. He felt an unreasoning antipathy toward the well-dressed women he saw coming out of big shops, or driving in the Park. If, on his way to the Art Museum, he noticed a pretty girl standing on the steps of one of the houses on upper Fifth Avenue, he frowned at her and went by with his shoulders hunched up as if he were cold. He had never known such girls, or heard them talk, or seen the inside of the houses in which they lived; but he believed them all to be artificial and, in an aesthetic sense, perverted. He saw them enslaved by desire of merchandise and manufactured articles, effective only in making life complicated and insincere and in embroidering it with ugly and meaningless trivialities. They were enough, he thought, to make one almost forget woman as she existed in art, in thought, and in the universe.

He had no desire to know the woman who had, for the time at least, so broken up his life,—no curiosity about her every-day personality. He shunned any revelation of it, and he listened for Miss Bower's coming and going, not to encounter, but to avoid her. He wished that the girl who wore shirt-waists and got letters from Chicago would keep out of his way, that she did not exist. With her he had naught to make. But in a room full of sun, before an old mirror, on a little enchanted rug of sleeping colours, he had seen a woman who emerged naked through a door, and disappeared naked. He thought of that body as never having been clad, or as having worn the stuffs and dyes of all the centuries but his own. And for him she had no geographical associations; unless with Crete, or Alexandria, or Veronese's Venice. She was the immortal conception, the perennial theme.

The first break in Hedger's lethargy occurred one afternoon when two young men came to take Eden Bower out to dine. They went into her music room, laughed and talked for a few minutes, and then took her away with them. They were gone a long while, but he did not go out for food himself; he waited for them to come back. At last he heard them coming down the hall, gayer and more talkative than when they left. One of them sat down at the piano, and they all began to sing. This Hedger found absolutely unendurable. He snatched up his hat and went running down the stairs. Caesar leaped beside him, hoping that old times were coming back. They had supper in the oysterman's basement and then sat down in front of their own doorway. The moon stood full over the Square, a thing of regal glory; but Hedger did not see the moon; he was looking, murderously, for men. Presently two, wearing straw hats and white trousers and carrying canes, came down the steps from his house. He rose and dogged them across the Square. They were laughing and seemed very much elated about something. As one stopped to light a cigarette, Hedger caught from the other:

"Don't you think she has a beautiful talent?"

His companion threw away his match. "She has a beautiful figure." They both ran to catch the stage.

Hedger went back to his studio. The light was shining from her transom. For the first time he violated her privacy at night, and peered through that fatal aperture. She was sitting, fully dressed, in the window, smoking a cigarette and looking out over the housetops. He watched her until she rose, looked about her with a disdainful, crafty smile, and turned out the light.

The next morning, when Miss Bower went out, Hedger followed her. Her white skirt gleamed ahead of him as she sauntered about the Square. She sat down behind the Garibaldi statue and opened a music book she carried. She turned the leaves carelessly, and several times glanced in his direction. He was on the point of going over to her, when she rose quickly and looked up at the sky. A flock of pigeons had risen from somewhere in the crowded Italian quarter to the south, and were wheeling rapidly up through the morning air, soaring and dropping, scattering and coming together, now grey, now white as silver, as they caught or intercepted the sunlight. She put up her hand to shade her eyes and followed them with a kind of defiant delight in her face.

Hedger came and stood beside her. "You've surely seen them before?"

"Oh, yes," she replied, still looking up. "I see them every day from my windows. They always come home about five o'clock. Where do they live?"

"I don't know. Probably some Italian raises them for the market. They were here long before I came, and I've been here four years."

"In that same gloomy room? Why didn't you take mine when it was vacant?"

"It isn't gloomy. That's the best light for painting."

"Oh, is it? I don't know anything about painting. I'd like to see your pictures sometime. You have such a lot in there. Don't they get dusty, piled up against the wall like that?"

"Not very. I'd be glad to show them to you. Is your name really Eden Bower? I've seen your letters on the table."

"Well, it's the name I'm going to sing under. My father's name is Bowers, but my friend Mr. Jones, a Chicago newspaper man who writes about music, told me to drop the 's.' He's crazy about my voice."

Miss Bower didn't usually tell the whole story,—about anything. Her first name, when she lived in Huntington, Illinois, was Edna, but Mr. Jones had persuaded her to change it to one which he felt would be worthy of her future. She was quick to take suggestions, though she told him she "didn't see what was the matter with 'Edna.' "

She explained to Hedger that she was going to Paris to study. She was waiting in New York for Chicago friends who were to take her over, but who had been detained. "Did you study in Paris?" she asked.

"No, I've never been in Paris. But I was in the south of France all last summer, studying with C———. He's the biggest man among the moderns,—at least I think so."

Miss Bower sat down and made room for him on the bench. "Do tell me about it. I expected to be there by this time, and I can't wait to find out what it's like."

Hedger began to relate how he had seen some of this Frenchman's work in an exhibition, and deciding at once that this was the man for him, he had taken a boat for Marseilles the next week, going over steerage. He proceeded at once to the little town on the coast where his painter lived, and presented himself. The man never took pupils, but because Hedger had come so far, he let him stay. Hedger lived at the master's house and every day they went out together to paint, sometimes on the blazing rocks down by the sea. They wrapped themselves in light woollen blankets and didn't feel the heat. Being there and working with C——— was being in Paradise, Hedger concluded; he learned more in three months than in all his life before.

Eden Bower laughed. "You're a funny fellow. Didn't you do anything but work? Are the women very beautiful? Did you have awfully good things to eat and drink?"

Hedger said some of the women were fine looking, especially one girl who went about selling fish and lobsters. About the food there was nothing remarkable,—except the ripe figs, he liked those. They drank sour wine, and used goat-butter, which was strong and full of hair, as it was churned in a goat skin.

"But don't they have parties or banquets? Aren't there any fine hotels down there?"

"Yes, but they are all closed in summer, and the country people are poor. It's a beautiful country, though."

"How, beautiful?" she persisted.

"If you want to go in, I'll show you some sketches, and you'll see."

Miss Bower rose. "All right. I won't go to my fencing lesson this morning. Do you fence? Here comes your dog. You can't move but he's after you. He always makes a face at me when I meet him in the hall, and shows his nasty little teeth as if he wanted to bite me."

In the studio Hedger got out his sketches, but to Miss Bower, whose favourite pictures were Christ Before Pilate and a redhaired Magdalen of Henner, these landscapes were not at all beautiful, and they gave her no idea of any country whatsoever. She was careful not to commit herself, however. Her vocal teacher had already convinced her that she had a great deal to learn about many things.

"Why don't we go out to lunch somewhere?" Hedger asked, and began to dust his fingers with a handkerchief—which he got out of sight as swiftly as possible.

"All right, the Brevoort," she said carelessly. "I think that's a good place, and they have good wine. I don't care for cocktails."

Hedger felt his chin uneasily. "I'm afraid I haven't shaved this morning. If you could wait for me in the Square? It won't take me ten minutes."

Left alone, he found a clean collar and handkerchief, brushed his coat and blacked his shoes, and last of all dug up ten dollars from the bottom of an old copper kettle he had brought from Spain. His winter hat was of such a complexion that the Brevoort hall boy winked at the porter as he took it and placed it on the rack in a row of fresh straw ones.

IV

That afternoon Eden Bower was lying on the coach in her music room, her face turned to the window, watching the pigeons. Reclining thus she could see none of the neighbouring roofs, only the sky itself and the birds that crossed and recrossed her field of vision, white as scraps of paper blowing in the wind. She was thinking that she was young and handsome and had had a good lunch, that a very easy-going, light-hearted city lay in the streets below her; and she was wondering why she found this queer painter chap, with his lean, bluish cheeks and heavy black eyebrows, more interesting than the smart young men she had met at her teacher's studio.

Eden Bower was, at twenty, very much the same person that we all know her to be at forty, except that she knew a great deal less. But one thing she knew: that she was to be Eden Bower. She was like some one standing before a great show window full of beautiful and costly things, deciding which she will order. She understands that they will arrive at her door. She already knew some of the many things that were to happen to her; for instance, that the Chicago millionaire who was going to take her abroad with his sister as chaperone, would eventually press his claim in quite another manner. He was the most circumspect of bachelors, afraid of everything obvious, even of women who were too flagrantly handsome. He was a nervous collector of pictures and furniture, a nervous patron of music, and a nervous host; very cautious about his health, and about any course of conduct that might make him ridiculous. But she knew that he would at last throw all his precautions to the winds.

People like Eden Bower are inexplicable. Her father sold farming machinery in Huntington, Illinois, and she had grown up with no acquaintances or experiences outside of that prairie town. Yet from her earliest childhood she had not one conviction or opinion in common with the people about her,—the only people she knew. Before she was out of short dresses she had made up her mind that she was going to be an actress, that she would live far away in great cities, that she would be much admired by men and would have everything she wanted. When she was thirteen, and was already singing and reciting for church entertainments, she read in some illustrated magazine a long article about the late Czar of Russia, then just come to the throne or about to come to it. After that, lying in the hammock on the front porch on summer evenings, or sitting through a long sermon in the family pew, she amused herself by trying to make up her mind whether she would or would not be the Czar's mistress when she played in his Capital. Now Edna had met this fascinating word only in the novels of Ouida,—her hard-worked little mother kept a long row of them in the upstairs storeroom, behind the linen chest. In Huntington, women who bore that relation to men were called by a very different name, and their lot was not an enviable one; of all the shabby and poor, they were the shabbiest. But then, Edna had never lived in Huntington, not even before she began to find books like "Sappho" and "Mademoiselle de Maupin," secretly sold in paper covers throughout Illinois. It was as if she had come into Huntington, into the Bowers family, on one of the trains that puffed over the marshes behind their back fence all day long, and was waiting for another train to take her out.

As she grew older and handsomer, she had many beaux, but these small-town boys didn't interest her. If a lad kissed her when he brought her home from a dance, she was indulgent and she rather liked it. But if he pressed her further, she slipped away from him, laughing. After she began to sing in Chicago, she was consistently discreet. She stayed as a guest in rich people's houses, and she knew that she was being watched like a rabbit in a laboratory. Covered up in bed, with the lights out, she thought her own thoughts, and laughed.

This summer in New York was her first taste of freedom. The Chicago capitalist, after all his arrangements were made for sailing, had been compelled to go to Mexico to look after oil interests. His sister knew an excellent singing master in New York. Why should not a discreet, well-balanced girl like Miss Bower spend the summer there, studying quietly? The capitalist suggested that his sister might enjoy a summer on Long Island; he would rent the Griffith's place for her, with all the servants, and Eden could stay there. But his sister met this proposal with a cold stare. So it fell out, that between selfishness and greed, Eden got a summer all her own,—which really did a great deal toward making her an artist and whatever else she was afterward to become. She had time to look about, to watch without being watched; to select diamonds in one window and furs in another, to select shoulders and moustaches in the big hotels where she went to lunch. She had the easy freedom of obscurity and the consciousness of power. She enjoyed both. She was in no hurry.

While Eden Bower watched the pigeons, Don Hedger sat on the other side of the bolted doors, looking into a pool of dark turpentine, at his idle brushes, wondering why a woman could do this to him. He, too, was sure of his future and knew that he was a chosen man. He could not know, of course, that he was merely the first to fall under a fascination which was to be disastrous to a few men and pleasantly stimulating to many thousands. Each of these two young people sensed the future, but not completely. Don Hedger knew that nothing much would ever happen to him. Eden Bower understood that to her a great deal would happen. But she did not guess that her neighbor would have more tempestuous adventures sitting in his dark studio than she would find in all the capitals of Europe, or in all the latitude of conduct she was prepared to permit herself.

V

One Sunday morning Eden was crossing the Square with a spruce young man in a white flannel suit and a panama hat. They had been breakfasting at the Brevoort and he was coaxing her to let him come up to her rooms and sing for an hour.

"No, I've got to write letters. You must run along now. I see a friend of mine over there, and I want to ask him about something before I go up."

"That fellow with the dog? Where did you pick him up?" the young man glanced toward the seat under a sycamore where Hedger was reading the morning paper.

"Oh, he's an old friend from the West," said Eden easily. "I won't introduce you, because he doesn't like people. He's a recluse. Good-bye. I can't be sure about Tuesday. I'll go with you if I have time after my lesson." She nodded, left him, and went over to the seat littered with newspapers. The young man went up the Avenue without looking back.

"Well, what are you going to do today? Shampoo this animal all morning?" Eden enquired teasingly.

Hedger made room for her on the seat. "No, at twelve o'clock I'm going out to Coney Island. One of my models is going up in a balloon this afternoon. I've often promised to go and see her, and now I'm going."

Eden asked if models usually did such stunts. No, Hedger told her, but Molly Welch added to her earnings in that way. "I believe," he added, "she likes the excitement of it. She's got a good deal of spirit. That's why I like to paint her. So many models have flaccid bodies."

"And she hasn't, eh? Is she the one who comes to see you? I can't help hearing her, she talks so loud."

"Yes, she has a rough voice, but she's a fine girl. I don't suppose you'd be interested in going?"

"I don't know," Eden sat tracing patterns on the asphalt with the end of her parasol. "Is it any fun? I got up feeling I'd like to do something different today. It's the first Sunday I've not had to sing in church. I had that engagement for breakfast at the Brevoort, but it wasn't very exciting. That chap can't talk about anything but himself."

Hedger warmed a little. "If you've never been to Coney Island, you ought to go. It's nice to see all the people; tailors and bar-tenders and prize-fighters with their best girls, and all sorts of folks taking a holiday."

Eden looked sidewise at him. So one ought to be interested in people of that kind, ought one? He was certainly a funny fellow. Yet he was never, somehow, tiresome. She had seen a good deal of him lately, but she kept wanting to know him better, to find out what made him different from men like the one she had just left—whether he really was as different as he seemed. "I'll go with you," she said at last, "if you'll leave that at home." She pointed to Caesar's flickering ears with her sunshade.

"But he's half the fun. You'd like to hear him bark at the waves when they come in."

"No, I wouldn't. He's jealous and disagreeable if he sees you talking to any one else. Look at him now."

"Of course, if you make a face at him. He knows what that means, and he makes a worse face. He likes Molly Welch, and she'll be disappointed if I don't bring him."

Eden said decidedly that he couldn't take both of them. So at twelve o'clock when she and Hedger got on the boat at Desbrosses Street, Caesar was lying on his pallet, with a bone.

Eden enjoyed the boat-ride. It was the first time she had been on the water, and she felt as if she were embarking for France. The light warm breeze and the plunge of the waves made her very wide awake, and she liked crowds of any kind. They went to the balcony of a big, noisy restaurant and had a shore dinner, with tall steins of beer. Hedger had got a big advance from his advertising firm since he first lunched with Miss Bower ten days ago, and he was ready for anything.

After dinner they went to the tent behind the bathing beach, where the tops of two balloons bulged out over the canvas. A red-faced man in a linen suit stood in front of the tent, shouting in a hoarse voice and telling the people that if the crowd was good for five dollars more, a beautiful young woman would risk her life for their entertainment. Four little boys in dirty red uniforms ran about taking contributions in their pill-box hats. One of the balloons was bobbing up and down in its tether and people were shoving forward to get nearer the tent.

"Is it dangerous, as he pretends?" Eden asked.

"Molly says it's simple enough if nothing goes wrong with the balloon. Then it would be all over, I suppose."

"Wouldn't you like to go up with her?"

"I? Of course not. I'm not fond of taking foolish risks."

Eden sniffed. "I shouldn't think sensible risks would be very much fun."

Hedger did not answer, for just then every one began to shove the other way and shout, "Look out. There she goes!" and a band of six pieces commenced playing furiously.

As the balloon rose from its tent enclosure, they saw a girl in green tights standing in the basket, holding carelessly to one of the ropes with one hand and with the other waving to the spectators. A long rope trailed behind to keep the balloon from blowing out to sea.

As it soared, the figure in green tights in the basket diminished to a mere spot, and the balloon itself, in the brilliant light, looked like a big silver-grey bat, with its wings folded. When it began to sink, the girl stepped through the hole in the basket to a trapeze that hung below, and gracefully descended through the air, holding to the rod with both hands, keeping her body taut and her feet close together. The crowd, which had grown very large by this time, cheered vociferously. The men took off their hats and waved, little boys shouted, and fat old women, shining with the heat and a beer lunch, murmured admiring comments upon the balloonist's figure. "Beautiful legs, she has!"

"That's so," Hedger whispered. "Not many girls would look well in that position." Then, for some reason, he blushed a slow, dark, painful crimson.

The balloon descended slowly, a little way from the tent, and the red-faced man in the linen suit caught Molly Welch before her feet touched the ground, and pulled her to one side. The band struck up "Blue Bell" by way of welcome, and one of the sweaty pages ran forward and presented the balloonist with a large bouquet of artificial flowers. She smiled and thanked him, and ran back across the sand to the tent.

"Can't we go inside and see her?" Eden asked. "You can explain to the door man. I want to meet her." Edging forward, she herself addressed the man in the linen suit and slipped something from her purse into his hand.

They found Molly seated before a trunk that had a mirror in the lid and a "make-up" outfit spread upon the tray. She was wiping the cold cream and powder from her neck with a discarded chemise.

"Hello, Don," she said cordially. "Brought a friend?"

Eden liked her. She had an easy, friendly manner, and there was something boyish and devil-may-care about her.

"Yes, it's fun. I'm mad about it," she said in reply to Eden's questions. "I always want to let go, when I come down on the bar. You don't feel your weight at all, as you would on a stationary trapeze."

The big drum boomed outside, and the publicity man began shouting to newly arrived boatloads. Miss Welch took a last pull at her cigarette. "Now you'll have to get out, Don. I change for the next act. This time I go up in a black evening dress, and lose the skirt in the basket before I start down."

"Yes, go along," said Eden. "Wait for me outside the door. I'll stay and help her dress."

Hedger waited and waited, while women of every build bumped into him and begged his pardon, and the red pages ran about holding out their caps for coins, and the people ate and perspired and shifted parasols against the sun. When the band began to play a two-step, all the bathers ran up out of the surf to watch the ascent. The second balloon bumped and rose, and the crowd began shouting to the girl in a black evening dress who stood leaning against the ropes and smiling. "It's a new girl," they called. "It ain't the Countess this time. You're a peach, girlie!"

The balloonist acknowledged these compliments, bowing and looking down over the sea of upturned faces,—but Hedger was determined she should not see him, and he darted behind the tent-fly. He was suddenly dripping with cold sweat, his mouth was full of the bitter taste of anger and his tongue felt stiff behind his teeth. Molly Welch, in a shirt-waist and a white tam-o'-shanter cap, slipped out from the tent under his arm and laughed up in his face. "She's a crazy one you brought along. She'll get what she wants!"

"Oh, I'll settle with you, all right!" Hedger brought out with difficulty.

"It's not my fault, Donnie. I couldn't do anything with her. She bought me off. What's the matter with you? Are you soft on her? She's safe enough. It's as easy as rolling off a log, if you keep cool." Molly Welch was rather excited herself, and she was chewing gum at a high speed as she stood beside him, looking up at the floating silver cone. "Now watch," she exclaimed suddenly. "She's coming down on the bar. I advised her to cut that out, but you see she does it first-rate. And she got rid of the skirt, too. Those black tights show off her legs very well. She keeps her feet together like I told her, and makes a good line along the back. See the light on those silver slippers,—that was a good idea I had. Come along to meet her. Don't be a grouch; she's done it fine!"

Molly tweaked his elbow, and then left him standing like a stump, while she ran down the beach with the crowd.

Though Hedger was sulking, his eye could not help seeing the low blue welter of the sea, the arrested bathers, standing in the surf, their arms and legs stained red by the dropping sun, all shading their eyes and gazing upward at the slowly falling silver star.

Molly Welch and the manager caught Eden under the arms and lifted her aside, a red page dashed up with a bouquet, and the band struck up "Blue Bell." Eden laughed and bowed, took Molly's arm, and ran up the sand in her black tights and silver slippers, dodging the friendly old women, and the gallant sports who wanted to offer their homage on the spot.

When she emerged from the tent, dressed in her own clothes, that part of the beach was almost deserted. She stepped to her companion's side and said carelessly: "Hadn't we better try to catch this boat? I hope you're not sore at me. Really, it was lots of fun."

Hedger looked at his watch. "Yes, we have fifteen minutes to get to the boat," he said politely.

As they walked toward the pier, one of the pages ran up panting. "Lady, you're carrying off the bouquet," he said, aggrievedly.

Eden stopped and looked at the bunch of spotty cotton roses in her hand. "Of course. I want them for a souvenir. You gave them to me yourself."

"I give 'em to you for looks, but you can't take 'em away. They belong to the show."

"Oh, you always use the same bunch?"

"Sure we do. There ain't too much money in this business."

She laughed and tossed them back to him. "Why are you angry?" she asked Hedger. "I wouldn't have done it if I'd been with some fellows, but I thought you were the sort who wouldn't mind. Molly didn't for a minute think you would."

"What possessed you to do such a fool thing?" he asked roughly.

"I don't know. When I saw her coming down, I wanted to try it. It looked exciting. Didn't I hold myself as well as she did?"

Hedger shrugged his shoulders, but in his heart he forgave her.

The return boat was not crowded, though the boats that passed them, going out, were packed to the rails. The sun was setting. Boys and girls sat on the long benches with their arms about each other, singing. Eden felt a strong wish to propitiate her companion, to be alone with him. She had been curiously wrought up by her balloon trip; it was a lark, but not very satisfying unless one came back to something after the flight. She wanted to be admired and adored. Though Eden said nothing, and sat with her arms limp on the rail in front of her, looking languidly at the rising silhouette of the city and the bright path of the sun, Hedger felt a strange drawing near to her. If he but brushed her white skirt with his knee, there was an instant communication between them, such as there had never been before. They did not talk at all, but when they went over the gangplank she took his arm and kept her shoulder close to his. He felt as if they were enveloped in a highly charged atmosphere, an invisible network of subtle, almost painful sensibility. They had some-how taken hold of each other.

An hour later, they were dining in the back garden of a little French hotel on Ninth Street, long since passed away. It was cool and leafy there, and the mosquitoes were not very numerous. A party of South Americans at another table were drinking champagne, and Eden murmured that she thought she would like some, if it were not too expensive. "Perhaps it will make me think I am in the balloon again. That was a very nice feeling. You've forgiven me, haven't you?"

Hedger gave her a quick straight look from under his black eye-brows, and something went over her that was like a chill, except that it was warm and feathery. She drank most of the wine; her companion was indifferent to it. He was talking more to her tonight than he had ever done before. She asked him about a new picture she had seen in his room; a queer thing full of stiff, supplicating female figures. "It's Indian, isn't it?"

"Yes. I call it Rain Spirits, or maybe, Indian Rain. In the Southwest, where I've been a good deal, the Indian traditions make women have to do with the rain-fall. They were supposed to control it, somehow, and to be able to find springs, and make moisture come out of the earth. You see I'm trying to learn to paint what people think and feel; to get away from all that photographic stuff. When I look at you, I don't see what a camera would see, do I?"

"How can I tell?"

"Well, if I should paint you, I could make you understand what I see." For the second time that day Hedger crimsoned unexpectedly, and his eyes fell and steadily contemplated a dish of little radishes. "That particular picture I got from a story a Mexican priest told me; he said he found it in an old manuscript book in a monastery down there, written by some Spanish Missionary, who got his stories from the Aztecs. This one he called 'The Forty Lovers of the Queen,' and it was more or less about rain-making."

"Aren't you going to tell it to me?" Eden asked.

Hedger fumbled among the radishes. "I don't know if it's the proper kind of story to tell a girl."

She smiled; "Oh, forget about that! I've been balloon riding today. I like to hear you talk."

Her low voice was flattering. She had seemed like clay in his hands ever since they got on the boat to come home. He leaned back in his chair, forgot his food, and, looking at her intently, began to tell his story, the theme of which he somehow felt was dangerous tonight.

The tale began, he said, somewhere in Ancient Mexico, and concerned the daughter of a king. The birth of this Princess was preceded by unusual portents. Three times her mother dreamed that she was delivered of serpents, which betokened that the child she carried would have power with the rain gods. The serpent was the symbol of water. The Princess grew up dedicated to the gods, and wise men taught her the rain-making mysteries. She was with difficulty restrained from men and was guarded at all times, for it was the law of the Thunder that she be maiden until her marriage. In the years of her adolescence, rain was abundant with her people. The oldest man could not remember such fertility. When the Princess had counted eighteen summers, her father went to drive out a war party that harried his borders on the north and troubled his prosperity. The King destroyed the invaders and brought home many prisoners. Among the prisoners was a young chief, taller than any of his captors, of such strength and ferocity that the King's people came a day's journey to look at him. When the Princess beheld his great stature, and saw that his arms and breast were covered with the figures of wild animals, bitten into the skin and coloured, she begged his life from her father. She desired that he should practise his art upon her, and prick upon her skin the signs of Rain and Lightning and Thunder, and stain the wounds with herb-juices, as they were upon his own

88

body. For many days, upon the roof of the King's house, the Princess submitted herself to the bone needle, and the women with her marvelled at her fortitude. But the Princess was without shame before the Captive, and it came about that he threw from him his needles and his stains, and fell upon the Princess to violate her honour; and her women ran down from the roof screaming, to call the guard which stood at the gateway of the King's house, and none stayed to protect their mistress. When the guard came, the Captive was thrown into bonds, and he was gelded, and his tongue was torn out, and he was given for a slave to the Rain Princess.

The country of the Aztecs to the east was tormented by thirst, and their king, hearing much of the rain-making arts of the Princess, sent an embassy to her father, with presents and an offer of marriage. So the Princess went from her father to be the Queen of the Aztecs, and she took with her the Captive, who served her in everything with entire fidelity and slept upon a mat before her door.

The King gave his bride a fortress on the outskirts of the city, whither she retired to entreat the rain gods. This fortress was called the Queen's House, and on the night of the new moon the Queen came to it from the palace. But when the moon waxed and grew toward the round, because the god of Thunder had had his will of her, then the Queen returned to the King. Drought abated in the country and rain fell abundantly by reason of the Queen's power with the stars.

When the Queen went to her own house she took with her no servant but the Captive, and he slept outside her door and brought her food after she had fasted. The Queen had a jewel of great value, a turquoise that had fallen from the sun, and had the image of the sun upon it. And when she desired a young man whom she had seen in the army or among the slaves, she sent the Captive to him with the jewel, for a sign that he should come to her secretly at the Queen's House upon business concerning the welfare of all. And some, after she had talked with them, she sent away with rewards; and some she took into her chamber and kept them by her for one night or two. Afterward she called the Captive and bade him conduct the youth by the secret way he had come, underneath the chambers of the fortress. But for the going away of the Queen's lovers the Captive took out the bar that was beneath a stone in the floor of the passage, and put in its stead a rush-reed, and the youth stepped upon it and fell through into a cavern that was the bed of an underground river, and whatever was thrown into it was not seen again. In this service nor in any other did the Captive fail the Queen.

But when the Queen sent for the Captain of the Archers, she detained him four days in her chamber, calling often for food and wine, and was greatly content with him. On the fourth day she went to the Captive outside her door and said: "Tomorrow take this man up by the sure way, by which the King comes, and let him live."

In the Queen's door were arrows, purple and white. When she desired the King to come to her publicly, with his guard, she sent him a white arrow; but when she sent the purple, he came secretly, and covered himself with his mantle to be hidden from the stone gods at the gate. On the fifth night that the Queen was with her lover, the Captive took a purple arrow to the King, and the King came secretly and found them together. He killed the Captain with his own hand, but the Queen he brought to public trial. The Captive, when he was put to the question, told on his fingers forty men that he had let through the underground passage into the river. The Captive and the Queen were put to death by fire, both on the same day, and afterward there was scarcity of rain.

Eden Bower sat shivering a little as she listened. Hedger was not trying to please her, she thought, but to antagonize and frighten her by his brutal story. She had often told herself that his lean, big-boned lower jaw was like his bull-dog's, but tonight his face made Caesar's most savage and determined expression seem an affectation. Now she was looking at the man he really was. Nobody's eyes had ever defied her like this. They were searching her and seeing everything; all she had concealed from Livingston, and from the millionaire and his friends, and from the newspaper men. He was testing her, trying her out, and she was more ill at ease than she wished to show.

"That's quite a thrilling story," she said at last, rising and winding her scarf about her throat. "It must be getting late. Almost every one has gone."

They walked down the Avenue like people who have quarrelled, or who wish to get rid of each other. Hedger did not take her arm at the street crossings, and they did not linger in the Square. At her door he tried none of the old devices of the Livingston boys. He stood like a post, having forgotten to take off his hat, gave her a harsh, threatening glance, muttered "goodnight," and shut his own door noisily.

There was no question of sleep for Eden Bower. Her brain was working like a machine that would never stop. After she undressed, she tried to calm her nerves by smoking a cigarette, lying on the divan by the open window. But she grew wider and wider awake, combating the challenge that had flamed all evening in Hedger's eyes. The balloon had been one kind of excitement, the wine another; but the thing that had roused her, as a blow rouses a proud man, was the doubt, the contempt, the sneering hostility with which the painter had looked at her when he told his savage story. Crowds and balloons were all very well, she reflected, but woman's chief adventure is man. With a mind over active and a sense of life over strong, she wanted to walk across the roofs in the starlight, to sail over the sea and face at once a world of which she had never been afraid.

Hedger must be asleep; his dog had stopped sniffing under the double doors. Eden put on her wrapper and slippers and stole softly down the hall over the old carpet; one loose board creaked just as she reached the ladder. The trapdoor was open, as always on hot nights. When she stepped out on the roof she drew a long breath and walked across it, looking up at the sky. Her foot touched something soft; she heard a low growl, and on the instant Caesar's sharp little teeth caught her ankle and waited. His breath was like steam on her leg. Nobody had ever intruded upon his roof before, and he panted for the movement or the word that would let him spring his jaw. Instead, Hedger's hand seized his throat.

"Wait a minute. I'll settle with him," he said grimly. He dragged the dog toward the manhole and disappeared. When he came back, he found Eden standing over by the dark chimney, looking away in an offended attitude.

"I caned him unmercifully," he panted. "Of course you didn't hear anything; he never whines when I beat him. He didn't nip you, did he?"

"I don't know whether he broke the skin or not," she answered aggrievedly, still looking off into the west.

"If I were one of your friends in white pants, I'd strike a match to find whether you were hurt, though I know you are not, and then I'd see your ankle, wouldn't I?"

"I suppose so."

He shook his head and stood with his hands in the pockets of his old painting jacket. "I'm not up to such boy-tricks. If you want the place to yourself, I'll clear out. There are plenty of places where I can spend the night, what's left of it. But if you stay here and I stay here——" He shrugged his shoulders.

Eden did not stir, and she made no reply. Her head drooped slightly, as if she were considering. But the moment he put his arms about her they began to talk, both at once, as people do in an opera. The instant avowal brought out a flood of trivial admissions. Hedger confessed his crime, was reproached and forgiven, and now Eden knew what it was in his look that she found so disturbing of late.

Standing against the black chimney, with the sky behind and blue shadows before, they looked like one of Hedger's own paintings of that period; two figures, one white and one dark, and nothing whatever distinguishable about them but that they were male and female. The faces were lost, the contours blurred in shadow, but the figures were a man and a woman, and that was their whole concern and their mysterious beauty,—it was the rhythm in which they moved, at last, along the roof and down into the dark hole; he first, drawing her gently after him. She came down very slowly. The excitement and bravado and uncertainty of that long day and night seemed all at once to tell upon her. When his feet were on the carpet and he reached up to lift her down, she twined her arms about his neck as after a long separation, and turned her face to him, and her lips, with their perfume of youth and passion.

One Saturday afternoon Hedger was sitting in the window of Eden's music room. They had been watching the pigeons come wheeling over the roofs from their unknown feeding grounds.

"Why," said Eden suddenly, "don't we fix those big doors into your studio so they will open? Then, if I want you, I won't have to go through the hall. That illustrator is loafing about a good deal of late."

"I'll open them, if you wish. The bolt is on your side."

"Isn't there one on yours, too?"

"No. I believe a man lived there for years before I came in, and the nurse used to have these rooms herself. Naturally, the lock was on the lady's side."

Eden laughed and began to examine the bolt. "It's all stuck up with paint." Looking about, her eye lighted upon a bronze Buddha which was one of the nurse's treasures. Taking him by his head, she struck the bolt a blow with his squatting posteriors. The two doors creaked, sagged, and swung weakly inward a little way, as if they were too old for such escapades. Eden tossed the heavy idol into a stuffed chair. "That's better," she exclaimed exultantly. "So the bolts are always on the lady's side? What a lot society takes for granted!"

Hedger laughed, sprang up and caught her arms roughly. "Whoever takes you for granted—Did anybody, ever?"

"Everybody does. That's why I'm here. You are the only one who knows anything about me. Now I'll have to dress if we're going out for dinner."

He lingered, keeping his hold on her. "But I won't always be the only one, Eden Bower. I won't be the last."

"No, I suppose not," she said carelessly. "But what does that matter? You are the first."

As a long, despairing whine broke in the warm stillness, they drew apart. Caesar, lying on his bed in the dark corner, had lifted his head at this invasion of sunlight, and realized that the side of his room was broken open, and his whole world shattered by change. There stood his master and this woman, laughing at him! The woman was pulling the long black hair of this mightiest of men, who bowed his head and permitted it.

VI

In time they quarrelled, of course, and about an abstraction,—as young people often do, as mature people almost never do. Eden came in late one afternoon. She had been with some of her musical friends to lunch at Burton Ives' studio, and she began telling Hedger about its splendours. He listened a moment and then threw down his brushes. "I know exactly what it's like," he said impatiently. "A very good department-store conception of a studio. It's one of the show places."

"Well, it's gorgeous, and he said I could bring you to see him. The boys tell me he's awfully kind about giving people a lift, and you might get something out of it."

Hedger started up and pushed his canvas out of the way. "What could I possibly get from Burton Ives? He's almost the worst painter in the world; the stupidest, I mean."

Eden was annoyed. Burton Ives had been very nice to her and had begged her to sit for him. "You must admit that he's a very successful one," she said coldly.

"Of course he is! Anybody can be successful who will do that sort of thing. I wouldn't paint his pictures for all the money in New York."

"Well, I saw a lot of them, and I think they are beautiful."

Hedger bowed stiffly.

"What's the use of being a great painter if nobody knows about you?" Eden went on persuasively. "Why don't you paint the kind of pictures people can understand, and then, after you're successful, do whatever you like?"

"As I look at it," said Hedger brusquely, "I am successful."

Eden glanced about. "Well, I don't see any evidences of it," she said, biting her lip. "He has a Japanese servant and a wine cellar, and keeps a riding horse."

Hedger melted a little. "My dear, I have the most expensive luxury in the world, and I am much more extravagant than Burton Ives, for I work to please nobody but myself."

"You mean you could make money and don't? That you don't try to get a public?"

"Exactly. A public only wants what has been done over and over. I'm painting for painters,—who haven't been born."

"What would you do if I brought Mr. Ives down here to see your things?"

"Well, for God's sake, don't! Before he left I'd probably tell him what I thought of him."

Eden rose. "I give you up. You know very well there's only one kind of success that's real."

"Yes, but it's not the kind you mean. So you've been thinking me a scrub painter, who needs a helping hand from some fashionable studio man? What the devil have you had anything to do with me for, then?"

"There's no use talking to you," said Eden walking slowly toward the door. "I've been trying to pull wires for you all afternoon, and this is what it comes to." She had expected that the tidings of a prospective call from the great man would be received very differently, and had been thinking as she came home in the stage how, as with a magic wand, she might gild Hedger's future, float him out of his dark hole on a tide of prosperity, see his name in the papers and his pictures in the windows on Fifth Avenue.

Hedger mechanically snapped the midsummer leash on Caesar's collar and they ran downstairs and hurried through Sullivan Street off toward the river. He wanted to be among rough, honest people, to get down where the big drays bumped over stone paving blocks and the men wore corduroy trowsers and kept their shirts open at the neck. He stopped for a drink in one of the sagging bar-rooms on the water front. He had never in his life been so deeply wounded; he did not know he could be so hurt. He had told this girl all his secrets. On the roof, in these warm, heavy summer nights, with her hands locked in his, he had been able to explain all his misty ideas about an unborn art the world was waiting for; had been able to explain them better than he had ever done to himself. And she had looked away to the chattels of this uptown studio and coveted them for him! To her he was only an unsuccessful Burton Ives.

Then why, as he had put it to her, did she take up with him? Young, beautiful, talented as she was, why had she wasted herself on a scrub? Pity? Hardly; she wasn't sentimental. There was no explaining her. But in this passion that had seemed so fearless and so fated to be, his own position now looked to him ridiculous; a poor dauber without money or fame,—it was her caprice to load him with favours.

Hedger ground his teeth so loud that his dog, trotting beside him, heard him and looked up.

While they were having supper at the oysterman's, he planned his escape. Whenever he saw her again, everything he had told her, that he should never have told any one, would come back to him; ideas he had never whispered even to the painter whom he worshipped and had gone all the way to France to see. To her they must seem his apology for not having horses and a valet, or merely the puerile boastfulness of a weak man. Yet if she slipped the bolt tonight and came through the doors and said, "Oh, weak man, I belong to you!" what could he do? That was the danger. He would catch the train out to Long Beach tonight, and tomorrow he would go on to the north end of Long Island, where an old friend of his had a summer studio among the sand dunes. He would stay until things came right in his mind. And she could find a smart painter, or take her punishment.

When he went home, Eden's room was dark; she was dining out somewhere. He threw his things into a hold-all he had carried about the world with him, strapped up some colours and canvases, and ran downstairs.

VII

Five days later Hedger was a restless passenger on a dirty, crowded Sunday train, coming back to town. Of course, he saw now how unreasonable he had been in expecting a Huntington girl to know anything about pictures; here was a whole continent full of people who knew nothing about pictures and he didn't hold it against them. What had such things to do with him and Eden Bower? When he lay out on the dunes, watching the moon come up out of the sea, it had seemed to him that there was no wonder in the world like the wonder of Eden Bower. He was going back to her because she was older than art, because she was the most overwhelming thing that had ever come into his life.

He had written her yesterday, begging her to be at home this evening, telling her that he was contrite, and wretched enough.

Now that he was on his way to her, his stronger feeling unac-
countably changed to a mood that was playful and tender. He wanted
to share everything with her, even the most trivial things. He wanted
to tell her about the people on the train, coming back tired from
their holiday with bunches of wilted flowers and dirty daisies; to tell
her that the fish-man, to whom she had often sent him for lobsters,
was among the passengers, disguised in a silk shirt and a spotted tie,
and how his wife looked exactly like a fish, even to her eyes, on
which cataracts were forming. He could tell her, too, that he hadn't
as much as unstrapped his canvases,—that ought to convince her.

In those days passengers from Long Island came into New York
by ferry. Hedger had to be quick about getting his dog out of the
express car in order to catch the first boat. The East River, and the
bridges, and the city to the west, were burning in the conflagration
of the sunset; there was that great home-coming reach of evening in
the air.

The car changes from Thirty-fourth Street were too many and too
perplexing; for the first time in his life Hedger took a hansom cab
for Washington Square. Caesar sat bolt upright on the worn leather
cushion beside him, and they jogged off, looking down on the rest
of the world.

It was twilight when they drove down lower Fifth Avenue into
the Square, and through the Arch behind them were the two long
rows of pale violet lights that used to bloom so beautifully against
the grey stone and asphalt. Here and yonder about the Square hung
globes that shed a radiance not unlike the blue mists of evening,
emerging softly when daylight died, as the stars emerged in the thin
blue sky. Under them the sharp shadows of the trees fell on the
cracked pavement and the sleeping grass. The first stars and the first
lights were growing silver against the gradual darkening, when Hedger
paid his driver and went into the house,—which, thank God, was
still there! On the hall table lay his letter of yesterday, unopened.

He went upstairs with every sort of fear and every sort of hope
clutching at his heart; it was as if tigers were tearing him. Why was
there no gas burning in the top hall? He found matches and the gas
bracket. He knocked, but got no answer; nobody was there. Before

his own door were exactly five bottles of milk, standing in a row. The milk-boy had taken spiteful pleasure in thus reminding him that he forgot to stop his order.

Hedger went down to the basement; it, too, was dark. The janitress was taking her evening airing on the basement steps. She sat waving a palm-leaf fan majestically, her dirty calico dress open at the neck. She told him at once that there had been "changes." Miss Bower's room was to let again, and the piano would go tomorrow. Yes, she left yesterday, she sailed for Europe with friends from Chicago. They arrived on Friday, heralded by many telegrams. Very rich people they were said to be, though the man had refused to pay the nurse a month's rent in lieu of notice,—which would have been only right, as the young lady had agreed to take the rooms until October. Mrs. Foley had observed, too, that he didn't overpay her or Willy for their trouble, and a great deal of trouble they had been put to, certainly. Yes, the young lady was very pleasant, but the nurse said there were rings on the mahogany table where she had put tumblers and wine glasses. It was just as well she was gone. The Chicago man was uppish in his ways, but not much to look at. She supposed he had poor health, for there was nothing to him inside his clothes.

Hedger went slowly up the stairs—never had they seemed so long, or his legs so heavy. The upper floor was emptiness and silence. He unlocked his room, lit the gas, and opened the windows. When he went to put his coat in the closet, he found, hanging among his clothes, a pale, flesh-tinted dressing gown he had liked to see her wear, with a perfume—oh, a perfume that was still Eden Bower! He shut the door behind him and there, in the dark, for a moment he lost his manliness. It was when he held this garment to him that he found a letter in the pocket.

The note was written with a lead pencil, in haste: She was sorry that he was angry, but she still didn't know just what she had done. She had thought Mr. Ives would be useful to him; she guessed he was too proud. She wanted awfully to see him again, but Fate came knocking at her door after he had left her. She believed in Fate. She would never forget him, and she knew he would become the greatest painter in the world. Now she must pack. She hoped he wouldn't mind her leaving the dressing gown; somehow, she could never wear it again.

After Hedger read this, standing under the gas, he went back into the closet and knelt down before the wall; the knot hole had been plugged up with a ball of wet paper,—the same blue note-paper on which her letter was written.

He was hard hit. Tonight he had to bear the loneliness of a whole lifetime. Knowing himself so well, he could hardly believe that such a thing had happened to him, that such a woman had lain happy and contented in his arms. And now it was over. He turned out the light and sat down on his painter's stool before the big window. Caesar, on the floor beside him, rested his head on his master's knee. We must leave Hedger thus, sitting in his tank with his dog, looking up at the stars.

COMING, APHRODITE! This legend, in electric lights over the Lexington Opera House, had long announced the return of Eden Bower to New York after years of spectacular success in Paris. She came at last, under the management of an American Opera Company, but bringing her own *chef d'orchestre*.

One bright December afternoon Eden Bower was going down Fifth Avenue in her car, on the way to her broker, in Williams Street. Her thoughts were entirely upon stocks,—Cerro de Pasco, and how much she should buy of it,—when she suddenly looked up and realized that she was skirting Washington Square. She had not seen the place since she rolled out of it in an old-fashioned four-wheeler to seek her fortune, eighteen years ago.

"Arrêtez, Alphonse. Attendez moi," she called, and opened the door before he could reach it. The children who were streaking over the asphalt on roller skates saw a lady in a long fur coat, and short, high-heeled shoes, alight from a French car and pace slowly about the Square, holding her muff to her chin. This spot, at least, had changed very little, she reflected; the same trees, the same fountain, the white arch, and over yonder, Garibaldi, drawing the sword for freedom. There, just opposite her, was the old red brick house.

"Yes, that is the place," she was thinking. "I can smell the carpets now, and the dog,—what was his name? That grubby bathroom at the end of the hall, and that dreadful Hedger—still, there was something about him, you know——" She glanced up and blinked against the sun. From somewhere in the crowded quarter south of the Square a flock of pigeons rose, wheeling quickly upward into the brilliant blue sky. She threw back her head, pressed her muff closer to her chin, and watched them with a smile of amazement and delight. So they still rose, out of all that dirt and noise and squalor, fleet and silvery, just as they used to rise that summer when she was twenty and went up in a balloon on Coney Island!

Alphonse opened the door and tucked her robes about her. All the way down town her mind wandered from Cerro de Pasco, and she kept smiling and looking up at the sky.

When she had finished her business with the broker, she asked him to look in the telephone book for the address of M. Gaston Jules, the picture dealer, and slipped the paper on which he wrote it into her glove. It was five o'clock when she reached the French Galleries, as they were called. On entering she gave the attendant her card, asking him to take it to M. Jules. The dealer appeared very promptly and begged her to come into his private office, where he pushed a great chair toward his desk for her and signalled his secretary to leave the room.

"How good your lighting is in here," she observed, glancing about. "I met you at Simon's studio, didn't I? Oh, no! I never forget anybody who interests me." She threw her muff on his writing table and sank into the deep chair. "I have come to you for some information that's not in my line. Do you know anything about an American painter named Hedger?"

He took the seat opposite her. "Don Hedger? But, certainly! There are some very interesting things of his in an exhibition at V——'s. If you would care to——"

She held up her hand. "No, no. I've no time to go to exhibitions. Is he a man of any importance?"

"Certainly. He is one of the first men among the moderns. That is to say, among the very moderns. He is always coming up with something different. He often exhibits in Paris, you must have seen——"

"No, I tell you I don't go to exhibitions. Has he had great success? That is what I want to know."

M. Jules pulled at his short grey moustache. "But, Madame, there are many kinds of success," he began cautiously.

Madame gave a dry laugh. "Yes, so he used to say. We once quarrelled on that issue. And how would you define his particular kind?"

M. Jules grew thoughtful. "He is a great name with all the young men, and he is decidedly an influence in art. But one can't definitely place a man who is original, erratic, and who is changing all the time."

She cut him short. "Is he much talked about at home? In Paris, I mean? Thanks. That's all I want to know." She rose and began buttoning her coat. "One doesn't like to have been an utter fool, even at twenty."

"*Mais, non!*" M. Jules handed her her muff with a quick, sympathetic glance. He followed her out through the carpeted showroom, now closed to the public and draped in cheesecloth, and put her into her car with words appreciative of the honour she had done him in calling.

Leaning back in the cushions, Eden Bower closed her eyes, and her face, as the street lamps flashed their ugly orange light upon it, became hard and settled, like a plaster cast; so a sail, that has been filled by a strong breeze, behaves when the wind suddenly dies. Tomorrow night the wind would blow again, and this mask would be the golden face of Aphrodite. But a "big" career takes its toll, even with the best of luck.

The Diamond Mine

I

I first became aware that Cressida Garnet was on board when I saw young men with cameras going up to the boat deck. In that exposed spot she was good-naturedly posing for them—amid fluttering lavender scarfs—wearing a most unseaworthy hat, her broad, vigorous face wreathed in smiles. She was too much an American not to believe in publicity. All advertising was good. If it was good for breakfast foods, it was good for prime donne,—especially for a prima donna who would never be any younger and who had just announced her intention of marrying a fourth time.

Only a few days before, when I was lunching with some friends at Sherry's, I had seen Jerome Brown come in with several younger men, looking so pleased and prosperous that I exclaimed upon it.

"His affairs," some one explained, "are looking up. He's going to marry Cressida Garnet. Nobody believed it at first, but since she confirms it he's getting all sorts of credit. That woman's a diamond mine."

If there was ever a man who needed a diamond mine at hand, immediately convenient, it was Jerome Brown. But as an old friend of Cressida Garnet, I was sorry to hear that mining operations were to be begun again.

I had been away from New York and had not seen Cressida for a year; now I paused on the gangplank to note how very like herself she still was, and with what undiminished zeal she went about even the most trifling things that pertained to her profession. From that distance I could recognize her "carrying" smile, and even what, in Columbus, we used to call "the Garnet look."

At the foot of the stairway leading up to the boat deck stood two of the factors in Cressida's destiny. One of them was her sister, Miss Julia; a woman of fifty with a relaxed, mournful face, an ageing skin that browned slowly, like meerschaum, and the unmistakable "look" by which one knew a Garnet. Beside her, pointedly ignoring her, smoking a cigarette while he ran over the passenger list with supercilious almond eyes, stood a youth in a pink shirt and a green plush hat, holding a French bull-dog on the leash. This was "Horace," Cressida's only son. He, at any rate, had not the Garnet look. He was rich and ruddy, indolent and insolent, with soft oval cheeks and the blooming complexion of twenty-two. There was the beginning of a silky shadow on his upper lip. He seemed like a ripe fruit grown out of a rich soil; "oriental," his mother called his peculiar lusciousness. His aunt's restless and aggrieved glance kept flecking him from the side, but the two were as motionless as the *bouledogue,* standing there on his bench legs and surveying his travelling basket with loathing. They were waiting, in constrained immobility, for Cressida to descend and reanimate them,—will them to do or to be something. Forward, by the rail, I saw the stooped, eager back for which I was unconsciously looking: Miletus Poppas, the Greek Jew, Cressida's accompanist and shadow. We were all there, I thought with a smile, except Jerome Brown.

The first member of Cressida's party with whom I had speech was Mr. Poppas. When we were two hours out I came upon him in the act of dropping overboard a steamer cushion made of American flags. Cressida never sailed, I think, that one of these vivid comforts of travel did not reach her at the dock. Poppas recognized me just as the striped object left his hand. He was standing with his arm still extended over the rail, his fingers contemptuously sprung back. "Lest we forgedt!" he said with a shrug. "Does Madame Cressida know we are to have the pleasure of your company for this voyage?" He spoke deliberate, grammatical English—he despised the American rendering of the language—but there was an indescribably foreign quality in his voice,—a something muted; and though he aspirated his "th's" with such conscientious thoroughness, there was always the thud of a "d" in them. Poppas stood before me in a short, tightly buttoned grey coat and cap, exactly the colour of his greyish skin and hair and waxed moustache; a monocle on a very wide black ribbon dangled over his chest. As to his age, I could not offer a conjecture. In the twelve years I had known his thin lupine face behind Cressida's shoulder, it had not changed. I was used to his cold, supercilious manner, to his alarming, deep-set eyes,—very close together, in colour a yellowish green, and always gleaming with something like defeated fury, as if he were actually on the point of having it out with you, or with the world, at last.

I asked him if Cressida had engagements in London.

"Quite so; the Manchester Festival, some concerts at Queen's Hall, and the Opera at Covent Garden; a rather special production of the operas of Mozart. That she can still do quite well,—which is not at all, of course, what we might have expected, and only goes to show that our Madame Cressida is now, as always, a charming exception to rules." Poppas' tone about his client was consistently patronizing, and he was always trying to draw one into a conspiracy of two, based on a mutual understanding of her shortcomings.

I approached him on the one subject I could think of which was more personal than his usefulness to Cressida, and asked him whether he still suffered from facial neuralgia as much as he had done in former years, and whether he was therefore dreading London, where the climate used to be so bad for him.

"And is still," he caught me up, "and is still! For me to go to London is martyrdom, *chère Madame*. In New York it is bad enough, but in London it is the *auto da fé,* nothing less. My nervous system is exotic in any country washed by the Atlantic ocean, and it shivers like a little hairless dog from Mexico. It never relaxes. I think I have told you about my favourite city in the middle of Asia, *la sainte Asie,* where the rainfall is absolutely nil, and you are protected on every side by hundreds of metres of warm, dry sand. I was there when I was a child once, and it is still my intention to retire there when I have finished with all this. I would be there now, n-ow-ow," his voice rose querulously, "if Madame Cressida did not imagine that she needs me,—and her fancies, you know," he flourished his hands, "one gives in to them. In humouring her caprices you and I have already played some together."

We were approaching Cressida's deck chairs, ranged under the open windows of her stateroom. She was already recumbent, swathed in lavender scarfs and wearing purple orchids—doubtless from Jerome Brown. At her left, Horace had settled down to a French novel, and Julia Garnet, at her right, was complainingly regarding the grey horizon. On seeing me, Cressida struggled under her fur-lined robes and got to her feet,—which was more than Horace or Miss Julia managed to do. Miss Julia, as I could have foretold, was not pleased. All the Garnets had an awkward manner with me. Whether it was that I reminded them of things they wished to forget, or whether they thought I esteemed Cressida too highly and the rest of them too lightly, I do not know; but my apppearance upon their scene always put them greatly on their dignity. After Horace had offered me his chair and Miss Julia had said doubtfully that she thought I was looking rather better than when she last saw me, Cressida took my arm and walked me off toward the stern.

"Do you know, Carrie, I half wondered whether I shouldn't find you here, or in London, because you always turn up at critical moments in my life." She pressed my arm confidentially, and I felt that she was once more wrought up to a new purpose. I told her that I had heard some rumour of her engagement.

"It's quite true, and it's all that it should be," she reassured me. "I'll tell you about it later, and you'll see that it's a real solution. They are against me, of course,—all except Horace. He has been such a comfort."

Horace's support, such as it was, could always be had in exchange for his mother's signature, I suspected. The pale May day had turned bleak and chilly, and we sat down by an open hatchway which emitted warm air from somewhere below. At this close range I studied Cressida's face, and felt reassured of her unabated vitality; the old force of will was still there, and with it her characteristic optimism, the old hope of a "solution."

"You have been in Columbus lately?" she was saying. "No, you needn't tell me about it," with a sigh. "Why is it, Caroline, that there is so little of my life I would be willing to live over again? So little that I can even think of without depression. Yet I've really not such a bad conscience. It may mean that I still belong to the future more than to the past, do you think?"

My assent was not warm enough to fix her attention, and she went on thoughtfully: "Of course, it was a bleak country and a bleak period. But I've sometimes wondered whether the bleakness may not have been in me, too; for it has certainly followed me. There, that is no way to talk!" she drew herself up from a momentary attitude of dejection. "Sea air always lets me down at first. That's why it's so good for me in the end."

"I think Julia always lets you down, too," I said bluntly. "But perhaps that depression works out in the same way."

Cressida laughed. "Julia is rather more depressing than Georgie, isn't she? But it was Julia's turn. I can't come alone, and they've grown to expect it. They haven't, either of them, much else to expect."

At this point the deck steward approached us with a blue envelope. "A wireless for you, Madame Garnet."

Cressida put out her hand with impatience, thanked him graciously, and with every indication of pleasure tore open the blue envelope. "It's from Jerome Brown," she said with some confusion, as she folded the paper small and tucked it between the buttons of her close-fitting gown, "Something he forgot to tell me. How long shall you be in London? Good; I want you to meet him. We shall probably be married there as soon as my engagements are over." She rose. "Now I must write some letters. Keep two places at your table, so that I can slip away from my party and dine with you sometimes."

I walked with her toward her chair, in which Mr. Poppas was now reclining. He indicated his readiness to rise, but she shook her head and entered the door of her deck suite. As she passed him, his eye went over her with assurance until it rested upon the folded bit of blue paper in her corsage. He must have seen the original rectangle in the steward's hand; having found it again, he dropped back between Horace and Miss Julia, whom I think he disliked no more than he did the rest of the world. He liked Julia quite as well as he liked me, and he liked me quite as well as he liked any of the women to whom he would be fitfully agreeable upon the voyage. Once or twice, during each crossing, he did his best and made himself very charming indeed, to keep his hand in,—for the same reason that he kept a dummy keyboard in his stateroom, somewhere down in the bowels of the boat. He practised all the small economies; paid the minimum rate, and never took a deck chair, because, as Horace was usually in the cardroom, he could sit in Horace's.

The three of them lay staring at the swell which was steadily growing heavier. Both men had covered themselves with rugs, after dutifully bundling up Miss Julia. As I walked back and forth on the deck, I was struck by their various degrees of in-expressiveness. Opaque brown eyes, almond-shaped and only half open; wolfish green eyes, close-set and always doing something, with a crooked gleam boring in this direction or in that; watery grey eyes, like the thick edges of broken skylight glass: I would have given a great deal to know what was going on behind each pair of them.

These three were sitting there in a row because they were all woven into the pattern of one large and rather splendid life. Each had a bond, and each had a grievance. If they could have their will, what would they do with the generous, credulous creature who nourished them, I wondered? How deep a humiliation would each egotism exact? They would scarcely have harmed her in fortune or in person (though I think Miss Julia looked forward to the day when Cressida would "break" and could be mourned over),—but the fire at which she warmed herself, the little secret hope,—the illusion, ridiculous or sublime, which kept her going,—that they would have stamped out on the instant, with the whole Garnet pack behind them to make extinction sure. All, except, perhaps, Miletus Poppas. He was a vulture of the vulture race, and he had the beak of one. But I always felt that if ever he had her thus at his mercy,—if ever he came upon the softness that was hidden under so much hardness, the warm credulity under a life so dated and scheduled and "reported" and generally exposed,—he would hold his hand and spare.

The weather grew steadily rougher. Miss Julia at last plucked Poppas by the sleeve and indicated that she wished to be released from her wrappings. When she disappeared, there seemed to be every reason to hope that she might be off the scene for awhile. As Cressida said, if she had not brought Julia, she would have had to bring Georgie, or some other Garnet. Cressida's family was like that of the unpopular Prince of Wales, of whom, when he died, some wag wrote:

> If it had been his brother,
> Better him than another.
> If it had been his sister,
> No one would have missed her.

Miss Julia was dampening enough, but Miss Georgie was aggressive and intrusive. She was out to prove to the world, and more especially to Ohio, that all the Garnets were as like Cressida as two peas. Both sisters were club-women, social service workers, and directors in musical societies, and they were continually travelling up and down the Middle West to preside at meetings or to deliver addresses. They reminded one of two sombre, bumping electrics, rolling about with no visible means of locomotion, always running out of power and lying beached in some inconvenient spot until they received a check or a suggestion from Cressy. I was only too well acquainted with the strained, anxious expression that the sight of their handwriting brought to Cressida's face when she ran over her morning mail at breakfast. She usually put their letters by to read "when she was feeling up to it" and hastened to open others which might possibly contain something gracious or pleasant. Sometimes these family unburdenings lay about unread for several days. Any other letters would have got themselves lost, but these bulky epistles, never properly fitted to their envelopes, seemed immune to mischance and unfailingly disgorged to Cressida long explanations as to why her sisters had to do and to have certain things precisely upon her account and because she was so much a public personage.

The truth was that all the Garnets, and particularly her two sisters, were consumed by an habitual, bilious, unenterprising envy of Cressy. They never forgot that, no matter what she did for them or how far she dragged them about the world with her, she would never take one of them to live with her in her Tenth Street house in New York. They thought that was the thing they most wanted. But what they wanted, in the last analysis, was to *be* Cressida. For twenty years she had been plunged in struggle; fighting for her life at first, then for a beginning, for growth, and at last for eminence and perfection; fighting in the dark, and afterward in the light,—which, with her bad preparation, and with her uninspired youth already behind her, took even more courage. During those twenty years the Garnets had been comfortable and indolent and vastly self-satisfied; and now they expected Cressida to make them equal sharers in the finer rewards of her struggle. When her brother Buchanan told me he thought Cressida ought "to make herself one of them," he stated the converse of what he meant. They coveted the qualities which had made her success, as well as the benefits which came from it. More than her furs or her fame or her fortune, they wanted her personal effectiveness, her brighter glow and stronger will to live.

"Sometimes," I have heard Cressida say, looking up from a bunch of those sloppily written letters, "sometimes I get discouraged."

For several days the rough weather kept Miss Julia cloistered in Cressida's deck suite with the maid, Luisa, who confided to me that the Signorina Garnet was "difficile." After dinner I usually found Cressida unincumbered, as Horace was always in the cardroom and Mr. Poppas either nursed his neuralgia or went through the exercise of making himself interesting to some one of the young women on board. One evening, the third night out, when the sea was comparatively quiet and the sky was full of broken black clouds, silvered by the moon at their ragged edges, Cressida talked to me about Jerome Brown.

I had known each of her former husbands. The first one, Charley Wilton, Horace's father, was my cousin. He was organist in a church in Columbus, and Cressida married him when she was nineteen. He died of tuberculosis two years after Horace was born. Cressida nursed him through a long illness and made the living besides. Her courage during the three years of her first marriage was fine enough to foreshadow her future to any discerning eye, and it had made me feel that she deserved any number of chances at marital happiness. There had, of course, been a particular reason for each subsequent experiment, and a sufficiently alluring promise of success. Her motives, in the case of Jerome Brown, seemed to me more vague and less convincing than those which she had explained to me on former occasions.

"It's nothing hasty," she assured me. "It's been coming on for several years. He has never pushed me, but he was always there— some one to count on. Even when I used to meet him at the Whitings, while I was still singing at the Metropolitan, I always felt that he was different from the others; that if I were in straits of any kind, I could call on him. You can't know what that feeling means to me, Carrie. If you look back, you'll see it's something I've never had."

I admitted that, in so far as I knew, she had never been much addicted to leaning on people.

"I've never had any one to lean on," she said with a short laugh. Then she went on, quite seriously: "Somehow, my relations with people always become business relations in the end. I suppose it's because,—except for a sort of professional personality, which I've had to get, just as I've had to get so many other things,—I've not very much that's personal to give people. I've had to give too much else. I've had to try too hard for people who wouldn't try at all."

"Which," I put in firmly, "has done them no good, and has robbed the people who really cared about you."

"By making me grubby, you mean?"

"By making you anxious and distracted so much of the time; empty."

She nodded mournfully. "Yes, I know. You used to warn me. Well, there's not one of my brothers and sisters who does not feel that I carried off the family success, just as I might have carried off the family silver,—if there'd been any! They take the view that there were just so many prizes in the bag; I reached in and took them, so there were none left for the others. At my age, that's a dismal truth to waken up to." Cressida reached for my hand and held it a moment, as if she needed courage to face the facts in her case. "When one remembers one's first success; how one hoped to go home like a Christmas tree full of presents—How much one learns in a life time! That year when Horace was a baby and Charley was dying, and I was touring the West with the Williams band, it was my feeling about my own people that made me go at all. Why I didn't drop myself into one of those muddy rivers, or turn on the gas in one of those dirty hotel rooms, I don't know to this day. At twenty-two you must hope for something more than to be able to bury your husband decently, and what I hoped for was to make my family happy. It was the same afterward in Germany. A young woman must live for human people. Horace wasn't enough. I might have had lovers, of course. I suppose you will say it would have been better if I had."

Though there seemed no need for me to say anything, I murmured that I thought there were more likely to be limits to the rapacity of a lover than to that of a discontented and envious family.

"Well," Cressida gathered herself up, "once I got out from under it all, didn't I? And perhaps, in a milder way, such a release can come again. You were the first person I told when I ran away with Charley, and for a long while you were the only one who knew about Blasius Bouchalka. That time, at least, I shook the Garnets. I wasn't distracted or empty. That time I was all there!"

"Yes," I echoed her, "that time you were all there. It's the greatest possible satisfaction to remember it."

"But even that," she sighed, "was nothing but lawyers and accounts in the end—and a hurt. A hurt that has lasted. I wonder what is the matter with me?"

The matter with Cressida was, that more than any woman I have ever known, she appealed to the acquisitive instinct in men; but this was not easily said, even in the brutal frankness of a long friendship.

We would probably have gone further into the Bouchalka chapter of her life, had not Horace appeared and nervously asked us if we did not wish to take a turn before we went inside. I pleaded indolence, but Cressida rose and disappeared with him. Later I came upon them, standing at the stern above the huddled steerage deck, which was by this time bathed in moonlight, under an almost clear sky. Down there on the silvery floor, little hillocks were scattered about under quilts and shawls; family units, presumably,—male, female, and young. Here and there a black shawl sat alone, nodding. They crouched submissively under the moonlight as if it were a spell. In one of those hillocks a baby was crying, but the sound was faint and thin, a slender protest which aroused no response. Everything was so still that I could hear snatches of the low talk between my friends. Cressida's voice was deep and entreating. She was remonstrating with Horace about his losses at bridge, begging him to keep away from the cardroom.

"But what else is there to do on a trip like this, my Lady?" he expostulated, tossing his spark of a cigarette-end overboard. "What is there, now, to do?"

"Oh, Horace!" she murmured, "how can you be so? If I were twenty-two, and a boy, with some one to back me—"

Horace drew his shoulders together and buttoned his top-coat. "Oh, I've not your energy, Mother dear. We make no secret of that. I am as I am. I didn't ask to be born into this charming world."

To this gallant speech Cressida made no answer. She stood with her hand on the rail and her head bent forward, as if she had lost herself in thought. The ends of her scarf, lifted by the breeze, fluttered upward, almost transparent in the argent light. Presently she turned away,—as if she had been alone and were leaving only the night sea behind her,—and walked slowly forward; a strong, solitary figure on the white deck, the smoke-like scarf twisting and climbing and falling back upon itself in the light over her head. She reached the door of her stateroom and disappeared. Yes, she was a Garnet, but she was also Cressida; and she had done what she had done.

II

My first recollections of Cressida Garnet have to do with the Columbus Public Schools; a little girl with sunny brown hair and eager bright eyes, looking anxiously at the teacher and reciting the names and dates of the Presidents: "James Buchanan, 1857–1861; Abraham Lincoln, 1861–1865"; etc. Her family came from North Carolina, and they had that to feel superior about before they had Cressy. The Garnet "look," indeed, though based upon a strong family resemblance, was nothing more than the restless, preoccupied expression of an inflamed sense of importance. The father was a Democrat, in the sense that other men were doctors or lawyers. He scratched up some sort of poor living for his family behind office windows inscribed with the words "Real Estate. Insurance. Investments." But it was his political faith that, in a Republican community, gave him his feeling of eminence and originality. The Garnet children were all in school then, scattered along from the first grade to the ninth. In almost any room of our school building you might chance to enter, you saw the self-conscious little face of one or another of them. They were restrained, uncomfortable children, not frankly boastful, but insinuating, and somehow forever demanding special consideration and holding grudges against teachers and classmates who did not show it them; all but Cressida, who was naturally as sunny and open as a May morning.

It was no wonder that Cressy ran away with young Charley Wilton, who hadn't a shabby thing about him except his health. He was her first music teacher, the choir-master of the church in which she sang. Charley was very handsome; the "romantic" son of an old, impoverished family. He had refused to go into a good business with his uncles and had gone abroad to study music when that was an extravagant and picturesque thing for an Ohio boy to do. His letters home were handed round among the members of his own family and of other families equally conservative. Indeed, Charley and what his mother called "his music" were the romantic expression of a considerable group of people; young cousins and old aunts and quiet-dwelling neighbours, allied by the amity of several generations. Nobody was properly married in our part of Columbus unless Charley Wilton, and no other, played the wedding march. The old ladies of the First Church used to say that he "hovered over the keys like a spirit." At nineteen Cressida was beautiful enough to turn a much harder head than the pale, ethereal one Charley Wilton bent above the organ.

That the chapter which began so gracefully ran on into such a stretch of grim, hard prose, was simply Cressida's relentless bad luck. In her undertakings, in whatever she could lay hold of with her two hands, she was successful; but whatever happened to her was almost sure to be bad. Her family, her husbands, her son, would have crushed any other woman I have ever known. Cressida lived, more than most of us, "for others"; and what she seemed to promote among her beneficiaries was indolence and envy and discord—even dishonesty and turpitude.

Her sisters were fond of saying—at club luncheons—that Cressida had remained "untouched by the breath of scandal," which was not strictly true. There were captious people who objected to her long and close association with Miletus Poppas. Her second husband, Ransome McChord, the foreign representative of the great McChord Harvester Company, whom she married in Germany, had so persistently objected to Poppas that she was eventually forced to choose between them. Any one who knew her well could easily understand why she chose Poppas.

While her actual self was the least changed, the least modified by experience that it would be possible to imagine, there had been, professionally, two Cressida Garnets; the big handsome girl, already a "popular favourite" of the concert stage, who took with her to

Germany the raw material of a great voice;—and the accomplished artist who came back. The singer that returned was largely the work of Miletus Poppas. Cressida had at least known what she needed, hunted for it, found it, and held fast to it. After experimenting with a score of teachers and accompanists, she settled down to work her problem out with Poppas. Other coaches came and went—she was always trying new ones—but Poppas survived them all. Cressida was not musically intelligent; she never became so. Who does not remember the countless rehearsals which were necessary before she first sang *Isolde* in Berlin; the disgust of the conductor, the sullenness of the tenor, the rages of the blonde *teufelin,* boiling with the impatience of youth and genius, who sang her *Brangaena?* Everything but her driving power Cressida had to get from the outside.

Poppas was, in his way, quite as incomplete as his pupil. He possessed a great many valuable things for which there is no market; intuitions, discrimination, imagination, a whole twilight world of intentions and shadowy beginnings which were dark to Cressida. I remember that when "Trilby" was published she fell into a fright and said such books ought to be prohibited by law; which gave me an intimation of what their relationship had actually become.

Poppas was indispensable to her. He was like a book in which she had written down more about herself than she could possibly remember—and it was information that she might need at any moment. He was the one person who knew her absolutely and who saw into the bottom of her grief. An artist's saddest secrets are those that have to do with his artistry. Poppas knew all the simple things that were so desperately hard for Cressida, all the difficult things in which she could count on herself; her stupidities and inconsistencies, the chiaroscuro of the voice itself and what could be expected from the mind somewhat mismated with it. He knew where she was sound and where she was mended. With him she could share the depressing knowledge of what a wretchedly faulty thing any productive faculty is.

But if Poppas was necessary to her career, she was his career. By the time Cressida left the Metropolitan Opera Company, Poppas was a rich man. He had always received a retaining fee and a percentage of her salary,—and he was a man of simple habits. Her liberality with Poppas was one of the weapons that Horace and the Garnets used against Cressida, and it was a point in the argument by which they justified to themselves their rapacity. Whatever they didn't get, they told themselves, Poppas would. What they got, therefore, they were only saving from Poppas. The Greek ached a good deal at the general pillage, and Cressida's conciliatory methods with her family made him sarcastic and spiteful. But he had to make terms, somehow, with the Garnets and Horace, and with the husband, if there happened to be one. He sometimes reminded them, when they fell to wrangling, that they must not, after all, overturn the boat under them, and that it would be better to stop just before they drove her wild than just after. As he was the only one among them who understood the sources of her fortune,—and they knew it,—he was able, when it came to a general set-to, to proclaim sanctuary for the goose that laid the golden eggs.

That Poppas had caused the break between Cressida and McChord was another stick her sisters held over her. They pretended to understand perfectly, and were always explaining what they termed her "separation"; but they let Cressida know that it cast a shadow over her family and took a good deal of living down.

A beautiful soundness of body, a seemingly exhaustless vitality, and a certain "squareness" of character as well as of mind, gave Cressida Garnet earning powers that were exceptional even in her lavishly rewarded profession. Managers chose her over the heads of singers much more gifted, because she was so sane, so conscientious, and above all, because she was so sure. Her efficiency was like a beacon to lightly anchored men, and in the intervals between her marriages she had as many suitors as Penelope. Whatever else they saw in her at first, her competency so impressed and delighted them that they gradually lost sight of everything else. Her sterling character was the subject of her story. Once, as she said, she very nearly escaped her destiny. With Blasius Bouchalka she became almost another woman, but not quite. Her "principles," or his lack of them, drove those two apart in the end. It was of Bouchalka that we talked upon that last voyage I ever made with Cressida Garnet, and not of Jerome Brown.

She remembered the Bohemian kindly, and since it was the passage in her life to which she most often reverted, it is the one I shall relate here.

III

Late one afternoon in the winter of 189–, Cressida and I were walking in Central Park after the first heavy storm of the year. The snow had been falling thickly all the night before, and all day, until about four o'clock. Then the air grew much warmer and the sky cleared. Overhead it was a soft, rainy blue, and to the west a smoky gold. All around the horizon everything became misty and silvery; even the big, brutal buildings looked like pale violet water-colours on a silver ground. Under the elm trees along the Mall the air was purple as wisterias. The sheep-field, toward Broadway, was smooth and white, with a thin gold wash over it. At five o'clock the carriage came for us, but Cressida sent the driver home to the Tenth Street house with the message that she would dine uptown, and that Horace and Mr. Poppas were not to wait for her. As the horses trotted away we turned up the Mall.

"I won't go indoors this evening for any one," Cressida declared. "Not while the sky is like that. Now we will go back to the laurel wood. They are so black, over the snow, that I could cry for joy. I don't know when I've felt so care-free as I feel tonight. Country winter, country stars—they always make me think of Charley Wilton."

She was singing twice a week, sometimes oftener, at the Metropolitan that season, quite at the flood-tide of her powers, and so enmeshed in operatic routine that to be walking in the park at an unaccustomed hour, unattended by one of the men of her entourage, seemed adventurous. As we strolled along the little paths among the snow banks and the bronze laurel bushes, she kept going back to my poor young cousin, dead so long. "Things happen out of season. That's the worst of living. It was untimely for both of us, and yet," she sighed softly, "since he had to die, I'm not sorry. There was one beautifully happy year, though we were so poor, and it gave him— something! It would have been too hard if he'd had to miss everything." (I remember her simplicity, which never changed any more than winter or Ohio change.) "Yes," she went on, "I always feel very tenderly about Charley. I believe I'd do the same thing right over again, even knowing all that had to come after. If I were nineteen tonight, I'd rather go sleigh-riding with Charley Wilton than anything else I've ever done."

We walked until the procession of carriages on the driveway, getting people home to dinner, grew thin, and then we went slowly toward the Seventh Avenue gate, still talking of Charley Wilton. We decided to dine at a place not far away, where the only access from the street was a narrow door, like a hole in the wall, between a tobacconist's and a flower shop. Cressida deluded herself into believing that her incognito was more successful in such non-descript places. She was wearing a long sable coat, and a deep fur hat, hung with red cherries, which she had brought from Russia. Her walk had given her a fine colour, and she looked so much a personage that no disguise could have been wholly effective.

The dining-rooms, frescoed with conventional Italian scenes, were built round a court. The orchestra was playing as we entered and selected our table. It was not a bad orchestra, and we were no sooner seated than the first violin began to speak, to assert itself, as if it were suddenly done with mediocrity.

"We have been recognized," Cressida said complacently. "What a good tone he has, quite unusual. What does he look like?" She sat with her back to the musicians.

The violinist was standing, directing his men with his head and with the beak of his violin. He was a tall, gaunt young man, big-boned and rugged, in skin-tight clothes. His high forehead had a kind of luminous pallour, and his hair was jet black and somewhat stringy. His manner was excited and dramatic. At the end of the number he acknowledged the applause, and Cressida looked at him graciously over her shoulder. He swept her with a brilliant glance and bowed again. Then I noticed his red lips and thick black eyebrows.

"He looks as if he were poor or in trouble," Cressida said. "See how short his sleeves are, and how he mops his face as if the least thing upset him. This is a hard winter for musicians."

The violinist rummaged among some music piled on a chair, turning over the sheets with flurried rapidity, as if he were searching for a lost article of which he was in desperate need. Presently he placed some sheets upon the piano and began vehemently to explain something to the pianist. The pianist stared at the music doubtfully—he was a plump old man with a rosy, bald crown, and his shiny linen and neat tie made him look as if he were on his way to a party. The violinist bent over him, suggesting rhythms with his shoulders and running his bony finger up and down the pages. When he stepped back to his place, I noticed that the other players sat at ease, without raising their instruments.

"He is going to try something unusual," I commented. "It looks as if it might be manuscript."

It was something, at all events, that neither of us had heard before, though it was very much in the manner of the later Russian composers who were just beginning to be heard in New York. The young man made a brilliant dash of it, despite a lagging, scrambling accompaniment by the conservative pianist. This time we both applauded him vigorously and again, as he bowed, he swept us with his eye.

The usual repertory of restaurant music followed, varied by a charming bit from Massenet's "Manon," then little known in this country. After we paid our check, Cressida took out one of her visiting cards and wrote across the top of it: *We thank you for the unusual music and the pleasure your playing has given us.* She folded the card in the middle, and asked the waiter to give it to the director of the orchestra. Pausing at the door, while the porter dashed out to call a cab, we saw, in the wall mirror, a pair of wild black eyes following us quite despairingly from behind the palms at the other end of the room. Cressida observed as we went out that the young man was probably having a hard struggle. "He never got those clothes here, surely. They were probably made by a country tailor in some little town in Austria. He seemed wild enough to grab at anything, and was trying to make himself heard above the dishes, poor fellow. There are so many like him. I wish I could help them all! I didn't quite have the courage to send him money. His smile, when he bowed to us, was not that of one who would take it, do you think?"

"No," I admitted, "it wasn't. He seemed to be pleading for recognition. I don't think it was money he wanted."

A week later I came upon some curious-looking manuscript songs on the piano in Cressida's music room. The text was in some Slavic tongue with a French translation written underneath. Both the handwriting and the musical script were done in a manner experienced, even distinguished. I was looking at them when Cressida came in.

"Oh, yes!" she exclaimed. "I meant to ask you to try them over. Poppas thinks they are very interesting. They are from that young violinist, you remember,—the one we noticed in the restaurant that evening. He sent them with such a nice letter. His name is Blasius Bouchalka (Boú-kal-ka), a Bohemian."

I sat down at the piano and busied myself with the manuscript, while Cressida dashed off necessary notes and wrote checks in a large square checkbook, six to a page. I supposed her immersed in sumptuary preoccupations when she suddenly looked over her shoulder and said, "Yes, that legend, *Sarka,* is the most interesting. Run it through a few times and I'll try it over with you."

There was another, *"Dans les ombres des forêts tristes,"* which I thought quite as beautiful. They were fine songs; very individual, and each had that spontaneity which makes a song seem inevitable and, once for all, "done." The accompaniments were difficult, but not unnecessarily so; they were free from fatuous ingenuity and fine writing.

"I wish he'd indicated his tempi a little more clearly," I remarked as I finished *Sarka* for the third time. "It matters, because he really has something to say. An orchestral accompaniment would be better, I should think."

"Yes, he sent the orchestral arrangement. Poppas has it. It works out beautifully,—so much colour in the instrumentation. The English horn comes in so effectively there," she rose and indicated the passage, "just right with the voice. I've asked him to come next Sunday, so please be here if you can. I want to know what you think of him."

Cressida was always at home to her friends on Sunday afternoon unless she was billed for the evening concert at the Opera House, in which case we were sufficiently advised by the daily press. Bouchalka must have been told to come early, for when I arrived on Sunday, at four, he and Cressida had the music-room quite to themselves and were standing by the piano in earnest conversation. In a few moments they were separated by other early comers, and I led Bouchalka across the hall to the drawing-room. The guests, as they came in, glanced at him curiously. He wore a dark blue suit, soft and rather baggy, with a short coat, and a high double-breasted vest with two rows of buttons coming up to the loops of his black tie. This costume was even more foreign-looking than his skin-tight dress clothes, but it was more becoming. He spoke hurried, elliptical English, and very good French. All his sympathies were French rather than German— the Czechs lean to the one culture or to the other. I found him a fierce, a transfixing talker. His brilliant eyes, his gaunt hands, his white, deeply-lined forehead, all entered into his speech.

I asked him whether he had not recognized Madame Garnet at once when we entered the restaurant that evening more than a week ago.

"*Mais, certainement!* I hear her twice when she sings in the afternoon, and sometimes at night for the last act. I have a friend who buys a ticket for the first part, and he comes out and gives to me his pass-back check, and I return for the last act. That is convenient if I am broke." He explained the trick with amusement but without embarrassment, as if it were a shift that we might any of us be put to.

I told him that I admired his skill with the violin, but his songs much more.

He threw out his red under-lip and frowned. "Oh, I have no instrument! The violin I play from necessity; the flute, the piano, as it happens. For three years now I write all the time, and it spoils the hand for violin."

When the maid brought him his tea, he took both muffins and cakes and told me that he was very hungry. He had to lunch and dine at the place where he played, and he got very tired of the food. "But since," his black eyebrows nearly met in an acute angle, "but since, before, I eat at a bakery, with the slender brown roach on the pie, I guess I better let alone well enough." He paused to drink his tea; as he tasted one of the cakes his face lit with sudden animation and he gazed across the hall after the maid with the tray—she was now holding it before the aged and ossified 'cellist of the Hempfstangle Quartette. "*Des gâteaux,*" he murmured feelingly, "*où est-ce qu'elle peut trouver de tels gâteaux ici à New York?*"

I explained to him that Madame Garnet had an accomplished cook who made them,—an Austrian, I thought.

He shook his head. *"Autrichienne? Je ne pense pas."*

Cressida was approaching with the new Spanish soprano, Mme. Bartolas, who was all black velvet and long black feathers, with a lace veil over her rich pallour and even a little black patch on her chin. I beckoned them. "Tell me, Cressida, isn't Ruzenka an Austrian?"

She looked surprised. "No, a Bohemian, though I got her in Vienna." Bouchalka's expression, and the remnant of a cake in his long fingers, gave her the connection. She laughed. "You like them? Of course, they are of your own country. You shall have more of them." She nodded and went away to greet a guest who had just come in.

A few moments later, Horace, then a beautiful lad in Eton clothes, brought another cup of tea and a plate of cakes for Bouchalka. We sat down in a corner, and talked about his songs. He was neither boastful nor deprecatory. He knew exactly in what respects they were excellent. I decided as I watched his face, that he must be under thirty. The deep lines in his forehead probably came there from his habit of frowning densely when he struggled to express himself, and suddenly elevating his coal-black eyebrows when his ideas cleared. His teeth were white, very irregular and interesting. The corrective methods of modern dentistry would have taken away half his good looks. His mouth would have been much less attractive for any re-arranging of those long, narrow, over-crowded teeth. Along with his frown and his way of thrusting out his lip, they contributed, somehow, to the engaging impetuousness of his conversation. As we talked about his songs, his manner changed. Before that he had seemed responsive and easily pleased. Now he grew abstracted, as if I had taken away his pleasant afternoon and wakened him to his miseries. He moved restlessly in his clothes. When I mentioned Puccini, he held his head in his hands. "Why is it they like that always and always? A little, oh yes, very nice. But so much, always the same thing! Why?" He pierced me with the despairing glance which had followed us out of the restaurant.

I asked him whether he had sent any of his songs to the publishers and named one whom I knew to be discriminating. He shrugged his shoulders. "They not want Bohemian songs. They not want my music. Even the street cars will not stop for me here, like for other people. Every time, I wait on the corner until somebody else make a signal to the car, and then it stop,—but not for me."

Most people cannot become utterly poor; whatever happens, they can right themselves a little. But one felt that Bouchalka was the sort of person who might actually starve or blow his brains out. Something very important had been left out either of his make-up or of his education; something that we are not accustomed to miss in people.

Gradually the parlour was filled with little groups of friends, and I took Bouchalka back to the music-room where Cressida was surrounded by her guests; feathered women, with large sleeves and hats, young men of no importance, in frock coats, with shining hair, and the smile which is intended to say so many flattering things but which really expresses little more than a desire to get on. The older men were standing about waiting for a word *à deux* with the hostess. To these people Bouchalka had nothing to say. He stood stiffly at the outer edge of the circle, watching Cressida with intent, impatient eyes, until, under the pretext of showing him a score, she drew him into the alcove at the back end of the long room, where she kept her musical library. The bookcases ran from the floor to the ceiling. There was a table and a reading-lamp, and a window seat looking upon the little walled garden. Two persons could be quite withdrawn there, and yet be a part of the general friendly scene. Cressida took a score from the shelf, and sat down with Bouchalka upon the window seat, the book open between them, though neither of them looked at it again. They fell to talking with great earnestness. At last the Bohemian pulled out a large, yellowing silver watch, held it up before him, and stared at it a moment as if it were an object of horror. He sprang up, bent over Cressida's hand and murmured something, dashed into the hall and out of the front door without waiting for the maid to open it. He had worn no overcoat, apparently. It was then seven o'clock; he would surely be late at his post in the up-town restaurant. I hoped he would have wit enough to take the elevated.

After supper Cressida told me his story. His parents, both poor musicians,—the mother a singer—died while he was yet a baby, and he was left to the care of an arbitrary uncle who resolved to make a priest of him. He was put into a monastery school and kept there. The organist and choir director, fortunately for Blasius, was an excellent musician, a man who had begun his career brilliantly, but who had met with crushing sorrows and disappointments in the world. He devoted himself to his talented pupil, and was the only teacher the young man ever had. At twenty-one, when he was ready for the novitiate, Blasius felt that the call of life was too strong for him, and he ran away out into a world of which he knew nothing. He tramped southward to Vienna, begging and playing his fiddle from town to town. In Vienna he fell in with a gipsy band which was being recruited for a Paris restaurant and went with them to Paris. He played in cafés and in cheap theatres, did transcribing for a music publisher, tried to get pupils. For four years he was the mouse, and hunger was the cat. She kept him on the jump. When he got work he did not understand why; when he lost a job he did not understand why. During the time when most of us acquire a practical sense, get a half-unconscious knowledge of hard facts and market values, he had been shut away from the world, fed like the pigeons in the bell-tower of his monastery. Bouchalka had now been in New York a year, and for all he knew about it, Cressida said, he might have landed the day before yesterday.

Several weeks went by, and as Bouchalka did not reappear on Tenth Street, Cressida and I went once more to the place where he had played, only to find another violinist leading the orchestra. We summoned the proprietor, a Swiss-Italian, polite and solicitous. He told us the gentleman was not playing there any more,—was playing somewhere else, but he had forgotten where. We insisted upon talking to the old pianist, who at last reluctantly admitted that the Bohemian had been dismissed. He had arrived very late one Sunday night three weeks ago, and had hot words with the proprietor. He had been late before, and had been warned. He was a very talented fellow, but wild and not to be depended upon. The old man gave us the address of a French boarding-house on Seventh Avenue where Bouchalka used to room. We drove there at once, but the woman who kept the place said that he had gone away two weeks before, leaving no address, as he never got letters. Another Bohemian, who did engraving on glass, had a room with her, and when he came home perhaps he could tell where Bouchalka was, for they were friends.

It took us several days to run Bouchalka down, but when we did find him Cressida promptly busied herself in his behalf. She sang his "*Sarka*" with the Metropolitan Opera orchestra at a Sunday night concert, she got him a position with the Symphony Orchestra, and persuaded the conservative Hempfstangle Quartette to play one of his chamber compositions from manuscript. She aroused the interest of a publisher in his work, and introduced him to people who were helpful to him.

By the new year Bouchalka was fairly on his feet. He had proper clothes now, and Cressida's friends found him attractive. He was usually at her house on Sunday afternoons; so usually, indeed, that Poppas began pointedly to absent himself. When other guests arrived, the Bohemian and his patroness were always found at the critical point of discussion,—at the piano, by the fire, in the alcove at the end of the room—both of them interested and animated. He was invariably respectful and admiring, deferring to her in every tone and gesture, and she was perceptibly pleased and flattered,—as if all this were new to her and she were tasting the sweetness of a first success.

One wild day in March Cressida burst tempestuously into my apartment and threw herself down, declaring that she had just come from the most trying rehearsal she had ever lived through. When I tried to question her about it, she replied absently and continued to shiver and crouch by the fire. Suddenly she rose, walked to the window, and stood looking out over the Square, glittering with ice and rain and strewn with the wrecks of umbrellas. When she turned again, she approached me with determination.

"I shall have to ask you to go with me," she said firmly. "That crazy Bouchalka has gone and got a pleurisy or something. It may be pneumonia; there is an epidemic of it just now. I've sent Dr. Brooks to him, but I can never tell anything from what a doctor says. I've got to see Bouchalka and his nurse, and what sort of place he's in. I've been rehearsing all day and I'm singing tomorrow night; I can't have so much on my mind. Can you come with me? It will save time in the end."

I put on my furs, and we went down to Cressida's carriage, waiting below. She gave the driver a number on Seventh Avenue, and then began feeling her throat with the alarmed expression which meant that she was not going to talk. We drove in silence to the address, and by this time it was growing dark. The French landlady was a cordial, comfortable person who took Cressida in at a glance and seemed much impressed. Cressida's incognito was never successful. Her black gown was inconspicuous enough, but over it she wore a dark purple velvet carriage coat, lined with fur and furred at the cuffs and collar. The Frenchwoman's eye ran over it delightedly and scrutinized the veil which only half-concealed the well-known face behind it. She insisted upon conducting us up to the fourth floor herself, running ahead of us and turning up the gas jets in the dark, musty-smelling halls. I suspect that she tarried outside the door after we sent the nurse for her walk.

We found the sick man in a great walnut bed, a relic of the better days which this lodging house must have seen. The grimy red plush carpet, the red velvet chairs with broken springs, the double gilt-framed mirror above the mantel, had all been respectable, substantial contributions to comfort in their time. The fireplace was now empty and grateless, and an ill-smelling gas stove burned in its sooty recess under the cracked marble. The huge arched windows were hung with heavy red curtains, pinned together and lightly stirred by the wind which rattled the loose frames.

I was examining these things while Cressida bent over Bouchalka. Her carriage cloak she threw over the foot of his bed, either from a protective impulse, or because there was no place else to put it. After she had greeted him and seated herself, the sick man reached down and drew the cloak up and over him, looking at it with weak, childish pleasure and stroking the velvet with his long fingers. *"Couleur de gloire, couleur des reines!"* I heard him murmur. He thrust the sleeve under his chin and closed his eyes. His loud, rapid breathing was the only sound in the room. If Cressida brushed back his hair or touched his hand, he looked up long enough to give her a smile of utter adoration, naïve and uninquiring, as if he were smiling at a dream or a miracle.

The nurse was gone for an hour, and we sat quietly, Cressida with her eyes fixed on Bouchalka, and I absorbed in the strange atmosphere of the house, which seemed to seep in under the door and through the walls. Occasionally we heard a call for *"de l'eau chaude!"* and the heavy trot of a serving woman on the stairs. On the floor below somebody was struggling with Schubert's Marche Militaire on a coarse-toned upright piano. Sometimes, when a door was opened, one could hear a parrot screaming, *"Voilà, voilà, tonnerre!"* The house was built before 1870, as one could tell from windows and mouldings, and the walls were thick. The sounds were not disturbing and Bouchalka was probably used to them.

When the nurse returned and we rose to go, Bouchalka still lay with his cheek on her cloak, and Cressida left it. "It seems to please him," she murmured as we went down the stairs. "I can go home without a wrap. It's not far." I had, of course, to give her my furs, as I was not singing *Donna Anna* tomorrow evening and she was.

After this I was not surprised by any devout attitude in which I happened to find the Bohemian when I entered Cressida's music-room unannounced, or by any radiance on her face when she rose from the window-seat in the alcove and came down the room to greet me.

Bouchalka was, of course, very often at the Opera now. On almost any night when Cressida sang, one could see his narrow black head— high above the temples and rather constrained behind the ears— peering from some part of the house. I used to wonder what he thought of Cressida as an artist, but probably he did not think seriously at all. A great voice, a handsome woman, a great prestige, all added together made a "great artist," the common synonym for success. Her success, and the material evidences of it, quite blinded him. I could never draw from him anything adequate about Anna Straka, Cressida's Slavic rival, and this perhaps meant that he considered comparison disloyal. All the while that Cressida was singing reliably, and satisfying the management, Straka was singing uncertainly and making history. Her voice was primarily defective, and her immediate vocal method was bad. Cressida was always living up to her contract, delivering the whole order in good condition; while the Slav was sometimes almost voiceless, sometimes inspired. She put you off with a hope, a promise, time after time. But she was quite as likely to put you off with a revelation,—with an interpretation that was inimitable, unrepeatable.

Bouchalka was not a reflective person. He had his own idea of what a great prima donna should be like, and he took it for granted that Mme. Garnet corresponded to his conception. The curious thing was that he managed to impress his idea upon Cressida herself. She began to see herself as he saw her, to try to be like the notion of her that he carried somewhere in that pointed head of his. She was exalted quite beyond herself. Things that had been chilled under the grind came to life in her that winter, with the breath of Bouchalka's adoration. Then, if ever in her life, she heard the bird sing on the branch outside her window; and she wished she were younger, lovelier, freer. She wished there were no Poppas, no Horace, no Garnets. She longed to be only the bewitching creature Bouchalka imagined her.

One April day when we were driving in the Park, Cressida, superb in a green-and-primrose costume hurried over from Paris, turned to me smiling and said: "Do you know, this is the first spring I haven't dreaded. It's the first one I've ever really had. Perhaps people never have more than one, whether it comes early or late." She told me that she was overwhelmingly in love.

Our visit to Bouchalka when he was ill had, of course, been reported, and the men about the Opera House had made of it the only story they have the wit to invent. They could no more change the pattern of that story than the spider could change the design of its web. But being, as she said, "in love" suggested to Cressida only one plan of action; to have the Tenth Street house done over, to put more money into her brothers' business, send Horace to school, raise Poppas' percentage, and then with a clear conscience be married in the Church of the Ascension. She went through this program with her usual thoroughness. She was married in June and sailed immediately with her husband. Poppas was to join them in Vienna in August, when she would begin to work again. From her letters I gathered that all was going well, even beyond her hopes.

When they returned in October, both Cressida and Blasius seemed changed for the better. She was preceptibly freshened and renewed.

She attacked her work at once with more vigour and more ease; did not drive herself so relentlessly. A little carelessness became her wonderfully. Bouchalka was less gaunt, and much less flighty and perverse. His frank pleasure in the comfort and order of his wife's establishment was ingratiating, even if it was a little amusing. Cressida had the sewing-room at the top of the house made over into a study for him. When I went up there to see him, I usually found him sitting before the fire or walking about with his hands in his coat pockets, admiring his new possessions. He explained the ingenious arrangement of his study to me a dozen times.

With Cressida's friends and guests, Bouchalka assumed nothing for himself. His deportment amounted to a quiet, unobtrusive appreciation of her and of his good fortune. He was proud to owe his wife so much. Cressida's Sunday afternoons were more popular than ever, since she herself had so much more heart for them. Bouchalka's picturesque presence stimulated her graciousness and charm. One still found them conversing together as eagerly as in the days when they saw each other but seldom. Consequently their guests were never bored. We felt as if the Tenth Street house had a pleasant climate quite its own. In the spring, when the Metropolitan company went on tour, Cressida's husband accompanied her, and afterward they again sailed for Genoa.

During the second winter people began to say that Bouchalka was becoming too thoroughly domesticated, and that since he was growing heavier in body he was less attractive. I noticed his increasing reluctance to stir abroad. Nobody could say that he was "wild" now. He seemed to dread leaving the house, even for an evening. Why should he go out, he said, when he had everything he wanted at home? He published very little. One was given to understand that he was writing an opera. He lived in the Tenth Street house like a tropical plant under glass. Nowhere in New York could he get such cookery as Ruzenka's. Ruzenka ("little Rose") had, like her mistress, bloomed afresh, now that she had a man and a compatriot to cook for. Her invention was tireless, and she took things with a high hand in the kitchen, confident of a perfect appreciation. She was a plump, fair, blue-eyed girl, giggly and easily flattered, with teeth like cream. She was passionately domestic, and her mind was full of homely stories and proverbs and superstitions which she somehow worked into her cookery. She and Bouchalka had between them a whole literature of traditions about sauces and fish and pastry. The cellar was full of the wines he liked, and Ruzenka always knew what wines to serve with the dinner. Blasius' monastery had been famous for good living.

That winter was a very cold one, and I think the even temperature of the house enslaved Bouchalka. "Imagine it," he once said to me when I dropped in during a blinding snowstorm and found him reading before the fire. "To be warm all the time, every day! It is like Aladdin. In Paris I have had weeks together when I was not warm once, when I did not have a bath once, like the cats in the street. The nights were a misery. People have terrible dreams when they are so cold. Here I waken up in the night so warm I do not know what it means. Her door is open, and I turn on my light. I cannot believe in myself until I see that she is there."

I began to think that Bouchalka's wildness had been the desperation which the tamest animals exhibit when they are tortured or terrorized. Naturally luxurious, he had suffered more than most men under the pinch of penury. Those first beautiful compositions, full of the folk-music of his own country, had been wrung out of him by home-sickness and heart-ache. I wondered whether he could compose only under the spur of hunger and loneliness, and whether his talent might not subside with his despair. Some such apprehension must have troubled Cressida, though his gratitude would have been propitiatory to a more exacting task-master. She had always liked to make people happy, and he was the first one who had accepted her bounty without sourness. When he did not accompany her upon her spring tour, Cressida said it was because travelling interfered with composition; but I felt that she was deeply disappointed. Blasius, or Blažej, as his wife had with difficulty learned to call him, was not showy or ex-travagant. He hated hotels, even the best of them. Cressida had always fought for the hearthstone and the fireside, and the humour of destiny is sometimes to give us too much of what we desire. I believe she would have preferred even enthusiasm about other women to his utter *oisiveté*. It was his old fire, not his docility, that had won her.

During the third season after her marriage Cressida had only twenty-five performances at the Metropolitan, and she was singing out of town a great deal. Her husband did not bestir himself to accompany her, but he attended, very faithfully, to her correspondence and to her business at home. He had no ambitious schemes to increase her fortune, and he carried out her directions exactly. Nevertheless, Cressida faced her concert tours somewhat grimly, and she seldom talked now about their plans for the future.

The crisis in this growing estrangement came about by accident,— one of those chance occurrences that affect our lives more than years of ordered effort,—and it came in an inverted form of a situation old to comedy. Cressida had been on the road for several weeks; singing in Minneapolis, Cleveland, St. Paul, then up into Canada and back to Boston. From Boston she was to go directly to Chicago, coming down on the five o'clock train and taking the eleven, over the Lake Shore, for the West. By her schedule she would have time to change cars comfortably at the Grand Central station.

On the journey down from Boston she was seized with a great desire to see Blasius. She decided, against her custom, one might say against her principles, to risk a performance with the Chicago orchestra without rehearsal, to stay the night in New York and go west by the afternoon train the next day. She telegraphed Chicago, but she did not telegraph Blasius, because she wished—the old fallacy of affection!—to "surprise" him. She could take it for granted that, at eleven on a cold winter night, he would be in the Tenth Street house and nowhere else in New York. She sent Poppas—paler than usual with accusing scorn—and her trunks on to Chicago, and with only her travelling bag and a sense of being very audacious in her behaviour and still very much in love, she took a cab for Tenth Street.

Since it was her intention to disturb Blasius as little as possible and to delight him as much as possible, she let herself in with her latch-key and went directly to his room. She did not find him there. Indeed, she found him where he should not have been at all. There must have been a trying scene.

Ruzenka was sent away in the morning, and the other two maids as well. By eight o'clock Cressida and Bouchalka had the house to themselves. Nobody had any breakfast. Cressida took the afternoon train to keep her engagement with Theodore Thomas, and to think over the situation. Blasius was left in the Tenth Street house with only the furnace man's wife to look after him. His explanation of his conduct was that he had been drinking too much. His digression, he swore, was casual. It had never occurred before, and he could only appeal to his wife's magnanimity. But it was, on the whole, easier for Cressida to be firm than to be yielding, and she knew herself too well to attempt a readjustment. She had never made shabby compromises, and it was too late for her to begin. When she returned to New York she went to a hotel, and she never saw Bouchalka alone again. Since he admitted her charge, the legal formalities were conducted so quietly that the granting of her divorce was announced in the morning papers before her friends knew that there was the least likelihood of one. Cressida's concert tours had interrupted the hospitalities of the house.

While the lawyers were arranging matters, Bouchalka came to see me. He was remorseful and miserable enough, and I think his perplexity was quite sincere. If there had been an intrigue with a woman of her own class, an infatuation, an affair, he said, he could understand. But anything so venial and accidental— He shook his head slowly back and forth. He assured me that he was not at all himself on that fateful evening, and that when he recovered himself he would have sent Ruzenka away, making proper provision for her, of course. It was an ugly thing, but ugly things sometimes happened in one's life, and one had to put them away and forget them. He could have overlooked any accident that might have occurred when his wife was on the road, with Poppas, for example. I cut him short, and he bent his head to my reproof.

"I know," he said, "such things are different with her. But when have I said that I am noble as she is? Never. But I have appreciated and I have adored. About me, say what you like. But if you say that in this there was any *méprise* to my wife, that is not true. I have lost all my place here. I came in from the streets; but I understand her, and all the fine things in her, better than any of you here. If that accident had not been, she would have lived happy with me for years. As for me, I have never believed in this happiness. I was not born under a good star. How did it come? By accident. It goes by accident. She tried to give good fortune to an unfortunate man, *un miserable;*

that was her mistake. It cannot be done in this world. The lucky should marry the lucky." Bouchalka stopped and lit a cigarette. He sat sunk in my chair as if he never meant to get up again. His large hands, now so much plumper than when I first knew him, hung limp. When he had consumed his cigarette he turned to me again.

"I, too, have tried. Have I so much as written one note to a lady since she first put out her hand to help me? Some of the artists who sing my compositions have been quite willing to plague my wife a little if I make the least sign. With the Española, for instance, I have had to be very stern, *farouche;* she is so very playful. I have never given my wife the slightest annoyance of this kind. Since I married her, I have not kissed the cheek of one lady! Then one night I am bored and drink too much champagne and I become a fool. What does it matter? Did my wife marry the fool of me? No, she married me, with my mind and my feelings all here, as I am today. But she is getting a divorce from the fool of me, which she would never see *anyhow!* The stupidity which excuse me is the thing she will not overlook. Even in her memory of me she will be harsh."

His view of his conduct and its consequences was fatalistic; he was meant to have just so much misery every day of his life; for three years it had been withheld, had been piling up somewhere, underground, overhead; now the accumulation burst over him. He had come to pay his respects to me, he said, to declare his undying gratitude to Madame Garnet, and to bid me farewell. He took up his hat and cane and kissed my hand. I have never seen him since. Cressida made a settlement upon him, but even Poppas, tortured by envy and curiosity, never discovered how much it was. It was very little, she told me. *"Pour des gâteaux,"* she added with a smile that was not forgiving. She could not bear to think of his being in want when so little could make him comfortable.

He went back to his own village in Bohemia. He wrote her that the old monk, his teacher, was still alive, and that from the windows of his room in the town he could see the pigeons flying forth from and back to the monastery bell-tower all day long. He sent her a song, with his own words, about those pigeons,—quite a lovely thing. He was the bell-tower, and *les colombes* were his memories of her.

IV

Jerome Brown proved, on the whole, the worst of Cressida's husbands, and, with the possible exception of her eldest brother, Buchanan Garnet, he was the most rapacious of the men with whom she had had to do. It was one thing to gratify every wish of a cake-loving fellow like Bouchalka, but quite another to stand behind a financier. And Brown would be a financier or nothing. After her marriage with him, Cressida grew rapidly older. For the first time in her life she wanted to go abroad and live—to get Jerome Brown away from the scene of his unsuccessful but undiscouraged activities. But Brown was not a man who could be amused and kept out of mischief in Continental hotels. He had to be a figure, if only a "mark," in Wall Street. Nothing else would gratify his peculiar vanity. The deeper he went in, the more affectionately he told Cressida that now all her cares and anxieties were over. To try to get related facts out of his optimism was like trying to find frame work in a feather bed. All Cressida knew was that she was perpetually "investing" to save investments. When she told me she had put a mortgage on the Tenth Street house, her eyes filled with tears. "Why is it? I have never cared about money, except to make people happy with it, and it has been the curse of my life. It has spoiled all my relations with people. Fortunately," she added irrelevantly, drying her eyes, "Jerome and Poppas get along well." Jerome could have got along with anybody; that is a promoter's business. His warm hand, his flushed face, his bright eye, and his newest funny story,—Poppas had no weapons that could do execution with a man like that.

Though Brown's ventures never came home, there was nothing openly disastrous until the outbreak of the revolution in Mexico jeopardized his interests there. Then Cressida went to England— where she could always raise money from a faithful public—for a winter concert tour. When she sailed, her friends knew that her husband's affairs were in a bad way; but we did not know how bad until after Cressida's death.

Cressida Garnet, as all the world knows, was lost on the *Titanic*. Poppas and Horace, who had been travelling with her, were sent on a week earlier and came as safely to port as if they had never stepped out of their London hotel. But Cressida had waited for the first trip of the sea monster—she still believed that all advertising was good—and she went down on the road between the old world and the new. She had been ill, and when the collision occurred she was in her stateroom, a modest one somewhere down in the boat, for she was travelling economically. Apparently she never left her cabin. She was not seen on the decks, and none of the survivors brought any word of her.

On Monday, when the wireless messages were coming from the *Carpathia* with the names of the passengers who had been saved, I went, with so many hundred others, down to the White Star offices. There I saw Cressida's motor, her redoubtable initials on the door, with four men sitting in the limousine. Jerome Brown, stripped of the promoter's joviality and looking flabby and old, sat behind with Buchanan Garnet, who had come on from Ohio. I had not seen him for years. He was now an old man, but he was still conscious of being in the public eye, and sat turning a cigar about in his face with that foolish look of importance which Cressida's achievement had stamped upon all the Garnets. Poppas was in front, with Horace. He was gnawing the finger of his chamois glove as it rested on the top of his cane. His head was sunk, his shoulders drawn together; he looked as old as Jewry. I watched him, wondering whether Cressida would come back to them if she could. After the last names were posted, the four men settled back into the powerful car—one of the best made—and the chauffeur backed off. I saw him dash away the tears from his face with the back of his driving glove. He was an Irish boy, and had been devoted to Cressida.

When the will was read, Henry Gilbert, the lawyer, an old friend of her early youth, and I, were named executors. A nice job we had of it. Most of her large fortune had been converted into stocks that were almost worthless. The marketable property realized only a hundred and fifty thousand dollars. To defeat the bequest of fifty thousand dollars to Poppas, Jerome Brown and her family contested the will. They brought Cressida's letters into court to prove that the will did not represent her intentions, often expressed in writing through many years, to "provide well" for them.

Such letters they were! The writing of a tired, over-driven woman; promising money, sending money herewith, asking for an acknowl-edgment of the draft sent last month, etc. In the letters to Jerome Brown she begged for information about his affairs and entreated him to go with her to some foreign city where they could live quietly and where she could rest; if they were careful, there would "be enough for all." Neither Brown nor her brothers and sisters had any sense of shame about these letters. It seemed never to occur to them that this golden stream, whether it rushed or whether it trickled, came out of the industry, out of the mortal body of a woman. They regarded her as a natural source of wealth; a copper vein, a diamond mine.

Henry Gilbert is a good lawyer himself, and he employed an able man to defend the will. We determined that in this crisis we would stand by Poppas, believing it would be Cressida's wish. Out of the lot of them, he was the only one who had helped her to make one penny of the money that had brought her so much misery. He was at least more deserving than the others. We saw to it that Poppas got his fifty thousand, and he actually departed, at last, for his city in *la sainte Asie,* where it never rains and where he will never again have to hold a hot water bottle to his face.

The rest of the property was fought for to a finish. Poppas out of the way, Horace and Brown and the Garnets quarrelled over her personal effects. They went from floor to floor of the Tenth Street house. The will provided that Cressida's jewels and furs and gowns were to go to her sisters. Georgie and Julia wrangled over them down to the last moleskin. They were deeply disappointed that some of the muffs and stoles which they remembered as very large, proved, when exhumed from storage and exhibited beside furs of a modern cut, to be ridiculously scant. A year ago the sisters were still reasoning with each other about pearls and opals and emeralds.

I wrote Poppas some account of these horrors, as during the court proceedings we had become rather better friends than of old. His reply arrived only a few days ago; a photograph of himself upon a camel, under which is written:

> Traulich und Treu
> ist's nur in der Tiefe:
> falsch und feig
> ist was dort oben sich freut!

His reply, and the memories it awakens—memories which have followed Poppas into the middle of Asia, seemingly,—prompted this informal narration.

A Gold Slipper

Marshall McKann followed his wife and her friend Mrs. Post down the aisle and up the steps to the stage of the Carnegie Music Hall with an ill-concealed feeling of grievance. Heaven knew he never went to concerts, and to be mounted upon the stage in this fashion, as if he were a "highbrow" from Sewickley, or some unfortunate with a musical wife, was ludicrous. A man went to concerts when he was courting, while he was a junior partner. When he became a person of substance he stopped that sort of nonsense. His wife, too, was a sensible person, the daughter of an old Pittsburgh family as solid and well-rooted as the McKanns. She would never have bothered him about this concert had not the meddlesome Mrs. Post arrived to pay her a visit. Mrs. Post was an old school friend of Mrs. McKann, and because she lived in Cincinnati she was always keeping up with the world and talking about things in which no one else was interested, music among them. She was an aggressive lady, with weighty opinions, and a deep voice like a jovial bassoon. She had arrived only last night, and at dinner she brought it out that she could on no account miss Kitty Ayrshire's recital; it was, she said, the sort of thing no one could afford to miss.

When McKann went into town in the morning he found that every seat in the music-hall was sold. He telephoned his wife to that effect, and, thinking he had settled the matter, made his reservation on the 11.25 train for New York. He was unable to get a drawing-room because this same Kitty Ayrshire had taken the last one. He had not intended going to New York until the following week, but he preferred to be absent during Mrs. Post's incumbency.

In the middle of the morning, when he was deep in his correspondence, his wife called him up to say the enterprising Mrs. Post had telephoned some musical friends in Sewickley and had found that two hundred folding-chairs were to be placed on the stage of the concert-hall, behind the piano, and that they would be on sale at noon. Would he please get seats in the front row? McKann asked if they would not excuse him, since he was going over to New York on the late train, would be tired, and would not have time to dress, etc. No, not at all. It would be foolish for two women to trail up to the stage unattended. Mrs. Post's husband always accompanied her to concerts, and she expected that much attention from her host. He needn't dress, and he could take a taxi from the concert-hall to the East Liberty station.

The outcome of it all was that, though his bag was at the station, here was McKann, in the worst possible humour, facing the large audience to which he was well known, and sitting among a lot of music students and excitable old maids. Only the desperately zealous or the morbidly curious would endure two hours in those wooden chairs, and he sat in the front row of this hectic body, somehow made a party to a transaction for which he had the utmost contempt.

When McKann had been in Paris, Kitty Ayrshire was singing at the Comique, and he wouldn't go to hear her—even there, where one found so little that was better to do. She was too much talked about, too much advertised; always being thrust in an American's face as if she were something to be proud of. Perfumes and petticoats and cutlets were named for her. Some one had pointed Kitty out to him one afternoon when she was driving in the Bois with a French composer—old enough, he judged, to be her father—who was said to be infatuated, carried away by her. McKann was told that this was one of the historic passions of old age. He had looked at her on that occasion, but she was so befrilled and befeathered that he caught nothing but a graceful outline and a small, dark head above a white ostrich boa. He had noted with disgust, however, the stooped shoulders and white imperial of the silk-hatted man beside her, and the senescent line of his back. McKann described to his wife this unpleasing picture only last night, while he was undressing, when he was making every possible effort to avert this concert party. But Bessie only looked superior and said she wished to hear Kitty Ayrshire sing, and that her "private life" was something in which she had no interest.

Well, here he was; hot and uncomfortable, in a chair much too small for him, with a row of blinding footlights glaring in his eyes. Suddenly the door at his right elbow opened. Their seats were at one end of the front row; he had thought they would be less conspicuous there than in the centre, and he had not foreseen that the singer would walk over him every time she came upon the stage. Her velvet train brushed against his trousers as she passed him. The applause which greeted her was neither overwhelming nor prolonged. Her conservative audience did not know exactly how to accept her toilette. They were accustomed to dignified concert gowns, like those which Pittsburgh matrons (in those days!) wore at their daughters' coming-out teas.

Kitty's gown that evening was really quite outrageous—the re-partée of a conscienceless Parisian designer who took her hint that she wished something that would be entirely novel in the States. Today, after we have all of us, even in the uttermost provinces, been educated by Bakst and the various Ballets Russes, we would accept such a gown without distrust; but then it was a little disconcerting, even to the well-disposed. It was constructed of a yard or two of green velvet—a reviling, shrieking green which would have made a fright of any woman who had not inextinguishable beauty—and it was made without armholes, a device to which we were then so unaccustomed that it was nothing less than alarming. The velvet skirt split back from a transparent gold-lace petticoat, gold stockings, gold slippers. The narrow train was, apparently, looped to both ankles, and it kept curling about her feet like a serpent's tail, turning up its gold lining as if it were squirming over on its back. It was not, we felt, a costume in which to sing Mozart and Handel and Beethoven.

Kitty sensed the chill in the air, and it amused her. She liked to be thought a brilliant artist by other artists, but by the world at large she liked to be thought a daring creature. She had every reason to believe, from experience and from example, that to shock the great crowd was the surest way to get its money and to make her name a household word. Nobody ever became a household word of being an artist, surely; and you were not a thoroughly paying proposition until your name meant something on the sidewalk and in the barber-shop. Kitty studied her audience with an appraising eye. She liked the stimulus of this disapprobation. As she faced this hard-shelled public she felt keen and interested; she knew that she would give such a recital as cannot often be heard for money. She nodded gaily to the young man at the piano, fell into an attitude of seriousness, and began the group of Beethoven and Mozart songs.

Though McKann would not have admitted it, there were really a great many people in the concert-hall who knew what the prodigal daughter of their country was singing, and how well she was doing it. They thawed gradually under the beauty of her voice and the subtlety of her interpretation. She had sung seldom in concert then, and they had supposed her very dependent upon the accessories of the opera. Clean singing, finished artistry, were not what they expected from her. They began to feel, even, the wayward charm of her personality.

McKann, who stared coldly up at the balconies during her first song, during the second glanced cautiously at the green apparition before him. He was vexed with her for having retained a débutante figure. He comfortably classed all singers—especially operatic singers—as "fat Dutchwomen" or "shifty Sadies," and Kitty would not fit into his clever generalization. She displayed, under his nose, the only kind of figure he considered worth looking at—that of a very young girl, supple and sinuous and quick-silverish; thin, eager shoulders, polished white arms that were nowhere too fat and nowhere too thin. McKann found it agreeable to look at Kitty, but when he saw that the authoritative Mrs. Post, red as a turkey-cock with opinions she was bursting to impart, was studying and appraising the singer through her lorgnette, he gazed indifferently out into the house again. He felt for his watch, but his wife touched him warningly with her elbow—which, he noticed, was not at all like Kitty's.

When Miss Ayrshire finished her first group of songs, her audience expressed its approval positively, but guardedly. She smiled bewitchingly upon the people in front, glanced up at the balconies, and then turned to the company huddled on the stage behind her. After her gay and careless bows, she retreated toward the stage door. As she passed McKann, she again brushed lightly against him, and this time she paused long enough to glance down at him and murmur, "Pardon!"

In the moment her bright, curious eyes rested upon him, McKann seemed to see himself as if she were holding a mirror up before him. He beheld himself a heavy, solid figure, unsuitably clad for the time and place, with a florid, square face, well-visored with good living and sane opinions—an inexpressive countenance. Not a rock face, exactly, but a kind of pressed-brick-and-cement face, a "business" face upon which years and feelings had made no mark—in which cocktails might eventually blast out a few hollows. He had never seen himself so distinctly in his shaving-glass as he did in that instant when Kitty Ayrshire's liquid eye held him, when her bright, inquiring glance roamed over his person. After her prehensile train curled over his boot and she was gone, his wife turned to him and said in the tone of approbation one uses when an infant manifests its groping intelligence, "Very gracious of her, I'm sure!" Mrs. Post nodded oracularly. McKann grunted.

Kitty began her second number, a group of romantic German songs which were altogether more her affair than her first number. When she turned once to acknowledge the applause behind her, she caught McKann in the act of yawning behind his hand—he of course wore no gloves—and he thought she frowned a little. This did not embarrass him; it somehow made him feel important. When she retired after the second part of the program, she again looked him over curiously as she passed, and she took marked precaution that her dress did not touch him. Mrs. Post and his wife again commented upon her consideration.

The final number was made up of modern French songs which Kitty sang enchantingly, and at last her frigid public was thoroughly aroused. While she was coming back again and again to smile and curtsy, McKann whispered to his wife that if there were to be encores he had better make a dash for his train.

"Not at all," put in Mrs. Post. "Kitty is going on the same train. She sings in *Faust* at the opera tomorrow night, so she'll take no chances."

McKann once more told himself how sorry he felt for Post. At last Miss Ayrshire returned, escorted by her accompanist, and gave the people what she of course knew they wanted: the most popular aria from the French opera of which the title-rôle had become synonymous with her name—an opera written for her and to her and round about her, by the veteran French composer who adored her,—the last and not the palest flash of his creative fire. This brought her audience all the way. They clamoured for more of it, but she was not to be coerced. She had been unyielding through storms to which this was a summer breeze. She came on once more, shrugged her shoulders, blew them a kiss, and was gone. Her last smile was for that uncomfortable part of her audience seated behind her, and she looked with recognition at McKann and his ladies as she nodded good night to the wooden chairs.

McKann hurried his charges into the foyer by the nearest exit and put them into his motor. Then he went over to the Schenley to have a glass of beer and a rarebit before train-time. He had not, he admitted to himself, been so much bored as he pretended. The minx herself was well enough, but it was absurd in his fellow-townsmen to look owlish and uplifted about her. He had no rooted dislike for pretty women; he even didn't deny that gay girls had their place in the world, but they ought to be kept in their place. He was born a Presbyterian, just as he was born a McKann. He sat in his pew in the First Church every Sunday, and he never missed a presbytery meeting when he was in town. His religion was not very spiritual, certainly, but it was substantial and concrete, made up of good, hard convictions and opinions. It had something to do with citizenship, with whom one ought to marry, with the coal business (in which his own name was powerful), with the Republican party, and with all majorities and established precedents. He was hostile to fads, to enthusiasms, to individualism, to all changes except in mining machinery and in methods of transportation.

His equanimity restored by his lunch at the Schenley, McKann lit a big cigar, got into his taxi, and bowled off through the sleet.

There was not a sound to be heard or a light to be seen. The ice glittered on the pavement and on the naked trees. No restless feet were abroad. At eleven o'clock the rows of small, comfortable houses looked as empty of the troublesome bubble of life as the Allegheny cemetery itself. Suddenly the cab stopped, and McKann thrust his head out of the window. A woman was standing in the middle of the street addressing his driver in a tone of excitement. Over against the curb a lone electric stood despondent in the storm. The young woman, her cloak blowing about her, turned from the driver to McKann himself, speaking rapidly and somewhat incoherently.

"Could you not be so kind as to help us? It is Mees Ayrshire, the singer. The juice is gone out and we cannot move. We must get to the station. Mademoiselle cannot miss the train; she sings tomorrow night in New York. It is very important. Could you not take us to the station at East Liberty?"

McKann opened the door. "That's all right, but you'll have to hurry. It's eleven-ten now. You've only got fifteen minutes to make the train. Tell her to come along."

The maid drew back and looked up at him in amazement. "But, the hand-luggage to carry, and Mademoiselle to walk! The street is like glass!"

McKann threw away his cigar and followed her. He stood silent by the door of the derelict, while the maid explained that she had found help. The driver had gone off somewhere to telephone for a car. Miss Ayrshire seemed not at all apprehensive; she had not doubted that a rescuer would be forthcoming. She moved deliberately; out of a whirl of skirts she thrust one fur-topped shoe—McKann saw the flash of the gold stocking above it—and alighted.

"So kind of you! So fortunate for us!" she murmured. One hand she placed upon his sleeve, and in the other she carried an armful of roses that had been sent up to the concert stage. The petals showered upon the sooty, sleety pavement as she picked her way along. They would be lying there tomorrow morning, and the children in those houses would wonder if there had been a funeral. The maid followed with two leather bags. As soon as he had lifted Kitty into his cab she exclaimed:

"My jewel-case! I have forgotten it. It is on the back seat, please. I am so careless!"

He dashed back, ran his hand along the cushions, and discovered a small leather bag. When he returned he found the maid and the luggage bestowed on the front seat, and a place left for him on the back seat beside Kitty and her flowers.

"Shall we be taking you far out of your way?" she asked sweetly. "I haven't an idea where the station is. I'm not even sure about the name. Céline thinks it is East Liberty, but I think it is West Liberty. An odd name, anyway. It is a Bohemian quarter, perhaps? A district where the law relaxes a trifle?"

McKann replied grimly that he didn't think the name referred to that kind of liberty.

"So much the better," sighed Kitty. "I am a Californian; that's the only part of America I know very well, and out there, when we called a place Liberty Hill or Liberty Hollow—well, we meant it. You will excuse me if I'm uncommunicative, won't you? I must not talk in this raw air. My throat is sensitive after a long program." She lay back in her corner and closed her eyes.

When the cab rolled down the incline at East Liberty station, the New York express was whistling in. A porter opened the door. McKann sprang out, gave him a claim check and his Pullman ticket, and told him to get his bag at the check-stand and rush it on that train.

Miss Ayrshire, having gathered up her flowers, put out her hand to take his arm. "Why, it's you!" she exclaimed, as she saw his face in the light. "What a coincidence!" She made no further move to alight, but sat smiling as if she had just seated herself in a drawing-room and were ready for talk and a cup of tea.

McKann caught her arm. "You must hurry, Miss Ayrshire, if you mean to catch that train. It stops here only a moment. Can you run?"

"Can I run!" she laughed. "Try me!"

As they raced through the tunnel and up the inside stairway, McKann admitted that he had never before made a dash with feet so quick and sure stepping out beside him. The white-furred boots chased each other like lambs at play, the gold stockings flashed like the spokes of a bicycle wheel in the sun. They reached the door of Miss Ayrshire's state-room just as the train began to pull out. McKann was ashamed of the way he was panting, for Kitty's breathing was as soft and regular as when she was reclining on the back seat of his taxi. It had somehow run in his head that all these stage women were a poor lot physically—unsound, overfed creatures, like canaries that are kept in a cage and stuffed with song-restorer. He retreated to escape her thanks. "Good night! Pleasant journey! Pleasant dreams!" With a friendly nod in Kitty's direction he closed the door behind him.

He was somewhat surprised to find his own bag, his Pullman ticket in the strap, on the seat just outside Kitty's door. But there was nothing strange about it. He had got the last section left on the train, No. 13, next to the drawing-room. Every other berth in the car was made up. He was just starting to look for the porter when the door of the state-room opened and Kitty Ayrshire came out. She seated herself carelessly in the front seat beside his bag.

"Please talk to me a little," she said coaxingly. "I'm always wakeful after I sing, and I have to hunt some one to talk to. Céline and I get so tired of each other. We can speak very low, and we shall not disturb any one." She crossed her feet and rested her elbow on his Gladstone. Though she still wore her gold slippers and stockings, she did not, he thanked Heaven, have on her concert gown, but a very demure black velvet with some sort of pearl trimming about the neck. "Wasn't it funny," she proceeded, "that it happened to be you who picked me up? I wanted a word with you, anyway."

McKann smiled in a way that meant he wasn't being taken in. "Did you? We are not very old acquaintances."

"No, perhaps not. But you disapproved tonight, and I thought I was singing very well. You are very critical in such matters?"

He had been standing, but now he sat down. "My dear young lady, I am not critical at all. I know nothing about 'such matters.'"

"And care less?" she said for him. "Well, then we know where we are, in so far as that is concerned. What did displease you? My gown, perhaps? It may seem a little *outré* here, but it's the sort of thing all the imaginative designers abroad are doing. You like the English sort of concert gown better?"

"About gowns," said McKann, "I know even less than about music. If I looked uncomfortable, it was probably because I was uncomfortable. The seats were bad and the lights were annoying."

Kitty looked up with solicitude. "I was sorry they sold those seats. I don't like to make people uncomfortable in any way. Did the lights give you a headache? They are very trying. They burn one's eyes out in the end, I believe." She paused and waved the porter away with a smile as he came toward them. Half-clad Pittsburghers were tramping up and down the aisle, casting sidelong glances at McKann and his companion. "How much better they look with all their clothes on," she murmured. Then, turning directly to McKann again: "I saw you were not well seated, but I felt something quite hostile and personal. You were displeased with me. Doubtless many people are, but I seldom get an opportunity to question them. It would be nice if you took the trouble to tell me why you were displeased."

She spoke frankly, pleasantly, without a shadow of challenge or hauteur. She did not seem to be angling for compliments. McKann settled himself in his seat. He thought he would try her out. She had come for it, and he would let her have it. He found, however, that it was harder to formulate the grounds of his disapproval than he would have supposed. Now that he sat face to face with her, now that she was leaning against his bag, he had no wish to hurt her.

"I'm a hard-headed business man," he said evasively, "and I don't much believe in any of you fluffy-ruffles people. I have a sort of natural distrust of them all, the men more than the women."

She looked thoughtful. "Artists, you mean?" drawing her words slowly. "What is your business?"

"Coal."

"I don't feel any natural distrust of business men, and I know ever so many. I don't know any coal-men, but I think I could become very much interested in coal. Am I larger-minded than you?"

McKann laughed. "I don't think you know when you are interested or when you are not. I don't believe you know what it feels like to be really interested. There is so much fake about your profession. It's an affectation on both sides. I know a great many of the people who went to hear you tonight, and I know that most of them neither know nor care anything about music. They imagine they do, because it's supposed to be the proper thing."

Kitty sat upright and looked interested. She was certainly a lovely creature—the only one of her tribe he had ever seen that he would cross the street to see again. Those were remarkable eyes she had— curious, penetrating, restless, somewhat impudent, but not at all dulled by self-conceit.

"But isn't that so in everything?" she cried. "How many of your clerks are honest because of a fine, individual sense of honour? They are honest because it is the accepted rule of good conduct in business. Do you know"—she looked at him squarely—"I thought you would have something quite definite to say to me; but this is funny-paper stuff, the sort of objection I'd expect from your office-boy."

"Then you don't think it silly for a lot of people to get together and pretend to enjoy something they know nothing about?"

"Of course I think it silly, but that's the way God made audiences. Don't people go to church in exactly the same way? If there were a spiritual-pressure test-machine at the door, I suspect not many of you would get to your pews."

"How do you know I go to church?"

She shrugged her shoulders. "Oh, people with these old, ready-made opinions usually go to church. But you can't evade me like that." She tapped the edge of his seat with the toe of her gold slipper. "You sat there all evening, glaring at me as if you could eat me alive. Now I give you a chance to state your objections, and you merely criticize my audience. What is it? Is it merely that you happen to dislike my personality? In that case, of course, I won't press you."

"No," McKann frowned, "I perhaps dislike your professional personality. As I told you, I have a natural distrust of your variety."

"Natural, I wonder?" Kitty murmured. "I don't see why you should naturally dislike singers any more than I naturally dislike coal-men. I don't classify people by their occupations. Doubtless I should find some coal-men repulsive, and you may find some singers so. But I have reason to believe that, at least, I'm one of the less repellent."

"I don't doubt it," McKann laughed, "and you're a shrewd woman to boot. But you are, all of you, according to my standards, light people. You're brilliant, some of you, but you've no depth."

Kitty seemed to assent, with a dive of her girlish head. "Well, it's a merit in some things to be heavy, and in others to be light. Some things are meant to go deep, and others to go high. Do you want all the women in the world to be profound?"

"You are all," he went on steadily, watching her with indulgence, "fed on hectic emotions. You are pampered. You don't help to carry the burdens of the world. You are self-indulgent and appetent."

"Yes, I am," she assented, with a candor which he did not expect. "Not all artists are, but I am. Why not? If I could once get a convincing statement as to why I should not be self-indulgent, I might change my ways. As for the burdens of the world—" Kitty rested her chin on her clasped hands and looked thoughtful. "One should give pleasure to others. My dear sir, granting that the great majority of people can't enjoy anything very keenly, you'll admit that I give pleasure to many more people than you do. One should help others who are less fortunate; at present I am supporting just eight people, besides those I hire. There was never another family in California that had so many cripples and hard-luckers as that into which I had the honour to be born. The only ones who could take care of themselves were ruined by the San Francisco earthquake some time ago. One should make personal sacrifices. I do; I give money and time and effort to talented students. Oh, I give something much more than that! something that you probably have never given to any one. I give, to the really gifted ones, my *wish,* my desire, my light, if I have any; and that, Mr. Worldly Wiseman, is like giving one's blood! It's the kind of thing you prudent people never give. That is what was in the box of precious ointment." Kitty drew off her fervour with a slight gesture, as if it were a scarf, and leaned back, tucking her slipper up on the edge of his seat. "If you saw the houses I keep up," she sighed, "and the people I employ, and the motor-cars I run— And, after all, I've only this to do it with." She indicated her slender person, which Marshall could almost have broken in two with his bare hands.

She was, he thought, very much like any other charming woman, except that she was more so. Her familiarity was natural and simple. She was at ease because she was not afraid of him or of herself, or of certain half-clad acquaintances of his who had been wandering up and down the car oftener than was necessary. Well, he was not afraid, either.

Kitty put her arms over her head and sighed again, feeling the smooth part in her black hair. Her head was small—capable of great agitation, like a bird's; or of great resignation, like a nun's. "I can't see why I shouldn't be self-indulgent, when I indulge others. I can't understand your equivocal scheme of ethics. Now I can understand Count Tolstoy's, perfectly. I had a long talk with him once, about his book 'What is Art?' As nearly as I could get it, he believes that we are a race who can exist only be gratifying appetites; the appetites are evil, and the existence they carry on is evil. We were always sad, he says, without knowing why; even in the Stone Age. In some miraculous way a divine ideal was disclosed to us, directly at variance with our appetites. It gave us a new craving, which we could only satisfy by starving all the other hungers in us. Happiness lies in ceasing to be and to cause being, because the thing revealed to us is dearer than any existence our appetites can ever get for us. I can understand that. It's something one often feels in art. It is even the subject of the greatest of all operas, which, because I can never hope to sing it, I love more than all the others." Kitty pulled herself up. "Perhaps you agree with Tolstoy?" she added languidly.

"No; I think he's a crank," said McKann, cheerfully.

"What do you mean by a crank?"

"I mean an extremist."

Kitty laughed. "Weighty word! You'll always have a world full of people who keep to the golden mean. Why bother yourself about me and Tolstoy?"

"I don't, except when you bother me."

"Poor man! It's true this isn't your fault. Still, you did provoke it by glaring at me. Why did you go to the concert?"

"I was dragged."

"I might have known!" she chuckled, and shook her head. "No, you don't give me any good reasons. Your morality seems to me the compromise of cowardice, apologetic and sneaking. When righteousness becomes alive and burning, you hate it as much as you do beauty. You want a little of each in your life, perhaps—adulterated, sterilized, with the sting taken out. It's true enough they are both fearsome things when they get loose in the world; they don't, often."

McKann hated tall talk. "My views on women," he said slowly, "are simple."

"Doubtless," Kitty responded dryly, "but are they consistent? Do you apply them to your stenographers as well as to me? I take it for granted you have unmarried stenographers. Their position, economically, is the same as mine."

McKann studied the toe of her shoe. "With a woman, everything comes back to one thing." His manner was judicial.

She laughed indulgently. "So we are getting down to brass tacks, eh? I have beaten you in argument, and now you are leading trumps." She put her hands behind her head and her lips parted in a half-yawn. "Does everything come back to one thing? I wish I knew! It's more than likely that, under the same conditions, I should have been very like your stenographers—if they are good ones. Whatever I was, I would have been a good one. I think people are very much alike. You are more different than any one I have met for some time, but I know that there are a great many more at home like you. And even you—I believe there is a real creature down under these custom-made prejudices that save you the trouble of thinking. If you and I were shipwrecked on a desert island, I have no doubt that we would come to a simple and natural understanding. I'm neither a coward nor a shirk. You would find, if you had to undertake any enterprise of danger or difficulty with a woman, that there are several qualifications quite as important as the one to which you doubtless refer."

McKann felt nervously for his watch-chain. "Of course," he brought out, "I am not laying down any generalizations——" His brows wrinkled.

"Oh, aren't you?" murmured Kitty. "Then I totally misunderstood. But remember"—holding up a finger—"it is you, not I, who are afraid to pursue this subject further. Now, I'll tell you something." She leaned forward and clasped her slim, white hands about her velvet knee. "I am as much a victim of these ineradicable prejudices as you. Your stenographer seems to you a better sort. Well, she does to me. Just because her life is, presumably, greyer than mine, she seems better. My mind tells me that dullness, and a mediocre order of ability, and poverty, are not in themselves admirable things. Yet in my heart I always feel that the sales-women in shops and the working girls in factories are more meritorious than I. Many of them, with my opportunities, would be more selfish than I am. Some of them, with their own opportunities, are more selfish. Yet I make this sentimental genuflection before the nun and the charwoman. Tell me, haven't you any weakness? Isn't there any foolish natural thing that unbends you a trifle and makes you feel gay?"

"I like to go fishing."

"To see how many fish you can catch?"

"No, I like the woods and the weather. I like to play a fish and work hard for him. I like the pussy-willows and the cold; and the sky, whether it's blue or grey—night coming on, every thing about it."

He spoke devoutly, and Kitty watched him through half-closed eyes. "And you like to feel that there are light-minded girls like me, who only care about the inside of shops and theatres and hotels, eh? You amuse me, you and your fish! But I mustn't keep you any longer. Haven't I given you every opportunity to state your case against me? I thought you would have more to say for yourself. Do you know, I believe it's not a case you have at all, but a grudge. I believe you are envious; that you'd like to be a tenor, and a perfect lady-killer!" She rose, smiling, and paused with her hand on the door of her state-room. "Anyhow, thank you for a pleasant evening. And, by the way, dream of me tonight, and not of either of those ladies who sat beside you. It does not matter much whom we live with in this world, but it matters a great deal whom we dream of." She noticed his bricky flush. "You are very naïf, after all, but, oh, so cautious! You are naturally afraid of everything new, just as I naturally want to try everything: new people, new religions—new miseries, even. If only there were more new things— If only you were really new! I might learn something. I'm like the Queen of Sheba—I'm not above learning. But you, my friend, would be afraid to try a new shaving soap. It isn't gravitation that holds the world in place; it's the lazy, obese cowardice of the people on it. All the same"—taking his hand and smiling encouragingly—"I'm going to haunt you a little. *Adios!*"

When Kitty entered her state-room, Céline, in her dressing-gown, was nodding by the window.

"Mademoiselle found the fat gentleman interesting?" she asked. "It is nearly one."

"Negatively interesting. His kind always say the same thing. If I could find one really intelligent man who held his views, I should adopt them."

"Monsieur did not look like an original," murmured Céline, as she began to take down her lady's hair.

McKann slept heavily, as usual, and the porter had to shake him in the morning. He sat up in his berth, and, after composing his hair with his fingers, began to hunt about for his clothes. As he put up the window-blind some bright object in the little hammock over his bed caught the sunlight and glittered. He stared and picked up a delicately turned gold slipper.

"Minx! hussy!" he ejaculated. "All that tall talk—! Probably got it from some man who hangs about; learned it off like a parrot. Did she poke this in here herself last night, or did she send that sneak-faced Frenchwoman? I like her nerve!" He wondered whether he might have been breathing audibly when the intruder thrust her head between his curtains. He was conscious that he did not look a Prince Charming in his sleep. He dressed as fast as he could, and, when he was ready to go to the wash-room, glared at the slipper. If the porter should start to make up his berth in his absence— He caught the slipper, wrapped it in his pajama jacket, and thrust it into his bag. He escaped from the train without seeing his tormentor again.

Later McKann threw the slipper into the wastebasket in his room at the Knickerbocker, but the chambermaid, seeing that it was new and mateless, thought there must be a mistake, and placed it in his clothes-closet. He found it there when he returned from the theatre that evening. Considerably mellowed by food and drink and cheerful company, he took the slipper in his hand and decided to keep it as a reminder that absurd things could happen to people of the most clocklike deportment. When he got back to Pittsburgh, he stuck it in a lock-box in his vault, safe from prying clerks.

McKann has been ill for five years now, poor fellow! He still goes to the office, because it is the only place that interests him, but his partners do most of the work, and his clerks find him sadly changed— "morbid," they call his state of mind. He has had the pine-trees in his yard cut down because they remind him of cemeteries. On Sundays or holidays, when the office is empty, and he takes his will or his insurance-policies out of his lock-box, he often puts the tarnished gold slipper on his desk and looks at it. Somehow it suggests life to his tired mind, as his pine-trees suggested death—life and youth. When he drops over some day, his executors will be puzzled by the slipper.

As for Kitty Ayrshire, she has played so many jokes, practical and impractical, since then, that she has long ago forgotten the night when she threw away a slipper to be a thorn in the side of a just man.

Scandal

Kitty Ayrshire had a cold, a persistent inflammation of the vocal cords which defied the throat specialist. Week after week her name was posted at the Opera, and week after week it was canceled, and the name of one of her rivals was substituted. For nearly two months she had been deprived of everything she liked, even of the people she liked, and had been shut up until she had come to hate the glass windows between her and the world, and the wintry stretch of the Park they looked out upon. She was losing a great deal of money, and, what was worse, she was losing life; days of which she wanted to make the utmost were slipping by, and nights which were to have crowned the days, nights of incalculable possibilities, were being stolen from her by women for whom she had no great affection. At first she had been courageous, but the strain of prolonged uncertainty was telling on her, and her nervous condition did not improve her larynx. Every morning Miles Creedon looked down her throat, only to put her off with evasions, to pronounce improvement that apparently never got her anywhere, to say that tomorrow he might be able to promise something definite.

Her illness, of course, gave rise to rumours—rumours that she had lost her voice, that at some time last summer she must have lost her discretion. Kitty herself was frightened by the way in which this cold hung on. She had had many sharp illnesses in her life, but always, before this, she had rallied quickly. Was she beginning to lose her resiliency? Was she, by any cursed chance, facing a bleak time when she would have to cherish herself? She protested as she wandered about her sunny, many-windowed rooms on the tenth floor, that if she was going to have to live frugally, she wouldn't live at all. She wouldn't live on any terms but the very generous ones she had always known. She wasn't going to hoard her vitality. It must be there when she wanted it, be ready for any strain she chose to put upon it, let her play fast and loose with it; and then, if necessary, she would be ill for a while and pay the piper. But be systematically prudent and parsimonious she would not.

When she attempted to deliver all this to Doctor Creedon, he merely put his finger on her lips and said they would discuss these things when she could talk without injuring her throat. He allowed her to see no one except the Director of the Opera, who did not shine in conversation and was not apt to set Kitty going. The Director was a glum fellow, indeed, but during this calamitous time he had tried to be soothing, and he agreed with Creedon that she must not risk a premature appearance. Kitty was tormented by a suspicion that he was secretly backing the little Spanish woman who had sung many of her parts since she had been ill. He furthered the girl's interests because his wife had a very special consideration for her, and Madame had that consideration because— But that was too long and too dreary a story to follow out in one's mind. Kitty felt a tonsilitis disgust for opera-house politics, which, when she was in health, she rather enjoyed, being no mean strategist herself. The worst of being ill was that it made so many things and people look base.

She was always afraid of being disillusioned. She wished to believe that everything for sale in Vanity Fair was worth the advertised price. When she ceased to believe in these delights, she told herself, her pulling power would decline and she would go to pieces. In some way the chill of her disillusionment would quiver through the long, black line which reached from the box-office down to Seventh Avenue on nights when she sang. They shivered there in the rain and cold, all those people, because they loved to believe in her inextinguishable zest. She was no prouder of what she drew in the boxes than she was of that long, oscillating tail; little fellows in thin coats, Italians, Frenchmen, South-Americans, Japanese.

When she had been cloistered like a Trappist for six weeks, with nothing from the outside world but notes and flowers and disquieting morning papers, Kitty told Miles Creedon that she could not endure complete isolation any longer.

"I simply cannot live through the evenings. They have become horrors to me. Every night is the last night of a condemned man. I do nothing but cry, and that makes my throat worse."

Miles Creedon, handsomest of his profession, was better looking with some invalids than with others. His athletic figure, his red cheeks, and splendid teeth always had a cheering effect upon this particular patient, who hated anything weak or broken.

"What can I do, my dear? What do you wish? Shall I come and hold your lovely hand from eight to ten? You have only to suggest it."

"Would you do that, even? No, *caro mio,* I take far too much of your time as it is. For an age now you have been the only man in the world to me, and you have been charming! But the world is big, and I am missing it. Let some one come tonight, some one interesting, but not too interesting. Pierce Tevis, for instance. He is just back from Paris. Tell the nurse I may see him for an hour tonight," Kitty finished pleadingly, and put her fingers on the doctor's sleeve. He looked down at them and smiled whimsically.

Like other people, he was weak to Kitty Ayrshire. He would do for her things that he would do for no one else; would break any engagement, desert a dinner-table, leaving an empty place and an offended hostess, to sit all evening in Kitty's dressing-room, spraying her throat and calming her nerves, using every expedient to get her through a performance. He had studied her voice like a singing master; knew all of its idiosyncracies and the emotional and nervous perturbations which affected it. When it was permissible, sometimes when it was not permissible, he indulged her caprices. On this sunny morning her wan, disconsolate face moved him.

"Yes, you may see Tevis this evening if you will assure me that you will not shed one tear for twenty-four hours. I may depend on your word?" He rose, and stood before the deep couch on which his patient reclined. Her arch look seemed to say, "On what could you depend more?" Creedon smiled, and shook his head. "If I find you worse tomorrow——"

He crossed to the writing-table and began to separate a bunch of tiny flame-coloured rosebuds. "May I?" Selecting one, he sat down on the chair from which he had lately risen, and leaned forward while Kitty pinched the thorns from the stem and arranged the flower in his buttonhole.

"Thank you. I like to wear one of yours. Now I must be off to the hospital. I've a nasty little operation to do this morning. I'm glad it's not you. Shall I telephone Tevis about this evening?"

Kitty hesitated. Her eyes ran rapidly about, seeking a likely pretext. Creedon laughed.

"Oh, I see. You've already asked him to come. You were so sure of me! Two hours in bed after lunch, with all the windows open, remember. Read something diverting, but not exciting; some homely British author; nothing *abandonné*. And don't make faces at me. Until tomorrow!"

When her charming doctor had disappeared through the doorway, Kitty fell back on her cushions and closed her eyes. Her mocking-bird, excited by the sunlight, was singing in his big gilt cage, and a white lilac-tree that had come that morning was giving out its faint sweetness in the warm room. But Kitty looked paler and wearier than when the doctor was with her. Even with him she rose to her part just a little; couldn't help it. And he took his share of her vivacity and sparkle, like every one else. He believed that his presence was soothing to her. But he admired; and whoever admired, blew on the flame, however lightly.

The mocking-bird was in great form this morning. He had the best bird-voice she had ever heard, and Kitty wished there were some way to note down his improvisations; but his intervals were not expressible in any scale she knew. Parker White had brought him to her, from Ojo Caliente, in New Mexico, where he had been trained in the pine forests by an old Mexican and an ill-tempered, lame master-bird, half thrush, that taught young birds to sing. This morning, in his song there were flashes of silvery Southern springtime; they opened inviting roads of memory. In half an hour he had sung his disconsolate mistress to sleep.

That evening Kitty sat curled up on the deep couch before the fire, awaiting Pierce Tevis. Her costume was folds upon folds of diaphanous white over equally diaphanous rose, with a line of white fur about her neck. Her beautiful arms were bare. Her tiny Chinese slippers were embroidered so richly that they resembled the painted porcelain of old vases. She looked like a sultan's youngest, newest bride; a beautiful little toy-woman, sitting at one end of the long room which composed about her,—which, in the soft light, seemed happily arranged for her. There were flowers everywhere: rose-trees; camellia-bushes, red and white; the first forced hyacinths of the season; a feathery mimosa-tree, tall enough to stand under.

The long front of Kitty's study was all windows. At one end was the fireplace, before which she sat. At the other end, back in a lighted alcove, hung a big, warm, sympathetic interior by Lucien Simon,— a group of Kitty's friends having tea in the painter's salon in Paris. The room in the picture was flooded with early lamplight, and one could feel the grey, chill winter twilight in the Paris streets outside. There stood the cavalier-like old composer, who had done much for Kitty, in his most characteristic attitude, before the hearth. Mme. Simon sat at the tea-table, B———, the historian, and H———, the philologist, stood in animated discussion behind the piano, while Mme. H———was tying on the bonnet of her lovely little daughter. Marcel Durand, the physicist, sat alone in a corner, his startling black-and-white profile lowered broodingly, his cold hands locked over his sharp knee. A genial, red-bearded sculptor stood over him, about to touch him on the shoulder and waken him from his dream.

This painting made, as it were, another room; so that Kitty's study on Central Park West seemed to open into that charming French interor, into one of the most highly harmonized and richly associated rooms in Paris. There her friends sat or stood about, men distinguished, women at once plain and beautiful, with their furs and bonnets, their clothes that were so distinctly not smart—all held together by the warm lamp-light, by an indescribable atmosphere of graceful and gracious human living.

Pierce Tevis, after he had entered noiselessly and greeted Kitty, stood before her fire and looked over her shoulder at this picture.

"It's nice that you have them there together, now that they are scattered, God knows where, fighting to preserve just that. But your own room, too, is charming," he added at last, taking his eyes from the canvas.

Kitty shrugged her shoulders.

"Bah! I can help to feed the lamp, but I can't supply the dear things it shines upon."

"Well, tonight it shines upon you and me, and we aren't so bad."

Tevis stepped forward and took her hand affectionately. "You've been over a rough bit of road. I'm so sorry. It's left you looking very lovely, though. Has it been very hard to get on?"

She brushed his hand gratefully against her cheek and nodded.

"Awfully dismal. Everything has been shut out from me but—gossip. That always get in. Often I don't mind, but this time I have. People do tell such lies about me."

"Of course we do. That's part of our fun, one of the many pleasures you give us. It only shows how hard up we are for interesting public personages; for a royal family, for romantic fiction, if you will. But I never hear any stories that wound me, and I'm very sensitive about you."

"I'm gossiped about rather more than the others, am I not?"

"I believe! Heaven send that the day when you are not gossiped about is far distant! Do you want to bite off your nose to spite your pretty face? You are the sort of person who makes myths. You can't turn around without making one. That's your singular good luck. A whole staff of publicity men, working day and night, couldn't do for you what you do for yourself. There is an affinity between you and the popular imagination."

"I suppose so," said Kitty, and sighed. "All the same, I'm getting almost as tired of the person I'm supposed to be as of the person I really am. I wish you would invent a new Kitty Ayrshire for me, Pierce. Can't I do something revolutionary? Marry, for instance?"

Tevis rose in alarm.

"Whatever you do, don't try to change your legend. You have now the one that gives the greatest satisfaction to the greatest number of people. Don't disappoint your public. The popular imagination, to which you make such a direct appeal, for some reason wished you to have a son, so it has given you one. I've heard a dozen versions of the story, but it is always a son, never by any chance a daughter. Your public gives you what is best for you. Let well enough alone."

Kitty yawned and dropped back on her cushions.

"He still persists, does he, in spite of never being visible?"

"Oh, but he has been seen by ever so many people. Let me think a moment." He sank into an attitude of meditative ease. "The best description I ever had of him was from a friend of my mother, an elderly woman, thoroughly truthful and matter-of-fact. She has seen him often. He is kept in Russia, in St. Petersburg, that was. He is about eight years old and of marvellous beauty. He is always that in every version. My old friend has seen him being driven in his sledge on the Nevskii Prospekt on winter afternoons; black horses with silver bells and a giant in uniform on the seat beside the driver. He is always attended by this giant, who is responsible to the Grand Duke Paul for the boy. This lady can produce no evidence beyond his beauty and his splendid furs and the fact that all the Americans in Petrograd know he is your son."

Kitty laughed mournfully.

"If the Grand Duke Paul had a son, any old rag of a son, the province of Moscow couldn't contain him! He may, for aught I know, actually pretend to have a son. It would be very like him." She looked at her finger-tips and her rings disapprovingly for a moment. "Do you know, I've been thinking that I would rather like to lay hands on that youngster. I believe he'd be interesting, I'm bored with the world."

Tevis looked up and said quickly:

"Would you like him, really?"

"Of course I should," she said indignantly. "But, then, I like other things, too; and one has to choose. When one has only two or three things to choose from, life is hard; when one has many, it is harder still. No, on the whole, I don't mind that story. It's rather pretty, except for the Grand Duke. But not all of them are pretty."

"Well, none of them are very ugly; at least I never heard but one that troubled me, and that was long ago."

She looked interested.

"That is what I want to know; how do the ugly ones get started? How did that one get going and what was it about? Is it too dreadful to repeat?"

"No, it's not especially dreadful; merely rather shabby. If you really wish to know, and won't be vexed, I can tell you exactly how it got going, for I took the trouble to find out. But it's a long story, and you really had nothing whatever to do with it."

"Then who did have to do with it? Tell me; I should like to know exactly how even one of them originated."

"Will you be comfortable and quiet and not get into a rage, and let me look at you as much as I please?"

Kitty nodded, and Tevis sat watching her indolently while he debated how much of his story he ought not to tell her. Kitty liked being looked at by intelligent persons. She knew exactly how good looking she was; and she knew, too, that, pretty as she was, some of those rather sallow women in the Simon painting had a kind of beauty which she would never have. This knowledge, Tevis was thinking, this important realization, contributed more to her loveliness than any other thing about her; more than her smooth, ivory skin or her changing grey eyes, the delicate forehead above them, or even the dazzling smile, which was gradually becoming too bright and too intentional,—out in the world, at least. Here by her own fire she still had for her friends a smile less electric than the one she flashed from stages. She could still be, in short, *intime,* a quality which few artists keep, which few ever had.

Kitty broke in on her friend's meditations.

"You may smoke. I had rather you did. I hate to deprive people of things they like."

"No, thanks. May I have those chocolates on the tea-table? They are quite as bad for me. May you? No, I suppose not." He settled himself by the fire, with the candy beside him, and began in the agreeable voice which always soothed his listener.

"As I said, it was a long while ago, when you first came back to this country and were singing at the Manhattan. I dropped in at the Metropolitan one evening to hear something new they were trying out. It was an off night, no pullers in the cast, and nobody in the boxes but governesses and poor relations. At the end of the first act two people entered one of the boxes in the second tier. The man was Siegmund Stein, the department-store millionaire, and the girl, so the men about me in the omnibus box began to whisper, was Kitty Ayrshire. I didn't know you then, but I was unwilling to believe that you were with Stein. I could not contradict them at that time, however, for the resemblance, if it was merely a resemblance, was absolute, and all the world knew that you were not singing at the Manhattan that night. The girl's hair was dressed just as you then wore yours. Moreover, her head was small and restless like yours,

and she had your colouring, your eyes, your chin. She carried herself
with the critical indifference one might expect in an artist who had
come for a look at a new production that was clearly doomed to
failure. She applauded lightly. She made comments to Stein when
comments were natural enough. I thought, as I studied her face with
the glass, that her nose was a trifle thinner than yours, a prettier
nose, my dear Kitty, but stupider and more inflexible. All the same,
I was troubled until I saw her laugh,—and then I knew she was a
counterfeit. I had never seen you laugh, but I knew that you would
not laugh like that. It was not boisterous; indeed, it was consciously
refined,—mirthless, meaningless. In short, it was not the laugh of
one whom our friends in there"—pointing to the Simon painting—
"would honour with their affection and admiration."

Kitty rose on her elbow and burst out indignantly:

"So you would really have been hood-winked except for that! You
may be sure that no woman, no intelligent woman, would have been.
Why do we ever take the trouble to look like anything for any of
you? I could count on my four fingers"—she held them up and shook
them at him—"the men I've known who had the least perception
of what any woman really looked like, and they were all dressmakers.
Even painters"—glancing back in the direction of the Simon picture—"never get more than one type through their thick heads; they
try to make all women look like some wife or mistress. You are all
the same; you never see our real faces. What you do see, is some
cheap conception of prettiness you got from a coloured supplement
when you were adolescents. It's too discouraging. I'd rather take vows
and veil my face for ever from such abominable eyes. In the kingdom
of the blind any petticoat is a queen." Kitty thumped the cushion
with her elbow. "Well, I can't do anything about it. Go on with your
story."

"Aren't you furious, Kitty! And I thought I was so shrewd. I've
quite forgotten where I was. Anyhow, I was not the only man fooled.
After the last curtain I met Villard, the press man of that management,
in the lobby, and asked him whether Kitty Ayrshire was in the house.
He said he thought so. Stein had telephoned for a box, and said he
was bringing one of the artists from the other company. Villard had
been too busy about the new production to go to the box, but he

was quite sure the woman was Ayrshire, whom he had met in Paris.

"Not long after that I met Dan Leland, a classmate of mine, at the Harvard Club. He's a journalist, and he used to keep such eccentric hours that I had not run across him for a long time. We got to talking about modern French music, and discovered that we both had a very lively interest in Kitty Ayrshire.

" 'Could you tell me,' Dan asked abruptly, 'why, with pretty much all the known world to choose her friends from, this young woman should flit about with Siegmund Stein? It prejudices people against her. He's a most objectionable person.'

" 'Have you,' I asked, 'seen her with him, yourself?'

"Yes, he had seen her driving with Stein, and some of the men on his paper had seen her dining with him at rather queer places down town. Stein was always hanging about the Manhattan on nights when Kitty sang. I told Dan that I suspected a masquerade. That interested him, and he said he thought he would look into the matter. In short, we both agreed to look into it. Finally, we got the story, though Dan could never use it, could never even hint at it, because Stein carries heavy advertising in his paper.

"To make you see the point, I must give you a little history of Siegmund Stein. Any one who has seen him never forgets him. He is one of the most hideous men in New York, but it's not at all the common sort of ugliness that comes from overeating and automobiles. He isn't one of the fat horrors. He has one of those rigid, horse-like faces that never tell anything; a long nose, flattened as if it had been tied down; a scornful chin; long, white teeth, flat cheeks, yellow as a Mongolian's; tiny, black eyes, with puffy lids and no lashes; dingy, dead-looking hair—looks as if it were glued on.

"Stein came here a beggar from somewhere in Austria. He began by working on the machines in old Rosenthal's garment factory. He became a speeder, a foreman, a salesman; worked his way ahead steadily until the hour when he rented an old dwelling-house on Seventh Avenue and began to make misses' and juniors' coats. I believe he was the first manufacturer to specialize in those particular articles. Dozens of garment manufacturers have come along the same road, but Stein is like none of the rest of them. He is, and always was, a personality. While he was still at the machine, a hideous, underfed little whippersnapper, he was already a youth of many-coloured ambitions, deeply concerned about his dress, his associates, his recreations. He haunted the old Astor Library and the Metropolitan Museum, learned something about pictures and porcelains, took singing lessons, though he had a voice like a crow's. When he sat down to his baked apple and doughnut in a basement lunch-room, he would prop a book up before him and address his food with as much leisure and ceremony as if he were dining at his club. He held himself at a distance from his fellow-workmen and somehow always managed to impress them with his superiority. He had inordinate vanity, and there are many stories about his foppishness. After his first promotion in Rosenthal's factory, he bought a new overcoat. A few days later, one of the men at the machines, which Stein had just quitted, appeared in a coat exactly like it. Stein could not discharge him, but he gave his own coat to a newly arrived Russian boy and got another. He was already magnificent.

"After he began to make headway with misses' and juniors' cloaks, he became a collector—etchings, china, old musical instruments. He had a dancing master, and engaged a beautiful Brazilian widow—she was said to be a secret agent for some South American republic—to teach him Spanish. He cultivated the society of the unknown great; poets, actors, musicians. He entertained them sumptuously, and they regarded him as a deep, mysterious Jew who had the secret of gold, which they had not. His business associates thought him a man of taste and culture, a patron of the arts, a credit to the garment trade.

"One of Stein's many ambitions was to be thought a success with women. He got considerable notoriety in the garment world by his attentions to an emotional actress who is now quite forgotten, but who had her little hour of expectation. Then there was a dancer; then, just after Gorky's visit here, a Russian anarchist woman. After that the coat-makers and shirtwaist-makers began to whisper that Stein's great success was with Kitty Ayrshire.

"It is the hardest thing in the world to disprove such a story, as Dan Leland and I discovered. We managed to worry down the girl's address through a taxi-cab driver who got next to Stein's chauffeur.

She had an apartment in a decent-enough house on Waverly Place. Nobody ever came to see her but Stein, her sisters, and a little Italian girl from whom we got the story.

"The counterfeit's name was Ruby Mohr. She worked in a shirt-waist factory, and this Italian girl, Margarita, was her chum. Stein came to the factory when he was hunting for living models for his new department store. He looked the girls over, and picked Ruby out from several hundred. He had her call at his office after business hours, tried her out in cloaks and evening gowns, and offered her a position. She never, however, appeared as a model in the Sixth Avenue store. Her likeness to the newly arrived prima donna suggested to Stein another act in the play he was always putting on. He gave two of her sisters positions as saleswomen, but Ruby he established in an apartment on Waverly Place.

"To the outside world Stein became more mysterious in his behaviour than ever. He dropped his Bohemian friends. No more suppers and theatre-parties. Whenever Kitty sang, he was in his box at the Manhattan, usually alone, but not always. Sometimes he took two or three good customers, large buyers from St. Louis or Kansas City. His coat factory is still the biggest earner of his properties. I've seen him there with these buyers, and they carried themselves as if they were being let in on something; took possession of the box with a proprietory air, smiled and applauded and looked wise as if each and every one of them were friends of Kitty Ayrshire. While they buzzed and trained their field-glasses on the prima donna, Stein was impassive and silent. I don't imagine he even told many lies. He is the most insinuating cuss, anyhow. He probably dropped his voice or lifted his eyebrows when he invited them, and let their own eager imaginations do the rest. But what tales they took back to their provincial capitals!

"Sometimes, before they left New York, they were lucky enough to see Kitty dining with their clever garment man at some restaurant, her back to the curious crowd, her face half concealed by a veil or a fur collar. Those people are like children; nothing that is true or probable interests them. They want the old, gaudy lies, told always in the same way. Siegmund Stein and Kitty Ayrshire—a story like that, once launched, is repeated unchallenged for years among New York factory sports. In St. Paul, St. Jo, Sioux City, Council Bluffs, there used to be clothing stores where a photograph of Kitty Ayrshire hung in the fitting-room or over the proprietor's desk.

"This girl impersonated you successfully to the lower manufacturing world of New York for two seasons. I doubt if it could have been put across anywhere else in the world except in this city, which pays you so magnificently and believes of you what it likes. Then you went over to the Metropolitan, stopped living in hotels, took this apartment, and began to know people. Stein discontinued his pantomime at the right moment, withdrew his patronage. Ruby, of course, did not go back to shirt-waists. A business friend of Stein's took her over, and she dropped out of sight. Last winter, one cold, snowy night, I saw her once again. She was going into a saloon hotel with a tough-looking young fellow. She had been drinking, she was shabby, and her blue shoes left stains in the slush. But she still looked amazingly, convincingly like a battered, hardened Kitty Ayrshire. As I saw her going up the brass-edged stairs, I said to myself—"

"Never mind that." Kitty rose quickly, took an impatient step to the hearth, and thrust one shining porcelain slipper out to the fire. "The girl doesn't interest me. There is nothing I can do about her, and of course she never looked like me at all. But what did Stein do without me?"

"Stein? Oh, he chose a new rôle. He married with great magnificence—married a Miss Mandelbaum, a California heiress. Her people have a line of department stores along the Pacific Coast. The Steins now inhabit a great house on Fifth Avenue that used to belong to people of a very different sort. To old New Yorkers, it's an historic house."

Kitty laughed, and sat down on the end of her couch nearest her guest; sat upright, without cushions.

"I imagine I know more about that house than you do. Let me tell you how I made the sequel to your story.

"It has to do with Peppo Amoretti. You may remember that I brought Peppo to this country, and brought him in, too, the year the war broke out, when it wasn't easy to get boys who hadn't done military service out of Italy. I had taken him to Munich to have some singing lessons. After the war came on we had to get from Munich to Naples in order to sail at all. We were told that we could take only hand luggage on the railways, but I took nine trunks and Peppo. I dressed Peppo in knickerbockers, made him brush his curls down over his ears like doughnuts, and carry a little violin-case. It took us eleven days to reach Naples. I got my trunks through purely by personal persuasion. Once at Naples, I had a frightful time getting Peppo on the boat. I declared him as hand-luggage; he was so travel-worn and so crushed by his absurd appearance that he did not look like much else. One inspector had a sense of humour, and passed him at that, but the other was inflexible. I had to be very dramatic. Peppo was frightened, and there is no fight in him, anyhow.

" '*Per me tutto e indifferente, Signorina,*' he kept whimpering. 'Why should I go without it? I have lost it.'

" 'Which?' I screamed. '*Not* the hat-trunk?'

" '*No, no; mia voce.* It is gone since Ravenna.'

"He thought he had lost his voice somewhere along the way. At last I told the inspector that I couldn't live without Peppo, and that I would throw myself into the bay. I took him into my confidence. Of course, when I found I had to play on that string, I wished I hadn't made the boy such a spectacle. But ridiculous as he was, I managed to make the inspector believe that I had kidnapped him, and that he was indispensable to my happiness. I found that incorruptible official, like most people, willing to aid one so utterly depraved. I could never have got that boy out for any proper, reasonable purpose, such as giving him a job or sending him to school. Well, it's a queer world! But I must cut all that and get to the Steins.

"That first winter Peppo had no chance at the Opera. There was an iron ring about him, and my interest in him only made it all the more difficult. We've become a nest of intrigues down there; worse than the Scala. Peppo had to scratch along just any way. One evening he came to me and said he could get an engagement to sing for the grand rich Steins, but the condition was that I should sing with him. They would pay, oh, anything! And the fact that I had sung a private engagement with him would give him other engagements of the same sort. As you know, I never sing private engagements; but to help the boy along, I consented.

"On the night of the party, Peppo and I went to the house together in a taxi. My car was ailing. At the hour when the music was about

to begin, the host and hostess appeared at my dressing-room, upstairs. Isn't he wonderful? Your description was most inadequate. I
never encountered such restrained, frozen, sculptured vanity. My
hostess struck me as extremely good natured and jolly, though somewhat intimate in her manner. Her reassuring pats and smiles puzzled
me at the time, I remember, when I didn't know that she had anything
in particular to be large-minded and charitable about. Her husband
made known his willingness to conduct me to the music-room, and
we ceremoniously descended a staircase blooming like the hanging-
gardens of Babylon. From there I had my first glimpse of the company.
They *were* strange people. The women glittered like Christmas-trees.
When we were half-way down the stairs, the buzz of conversation
stopped so suddenly that some foolish remark I happened to be making
rang out like oratory. Every face was lifted toward us. My host and
I completed our descent and went the length of the drawing-room
through a silence which somewhat awed me. I couldn't help wishing
that one could ever get that kind of attention in a concert-hall. In
the music-room Stein insisted upon arranging things for me. I must
say that he was neither awkward nor stupid, not so wooden as most
rich men who rent singers. I was properly affable. One has, under
such circumstances, to be either gracious or pouty. Either you have
to stand and sulk, like an old-fashioned German singer who wants
the piano moved about for her like a tea-wagon, and the lights turned
up and the lights turned down,—or you have to be a trifle forced,
like a débutante trying to make good. The fixed attention of my
audience affected me. I was aware of unusual interest, of a thoroughly
enlisted public. When, however, my host at last left me, I felt the
tension relax to such an extent that I wondered whether by any
chance he, and not I, was the object of so much curiosity. But, at
any rate, their cordiality pleased me so well that after Peppo and I
had finished our numbers I sang an encore or two, and I stayed
through Peppo's performance because I felt that they liked to look
at me.

"I had asked not to be presented to people, but Mrs. Stein, of
course, brought up a few friends. The throng began closing in upon
me, glowing faces bore down from every direction, and I realized
that, among people of such unscrupulous cordiality, I must look out

for myself. I ran through the drawing-room and fled up the stairway, which was thronged with Old Testament characters. As I passed them, they all looked at me with delighted, cherishing eyes, as if I had at last come back to my native hamlet. At the top of the stairway a young man, who looked like a camel with its hair parted on the side, stopped me, seized my hands and said he must present himself, as he was such an old friend of Siegmund's bachelor days. I said, 'Yes, how interesting!' The atmosphere was somehow so thick and personal that I felt uncomfortable.

"When I reached my dressing-room Mrs. Stein followed me to say that I would, of course, come down to supper, as a special table had been prepared for me. I replied that it was not my custom.

" 'But here it is different. With us you must feel perfect freedom. Siegmund will never forgive me if you do not stay. After supper our car will take you home.' She was overpowering. She had the manner of an intimate and indulgent friend of long standing. She seemed to have come to make me a visit. I could only get rid of her by telling her that I must see Peppo at once, if she would be good enough to send him to me. She did not come back, and I began to fear that I would actually be dragged down to supper. It was as if I had been kidnapped. I felt like *Gulliver* among the giants. These people were all too—well, too much what they were. No chill of manner could hold them off. I was defenceless. I must get away. I ran to the top of the staircase and looked down. There was that fool Peppo, belea-guered by a bevy of fair women. They were simply looting him, and he was grinning like an idiot. I gathered up my train, ran down, and made a dash at him, yanked him out of that circle of rich contours, and dragged him by a limp cuff up the stairs after me. I told him that I must escape from that house at once. If he could get to the telephone, well and good; but if he couldn't get past so many deep-breathing ladies, then he must break out of the front door and hunt me a cab on foot. I felt as if I were about to be immured within a harem.

"He had scarcely dashed off when the host called my name several times outside the door. Then he knocked and walked in, uninvited. I told him that I would be inflexible about supper. He must make my excuses to his charming friends; any pretext he chose. He did not insist. He took up his stand by the fireplace and began to talk; said rather intelligent things. I did not drive him out; it was his own house, and he made himself agreeable. After a time a deputation of his friends came down the hall, somewhat boisterously, to say that supper could not be served until we came down. Stein was still standing by the mantel, I remember. He scattered them, without moving or speaking to them, by a portentous look. There is something hideously forceful about him. He took a very profound leave of me, and said he would order his car at once. In a moment Peppo arrived, splashed to the ankles, and we made our escape together.

"A week later Peppo came to me in a rage, with a paper called *The American Gentleman,* and showed me a page devoted to three photographs: Mr. and Mrs. Siegmund Stein, lately married in New York City, and Kitty Ayrshire, operatic soprano, who sang at their house-warming. Mrs. Stein and I were grinning our best, looked frantic with delight, and Siegmund frowned inscrutably between us. Poor Peppo wasn't mentioned. Stein has a publicity sense."

Tevis rose.

"And you have enormous publicity value and no discretion. It was just like you to fall for such a plot, Kitty. You'd be sure to."

"What's the use of discretion?" She murmured behind her hand. "If the Steins want to adopt you into their family circle, they'll get you in the end. That's why I don't feel compassionate about your Ruby. She and I are in the same boat. We are both the victims of circumstance, and in New York so many of the circumstances are Steins."

Paul's Case

It was Paul's afternoon to appear before the faculty of the Pittsburgh High School to account for his various misdemeanours. He had been suspended a week ago, and his father had called at the Principal's office and confessed his perplexity about his son. Paul entered the faculty room suave and smiling. His clothes were a trifle outgrown, and the tan velvet on the collar of his open overcoat was frayed and worn; but for all that there was something of the dandy about him, and he wore an opal pin in his neatly knotted black four-in-hand, and a red carnation in his button-hole. This latter adornment the faculty somehow felt was not properly significant of the contrite spirit befitting a boy under the ban of suspension.

Paul was tall for his age and very thin, with high, cramped shoulders and a narrow chest. His eyes were remarkable for a certain hysterical brilliancy, and he continually used them in a conscious, theatrical sort of way, peculiarly offensive in a boy. The pupils were abnormally large, as though he were addicted to belladonna, but there was a glassy glitter about them which that drug does not produce.

When questioned by the Principal as to why he was there, Paul stated, politely enough, that he wanted to come back to school. This was a lie, but Paul was quite accustomed to lying; found it, indeed, indispensable for overcoming friction. His teachers were asked to state their respective charges against him, which they did with such a rancour and aggrievedness as evinced that this was not a usual case. Disorder and impertinence were among the offences named, yet each of his instructors felt that it was scarcely possible to put into words the real cause of the trouble, which lay in a sort of hysterically defiant manner of the boy's; in the contempt which they all knew he felt for them, and which he seemingly made not the least effort to conceal. Once, when he had been making a synopsis of a paragraph at the blackboard, his English teacher had stepped to his side and attempted to guide his hand. Paul had started back with a shudder and thrust his hands violently behind him. The astonished woman could scarcely have been more hurt and embarrassed had he struck at her. The insult was so involuntary and definitely personal as to be unforgettable. In one way and another, he had made all his teachers, men and women alike, conscious of the same feeling of physical aversion. In one class he habitually sat with his hand shading his eyes; in another he always looked out of the window during the recitation; in another he made a running commentary on the lecture, with humorous intent.

His teachers felt this afternoon that his whole attitude was symbolized by his shrug and his flippantly red carnation flower, and they fell upon him without mercy, his English teacher leading the pack. He stood through it smiling, his pale lips parted over his white teeth. (His lips were continually twitching, and he had a habit of raising his eyebrows that was contemptuous and irritating to the last degree.) Older boys than Paul had broken down and shed tears under that ordeal, but his set smile did not once desert him, and his only sign of discomfort was the nervous trembling of the fingers that toyed with the buttons of his overcoat, and an occasional jerking of the other hand which held his hat. Paul was always smiling, always glancing about him, seeming to feel that people might be watching him and trying to detect something. This conscious expression, since it was as far as possible from boyish mirthfulness, was usually attributed to insolence or "smartness."

As the inquisition proceeded, one of his instructors repeated an impertinent remark of the boy's, and the Principal asked him whether he thought that a courteous speech to make to a woman. Paul shrugged his shoulders slightly and his eyebrows twitched.

"I don't know," he replied. "I didn't mean to be polite or impolite, either. I guess it's a sort of way I have, of saying things regardless."

The Principal asked him whether he didn't think that a way it would be well to get rid of. Paul grinned and said he guessed so. When he was told that he could go, he bowed gracefully and went out. His bow was like a repetition of the scandalous red carnation.

His teachers were in despair, and his drawing master voiced the feeling of them all when he declared there was something about the boy which none of them understood. He added: "I don't really believe that smile of his comes altogether from insolence; there's something sort of haunted about it. The boy is not strong, for one thing. There is something wrong about the fellow."

The drawing master had come to realize that, in looking at Paul, one saw only his white teeth and the forced animation of his eyes. One warm afternoon the boy had gone to sleep at his drawing-board, and his master had noted with amazement what a white, blue-veined face it was; drawn and wrinkled like an old man's about the eyes, the lips twitching even in his sleep.

His teachers left the building dissatisfied and unhappy; humiliated to have felt so vindictive toward a mere boy, to have uttered this feeling in cutting terms, and to have set each other on, as it were, in the grewsome game of intemperate reproach. One of them remembered having seen a miserable street cat set at bay by a ring of tormentors.

As for Paul, he ran down the hill whistling the Soldiers' Chorus from *Faust,* looking wildly behind him now and then to see whether some of his teachers were not there to witness his light-heartedness. As it was now late in the afternoon and Paul was on duty that evening as usher at Carnegie Hall, he decided that he would not go home to supper.

When he reached the concert hall the doors were not yet open. It was chilly outside, and he decided to go up into the picture gallery— always deserted at this hour—where there were some of Raffelli's gay studies of Paris streets and an airy blue Venetian scene or two that always exhilarated him. He was delighted to find no one in the gallery but the old guard, who sat in the corner, a newspaper on his knee, a black patch over one eye and the other closed. Paul possessed himself of the place and walked confidently up and down, whistling under his breath. After a while he sat down before a blue Rico and lost himself. When he bethought him to look at his watch, it was after seven o'clock, and he rose with a start and ran downstairs, making a face at Augustus Cæsar, peering out from the cast-room, and an evil gesture at the Venus of Milo as he passed her on the stairway.

When Paul reached the ushers' dressing-room half-a-dozen boys were there already, and he began excitedly to tumble into his uniform.

It was one of the few that at all approached fitting, and Paul thought it very becoming—though he knew the tight, straight coat accentuated his narrow chest, about which he was exceedingly sensitive. He was always excited while he dressed, twanging all over to the tuning of the strings and the preliminary flourishes of the horns in the music-room; but tonight he seemed quite beside himself, and he teased and plagued the boys until, telling him that he was crazy, they put him down on the floor and sat on him.

Somewhat calmed by his suppression, Paul dashed out to the front of the house to seat the early comers. He was a model usher. Gracious and smiling he ran up and down the aisles. Nothing was too much trouble for him; he carried messages and brought programs as though it were his greatest pleasure in life, and all the people in his section thought him a charming boy, feeling that he remembered and admired them. As the house filled, he grew more and more vivacious and animated, and the colour came to his cheeks and lips. It was very much as though this were a great reception and Paul were the host. Just as the musicians came out to take their places, his English teacher arrived with checks for the seats which a prominent manufacturer had taken for the season. She betrayed some embarrassment when she handed Paul the tickets, and a *hauteur* which subsequently made her feel very foolish. Paul was startled for a moment, and had the feeling of wanting to put her out; what business had she here among all these fine people and gay colours? He looked her over and decided that she was not appropriately dressed and must be a fool to sit downstairs in such togs. The tickets had probably been sent her out of kindness, he reflected, as he put down a seat for her, and she had about as much right to sit there as he had.

When the symphony began Paul sank into one of the rear seats with a long sigh of relief, and lost himself as he had done before the Rico. It was not that symphonies, as such, meant anything in particular to Paul, but the first sigh of the instruments seemed to free some hilarious spirit within him; something that struggled there like the Genius in the bottle found by the Arab fisherman. He felt a sudden zest of life; the lights danced before his eyes and the concert hall blazed into unimaginable splendour. When the soprano soloist came on, Paul forgot even the nastiness of his teacher's being there, and gave himself up to the peculiar intoxication such personages always had for him. The soloist chanced to be a German woman, by no means in her first youth, and the mother of many children; but she wore a satin gown and a tiara, and she had that indefinable air of achievement, that world-shine upon her, which always blinded Paul to any possible defects.

After a concert was over, Paul was often irritable and wretched until he got to sleep,—and tonight he was even more than usually restless. He had the feeling of not being able to let down; of its being impossible to give up this delicious excitement which was the only thing that could be called living at all. During the last number he withdrew and, after hastily changing his clothes in the dressing-room, slipped out to the side door where the singer's carriage stood. Here he began pacing rapidly up and down the walk, waiting to see her come out.

Over yonder the Schenley, in its vacant stretch, loomed big and square through the fine rain, the windows of its twelve stories glowing like those of a lighted card-board house under a Christmas tree. All the actors and singers of any importance stayed there when they were in the city, and a number of the big manufacturers of the place lived there in the winter. Paul had often hung about the hotel, watching the people go in and out, longing to enter and leave school-masters and dull care behind him for ever.

At last the singer came out, accompanied by the conductor, who helped her into her carriage and closed the door with a cordial *auf wiedersehen,*—which set Paul to wondering whether she was not an old sweetheart of his. Paul followed the carriage over to the hotel, walking so rapidly as not to be far from the entrance when the singer alighted and disappeared behind the swinging glass doors which were opened by a negro in a tall hat and a long coat. In the moment that the door was ajar, it seemed to Paul that he, too, entered. He seemed to feel himself go after her up the steps, into the warm, lighted building, into an exotic, a tropical world of shiny, glistening surfaces and basking ease. He reflected upon the mysterious dishes that were brought into the dining-room, the green bottles in buckets of ice, as he had seen them in the supper party pictures of the Sunday sup-plement. A quick gust of wind brought the rain down with sudden vehemence, and Paul was startled to find that he was still outside in the slush of the gravel driveway; that his boots were letting in the water and his scanty overcoat was clinging wet about him; that the lights in front of the concert hall were out, and that the rain was driving in sheets between him and the orange glow of the windows above him. There it was, what he wanted—tangibly before him, like the fairy world of a Christmas pantomime; as the rain beat in his face, Paul wondered whether he were destined always to shiver in the black night outside, looking up at it.

He turned and walked reluctantly toward the car tracks. The end had to come sometime; his father in his night-clothes at the top of the stairs, explanations that did not explain, hastily improvised fictions that were forever tripping him up, his up-stairs room and its horrible yellow wallpaper, the creaking bureau with the greasy plush collar-box, and over his painted wooden bed the pictures of George Washington and John Calvin, and the framed motto, "Feed my Lambs," which had been worked in red worsted by his mother, whom Paul could not remember.

Half an hour later, Paul alighted from the Negley Avenue car and went slowly down one of the side streets off the main thoroughfare. It was a highly respectable street, where all the houses were exactly alike, and where business men of moderate means begot and reared large families of children, all of whom went to Sabbath-school and learned the shorter catechism, and were interested in arithmetic; all of whom were as exactly alike as their homes, and of a piece with the monotony in which they lived. Paul never went up Cordelia Street without a shudder of loathing. His home was next the house of the Cumberland minister. He approached it tonight with the nerveless sense of defeat, the hopeless feeling of sinking back forever into ugliness and commonness that he had always had when he came home. The moment he turned into Cordelia Street he felt the waters close above his head. After each of these orgies of living, he experienced all the physical depression which follows a debauch; the loathing of respectable beds, of common food, of a house permeated by kitchen odours; a shuddering repulsion for the flavourless, colourless mass of every-day existence, a morbid desire for cool things and soft lights and fresh flowers.

The nearer he approached the house, the more absolutely unequal Paul felt to the sight of it all; his ugly sleeping chamber; the cold bath-room with the grimy zinc tub, the cracked mirror, the dripping spiggots; his father, at the top of the stairs, his hairy legs sticking out from his nightshirt, his feet thrust into carpet slippers. He was so much later than usual that there would certainly be inquiries and reproaches. Paul stopped short before the door. He felt that he could not be accosted by his father tonight; that he could not toss again on that miserable bed. He would not go in. He would tell his father that he had no car fare, and it was raining so hard he had gone home with one of the boys and stayed all night.

Meanwhile, he was wet and cold. He went around to the back of the house and tried one of the basement windows, found it open, raised it cautiously, and scrambled down the cellar wall to the floor. There he stood, holding his breath, terrified by the noise he had made; but the floor above him was silent, and there was no creak on the stairs. He found a soap-box, and carried it over to the soft ring of light that streamed from the furnace door, and sat down. He was horribly afraid of rats, so he did not try to sleep, but sat looking distrustfully at the dark, still terrified lest he might have awakened his father. In such reactions, after one of the experiences which made days and nights out of the dreary blanks of the calendar, when his senses were deadened, Paul's head was always singularly clear. Suppose his father had heard him getting in at the window and had come down and shot him for a burglar? Then, again, suppose his father had come down, pistol in hand, and he had cried out in time to save himself, and his father had been horrified to think how nearly he had killed him? Then, again, suppose a day should come when his father would remember that night, and wish there had been no warning cry to stay his hand? With this last supposition Paul entertained himself until daybreak.

The following Sunday was fine; the sodden November chill was broken by the last flash of autumnal summer. In the morning Paul had to go to church and Sabbath-school, as always. On seasonable Sunday afternoons the burghers of Cordelia Street usually sat out on their front "stoops," and talked to their neighbours on the next stoop, or called to those across the street in neighbourly fashion. The men sat placidly on gay cushions placed upon the steps that led down to the sidewalk, while the women, in their Sunday "waists," sat in rockers on the cramped porches, pretending to be greatly at their ease. The children played in the streets; there were so many of them that the place resembled the recreation grounds of a kindergarten. The men on the steps—all in their shirt sleeves, their vests unbuttoned—sat with their legs well apart, their stomachs comfortably protruding, and talked of the prices of things, or told anecdotes of the sagacity of their various chiefs and overlords. They occasionally looked over the multitude of squabbling children, listened affectionately to their high-pitched, nasal voices, smiling to see their own proclivities reproduced in their offspring, and interspersed their legends of the iron kings with remarks about their sons' progress at school, their grades in arithmetic, and the amounts they had saved in their toy banks.

On this last Sunday of November, Paul sat all the afternoon on the lowest step of his "stoop," staring into the street, while his sisters, in their rockers, were talking to the minister's daughters next door about how many shirt-waists they had made in the last week, and how many waffles some one had eaten at the last church supper. When the weather was warm, and his father was in a particularly jovial frame of mind, the girls made lemonade, which was always brought out in a red-glass pitcher, ornamented with forget-me-nots in blue enamel. This the girls thought very fine, and the neighbours joked about the suspicious colour of the pitcher.

Today Paul's father, on the top step, was talking to a young man who shifted a restless baby from knee to knee. He happened to be the young man who was daily held up to Paul as a model, and after whom it was his father's dearest hope that he would pattern. This young man was of a ruddy complexion, with a compressed, red mouth, and faded, near-sighted eyes, over which he wore thick spectacles, with gold bows that curved about his ears. He was clerk to one of the magnates of a great steel corporation, and was looked upon in Cordelia Street as a young man with a future. There was a story that, some five years ago—he was now barely twenty-six—he had been a trifle "dissipated," but in order to curb his appetites and save the loss of time and strength that a sowing of wild oats might have entailed, he had taken his chief's advice, oft reiterated to his employés, and at twenty-one had married the first woman whom he could persuade to share his fortunes. She happened to be an angular school-mistress, much older than he, who also wore thick glasses, and who had now borne him four children, all near-sighted, like herself.

The young man was relating how his chief, now cruising in the Mediterranean, kept in touch with all the details of the business, arranging his office hours on his yacht just as though he were at home, and "knocking off work enough to keep two stenographers busy." His father told, in turn, the plan his corporation was consid-ering, of putting in an electric railway plant at Cairo. Paul snapped his teeth; he had an awful apprehension that they might spoil it all before he got there. Yet he rather liked to hear these legends of the iron kings, that were told and retold on Sundays and holidays; these stories of palaces in Venice, yachts on the Mediterranean, and high play at Monte Carlo appealed to his fancy, and he was interested in the triumphs of cash boys who had become famous, though he had no mind for the cashboy stage.

After supper was over, and he had helped to dry the dishes, Paul nervously asked his father whether he could go to George's to get some help in his geometry, and still more nervously asked for car-fare. This latter request he had to repeat, as his father, on principle, did not like to hear requests for money, whether much or little. He asked Paul whether he could not go to some boy who lived nearer, and told him that he ought not to leave his school work until Sunday; but he gave him the dime. He was not a poor man, but he had a worthy ambition to come up in the world. His only reason for allowing Paul to usher was that he thought a boy ought to be earning a little.

Paul bounded upstairs, scrubbed the greasy odour of the dish-water from his hands with the ill-smelling soap he hated, and then shook over his fingers a few drops of violet water from the bottle he kept hidden in his drawer. He left the house with his geometry conspicuously under his arm, and the moment he got out of Cordelia Street and boarded a downtown car, he shook off the lethargy of two deadening days, and began to live again.

The leading juvenile of the permanent stock company which played at one of the downtown theatres was an acquaintance of Paul's, and the boy had been invited to drop in at the Sunday-night rehearsals whenever he could. For more than a year Paul had spent every available moment loitering about Charley Edwards's dressing-room. He had won a place among Edwards's following not only because the young actor, who could not afford to employ a dresser, often found him useful, but because he recognized in Paul something akin to what churchmen term "vocation."

It was at the theatre and at Carnegie Hall that Paul really lived; the rest was but a sleep and a forgetting. This was Paul's fairy tale, and it had for him all the allurement of a secret love. The moment he inhaled the gassy, painty, dusty odour behind the scenes, he breathed like a prisoner set free, and felt within him the possibility of doing or saying splendid, brilliant things. The moment the cracked orchestra beat out the overture from *Martha*, or jerked at the serenade from *Rigoletto*, all stupid and ugly things slid from him, and his senses were deliciously, yet delicately fired.

Perhaps it was because, in Paul's world, the natural nearly always wore the guise of ugliness, that a certain element of artificiality seemed to him necessary in beauty. Perhaps it was because his experience of life elsewhere was so full of Sabbath-school picnics, petty economies, wholesome advice as to how to succeed in life, and the unescapable odours of cooking, that he found this existence so alluring, these smartly-clad men and women so attractive, that he was so moved by these starry apple orchards that bloomed perennially under the lime-light.

It would be difficult to put it strongly enough how convincingly the stage entrance of that theatre was for Paul the actual portal of Romance. Certainly none of the company ever suspected it, least of all Charley Edwards. It was very like the old stories that used to float about London of fabulously rich Jews, who had subterranean halls, with palms, and fountains, and soft lamps and richly apparelled women who never saw the disenchanting light of London day. So, in the midst of that smoke-palled city, enamoured of figures and grimy toil, Paul had his secret temple, his wishing-carpet, his bit of blue-and-white Mediterranean shore bathed in perpetual sunshine.

Several of Paul's teachers had a theory that his imagination had been perverted by garish fiction; but the truth was, he scarcely ever read at all. The books at home were not such as would either tempt or corrupt a youthful mind, and as for reading the novels that some of his friends urged upon him—well, he got what he wanted much more quickly from music; any sort of music, from an orchestra to a barrel organ. He needed only the spark, the indescribable thrill that made his imagination master of his senses, and he could make plots and pictures enough of his own. It was equally true that he was not stage-struck—not, at any rate, in the usual acceptation of that expression. He had no desire to become an actor, any more than he had to become a musician. He felt no necessity to do any of these things; what he wanted was to see, to be in the atmosphere, float on the wave of it, to be carried out, blue league after blue league, away from everything.

After a night behind the scenes, Paul found the school-room more than ever repulsive; the bare floors and naked walls; the prosy men who never wore frock coats, or violets in their button-holes; the women with their dull gowns, shrill voices, and pitiful seriousness about prepositions that govern the dative. He could not bear to have the other pupils think, for a moment, that he took these people seriously; he must convey to them that he considered it all trivial, and was there only by way of a joke, anyway. He had autograph pictures of all the members of the stock company which he showed his class-mates, telling them the most incredible stories of his familiarity with these people, of his acquaintance with the soloists who came to Carnegie Hall, his suppers with them and the flowers he sent them. When these stories lost their effect, and his audience grew listless, he would bid all the boys good-bye, announcing that he was going to travel for awhile; going to Naples, to California, to Egypt. Then, next Monday, he would slip back, conscious and nervously smiling; his sister was ill, and he would have to defer his voyage until spring.

Matters went steadily worse with Paul at school. In the itch to let his instructors know how heartily he despised them, and how thoroughly he was appreciated elsewhere, he mentioned once or twice that he had no time to fool with theorems; adding—with a twitch of the eyebrows and a touch of that nervous bravado which so perplexed them—that he was helping the people down at the stock company; they were old friends of his.

The upshot of the matter was, that the Principal went to Paul's father, and Paul was taken out of school and put to work. The manager at Carnegie Hall was told to get another usher in his stead; the doorkeeper at the theatre was warned not to admit him to the house; and Charley Edwards remorsefully promised the boy's father not to see him again.

The members of the stock company were vastly amused when some of Paul's stories reached them—especially the women. They were hard-working women, most of them supporting indolent husbands or brothers, and they laughed rather bitterly at having stirred the boy to such fervid and florid inventions. They agreed with the faculty and with his father, that Paul's was a bad case.

The east-bound train was ploughing through a January snow-storm; the dull dawn was beginning to show grey when the engine whistled a mile out of Newark. Paul started up from the seat where he had lain curled in uneasy slumber, rubbed the breath-misted window glass with his hand, and peered out. The snow was whirling in curling eddies above the white bottom lands, and the drifts lay already deep in the fields and along the fences, while here and there the long dead grass and dried weed stalks protruded black above it. Lights shone from the scattered houses, and a gang of labourers who stood beside the track waved their lanterns.

Paul had slept very little, and he felt grimy and uncomfortable. He had made the all-night journey in a day coach because he was afraid if he took a Pullman he might be seen by some Pittsburgh business man who had noticed him in Denny & Carson's office. When the whistle woke him, he clutched quickly at his breast pocket, glancing about him with an uncertain smile. But the little, clay-bespattered Italians were still sleeping, the slatternly women across the aisle were in open-mouthed oblivion, and even the crumby, crying babies were for the nonce stilled. Paul settled back to struggle with his impatience as best he could.

When he arrived at the Jersey City station, he hurried through his breakfast, manifestly ill at ease and keeping a sharp eye about him. After he reached the Twenty-third Street station, he consulted a cabman, and had himself driven to a men's furnishing establishment which was just opening for the day. He spent upward of two hours there, buying with endless reconsidering and great care. His new street suit he put on in the fitting-room; the frock coat and dress clothes he had bundled into the cab with his new shirts. Then he drove to a hatter's and a shoe house. His next errand was at Tiffany's, where he selected silver mounted brushes and a scarf-pin. He would not wait to have his silver marked, he said. Lastly, he stopped at a trunk shop on Broadway, and had his purchases packed into various travelling bags.

It was a little after one o'clock when he drove up to the Waldorf, and, after settling with the cabman, went into the office. He registered from Washington; said his mother and father had been abroad, and that he had come down to await the arrival of their steamer. He told his story plausibly and had no trouble, since he offered to pay for them in advance, in engaging his rooms; a sleeping-room, sitting-room and bath.

Not once, but a hundred times Paul had planned this entry into New York. He had gone over every detail of it with Charley Edwards, and in his scrap book at home there were pages of description about New York hotels, cut from the Sunday papers.

When he was shown to his sitting-room on the eighth floor, he saw at a glance that everything was as it should be; there was but one detail in his mental picture that the place did not realize, so he rang for the bell boy and sent him down for flowers. He moved about nervously until the boy returned, putting away his new linen and fingering it delightedly as he did so. When the flowers came, he put them hastily into water, and then tumbled into a hot bath. Presently he came out of his white bath-room, resplendent in his new silk underwear, and playing with the tassels of his red robe. The snow was whirling so fiercely outside his windows that he could scarcely see across the street; but within, the air was deliciously soft and fragrant. He put the violets and jonquils on the tabouret beside the couch, and threw himself down with a long sigh, covering himself with a Roman blanket. He was thoroughly tired; he had been in such haste, he had stood up to such a strain, covered so much ground in the last twenty-four hours, that he wanted to think how it had all come about. Lulled by the sound of the wind, the warm air, and the cool fragrance of the flowers, he sank into deep, drowsy retrospection.

It had been wonderfully simple; when they had shut him out of the theatre and concert hall, when they had taken away his bone, the whole thing was virtually determined. The rest was a mere matter of opportunity. The only thing that at all surprised him was his own courage—for he realized well enough that he had always been tormented by fear, a sort of apprehensive dread that, of late years, as the meshes of the lies he had told closed about him, had been pulling the muscles of his body tighter and tighter. Until now, he could not remember a time when he had not been dreading something. Even when he was a little boy, it was always there—behind him, or before, or on either side. There had always been the shadowed corner, the dark place into which he dared not look, but from which something seemed always to be watching him—and Paul had done things that were not pretty to watch, he knew.

But now he had a curious sense of relief, as though he had at last thrown down the gauntlet to the thing in the corner.

Yet it was but a day since he had been sulking in the traces; but yesterday afternoon that he had been sent to the bank with Denny & Carson's deposit, as usual—but this time he was instructed to leave the book to be balanced. There was above two thousand dollars in checks, and nearly a thousand in the bank notes which he had taken from the book and quietly transferred to his pocket. At the bank he had made out a new deposit slip. His nerves had been steady enough to permit of his returning to the office, where he had finished his work and asked for a full day's holiday tomorrow, Saturday, giving a perfectly reasonable pretext. The bank book, he knew, would not be returned before Monday or Tuesday, and his father would be out of town for the next week. From the time he slipped the bank notes into his pocket until he boarded the night train for New York, he had not known a moment's hesitation.

How astonishingly easy it had all been; here he was, the thing done; and this time there would be no awakening, no figure at the top of the stairs. He watched the snow flakes whirling by his window until he fell asleep.

When he awoke, it was four o'clock in the afternoon. He bounded up with a start; one of his precious days gone already! He spent nearly an hour in dressing, watching every stage of his toilet carefully in the mirror. Everything was quite perfect; he was exactly the kind of boy he had always wanted to be.

When he went downstairs, Paul took a carriage and drove up Fifth Avenue toward the Park. The snow had somewhat abated; carriages and tradesmen's wagons were hurrying soundlessly to and fro in the winter twilight; boys in woollen mufflers were shovelling off the doorsteps; the avenue stages made fine spots of colour against the white street. Here and there on the corners whole flower gardens blooming behind glass windows, against which the snow flakes stuck and melted; violets, roses, carnations, lilies of the valley—somehow vastly more lovely and alluring that they blossomed thus unnaturally in the snow. The Park itself was a wonderful stage winterpiece.

When he returned, the pause of the twilight had ceased, and the tune of the streets had changed. The snow was falling faster, lights streamed from the hotels that reared their many stories fearlessly up into the storm, defying the raging Atlantic winds. A long, black stream of carriages poured down the avenue, intersected here and there by other streams, tending horizontally. There were a score of cabs about the entrance of his hotel, and his driver had to wait. Boys in livery were running in and out of the awning stretched across the sidewalk, up and down the red velvet carpet laid from the door to the street. Above, about, within it all, was the rumble and roar, the hurry and toss of thousands of human beings as hot for pleasure as himself, and on every side of him towered the glaring affirmation of the omnipotence of wealth.

The boy set his teeth and drew his shoulders together in a spasm of realization; the plot of all dramas, the text of all romances, the nerve-stuff of all sensations was whirling about him like the snow flakes. He burnt like a faggot in a tempest.

When Paul came down to dinner, the music of the orchestra floated up the elevator shaft to greet him. As he stepped into the thronged corridor, he sank back into one of the chairs against the wall to get his breath. The lights, the chatter, the perfumes, the bewildering medley of colour—he had, for a moment, the feeling of not being able to stand it. But only for a moment; these were his own people, he told himself. He went slowly about the corridors, through the writing-rooms, smoking-rooms, reception-rooms, as though he were exploring the chambers of an enchanted palace, built and peopled for him alone.

When he reached the dining-room he sat down at a table near a window. The flowers, the white linen, the many-coloured wine glasses, the gay toilettes of the women, the low popping of corks, the undulating repetitions of the *Blue Danube* from the orchestra, all flooded Paul's dream with bewildering radiance. When the roseate tinge of his champagne was added—that cold, precious, bubbling stuff that creamed and foamed in his glass—Paul wondered that there were honest men in the world at all. This was what all the world was fighting for, he reflected; this was what all the struggle was about. He doubted the reality of his past. Had he ever known a place called Cordelia Street, a place where fagged looking business men boarded the early car? Mere rivets in a machine they seemed to Paul,—sickening men, with combings of children's hair always hanging to their coats, and the smell of cooking in their clothes. Cordelia Street—Ah, that belonged to another time and country! Had he not always been thus, had he not sat here night after night, from as far back as he could remember, looking pensively over just such shimmering textures, and slowly twirling the stem of a glass like this one between his thumb and middle finger? He rather thought he had.

He was not in the least abashed or lonely. He had no especial desire to meet or to know any of these people; all he demanded was the right to look on and conjecture, to watch the pageant. The mere stage properties were all he contended for. Nor was he lonely later in the evening, in his loge at the Opera. He was entirely rid of his nervous misgivings, of his forced aggressiveness, of the imperative desire to show himself different from his surroundings. He felt now that his surroundings explained him. Nobody questioned the purple; he had only to wear it passively. He had only to glance down at his dress coat to reassure himself that here it would be impossible for anyone to humiliate him.

He found it hard to leave his beautiful sitting-room to go to bed that night, and sat long watching the raging storm from his turret window. When he went to sleep, it was with the lights turned on in his bedroom; partly because of his old timidity, and partly so that, if he should wake in the night, there would be no wretched moment of doubt, no horrible suspicion of yellow wall-paper, or of Washington and Calvin above his bed.

On Sunday morning the city was practically snowbound. Paul breakfasted late, and in the afternoon he fell in with a wild San Francisco boy, a freshman at Yale, who said he had run down for a "little flyer" over Sunday. The young man offered to show Paul the night side of the town, and the two boys went off together after dinner, not returning to the hotel until seven o'clock the next morning. They had started out in the confiding warmth of a champagne friendship, but their parting in the elevator was singularly cool. The freshman pulled himself together to make his train, and Paul went to bed. He awoke at two o'clock in the afternoon, very thirsty and dizzy, and rang for ice-water, coffee, and the Pittsburgh papers.

On the part of the hotel management, Paul excited no suspicion. There was this to be said for him, that he wore his spoils with dignity and in no way made himself conspicuous. His chief greediness lay in his ears and eyes, and his excesses were not offensive ones. His dearest pleasures were the grey winter twilights in his sitting-room; his quiet enjoyment of his flowers, his clothes, his wide divan, his cigarette and his sense of power. He could not remember a time when he had felt so at peace with himself. The mere release from the necessity of petty lying, lying every day and every day, restored his self-respect. He had never lied for pleasure, even at school; but to make himself noticed and admired, to assert his difference from other Cordelia Street boys; and he felt a good deal more manly, more honest, even, now that he had no need for boastful pretensions, now that he could, as his actor friends used to say, "dress the part." It was characteristic that remorse did not occur to him. His golden days went by without a shadow, and he made each as perfect as he could.

On the eighth day after his arrival in New York, he found the whole affair exploited in the Pittsburgh papers, exploited with a wealth of detail which indicated that local news of a sensational nature was at a low ebb. The firm of Denny & Carson announced that the boy's father had refunded the full amount of his theft, and that they had no intention of prosecuting. The Cumberland minister had been interviewed, and expressed his hope of yet reclaiming the motherless lad, and Paul's Sabbath-school teacher declared that she would spare no effort to that end. The rumour had reached Pittsburgh that the boy had been seen in a New York hotel, and his father had gone East to find him and bring him home.

Paul had just come in to dress for dinner; he sank into a chair, weak in the knees, and clasped his head in his hands. It was to be worse than jail, even; the tepid waters of Cordelia Street were to close over him finally and forever. The grey monotony stretched before him in hopeless, unrelieved years; Sabbath-school, Young People's Meeting, the yellow-papered room, the damp dish-towels; it all rushed back upon him with sickening vividness. He had the old feeling that the orchestra had suddenly stopped, the sinking sensation that the play was over. The sweat broke out on his face, and he sprang to his feet, looked about him with his white, conscious smile, and winked at himself in the mirror. With something of the childish belief in miracles with which he had so often gone to class, all his lessons unlearned, Paul dressed and dashed whistling down the corridor to the elevator.

He had no sooner entered the dining-room and caught the measure of the music, than his remembrance was lightened by his old elastic power of claiming the moment, mounting with it, and finding it all sufficient. The glare and glitter about him, the mere scenic accessories had again, and for the last time, their old potency. He would show himself that he was game, he would finish the thing splendidly. He doubted, more than ever, the existence of Cordelia Street, and for the first time he drank his wine recklessly. Was he not, after all, one of these fortunate beings? Was he not still himself, and in his own place? He drummed a nervous accompaniment to the music and looked about him, telling himself over and over that it had paid.

He reflected drowsily, to the swell of the violin and the chill sweetness of his wine, that he might have done it more wisely. He might have caught an outbound steamer and been well out of their clutches before now. But the other side of the world had seemed too far away and too uncertain then; he could not have waited for it; his need had been too sharp. If he had to choose over again, he would do the same thing tomorrow. He looked affectionately about the dining-room, now gilded with a soft mist. Ah, it had paid indeed!

Paul was awakened next morning by a painful throbbing in his head and feet. He had thrown himself across the bed without undressing, and had slept with his shoes on. His limbs and hands were lead heavy, and his tongue and throat were parched. There came upon him one of those fateful attacks of clear-headedness that never occurred except when he was physically exhausted and his nerves hung loose. He lay still and closed his eyes and let the tide of realities wash over him.

His father was in New York; "stopping at some joint or other," he told himself. The memory of successive summers on the front stoop fell upon him like a weight of black water. He had not a hundred dollars left; and he knew now, more than ever, that money was everything, the wall that stood between all he loathed and all he wanted. The thing was winding itself up; he had thought of that on his first glorious day in New York, and had even provided a way to snap the thread. It lay on his dressing-table now; he had got it out last night when he came blindly up from dinner—but the shiny metal hurt his eyes, and he disliked the look of it, anyway.

He rose and moved about with a painful effort, succumbing now and again to attacks of nausea. It was the old depression exaggerated; all the world had become Cordelia Street. Yet somehow he was not afraid of anything, was absolutely calm; perhaps because he had looked into the dark corner at last, and knew. It was bad enough, what he saw there; but somehow not so bad as his long fear of it had been. He saw everything clearly now. He had a feeling that he had made the best of it, that he had lived the sort of life he was meant to live, and for half an hour he sat staring at the revolver. But he told himself that was not the way, so he went downstairs and took a cab to the ferry.

When Paul arrived at Newark, he got off the train and took another cab, directing the driver to follow the Pennsylvania tracks out of the town. The snow lay heavy on the roadways and had drifted deep in the open fields. Only here and there the dead grass or dried weed stalks projected, singularly black, above it. Once well into the country, Paul dismissed the carriage and walked, floundering along the tracks, his mind a medley of irrelevant things. He seemed to hold in his brain an actual picture of everything he had seen that morning. He remembered every feature of both his drivers, the toothless old woman from whom he had bought the red flowers in his coat, the agent from whom he had got his ticket, and all of his fellow-passengers on the ferry. His mind, unable to cope with vital matters near at hand, worked feverishly and deftly at sorting and grouping these images. They made for him a part of the ugliness of the world, of the ache in his head, and the bitter burning on his tongue. He stooped and put a handful of snow into his mouth as he walked, but that, too, seemed hot. When he reached a little hillside, where the tracks ran through a cut some twenty feet below him, he stopped and sat down.

The carnations in his coat were drooping with the cold, he noticed; all their red glory over. It occurred to him that all the flowers he had seen in the show windows that first night must have gone the same way, long before this. It was only one splendid breath they had, in spite of their brave mockery at the winter outside the glass. It was a losing game in the end, it seemed, this revolt against the homilies by which the world is run. Paul took one of the blossoms carefully from his coat and scooped a little hole in the snow, where he covered it up. Then he dozed a while, from his weak condition, seeming insensible to the cold.

The sound of an approaching train woke him, and he started to his feet, remembering only his resolution, and afraid lest he should be too late. He stood watching the approaching locomotive, his teeth chattering, his lips drawn away from them in a frightened smile; once or twice he glanced nervously sidewise, as though he were being watched. When the right moment came, he jumped. As he fell, the folly of his haste occurred to him with merciless clearness, the vastness of what he had left undone. There flashed through his brain, clearer than ever before, the blue of Adriatic water, the yellow of Algerian sands.

He felt something strike his chest,—his body was being thrown swiftly through the air, on and on, immeasurably far and fast, while his limbs gently relaxed. Then, because the picture making mechanism was crushed, the disturbing visions flashed into black, and Paul dropped back into the immense design of things.

A Wagner Matinée

I received one morning a letter, written in pale ink on glassy, blue-lined note-paper, and bearing the postmark of a little Nebraska village. This communication, worn and rubbed, looking as if it had been carried for some days in a coat pocket that was none too clean, was from my uncle Howard, and informed me that his wife had been left a small legacy by a bachelor relative, and that it would be necessary for her to go to Boston to attend to the settling of the estate. He requested me to meet her at the station and render her whatever services might be necessary. On examining the date indicated as that of her arrival, I found it to be no later than tomorrow. He had characteristically delayed writing until, had I been away from home for a day, I must have missed my aunt altogether.

The name of my Aunt Georgiana opened before me a gulf of recollection so wide and deep that, as the letter dropped from my hand, I felt suddenly a stranger to all the present conditions of my existence, wholly ill at ease and out of place amid the familiar sur-roundings of my study. I became, in short, the gangling farmer-boy my aunt had known, scourged with chilblains and bashfulness, my hands cracked and sore from the corn husking. I sat again before her parlour organ, fumbling the scales with my stiff, red fingers, while she, beside me, made canvas mittens for the huskers.

The next morning, after preparing my landlady for a visitor, I set out for the station. When the train arrived I had some difficulty in finding my aunt. She was the last of the passengers to alight, and it was not until I got her into the carriage that she seemed really to recognize me. She had come all the way in a day coach; her linen duster had become black with soot and her black bonnet grey with dust during the journey. When we arrived at my boarding-house the landlady put her to bed at once and I did not see her again until the next morning.

Whatever shock Mrs. Springer experienced at my aunt's appear-ance, she considerately concealed. As for myself, I saw my aunt's battered figure with that feeling of awe and respect with which we behold explorers who have left their ears and fingers north of Franz-Joseph-Land, or their health somewhere along the Upper Congo. My Aunt Georgiana had been a music teacher at the Boston Conservatory, somewhere back in the latter sixties. One summer, while visiting in the little village among the Green Mountains where her ancestors had dwelt for generations, she had kindled the callow fancy of my uncle, Howard Carpenter, then an idle, shiftless boy of twenty-one. When she returned to her duties in Boston, Howard followed her, and the upshot of this infatuation was that she eloped with him, eluding the reproaches of her family and the criticism of her friends by going with him to the Nebraska frontier. Carpenter, who, of course, had no money, took up a homestead in Red Willow County, fifty miles from the railroad. There they had measured off their land themselves, driving across the prairie in a wagon, to the wheel of which they had tied a red cotton handkerchief, and counting its revolutions. They built a dug-out in the red hillside, one of those cave dwellings whose inmates so often reverted to primitive conditions. Their water they got from the lagoons where the buffalo drank, and their slender stock of provisions was always at the mercy of bands of roving Indians. For thirty years my aunt had not been farther than fifty miles from the homestead.

I owed to this woman most of the good that ever came my way in my boyhood, and had a reverential affection for her. During the years when I was riding herd for my uncle, my aunt, after cooking the three meals—the first of which was ready at six o'clock in the morning—and putting the six children to bed, would often stand until midnight at her ironing-board, with me at the kitchen table beside her, hearing me recite Latin declensions and conjugations, gently shaking me when my drowsy head sank down over a page of irregular verbs. It was to her, at her ironing or mending, that I read my first Shakspere, and her old text-book on mythology was the first that ever came into my empty hands. She taught me my scales and exercises on the little parlour organ which her husband had bought her after fifteen years during which she had not so much as seen a musical instrument. She would sit beside me by the hour, darning and counting, while I struggled with the "Joyous Farmer." She seldom talked to me about music, and I understood why. Once when I had been doggedly beating out some easy passages from an old score of *Euryanthe* I had found among her music books, she came up to me and, putting her hands over my eyes, gently drew my head back upon her shoulder, saying tremulously, "Don't love it so well, Clark, or it may be taken from you."

When my aunt appeared on the morning after her arrival in Boston, she was still in a semi-somnambulant state. She seemed not to realize that she was in the city where she had spent her youth, the place longed for hungrily half a lifetime. She had been so wretchedly train-sick throughout the journey that she had no recollection of anything but her discomfort, and, to all intents and purposes, there were but a few hours of nightmare between the farm in Red Willow County and my study on Newbury Street. I had planned a little pleasure for her that afternoon, to repay her for some of the glorious moments she had given me when we used to milk together in the straw-thatched cowshed and she, because I was more than usually tired, or because her husband had spoken sharply to me, would tell me of the splendid performance of the *Huguenots* she had seen in Paris, in her youth.

At two o'clock the Symphony Orchestra was to give a Wagner program, and I intended to take my aunt; though, as I conversed with her, I grew doubtful about her enjoyment of it. I suggested our visiting the Conservatory and the Common before lunch, but she seemed altogether too timid to wish to venture out. She questioned me absently about various changes in the city, but she was chiefly concerned that she had forgotten to leave instructions about feeding half-skimmed milk to a certain weakling calf, "old Maggie's calf, you know, Clark," she explained, evidently having forgotten how long I had been away. She was further troubled because she had neglected to tell her daughter about the freshly-opened kit of mackerel in the cellar, which would spoil if it were not used directly.

I asked her whether she had ever heard any of the Wagnerian operas, and found that she had not, though she was perfectly familiar with their respective situations, and had once possessed the piano score of *The Flying Dutchman*. I began to think it would be best to get her back to Red Willow County without waking her, and regretted having suggested the concert.

From the time we entered the concert hall, however, she was a trifle less passive and inert, and for the first time seemed to perceive her surroundings. I had felt some trepidation lest she might become aware of her queer, country clothes, or might experience some painful embarrassment at stepping suddenly into the world to which she had been dead for a quarter of a century. But, again, I found how superficially I had judged her. She sat looking about her with eyes as impersonal, almost as stony, as those with which the granite Rameses in a museum watches the froth and fret that ebbs and flows about his pedestal. I have seen this same aloofness in old miners who drift into the Brown hotel at Denver, their pockets full of bullion, their linen soiled, their haggard faces unshaven; standing in the thronged corridors as solitary as though they were still in a frozen camp on the Yukon.

The matinée audience was made up chiefly of women. One lost the contour of faces and figures, indeed any effect of line whatever, and there was only the colour of bodices past counting, the shimmer of fabrics soft and firm, silky and sheer; red, mauve, pink, blue, lilac, purple, écru, rose, yellow, cream, and white, all the colours that an impressionist finds in a sunlit landscape, with here and there the dead shadow of a frock coat. My Aunt Georgiana regarded them as though they had been so many daubs of tube-paint on a palette.

When the musicians came out and took their places, she gave a little stir of anticipation, and looked with quickening interest down over the rail at that invariable grouping, perhaps the first wholly familiar thing that had greeted her eye since she had left old Maggie and her weakling calf. I could feel how all those details sank into her soul, for I had not forgotten how they had sunk into mine when I came fresh from ploughing forever and forever between green aisles of corn, where, as in a treadmill, one might walk from daybreak to dusk without perceiving a shadow of change. The clean profiles of the musicians, the gloss of their linen, the dull black of their coats, the beloved shapes of the instruments, the patches of yellow light on the smooth, varnished bellies of the 'cellos and the bass viols in

the rear, the restless, wind-tossed forest of fiddle necks and bows—
I recalled how, in the first orchestra I ever heard, those long bow-
strokes seemed to draw the heart out of me, as a conjurer's stick
reels out yards of paper ribbon from a hat.

The first number was the *Tannhäuser* overture. When the horns
drew out the first strain of the Pilgrim's chorus, Aunt Georgiana
clutched my coat sleeve. Then it was I first realized that for her this
broke a silence of thirty years. With the battle between the two
motives, with the frenzy of the Venusberg theme and its ripping of
strings, there came to me an overwhelming sense of the waste and
wear we are so powerless to combat; and I saw again the tall, naked
house on the prairie, black and grim as a wooden fortress; the black
pond where I had learned to swim, its margin pitted with sun-dried
cattle tracks; the rain gullied clay banks about the naked house, the
four dwarf ash seedlings where the dish-cloths were always hung to
dry before the kitchen door. The world there was the flat world of
the ancients; to the east, a cornfield that stretched to daybreak; to
the west, a corral that reached to sunset; between, the conquests of
peace, dearer-bought than those of war.

The overture closed, my aunt released my coat sleeve, but she said
nothing. She sat staring dully at the orchestra. What, I wondered,
did she get from it? She had been a good pianist in her day, I knew,
and her musical education had been broader than that of most music
teachers of a quarter of a century ago. She had often told me of
Mozart's operas and Meyerbeer's, and I could remember hearing her
sing, years ago, certain melodies of Verdi. When I had fallen ill with
a fever in her house she used to sit by my cot in the evening—when
the cool, night wind blew in through the faded mosquito netting
tacked over the window and I lay watching a certain bright star that
burned red above the cornfield—and sing "Home to our mountains,
O, let us return!" in a way fit to break the heart of a Vermont boy
near dead of home-sickness already.

I watched her closely through the prelude to *Tristan and Isolde,*
trying vainly to conjecture what that seething turmoil of strings and
winds might mean to her, but she sat mutely staring at the violin
bows that drove obliquely downward, like the pelting streaks of rain
in a summer shower. Had this music any message for her? Had she

enough left to at all comprehend this power which had kindled the world since she had left it? I was in a fever of curiosity, but Aunt Georgiana sat silent upon her peak in Darien. She preserved this utter immobility throughout the number from *The Flying Dutchman,* though her fingers worked mechanically upon her black dress, as if, of themselves, they were recalling the piano score they had once played. Poor hands! They had been stretched and twisted into mere tentacles to hold and lift and knead with;—on one of them a thin, worn band that had once been a wedding ring. As I pressed and gently quieted one of those groping hands, I remembered with quivering eyelids their services for me in other days.

Soon after the tenor began the "Prize Song," I heard a quick drawn breath and turned to my aunt. Her eyes were closed, but the tears were glistening on her cheeks, and I think, in a moment more, they were in my eyes as well. It never really died, then—the soul which can suffer so excruciatingly and so interminably; it withers to the outward eye only; like that strange moss which can lie on a dusty shelf half a century and yet, if placed in water, grows green again. She wept so throughout the development and elaboration of the melody.

During the intermission before the second half, I questioned my aunt and found that the "Prize Song" was not new to her. Some years before there had drifted to the farm in Red Willow County a young German, a tramp cow-puncher, who had sung in the chorus at Bayreuth when he was a boy, along with the other peasant boys and girls. Of a Sunday morning he used to sit on his gingham-sheeted bed in the hands' bedroom which opened off the kitchen, cleaning the leather of his boots and saddle, singing the "Prize Song," while my aunt went about her work in the kitchen. She had hovered over him until she had prevailed upon him to join the country church, though his sole fitness for this step, in so far as I could gather, lay in his boyish face and his possession of this divine melody. Shortly afterward, he had gone to town on the Fourth of July, been drunk for several days, lost his money at a faro table, ridden a saddled Texas steer on a bet, and disappeared with a fractured collar-bone. All this my aunt told me huskily, wanderingly, as though she were talking in the weak lapses of illness.

"Well, we have come to better things than the old *Trovatore* at any rate, Aunt Georgie?" I queried, with a well meant effort at jocularity.

Her lip quivered and she hastily put her handkerchief up to her mouth. From behind it she murmured, "And you have been hearing this ever since you left me, Clark?" Her question was the gentlest and saddest of reproaches.

The second half of the program consisted of four numbers from the *Ring,* and closed with Siegfried's funeral march. My aunt wept quietly, but almost continuously, as a shallow vessel overflows in a rain-storm. From time to time her dim eyes looked up at the lights, burning softly under their dull glass globes.

The deluge of sound poured on and on; I never knew what she found in the shining current of it; I never knew how far it bore her, or past what happy islands. From the trembling of her face I could well believe that before the last number she had been carried out where the myriad graves are, into the grey, nameless burying grounds of the sea; or into some world of death vaster yet, where, from the beginning of the world, hope has lain down with hope and dream with dream and, renouncing, slept.

The concert was over; the people filed out of the hall chattering and laughing, glad to relax and find the living level again, but my kinswoman made no effort to rise. The harpist slipped the green felt cover over his instrument; the flute-players shook the water from their mouth-pieces; the men of the orchestra went out one by one, leaving the stage to the chairs and music stands, empty as a winter cornfield.

I spoke to my aunt. She burst into tears and sobbed pleadingly. "I don't want to go, Clark, I don't want to go!"

I understood. For her, just outside the concert hall, lay the black pond with the cattle-tracked bluffs; the tall, unpainted house, with weather-curled boards, naked as a tower; the crook-backed ash seedlings where the dish-cloths hung to dry; the gaunt, moulting turkeys picking up refuse about the kitchen door.

The Sculptor's Funeral

A group of the townspeople stood on the station siding of a little
Kansas town, awaiting the coming of the night train, which was
already twenty minutes overdue. The snow had fallen thick over
everything; in the pale starlight the line of bluffs across the wide,
white meadows south of the town made soft, smoke-coloured curves
against the clear sky. The men on the siding stood first on one foot
and then on the other, their hands thrust deep into their trousers
pockets, their overcoats open, their shoulders screwed up with the
cold; and they glanced from time to time toward the southeast, where
the railroad track wound along the river shore. They conversed in
low tones and moved about restlessly, seeming uncertain as to what
was expected of them. There was but one of the company who looked
as if he knew exactly why he was there, and he kept conspicuously
apart; walking to the far end of the platform, returning to the station
door, then pacing up the track again, his chin sunk in the high collar
of his overcoat, his burly shoulders drooping forward, his gait heavy
and dogged. Presently he was approached by a tall, spare, grizzled
man clad in a faded Grand Army suit, who shuffled out from the
group and advanced with a certain deference, craning his neck forward
until his back made the angle of a jack-knife three-quarters open.

"I reckon she's a goin' to be pretty late again tonight, Jim," he
remarked in a squeaky falsetto. "S'pose it's the snow?"

"I don't know," responded the other man with a shade of annoyance, speaking from out an astonishing cataract of red beard that
grew fiercely and thickly in all directions.

The spare man shifted the quill toothpick he was chewing to the
other side of his mouth. "It ain't likely that anybody from the East
will come with the corpse, I s'pose," he went on reflectively.

"I don't know," responded the other, more curtly than before.

"It's too bad he didn't belong to some lodge or other. I like an
order funeral myself. They seem more appropriate for people of some
repytation," the spare man continued, with an ingratiating concession

in his shrill voice, as he carefully placed his toothpick in his vest pocket. He always carried the flag at the G.A.R. funerals in the town.

The heavy man turned on his heel, without replying, and walked up the siding. The spare man rejoined the uneasy group. "Jim's ez full ez a tick, ez ushel," he commented commiseratingly.

Just then a distant whistle sounded, and there was a shuffling of feet on the platform. A number of lanky boys, of all ages, appeared as suddenly and slimily as eels wakened by the crack of thunder; some came from the waiting-room, where they had been warming themselves by the red stove, or half asleep on the slat benches; others uncoiled themselves from baggage trucks or slid out of express wagons. Two clambered down from the driver's seat of a hearse that stood backed up against the siding. They straightened their stooping shoulders and lifted their heads, and a flash of momentary animation kindled their dull eyes at that cold, vibrant scream, the world-wide call for men. It stirred them like the note of a trumpet; just as it had often stirred the man who was coming home tonight, in his boyhood.

The night express shot, red as a rocket, from out the eastward marsh lands and wound along the river shore under the long lines of shivering poplars that sentinelled the meadows, the escaping steam hanging in grey masses against the pale sky and blotting out the Milky Way. In a moment the red glare from the headlight streamed up the snow-covered track before the siding and glittered on the wet, black rails. The burly man with the dishevelled red beard walked swiftly up the platform toward the approaching train, uncovering his head as he went. The group of men behind him hesitated, glanced questioningly at one another, and awkwardly followed his example. The train stopped, and the crowd shuffled up to the express car just as the door was thrown open, the man in the G.A.R. suit thrusting his head forward with curiosity. The express messenger appeared in the doorway, accompanied by a young man in a long ulster and travelling cap.

"Are Mr. Merrick's friends here?" inquired the young man.

The group on the platform swayed uneasily. Philip Phelps, the banker, responded with dignity: "We have come to take charge of the body. Mr. Merrick's father is very feeble and can't be about."

"Send the agent out here," growled the express messenger, "and tell the operator to lend a hand."

The coffin was got out of its rough-box and down on the snowy platform. The townspeople drew back enough to make room for it and then formed a close semicircle about it, looking curiously at the palm leaf which lay across the black cover. No one said anything. The baggage man stood by his truck, waiting to get at the trunks. The engine panted heavily, and the fireman dodged in and out among the wheels with his yellow torch and long oil-can, snapping the spindle boxes. The young Bostonian, one of the dead sculptor's pupils who had come with the body, looked about him helplessly. He turned to the banker, the only one of that black, uneasy, stoop-shouldered group who seemed enough of an individual to be addressed.

"None of Mr. Merrick's brothers are here?" he asked uncertainly.

The man with the red beard for the first time stepped up and joined the others. "No, they have not come yet; the family is scattered. The body will be taken directly to the house." He stooped and took hold of one of the handles of the coffin.

"Take the long hill road up, Thompson, it will be easier on the horses," called the liveryman as the undertaker snapped the door of the hearse and prepared to mount to the driver's seat.

Laird, the red-bearded lawyer, turned again to the stranger: "We didn't know whether there would be any one with him or not," he explained. "It's a long walk, so you'd better go up in the hack." He pointed to a single battered conveyance, but the young man replied stiffly: "Thank you, but I think I will go up with the hearse. If you don't object," turning to the undertaker, "I'll ride with you."

They clambered up over the wheels and drove off in the starlight up the long, white hill toward the town. The lamps in the still village were shining from under the low, snow-burdened roofs; and beyond, on every side, the plains reached out into emptiness, peaceful and wide as the soft sky itself, and wrapped in a tangible, white silence.

When the hearse backed up to a wooden sidewalk before a naked, weather-beaten frame house, the same composite, ill-defined group that had stood upon the station siding was huddled about the gate. The front yard was an icy swamp, and a couple of warped planks, extending from the sidewalk to the door, made a sort of rickety foot-bridge. The gate hung on one hinge, and was opened wide with difficulty. Steavens, the young stranger, noticed that something black was tied to the knob of the front door.

The grating sound made by the casket, as it was drawn from the hearse, was answered by a scream from the house; the front door was wrenched open, and a tall, corpulent woman rushed out bare-headed into the snow and flung herself upon the coffin, shrieking: "My boy, my boy! And this is how you've come home to me!"

As Steavens turned away and closed his eyes with a shudder of unutterable repulsion, another woman, also tall, but flat and angular, dressed entirely in black, darted out of the house and caught Mrs. Merrick by the shoulders, crying sharply: "Come, come, mother; you mustn't go on like this!" Her tone changed to one of obsequious solemnity as she turned to the banker: "The parlour is ready, Mr. Phelps."

The bearers carried the coffin along the narrow boards, while the undertaker ran ahead with the coffin-rests. They bore it into a large, unheated room that smelled of dampness and disuse and furniture polish, and set it down under a hanging lamp ornamented with jingling glass prisms and before a "Rogers group" of John Alden and Priscilla, wreathed with smilax. Henry Steavens stared about him with the sickening conviction that there had been a mistake, and that he had somehow arrived at the wrong destination. He looked at the clover-green Brussels, the fat plush upholstery, among the hand-painted china placques and panels and vases, for some mark of identifica-tion,—for something that might once conceivably have belonged to Harvey Merrick. It was not until he recognized his friend in the crayon portrait of a little boy in kilts and curls, hanging above the piano, that he felt willing to let any of these people approach the coffin.

"Take the lid off, Mr. Thompson; let me see my boy's face," wailed the elder woman between her sobs. This time Steavens looked fear-fully, almost beseechingly into her face, red and swollen under its masses of strong, black, shiny hair. He flushed, dropped his eyes, and then, almost incredulously, looked again. There was a kind of power about her face—a kind of brutal handsomeness, even; but it was scarred and furrowed by violence, and so coloured and coarsened by fiercer passions that grief seemed never to have laid a gentle finger there. The long nose was distended and knobbed at the end, and there were deep lines on either side of it; her heavy, black brows almost met across her forehead, her teeth were large and square, and set far apart—teeth that could tear. She filled the room; the men were obliterated, seemed tossed about like twigs in an angry water, and even Steavens felt himself being drawn into the whirlpool.

The daughter—the tall, raw-boned woman in crêpe, with a mourning comb in her hair which curiously lengthened her long face—sat stiffly upon the sofa, her hands, conspicuous for their large knuckles, folded in her lap, her mouth and eyes drawn down, solemnly awaiting the opening of the coffin. Near the door stood a mulatto woman, evidently a servant in the house, with a timid bearing and an emaciated face pitifully sad and gentle. She was weeping silently, the corner of her calico apron lifted to her eyes, occasionally suppressing a long, quivering sob. Steavens walked over and stood beside her.

Feeble steps were heard on the stairs, and an old man, tall and frail, odorous of pipe smoke, with shaggy, unkept grey hair and a dingy beard, tobacco stained about the mouth, entered uncertainly. He went slowly up to the coffin and stood rolling a blue cotton handkerchief between his hands, seeming so pained and embarrassed by his wife's orgy of grief that he had no consciousness of anything else.

"There, there, Annie, dear, don't take on so," he quavered timidly, putting out a shaking hand and awkwardly patting her elbow. She turned and sank upon his shoulder with such violence that he tottered a little. He did not even glance toward the coffin, but continued to look at her with a dull, frightened, appealing expression, as a spaniel looks at the whip. His sunken cheeks slowly reddened and burned with miserable shame. When his wife rushed from the room, her daughter strode after her with set lips. The servant stole up to the coffin, bent over it for a moment, and then slipped away to the kitchen, leaving Steavens, the lawyer, and the father to themselves. The old man stood looking down at his dead son's face. The sculptor's splendid head seemed even more noble in its rigid stillness than in life. The dark hair had crept down upon the wide forehead; the face seemed strangely long, but in it there was not that repose we expect to find in the faces of the dead. The brows were so drawn that there were two deep lines above the beaked nose, and the chin was thrust forward defiantly. It was as though the strain of life had been so sharp and bitter that death could not at once relax the tension and smooth the countenance into perfect peace—as though he were still guarding something precious, which might even yet be wrested from him.

The old man's lips were working under his stained beard. He turned to the lawyer with timid deference: "Phelps and the rest are comin' back to set up with Harve, ain't they?" he asked. "Thank 'ee, Jim, thank 'ee." He brushed the hair back gently from his son's forehead. "He was a good boy, Jim; always a good boy. He was ez gentle ez a child and the kindest of 'em all—only we didn't none of us ever onderstand him." The tears trickled slowly down his beard and dropped upon the sculptor's coat.

"Martin, Martin! Oh, Martin! come here," his wife wailed from the top of the stairs. The old man started timorously: "Yes, Annie, I'm coming." He turned away, hesitated, stood for a moment in miserable indecision; then reached back and patted the dead man's hair softly, and stumbled from the room.

"Poor old man, I didn't think he had any tears left. Seems as if his eyes would have gone dry long ago. At his age nothing cuts very deep," remarked the lawyer.

Something in his tone made Steavens glance up. While the mother had been in the room, the young man had scarcely seen any one else; but now, from the moment he first glanced into Jim Laird's florid face and bloodshot eyes, he knew that he had found what he had been heartsick at not finding before—the feeling, the understanding, that must exist in some one, even here.

The man was red as his beard, with features swollen and blurred by dissipation, and a hot, blazing blue eye. His face was strained—that of a man who is controlling himself with difficulty—and he kept plucking at his beard with a sort of fierce resentment. Steavens, sitting by the window, watched him turn down the glaring lamp, still its jangling pendants with an angry gesture, and then stand with his hands locked behind him, staring down into the master's face. He could not help wondering what link there had been between the porcelain vessel and so sooty a lump of potter's clay.

From the kitchen an uproar was sounding; when the dining-room door opened, the import of it was clear. The mother was abusing the maid for having forgotten to make the dressing for the chicken salad which had been prepared for the watchers. Steavens had never heard anything in the least like it; it was injured, emotional, dramatic abuse, unique and masterly in its excruciating cruelty, as violent and unrestrained as had been her grief of twenty minutes before. With a shudder of disgust the lawyer went into the dining-room and closed the door into the kitchen.

"Poor Roxy's getting it now," he remarked when he came back. "The Merricks took her out of the poor-house years ago; and if her loyalty would let her, I guess the poor old thing could tell tales that would curdle your blood. She's the mulatto woman who was standing in here a while ago, with her apron to her eyes. The old woman is a fury; there never was anybody like her. She made Harvey's life a hell for him when he lived at home; he was so sick ashamed of it. I never could see how he kept himself sweet."

"He was wonderful," said Steavens slowly, "wonderful; but until tonight I have never known how wonderful."

"That is the eternal wonder of it, anyway; that it can come even from such a dung heap as this," the lawyer cried, with a sweeping gesture which seemed to indicate much more than the four walls within which they stood.

"I think I'll see whether I can get a little air. The room is so close I am beginning to feel rather faint," murmured Steavens, struggling with one of the windows. The sash was stuck, however, and would not yield, so he sat down dejectedly and began pulling at his collar. The lawyer came over, loosened the sash with one blow of his red fist and sent the window up a few inches. Steavens thanked him, but the nausea which had been gradually climbing into his throat for the last half hour left him with but one desire—a desperate feeling that he must get away from this place with what was left of Harvey Merrick. Oh, he comprehended well enough now the quiet bitterness of the smile that he had seen so often on his master's lips!

Once when Merrick returned from a visit home, he brought with him a singularly feeling and suggestive bas-relief of a thin, faded old woman, sitting and sewing something pinnned to her knee; while a full-lipped, full-blooded little urchin, his trousers held up by a single gallows, stood beside her, impatiently twitching her gown to call her attention to a butterfly he had caught. Steavens, impressed by the tender and delicate modelling of the thin, tired face, had asked him if it were his mother. He remembered the dull flush that had burned up in the sculptor's face.

The lawyer was sitting in a rocking-chair beside the coffin, his head thrown back and his eyes closed. Steavens looked at him earnestly, puzzled at the line of the chin, and wondering why a man should conceal a feature of such distinction under that disfiguring shock of beard. Suddenly, as though he felt the young sculptor's keen glance, Jim Laird opened his eyes.

"Was he always a good deal of an oyster?" he asked abruptly. "He was terribly shy as a boy."

"Yes, he was an oyster, since you put it so," rejoined Steavens. "Although he could be very fond of people, he always gave one the impression of being detached. He disliked violent emotion; he was reflective, and rather distrustful of himself—except, of course, as regarded his work. He was sure enough there. He distrusted men pretty thoroughly and women even more, yet somehow without believing ill of them. He was determined, indeed, to believe the best; but he seemed afraid to investigate."

"A burnt dog dreads the fire," said the lawyer grimly, and closed his eyes.

Steavens went on and on, reconstructing that whole miserable boyhood. All this raw, biting ugliness had been the portion of the man whose mind was to become an exhaustless gallery of beautiful impressions—so sensitive that the mere shadow of a poplar leaf flickering against a sunny wall would be etched and held there for ever. Surely, if ever a man had the magic word in his finger tips, it was Merrick. Whatever he touched, he revealed its holiest secret; liberated it from enchantment and restored it to its pristine loveliness. Upon whatever he had come in contact with, he had left a beautiful record of the experience—a sort of ethereal signature; a scent, a sound, a colour that was his own.

Steavens understood now the real tragedy of his master's life; neither love nor wine, as many had conjectured; but a blow which had fallen earlier and cut deeper than anything else could have done— a shame not his, and yet so unescapably his, to hide in his heart from his very boyhood. And without—the frontier warfare; the yearning of a boy, cast ashore upon a desert of newness and ugliness and sordidness, for all that is chastened and old, and noble with traditions.

At eleven o'clock the tall, flat woman in black announced that the watchers were arriving, and asked them to "step into the dining-room." As Steavens rose, the lawyer said dryly: "You go on—it'll be a good experience for you. I'm not equal to that crowd tonight; I've had twenty years of them."

As Steavens closed the door after him he glanced back at the lawyer, sitting by the coffin in the dim light, with his chin resting on his hand.

The same misty group that had stood before the door of the express car shuffled into the dining-room. In the light of the kerosene lamp they separated and became individuals. The minister, a pale, feeble-looking man with white hair and blond chin-whiskers, took his seat beside a small side table and placed his Bible upon it. The Grand Army man sat down behind the stove and tilted his chair back comfortably against the wall, fishing his quill toothpick from his waistcoat pocket. The two bankers, Phelps and Elder, sat off in a corner behind the dinner-table, where they could finish their discussion of the new usury law and its effect on chattel security loans. The real estate agent, an old man with a smiling, hypocritical face, soon joined them. The coal and lumber dealer and the cattle shipper sat on opposite sides of the hard coal-burner, their feet on the nickel-work. Steavens took a book from his pocket and began to read. The talk around him ranged through various topics of local interest while the house was quieting down. When it was clear that the members of the family were in bed, the Grand Army man hitched his shoulders and, untangling his long legs, caught his heels on the rounds of his chair.

"S'pose there'll be a will, Phelps?" he queried in his weak falsetto.

The banker laughed disagreeably, and began trimming his nails with a pearl-handled pocket-knife.

"There'll scarcely be any need for one, will there?" he queried in his turn.

The restless Grand Army man shifted his position again, getting his knees still nearer his chin. "Why, the ole man says Harve's done right well lately," he chirped.

The other banker spoke up. "I reckon he means by that Harve ain't asked him to mortgage any more farms lately, so as he could go on with his education."

'Seems like my mind don't reach back to a time when Harve wasn't bein' edycated," tittered the Grand Army man.

There was a general chuckle. The minister took out his handkerchief and blew his nose sonorously. Banker Phelps closed his knife with a snap. "It's too bad the old man's sons didn't turn out better," he remarked with reflective authority. "They never hung together. He spent money enough on Harve to stock a dozen cattle-farms, and he might as well have poured it into Sand Creek. If Harve had stayed at home and helped nurse what little they had, and gone into stock on the old man's bottom farm, they might all have been well fixed. But the old man had to trust everything to tenants and was cheated right and left."

"Harve never could have handled stock none," interposed the cattleman. "He hadn't it in him to be sharp. Do you remember when he bought Sander's mules for eight-year olds, when everybody in town knew that Sander's father-in-law give 'em to his wife for a wedding present eighteen years before, an' they was full-grown mules then?"

The company laughed discreetly, and the Grand Army man rubbed his knees with a spasm of childish delight.

"Harve never was much account for anything practical, and he shore was never fond of work," began the coal and lumber dealer. "I mind the last time he was home; the day he left, when the old man was out to the barn helpin' his hand hitch up to take Harve to the train, and Cal Moots was patchin' up the fence; Harve, he come out on the step and sings out, in his ladylike voice: 'Cal Moots, Cal Moots! please come cord my trunk.' "

"That's Harve for you," approved the Grand Army man. "I kin

hear him howlin' yet, when he was a big feller in long pants and his mother used to whale him with a rawhide in the barn for lettin' the cows git foundered in the cornfield when he was drivin' 'em home from pasture. He killed a cow of mine that-a-way onct—a pure Jersey and the best milker I had, an' the ole man had to put up for her. Harve, he was watchin' the sun set acrost the marshes when the anamile got away."

"Where the old man made his mistake was in sending the boy East to school," said Phelps, stroking his goatee and speaking in a deliberate, judicial tone. "There was where he got his head full of nonsense. What Harve needed, of all people, was a course in some first-class Kansas City business college."

The letters were swimming before Steavens's eyes. Was it possible that these men did not understand, that the palm on the coffin meant nothing to them? The very name of their town would have remained for ever buried in the postal guide had it not been now and again mentioned in the world in connection with Harvey Merrick's. He remembered what his master had said to him on the day of his death, after the congestion of both lungs had shut off any probability of recovery, and the sculptor had asked his pupil to send his body home. "It's not a pleasant place to be lying while the world is moving and doing and bettering," he had said with a feeble smile, "but it rather seems as though we ought to go back to the place we came from, in the end. The townspeople will come in for a look at me; and after they have had their say, I shan't have much to fear from the judgment of God!"

The cattleman took up the comment. "Forty's young for a Merrick to cash in; they usually hang on pretty well. Probably he helped it along with whisky."

"His mother's people were not long lived, and Harvey never had a robust constitution," said the minister mildly. He would have liked to say more. He had been the boy's Sunday-school teacher, and had been fond of him; but he felt that he was not in a position to speak. His own sons had turned out badly, and it was not a year since one of them had made his last trip home in the express car, shot in a gambling-house in the Black Hills.

"Nevertheless, there is no disputin' that Harve frequently looked upon the wine when it was red, also variegated, and it shore made an oncommon fool of him," moralized the cattleman.

Just then the door leading into the parlour rattled loudly and every one started involuntarily, looking relieved when only Jim Laird came out. The Grand Army man ducked his head when he saw the spark in his blue, blood-shot eye. They were all afraid of Jim; he was a drunkard, but he could twist the law to suit his client's needs as no other man in all western Kansas could do, and there were many who tried. The lawyer closed the door behind him, leaned back against it and folded his arms, cocking his head a little to one side. When he assumed this attitude in the court-room, ears were always pricked up, as it usually foretold a flood of withering sarcasm.

"I've been with you gentlemen before," he began in a dry, even tone, "when you've sat by the coffins of boys born and raised in this town; and, if I remember rightly, you were never any too well satisfied when you checked them up. What's the matter, anyhow? Why is it that reputable young men are as scarce as millionaires in Sand City? It might almost seem to a stranger that there was some way something the matter with your progressive town. Why did Ruben Sayer, the brightest young lawyer you ever turned out, after he had come home from the university as straight as a die, take to drinking and forge a check and shoot himself? Why did Bill Merrit's son die of the shakes in a saloon in Omaha? Why was Mr. Thomas's son, here, shot in a gambling-house? Why did young Adams burn his mill to beat the insurance companies and go to the pen?"

The lawyer paused and unfolded his arms, laying one clenched fist quietly on the table. "I'll tell you why. Because you drummed nothing but money and knavery into their ears from the time they wore knickerbockers; because you carped away at them as you've been carping here tonight, holding our friends Phelps and Elder up to them for their models, as our grandfathers held up George Washington and John Adams. But the boys were young, and raw at the business you put them to, and how could they match coppers with such artists as Phelps and Elder? You wanted them to be successful rascals; they were only unsuccessful ones—that's all the difference. There was only one boy ever raised in this borderland between ruffianism and civilization who didn't come to grief, and you hated Harvey Merrick more for winning out than you hated all the other boys who got under the wheels. Lord, Lord, how you did hate him! Phelps, here, is fond of saying that he could buy and sell us all out any time he's a mind to; but he knew Harve wouldn't have given a tinker's damn for his bank and all his cattlefarms put together; and a lack of appreciation, that way, goes hard with Phelps.

"Old Nimrod thinks Harve drank too much; and this from such as Nimrod and me!

"Brother Elder says Harve was too free with the old man's money—fell short in filial consideration, maybe. Well, we can all remember the very tone in which brother Elder swore his own father was a liar, in the county court; and we all know that the old man came out of that partnership with his son as bare as a sheared lamb. But maybe I'm getting personal, and I'd better be driving ahead at what I want to say."

The lawyer paused a moment, squared his heavy shoulders, and went on: "Harvey Merrick and I went to school together, back East. We were dead in earnest, and we wanted you all to be proud of us some day. We meant to be great men. Even I, and I haven't lost my sense of humour, gentlemen, I meant to be a great man. I came back here to practise, and I found you didn't in the least want me to be a great man. You wanted me to be a shrewd lawyer—oh, yes! Our veteran here wanted me to get him an increase of pension, because he had dyspepsia; Phelps wanted a new county survey that would put the widow Wilson's little bottom farm inside his south line; Elder wanted to lend money at 5 per cent. a month, and get it collected; and Stark here wanted to wheedle old women up in Vermont into investing their annuities in real-estate mortgages that are not worth the paper they are written on. Oh, you needed me hard enough, and you'll go on needing me!

"Well, I came back here and became the damned shyster you wanted me to be. You pretend to have some sort of respect for me; and yet you'll stand up and throw mud at Harvey Merrick, whose soul you couldn't dirty and whose hands you couldn't tie. Oh, you're a discriminating lot of Christians! There have been times when the sight of Harvey's name in some Eastern paper has made me hang my head like a whipped dog; and, again, times when I liked to think of him off there in the world, away from all this hog-wallow, climbing the big, clean up-grade he'd set for himself.

"And we? Now that we've fought and lied and sweated and stolen, and hated as only the disappointed strugglers in a bitter, dead little Western town know how to do, what have we got to show for it? Harvey Merrick wouldn't have given one sunset over your marshes for all you've got put together, and you know it. It's not for me to say why, in the inscrutable wisdom of God, a genius should ever have been called from this place of hatred and bitter waters; but I want this Boston man to know that the drivel he's been hearing here tonight is the only tribute any truly great man could have from such a lot of sick, side-tracked, burnt-dog, land-poor sharks as the here-present financiers of Sand City—upon which town may God have mercy!"

The lawyer thrust out his hand to Steavens as he passed him, caught up his overcoat in the hall, and had left the house before the Grand Army man had had time to lift his ducked head and crane his long neck about at his fellows.

Next day Jim Laird was drunk and unable to attend the funeral services. Steavens called twice at his office, but was compelled to start East without seeing him. He had a presentiment that he would hear from him again, and left his address on the lawyer's table; but if Laird found it, he never acknowledged it. The thing in him that Harvey Merrick had loved must have gone under ground with Harvey Merrick's coffin; for it never spoke again, and Jim got the cold he died of driving across the Colorado mountains to defend one of Phelps's sons who had got into trouble out there by cutting government timber.

"A Death in the Desert"

Everett Hilgarde was conscious that the man in the seat across the aisle was looking at him intently. He was a large, florid man, wore a conspicuous diamond solitaire upon his third finger, and Everett judged him to be a travelling salesman of some sort. He had the air of an adaptable fellow who had been about the world and who could keep cool and clean under almost any circumstances.

The "High Line Flyer," as this train was derisively called among railroad men, was jerking along through the hot afternoon over the monotonous country between Holdredge and Cheyenne. Besides the blond man and himself the only occupants of the car were two dusty, bedraggled-looking girls who had been to the Exposition at Chicago, and who were earnestly discussing the cost of their first trip out of Colorado. The four uncomfortable passengers were covered with a sediment of fine, yellow dust which clung to their hair and eyebrows like gold powder. It blew up in clouds from the bleak, lifeless country through which they passed, until they were one colour with the sage-brush and sand-hills. The grey and yellow desert was varied only by occasional ruins of deserted towns, and the little red boxes of station-houses, where the spindling trees and sickly vines in the blue-grass yards made little green reserves fenced off in that confusing wilderness of sand.

As the slanting rays of the sun beat in stronger and stronger through the car-windows, the blond gentleman asked the ladies' permission to remove his coat, and sat in his lavender striped shirt-sleeves, with a black silk handkerchief tucked about his collar. He had seemed interested in Everett since they had boarded the train at Holdredge; kept glancing at him curiously and then looking reflectively out of the window, as though he were trying to recall something. But wherever Everett went, some one was almost sure to look at him with that curious interest, and it had ceased to embarrass or annoy him. Presently the stranger, seeming satisfied with his observation, leaned back in his seat, half closed his eyes, and began softly to whistle the Spring Song from *Proserpine,* the cantata that a dozen years before had made its young composer famous in a night. Everett had heard that air on guitars in Old Mexico, on mandolins at college glees, on cottage organs in New England hamlets, and only two weeks ago he had heard it played on sleigh bells at a variety theatre in Denver. There was literally no way of escaping his brother's precocity. Adriance could live on the other side of the Atlantic, where his youthful indiscretions were forgotten in his mature achievements, but his brother had never been able to outrun *Proserpine,*—and here he found it again, in the Colorado sand-hills. Not that Everett was exactly ashamed of *Proserpine;* only a man of genius could have written it, but it was the sort of thing that a man of genius outgrows as soon as he can.

Everett unbent a trifle, and smiled at his neighbour across the aisle. Immediately the large man rose and coming over dropped into the seat facing Hilgarde, extending his card.

"Dusty ride, isn't it? I don't mind it myself; I'm used to it. Born and bred in de briar patch, like Br'er Rabbit. I've been trying to place you for a long time; I think I must have met you before."

"Thank you," said Everett, taking the card; "my name is Hilgarde. You've probably met my brother, Adriance; people often mistake me for him."

The travelling-man brought his hand down upon his knee with such vehemence that the solitaire blazed.

"So I was right after all, and if you're not Adriance Hilgarde you're his double. I thought I couldn't be mistaken. Seen him? Well, I guess! I never missed one of his recitals at the Auditorium, and he played the piano score of *Proserpine* through to us once at the Chicago Press Club. I used to be on the *Commercial* there before I began to travel for the publishing department of the concern. So you're Hilgarde's brother, and here I've run into you at the jumping-off place. Sounds like a newspaper yarn, doesn't it?"

The travelling-man laughed and offering Everett a cigar plied him with questions on the only subject that people ever seemed to care to talk to him about. At length the salesman and the two girls alighted at a Colorado way station, and Everett went on to Cheyenne alone.

The train pulled into Cheyenne at nine o'clock, late by a matter of four hours or so; but no one seemed particularly concerned at its tardiness except the station agent, who grumbled at being kept in the office over time on a summer night. When Everett alighted from the train he walked down the platform and stopped at the track crossing, uncertain as to what direction he should take to reach a hotel. A phaeton stood near the crossing and a woman held the reins. She was dressed in white, and her figure was clearly silhouetted against the cushions, though it was too dark to see her face. Everett had scarcely noticed her, when the switch-engine came puffing up from the opposite direction, and the head-light threw a strong glare of light on his face. The woman in the phaeton uttered a low cry and dropped the reins. Everett started forward and caught the horse's head, but the animal only lifted its ears and whisked its tail in impatient surprise. The woman sat perfectly still, her head sunk between her shoulders and her handkerchief pressed to her face. Another woman came out of the depot and hurried toward the phaeton, crying, "Katherine, dear, what is the matter?"

Everett hesitated a moment in painful embarrassment, then lifted his hat and passed on. He was accustomed to sudden recognitions in the most impossible places, especially from women.

While he was breakfasting the next morning, the head waiter leaned over his chair to murmur that there was a gentleman waiting to see him in the parlour. Everett finished his coffee, and went in the direction indicated, where he found his visitor restlessly pacing the floor. His whole manner betrayed a high degree of agitation, though his physique was not that of a man whose nerves lie near the surface. He was something below medium height, square-shouldered and solidly built. His thick, closely cut hair was beginning to show grey about the ears, and his bronzed face was heavily lined. His square brown hands were locked behind him, and he held his shoulders like a man conscious of responsibilities, yet, as he turned to greet Everett, there was an incongruous diffidence in his address.

"Good-morning, Mr. Hilgarde," he said, extending his hand; "I found your name on the hotel register. My name is Gaylord. I'm afraid my sister startled you at the station last night, and I've come around to explain."

"Ah! the young lady in the phaeton? I'm sure I didn't know whether

I had anything to do with her alarm or not. If I did, it is I who owe an apology."

The man coloured a little under the dark brown of his face.

"Oh, it's nothing you could help, sir, I fully understand that. You see, my sister used to be a pupil of your brother's, and it seems you favour him; when the switch-engine threw a light on your face, it startled her."

Everett wheeled about in his chair. "Oh! *Katharine* Gaylord! Is it possible! Why, I used to know her when I was a boy. What on earth——"

"Is she doing here?" Gaylord grimly filled out the pause. "You've got at the heart of the matter. You know my sister had been in bad health for a long time?"

"No. The last I knew of her she was singing in London. My brother and I correspond infrequently, and seldom get beyond family matters. I am deeply sorry to hear this."

The lines in Charley Gaylord's brow relaxed a little.

"What I'm trying to say, Mr. Hilgarde, is that she wants to see you. She's set on it. We live several miles out of town, but my rig's below, and I can take you out any time you can go."

"At once, then. I'll get my hat and be with you in a moment."

When he came downstairs Everett found a cart at the door, and Charley Gaylord drew a long sigh of relief as he gathered up the reins and settled back into his own element.

"I think I'd better tell you something about my sister before you see her, and I don't know just where to begin. She travelled in Europe with your brother and his wife, and sang at a lot of his concerts; but I don't know just how much you know about her."

"Very little, except that my brother always thought her the most gifted of his pupils. When I knew her she was very young and very beautiful, and quite turned my head for a while."

Everett saw that Gaylord's mind was entirely taken up by his grief. "That's the whole thing," he went on, flecking his horses with a whip.

"She was a great woman, as you say, and she didn't come of a great family. She had to fight her own way from the first. She got to Chicago, and then to New York, and then to Europe, and got a taste for it all; and now she's dying here like a rat in a hole, out of her own world, and she can't fall back into ours. We've grown apart, some way—miles and miles apart—and I'm afraid she's fearfully unhappy."

"It's a tragic story you're telling me, Gaylord," said Everett. They were well out into the country now, spinning along over the dusty plains of red grass, with the ragged blue outline of the mountains before them.

"Tragic!" cried Gaylord, starting up in his seat, "my God, nobody will ever know how tragic! It's a tragedy I live with and eat with and sleep with, until I've lost my grip on everything. You see she had made a good bit of money, but she spent it all going to health resorts. It's her lungs. I've got money enough to send her anywhere, but the doctors all say it's no use. She hasn't the ghost of a chance. It's just getting through the days now. I had no notion she was half so bad before she came to me. She just wrote that she was run down. Now that she's here, I think she'd be happier anywhere under the sun, but she won't leave. She says it's easier to let go of life here. There was a time when I was a brakeman with a run out of Bird City, Iowa, and she was a little thing I could carry on my shoulder, when I could get her everything on earth she wanted, and she hadn't a wish my $80 a month didn't cover; and now, when I've got a little property together, I can't buy her a night's sleep!"

Everett saw that, whatever Charley Gaylord's present status in the world might be, he had brought the brakeman's heart up the ladder with him.

The reins slackened in Gaylord's hand as they drew up before a showily painted house with many gables and a round tower. "Here we are," he said, turning to Everett, "and I guess we understand each other."

They were met at the door by a thin, colourless woman, whom Gaylord introduced as "My sister, Maggie." She asked her brother to show Mr. Hilgarde into the music-room, where Katharine would join him.

When Everett entered the music-room he gave a little start of surprise, feeling that he had stepped from the glaring Wyoming sunlight into some New York studio that he had always known. He looked incredulously out of the window at the grey plain that ended in the great upheaval of the Rockies.

The haunting air of familiarity perplexed him. Suddenly his eye fell upon a large photograph of his brother above the piano. Then it all became clear enough: this was veritably his brother's room. If it were not an exact copy of one of the many studios that Adriance had fitted up in various parts of the world, wearying of them and leaving almost before the renovator's varnish had dried, it was at least in the same tone. In every detail Adriance's taste was so manifest that the room seemed to exhale his personality.

Among the photographs on the wall there was one of Katharine Gaylord, taken in the days when Everett had known her, and when the flash of her eye or the flutter of her skirt was enough to set his boyish heart in a tumult. Even now, he stood before the portrait with a certain degree of embarrassment. It was the face of a woman already old in her first youth, a trifle hard, and it told of what her brother had called her fight. The *camaraderie* of her frank, confident eyes was qualified by the deep lines about her mouth and the curve of the lips, which was both sad and cynical. Certainly she had more good-will than confidence toward the world. The chief charm of the woman, as Everett had known her, lay in her superb figure and in her eyes, which possessed a warm, life-giving quality like the sunlight; eyes which glowed with a perpetual *salutat* to the world.

Everett was still standing before the picture, his hands behind him and his head inclined, when he heard the door open. A tall woman advanced toward him, holding out her hand. As she started to speak she coughed slightly, then, laughing, said, in a low, rich voice, a trifle husky: "You see I make the traditional Camille entrance. How good of you to come, Mr. Hilgarde."

Everett was acutely conscious that while addressing him she was not looking at him at all, and, as he assured her of his pleasure in coming, he was glad to have an opportunity to collect himself. He had not reckoned upon the ravages of a long illness. The long, loose folds of her white gown had been especially designed to conceal the sharp outlines of her body, but the stamp of her disease was there; simple and ugly and obtrusive, a pitiless fact that could not be disguised or evaded. The splendid shoulders were stooped, there was a swaying unevenness in her gait, her arms seemed disproportionately long, and her hands were transparently white, and cold to the touch. The changes in her face were less obvious; the proud carriage of the head, the warm, clear eyes, even the delicate flush of colour in her cheeks, all defiantly remained, though they were all in a lower key—older, sadder, softer.

She sat down upon the divan and began nervously to arrange the pillows. "Of course I'm ill, and I look it, but you must be quite frank and sensible about that and get used to it at once, for we've no time to lose. And if I'm a trifle irritable you won't mind?—for I'm more than usually nervous."

"Don't bother with me this morning, if you are tired," urged Everett. "I can come quite as well tomorrow."

"Gracious, no!" she protested, with a flash of that quick, keen humour that he remembered as a part of her. "It's solitude that I'm tired to death of—solitude and the wrong kind of people. You see, the minister called on me this morning. He happened to be riding by on his bicycle and felt it his duty to stop. The funniest feature of his conversation is that he is always excusing my own profession to me. But how we are losing time! Do tell me about New York; Charley says you're just on from there. How does it look and taste and smell just now? I think a whiff of the Jersey ferry would be as flagons of cod-liver oil to me. Are the trees still green in Madison Square, or have they grown brown and dusty? Does the chaste Diana still keep her vows through all the exasperating changes of weather? Who has your brother's old studio now, and what misguided aspirants practise their scales in the rookeries about Carnegie Hall? What do people go to see at the theatres, and what do they eat and drink in the world nowadays? Oh, let me die in Harlem!" she was interrupted by a violent attack of coughing, and Everett, embarrassed by her discomfort, plunged into gossip about the professional people he had met in town during the summer, and the musical outlook for the winter. He was diagramming with his pencil some new mechanical device to be used at the Metropolitan in the production of the *Rheingold,* when he became conscious that she was looking at him intently, and that he was talking to the four walls.

Katharine was lying back among the pillows, watching him through half-closed eyes, as a painter looks at a picture. He finished his explanation vaguely enough and put the pencil back in his pocket. As he did so, she said, quietly: "How wonderfully like Adriance you are!"

He laughed, looking up at her with a touch of pride in his eyes that made them seem quite boyish. "Yes, isn't it absurd? It's almost as awkward as looking like Napoleon— But, after all, there are some advantages. It has made some of his friends like me, and I hope it will make you."

Katharine gave him a quick, meaning glance from under her lashes. "Oh, it did that long ago. What a haughty, reserved youth you were then, and how you used to stare at people, and then blush and look cross. Do you remember that night you took me home from a rehearsal, and scarcely spoke a word to me?"

"It was the silence of admiration," protested Everett, "very crude and boyish, but certainly sincere. Perhaps you suspected something of the sort?"

"I believe I suspected a pose; the one that boys often affect with singers. But it rather surprised me in you, for you must have seen a good deal of your brother's pupils." Everett shook his head. "I saw my brother's pupils come and go. Sometimes I was called on to play accompaniments, or to fill out a vacancy at a rehearsal, or to order a carriage for an infuriated soprano who had thrown up her part. But they never spent any time on me, unless it was to notice the resemblance you speak of."

"Yes," observed Katharine, thoughtfully, "I noticed it then, too; but it has grown as you have grown older. That is rather strange, when you have lived such different lives. It's not merely an ordinary family likeness of features, you know, but the suggestion of the other man's personality in your face—like an air transposed to another key. But I'm not attempting to define it; it's beyond me; something altogether unusual and a trifle—well, uncanny," she finished, laughing.

Everett sat looking out under the red window-blind which was raised just a little. As it swung back and forth in the wind it revealed the glaring panorama of the desert—a blinding stretch of yellow, flat as the sea in dead calm, splotched here and there with deep purple shadows; and, beyond, the ragged blue outline of the mountains and the peaks of snow, white as the white clouds. "I remember, when I was a child I used to be very sensitive about it. I don't think it exactly displeased me, or that I would have had it otherwise, but it seemed like a birthmark, or something not to be lightly spoken of. It came into even my relations with my mother. Ad went abroad to study when he was very young, and mother was all broken up over it. She did her whole duty by each of us, but it was generally understood among us that she'd have made burnt-offerings of us all for him any day. I was a little fellow then, and when she sat alone on the porch on summer evenings, she used sometimes to call me to her and turn my face up in the light that streamed out through the shutters and kiss me, and then I always knew she was thinking of Adriance."

"Poor little chap," said Katharine, in her husky voice. "How fond people have always been of Adriance! Tell me the latest news of him. I haven't heard, except through the press, for a year or more. He was in Algiers then, in the valley of the Chelif, riding horseback, and he had quite made up his mind to adopt the Mahometan faith and become an Arab. How many countries and faiths has he adopted, I wonder?"

"Oh, that's Adriance," chuckled Everett. "He is himself barely long enough to write checks and be measured for his clothes. I didn't hear from him while he was an Arab; I missed that."

"He was writing an Algerian *suite* for the piano then; it must be in the publisher's hands by this time. I have been too ill to answer his letter, and have lost touch with him."

Everett drew an envelope from his pocket. "This came a month ago. Read it at your leisure."

"Thanks. I shall keep it as a hostage. Now I want you to play for me. Whatever you like; but if there is anything new in the world, in mercy let me hear it."

He sat down at the piano, and Katharine sat near him, absorbed in his remarkable physical likeness to his brother, and trying to discover in just what it consisted. He was of a larger build than Adriance, and much heavier. His face was of the same oval mould, but it was grey, and darkened about the mouth by continual shaving. His eyes were of the same inconstant April colour, but they were reflective and rather dull; while Adriance's were always points of high light, and always meaning another thing than the thing they meant yesterday. It was hard to see why this earnest man should so continually suggest that lyric, youthful face, as gay as his was grave. For Adriance, though he was ten years the elder, and though his hair was streaked with silver, had the face of a boy of twenty, so mobile that it told his thoughts before he could put them into words. A contralto, famous for the extravagance of her vocal methods and of her affections, once said that the shepherd-boys who sang in the Vale of Tempe must certainly have looked like young Hilgarde.

Everett sat smoking on the veranda of the Inter-Ocean House that night, the victim of mournful recollections. His infatuation for Katharine Gaylord, visionary as it was, had been the most serious of his boyish love-affairs. The fact that it was all so done and dead and far behind him, and that the woman had lived her life out since then, gave him an oppressive sense of age and loss.

He remembered how bitter and morose he had grown during his stay at his brother's studio when Katharine Gaylord was working there, and how he had wounded Adriance on the night of his last concert in New York. He had sat there in the box—while his brother and Katharine were called back again and again, and the flowers went up over the footlights until they were stacked half as high as the piano—brooding in his sullen boy's heart upon the pride those two felt in each other's work—spurring each other to their best and beautifully contending in song. The footlights had seemed a hard, glittering line drawn sharply between their life and his. He walked back to his hotel alone, and sat in his window staring out on Madison Square until long after midnight, resolved to beat no more at doors that he could never enter.

Everett's week in Cheyenne stretched to three, and he saw no prospect of release except through the thing he dreaded. The bright, windy days of the Wyoming autumn passed swiftly. Letters and telegrams came urging him to hasten his trip to the coast, but he resolutely postponed his business engagements. The mornings he spent on one of Charley Gaylord's ponies, or fishing in the mountains. In the afternoon he was usually at his post of duty. Destiny, he reflected, seems to have very positive notions about the sort of parts we are fitted to play. The scene changes and the compensation varies, but in the end we usually find that we have played the same class of business from first to last. Everett had been a stop-gap all his life. He remembered going through a looking-glass labyrinth when he was a boy, and trying gallery after gallery, only at every turn to bump his nose against his own face—which, indeed, was not his own, but his brother's. No matter what his mission, east or west, by land or sea, he was sure to find himself employed in his brother's business, one of the tributary lives which helped to swell the shining current of Adriance Hilgarde's. It was not the first time that his duty had been to comfort, as best he could, one of the broken things his brother's imperious speed had cast aside and forgotten. He made no attempt to analyse the situation or to state it in exact terms; but he accepted it as a commission from his brother to help this woman to die. Day by day he felt her need for him grow more acute and positive; and day by day he felt that in his peculiar relation to her, his own individuality played a smaller part. His power to minister to her comfort lay solely in his link with his brother's life. He knew that she sat by him always watching for some trick of gesture, some familiar play of expression, some illusion of light and shadow, in which he should seem wholly Adriance. He knew that she lived upon this, and that in the exhaustion which followed this turmoil of her dying senses, she slept deep and sweet, and dreamed of youth and art and days in a certain old Florentine garden, and not of bitterness and death.

A few days after his first meeting with Katharine Gaylord, he had cabled his brother to write her. He merely said that she was mortally ill; he could depend on Adriance to say the right thing—that was a part of his gift. Adriance always said not only the right thing, but the opportune, graceful, exquisite thing. He caught the lyric essence of the moment, the poetic suggestion of every situation. Moreover, he usually did the right thing—except, when he did very cruel things—bent upon making people happy when their existence touched his, just as he insisted that his material environment should be beautiful; lavishing upon those near him all the warmth and ra-diance of his rich nature, all the homage of the poet and troubadour, and, when they were no longer near, forgetting—for that also was a part of Adriance's gift.

Three weeks after Everett had sent his cable, when he made his daily call at the gaily painted ranch-house, he found Katharine laughing like a girl. "Have you ever thought," she said, as he entered the music-room, "how much these séances of ours are like Heine's 'Florentine Nights,' except that I don't give you an opportunity to monopolize the conversation?" She held his hand longer than usual as she greeted him. "You are the kindest man living, the kindest," she added, softly.

Everett's grey face coloured faintly as he drew his hand away, for he felt that this time she was looking at him, and not at a whimsical caricature of his brother.

She drew a letter with a foreign postmark from between the leaves of a book and held it out, smiling. "You got him to write it. Don't say you didn't, for it came direct, you see, and the last address I gave him was a place in Florida. This deed shall be remembered of you when I am with the just in Paradise. But one thing you did not ask him to do, for you didn't know about it. He has sent me his latest work, the new sonata, and you are to play it for me directly. But first for the letter; I think you would better read it aloud to me."

Everett sat down in a low chair facing the window-seat in which she reclined with a barricade of pillows behind her. He opened the letter, his lashes half-veiling his kind eyes, and saw to his satisfaction that it was a long one; wonderfully tactful and tender, even for Adriance, who was tender with his valet and his stable-boy, with his old gondolier and the beggar-women who prayed to the saints for him.

The letter was from Granada, written in the Alhambra, as he sat by the fountain of the Patio di Lindaraxa. The air was heavy with the warm fragrance of the South and full of the sound of splashing, running water, as it had been in a certain old garden in Florence, long ago. The sky was one great turquoise, heated until it glowed. The wonderful Moorish arches threw graceful blue shadows all about him. He had sketched an outline of them on the margin of his note-paper. The letter was full of confidences about his work, and delicate allusions to their old happy days of study and comradeship.

As Everett folded it he felt that Adriance had divined the thing needed and had risen to it in his own wonderful way. The letter was consistently egotistical, and seemed to him even a trifle patronizing, yet it was just what she had wanted. A strong realization of his brother's charm and intensity and power came over him; he felt the breath of that whirlwind of flame in which Adriance passed, consuming all in his path, and himself even more resolutely than he consumed others. Then he looked down at this white, burnt-out brand that lay before him.

"Like him, isn't it?" she said quietly. "I think I can scarcely answer his letter, but when you see him next you can do that for me. I want you to tell him many things for me, yet they can all be summed up in this: I want him to grow wholly into his best and greatest self, even at the cost of what is half his charm to you and me. Do you understand me?"

"I know perfectly well what you mean," answered Everett, thoughtfully. "And yet it's difficult to prescribe for those fellows; so little makes, so little mars."

Katharine raised herelf upon her elbow, and her face flushed with feverish earnestness. "Ah, but it is the waste of himself that I mean; his lashing himself out on stupid and uncomprehending people until they take him at their own estimate."

"Come, come," expostulated Everett, now alarmed at her excitement. "Where is the new sonata? Let him speak for himself."

He sat down at the piano and began playing the first movement, which was indeed the voice of Adriance, his proper speech. The sonata was the most ambitious work he had done up to that time, and marked the transition from his early lyric vein to a deeper and nobler style. Everett played intelligently and with that sympathetic comprehension which seems peculiar to a certain lovable class of men who never accomplish anything in particular. When he had finished he turned to Katharine.

"How he has grown!" she cried. "What the three last years have done for him! He used to write only the tragedies of passion; but this is the tragedy of effort and failure, the thing Keats called hell. This is my tragedy, as I lie here, listening to the feet of the runners as they pass me—ah, God! the swift feet of the runners!"

She turned her face away and covered it with her hands. Everett crossed over to her and knelt beside her. In all the days he had known her she had never before, beyond an occasional ironical jest, given voice to the bitterness of her own defeat. Her courage had become a point of pride with him.

"Don't do it," he gasped. "I can't stand it, I really can't, I feel it too much."

When she turned her face back to him there was a ghost of the old, brave, cynical smile on it, more bitter than the tears she could not shed. "No, I won't; I will save that for the night, when I have no better company. Run over that theme at the beginning again, will you? It was running in his head when we were in Venice years ago, and he used to drum it on his glass at the dinner-table. He had just begun to work it out when the late autumn came on, and he decided to go to Florence for the winter. He lost touch with his idea, I suppose, during his illness. Do you remember those frightful days? All the people who have loved him are not strong enough to save him from himself! When I got word from Florence that he had been ill, I was singing at Monte Carlo. His wife was hurrying to him from Paris, but I reached him first. I arrived at dusk, in a terrific storm. They had taken an old palace there for the winter, and I found him in the library—a long, dark room full of old Latin books and heavy furniture and bronzes. He was sitting by a wood fire at one end of the room, looking, oh, so worn and pale!—as he always does when he is ill, you know. Ah, it is so good that you *do* know! Even his red smoking-jacket lent no colour to his face. His first words were not to tell me how ill he had been, but that that morning he had been well enough to put the last strokes to the score of his '*Souvenirs d' Automne,*' and he was as I most like to remember him; calm and happy, and tired with that heavenly tiredness that comes after a good work done at last. Outside, the rain poured down in torrents, and the wind moaned and sobbed in the garden and about the walls of that desolated old palace. How that night comes back to me! There were no lights in the room, only the wood fire. It glowed on the black walls and floor like the reflection of purgatorial flame. Beyond us it scarcely penetrated the gloom at all. Adriance sat staring at the fire with the weariness of all his life in his eyes, and of all the other lives that must aspire and suffer to make up one such life as his. Somehow the wind with all its world-pain had got into the room, and the cold rain was in our eyes, and the wave came up in both of us at once—that awful vague, universal pain, that cold fear of life and death and God and hope—and we were like two clinging together on a spar in mid-ocean after the shipwreck of everything. Then we heard the front door open with a great gust of wind that shook even the walls, and the servants came running with lights, announcing that Madame had returned, *'and in the book we read no more than night.'* "

She gave the old line with a certain bitter humour, and with the hard, bright smile in which of old she had wrapped her weakness as in a glittering garment. That ironical smile, worn through so many years, had gradually changed the lines of her face, and when she looked in the mirror she saw not herself, but the scathing critic, the amused observer and satirist of herself.

Everett dropped his head upon his hand. "How much you have cared!" he said.

"Ah, yes, I cared," she replied, closing her eyes. "You can't imagine what a comfort it is to have you know how I cared, what a relief it is to be able to tell it to some one."

Everett continued to look helplessly at the floor. "I was not sure how much you wanted me to know," he said.

"Oh, I intended you should know from the first time I looked into your face, when you came that day with Charley. You are so like him, that it is almost like telling him himself. At least, I feel now that he will know some day, and then I will be quite sacred from his compassion."

"And has he never known at all?" asked Everett, in a thick voice.

"Oh! never at all in the way that you mean. Of course, he is accustomed to looking into the eyes of women and finding love there; when he doesn't find it there he thinks he must have been guilty of some discourtesy. He has a genuine fondness for every woman who is not stupid or gloomy, or old or preternaturally ugly. I shared with the rest; shared the smiles and the gallantries and the droll little sermons. It was quite like a Sunday-school picnic; we wore our best clothes and a smile and took our turns. It was his kindness that was hardest."

"Don't; you'll make me hate him," groaned Everett.

Katharine laughed and began to play nervously with her fan. "It wasn't in the slightest degree his fault; that is the most grotesque part of it. Why, it had really begun before I ever met him. I fought my way to him, and I drank my doom greedily enough."

Everett rose and stood hesitating. "I think I must go. You ought to be quiet, and I don't think I can hear any more just now."

She put out her hand and took his playfully. "You've put in three weeks at this sort of thing, haven't you? Well, it ought to square accounts for a much worse life than yours will ever be."

He knelt beside her, saying, brokenly: "I stayed because I wanted to be with you, that's all. I have never cared about other women since I knew you in New York when I was a lad. You are a part of my destiny, and I could not leave you if I would."

She put her hands on his shoulders and shook her head. "No, no; don't tell me that. I have seen enough tragedy. It was only a boy's fancy, and your divine pity and my utter pitiableness have recalled it for a moment. One does not love the dying, dear friend. Now go, and you will come again tomorrow, as long as there are tomorrows." She took his hand with a smile that was both courage and despair, and full of infinite loyalty and tenderness, as she said softly:

> "For ever and for ever, farewell, Cassius;
> If we do meet again, why, we shall smile;
> If not, why then, this parting was well made."

The courage in her eyes was like the clear light of a star to him as he went out.

On the night of Adriance Hilgarde's opening concert in Paris, Everett sat by the bed in the ranch-house in Wyoming, watching over the last battle that we have with the flesh before we are done with it and free of it for ever. At times it seemed that the serene soul of her must have left already and found some refuge from the storm, and only the tenacious animal life were left to do battle with death. She laboured under a delusion at once pitiful and merciful, thinking that she was in the Pullman on her way to New York, going back to her life and her work. When she roused from her stupor, it was only to ask the porter to waken her half an hour out of Jersey City, or to remonstrate about the delays and the roughness of the road. At midnight Everett and the nurse were left alone with her. Poor Charley Gaylord had lain down on a couch outside the door. Everett sat looking at the sputtering night-lamp until it made his eyes ache. His head dropped forward, and he sank into heavy, distressful slumber. He was dreaming of Adriance's concert in Paris, and of Adriance, the troubadour. He heard the applause and he saw the flowers going up over the foot-lights until they were stacked half as high as the piano, and the petals fell and scattered, making crimson splotches on the floor. Down this crimson pathway came Adriance with his youthful step, leading his singer by the hand; a dark woman this time, with Spanish eyes.

The nurse touched him on the shoulder, he started and awoke. She screened the lamp with her hand. Everett saw that Katharine was awake and conscious, and struggling a little. He lifted her gently on his arm and began to fan her. She looked into his face with eyes that seemed never to have wept or doubted. "Ah, dear Adriance, dear, dear!" she whispered.

Everett went to call her brother, but when they came back the madness of art was over for Katharine.

Two days later Everett was pacing the station siding, waiting for the west-bound train. Charley Gaylord walked beside him, but the two men had nothing to say to each other. Everett's bags were piled on the truck, and his step was hurried and his eyes were full of impatience, as he gazed again and again up the track, watching for the train. Gaylord's impatience was not less than his own; these two, who had grown so close, had now become painful and impossible to each other, and longed for the wrench of farewell.

As the train pulled in, Everett wrung Gaylord's hand among the crowd of alighting passengers. The people of a German opera company, *en route* for the coast, rushed by them in frantic haste to snatch their breakfast during the stop. Everett heard an exclamation, and a stout woman rushed up to him, glowing with joyful surprise and caught his coat-sleeve with her tightly gloved hands.

"*Herr Gott,* Adriance, *lieber Freund,*" she cried.

Everett lifted his hat, blushing. "Pardon me, madame. I see that you have mistaken me for Adriance Hilgarde. I am his brother." Turning from the crestfallen singer he hurried into the car.

Obscure
Destinies

Neighbour Rosicky

I

When Doctor Burleigh told neighbour Rosicky he had a bad heart, Rosicky protested.

"So? No, I guess my heart was always pretty good. I got a little asthma, maybe. Just a awful short breath when I was pitchin' hay last summer, dat's all."

"Well now, Rosicky, if you know more about it than I do, what did you come to me for? It's your heart that makes you short of breath, I tell you. You're sixty-five years old, and you've always worked hard, and your heart's tired. You've got to be careful from now on, and you can't do heavy work any more. You've got five boys at home to do it for you."

The old farmer looked up at the Doctor with a gleam of amusement in his queer triangular-shaped eyes. His eyes were large and lively, but the lids were caught up in the middle in a curious way, so that they formed a triangle. He did not look like a sick man. His brown face was creased but not wrinkled, he had a ruddy colour in his smooth-shaven cheeks and in his lips, under his long brown moustache. His hair was thin and ragged around his ears, but very little grey. His forehead, naturally high and crossed by deep parallel lines, now ran all the way up to his pointed crown. Rosicky's face had the habit of looking interested,—suggested a contented disposition and a reflective quality that was gay rather than grave. This gave him a certain detachment, the easy manner of an onlooker and observer.

"Well, I guess you ain't got no pills fur a bad heart, Doctor Ed. I guess the only thing is fur me to git me a new one."

Doctor Burleigh swung round in his deskchair and frowned at the old farmer. "I think if I were you I'd take a little care of the old one, Rosicky."

Rosicky shrugged. "Maybe I don't know how. I expect you mean fur me not to drink my coffee no more."

"I wouldn't, in your place. But you'll do as you choose about that. I've never yet been able to separate a Bohemian from his coffee or his pipe. I've quit trying. But the sure thing is you've got to cut out farm work. You can feed the stock and do chores about the barn, but you can't do anything in the fields that makes you short of breath."

"How about shelling corn?"

"Of course not!"

Rosicky considered with puckered brows.

"I can't make my heart go no longer'n it wants to, can I, Doctor Ed?"

"I think it's good for five or six years yet, maybe more, if you'll take the strain off it. Sit around the house and help Mary. If I had a good wife like yours, I'd want to stay around the house."

His patient chuckled. "It ain't no place fur a man. I don't like no old man hanging round the kitchen too much. An' my wife, she's a awful hard worker her own self."

"That's it; you can help her a little. My Lord, Rosicky, you are one of the few men I know who has a family he can get some comfort out of; happy dispositions, never quarrel among themselves, and they treat you right. I want to see you live a few years and enjoy them."

"Oh, they're good kids, all right," Rosicky assented.

The Doctor wrote him a prescription and asked him how his oldest son, Rudolph, who had married in the spring, was getting on. Rudolph had struck out for himself, on rented land. "And how's Polly? I was afraid Mary mightn't like an American daughter-in-law, but it seems to be working out all right."

"Yes, she's a fine girl. Dat widder woman bring her daughters up very nice. Polly got lots of spunk, an' she got some style, too. Da's nice, for young folks to have some style." Rosicky inclined his head gallantly. His voice and his twinkly smile were an affectionate compliment to his daughter-in-law.

"It looks like a storm, and you'd better be getting home before it comes. In town in the car?" Doctor Burleigh rose.

"No, I'm in de wagon. When you got five boys, you ain't got much chance to ride round in de Ford. I ain't much for cars, noway."

"Well, it's a good road out to your place; but I don't want you bumping around in a wagon much. And never again on a hay-rake, remember!"

Rosicky placed the Doctor's fee delicately behind the desk-telephone, looking the other way, as if this were an absent-minded gesture. He put on his plush cap and his corduroy jacket with a sheepskin collar, and went out.

The Doctor picked up his stethoscope and frowned at it as if he were seriously annoyed with the instrument. He wished it had been telling tales about some other man's heart, some old man who didn't look the Doctor in the eye so knowingly, or hold out such a warm brown hand when he said good-bye. Doctor Burleigh had been a poor boy in the country before he went away to medical school; he had known Rosicky almost ever since he could remember, and he had a deep affection for Mrs. Rosicky.

Only last winter he had had such a good breakfast at Rosicky's, and that when he needed it. He had been out all night on a long, hard confinement case at Tom Marshall's—a big rich farm where there was plenty of stock and plenty of feed and a great deal of expensive farm machinery of the newest model, and no comfort whatever. The woman had too many children and too much work, and she was no manager. When the baby was born at last, and handed over to the assisting neighbour woman, and the mother was properly attended to, Burleigh refused any breakfast in that slovenly house, and drove his buggy—the snow was too deep for a car—eight miles to Anton Rosicky's place. He didn't know another farm-house where a man could get such a warm welcome, and such good strong coffee with rich cream. No wonder the old chap didn't want to give up his coffee!

He had driven in just when the boys had come back from the barn and were washing up for breakfast. The long table, covered with a bright oilcloth, was set out with dishes waiting for them, and the warm kitchen was full of the smell of coffee and hot biscuit and sausage. Five big handsome boys, running from twenty to twelve, all with what Burleigh called natural good manners,—they hadn't a bit of the painful self-consciousness he himself had to struggle with when he was a lad. One ran to put his horse away, another helped him off with his fur coat and hung it up, and Josephine, the youngest child and the only daughter, quickly set another place under her mother's direction.

With Mary, to feed creatures was the natural expression of affection,—her chickens, the calves, her big hungry boys. It was a rare pleasure to feed a young man whom she seldom saw and of whom she was as proud as if he belonged to her. Some country housekeepers would have stopped to spread a white cloth over the oilcloth, to change the thick cups and plates for their best china, and the wooden-handled knives for plated ones. But not Mary.

"You must take us as you find us, Doctor Ed. I'd be glad to put out my good things for you if you was expected, but I'm glad to get you any way at all."

He knew she was glad,—she threw back her head and spoke out as if she were announcing him to the whole prairie. Rosicky hadn't said anything at all; he merely smiled his twinkling smile, put some more coal on the fire, and went into his own room to pour the Doctor a little drink in a medicine glass. When they were all seated, he watched his wife's face from his end of the table and spoke to her in Czech. Then, with the instinct of politeness which seldom failed him, he turned to the Doctor and said slyly; "I was just tellin' her not to ask you no questions about Mrs. Marshall till you eat some breakfast. My wife, she's terrible fur to ask questions."

The boys laughed, and so did Mary. She watched the Doctor devour her biscuit and sausage, too much excited to eat anything herself. She drank her coffee and sat taking in everything about her visitor. She had known him when he was a poor country boy, and was boastfully proud of his success, always saying: "What do people go to Omaha for, to see a doctor, when we got the best one in the State right here?" If Mary liked people at all, she felt physical pleasure in the sight of them, personal exultation in any good fortune that came to them. Burleigh didn't know many women like that, but he knew she was like that.

When his hunger was satisfied, he did, of course, have to tell them about Mrs. Marshall, and he noticed what a friendly interest the boys took in the matter.

Rudolph, the oldest one (he was still living at home then), said:

"The last time I was over there, she was lifting them big heavy milk-cans, and I knew she oughtn't to be doing it."

"Yes, Rudolph told me about that when he come home, and I said it wasn't right," Mary put in warmly. "It was all right for me to do them things up to the last, for I was terrible strong, but that woman's weakly. And do you think she'll be able to nurse it, Ed?" She sometimes forgot to give him the title she was so proud of. "And to think of your being up all night and then not able to get a decent breakfast! I don't know what's the matter with such people."

"Why, Mother," said one of the boys, "if Doctor Ed had got breakfast there, we wouldn't have him here. So you ought to be glad."

"He knows I'm glad to have him, John, any time. But I'm sorry for that poor woman, how bad she'll feel the Doctor had to go away in the cold without his breakfast."

"I wish I'd been in practice when these were getting born." The doctor looked down the row of close-clipped heads. "I missed some good breakfasts by not being."

The boys began to laugh at their mother because she flushed so red, but she stood her ground and threw up her head. "I don't care, you wouldn't have got away from this house without breakfast. No doctor ever did. I'd have had something ready fixed that Anton could warm up for you."

The boys laughed harder than ever, and exclaimed at her: "I'll bet you would!" "She would, that!"

"Father, did you get breakfast for the doctor when we were born?"

"Yes, and he used to bring me my breakfast, too, mighty nice. I was always awful hungry!" Mary admitted with a guilty laugh.

While the boys were getting the Doctor's horse, he went to the window to examine the house plants. "What do you do to your geraniums to keep them blooming all winter, Mary? I never pass this house that from the road I don't see your windows full of flowers."

She snapped off a dark red one, and a ruffled new green leaf, and put them in his button-hole. "There, that looks better. You look too solemn for a young man, Ed. Why don't you git married? I'm worried about you. Settin' at breakfast, I looked at you real hard, and I seen you've got some grey hairs already."

"Oh, yes! They're coming. Maybe they'd come faster if I married."

"Don't talk so. You'll ruin your health eating at the hotel. I could send your wife a nice loaf of nut bread, if you only had one. I don't like to see a young man getting grey. I'll tell you something, Ed; you make some strong black tea and keep it handy in a bowl, and every morning just brush it into your hair, an' it'll keep the grey from showin' much. That's the way I do!"

Sometimes the Doctor heard the gossipers in the drug-store wondering why Rosicky didn't get on faster. He was industrious, and so were his boys, but they were rather free and easy, weren't pushers, and they didn't always show good judgment. They were comfortable, they were out of debt, but they didn't get much ahead. Maybe, Doctor Burleigh reflected, people as generous and warm-hearted and affectionate as the Rosickys never got ahead much; maybe you couldn't enjoy your life and put it into the bank, too.

II

When Rosicky left Doctor Burleigh's office he went into the farm-implement store to light his pipe and put on his glasses and read over the list Mary had given him. Then he went into the general merchandise place next door and stood about until the pretty girl with the plucked eyebrows, who always waited on him, was free. Those eyebrows, two thin India-ink strokes, amused him, because he remembered how they used to be. Rosicky always prolonged his shopping by a little joking; the girl knew the old fellow admired her, and she liked to chaff with him.

"Seems to me about every other week you buy ticking, Mr. Rosicky, and always the best quality," she remarked as she measured off the heavy bolt with red stripes.

"You see, my wife is always makin' goose-fedder pillows, an' de thin stuff don't hold in dem little down-fedders."

"You must have lots of pillows at your house."

"Sure. She makes quilts of dem, too. We sleeps easy. Now she's makin' a fedder quilt for my son's wife. You know Polly, that married my Rudolph. How much my bill, Miss Pearl?"

"Eight eighty-five."

"Chust make it nine, and put in some candy fur de women."

"As usual. I never did see a man buy so much candy for his wife. First thing you know, she'll be getting too fat."

"I'd like dat. I ain't much fur all dem slim women like what de style is now."

"That's one for me, I suppose, Mr. Bohunk!" Pearl sniffed and elevated her India-ink strokes.

When Rosicky went out to his wagon, it was beginning to snow,— the first snow of the season, and he was glad to see it. He rattled out of town and along the highway through a wonderfully rich stretch of country, the finest farms in the county. He admired this High Prairie, as it was called, and always liked to drive through it. His own place lay in a rougher territory, where there was some clay in the soil and it was not so productive. When he bought his land, he hadn't the money to buy on High Prairie; so he told his boys, when they grumbled, that if their land hadn't some clay in it, they wouldn't own it at all. All the same, he enjoyed looking at these fine farms, as he enjoyed looking at a prize bull.

After he had gone eight miles, he came to the graveyard, which lay just at the edge of his own hay-land. There he stopped his horses and sat still on his wagon seat, looking about at the snowfall. Over yonder on the hill he could see his own house, crouching low, with the clump of orchard behind and the windmill before, and all down the gentle hill-slope the rows of pale gold cornstalks stood out against the white field. The snow was falling over the cornfield and the pasture and the hay-land, steadily, with very little wind,—a nice dry snow. The graveyard had only a light wire fence about it and was all overgrown with long red grass. The fine snow, settling into this red grass and upon the few little evergreens and the headstones, looked very pretty.

It was a nice graveyard, Rosicky reflected, sort of snug and home-like, not cramped or mournful,—a big sweep all round it. A man could lie down in the long grass and see the complete arch of the sky over him, hear the wagons go by; in summer the mowing-machine rattled right up to the wire fence. And it was so near home. Over there across the cornstalks his own roof and windmill looked so good to him that he promised himself to mind the Doctor and take care of himself. He was awful fond of his place, he admitted. He wasn't anxious to leave it. And it was a comfort to think that he would never have to go farther than the edge of his own hayfield. The snow, falling over his barnyard and the graveyard, seemed to draw things together like. And they were all old neighbours in the graveyard, most of them friends; there was nothing to feel awkward or embarrassed about. Embarrassment was the most disagreeable feeling Rosicky knew. He didn't often have it,—only with certain people whom he didn't understand at all.

Well, it was a nice snowstorm; a fine sight to see the snow falling so quietly and graciously over so much open country. On his cap and shoulders, on the horses' backs and manes, light, delicate, mysterious it fell; and with it a dry cool fragrance was released into the air. It meant rest for vegetation and men and beasts, for the ground itself; a season of long nights for sleep, leisurely breakfasts, peace by the fire. This and much more went through Rosicky's mind, but he merely told himself that winter was coming, clucked to his horses, and drove on.

When he reached home, John, the youngest boy, ran out to put away his team for him, and he met Mary coming up from the outside cellar with her apron full of carrots. They went into the house together. On the table, covered with oilcloth figured with clusters of blue grapes, a place was set, and he smelled hot coffee-cake of some kind. Anton never lunched in town; he thought that extravagant, and anyhow he didn't like the food. So Mary always had something ready for him when he got home.

After he was settled in his chair, stirring his coffee in a big cup, Mary took out of the oven a pan of *kolache* stuffed with apricots, examined them anxiously to see whether they had got too dry, put them beside his plate, and then sat down opposite him.

Rosicky asked her in Czech if she wasn't going to have any coffee.

She replied in English, as being somehow the right language for transacting business: "Now what did Doctor Ed say, Anton? You tell me just what."

"He said I was to tell you some compliments, but I forgot 'em." Rosicky's eyes twinkled.

"About you, I mean. What did he say about your asthma?"

"He says I ain't got no asthma." Rosicky took one of the little rolls in his broad brown fingers. The thickened nail of his right thumb told the story of his past.

"Well, what is the matter? And don't try to put me off."

"He don't say nothing much, only I'm a little older, and my heart ain't so good like it used to be."

Mary started and brushed her hair back from her temples with both hands as if she were a little out of her mind. From the way she glared, she might have been in a rage with him.

"He says there's something the matter with your heart? Doctor Ed says so?"

"Now don't yell at me like I was a hog in de garden, Mary. You know I always did like to hear a woman talk soft. He didn't say anything de matter wid my heart, only it ain't so young like it used to be, an' he tell me not to pitch hay or run de corn-sheller."

Mary wanted to jump up, but she sat still. She admired the way he never under any circumstances raised his voice or spoke roughly. He was city-bred, and she was country-bred; she often said she wanted her boys to have their papa's nice ways.

"You never have no pain there, do you? It's your breathing and your stomach that's been wrong. I wouldn't believe nobody but Doctor Ed about it. I guess I'll go see him myself. Didn't he give you no advice?"

"Chust to take it easy like, an' stay round de house dis winter. I guess you got some carpenter work for me to do. I kin make some new shelves for you, and I want dis long time to build a closet in de boys' room and make dem two little fellers keep der clo'es hung up."

Rosicky drank his coffee from time to time, while he considered. His moustache was of the soft long variety and came down over his mouth like the teeth of a buggy-rake over a bundle of hay. Each time he put down his cup, he ran his blue handkerchief over his lips. When he took a drink of water, he managed very neatly with the back of his hand.

Mary sat watching him intently, trying to find any change in his face. It is hard to see anyone who has become like your own body to you. Yes, his hair had got thin, and his high forehead had deep lines running from left to right. But his neck, always clean shaved except in the busiest seasons, was not loose or baggy. It was burned a dark reddish brown, and there were deep creases in it, but it looked firm and full of blood. His cheeks had a good colour. On either side of his mouth there was a half-moon down the length of his cheek, not wrinkles, but two lines that had come there from his habitual expression. He was shorter and broader than when she married him; his back had grown broad and curved, a good deal like the shell of an old turtle, and his arms and legs were short.

He was fifteen years older than Mary, but she had hardly ever thought about it before. He was her man, and the kind of man she liked. She was rough, and he was gentle,—city-bred, as she always said. They had been shipmates on a rough voyage and had stood by each other in trying times. Life had gone well with them because, at bottom, they had the same ideas about life. They agreed, without discussion, as to what was most important and what was secondary. They didn't often exchange opinions, even in Czech,—it was as if they had thought the same thought together. A good deal had to be sacrificed and thrown overboard in a hard life like theirs, and they had never disagreed as to the things that could go. It had been a hard life, and a soft life, too. There wasn't anything brutal in the short, broad-backed man with the three-cornered eyes and the fore-head that went on to the top of his skull. He was a city man, a gentle man, and though he had married a rough farm girl, he had never touched her without gentleness.

They had been at one accord not to hurry through life, not to be always skimping and saving. They saw their neighbours buy more land and feed more stock than they did, without discontent. Once when the creamery agent came to the Rosickys to persuade them to sell him their cream, he told them how much money the Fasslers, their nearest neighbours, had made on their cream last year.

"Yes," said Mary, "and look at them Fassler children! Pale, pinched little things, they look like skimmed milk. I'd rather put some colour into my children's faces than put money into the bank."

The agent shrugged and turned to Anton.

"I guess we'll do like she says," said Rosicky.

III

Mary very soon got into town to see Doctor Ed, and then she had a talk with her boys and set a guard over Rosicky. Even John, the youngest, had his father on his mind. If Rosicky went to throw hay down from the loft, one of the boys ran up the ladder and took the fork from him. He sometimes complained that though he was getting to be an old man, he wasn't an old woman yet.

That winter he stayed in the house in the afternoons and carpentered, or sat in the chair between the window full of plants and the wooden bench where the two pails of drinking-water stood. This spot was called "Father's corner," though it was not a corner at all. He had a shelf there, where he kept his Bohemian papers and his pipes and tobacco, and his shears and needles and thread and tailor's thimble. Having been a tailor in his youth, he couldn't bear to see a woman patching at his clothes, or at the boys'. He liked tailoring, and always patched all the overalls and jackets and work shirts. Occasionally he made over a pair of pants one of the older boys had outgrown, for the little fellow.

While he sewed, he let his mind run back over his life. He had a good deal to remember, really; life in three countries. The only part of his youth he didn't like to remember was the two years he had spent in London, in Cheapside, working for a German tailor who was wretchedly poor. Those days, when he was nearly always hungry, when his clothes were dropping off him for dirt, and the sound of a strange language kept him in continual bewilderment, had left a sore spot in his mind that wouldn't bear touching.

He was twenty when he landed at Castle Garden in New York, and he had a protector who got him work in a tailor shop in Vesey Street, down near the Washington Market. He looked upon that part of his life as very happy. He became a good workman, he was industrious, and his wages were increased from time to time. He minded his own business and envied nobody's good fortune. He went to night school and learned to read English. He often did over-time work and was well paid for it, but somehow he never saved anything. He couldn't refuse a loan to a friend, and he was self-indulgent. He liked a good dinner, and a little went for beer, a little for tobacco; a good deal went to the girls. He often stood through an opera on Saturday nights; he could get standing-room for a dollar. Those were the great days of opera in New York, and it gave a fellow something to think about for the rest of the week. Rosicky had a quick ear, and a childish love of all the stage splendour; the scenery, the costumes, the ballet. He usually went with a chum, and after the performance they had beer and maybe some oysters somewhere. It was a fine life; for the first five years or so it satisfied him completely. He was never hungry or cold or dirty, and everything amused him: a fire, a dog fight, a parade, a storm, a ferry ride. He thought New York the finest, richest, friendliest city in the world.

Moreover, he had what he called a happy home life. Very near the tailor shop was a small furniture-factory, where an old Austrian, Loeffler, employed a few skilled men and made unusual furniture, most of it to order, for the rich German housewives up-town. The top floor of Loeffler's five-storey factory was a loft, where he kept his choice lumber and stored the odd pieces of furniture left on his hands. One of the young workmen he employed was a Czech, and he and Rosicky became fast friends. They persuaded Loeffler to let them have a sleeping-room in one corner of the loft. They bought good beds and bedding and had their pick of the furniture kept up there. The loft was low-pitched, but light and airy, full of windows, and good-smelling by reason of the fine lumber put up there to season. Old Loeffler used to go down to the docks and buy wood from South America and the East from the sea captains. The young men were as foolish about their house as a bridal pair. Zichec, the young cabinet-maker, devised every sort of convenience, and Rosicky kept their clothes in order. At night and on Sundays, when the quiver of machinery underneath was still, it was the quietest place in the world, and on summer nights all the sea winds blew in. Zichec often practised on his flute in the evening. They were both fond of music and went to the opera together. Rosicky thought he wanted to live like that for ever.

But as the years passed, all alike, he began to get a little restless. When spring came round, he would begin to feel fretted, and he got to drinking. He was likely to drink too much of a Saturday night.

On Sunday he was languid and heavy, getting over his spree. On Monday he plunged into work again. So he never had time to figure out what ailed him, though he knew something did. When the grass turned green in Park Place, and the lilac hedge at the back of Trinity churchyard put out its blossoms, he was tormented by a longing to run away. That was why he drank too much; to get a temporary illusion of freedom and wide horizons.

Rosicky, the old Rosicky, could remember as if it were yesterday the day when the young Rosicky found out what was the matter with him. It was on a Fourth of July afternoon, and he was sitting in Park Place in the sun. The lower part of New York was empty. Wall Street, Liberty Street, Broadway, all empty. So much stone and asphalt with nothing going on, so many empty windows. The emptiness was intense, like the stillness in a great factory when the machinery stops and the belts and bands cease running. It was too great a change, it took all the strength out of one. Those blank buildings, without the stream of life pouring through them, were like empty jails. It struck young Rosicky that this was the trouble with big cities; they built you in from the earth itself, cemented you away from any contact with the ground. You lived in an unnatural world, like the fish in an aquarium, who were probably much more comfortable than they ever were in the sea.

On that very day he began to think seriously about the articles he had read in the Bohemian papers, describing prosperous Czech farming communities in the West. He believed he would like to go out there as a farm hand; it was hardly possible that he could ever have land of his own. His people had always been workmen; his father and grandfather had worked in shops. His mother's parents had lived in the country, but they rented their farm and had a hard time to get along. Nobody in his family had ever owned any land,—that belonged to a different station of life altogether. Anton's mother died when he was little, and he was sent into the country to her parents. He stayed with them until he was twelve, and formed those ties with the earth and the farm animals and growing things which are never made at all unless they are made early. After his grandfather died, he went back to live with his father and stepmother, but she was very hard on him, and his father helped him to get passage to London.

After that Fourth of July day in Park Place, the desire to return to the country never left him. To work on another man's farm would be all he asked; to see the sun rise and set and to plant things and watch them grow. He was a very simple man. He was like a tree that has not many roots, but one tap-root that goes down deep. He subscribed for a Bohemian paper printed in Chicago, then for one printed in Omaha. His mind got farther and farther west. He began to save a little money to buy his liberty. When he was thirty-five, there was a great meeting in New York of Bohemian athletic societies, and Rosicky left the tailor shop and went home with the Omaha delegates to try his fortune in another part of the world.

IV

Perhaps the fact that his own youth was well over before he began to have a family was one reason why Rosicky was so fond of his boys. He had almost a grandfather's indulgence for them. He had never had to worry about any of them—except, just now, a little about Rudolph.

On Saturday night the boys always piled into the Ford, took little Josephine, and went to town to the moving-picture show. One Saturday morning they were talking at the breakfast table about starting early that evening, so that they would have an hour or so to see the Christmas things in the stores before the show began. Rosicky looked down the table.

"I hope you boys ain't disappointed, but I want you to let me have de car tonight. Maybe some of you can go in with de neighbours."

Their faces fell. They worked hard all week, and they were still like children. A new jack-knife or a box of candy pleased the older ones as much as the little fellow.

"If you and Mother are going to town," Frank said, "maybe you could take a couple of us along with you, anyway."

"No, I want to take de car down to Rudolph's, and let him an' Polly go in to de show. She don't git into town enough, an' I'm afraid she's gettin' lonesome, an' he can't afford no car yet."

That settled it. The boys were a good deal dashed. Their father took another piece of apple-cake and went on: "Maybe next Saturday night de two little fellers can go along wid dem."

"Oh, is Rudolph going to have the car every Saturday night?"

Rosicky did not reply at once; then he began to speak seriously: "Listen, boys; Polly ain't lookin' so good. I don't like to see nobody lookin' sad. It comes hard fur a town girl to be a farmer's wife. I don't want no trouble to start in Rudolph's family. When it starts, it ain't so easy to stop. An American girl don't git used to our ways all at once. I like to tell Polly she and Rudolph can have the car every Saturday night till after New Year's, if it's all right with you boys."

"Sure it's all right, Papa," Mary cut in. "And it's good you thought about that. Town girls is used to more than country girls. I lay awake nights, scared she'll make Rudolph discontented with the farm."

The boys put as good a face on it as they could. They surely looked forward to their Saturday nights in town. That evening Rosicky drove the car the half-mile down to Rudolph's new, bare little house.

Polly was in a short-sleeved gingham dress, clearing away the supper dishes. She was a trim, slim little thing, with blue eyes and shingled yellow hair, and her eyebrows were reduced to a mere brush-stroke, like Miss Pearl's.

"Good evening, Mr. Rosicky. Rudolph's at the barn, I guess." She never called him father, or Mary mother. She was sensitive about having married a foreigner. She never in the world would have done it if Rudolph hadn't been such a handsome, persuasive fellow and such a gallant lover. He had graduated in her class in high school in town, and their friendship began in the ninth grade.

Rosicky went in, though he wasn't exactly asked. "My boys ain't goin' to town tonight, an' I brought de car over fur you two to go in to de picture show."

Polly, carrying dishes to the sink, looked over her shoulder at him. "Thank you. But I'm late with my work tonight, and pretty tired. Maybe Rudolph would like to go in with you."

"Oh, I don't go to de shows! I'm too old-fashioned. You won't feel so tired after you ride in de air a ways. It's a nice clear night, an' it ain't cold. You go an' fix yourself up, Polly, an' I'll wash de dishes an' leave everything nice fur you."

Polly blushed and tossed her bob. "I couldn't let you do that, Mr. Rosicky. I wouldn't think of it."

Rosicky said nothing. He found a bib apron on a nail behind the kitchen door. He slipped it over his head and then took Polly by her two elbows and pushed her gently toward the door of her own room. "I washed up de kitchen many times for my wife, when de babies was sick or somethin'. You go an' make yourself look nice. I like you to look prettier'n any of dem town girls when you go in. De young folks must have some fun, an' I'm goin' to look out fur you, Polly."

That kind, reassuring grip on her elbows, the old man's funny bright eyes, made Polly want to drop her head on his shoulder for a second. She restrained herself, but she lingered in his grasp at the door of her room, murmuring tearfully: "You always lived in the city when you were young, didn't you? Don't you ever get lonesome out here?"

As she turned round to him, her hand fell naturally into his, and he stood holding it and smiling into her face with his peculiar, knowing, indulgent smile without a shadow of reproach in it. "Dem big cities is all right fur de rich, but dey is terrible hard fur de poor."

"I don't know. Sometimes I think I'd like to take a chance. You lived in New York, didn't you?"

"An' London. Da's bigger still. I learned my trade dere. Here's Rudolph comin', you better hurry."

"Will you tell me about London some time?"

"Maybe. Only I ain't no talker, Polly. Run an' dress yourself up."

The bedroom door closed behind her, and Rudolph came in from the outside, looking anxious. He had seen the car and was sorry any of his family should come just then. Supper hadn't been a very pleasant occasion. Halting in the doorway, he saw his father in a kitchen apron, carrying dishes to the sink. He flushed crimson and something flashed in his eye. Rosicky held up a warning finger.

"I brought de car over fur you an' Polly to go to de picture show, an' I made her let me finish here so you won't be late. You go put on a clean shirt, quick!"

"But don't the boys want the car, Father?"

"Not tonight dey don't." Rosicky fumbled under his apron and found his pants pocket. He took out a silver dollar and said in a hurried whisper: "You go an' buy dat girl some ice cream an' candy tonight, like you was courtin'. She's awful good friends wid me."

Rudolph was very short of cash, but he took the money as if it hurt him. There had been a crop failure all over the county. He had more than once been sorry he'd married this year.

In a few minutes the young people came out, looking clean and a little stiff. Rosicky hurried them off, and then he took his own time with the dishes. He scoured the pots and pans and put away the milk and swept the kitchen. He put some coal in the stove and shut off the draughts, so the place would be warm for them when they got home late at night. Then he sat down and had a pipe and listened to the clock tick.

Generally speaking, marrying an American girl was certainly a risk. A Czech should marry a Czech. It was lucky that Polly was the daughter of a poor widow woman; Rudolph was proud, and if she had a prosperous family to throw up at him, they could never make it go. Polly was one of four sisters, and they all worked; one was book-keeper in the bank, one taught music, and Polly and her younger sister had been clerks, like Miss Pearl. All four of them were musical, had pretty voices, and sang in the Methodist choir, which the eldest sister directed.

Polly missed the sociability of a store position. She missed the choir, and the company of her sisters. She didn't dislike housework, but she disliked so much of it. Rosicky was a little anxious about this pair. He was afraid Polly would grow so discontented that Rudy would quit the farm and take a factory job in Omaha. He had worked for a winter up there, two years ago, to get money to marry on. He had done very well, and they would always take him back at the stockyards. But to Rosicky that meant the end of everything for his son. To be a landless man was to be a wage-earner, a slave, all your life; to have nothing, to be nothing.

Rosicky thought he would come over and do a little carpentering for Polly after the New Year. He guessed she needed jollying. Rudolph was a serious sort of chap, serious in love and serious about his work.

Rosicky shook out his pipe and walked home across the fields. Ahead of him the lamplight shone from his kitchen windows. Suppose he were still in a tailor shop in Vesey Street, with a bunch of pale, narrow-chested sons working on machines, all coming home tired and sullen to eat supper in a kitchen that was a parlour also; with another crowded, angry family quarrelling just across the dumb-waiter shaft, and squeaking pulleys at the windows where dirty washings hung on dirty lines above a court full of old brooms and mops and ash-cans. . . .

He stopped by the windmill to look up at the frosty winter stars and draw a long breath before he went inside. That kitchen with the shining windows was dear to him; but the sleeping fields and bright stars and the noble darkness were dearer still.

V

On the day before Christmas the weather set in very cold; no snow, but a bitter, biting wind that whistled and sang over the flat land and lashed one's face like fine wires. There was baking going on in the Rosicky kitchen all day, and Rosicky sat inside, making over a coat that Albert had outgrown into an overcoat for John. Mary had a big red geranium in bloom for Christmas, and a row of Jerusalem cherry trees, full of berries. It was the first year she had ever grown these; Doctor Ed brought her the seeds from Omaha when he went to some medical convention. They reminded Rosicky of plants he had seen in England; and all afternoon, as he stitched, he sat thinking about those two years in London, which his mind usually shrank from even after all this while.

He was a lad of eighteen when he dropped down into London, with no money and no connexions except the address of a cousin who was supposed to be working at a confectioner's. When he went to the pastry shop, however, he found that the cousin had gone to America. Anton tramped the streets for several days, sleeping in doorways and on the Embankment, until he was in utter despair. He knew no English, and the sound of the strange language all about him confused him. By chance he met a poor German tailor who had learned his trade in Vienna, and could speak a little Czech. This tailor, Lifschnitz, kept a repair shop in a Cheapside basement, underneath a cobbler. He didn't much need an apprentice, but he was sorry for the boy and took him in for no wages but his keep and what he could pick up. The pickings were supposed to be coppers given you when you took work home to a customer. But most of the customers called for their clothes themselves, and the coppers that came Anton's way were very few. He had, however, a place to sleep. The tailor's family lived upstairs in three rooms; a kitchen, a bedroom, where Lifschnitz and his wife and five children slept, and a living-room. Two corners of this living-room were curtained off for lodgers; in one Rosicky slept on an old horsehair sofa, with a feather quilt to wrap himself in. The other corner was rented to a wretched, dirty boy, who was studying the violin. He actually practised there. Rosicky was dirty, too. There was no way to be anything else. Mrs. Lifschnitz got the water she cooked and washed with from a pump in a brick court, four flights down. There were bugs in the place, and multitudes of fleas, though the poor woman did the best she could. Rosicky knew she often went empty to give another potato or a spoonful of dripping to the two hungry, sad-eyed boys who lodged with her. He used to think he would never get out of there, never get a clean shirt to his back again. What would he do, he wondered, when his clothes actually dropped to pieces and the worn cloth wouldn't hold patches any longer?

It was still early when the old farmer put aside his sewing and his recollections. The sky had been a dark grey all day, with not a gleam of sun, and the light failed at four o'clock. He went to shave and change his shirt while the turkey was roasting. Rudolph and Polly were coming over for supper.

After supper they sat round in the kitchen, and the younger boys were saying how sorry they were it hadn't snowed. Everybody was sorry. They wanted a deep snow that would lie long and keep the wheat warm, and leave the ground soaked when it melted.

"Yes, sir!" Rudolph broke out fiercely; "if we have another dry year like last year, there's going to be hard times in this country."

Rosicky filled his pipe. "You boys don't know what hard times is. You don't owe nobody, you got plenty to eat an' keep warm, an' plenty water to keep clean. When you got them, you can't have it very hard."

Rudolph frowned, opened and shut his big right hand, and dropped it clenched upon his knee. "I've got to have a good deal more than that, Father, or I'll quit this farming gamble. I can always make good wages railroading, or at the packing house, and be sure of my money."

"Maybe so," his father answered dryly.

Mary, who had just come in from the pantry and was wiping her hands on the roller towel, thought Rudy and his father were getting too serious. She brought her darning-basket and sat down in the middle of the group.

"I ain't much afraid of hard times, Rudy," she said heartily. "We've had a plenty, but we've always come through. Your father wouldn't never take nothing very hard, not even hard times. I got a mind to tell you a story on him. Maybe you boys can't hardly remember the year we had that terrible hot wind, that burned everything up on the Fourth of July? All the corn an' the gardens. An' that was in the days when we didn't have alfalfa yet,—I guess it wasn't invented.

"Well, that very day your father was out cultivatin' corn, and I was here in the kitchen makin' plum preserves. We had bushels of plums that year. I noticed it was terrible hot, but it's always hot in the kitchen when you're preservin', an' I was too busy with my plums to mind. Anton come in from the field about three o'clock, an' I asked him what was the matter.

" 'Nothin',' he says, 'but it's pretty hot, an' I think I won't work no more today.' He stood round for a few minutes, an' then he says: 'Ain't you near through? I want you should git up a nice supper for us tonight. It's Fourth of July.'

"I told him to git along, that I was right in the middle of preservin', but the plums would taste good on hot biscuit. 'I'm goin' to have fried chicken, too,' he says, and he went off an' killed a couple. You three oldest boys was little fellers, playin' round outside, real hot an' sweaty, an' your father took you to the horse tank down by the windmill an' took off your clothes an' put you in. Them two box-elder trees was little then, but they made shade over the tank. Then he took off all his own clothes, an' got in with you. While he was playin' in the water with you, the Methodist preacher drove into our place to say how all the neighbours was goin' to meet at the school-house that night, to pray for rain. He drove right to the windmill, of course, and there was your father and you three with no clothes on. I was in the kitchen door, an' I had to laugh, for the preacher acted like he ain't never seen a naked man before. He surely was embarrassed, an' your father couldn't git to his clothes; they was all hangin' up on the windmill to let the sweat dry out of 'em. So he laid in the tank where he was, an' put one of you boys on top of him to cover him up a little, an' talked to the preacher.

"When you got through playin' in the water, he put clean clothes on you and a clean shirt on himself, an' by that time I'd begun to get supper. He says: 'It's too hot in here to eat comfortable. Let's have a picnic in the orchard. We'll eat our supper behind the mulberry hedge, under them linden trees.'

"So he carried our supper down, an' a bottle of my wild-grape wine, an' everything tasted good, I can tell you. The wind got cooler as the sun was goin' down, and it turned out pleasant, only I noticed how the leaves was curled up on the linden trees. That made me think, an' I asked your father if that hot wind all day hadn't been terrible hard on the gardens an' the corn.

" 'Corn,' he says, 'there ain't no corn.'

" 'What you talkin' about?' I said. 'Ain't we got forty acres?'

" 'We ain't got an ear,' he says, 'nor nobody else ain't got none. All the corn in this country was cooked by three o'clock today, like you'd roasted it in an oven.'

" 'You mean you won't get no crop at all?' I asked him. I couldn't believe it, after he'd worked so hard.

" 'No crop this year,' he says. 'That's why we're havin' a picnic. We might as well enjoy what we got.'

"An' that's how your father behaved, when all the neighbours was so discouraged they couldn't look you in the face. An' we enjoyed ourselves that year, poor as we was, an' our neighbours wasn't a bit better off for bein' miserable. Some of 'em grieved till they got poor digestions and couldn't relish what they did have."

The younger boys said they thought their father had the best of it. But Rudolf was thinking that, all the same, the neighbours had managed to get ahead more, in the fifteen years since that time. There must be something wrong about his father's way of doing things. He wished he knew what was going on in the back of Polly's mind. He knew she liked his father, but he knew, too, that she was afraid of something. When his mother sent over coffee-cake or prune tarts or a loaf of fresh bread, Polly seemed to regard them with a certain suspicion. When she observed to him that his brothers had nice manners, her tone implied that it was remarkable they should have. With his mother she was stiff and on her guard. Mary's hearty frankness and gusts of good humour irritated her. Polly was afraid of being unusual or conspicuous in any way, of being "ordinary," as she said!

When Mary had finished her story, Rosicky laid aside his pipe.

"You boys like me to tell you about some of dem hard times I been through in London?" Warmly encouraged, he sat rubbing his forehead along the deep creases. It was bothersome to tell a long story in English (he nearly always talked to the boys in Czech), but he wanted Polly to hear this one.

"Well, you know about dat tailor shop I worked in in London? I had one Christmas dere I ain't never forgot. Times was awful bad before Christmas; de boss ain't got much work, an' have it awful hard to pay his rent. It ain't so much fun, bein' poor in a big city like London, I'll say! All de windows is full of good t'ings to eat, an' all de pushcarts in de streets is full, an' you smell 'em all de time, an' you ain't got no money,—not a damn bit. I didn't mind de cold so much, though I didn't have no overcoat, chust a short jacket I'd outgrowed so it wouldn't meet on me, an' my hands was chapped raw. But I always had a good appetite, like you all know, an' de sight of dem pork pies in de windows was awful fur me!

"Day before Christmas was terrible foggy dat year, an' dat fog gits into your bones and makes you all damp like. Mrs. Lifschnitz didn't give us nothin' but a little bread an' drippin' for supper, because she was savin' to try for to give us a good dinner on Christmas Day. After supper de boss say I can go an' enjoy myself, so I went into de streets to listen to de Christmas singers. Dey sing old songs an' make very nice music, an' I run round after dem a good ways, till I got awful hungry. I t'ink maybe if I go home, I can sleep till morning an' forgit my belly.

"I went into my corner real quiet, and roll up in my fedder quilt. But I ain't got my head down, till I smell somet'ing good. Seem like it git stronger an' stronger, an' I can't git to sleep noway. I can't understand dat smell. Dere was a gas light in a hall across de court, dat always shine in at my window a little. I got up an' look round. I got a little wooden box in my corner fur a stool, 'cause I ain't got no chair. I picks up dat box, and under it dere is a roast goose on a platter! I can't believe my eyes. I carry it to de window where de light comes in, an' touch it and smell it to find out, an' den I taste it to be sure. I say, I will eat chust one little bite of dat goose, so I can go to sleep, and tomorrow I won't eat none at all. But I tell you, boys, when I stop, one half of dat goose was gone!"

The narrator bowed his head, and the boys shouted. But little Josephine slipped behind his chair and kissed him on the neck beneath his ear.

"Poor little Papa, I don't want him to be hungry!"

"Da's long ago, child. I ain't never been hungry since I had your mudder to cook fur me."

"Go on and tell us the rest, please," said Polly.

"Well, when I come to realize what I done, of course, I felt terrible. I felt better in de stomach, but very bad in de heart. I set on my bed wid dat platter on my knees, an' it all come to me; how hard dat poor woman save to buy dat goose, and how she get some neighbour to cook it dat got more fire, an' how she put it in my corner to keep it away from dem hungry children. Dey was a old carpet hung up to shut my corner off, an' de children wasn't allowed to go in dere. An' I know she put it in my corner because she trust me more'n she did de violin boy. I can't stand it to face her after I spoil de Christmas. So I put on my shoes and go out into de city. I tell myself I better throw myself in de river; but I guess I ain't dat kind of a boy.

"It was after twelve o'clock, an' terrible cold, an' I start out to walk about London all night. I walk along de river awhile, but dey was lots of drunks all along; men, and women too. I chust move along to keep away from de police. I git onto de Strand, an' den over to New Oxford Street, where dere was a big German restaurant on de ground floor, wid big windows all fixed up fine, an' I could see de people havin' parties inside. While I was lookin' in, two men and two ladies come out, laughin' and talkin' and feelin' happy about all dey been eatin' an' drinkin', and dey was speakin' Czech,—not like de Austrians, but like de home folks talk it.

"I guess I went crazy, an' I done what I ain't never done before nor since. I went right up to dem gay people an' begun to beg dem: 'Fellow-countrymen, for God's sake give me money enough to buy a goose!'

"Dey laugh, of course, but de ladies speak awful kind to me, an' dey take me back into de restaurant and give me hot coffee and cakes, an' make me tell all about how I happened to come to London, an' what I was doin' dere. Dey take my name and where I work down on paper, an' both of dem ladies give me ten shillings.

"De big market at Covent Garden ain't very far away, an' by dat time it was open. I go dere an' buy a big goose an' some pork pies, an' potatoes and onions, an' cakes an' oranges fur de children,—all I could carry! When I git home, everybody is still asleep. I pile all I bought on de kitchen table, an' go in an' lay down on my bed, an' I ain't waken up till I hear dat woman scream when she come out into her kitchen. My goodness, but she was surprise! She laugh an' cry at de same time, an' hug me and waken all de children. She ain't stop fur no breakfast; she git de Christmas dinner ready dat morning, and we all sit down an' eat all we can hold. I ain't never seen dat violin boy have all he can hold before.

"Two three days after dat, de two men come to hunt me up, an' dey ask my boss, and he give me a good report an' tell dem I was a steady boy all right. One of dem Bohemians was very smart an' run a Bohemian newspaper in New York, an' de odder was a rich man, in de importing business, an' dey been travelling togedder. Dey told me how t'ings was easier in New York, an' offered to pay my passage when dey was goin' home soon on a boat. My boss say to me: 'You go. You ain't got no chance here, an' I like to see you git ahead, fur you always been a good boy to my woman, and fur dat fine Christmas dinner you give us all.' An' da's how I got to New York."

That night when Rudolph and Polly, arm in arm, were running home across the fields with the bitter wind at their backs, his heart leaped for joy when she said she thought they might have his family come over for supper on New Year's Eve. "Let's get up a nice supper, and not let your mother help at all; make her be company for once."

"That would be lovely of you, Polly," he said humbly. He was a very simple, modest boy, and he, too, felt vaguely that Polly and her sisters were more experienced and worldly than his people.

VI

The winter turned out badly for farmers. It was bitterly cold, and after the first light snows before Christmas there was no snow at all,—and no rain. March was as bitter as February. On those days when the wind fairly punished the country, Rosicky sat by his window. In the fall he and the boys had put in a big wheat planting, and now the seed had frozen in the ground. All that land would have to be ploughed up and planted over again, planted in corn. It had happened before, but he was younger then, and he never worried about what had to be. He was sure of himself and of Mary; he knew they could bear what they had to bear, that they would always pull through somehow. But he was not so sure about the young ones, and he felt troubled because Rudolph and Polly were having such a hard start.

Sitting beside his flowering window while the panes rattled and the wind blew in under the door, Rosicky gave himself to reflection as he had not done since those Sundays in the loft of the furniture-factory in New York, long ago. Then he was trying to find what he wanted in life for himself; now he was trying to find what he wanted for his boys, and why it was he so hungered to feel sure they would be here, working this very land, after he was gone.

They would have to work hard on the farm, and probably they would never do much more than make a living. But if he could think of them as staying here on the land, he wouldn't have to fear any great unkindness for them. Hardships, certainly; it was a hardship to have the wheat freeze in the ground when seed was so high; and to have to sell your stock because you had no feed. But there would be other years when everything came along right, and you caught up. And what you had was your own. You didn't have to choose between bosses and strikers, and go wrong either way. You didn't have to do with dishonest and cruel people. They were the only things in his experience he had found terrifying and horrible; the look in the eyes of a dishonest and crafty man, of a scheming and rapacious woman.

In the country, if you had a mean neighbour, you could keep off his land and make him keep off yours. But in the city, all the foulness and misery and brutality of your neighbours was part of your life. The worst things he had come upon in his journey through the world were human,—depraved and poisonous specimens of man. To this day he could recall certain terrible faces in the London streets. There were mean people everywhere, to be sure, even in their own country town here. But they weren't tempered, hardened, sharpened, like the treacherous people in cities who live by grinding or cheating or poisoning their fellow-men. He had helped to bury two of his fellow-workmen in the tailoring trade, and he was distrustful of the organized industries that see one out of the world in big cities. Here, if you were sick, you had Doctor Ed to look after you; and if you died, fat Mr. Haycock, the kindest man in the world, buried you.

It seemed to Rosicky that for good, honest boys like his, the worst they could do on the farm was better than the best they would be likely to do in the city. If he'd had a mean boy, now, one who was crooked and sharp and tried to put anything over on his brothers, then town would be the place for him. But he had no such boy. As for Rudolph, the discontented one, he would give the shirt off his back to anyone who touched his heart. What Rosicky really hoped for his boys was that they could get through the world without ever knowing much about the cruelty of human beings. "Their mother and me ain't prepared them for that," he sometimes said to himself.

These thoughts brought him back to a grateful consideration of his own case. What an escape he had had, to be sure! He, too, in his time, had had to take money for repair work from the hand of a hungry child who let it go so wistfully; because it was money due his boss. And now, in all these years, he had never had to take a cent from anyone in bitter need,—never had to look at the face of a woman become like a wolf's from struggle and famine. When he thought of these things, Rosicky would put on his cap and jacket and slip down to the barn and give his work-horses a little extra oats, letting them eat it out of his hand in their slobbery fashion. It was his way of expressing what he felt, and made him chuckle with pleasure.

The spring came warm, with blue skies,—but dry, dry as a bone. The boys began ploughing up the wheat-fields to plant them over in corn. Rosicky would stand at the fence corner and watch them, and the earth was so dry it blew up in clouds of brown dust that hid the horses and the sulky plough and the driver. It was a bad outlook.

The big alfalfa-field that lay between the home place and Rudolph's came up green, but Rosicky was worried because during that open windy winter a great many Russian thistle plants had blown in there and lodged. He kept asking the boys to rake them out; he was afraid their seed would root and "take the alfalfa." Rudolph said that was nonsense. The boys were working so hard planting corn, their father felt he couldn't insist about the thistles, but he set great store by that big alfalfa field. It was a feed you could depend on,—and there was some deeper reason, vague, but strong. The peculiar green of that clover woke early memories in old Rosicky, went back to something in his childhood in the old world. When he was a little boy, he had played in fields of that strong blue-green colour.

One morning, when Rudolph had gone to town in the car, leaving a work-team idle in his barn, Rosicky went over to his son's place, put the horses to the buggy-rake, and set about quietly raking up those thistles. He behaved with guilty caution, and rather enjoyed stealing a march on Doctor Ed, who was just then taking his first vacation in seven years of practice and was attending a clinic in Chicago. Rosicky got the thistles raked up, but did not stop to burn them. That would take some time, and his breath was pretty short, so he thought he had better get the horses back to the barn.

He got them into the barn and to their stalls, but the pain had come on so sharp in his chest that he didn't try to take the harness off. He started for the house, bending lower with every step. The cramp in his chest was shutting him up like a jack-knife. When he reached the windmill, he swayed and caught at the ladder. He saw Polly coming down the hill, running with the swiftness of a slim greyhound. In a flash she had her shoulder under his armpit.

"Lean on me, Father, hard! Don't be afraid. We can get to the house all right."

Somehow they did, though Rosicky became blind with pain; he could keep on his legs, but he couldn't steer his course. The next thing he was conscious of was lying on Polly's bed, and Polly bending over him wringing out bath towels in hot water and putting them on his chest. She stopped only to throw coal into the stove, and she kept the tea-kettle and the black pot going. She put these hot applications on him for nearly an hour, she told him afterwards, and all that time he was drawn up stiff and blue, with the sweat pouring off him.

As the pain gradually loosed its grip, the stiffness went out of his jaws, the black circles round his eyes disappeared, and a little of his natural colour came back. When his daughter-in-law buttoned his shirt over his chest at last, he sighed.

"Da's fine, de way I feel now, Polly. It was a awful bad spell, an' I was so sorry it all come on you like it did."

Polly was flushed and excited. "Is the pain really gone? Can I leave you long enough to telephone over to your place?"

Rosicky's eyelids fluttered. "Don't telephone, Polly. It ain't no use to scare my wife. It's nice and quiet here, an' if I ain't too much trouble to you, just let me lay still till I feel like myself. I ain't got no pain now. It's nice here."

Polly bent over him and wiped the moisture from his face. "Oh, I'm so glad it's over!" she broke out impulsively. "It just broke my heart to see you suffer so, Father."

Rosicky motioned her to sit down on the chair where the tea-kettle had been, and looked up at her with that lively affectionate gleam in his eyes. "You was awful good to me, I won't never forget dat. I hate it to be sick on you like dis. Down at de barn I say to myself, dat young girl ain't had much experience in sickness, I don't want to scare her, an' maybe she's got a baby comin' or somet'ing."

Polly took his hand. He was looking at her so intently and affectionately and confidingly; his eyes seemed to caress her face, to regard it with pleasure. She frowned with her funny streaks of eyebrows, and then smiled back at him.

"I guess maybe there is something of that kind going to happen. But I haven't told anyone yet, not my mother or Rudolph. You'll be the first to know."

His hand pressed hers. She noticed that it was warm again. The twinkle in his yellow-brown eyes seemed to come nearer.

"I like mighty well to see dat little child, Polly," was all he said. Then he closed his eyes and lay half-smiling. But Polly sat still, thinking hard. She had a sudden feeling that nobody in the world, not her mother, not Rudolph, or anyone, really loved her as much as old Rosicky did. It perplexed her. She sat frowning and trying to puzzle it out. It was as if Rosicky had a special gift for loving people, something that was like an ear for music or an eye for colour. It was quiet, unobtrusive; it was merely there. You saw it in his eyes,— perhaps that was why they were merry. You felt it in his hands, too. After he dropped off to sleep, she sat holding his warm, broad, flexible brown hand. She had never seen another in the least like it. She wondered if it wasn't a kind of gypsy hand, it was so alive and quick and light in its communications,—very strange in a farmer. Nearly all the farmers she knew had huge lumps of fists, like mauls, or they were knotty and bony and uncomfortable-looking, with stiff fingers. But Rosicky's was like quick-silver, flexible, muscular, about the colour of a pale cigar, with deep, deep creases across the palm. It wasn't nervous, it wasn't a stupid lump; it was a warm brown human hand, with some cleverness in it, a great deal of generosity, and something else which Polly could only call "gypsy-like,"—something nimble and lively and sure, in the way that animals are.

Polly remembered that hour long afterwards; it had been like an awakening to her. It seemed to her that she had never learned so much about life from anything as from old Rosicky's hand. It brought her to herself; it communicated some direct and untranslatable message.

When she heard Rudolph coming in the car, she ran out to meet him.

"Oh, Rudy, your father's been awful sick! He raked up those thistles he's been worrying about, and afterwards he could hardly get to the house. He suffered so I was afraid he was going to die."

Rudolph jumped to the ground. "Where is he now?"

"On the bed. He's asleep. I was terribly scared, because, you know, I'm so fond of your father." She slipped her arm through his and they went into the house. That afternoon they took Rosicky home and put him to bed, though he protested that he was quite well again.

The next morning he got up and dressed and sat down to breakfast with his family. He told Mary that his coffee tasted better than usual to him, and he warned the boys not to bear any tales to Doctor Ed when he got home. After breakfast he sat down by his window to do some patching and asked Mary to thread several needles for him before she went to feed her chickens,—her eyes were better than his, and her hands steadier. He lit his pipe and took up John's overalls. Mary had been watching him anxiously all morning, and as she went out of the door with her bucket of scraps, she saw that he was smiling. He was thinking, indeed, about Polly, and how he might never have known what a tender heart she had if he hadn't got sick over there. Girls nowadays didn't wear their heart on their sleeve. But now he knew Polly would make a fine woman after the foolishness wore off. Either a woman had that sweetness at her heart or she hadn't. You couldn't always tell by the look of them; but if they had that, everything came out right in the end.

After he had taken a few stitches, the cramp began in his chest, like yesterday. He put his pipe cautiously down on the window-sill and bent over to ease the pull. No use,—he had better try to get to his bed if he could. He rose and groped his way across the familiar floor, which was rising and falling like the deck of a ship. At the door he fell. When Mary came in, she found him lying there, and the moment she touched him she knew that he was gone.

Doctor Ed was away when Rosicky died, and for the first few weeks after he got home he was hard driven. Every day he said to himself that he must get out to see that family that had lost their father. One soft, warm moonlight night in early summer he started for the farm. His mind was on other things, and not until his road ran by the graveyard did he realize that Rosicky wasn't over there on the hill where the red lamplight shone, but here, in the moonlight. He stopped his car, shut off the engine, and sat there for a while.

A sudden hush had fallen on his soul. Everything here seemed strangely moving and significant, though signifying what, he did not know. Close by the wire fence stood Rosicky's mowing-machine, where one of the boys had been cutting hay that afternoon; his own work-horses had been going up and down there. The new-cut hay perfumed all the night air. The moonlight silvered the long, billowy grass that grew over the graves and hid the fence; the few little evergreens stood out black in it, like shadows in a pool. The sky was very blue and soft, the stars rather faint because the moon was full.

For the first time it struck Doctor Ed that this was really a beautiful graveyard. He thought of city cemeteries; acres of shrubbery and heavy stone, so arranged and lonely and unlike anything in the living world. Cities of the dead, indeed; cities of the forgotten, of the "put away." But this was open and free, this little square of long grass which the wind for ever stirred. Nothing but the sky overhead, and the many-coloured fields running on until they met that sky. The horses worked here in summer; the neighbours passed on their way to town; and over yonder, in the cornfield, Rosicky's own cattle would be eating fodder as winter came on. Nothing could be more undeathlike than this place; nothing could be more right for a man who had helped to do the work of great cities and had always longed for the open country and had got to it at last. Rosicky's life seemed to him complete and beautiful.

Old Mrs. Harris

I

Mrs. David Rosen, cross-stitch in hand, sat looking out of the window across her own green lawn to the ragged, sunburned back yard of her neighbours on the right. Occasionally she glanced anxiously over her shoulder toward her shining kitchen, with a black and white linoleum floor in big squares, like a marble pavement.

"Will dat woman never go?" she muttered impatiently, just under her breath. She spoke with a slight accent—it affected only her *th*'s, and, occasionally, the letter *v*. But people in Skyline thought this unfortunate, in a woman whose superiority they recognized.

Mrs. Rosen ran out to move the sprinkler to another spot on the lawn, and in doing so she saw what she had been waiting to see. From the house next door a tall, handsome woman emerged, dressed in white broadcloth and a hat with white lilacs; she carried a sunshade and walked with a free, energetic step, as if she were going out on a pleasant errand.

Mrs. Rosen darted quickly back into the house, lest her neighbour should hail her and stop to talk. She herself was in her kitchen housework dress, a crisp blue chambray which fitted smoothly over her tightly corseted figure, and her lustrous black hair was done in two smooth braids, wound flat at the back of her head, like a braided rug. She did not stop for a hat—her dark, ruddy, salmon-tinted skin had little to fear from the sun. She opened the half-closed oven door and took out a symmetrically plaited coffee-cake, beautifully browned, delicately peppered over with poppy seeds, with sugary margins about the twists. On the kitchen table a tray stood ready with cups and saucers. She wrapped the cake in a napkin, snatched up a little French coffee-pot with a black wooden handle, and ran across her green lawn, through the alley-way and the sandy, unkept yard next door, and entered her neighbour's house by the kitchen.

The kitchen was hot and empty, full of the untempered afternoon sun. A door stood open into the next room; a cluttered, hideous room, yet somehow homely. There, beside a goods-box covered with figured oilcloth, stood an old woman in a brown calico dress, washing her hot face and neck at a tin basin. She stood with her feet wide apart, in an attitude of profound weariness. She started guiltily as the visitor entered.

"Don't let me disturb you, Grandma," called Mrs. Rosen. "I always have my coffee at dis hour in the afternoon. I was just about to sit down to it when I thought: 'I will run over and see if Grandma Harris won't take a cup with me.' I hate to drink my coffee alone."

Grandma looked troubled,—at a loss. She folded her towel and concealed it behind a curtain hung across the corner of the room to make a poor sort of closet. The old lady was always composed in manner, but it was clear that she felt embarrassment.

"Thank you, Mrs. Rosen. What a pity Victoria just this minute went down town!"

"But dis time I came to see you yourself, Grandma. Don't let me disturb you. Sit down there in your own rocker, and I will put my tray on this little chair between us, so!"

Mrs. Harris sat down in her black wooden rocking-chair with curved arms and a faded cretonne pillow on the wooden seat. It stood in the corner beside a narrow spindle-frame lounge. She looked on silently while Mrs. Rosen uncovered the cake and delicately broke it with her plump, smooth, dusky-red hands. The old lady did not seem pleased,—seemed uncertain and apprehensive, indeed. But she was not fussy or fidgety. She had the kind of quiet, intensely quiet, dignity that comes from complete resignation to the chances of life. She watched Mrs. Rosen's deft hands out of grave, steady brown eyes.

"Dis is Mr. Rosen's favourite coffee-cake, Grandma, and I want you to try it. You are such a good cook yourself, I would like your opinion of my cake."

"It's very nice, ma'am," said Mrs. Harris politely, but without enthusiasm.

"And you aren't drinking your coffee; do you like more cream in it?"

"No, thank you. I'm letting it cool a little. I generally drink it that way."

"Of course she does," thought Mrs. Rosen, "since she ne␣ r has her coffee until all the family are done breakfast!"

Mrs. Rosen had brought Grandma Harris coffee-cake time and again, but she knew that Grandma merely tasted it and saved it for her daughter Victoria, who was as fond of sweets as her own children, and jealous about them, moreover,—couldn't bear that special dainties should come into the house for anyone but herself. Mrs. Rosen, vexed at her failures, had determined that just once she would take a cake to "de old lady Harris," and with her own eyes see her eat it. The result was not all she had hoped. Receiving a visitor alone, unsupervised by her daughter, having cake and coffee that should properly be saved for Victoria, was all so irregular that Mrs. Harris could not enjoy it. Mrs. Rosen doubted if she tasted the cake as she swallowed it,—certainly she ate it without relish, as a hollow form. But Mrs. Rosen enjoyed her own cake, at any rate, and she was glad of an opportunity to sit quietly and look at Grandmother, who was more interesting to her than the handsome Victoria.

It was a queer place to be having coffee, when Mrs. Rosen liked order and comeliness so much: a hideous, cluttered room, furnished with a rocking-horse, a sewing-machine, an empty baby-buggy. A walnut table stood against a blind window, piled high with old magazines and tattered books, and children's caps and coats. There was a wash-stand (two wash-stands, if you counted the oilcloth-covered box as one). A corner of the room was curtained off with some black-and-red-striped cotton goods, for a clothes closet. In another corner was the wooden lounge with a thin mattress and a red calico spread which was Grandma's bed. Beside it was her wooden rocking-chair, and the little splint-bottom chair with the legs sawed short on which her darning-basket usually stood, but which Mrs. Rosen was now using for a tea-table.

The old lady was always impressive, Mrs. Rosen was thinking,— one could not say why. Perhaps it was the way she held her head,— so simply, unprotesting and unprotected; or the gravity of her large, deep-set brown eyes, a warm, reddish brown, though their look, always direct, seemed to ask nothing and hope for nothing. They were not cold, but inscrutable, with no kindling gleam of intercourse in them. There was the kind of nobility about her head that there is

about an old lion's: an absence of self-consciousness, vanity, preoccupation—something absolute. Her grey hair was parted in the middle, wound in two little horns over her ears, and done in a little flat
knot behind. Her mouth was large and composed,—resigned, the
corners drooping. Mrs. Rosen had very seldom heard her laugh (and
then it was a gentle, polite laugh which meant only politeness). But
she had observed that whenever Mrs. Harris's grandchildren were
about, tumbling all over her, asking for cookies, teasing her to read
to them, the old lady looked happy.

As she drank her coffee, Mrs. Rosen tried one subject after another
to engage Mrs. Harris's attention.

"Do you feel this hot weather, Grandma? I am afraid you are over
the stove too much. Let those naughty children have a cold lunch
occasionally."

"No'm, I don't mind the heat. It's apt to come on like this for a
spell in May. I don't feel the stove. I'm accustomed to it."

"Oh, so am I! But I get very impatient with my cooking in hot
weather. Do you miss your old home in Tennessee very much,
Grandma?"

"No'm, I can't say I do. Mr. Templeton thought Colorado was a
better place to bring up the children."

"But you had things much more comfortable down there, I'm sure.
These little wooden houses are too hot in summer."

"Yes'm, we were more comfortable. We had more room."

"And a flower-garden, and beautiful old trees, Mrs. Templeton
told me."

"Yes'm, we had a great deal of shade."

Mrs. Rosen felt that she was not getting anywhere. She almost
believed that Grandma thought she had come on an equivocal errand,
to spy out something in Victoria's absence. Well, perhaps she had!
Just for once she would like to get past the others to the real
grandmother,—and the real grandmother was on her guard, as always.
At this moment she heard a faint miaow. Mrs. Harris rose, lifting
herself by the wooden arms of her chair, said: "Excuse me," went
into the kitchen, and opened the screen door.

In walked a large, handsome, thickly furred Maltese cat, with long
whiskers and yellow eyes and a white star on his breast. He preceded

Grandmother, waited until she sat down. Then he sprang up into her lap and settled himself comfortably in the folds of her full-gathered calico skirt. He rested his chin in his deep bluish fur and regarded Mrs. Rosen. It struck her that he held his head in just the way Grandmother held hers. And Grandmother now became more alive, as if some missing part of herself were restored.

"This is Blue Boy," she said, stroking him. "In winter, when the screen door ain't on, he lets himself in. He stands up on his hind legs and presses the thumb-latch with his paw, and just walks in like anybody."

"He's your cat, isn't he, Grandma?" Mrs. Rosen couldn't help prying just a little; if she could find but a single thing that was Grandma's own!

"He's our cat," replied Mrs. Harris. "We're all very fond of him. I expect he's Vickie's more'n anybody's."

"Of course!" groaned Mrs. Rosen to herself. "Dat Vickie is her mother over again."

Here Mrs. Harris made her first unsolicited remark. "If you was to be troubled with mice at any time, Mrs. Rosen, ask one of the boys to bring Blue Boy over to you, and he'll clear them out. He's a master mouser." She scratched the thick blue fur at the back of his neck, and he began a deep purring. Mrs. Harris smiled. "We call that spinning, back with us. Our children still say: 'Listen to the Blue Boy spin,' though none of 'em is ever heard a spinning-wheel—except maybe Vickie remembers."

"Did you have a spinning-wheel in your own house, Grandma Harris?"

"Yes'm. Miss Sadie Crummer used to come and spin for us. She was left with no home of her own, and it was to give her something to do, as much as anything, that we had her. I spun a good deal myself, in my young days." Grandmother stopped and put her hands on the arms of her chair, as if to rise. "Did you hear a door open? It might be Victoria."

"No, it was the wind shaking the screen door. Mrs. Templeton won't be home yet. She is probably in my husband's store this minute, ordering him about. All the merchants down town will take anything from your daughter. She is very popular wid de gentlemen, Grandma."

Mrs. Harris smiled complacently. "Yes'm. Victoria was always much admired."

At this moment a chorus of laughter broke in upon the warm silence, and a host of children, as it seemed to Mrs. Rosen, ran through the yard. The hand-pump on the back porch, outside the kitchen door, began to scrape and gurgle.

"It's the children, back from school," said Grandma. "They are getting a cool drink."

"But where is the baby, Grandma?"

"Vickie took Hughie in his cart over to Mr. Holliday's yard, where she studies. She's right good about minding him."

Mrs. Rosen was glad to hear that Vickie was good for something.

Three little boys came running in through the kitchen; the twins, aged ten, and Ronald, aged six, who went to kindergarten. They snatched off their caps and threw their jackets and school bags on the table, the sewing-machine, the rocking-horse.

"Howdy do, Mrs. Rosen." They spoke to her nicely. They had nice voices, nice faces, and were always courteous, like their father. "We are going to play in our back yard with some of the boys, Gram'ma," said one of the twins respectfully, and they ran out to join a troop of schoolmates who were already shouting and racing over that poor trampled back yard, strewn with velocipedes and croquet mallets and toy wagons, which was such an eyesore to Mrs. Rosen.

Mrs. Rosen got up and took her tray.

"Can't you stay a little, ma'am? Victoria will be here any minute."

But her tone let Mrs. Rosen know that Grandma really wished her to leave before Victoria returned.

A few moments after Mrs. Rosen had put the tray down in her own kitchen, Victoria Templeton came up the wooden sidewalk, attended by Mr. Rosen, who had quitted his store half an hour earlier than usual for the pleasure of walking home with her. Mrs. Templeton stopped by the picket fence to smile at the children playing in the back yard,—and it was a real smile, she was glad to see them. She called Ronald over to the fence to give him a kiss. He was hot and sticky.

"Was your teacher nice today? Now run in and ask Grandma to wash your face and put a clean waist on you."

II

That night Mrs. Harris got supper with an effort—had to drive herself harder than usual. Mandy, the bound girl they had brought with them from the South, noticed that the old lady was uncertain and short of breath. The hours from two to four, when Mrs. Harris usually rested, had not been at all restful this afternoon. There was an understood rule that Grandmother was not to receive visitors alone. Mrs. Rosen's call, and her cake and coffee, were too much out of the accepted order. Nervousness had prevented the old lady from getting any repose during her visit.

After the rest of the family had left the supper table, she went into the dining-room and took her place, but she ate very little. She put away the food that was left, and then, while Mandy washed the dishes, Grandma sat down in her rocking-chair in the dark and dozed.

The three little boys came in from playing under the electric light (arc lights had been but lately installed in Skyline) and began begging Mrs. Harris to read *Tom Sawyer* to them. Grandmother loved to read, anything at all, the Bible or the continued story in the Chicago weekly paper. She roused herself, lit her brass "safety lamp," and pulled her black rocker out of its corner to the wash-stand (the table was too far away from her corner, and anyhow it was completely covered with coats and school satchels). She put on her old-fashioned silver-rimmed spectacles and began to read. Ronald lay down on Grandmother's lounge bed, and the twins, Albert and Adelbert, called Bert and Del, sat down against the wall, one on a low box covered with felt, and the other on the little sawed-off chair upon which Mrs. Rosen had served coffee. They looked intently at Mrs. Harris, and she looked intently at the book.

Presently Vickie, the oldest grandchild, came in. She was fifteen. Her mother was entertaining callers in the parlour, callers who didn't interest Vickie, so she was on her way up to her own room by the kitchen stairway.

Mrs. Harris looked up over her glasses. "Vickie, maybe you'd take the book awhile, and I can do my darning."

"All right," said Vickie. Reading aloud was one of the things she would always do toward the general comfort. She sat down by the wash-stand and went on with the story. Grandmother got her darning-basket and began to drive her needle across great knee-holes in the boys' stockings. Sometimes she nodded for a moment, and her hands fell into her lap. After a while the little boy on the lounge went to sleep. But the twins sat upright, their hands on their knees, their round brown eyes fastened upon Vickie, and when there was anything funny, they giggled. They were chubby, dark-skinned little boys, with round jolly faces, white teeth, and yellow-brown eyes that were always bubbling with fun unless they were sad,—even then their eyes never got red or weepy. Their tears sparkled and fell; left no trace but a streak on the cheeks, perhaps.

Presently old Mrs. Harris gave out a long snore of utter defeat. She had been overcome at last. Vickie put down the book. "That's enough for tonight. Grandmother's sleepy, and Ronald's fast asleep. What'll we do with him?"

"Bert and me'll get him undressed," said Adelbert. The twins roused the sleepy little boy and prodded him up the back stairway to the bare room without window blinds, where he was put into his cot beside their double bed. Vickie's room was across the narrow hall-way; not much bigger than a closet, but, anyway, it was her own. She had a chair and an old dresser, and beside her bed was a high stool which she used as a lamp-table,—she always read in bed.

After Vickie went upstairs, the house was quiet. Hughie, the baby, was asleep in his mother's room, and Victoria herself, who still treated her husband as if he were her "beau," had persuaded him to take her down town to the ice-cream parlour. Grandmother's room, be-tween the kitchen and the dining-room, was rather like a passage-way; but now that the children were upstairs and Victoria was off enjoying herself somewhere, Mrs. Harris could be sure of enough privacy to undress. She took off the calico cover from her lounge bed and folded it up, put on her nightgown and white nightcap.

Mandy, the bound girl, appeared at the kitchen door.

"Miz' Harris," she said in a guarded tone, ducking her head, "you want me to rub your feet for you?"

For the first time in the long day the old woman's low composure broke a little. "Oh, Mandy, I would take it kindly of you!" she breathed gratefully.

That had to be done in the kitchen; Victoria didn't like anybody slopping about. Mrs. Harris put an old checked shawl round her shoulders and followed Mandy. Beside the kitchen stove Mandy had a little wooden tub full of warm water. She knelt down and untied Mrs. Harris's garter strings and took off her flat cloth slippers and stockings.

"Oh, Miz' Harris, your feet an' legs is swelled turrible tonight!"

"I expect they air, Mandy. They feel like it."

"Pore soul!" murmured Mandy. She put Grandma's feet in the tub and, crouching beside it, slowly, slowly rubbed her swollen legs. Mandy was tired, too. Mrs. Harris sat in her nightcap and shawl, her hands crossed in her lap. She never asked for this greatest solace of the day; it was something that Mandy gave, who had nothing else to give. If there could be a comparison in absolutes, Mandy was the needier of the two,—but she was younger. The kitchen was quiet and full of shadow, with only the light from an old lantern. Neither spoke. Mrs. Harris dozed from comfort, and Mandy herself was half asleep as she performed one of the oldest rites of compassion.

Although Mrs. Harris's lounge had no springs, only a thin cotton mattress between her and the wooden slats, she usually went to sleep as soon as she was in bed. To be off her feet, to lie flat, to say over the psalm beginning: "*The Lord is my shepherd,*" was comfort enough. About four o'clock in the morning, however, she would begin to feel the hard slats under her, and the heaviness of the old home-made quilts, with weight but little warmth, on top of her. Then she would reach under her pillow for her little comforter (she called it that to herself) that Mrs. Rosen had given her. It was a tan sweater of very soft brushed wool, with one sleeve torn and ragged. A young nephew from Chicago had spent a fortnight with Mrs. Rosen last summer and had left this behind him. One morning, when Mrs. Harris went out to the stable at the back of the yard to pat Buttercup, the cow, Mrs. Rosen ran across the alley-way.

"Grandma Harris," she said, coming into the shelter of the stable, "I wonder if you could make any use of this sweater Sammy left? The yarn might be good for your darning."

Mrs. Harris felt of the article gravely. Mrs. Rosen thought her face brightened. "Yes'm, indeed I could use it. I thank you kindly."

She slipped it under her apron, carried it into the house with her, and concealed it under her mattress. There she had kept it ever since. She knew Mrs. Rosen understood how it was; that Victoria couldn't bear to have anything come into the house that was not for her to dispose of.

On winter nights, and even on summer nights after the cocks began to crow, Mrs. Harris often felt cold and lonely about the chest. Sometimes her cat, Blue Boy, would creep in beside her and warm that aching spot. But on spring and summer nights he was likely to be abroad skylarking, and this little sweater had become the dearest of Grandmother's few possessions. It was kinder to her, she used to think, as she wrapped it about her middle, than any of her own children had been. She had married at eighteen and had had eight children; but some died, and some were, as she said, scattered.

After she was warm in that tender spot under the ribs, the old woman could lie patiently on the slats, waiting for daybreak; thinking about the comfortable rambling old house in Tennessee, its feather beds and hand-woven rag carpets and splint-bottom chairs, the mahogany sideboard, and the marble-top parlour table; all that she had left behind to follow Victoria's fortunes.

She did not regret her decision; indeed, there had been no decision. Victoria had never once thought it possible that Ma should not go wherever she and the children went, and Mrs. Harris had never thought it possible. Of course she regretted Tennessee, though she would never admit it to Mrs. Rosen:—the old neighbours, the yard and garden she had worked in all her life, the apple trees she had planted, the lilac arbour, tall enough to walk in, which she had clipped and shaped so many years. Especially she missed her lemon tree, in a tub on the front porch, which bore little lemons almost every summer, and folks would come for miles to see it.

But the road had led westward, and Mrs. Harris didn't believe that women, especially old women, could say when or where they would stop. They were tied to the chariot of young life, and had to go where it went, because they were needed. Mrs. Harris had gathered from Mrs. Rosen's manner, and from comments she occasionally dropped, that the Jewish people had an altogether different attitude toward their old folks; therefore her friendship with this kind neighbour was almost as disturbing as it was pleasant. She didn't want Mrs. Rosen to think that she was "put upon," that there was anything unusual or pitiful in her lot. To be pitied was the deepest hurt anybody could know. And if Victoria once suspected Mrs. Rosen's indignation, it would be all over. She would freeze her neighbour out, and that friendly voice, that quick pleasant chatter with the little foreign twist, would thenceforth be heard only at a distance, in the alley-way or across the fence. Victoria had a good heart, but she was terribly proud and could not bear the least criticism.

As soon as the grey light began to steal into the room, Mrs. Harris would get up softly and wash at the basin on the oilcloth-covered box. She would wet her hair above her forehead, comb it with a little bone comb set in a tin rim, do it up in two smooth little horns over her ears, wipe the comb dry, and put it away in the pocket of her full-gathered calico skirt. She left nothing lying about. As soon as she was dressed, she made her bed, folding her nightgown and nightcap under the pillow, the sweater under the mattress. She smoothed the heavy quilts, and drew the red calico spread neatly over all. Her towel was hung on its special nail behind the curtain. Her soap she kept in a tin tobacco-box; the children's soap was in a crockery saucer. If her soap or towel got mixed up with the children's, Victoria was always sharp about it. The little rented house was much too small for the family, and Mrs. Harris and her "things" were almost required to be invisible. Two clean calico dresses hung in the curtained corner; another was on her back, and a fourth was in the wash. Behind the curtain there was always a good supply of aprons; Victoria bought them at church fairs, and it was a great satisfaction to Mrs. Harris to put on a clean one whenever she liked. Upstairs, in Mandy's attic room over the kitchen, hung a black cashmere dress and a black bonnet with a long crêpe veil, for the rare occasions when Mr. Templeton hired a double buggy and horses and drove the family to

a picnic or to Decoration Day exercises. Mrs. Harris rather dreaded
these drives, for Victoria was usually cross afterwards.

When Mrs. Harris went out into the kitchen to get breakfast,
Mandy always had the fire started and the water boiling. They enjoyed
a quiet half-hour before the little boys came running down the stairs,
always in a good humour. In winter the boys had their breakfast in
the kitchen, with Vickie. Mrs. Harris made Mandy eat the cakes and
fried ham the children left, so that she would not fast so long. Mr.
and Mrs. Templeton breakfasted rather late, in the dining-room, and
they always had fruit and thick cream,—a small pitcher of the very
thickest was for Mrs. Templeton. The children were never fussy about
their food. As Grandmother often said feelingly to Mrs. Rosen, they
were as little trouble as children could possibly be. They sometimes
tore their clothes, of course, or got sick. But even when Albert had
an abscess in his ear and was in such pain, he would lie for hours
on Grandmother's lounge with his cheek on a bag of hot salt, if only
she or Vickie would read aloud to him.

"It's true, too, what de old lady says," remarked Mrs. Rosen to
her husband one night at supper, "dey are nice children. No one ever
taught them anything, but they have good instincts, even dat Vickie.
And think, if you please, of all the self-sacrificing mothers we know,—
Fannie and Esther, to come near home; how they have planned for
those children from infancy and given them every advantage. And
now ingratitude and coldness is what dey meet with."

Mr. Rosen smiled his teasing smile. "Evidently your sister and mine
have the wrong method. The way to make your children unselfish is
to be comfortably selfish yourself."

"But dat woman takes no more responsibility for her children than
a cat takes for her kittens. Nor does poor young Mr. Templeton, for
dat matter. How can he expect to get so many children started in
life, I ask you? It is not at all fair!"

Mr. Rosen sometimes had to hear altogether too much about the
Templetons, but he was patient, because it was a bitter sorrow to
Mrs. Rosen that she had no children. There was nothing else in the
world she wanted so much.

III

Mrs. Rosen in one of her blue working dresses, the indigo blue that became a dark skin and dusky red cheeks with a tone of salmon colour, was in her shining kitchen, washing her beautiful dishes—her neighbours often wondered why she used her best china and linen every day—when Vickie Templeton came in with a book under her arm.

"Good day, Mrs. Rosen. Can I have the second volume?"

"Certainly. You know where the books are." She spoke coolly, for it always annoyed her that Vickie never suggested wiping the dishes or helping with such household work as happened to be going on when she dropped in. She hated the girl's bringing-up so much that sometimes she almost hated the girl.

Vickie strolled carelessly through the dining-room into the parlour and opened the doors of one of the big bookcases. Mr. Rosen had a large library, and a great many unusual books. There was a complete set of the Waverley Novels in German, for example; thick, dumpy little volumes bound in tooled leather, with very black type and dramatic engravings printed on wrinkled, yellowing pages. There were many French books, and some of the German classics done into English, such as Coleridge's translation of Schiller's *Wallenstein.*

Of course no other house in Skyline was in the least like Mrs. Rosen's; it was the nearest thing to an art gallery and a museum that the Templetons had ever seen. All the rooms were carpeted alike (that was very unusual), with a soft velvet carpet, little blue and rose flowers scattered on a rose-grey ground. The deep chairs were upholstered in dark blue velvet. The walls were hung with engravings in pale gold frames: some of Raphael's "Hours," a large soft engraving of a castle on the Rhine, and another of cypress trees about a Roman ruin, under a full moon. There were a number of water-colour sketches, made in Italy by Mr. Rosen himself when he was a boy. A rich uncle had taken him abroad as his secretary. Mr. Rosen was a reflective, unambitious man, who didn't mind keeping a clothing-store in a little Western town, so long as he had a great deal of time to read philosophy. He was the only unsuccessful member of a large, rich Jewish family.

Last August, when the heat was terrible in Skyline, and the crops were burned up on all the farms to the north, and the wind from the pink and yellow sand-hills to the south blew so hot that it singed the few green lawns in the town, Vickie had taken to dropping in upon Mrs. Rosen at the very hottest part of the afternoon. Mrs. Rosen knew, of course, that it was probably because the girl had no other cool and quiet place to go——her room at home under the roof would be hot enough! Now, Mrs. Rosen liked to undress and take a nap from three to five,——if only to get out of her tight corsets, for she would have an hour-glass figure at any cost. She told Vickie firmly that she was welcome to come if she would read in the parlour with the blind up only a little way, and would be as still as a mouse. Vickie came, meekly enough, but she seldom read. She would take a sofa pillow and lie down on the soft carpet and look up at the pictures in the dusky room, and feel a happy, pleasant excitement from the heat and glare outside and the deep shadow and quiet within. Curiously enough, Mrs. Rosen's house never made her dissatisfied with her own; she thought that very nice, too.

Mrs. Rosen, leaving her kitchen in a state of such perfection as the Templetons were unable to sense or to admire, came into the parlour and found her visitor sitting cross-legged on the floor before one of the bookcases.

"Well, Vickie, and how did you get along with *Wilhelm Meister?*"

"I like it," said Vickie.

Mrs. Rosen shrugged. The Templetons always said that; quite as if a book or a cake were lucky to win their approbation.

"Well, *what* did you like?"

"I guess I liked all that about the theatre and Shakspere best."

"It's rather celebrated," remarked Mrs. Rosen dryly. "And are you studying every day? Do you think you will be able to win that scholarship?"

"I don't know. I'm going to try awful hard."

Mrs. Rosen wondered whether any Templeton knew how to try very hard. She reached for her work-basket and began to do cross-stitch. It made her nervous to sit with folded hands.

Vickie was looking at a German book in her lap, an illustrated edition of *Faust*. She had stopped at a very German picture of Gretchen entering the church, with Faustus gazing at her from behind a rose tree, Mephisto at his shoulder.

"I wish I could read this," she said, frowning at the black Gothic text. "It's splendid, isn't it?"

Mrs. Rosen rolled her eyes upward and sighed. "Oh, my dear, one of de world's masterpieces!"

That meant little to Vickie. She had not been taught to respect masterpieces, she had no scale of that sort in her mind. She cared about a book only because it took hold of her.

She kept turning over the pages. Between the first and second parts, in this edition, there was inserted the *Dies Iræ* hymn in full. She stopped and puzzled over it for a long while.

"Here is something I can read," she said, showing the page to Mrs. Rosen.

Mrs. Rosen looked up from her cross-stitch. "There you have the advantage of me. I do not read Latin. You might translate it for me."

Vickie began:

> "Day of wrath, upon that day
> The world to ashes melts away,
> As David and the Sibyl say.

"But that don't give you the rhyme; every line ought to end in two syllables."

"Never mind if it doesn't give the metre," corrected Mrs. Rosen kindly; "go on, if you can."

Vickie went on stumbling through the Latin verses, and Mrs. Rosen sat watching her. You couldn't tell about Vickie. She wasn't pretty, yet Mrs. Rosen found her attractive. She liked her sturdy build and the steady vitality that glowed in her rosy skin and dark blue eyes,— even gave a springy quality to her curly reddish-brown hair, which she still wore in a single braid down her back. Mrs. Rosen liked to have Vickie about because she was never listless or dreamy or apathetic. A half-smile nearly always played about her lips and eyes, and it was there because she was pleased with something, not because she wanted to be agreeable. Even a half-smile made her cheeks dimple. She had what her mother called "a happy disposition."

When she finished the verses, Mrs. Rosen nodded approvingly. "Thank you, Vickie. The very next time I go to Chicago, I will try to get an English translation of *Faust* for you."

"But I want to read this one." Vickie's open smile darkened. "What I want is to pick up any of these books and just read them, like you and Mr. Rosen do."

The dusky red of Mrs. Rosen's cheeks grew a trifle deeper. Vickie never paid compliments, absolutely never; but if she really admired anyone, something in her voice betrayed it so convincingly that one felt flattered. When she dropped a remark of this kind, she added another link to the chain of responsibility which Mrs. Rosen unwillingly bore and tried to shake off—the irritating sense of being somehow responsible for Vickie, since, God knew, no one else felt responsible.

Once or twice, when she happened to meet pleasant young Mr. Templeton alone, she had tried to talk to him seriously about his daughter's future. "She has finished de school here, and she should be getting training of some sort; she is growing up," she told him severely.

He laughed and said in his way that was so honest, and so disarmingly sweet and frank: "Oh, don't remind me, Mrs. Rosen! I just pretend to myself she isn't. I want to keep my little daughter as long as I can." And there it ended.

Sometimes Vickie Templeton seemed so dense, so utterly unperceptive, that Mrs. Rosen was ready to wash her hands of her. Then some queer streak of sensibility in the child would make her change her mind. Last winter, when Mrs. Rosen came home from a visit to her sister in Chicago, she brought with her a new cloak of the sleeveless dolman type, black velvet, lined with grey and white squirrel skins, a grey skin next a white. Vickie, so indifferent to clothes, fell in love with that cloak. Her eyes followed it with delight whenever Mrs. Rosen wore it. She found it picturesque, romantic. Mrs. Rosen had been captivated by the same thing in the cloak, and had bought it with a shrug, knowing it would be quite out of place in Skyline; and Mr. Rosen, when she first produced it from her trunk, had laughed and said; "Where did you get that?—out of *Rigoletto*?" It looked like that—but how could Vickie know?

Vickie's whole family puzzled Mrs. Rosen; their feelings were so much finer than their way of living. She bought milk from the Templetons because they kept a cow—which Mandy milked,—and every night one of the twins brought the milk to her in a tin pail. Whichever boy brought it, she always called him Albert—she thought Adelbert a silly, Southern name.

One night when she was fitting the lid on an empty pail, she said severely:

"Now, Albert, I have put some cookies for Grandma in this pail, wrapped in a napkin. And they are for Grandma, remember, not for your mother or Vickie."

"Yes'm."

When she turned to him to give him the pail, she saw two full crystal globes in the little boy's eyes, just ready to break. She watched him go softly down the path and dash those tears away with the back of his hand. She was sorry. She hadn't thought the little boys realized that their household was somehow a queer one.

Queer or not, Mrs. Rosen liked to go there better than to most houses in the town. There was something easy, cordial, and carefree in the parlour that never smelled of being shut up, and the ugly furniture looked hospitable. One felt a pleasantness in the human relationships. These people didn't seem to know there were such things as struggle or exactness or competition in the world. They were always genuinely glad to see you, had time to see you, and were usually gay in mood—all but Grandmother, who had the kind of gravity that people who take thought of human destiny must have. But even she liked light-heartedness in others; she drudged, indeed, to keep it going.

There were houses that were better kept, certainly, but the housekeepers had no charm, no gentleness of manner, were like hard little machines, most of them; and some were grasping and narrow. The Templetons were not selfish or scheming. Anyone could take advantage of them, and many people did. Victoria might eat all the cookies her neighbour sent in, but she would give away anything she had. She was always ready to lend her dresses and hats and bits of jewellery for the school theatricals, and she never worked people for favours.

As for Mr. Templeton (people usually called him "young Mr.

Templeton"), he was too delicate to collect his just debts. His boyish, eager-to-please manner, his fair complexion and blue eyes and young face, made him seem very soft to some of the hard old money-grubbers on Main Street, and the fact that he always said "Yes, sir," and "No, sir," to men older than himself furnished a good deal of amusement to by-standers.

Two years ago, when this Templeton family came to Skyline and moved into the house next door, Mrs. Rosen was inconsolable. The new neighbours had a lot of children, who would always be making a racket. They put a cow and a horse into the empty barn, which would mean dirt and flies. They strewed their back yard with packing-cases and did not pick them up.

She first met Mrs. Templeton at an afternoon card party, in a house at the extreme north end of the town, fully half a mile away, and she had to admit that her new neighbour was an attractive woman, and that there was something warm and genuine about her. She wasn't in the least willowy or languishing, as Mrs. Rosen had usually found Southern ladies to be. She was high-spirited and direct; a trifle imperious, but with a shade of diffidence, too, as if she was trying to adjust herself to a new group of people and to do the right thing.

While they were at the party, a blinding snowstorm came on, with a hard wind. Since they lived next door to each other, Mrs. Rosen and Mrs. Templeton struggled homeward together through the blizzard. Mrs. Templeton seemed delighted with the rough weather; she laughed like a big country girl whenever she made a mis-step off the obliterated sidewalk and sank up to her knees in a snow-drift.

"Take care, Mrs. Rosen," she kept calling, "keep to the right! Don't spoil your nice coat. My, ain't this real winter? We never had it like this back with us."

When they reached the Templeton's gate, Victoria wouldn't hear of Mrs. Rosen's going farther. "No, indeed, Mrs. Rosen, you come right in with me and get dry, and Ma'll make you a hot toddy while I take the baby."

By this time Mrs. Rosen had begun to like her neighbour, so she went in. To her surprise, the parlour was neat and comfortable—the children did not strew things about there, apparently. The hard-coal burner threw out a warm red glow. A faded, respectable Brussels carpet covered the floor, an old-fashioned wooden clock ticked on the walnut bookcase. There were a few easy chairs, and no hideous ornaments about. She rather liked the old oil-chromos on the wall: "Hagar and Ishmael in the Wilderness," and "The Light of the World." While Mrs. Rosen dried her feet on the nickel base of the stove, Mrs. Templeton excused herself and withdrew to the next room,—her bedroom,—took off her silk dress and corsets, and put on a white challis négligée. She reappeared with the baby, who was not crying, exactly, but making eager, passionate, gasping entreaties,— faster and faster, tenser and tenser, as he felt his dinner nearer and nearer and yet not his.

Mrs. Templeton sat down in a low rocker by the stove and began to nurse him, holding him snugly but carelessly, still talking to Mrs. Rosen about the card party, and laughing about their wade home through the snow. Hughie, the baby, fell to work so fiercely that beads of sweat came out all over his flushed forehead. Mrs. Rosen could not help admiring him and his mother. They were so comfortable and complete. When he was changed to the other side, Hughie resented the interruption a little; but after a time he became soft and bland, as smooth as oil, indeed; began looking about him as he drew in his milk. He finally dropped the nipple from his lips altogether, turned on his mother's arm, and looked inquiringly at Mrs. Rosen.

"What a beautiful baby!" she exclaimed from her heart. And he was. A sort of golden baby. His hair was like sunshine, and his long lashes were gold over such gay blue eyes. There seemed to be a gold glow in his soft pink skin, and he had the smile of a cherub.

"We think he's a pretty boy," said Mrs. Templeton. "He's the prettiest of my babies. Though the twins were mighty cunning little fellows. I hated the idea of twins, but the minute I saw them, I couldn't resist them."

Just then old Mrs. Harris came in, walking widely in her full-gathered skirt and felt-soled shoes, bearing a tray with two smoking goblets upon it.

"This is my mother, Mrs. Harris, Mrs. Rosen," said Mrs. Templeton.

"I'm glad to know you, ma'am," said Mrs. Harris. "Victoria, let me take the baby, while you two ladies have your toddy."

"Oh, don't take him away, Mrs. Harris, please!" cried Mrs. Rosen.

The old lady smiled. "I won't. I'll set right here. He never frets with his grandma."

When Mrs. Rosen had finished her excellent drink she asked if she might hold the baby, and Mrs. Harris placed him on her lap. He made a few rapid boxing motions with his two fists, then braced himself on his heels and the back of his head, and lifted himself up in an arc. When he dropped back, he looked up at Mrs. Rosen with his most intimate smile. "See what a smart boy I am!"

When Mrs. Rosen walked home, feeling her way through the snow by following the fence, she knew she could never stay away from a house where there was a baby like that one.

IV

Vickie did her studying in a hammock hung between two tall cottonwood trees over in the Roadmaster's green yard. The Roadmaster had the finest yard in Skyline, on the edge of the town, just where the sandy plain and the sage-brush began. His family went back to Ohio every summer, and Bert and Del Templeton were paid to take care of his lawn, to turn the sprinkler on at the right hours and to cut the grass. They were really too little to run the heavy lawn-mower very well, but they were able to manage because they were twins. Each took one end of the handle-bar, and they pushed together like a pair of fat Shetland ponies. They were very proud of being able to keep the lawn so nice, and worked hard on it. They cut Mrs. Rosen's grass once a week, too, and did it so well that she wondered why in the world they never did anything about their own yard. They didn't have city water, to be sure (it was expensive), but she thought they might pick up a few velocipedes and iron hoops, and dig up the messy "flower-bed," that was even uglier than the naked gravel spots. She was particularly offended by a deep ragged ditch, a miniature arroyo, which ran across the back yard, serving no purpose and looking very dreary.

One morning she said craftily to the twins, when she was paying them for cutting her grass:

"And, boys, why don't you just shovel the sand-pile by your fence into dat ditch, and make your back yard smooth?"

"Oh, no, ma'am," said Adelbert with feeling. "We like to have the ditch to build bridges over!"

Ever since vacation began, the twins had been busy getting the Roadmaster's yard ready for the Methodist lawn party. When Mrs. Holliday, the Roadmaster's wife, went away for the summer, she always left a key with the Ladies' Aid Society and invited them to give their ice-cream social at her place.

This year the date set for the party was June fifteenth. The day was a particularly fine one, and as Mr. Holliday himself had been called to Cheyenne on railroad business, the twins felt personally responsible for everything. They got out to the Holliday place early in the morning, and stayed on guard all day. Before noon the drayman brought a wagonload of card-tables and folding chairs, which the boys placed in chosen spots under the cottonwood trees. In the afternoon the Methodist ladies arrived and opened up the kitchen to receive the freezers of home-made ice-cream, and the cakes which the congregation donated. Indeed, all the good cake-bakers in town were expected to send a cake. Grandma Harris baked a white cake, thickly iced and covered with freshly grated coconut, and Vickie took it over in the afternoon.

Mr. and Mrs. Rosen, because they belonged to no church, con-tributed to the support of all, and usually went to the church suppers in winter and the socials in summer. On this warm June evening they set out early, in order to take a walk first. They strolled along the hard gravelled road that led out through the sage toward the sand-hills; tonight it led toward the moon, just rising over the sweep of dunes. The sky was almost as blue as at midday, and had that look of being very near and very soft which it has in desert countries. The moon, too, looked very near, soft and bland and innocent. Mrs. Rosen admitted that in the Adirondacks, for which she was always secretly homesick in summer, the moon had a much colder brilliance, seemed farther off and made of a harder metal. This moon gave the sage-brush plain and the drifted sand-hills the softness of velvet. All countries were beautiful to Mr. Rosen. He carried a country of his own in his mind, and was able to unfold it like a tent in any wilderness.

When they at last turned back toward the town, they saw groups of people, women in white dresses, walking toward the dark spot where the paper lanterns made a yellow light underneath the cottonwoods. High above, the rustling tree-tops stirred free in the flood of moonlight.

The lighted yard was surrounded by a low board fence, painted the dark red Burlington colour, and as the Rosens drew near, they noticed four children standing close together in the shadow of some tall elder bushes just outside the fence. They were the poor Maude children; their mother was the washwoman, the Rosens' laundress and the Templetons'. People said that every one of those children had a different father. But good laundresses were few, and even the members of the Ladies' Aid were glad to get Mrs. Maude's services at a dollar a day, though they didn't like their children to play with hers. Just as the Rosens approached, Mrs. Templeton came out from the lighted square, leaned over the fence, and addressed the little Maudes.

"I expect you children forgot your dimes, now didn't you? Never mind, here's a dime for each of you, so come along and have your ice-cream."

The Maudes put out small hands and said: "Thank you," but not one of them moved.

"Come along, Francie" (the oldest girl was named Frances). "Climb right over the fence." Mrs. Templeton reached over and gave her a hand, and the little boys quickly scrambled after their sister. Mrs. Templeton took them to a table which Vickie and the twins had just selected as being especially private—they liked to do things together.

"Here, Vickie, let the Maudes sit at your table, and take care they get plenty of cake."

The Rosens had followed close behind Mrs. Templeton, and Mr. Rosen now overtook her and said in his most courteous and friendly manner: "Good evening, Mrs. Templeton. Will you have ice-cream with us?" He always used the local idioms, though his voice and enunciation made them sound altogether different from Skyline speech.

"Indeed I will, Mr. Rosen. Mr. Templeton will be late. He went out to his farm yesterday, and I don't know just when to expect him."

Vickie and the twins were disappointed at not having their table to themselves, when they had come early and found a nice one; but they knew it was right to look out for the dreary little Maudes, so they moved close together and made room for them. The Maudes didn't cramp them long. When the three boys had eaten the last crumb of cake and licked their spoons, Francie got up and led them to a green slope by the fence, just outside the lighted circle. "Now set down, and watch and see how folks do," she told them. The boys looked to Francie for commands and support. She was really Amos Maude's child, born before he ran away to the Klondike, and it had been rubbed into them that this made a difference.

The Templeton children made their ice-cream linger out, and sat watching the crowd. They were glad to see their mother go to Mr. Rosen's table, and noticed how nicely he placed a chair for her and insisted upon putting a scarf about her shoulders. Their mother was wearing her new dotted Swiss, with many ruffles, all edged with black ribbon, and wide ruffly sleeves. As the twins watched her over their spoons, they thought how much prettier their mother was than any of the other women, and how becoming her new dress was. The children got as much satisfaction as Mrs. Harris out of Victoria's good looks.

Mr. Rosen was well pleased with Mrs. Templeton and her new dress, and with her kindness to the little Maudes. He thought her manner with them just right,—warm, spontaneous, without anything patronizing. He always admired her way with her own children, though Mrs. Rosen thought it too casual. Being a good mother, he believed, was much more a matter of physical poise and richness than of sentimentalizing and reading doctor-books. Tonight he was more talkative than usual, and in his quiet way made Mrs. Templeton feel his real friendliness and admiration. Unfortunately, he made other people feel it, too.

Mrs. Jackson, a neighbour who didn't like the Templetons, had been keeping an eye on Mr. Rosen's table. She was a stout square

woman of imperturbable calm, effective in regulating the affairs of
the community because she never lost her temper, and could say the
most cutting things in calm, even kindly, tones. Her face was smooth
and placid as a mask, rather good-humoured, and the fact that one
eye had a cast and looked askance made it the more difficult to see
through her intentions. When she had been lingering about the Rosens' table for some time, studying Mr. Rosen's pleasant attentions
to Mrs. Templeton, she brought up a trayful of cake.

"You folks are about ready for another helping," she remarked
affably.

Mrs. Rosen spoke. "I want some of Grandma Harris's cake. It's a
white coconut, Mrs. Jackson."

"How about you, Mrs. Templeton, would you like some of your
own cake?"

"Indeed I would," said Mrs. Templeton heartily. "Ma said she had
good luck with it. I didn't see it. Vickie brought it over."

Mrs. Jackson deliberately separated the slices on her tray with two
forks. "Well," she remarked with a chuckle that really sounded
amiable, "I don't know but I'd like my cakes, if I kept somebody in
the kitchen to bake them for me."

Mr. Rosen for once spoke quickly. "If I had a cook like Grandma
Harris in my kitchen, I'd live in it!" he declared.

Mrs. Jackson smiled. "I don't know as we feel like that, Mrs.
Templeton? I tell Mr. Jackson that my idea of coming up in the world
would be to forget I had a cook-stove, like Mrs. Templeton. But we
can't all be lucky."

Mr. Rosen could not tell how much was malice and how much
was stupidity. What he chiefly detected was self-satisfaction; the
craftiness of the coarse-fibred country girl putting catch questions to
the teacher. Yes, he decided, the woman was merely showing off—
she regarded it as an accomplishment to make people uncomfortable.

Mrs. Templeton didn't at once take it in. Her training was all to
the end that you must give a guest everything you have, even if he
happens to be your worst enemy, and that to cause anyone embarrassment is a frightful and humiliating blunder. She felt hurt without
knowing just why, but all evening it kept growing clearer to her that

this was another of those thrusts from the outside which she couldn't understand. The neighbours were sure to take sides against her, apparently, if they came often to see her mother.

Mr. Rosen tried to distract Mrs. Templeton but he could feel the poison working. On the way home the children knew something had displeased or hurt their mother. When they went into the house, she told them to go upstairs at once, as she had a headache. She was severe and distant. When Mrs. Harris suggested making her some peppermint tea, Victoria threw up her chin.

"I don't want anybody waiting on me. I just want to be let alone." And she withdrew without saying good-night, or "Are you all right, Ma?" as she usually did.

Left alone, Mrs. Harris sighed and began to turn down her bed. She knew, as well as if she had been at the social, what kind of thing had happened. Some of those prying ladies of the Woman's Relief Corps, or the Woman's Christian Temperance Union, had been intimating to Victoria that her mother was "put upon." Nothing ever made Victoria cross but criticism. She was jealous of small attentions paid to Mrs. Harris, because she felt they were paid "behind her back" or "over her head," in a way that implied reproach to her. Victoria had been a belle in their own town in Tennessee, but here she was not very popular, no matter how many pretty dresses she wore, and she couldn't bear it. She felt as if her mother and Mr. Templeton must be somehow to blame; at least they ought to protect her from whatever was disagreeable—they always had!

V

Mrs. Harris wakened at about four o'clock, as usual, before the house was stirring, and lay thinking about their position in this new town. She didn't know why the neighbours acted so; she was as much in the dark as Victoria. At home, back in Tennessee, her place in the family was not exceptional, but perfectly regular. Mrs. Harris had replied to Mrs. Rosen, when that lady asked why in the world she didn't break Vickie in to help her in the kitchen: "We are only young once, and trouble comes soon enough." Young girls, in the South, were supposed to be carefree and foolish; the fault Grandmother found in Vickie was that she wasn't foolish enough. When the foolish girl married and began to have children, everything else must give way to that. She must be humoured and given the best of everything, because having children was hard on a woman, and it was the most important thing in the world. In Tennessee every young married woman in good circumstances had an older woman in the house, a mother or mother-in-law or an old aunt, who managed the household economies and directed the help.

That was the great difference; in Tennessee there had been plenty of helpers. There was old Miss Sadie Crummer, who came to the house to spin and sew and mend; old Mrs. Smith, who always arrived to help at butchering- and preserving-time; Lizzie, the coloured girl, who did the washing and who ran in every day to help Mandy. There were plenty more, who came whenever one of Lizzie's bare-foot boys ran to fetch them. The hills were full of solitary old women, or women but slightly attached to some household, who were glad to come to Miz' Harris's for good food and a warm bed, and the little present that either Mrs. Harris or Victoria slipped into their carpet-sack when they went away.

To be sure, Mrs. Harris, and the other women of her age who managed their daughter's house, kept in the background; but it was their own background, and they ruled it jealously. They left the front porch and the parlour to the young married couple and their young friends; the old women spent most of their lives in the kitchen and pantries and back dining-room. But there they ordered life to their own taste, entertained their friends, dispensed charity, and heard the troubles of the poor. Moreover, back there it was Grandmother's own house they lived in. Mr. Templeton came of a superior family and had what Grandmother called "blood," but no property. He never so much as mended one of the steps to the front porch without consulting Mrs. Harris. Even "back home," in the aristocracy, there were old women who went on living like young ones—gave parties and drove out in their carriage and "went North" in the summer. But among the middle-class people and the country-folk, when a woman was a widow and had married daughters, she considered herself an old woman and wore full-gathered black dresses and a black bonnet and became a housekeeper. She accepted this estate unprotestingly, almost gratefully.

The Templetons' troubles began when Mr. Templeton's aunt died and left him a few thousand dollars, and he got the idea of bettering himself. The twins were little then, and he told Mrs. Harris his boys would have a better chance in Colorado—everybody was going West. He went alone first, and got a good position with a mining company in the mountains of southern Colorado. He had been book-keeper in the bank in his home town, had "grown up in the bank," as they said. He was industrious and honourable, and the managers of the mining company liked him, even if they laughed at his polite, soft-spoken manners. He could have held his position indefinitely, and maybe got a promotion. But the altitude of that mountain town was too high for his family. All the children were sick there; Mrs. Templeton was ill most of the time and nearly died when Ronald was born. Hillary Templeton lost his courage and came north to the flat, sunny, semi-arid country between Wray and Cheyenne, to work for an irrigation project. So far, things had not gone well with him. The pinch told on everyone, but most on Grandmother. Here, in Skyline, she had all her accustomed responsibilities, and no helper but Mandy. Mrs. Harris was no longer living in a feudal society, where there were plenty of landless people, glad to render service to the more fortunate, but in a snappy little Western democracy, where every man was as good as his neighbour and out to prove it.

Neither Mrs. Harris nor Mrs. Templeton understood just what was the matter; they were hurt and dazed, merely. Victoria knew that here she was censured and criticized, she who had always been so admired and envied! Grandmother knew that these meddlesome "Northerners" said things that made Victoria suspicious and unlike herself; made her unwilling that Mrs. Harris should receive visitors alone, or accept marks of attention that seemed offered in compassion for her state.

These women who belonged to clubs and Relief Corps lived differently, Mrs. Harris knew, but she herself didn't like the way they lived. She believed that somebody ought to be in the parlour, and somebody in the kitchen. She wouldn't for the world have had Victoria go about every morning in a short gingham dress, with bare arms, and a dust-cap on her head to hide the curling-kids, as these brisk housekeepers did. To Mrs. Harris that would have meant real poverty, coming down in the world so far that one could no longer keep up appearances. Her life was hard now, to be sure, since the family went on increasing and Mr. Templeton's means went on decreasing; but she certainly valued respectability above personal comfort, and she could go on a good way yet if they always had a cool pleasant parlour, with Victoria properly dressed to receive visitors. To keep Victoria different from these "ordinary" women meant everything to Mrs. Harris. She realized that Mrs. Rosen managed to be mistress of any situation, either in kitchen or parlour, but that was because she was "foreign." Grandmother perfectly understood that their neighbour had a superior cultivation which made everything she did an exercise of skill. She knew well enough that their own ways of cooking and cleaning were primitive beside Mrs. Rosen's.

If only Mr. Templeton's business affairs would look up, they could rent a larger house, and everything would be better. They might even get a German girl to come in and help—but now there was no place to put her. Grandmother's own lot could improve only with the family fortunes—any comfort for herself, aside from that of the family, was inconceivable to her; and on the other hand she could have no real unhappiness while the children were well, and good, and fond of her and their mother. That was why it was worth while to get up early in the morning and make her bed neat and draw the red spread smooth. The little boys loved to lie on her lounge and her pillows when they were tired. When they were sick, Ronald and Hughie wanted to be in her lap. They had no physical shrinking from her because she was old. And Victoria was never jealous of the children's wanting to be with her so much; that was a mercy!

Sometimes, in the morning, if her feet ached more than usual, Mrs. Harris felt a little low. (Nobody did anything about broken arches in those days, and the common endurance test of old age was to keep going after every step cost something.) She would hang up her towel with a sigh and go into the kitchen, feeling that it was hard to make a start. But the moment she heard the children running down the uncarpeted back stairs, she forgot to be low. Indeed, she ceased to be an individual, an old woman with aching feet; she became part of a group, became a relationship. She was drunk up into their freshness when they burst in upon her, telling her about their dreams, explaining their troubles with buttons and shoe-laces and underwear shrunk too small. The tired, solitary old woman Grandmother had been at daybreak vanished; suddenly the morning seemed as important to her as it did to the children, and the morning ahead stretched out sunshiny, important.

VI

The day after the Methodist social, Blue Boy didn't come for his morning milk; he always had it in a clean saucer on the covered back porch, under the long bench where the tin wash-tubs stood ready for Mrs. Maude. After the children had finished breakfast, Mrs. Harris sent Mandy out to look for the cat.

The girl came back in a minute, her eyes big.

"Law me, Miz' Harris, he's awful sick. He's a-layin' in the straw in the barn. He's swallered a bone, or havin' a fit or somethin.' "

Grandmother threw an apron over her head and went out to see for herself. The children went with her. Blue Boy was retching and choking, and his yellow eyes were filled up with rheum.

"Oh, Gram'ma, what's the matter?" the boys cried.

"It's the distemper. How could he have got it?" Her voice was so harsh that Ronald began to cry. "Take Ronald back to the house, Del. He might get bit. I wish I'd kept my word and never had a cat again!"

"Why, Gram'ma!" Albert looked at her. "Won't Blue Boy get well?"

"Not from the distemper, he won't."

"But Gram'ma, can't I run for the veter'nary?"

"You gether up an armful of hay. We'll take him into the coal-house, where I can watch him."

Mrs. Harris waited until the spasm was over, then picked up the limp cat and carried him to the coal-shed that opened off the back porch. Albert piled the hay in one corner—the coal was low, since it was summer—and they spread a piece of old carpet on the hay and made a bed for Blue Boy. "Now you run along with Adelbert.

There'll be a lot of work to do on Mr. Holliday's yard, cleaning up after the sociable. Mandy an' me'll watch Blue Boy. I expect he'll sleep for a while."

Albert went away regretfully, but the dray-man and some of the Methodist ladies were in Mr. Holliday's yard, packing chairs and tables and ice-cream freezers into the wagon, and the twins forgot the sick cat in their excitement. By noon they had picked up the last paper napkin, raked over the gravel walks where the salt from the freezers had left white patches, and hung the hammock in which Vickie did her studying back in its place. Mr. Holliday paid the boys a dollar a week for keeping up the yard, and they gave the money to their mother—it didn't come amiss in a family where actual cash was so short. She let them keep half the sum Mrs. Rosen paid for her milk every Saturday, and that was more spending money than most boys had. They often made a few extra quarters by cutting grass for other people, or by distributing handbills. Even the disagreeable Mrs. Jackson next door had remarked over the fence to Mrs. Harris: "I do believe Bert and Del are going to be industrious. They must have got it from you, Grandma."

The day came on very hot, and when the twins got back from the Roadmaster's yard, they both lay down on Grandmother's lounge and went to sleep. After dinner they had a rare opportunity; the Roadmaster himself appeared at the front door and invited them to go up to the next town with him on his railroad velocipede. That was great fun: the velocipede always whizzed along so fast on the bright rails, the gasoline engine puffing; and grasshoppers jumped up out of the sage-brush and hit you in the face like sling-shot bullets. Sometimes the wheels cut in two a lazy snake who was sunning himself on the track, and the twins always hoped it was a rattler and felt they had done a good work.

The boys got back from their trip with Mr. Holliday late in the afternoon. The house was cool and quiet. Their mother had taken Ronald and Hughie down town with her, and Vickie was off somewhere. Grandmother was not in her room, and the kitchen was empty. The boys went out to the back porch to pump a drink. The coal-shed door was open, and inside, on a low stool, sat Mrs. Harris beside her cat. Bert and Del didn't stop to get a drink; they felt ashamed that they had gone off for a gay ride and forgotten Blue Boy. They sat down on a big lump of coal beside Mrs. Harris. They would never have known that this miserable rumpled animal was their proud tom. Presently he went off into a spasm and began to froth at the mouth.

"Oh, Gram'ma, can't you do anything?" cried Albert, struggling with his tears. "Blue Boy was such a good cat,—why has he got to suffer?"

"Everything that's alive has got to suffer," said Mrs. Harris. Albert put out his hand and caught her skirt, looking up at her beseechingly, as if to make her unsay that saying, which he only half understood. She patted his hand. She had forgot she was speaking to a little boy.

"Where's Vickie?" Adelbert asked aggrievedly. "Why don't she do something! He's part her cat."

Mrs. Harris sighed. "Vickie's got her head full of things lately; that makes people kind of heartless."

The boys resolved they would never put anything into their heads, then!

Blue Boy's fit passed, and the three sat watching their pet that no longer knew them. The twins had not seen much suffering; Grandmother had seen a great deal. Back in Tennessee, in her own neighbourhood, she was accounted a famous nurse. When any of the poor mountain people were in great distress, they always sent for Miz' Harris. Many a time she had gone into a house where five or six children were all down with scarlet fever or diphtheria, and done what she could. Many a child and many a woman she had laid out and got ready for the grave. In her primitive community the undertaker made the coffin—he did nothing more. She had seen so much misery that she wondered herself why it hurt so to see her tom-cat die. She had taken her leave of him, and she got up from her stool. She didn't want the boys to be too much distressed.

"Now you boys must wash and put on clean shirts. Your mother will be home pretty soon. We'll leave Blue Boy; he'll likely be easier in the morning." She knew the cat would die at sundown.

After supper, when Bert looked into the coal-shed and found the cat dead, all the family were sad. Ronald cried miserably, and Hughie cried because Ronald did. Mrs. Templeton herself went out and looked into the shed, and she was sorry, too. Though she didn't like cats, she had been fond of this one.

"Hillary," she told her husband, "when you go down town tonight, tell the Mexican to come and get that cat early in the morning, before the children are up."

The Mexican had a cart and two mules, and he hauled away tin cans and refuse to a gully out in the sage-brush.

Mrs. Harris gave Victoria an indignant glance when she heard this, and turned back to the kitchen. All evening she was gloomy and silent. She refused to read aloud, and the twins took Ronald and went mournfully out to play under the electric light. Later, when they had said good-night to their parents in the parlour and were on their way upstairs, Mrs. Harris followed them into the kitchen, shut the door behind her, and said indignantly:

"Air you two boys going to let that Mexican take Blue Boy and throw him onto some trash-pile?"

The sleepy boys were frightened at the anger and bitterness in her tone. They stood still and looked up at her, while she went on:

"You git up early in the morning, and I'll put him in a sack, and one of you take a spade and go to that crooked old willer tree that grows just where the sand creek turns off the road, and you dig a little grave for Blue Boy, an' bury him right."

They had seldom seen such resentment in their grandmother. Albert's throat choked up, he rubbed the tears away with his fist.

"Yes'm, Gram'ma, we will, we will," he gulped.

VII

Only Mrs. Harris saw the boys go out next morning. She slipped a bread-and-butter sandwich into the hand of each, but she said nothing, and they said nothing.

The boys did not get home until their parents were ready to leave the table. Mrs. Templeton made no fuss, but told them to sit down and eat their breakfast. When they had finished, she said commandingly:

"Now you march into my room." That was where she heard

explanations and administered punishment. When she whipped them, she did it thoroughly.

She followed them and shut the door.

"Now, what were you boys doing this morning?"

"We went off to bury Blue Boy."

"Why didn't you tell me you were going?"

They looked down at their toes, but said nothing. Their mother studied their mournful faces, and her overbearing expression softened.

"The next time you get up and go off anywhere, you come and tell me beforehand, do you understand?"

"Yes'm."

She opened the door, motioned them out, and went with them into the parlour. "I'm sorry about your cat, boys," she said. "That's why I don't like to have cats around; they're always getting sick and dying. Now run along and play. Maybe you'd like to have a circus in the back yard this afternoon? And we'll all come."

The twins ran out in a joyful frame of mind. Their grandmother had been mistaken; their mother wasn't indifferent about Blue Boy, she was sorry. Now everything was all right, and they could make a circus ring.

They knew their grandmother got put out about strange things, anyhow. A few months ago it was because their mother hadn't asked one of the visiting preachers who came to the church conference to stay with them. There was no place for the preacher to sleep except on the folding lounge in the parlour, and no place for him to wash— he would have been very uncomfortable, and so would all the household. But Mrs. Harris was terribly upset that there should be a conference in the town, and they not keeping a preacher! She was quite bitter about it.

The twins called in the neighbour boys, and they made a ring in the back yard, around their turning-bar. Their mother came to the show and paid admission, bringing Mrs. Rosen and Grandma Harris. Mrs. Rosen thought if all the children in the neighbourhood were to be howling and running in a circle in the Templetons' back yard, she might as well be there, too, for she would have no peace at home.

After the dog races and the Indian fight were over, Mrs. Templeton took Mrs. Rosen into the house to revive her with cake and lemonade.

The parlour was cool and dusky. Mrs. Rosen was glad to get into it after sitting on a wooden bench in the sun. Grandmother stayed in the parlour with them, which was unusual. Mrs. Rosen sat waving a palm-leaf fan,—she felt the heat very much, because she wore her stays so tight—while Victoria went to make the lemonade.

"De circuses are not so good, widout Vickie to manage them, Grandma," she said.

"No'm. The boys complain right smart about losing Vickie from their plays. She's at her books all the time now. I don't know what's got into the child."

"If she wants to go to college, she must prepare herself, Grandma. I am agreeably surprised in her. I didn't think she'd stick to it."

Mrs. Templeton came in with a tray of tumblers and the glass pitcher all frosted over. Mrs. Rosen wistfully admired her neighbour's tall figure and good carriage; she was wearing no corsets at all today under her flowered organdie afternoon dress, Mrs. Rosen had noticed, and yet she could carry herself so smooth and straight,—after having had so many children, too! Mrs. Rosen was envious, but she gave credit where credit was due.

When Mrs. Templeton brought in the cake, Mrs. Rosen was still talking to Grandmother about Vickie's studying. Mrs. Templeton shrugged carelessly.

"There's such a thing as overdoing it, Mrs. Rosen," she observed as she poured the lemonade. "Vickie's very apt to run to extremes."

"But, my dear lady, she can hardly be too extreme in dis matter. If she is to take a competitive examination with girls from much better schools than ours, she will have to do better than the others, or fail; no two ways about it. We must encourage her."

Mrs. Templeton bridled a little. "I'm sure I don't interfere with her studying, Mrs. Rosen. I don't see where she got this notion, but I let her alone."

Mrs. Rosen accepted a second piece of chocolate cake. "And what do you think about it, Grandma?"

Mrs. Harris smiled politely. "None of our people, or Mr. Templeton's either, ever went to college. I expect it is all on account of the young gentleman who was here last summer."

Mrs. Rosen laughed and lifted her eyebrows. "Something very

personal in Vickie's admiration for Professor Chalmers we think, Grandma? A very sudden interest in de sciences, I should say!"

Mrs. Templeton shrugged. "You're mistaken, Mrs. Rosen. There ain't a particle of romance in Vickie."

"But there are several kinds of romance, Mrs. Templeton. She may not have your kind."

"Yes'm, that's so," said Mrs. Harris in a low, grateful voice. She thought that a hard word Victoria had said of Vickie.

"I didn't see a thing in that Professor Chalmers, myself," Victoria remarked. "He was a gawky kind of fellow, and never had a thing to say in company. Did you think he amounted to much?"

"Oh, widout doubt Doctor Chalmers is a very scholarly man. A great many brilliant scholars are widout de social graces, you know." When Mrs. Rosen, from a much wider experience, corrected her neighbour, she did so somewhat playfully, as if insisting upon something Victoria capriciously chose to ignore.

At this point old Mrs. Harris put her hands on the arms of the chair in preparation to rise. "If you ladies will excuse me, I think I will go and lie down a little before supper." She rose and went heavily out on her felt soles. She never really lay down in the afternoon, but she dozed in her own black rocker. Mrs. Rosen and Victoria sat chatting about Professor Chalmers and his boys.

Last summer the young professor had come to Skyline with four of his students from the University of Michigan, and had stayed three months, digging for fossils out in the sandhills. Vickie had spent a great many mornings at their camp. They lived at the town hotel, and drove out to their camp every day in a light spring-wagon. Vickie used to wait for them at the edge of the town, in front of the Roadmaster's house, and when the spring-wagon came rattling along, the boys would call: "There's our girl!" slow the horses, and give her a hand up. They said she was their mascot, and were very jolly with her. They had a splendid summer,—found a great bed of fossil elephant bones, where a whole herd must once have perished. Later on they came upon the bones of a new kind of elephant, scarcely larger than a pig. They were greatly excited about their finds, and so was Vickie. That was why they liked her. It was they who told

her about a memorial scholarship at Ann Arbor, which was open to
any girl from Colorado.

VIII

In August Vickie went down to Denver to take her examinations.
Mr. Holliday, the Roadmaster, got her a pass, and arranged that she
should stay with the family of one of his passenger conductors.

For three days she wrote examination papers along with other
contestants, in one of the Denver high schools, proctored by a teacher.
Her father had given her five dollars for incidental expenses, and she
came home with a box of mineral specimens for the twins, a singing
top for Ronald, and a toy burro for Hughie.

Then began days of suspense that stretched into weeks. Vickie
went to the post-office every morning, opened her father's combination box, and looked over the letters, long before he got down
town,—always hoping there might be a letter from Ann Arbor. The
night mail came in at six, and after supper she hurried to the post-
office and waited about until the shutter at the general-delivery
window was drawn back, a signal that the mail had all been "dis-
tributed." While the tedious process of distribution was going on,
she usually withdrew from the office, full of joking men and cigar
smoke, and walked up and down under the big cottonwood trees
that overhung the side street. When the crowd of men began to come
out, then she knew the mail-bags were empty, and she went in to
get whatever letters were in the Templeton box and take them home.

After two weeks went by, she grew down-hearted. Her young
professor, she knew, was in England for his vacation. There would
be no one at the University of Michigan who was interested in her
fate. Perhaps the fortunate contestant had already been notified of
her success. She never asked herself, as she walked up and down
under the cottonwoods on those summer nights, what she would do
if she didn't get the scholarship. There was no alternative. If she
didn't get it, then everything was over.

During the weeks when she lived only to go to the post-office,
she managed to cut her finger and get ink into the cut. As a result,

she had a badly infected hand and had to carry it in a sling. When she walked her nightly beat under the cottonwoods, it was a kind of comfort to feel that finger throb; it was companionship, made her case more complete.

The strange thing was that one morning a letter came, addressed to Miss Victoria Templeton; in a long envelope such as her father called "legal size," with *"University of Michigan"* in the upper left-hand corner. When Vickie took it from the box, such a wave of fright and weakness went through her that she could scarcely get out of the post-office. She hid the letter under her striped blazer and went a weak, uncertain trail down the sidewalk under the big trees. Without seeing anything or knowing what road she took, she got to the Roadmaster's green yard and her hammock, where she always felt not on the earth, yet of it.

Three hours later, when Mrs. Rosen was just tasting one of those clear soups upon which the Templetons thought she wasted so much pains and good meat, Vickie walked in at the kitchen door and said in a low but somewhat unnatural voice:

"Mrs. Rosen, I got the scholarship."

Mrs. Rosen looked up at her sharply, then pushed the soup back to a cooler part of the stove.

"What is dis you say, Vickie? You have heard from de University?"

"Yes'm. I got the letter this morning." She produced it from under her blazer.

Mrs. Rosen had been cutting noodles. She took Vickie's face in two hot, plump hands that were still floury, and looked at her intently. "Is dat true, Vickie? No mistake? I am delighted—and surprised! Yes, surprised. Den you will *be* something, you won't just sit on de front porch." She squeezed the girl's round, good-natured cheeks, as if she could mould them into something definite then and there. "Now you must stay for lunch and tell us all about it. Go in and announce yourself to Mr. Rosen."

Mr. Rosen had come home for lunch and was sitting, a book in his hand, in a corner of the darkened front parlour where a flood of yellow sun streamed in under the dark green blind. He smiled his friendly smile at Vickie and waved her to a seat, making her understand that he wanted to finish his paragraph. The dark engraving of the pointed cypresses and the Roman tomb was on the wall just behind him.

Mrs. Rosen came into the back parlour, which was the dining-room, and began taking things out of the silver-drawer to lay a place for their visitor. She spoke to her husband rapidly in German.

He put down his book, came over, and took Vickie's hand.

"Is it true, Vickie? Did you really win the scholarship?"

"Yes, sir."

He stood looking down at her through his kind, remote smile,— a smile in the eyes, that seemed to come up through layers and layers of something—gentle doubts, kindly reservations.

"Why do you want to go to college, Vickie?" he asked playfully.

"To learn," she said with surprise.

"But why do you want to learn? What do you want to do with it?"

"I don't know. Nothing, I guess."

"Then what do you want it for?"

"I don't know. I just want it."

For some reason Vickie's voice broke there. She had been terribly strung up all morning, lying in the hammock with her eyes tight shut. She had not been home at all, she had wanted to take her letter to the Rosens first. And now one of the gentlest men she knew made her choke by something strange and presageful in his voice.

"Then if you want it without any purpose at all, you will not be disappointed." Mr. Rosen wished to distract her and help her to keep back the tears. "Listen: a great man once said: *'Le but n'est rien; le chemin, c'est tout.'* That means: The end is nothing, the road is all. Let me write it down for you and give you your first French lesson."

He went to the desk with its big silver ink-well, where he and his wife wrote so many letters in several languages, and inscribed the sentence on a sheet of purple paper, in his delicately shaded foreign script, signing under it a name: *J. Michelet.* He brought it back and shook it before Vickie's eyes. "There, keep it to remember me by. Slip it into the envelope with your college credentials,—that is a good place for it." From his delicate smile and the twitch of one eyebrow,

Vickie knew he meant her to take it along as an antidote, a corrective for whatever colleges might do to her. But she had always known that Mr. Rosen was wiser than professors.

Mrs. Rosen was frowning, she thought that sentence a bad precept to give any Templeton. Moreover, she always promptly called her husband back to earth when he soared a little; though it was exactly for this transcendental quality of mind that she reverenced him in her heart, and thought him so much finer than any of his successful brothers.

"Luncheon is served," she said in the crisp tone that put people in their places. "And Miss Vickie, you are to eat your tomatoes with an oil dressing, as we do. If you are going off into the world, it is quite time you learn to like things that are everywhere accepted."

Vickie said: "Yes'm," and slipped into the chair Mr. Rosen had placed for her. Today she didn't care what she ate, though ordinarily she thought a French dressing tasted a good deal like castor oil.

IX

Vickie was to discover that nothing comes easily in this world. Next day she got a letter from one of the jolly students of Professor Chalmers's party, who was watching over her case in his chief's absence. He told her the scholarship meant admission to the freshman class without further examinations, and two hundred dollars toward her expenses; she would have to bring along about three hundred more to put her through the year.

She took this letter to her father's office. Seated in his revolving desk-chair, Mr. Templeton read it over several times and looked embarrassed.

"I'm sorry, daughter," he said at last, "but really, just now, I couldn't spare that much. Not this year. I expect next year will be better for us."

"But the scholarship is for this year, Father. It wouldn't count next year. I just have to go in September."

"I really ain't got it, daughter." He spoke, oh so kindly! He had lovely manners with his daughter and his wife. "It's just all I can do to keep the store bills paid up. I'm away behind with Mr. Rosen's bill. Couldn't you study here this winter and get along about as fast? It isn't that I wouldn't like to let you have the money if I had it. And with young children, I can't let my life insurance go."

Vickie didn't say anything more. She took her letter and wandered down Main Street with it, leaving young Mr. Templeton to a very bad half-hour.

At dinner Vickie was silent, but everyone could see she had been crying. Mr. Templeton told *Uncle Remus* stories to keep up the family morale and make the giggly twins laugh. Mrs. Templeton glanced covertly at her daughter from time to time. She was sometimes a little afraid of Vickie, who seemed to her to have a hard streak. If it were a love-affair that the girl was crying about, that would be so much more natural—and more hopeful!

At two o'clock Mrs. Templeton went to the Afternoon Euchre Club, the twins were to have another ride with the Roadmaster on his velocipede, the little boys took their nap on their mother's bed. The house was empty and quiet. Vickie felt an aversion for the hammock under the cottonwoods where she had been betrayed into such bright hopes. She lay down on her grandmother's lounge in the cluttered play-room and turned her face to the wall.

When Mrs. Harris came in for her rest, and began to wash her face at the tin basin, Vickie got up. She wanted to be alone. Mrs. Harris came over to her while she was still sitting on the edge of the lounge.

"What's the matter, Vickie child?" She put her hand on her granddaughter's shoulder, but Vickie shrank away. Young misery is like that, sometimes.

"Nothing. Except that I can't go to college after all. Papa can't let me have the money."

Mrs. Harris settled herself on the faded cushions of her rocker. "How much is it? Tell me about it, Vickie. Nobody's around."

Vickie told her what the conditions were, briefly and dryly, as if she were talking to an enemy. Everyone was an enemy; all society was against her. She told her grandmother the facts and then went upstairs, refusing to be comforted.

Mrs. Harris saw her disappear through the kitchen door, and then sat looking at the door, her face grave, her eyes stern and sad. A poor factory-made piece of joiner's work seldom has to bear a look of such intense, accusing sorrow; as if that flimsy pretence of "grained" yellow pine were the door shut against all young aspiration.

X

Mrs. Harris had decided to speak to Mr. Templeton, but opportunities for seeing him alone were not frequent. She watched out of the kitchen window, and when she next saw him go into the barn to fork down hay for his horse, she threw an apron over her head and followed him. She waylaid him as he came down from the hayloft.

"Hillary, I want to see you about Vickie. I was wondering if you could lay hand on any of the money you got for the sale of my house back home."

Mr. Templeton was nervous. He began brushing his trousers with a little whisk-broom he kept there, hanging on a nail.

"Why, no'm, Mrs. Harris. I couldn't just conveniently call in any of it right now. You know we had to use part of it to get moved up here from the mines."

"I know. But I thought if there was any left you could get at, we could let Vickie have it. A body'd like to help the child."

"I'd like to, powerful well, Mrs. Harris. I would, indeedy. But I'm afraid I can't manage it right now. The fellers I've loaned to can't pay up this year. Maybe next year——" He was like a little boy trying to escape a scolding, though he had never had a nagging word from Mrs. Harris.

She looked downcast, but said nothing.

"It's all right, Mrs. Harris," he took on his brisk business tone and hung up the brush. "The money's perfectly safe. It's well invested."

Invested; that was a word men always held over women, Mrs. Harris thought, and it always meant they could have none of their own money. She sighed deeply.

"Well, if that's the way it is——" She turned away and went back to the house on her flat heelless slippers, just in time; Victoria was at that moment coming out to the kitchen with Hughie.

"Ma," she said, "can the little boy play out here, while I go down town?"

XI

For the next few days Mrs. Harris was very sombre, and she was not well. Several times in the kitchen she was seized with what she called giddy spells, and Mandy had to help her to a chair and give her a little brandy.

"Don't you say nothin', Mandy," she warned the girl. But Mandy knew enough for that.

Mrs. Harris scarcely noticed how her strength was failing, because she had so much on her mind. She was very proud, and she wanted to do something that was hard for her to do. The difficulty was to catch Mrs. Rosen alone.

On the afternoon when Victoria went to her weekly euchre, the old lady beckoned Mandy and told her to run across the alley and fetch Mrs. Rosen for a minute.

Mrs. Rosen was packing her trunk, but she came at once. Grandmother awaited her in her chair in the play-room.

"I take it very kindly of you to come, Mrs. Rosen. I'm afraid it's warm in here. Won't you have a fan?" She extended the palm leaf she was holding.

"Keep it yourself, Grandma. You are not looking very well. Do you feel badly, Grandma Harris?" She took the old lady's hand and looked at her anxiously.

"Oh, no, ma'am! I'm as well as usual. The heat wears on me a little, maybe. Have you seen Vickie lately, Mrs. Rosen?"

"Vickie? No. She hasn't run in for several days. These young people are full of their own affairs, you know."

"I expect she's backward about seeing you, now that she's so discouraged."

"Discouraged? Why, didn't the child get her scholarship after all?"

"Yes'm, she did. But they write her she has to bring more money to help her out; three hundred dollars. Mr. Templeton can't raise it just now. We had so much sickness in that mountain town before we moved up here, he got behind. Pore Vickie's downhearted."

"Oh, that is too bad! I expect you've been fretting over it, and that is why you don't look like yourself. Now what can we do about it?"

Mrs. Harris sighed and shook her head. "Vickie's trying to muster courage to go around to her father's friends and borrow from one and another. But we ain't been here long,—it ain't like we had old friends here. I hate to have the child do it."

Mrs. Rosen looked perplexed. "I'm sure Mr. Rosen would help her. He takes a great interest in Vickie."

"I thought maybe he could see his way to. That's why I sent Mandy to fetch you."

"That was right, Grandma. Now let me think." Mrs. Rosen put up her plump red-brown hand and leaned her chin upon it. "Day after tomorrow I am going to run on to Chicago for my niece's wedding." She saw her old friend's face fall. "Oh, I shan't be gone long; ten days, perhaps. I will speak to Mr. Rosen tonight, and if Vickie goes to him after I am off his hands, I'm sure he will help her."

Mrs. Harris looked up at her with solemn gratitude. "Vickie ain't the kind of girl would forget anything like that, Mrs. Rosen. Nor I wouldn't forget it."

Mrs. Rosen patted her arm. "Grandma Harris," she exclaimed, "I will just ask Mr. Rosen to do it for you! You know I care more about the old folks than the young. If I take this worry off your mind, I shall go away to the wedding with a light heart. Now dismiss it. I am sure Mr. Rosen can arrange this himself for you, and Vickie won't have to go about to these people here, and our gossipy neighbours will never be the wiser." Mrs. Rosen poured this out in her quick, authoritative tone, converting her *th*'s into *d*'s, as she did when she was excited.

Mrs. Harris's red-brown eyes slowly filled with tears,—Mrs. Rosen had never seen that happen before. But she simply said, with quiet dignity: "Thank you, ma'am. I wouldn't have turned to nobody else."

"That means I am an old friend already, doesn't it, Grandma? And that's what I want to be. I am very jealous where Grandma Harris is concerned!" She lightly kissed the back of the purple-veined hand she had been holding, and ran home to her packing. Grandma sat looking down at her hand. How easy it was for these foreigners to say what they felt!

XII

Mrs. Harris knew she was failing. She was glad to be able to conceal it from Mrs. Rosen when that kind neighbour dashed in to kiss her good-bye on the morning of her departure for Chicago. Mrs. Templeton was, of course, present, and secrets could not be discussed. Mrs. Rosen, in her stiff little brown travelling-hat, her hands tightly gloved in brown kid, could only wink and nod to Grandmother to tell her all was well. Then she went out and climbed into the "hack" bound for the depot, which had stopped for a moment at the Templetons' gate.

Mrs. Harris was thankful that her excitable friend hadn't noticed anything unusual about her looks, and, above all, that she had made no comment. She got through the day, and that evening, thank goodness, Mr. Templeton took his wife to hear a company of strolling players sing *The Chimes of Normandy* at the Opera House. He loved music, and just now he was very eager to distract and amuse Victoria. Grandma sent the twins out to play and went to bed early.

Next morning, when she joined Mandy in the kitchen, Mandy noticed something wrong.

"You set right down, Miz' Harris, an' let me git you some whisky. Deed, ma'am, you look awful porely. You ought to tell Miss Victoria an' let her send for the doctor."

"No, Mandy, I don't want no doctor. I've seen more sickness than ever he has. Doctors can't do no more than linger you out, an' I've always prayed I wouldn't last to be a burden. You git me some whisky in hot water, and pour it on a piece of toast. I feel real empty."

That afternoon when Mrs. Harris was taking her rest, for once she lay down upon her lounge. Vickie came in, tense and excited, and stopped for a moment.

"It's all right, Grandma. Mr. Rosen is going to lend me the money. I won't have to go to anybody else. He won't ask Father to endorse my note, either. He'll just take my name." Vickie rather shouted this news at Mrs. Harris, as if the old lady were deaf, or slow of understanding. She didn't thank her; she didn't know her grandmother was in any way responsible for Mr. Rosen's offer, though at the close of their interview he had said: "We won't speak of our arrangement to anyone but your father. And I want you to mention it to the old lady Harris. I know she has been worrying about you."

Having brusquely announced her news, Vickie hurried away. There was so much to do about getting ready, she didn't know where to begin. She had no trunk and no clothes. Her winter coat, bought two years ago, was so outgrown that she couldn't get into it. All her shoes were run over at the heel and must go to the cobbler. And she had only two weeks in which to do everything! She dashed off.

Mrs. Harris sighed and closed her eyes happily. She thought with modest pride that with people like the Rosens she had always "got along nicely." It was only with the ill-bred and unclassified, like this Mrs. Jackson next door, that she had disagreeable experiences. Such folks, she told herself, had come out of nothing and knew no better. She was afraid this inquisitive woman might find her ailing and come prying round with unwelcome suggestions.

Mrs. Jackson did, indeed, call that very afternoon, with a miserable contribution of veal-loaf as an excuse (all the Templetons hated veal), but Mandy had been forewarned, and she was resourceful. She met Mrs. Jackson at the kitchen door and blocked the way.

"Sh-h-h, ma'am, Miz' Harris is asleep, havin' her nap. No'm, she ain't porely, she's as usual. But Hughie had the colic last night when Miss Victoria was at the show, an' kep' Miz' Harris awake."

Mrs. Jackson was loath to turn back. She had really come to find out why Mrs. Rosen drove away in the depot hack yesterday morning. Except at church socials, Mrs. Jackson did not meet people in Mrs. Rosen's set.

The next day, when Mrs. Harris got up and sat on the edge of her bed, her head began to swim, and she lay down again. Mandy peeped into the play-room as soon as she came down-stairs, and found the old lady still in bed. She leaned over her and whispered:

"Ain't you feelin' well, Miz' Harris?"

"No, Mandy, I'm right porely," Mrs. Harris admitted.

"You stay where you air, ma'am. I'll git the breakfast fur the chillun, an' take the other breakfast in fur Miss Victoria an' Mr. Templeton." She hurried back to the kitchen, and Mrs. Harris went to sleep.

Immediately after breakfast Vickie dashed off about her own concerns, and the twins went to cut grass while the dew was still on it. When Mandy was taking the other breakfast into the dining-room, Mrs. Templeton came through the play-room.

"What's the matter, Ma? Are you sick?" she asked in an accusing tone.

"No, Victoria, I ain't sick. I had a little giddy spell, and I thought I'd lay still."

"You ought to be more careful what you eat, Ma. If you're going to have another bilious spell, when everything is so upset anyhow, I don't know what I'll do!" Victoria's voice broke. She hurried back into her bedroom, feeling bitterly that there was no place in that house to cry in, no spot where one could be alone, even with misery; that the house and the people in it were choking her to death.

Mrs. Harris sighed and closed her eyes. Things did seem to be upset, though she didn't know just why. Mandy, however, had her suspicions. While she waited on Mr. and Mrs. Templeton at breakfast, narrowly observing their manner toward each other and Victoria's swollen eyes and desperate expression, her suspicions grew stronger.

Instead of going to his office, Mr. Templeton went to the barn and ran out the buggy. Soon he brought out Cleveland, the black horse, with his harness on. Mandy watched from the back window. After he had hitched the horse to the buggy, he came into the kitchen to wash his hands. While he dried them on the roller towel, he said in his most business-like tone:

"I likely won't be back tonight, Mandy. I have to go out to my farm, and I'll hardly get through my business there in time to come home."

Then Mandy was sure. She had been through these times before, and at such a crisis poor Mr. Templeton was always called away on important business. When he had driven out through the alley and up the street past Mrs. Rosen's, Mandy left her dishes and went in to Mrs. Harris. She bent over and whispered low:

"Miz' Harris, I 'spect Miss Victoria's done found out she's goin' to have another baby! It looks that way. She's gone back to bed."

Mrs. Harris lifted a warning finger. "Sh-h-h!"

"Oh yes'm, I won't say nothin'. I never do."

Mrs. Harris tried to face this possibility, but her mind didn't seem strong enough—she dropped off into another doze.

All that morning Mrs. Templeton lay on her bed alone, the room darkened and a handkerchief soaked in camphor tied round her forehead. The twins had taken Ronald off to watch them cut grass, and Hughie played in the kitchen under Mandy's eye.

Now and then Victoria sat upright on the edge of the bed, beat her hands together softly and looked desperately at the ceiling, then about at those frail, confining walls. If only she could meet the situation with violence, fight it, conquer it! But there was nothing for it but stupid animal patience. She would have to go through all that again, and nobody, not even Hillary, wanted another baby,—poor as they were, and in this overcrowded house. Anyhow, she told herself, she was ashamed to have another baby, when she had a daughter old enough to go to college! She was sick of it all; sick of dragging this chain of life that never let her rest and periodically knotted and overpowered her; made her ill and hideous for months, and then dropped another baby into her arms. She had had babies enough; and there ought to be an end to such apprehensions some time before you were old and ugly.

She wanted to run away, back to Tennessee, and lead a free, gay life, as she had when she was first married. She could do a great deal more with freedom than ever Vickie could. She was still young, and she was still handsome; why must she be for ever shut up in a little cluttered house with children and fresh babies and an old woman and a stupid bound girl and a husband who wasn't very successful? Life hadn't brought her what she expected when she married Hillary Templeton; life hadn't used her right. She had tried to keep up appearances, to dress well with very little to do it on, to keep young for her husband and children. She had tried, she had tried! Mrs. Templeton buried her face in the pillow and smothered the sobs that shook the bed.

Hillary Templeton, on his drive out through the sage-brush, up into the farming country that was irrigated from the North Platte, did not feel altogether cheerful, though he whistled and sang to himself on the way. He was sorry Victoria would have to go through another time. It was awkward just now, too, when he was so short of money. But he was naturally a cheerful man, modest in his demands upon fortune, and easily diverted from unpleasant thoughts. Before Cleveland had travelled half the eighteen miles to the farm, his master was already looking forward to a visit with his tenants, an old German couple who were fond of him because he never pushed them in a hard year—so far, all the years had been hard—and he sometimes brought them bananas and such delicacies from town.

Mrs. Heyse would open her best preserves for him, he knew, and kill a chicken, and tonight he would have a clean bed in her spare room. She always put a vase of flowers in his room when he stayed overnight with them, and that pleased him very much. He felt like a youth out there, and forgot all the bills he had somehow to meet, and the loans he had made and couldn't collect. The Heyses kept bees and raised turkeys, and had honeysuckle vines running over the front porch. He loved all those things. Mr. Templeton touched Cleveland with the whip, and as they sped along into the grass country, sang softly:

> "Old Jesse was a gem'man
> Way down in Tennessee."

XIII

Mandy had to manage the house herself that day, and she was not at all sorry. There wasn't a great deal of variety in her life, and she felt very important taking Mrs. Harris's place, giving the children their dinner, and carrying a plate of milk toast to Mrs. Templeton. She was worried about Mrs. Harris, however, and remarked to the children at noon that she thought somebody ought to "set" with their grandma. Vickie wasn't home for dinner. She had her father's office to herself for the day and was making the most of it, writing a long letter to Professor Chalmers. Mr. Rosen had invited her to have dinner with him at the hotel (he boarded there when his wife was away), and that was a great honour.

When Mandy said someone ought to be with the old lady, Bert and Del offered to take turns. Adelbert went off to rake up the grass they had been cutting all morning, and Albert sat down in the playroom. It seemed to him his grandmother looked pretty sick. He watched her while Mandy gave her toast-water with whisky in it, and thought he would like to make the room look a little nicer. While Mrs. Harris lay with her eyes closed, he hung up the caps and coats lying about, and moved away the big rocking-chair that stood by the head of Grandma's bed. There ought to be a table there, he believed, but the small tables in the house all had something on them. Upstairs, in the room where he and Adelbert and Ronald slept, there was a nice clean wooden cracker-box, on which they sat in the morning to put on their shoes and stockings. He brought this down and stood it on end at the head of Grandma's lounge, and put a clean napkin over the top of it.

She opened her eyes and smiled at him. "Could you git me a tin of fresh water, honey?"

He went to the back porch and pumped till the water ran cold. He gave it to her in a tin cup as she had asked, but he didn't think that was the right way. After she dropped back on the pillow, he fetched a glass tumbler from the cupboard, filled it, and set it on the table he had just manufactured. When Grandmother drew a red cotton handkerchief from under her pillow and wiped the moisture from her face, he ran upstairs again and got one of his Sunday-school handkerchiefs, linen ones, that Mrs. Rosen had given him and Del for Christmas. Having put this in Grandmother's hand and taken away the crumpled red one, he could think of nothing else to do—except to darken the room a little. The windows had no blinds, but flimsy cretonne curtains tied back,—not really tied, but caught back over nails driven into the sill. He loosened them and let them hang down over the bright afternoon sunlight. Then he sat down on the low sawed-off chair and gazed about, thinking that now it looked quite like a sick-room.

It was hard for a little boy to keep still. "Would you like me to read *Joe's Luck* to you, Gram'ma?" he said presently.

"You might, Bertie."

He got the "boy's book" she had been reading aloud to them, and began where she had left off. Mrs. Harris liked to hear his voice, and she liked to look at him when she opened her eyes from time to time. She did not follow the story. In her mind she was repeating a passage from the second part of *Pilgrim's Progress,* which she had read aloud to the children so many times; the passage where Christiana and her band come to the arbour on the Hill of Difficulty: *"Then said Mercy, how sweet is rest to them that labour."*

At about four o'clock Adelbert came home, hot and sweaty from raking. He said he had got in the grass and taken it to their cow, and if Bert was reading, he guessed he'd like to listen. He dragged the wooden rocking-chair up close to Grandma's bed and curled up in it.

Grandmother was perfectly happy. She and the twins were about the same age; they had in common all the realest and truest things. The years between them and her, it seemed to Mrs. Harris, were full of trouble and unimportant. The twins and Ronald and Hughie were important. She opened her eyes.

"Where is Hughie?" she asked.

"I guess he's asleep. Mother took him into her bed."

"And Ronald?"

"He's upstairs with Mandy. There ain't nobody in the kitchen now."

"Then you might git me a fresh drink, Del."

"Yes'm, Gram'ma." He tiptoed out to the pump in his brown canvas sneakers.

When Vickie came home at five o'clock, she went to her mother's room, but the door was locked—a thing she couldn't remember ever happening before. She went into the play-room,—old Mrs. Harris was asleep, with one of the twins on guard, and he held up a warning finger. She went into the kitchen. Mandy was making biscuits, and Ronald was helping her to cut them out.

"What's the matter, Mandy? Where is everybody?"

"You know your papa's away, Miss Vickie; an' your mama's got a headache, an' Miz' Harris has had a bad spell. Maybe I'll just fix supper for you an' the boys in the kitchen, so you won't all have to be runnin' through her room."

"Oh, very well," said Vickie bitterly, and she went upstairs. Wasn't it just like them all to go and get sick, when she had now only two weeks to get ready for school, and no trunk and no clothes or anything?

Nobody but Mr. Rosen seemed to take the least interest, "when my whole life hangs by a thread," she told herself fiercely. What were families for, anyway?

After supper Vickie went to her father's office to read; she told Mandy to leave the kitchen door open, and when she got home she would go to bed without disturbing anybody. The twins ran out to play under the electric light with the neighbour boys for a little while, then slipped softly up the back stairs to their room. Mandy came to Mrs. Harris after the house was still.

"Kin I rub your legs fur you, Miz' Harris?"

"Thank you, Mandy. And you might get me a clean nightcap out of the press."

Mandy returned with it.

"Lawsie me! But your legs is cold, ma'am!"

"I expect it's about time, Mandy," murmured the old lady. Mandy knelt on the floor and set to work with a will. It brought the sweat out on her, and at last she sat up and wiped her face with the back of her hand.

"I can't seem to git no heat into 'em, Miz' Harris. I got a hot flat-iron on the stove; I'll wrap it in a piece of old blanket and put it to your feet. Why didn't you have the boys tell me you was cold, pore soul?"

Mrs. Harris did not answer. She thought it was probably a cold that neither Mandy nor the flat-iron could do much with. She hadn't nursed so many people back in Tennessee without coming to know certain signs.

After Mandy was gone, she fell to thinking of her blessings. Every night for years, when she said her prayers, she had prayed that she might never have a long sickness or be a burden. She dreaded the heart-ache and humiliation of being helpless on the hands of people who would be impatient under such a care. And now she felt certain that she was going to die tonight, without troubling anybody.

She was glad Mrs. Rosen was in Chicago. Had she been at home, she would certainly have come in, would have seen that her old neighbour was very sick, and bustled about. Her quick eye would have found out all Grandmother's little secrets: how hard her bed was, that she had no proper place to wash, and kept her comb in her pocket; that her nightgowns were patched and darned. Mrs. Rosen would have been indignant, and that would have made Victoria cross. She didn't have to see Mrs. Rosen again to know that Mrs. Rosen thought highly of her and admired her—yes, admired her. Those funny little pats and arch pleasantries had meant a great deal to Mrs. Harris.

It was a blessing that Mr. Templeton was away, too. Appearances had to be kept up when there was a man in the house; and he might have taken it into his head to send for the doctor, and stir everybody up. Now everything would be so peaceful. *"The Lord is my shepherd,"* she whispered gratefully. "Yes, Lord, I always spoiled Victoria. She was so much the prettiest. But nobody won't ever be the worse for it: Mr. Templeton will always humour her, and the children love her more than most. They'll always be good to her; she has that way with her."

Grandma fell to remembering the old place at home: what a dashing, high-spirited girl Victoria was, and how proud she had always been of her; how she used to hear her laughing and teasing out in the lilac arbour when Hillary Templeton was courting her. Toward morning all these pleasant reflections faded out. Mrs. Harris felt that she and her bed were softly sinking, through the darkness to a deeper darkness.

Old Mrs. Harris did not really die that night, but she believed she did. Mandy found her unconscious in the morning. Then there was a great stir and bustle; Victoria, and even Vickie, were startled out of their intense self-absorption. Mrs. Harris was hastily carried out of the play-room and laid in Victoria's bed, put into one of Victoria's best nightgowns. Mr. Templeton was sent for, and the doctor was sent for. The inquisitive Mrs. Jackson from next door got into the house at last,—installed herself as nurse, and no one had the courage to say her nay. But Grandmother was out of it all, never knew that she was the object of so much attention and excitement. She died a little while after Mr. Templeton got home.

Thus Mrs. Harris slipped out of the Templetons' story; but Victoria and Vickie had still to go on, to follow the long road that leads through things unguessed at and unforeseeable. When they are old, they will come closer and closer to Grandma Harris. They will think a great deal about her, and remember things they never noticed; and their lot will be more or less like hers. They will regret that they heeded her so little; but they, too, will look into the eager, unseeing eyes of young people and feel themselves alone. They will say to themselves: "I was heartless, because I was young and strong and wanted things so much. But now I know."

Two Friends

I

Even in early youth, when the mind is so eager for the new and untried, while it is still a stranger to faltering and fear, we yet like to think that there are certain unalterable realities, somewhere at the bottom of things. These anchors may be ideas; but more often they are merely pictures, vivid memories, which in some unaccountable and very personal way give us courage. The sea-gulls, that seem so much creatures of the free wind and waves, that are as homeless as the sea (able to rest upon the tides and ride the storm, needing nothing but water and sky), at certain seasons even they go back to something they have known before; to remote islands and lonely ledges that are their breeding-grounds. The restlessness of youth has such retreats, even though it may be ashamed of them.

Long ago, before the invention of the motor-car (which has made more changes in the world than the War, which indeed produced the particular kind of war that happened just a hundred years after Waterloo), in a little wooden town in a shallow Kansas river valley, there lived two friends. They were "business men," the two most prosperous and influential men in our community, the two men whose affairs took them out into the world to big cities, who had "connections" in St. Joseph and Chicago. In my childhood they represented to me success and power.

R. E. Dillon was of Irish extraction, one of the dark Irish, with glistening jet-black hair and moustache, and thick eyebrows. His skin was very white, bluish on his shaven cheeks and chin. Shaving must have been a difficult process for him, because there were no smooth expanses for the razor to glide over. The bony structure of his face was prominent and unusual; high cheek-bones, a bold Roman nose, a chin cut by deep lines, with a hard dimple at the tip, a jutting ridge over his eyes where his curly black eyebrows grew and met. It was a face in many planes, as if the carver had whittled and modelled and indented to see how far he could go. Yet on meeting him what you saw was an imperious head on a rather small, wiry man, a head held conspicuously and proudly erect, with a carriage unmistakably arrogant and consciously superior. Dillon had a musical, vibrating voice, and the changeable grey eye that is peculiarly Irish. His full name, which he never used, was Robert Emmet Dillon, so there must have been a certain feeling somewhere back in his family.

He was the principal banker in our town, and proprietor of the large general store next the bank; he owned farms up in the grass country, and a fine ranch in the green timbered valley of the Caw. He was, according to our standards, a rich man.

His friend, J. H. Trueman, was what we called a big cattleman. Trueman was from Buffalo; his family were old residents there, and he had come West as a young man because he was restless and unconventional in his tastes. He was fully ten years older than Dillon,—in his early fifties, when I knew him; large, heavy, very slow in his movements, not given to exercise. His countenance was as unmistakably American as Dillon's was not,—but American of that period, not of this. He did not belong to the time of efficiency and advertising and progressive methods. For any form of pushing or boosting he had a cold, unqualified contempt. All this was in his face,—heavy, immobile, rather melancholy, not remarkable in any particular. But the moment one looked at him one felt solidity, an entire absence of anything mean or small, easy carelessness, courage, a high sense of honour.

These two men had been friends for ten years before I knew them, and I knew them from the time I was ten until I was thirteen. I saw them as often as I could, because they led more varied lives than the other men in our town; one could look up to them. Dillon, I believe, was the more intelligent. Trueman had, perhaps, a better tradition, more background.

Dillon's bank and general store stood at the corner of Main Street and a cross-street, and on this cross-street, two short blocks away, my family lived. On my way to and from school, and going on the countless errands that I was sent upon day and night, I always passed Dillon's store. Its long, red brick wall, with no windows except high overhead, ran possibly a hundred feet along the sidewalk of the cross-street. The front door and show windows were on Main Street, and the bank was next door. The board sidewalk along that red brick wall was wider than any other piece of walk in town, smoother, better laid, kept in perfect repair; very good to walk on in a community where most things were flimsy. I liked the store and the brick wall and the sidewalk because they were solid and well built, and possibly I admired Dillon and Trueman for much the same reason. They were secure and established. So many of our citizens were nervous little hopper men, trying to get on. Dillon and Trueman had got on; they stood with easy assurance on a deck that was their own.

In the daytime one did not often see them together—each went about his own affairs. But every evening they were both to be found at Dillon's store. The bank, of course, was locked and dark before the sun went down, but the store was always open until ten o'clock; the clerks put in a long day. So did Dillon. He and his store were one. He never acted as sales-man, and he kept a cashier in the wire-screened office at the back end of the store; but he was there to be called on. The thrifty Swedes to the north, who were his best customers, usually came to town and did their shopping after dark—they didn't squander daylight hours in farming season. In these evening visits with his customers, and on his drives in his buckboard among the farms, Dillon learned all he needed to know about how much money it was safe to advance a farmer who wanted to feed cattle, or to buy a steam thrasher or build a new barn.

Every evening in winter, when I went to the post-office after supper, I passed through Dillon's store instead of going round it,— for the warmth and cheerfulness, and to catch sight of Mr. Dillon and Mr. Trueman playing checkers in the office behind the wire screening; both seated on high accountant's stools, with the checker-board on the cashier's desk before them. I knew all Dillon's clerks, and if they were not busy, I often lingered about to talk to them; sat on one of the grocery counters and watched the checker-players from a distance. I remember Mr. Dillon's hand used to linger in the air above the board before he made a move; a well-kept hand, white, marked with blue veins and streaks of strong black hair. Trueman's hands rested on his knees under the desk while he considered; he took a checker, set it down, then dropped his hand on his knee again.

He seldom made an unnecessary movement with his hands or feet. Each of the men wore a ring on his little finger. Mr. Dillon's was a large diamond solitaire set in a gold claw, Trueman's the head of a Roman soldier cut in onyx and set in pale twisted gold; it had been his father's, I believe.

Exactly at ten o'clock the store closed. Mr. Dillon went home to his wife and family, to his roomy, comfortable house with a garden and orchard and big stables. Mr. Trueman, who had long been a widower, went to his office to begin the day over. He led a double life, and until one or two o'clock in the morning entertained the poker-players of our town. After everything was shut for the night, a queer crowd drifted into Trueman's back office. The company was seldom the same on two successive evenings, but there were three tireless poker-players who always came: the billiard-hall proprietor, with green-gold moustache and eyebrows, and big white teeth; the horse-trader, who smelled of horses; the dandified cashier of the bank that rivalled Dillon's. The gamblers met in Trueman's place because a game that went on there was respectable, was a social game, no matter how much money changed hands. If the horse-trader or the crooked money-lender got over-heated and broke loose a little, a look or a remark from Mr. Trueman would freeze them up. And his remark was always the same:

"Careful of the language around here."

It was never "your" language, but "the" language,—though he certainly intended no pleasantry. Trueman himself was not a lucky poker man; he was never ahead of the game on the whole. He played because he liked it, and he was willing to pay for his amusement. In general he was large and indifferent about money matters,—always carried a few hundred-dollar bills in his inside coat-pocket, and left his coat hanging anywhere,—in his office, in the bank, in the barber shop, in the cattle-sheds behind the freight yard.

Now, R. E. Dillon detested gambling, often dropped a contemptuous word about "poker bugs" before the horse-trader and the billiard-hall man and the cashier of the other bank. But he never made remarks of that sort in Trueman's presence. He was a man who voiced his prejudices fearlessly and cuttingly, but on this and other matters he held his peace before Trueman. His regard for him must have been very strong.

During the winter, usually in March, the two friends always took a trip together, to Kansas City and St. Joseph. When they got ready, they packed their bags and stepped aboard a fast Santa Fé train and went; the Limited was often signalled to stop for them. Their excursions made some of the rest of us feel less shut away and small-townish, just as their fur overcoats and silk shirts did. They were the only men in Singleton who wore silk shirts. The other business men wore white shirts with detachable collars, high and stiff or low and sprawling, which were changed much oftener than the shirts. Neither of my heroes was afraid of laundry bills. They did not wear waistcoats, but went about in their shirt-sleeves in hot weather; their suspenders were chosen with as much care as their neckties and handkerchiefs. Once when a bee stung my hand in the store (a few of them had got into the brown-sugar barrel), Mr. Dillon himself moistened the sting, put baking soda on it, and bound my hand up with his pocket handkerchief. It was of the smoothest linen, and in one corner was a violet square bearing his initials, R. E. D., in white. There were never any handkerchiefs like that in my family. I cherished it until it was laundered, and I returned it with regret.

It was in the spring and summer that one saw Mr. Dillon and Mr. Trueman at their best. Spring began early with us,—often the first week of April was hot. Every evening when he came back to the store after supper, Dillon had one of his clerks bring two arm-chairs out to the wide sidewalk that ran beside the red brick wall,—office chairs of the old-fashioned sort, with a low round back which formed a half-circle to enclose the sitter, and spreading legs, the front ones slightly higher. In those chairs the two friends would spend the evening. Dillon would sit down and light a good cigar. In a few moments Mr. Trueman would come across from Main Street, walking slowly, spaciously, as if he were used to a great deal of room. As he approached, Mr. Dillon would call out to him:

"Good evening, J. H. Fine weather."

J. H. would take his place in the empty chair.

"Spring in the air," he might remark, if it were April. Then he would relight a dead cigar which was always in his hand,—seemed to belong there, like a thumb or finger.

"I drove up north today to see what the Swedes are doing," Mr. Dillon might begin. "They're the boys to get the early worm. They never let the ground go to sleep. Whatever moisture there is, they get the benefit of it."

"The Swedes are good farmers. I don't sympathize with the way they work their women."

"The women like it, J. H. It's the old-country way; they're accustomed to it, and they like it."

"Maybe. I don't like it," Trueman would reply with something like a grunt.

They talked very much like this all evening; or, rather, Mr. Dillon talked, and Mr. Trueman made an occasional observation. No one could tell just how much Mr. Trueman knew about anything, because he was so consistently silent. Not from diffidence, but from superiority; from a contempt for chatter, and a liking for silence, a taste for it. After they had exchanged a few remarks, he and Dillon often sat in an easy quiet for a long time, watching the passers-by, watching the wagons on the road, watching the stars. Sometimes, very rarely, Mr. Trueman told a long story, and it was sure to be an interesting and unusual one.

But on the whole it was Mr. Dillon who did the talking; he had a wide-awake voice with much variety in it. Trueman's was thick and low,—his speech was rather indistinct and never changed in pitch or tempo. Even when he swore wickedly at the hands who were loading his cattle into freight cars, it was a mutter, a low, even growl. There was a curious attitude in men of his class and time, that of being rather above speech, as they were above any kind of fussiness or eagerness. But I knew he liked to hear Mr. Dillon talk,— anyone did. Dillon had such a crisp, clear enunciation, and he could say things so neatly. People would take a reprimand from him they wouldn't have taken from anyone else, because he put it so well. His voice was never warm or soft—it had a cool, sparkling quality; but it could be very humorous, very kind and considerate, very teasing and stimulating. Every sentence he uttered was alive, never languid, perfunctory, slovenly, unaccented. When he made a remark, it not only meant something, but sounded like something,—sounded like the thing he meant.

When Mr. Dillon was closeted with a depositor in his private room in the bank, and you could not hear his words through the closed door, his voice told you exactly the degree of esteem in which he held that customer. It was interested, encouraging, deliberative, humorous, satisfied, admiring, cold, critical, haughty, contemptuous, according to the deserts and pretensions of his listener. And one could tell when the person closeted with him was a woman; a farmer's wife, or a woman who was trying to run a little business, or a country girl hunting a situation. There was a difference; something peculiarly kind and encouraging. But if it were a foolish, extravagant woman, or a girl he didn't approve of, oh, then one knew it well enough! The tone was courteous, but cold; relentless as the multiplication table.

All these possibilities of voice made his evening talk in the spring dusk very interesting; interesting for Trueman and for me. I found many pretexts for lingering near them, and they never seemed to mind my hanging about. I was very quiet. I often sat on the edge of the sidewalk with my feet hanging down and played jacks by the hour when there was moonlight. On dark nights I sometimes perched on top of one of the big goods-boxes—we called them "store boxes,"—there were usually several of these standing empty on the sidewalk against the red brick wall.

I liked to listen to those two because theirs was the only "conversation" one could hear about the streets. The older men talked of nothing but politics and their business, and the very young men's talk was entirely what they called "josh"; very personal, supposed to be funny, and really not funny at all. It was scarcely speech, but noises, snorts, giggles, yawns, sneezes, with a few abbreviated words and slang expressions which stood for a hundred things. The original Indians of the Kansas plains had more to do with articulate speech than had our promising young men.

To be sure my two aristocrats sometimes discussed politics, and joked each other about the policies and pretentions of their respective parties. Mr. Dillon, of course, was a Democrat,—it was in the very frosty sparkle of his speech,—and Mr. Trueman was a Republican;

his rear, as he walked about the town, looked a little like the walking elephant labelled "G. O. P." in *Puck*. But each man seemed to enjoy hearing his party ridiculed, took it as a compliment.

In the spring their talk was usually about weather and planting and pasture and cattle. Mr. Dillon went about the country in his light buckboard a great deal at that season, and he knew what every farmer was doing and what his chances were, just how much he was falling behind or getting ahead.

"I happened to drive by Oscar Ericson's place today, and I saw as nice a lot of calves as you could find anywhere," he would begin, and Ericson's history and his family would be pretty thoroughly discussed before they changed the subject.

Or he might come out with something sharp: "By the way, J. H., I saw an amusing sight today. I turned in at Sandy Bright's place to get water for my horse, and he had a photographer out there taking pictures of his house and barn. It would be more to the point if he had a picture taken of the mortgages he's put on that farm."

Trueman would give a short, mirthless response, more like a cough than a laugh.

Those April nights, when the darkness itself tasted dusty (or, by the special mercy of God, cool and damp), when the smell of burning grass was in the air, and a sudden breeze brought the scent of wild plum blossoms,—those evenings were only a restless preparation for the summer nights,—nights of full liberty and perfect idleness. Then there was no school, and one's family never bothered about where one was. My parents were young and full of life, glad to have the children out of the way. All day long there had been the excitement that intense heat produces in some people,—a mild drunkenness made of sharp contrasts; thirst and cold water, the blazing stretch of Main Street and the cool of the brick stores when one dived into them. By nightfall one was ready to be quiet. My two friends were always in their best form on those moonlit summer nights, and their talk covered a wide range.

I suppose there were moonless nights, and dark ones with but a silver shaving and pale stars in the sky, just as in the spring. But I remember them all as flooded by the rich indolence of a full moon, or a half-moon set in uncertain blue. Then Trueman and Dillon would sit with their coats off and have a supply of fresh handkerchiefs to mop their faces; they were more largely and positively themselves. One could distinguish their features, the stripes on their shirts, the flash of Mr. Dillon's diamond; but their shadows made two dark masses on the white sidewalk. The brick wall behind them, faded almost pink by the burning of successive summers, took on a carnelian hue at night. Across the street, which was merely a dusty road, lay an open space, with a few stunted box-elder trees, where the farmers left their wagons and teams when they came to town. Beyond this space stood a row of frail wooden buildings, due to be pulled down any day; tilted, crazy, with outside stairs going up to rickety second-storey porches that sagged in the middle. They had once been white, but were now grey, with faded blue doors along the wavy upper porches. These abandoned buildings, an eyesore by day, melted together into a curious pile in the moonlight, became an immaterial structure of velvet-white and glossy blackness, with here and there a faint smear of blue door, or a tilted patch of sage-green that had once been a shutter.

The road, just in front of the sidewalk where I sat and played jacks, would be ankle-deep in dust, and seemed to drink up the moonlight like folds of velvet. It drank up sound, too; muffled the wagon-wheels and hoof-beats; lay soft and meek like the last residuum of material things,—the soft bottom resting-place. Nothing in the world, not snow mountains or blue seas, is so beautiful in moonlight as the soft, dry summer roads in a farming country, roads where the white dust falls back from the slow wagon-wheel.

Wonderful things do happen even in the dullest places—in the corn-fields and the wheat-fields. Sitting there on the edge of the sidewalk one summer night, my feet hanging in the warm dust, I saw an occultation of Venus. Only the three of us were there. It was a hot night, and the clerks had closed the store and gone home. Mr. Dillon and Mr. Trueman waited on a little while to watch. It was a very blue night, breathless and clear, not the smallest cloud from horizon to horizon. Everything up there overhead seemed as usual, it was the familiar face of a summer-night sky. But presently we saw one bright star moving. Mr. Dillon called to me; told me to watch what was going to happen, as I might never chance to see it again in my lifetime.

That big star certainly got nearer and nearer the moon,—very rapidly, too, until there was not the width of your hand between them—now the width of two fingers—then it passed directly into the moon at about the middle of its girth; absolutely disappeared. The star we had been watching was gone. We waited, I do not know how long, but it seemed to me about fifteen minutes. Then we saw a bright wart on the other edge of the moon, but for a second only,— the machinery up there worked fast. While the two men were exclaiming and telling me to look, the planet swung clear of the golden disk, a rift of blue came between them and widened very fast. The planet did not seem to move, but that inky blue space between it and the moon seemed to spread. The thing was over.

My friends stayed on long past their usual time and talked about eclipses and such matters.

"Let me see," Mr. Trueman remarked slowly, "they reckon the moon's about two hundred and fifty thousand miles away from us. I wonder how far that star is."

"I don't know, J. H., and I really don't much care. When we can get the tramps off the railroad, and manage to run this town with one fancy house instead of two, and have a Federal Government that is as honest as a good banking business, then it will be plenty of time to turn our attention to the star."

Mr. Trueman chuckled and took his cigar from between his teeth. "Maybe the stars will throw some light on all that, if we get the run of them," he said humorously. Then he added: "Mustn't be a reformer, R. E. Nothing in it. That's the only time you ever get off on the wrong foot. Life is what it always has been, always will be. No use to make a fuss." He got up, said: "Good-night, R. E.," said good-night to me, too, because this had been an unusual occasion, and went down the sidewalk with his wide, sailor-like tread, as if he were walking the deck of his own ship.

When Dillon and Trueman went to St. Joseph, or, as we called it, St. Joe, they stopped at the same hotel, but their diversions were very dissimilar. Mr. Dillon was a family man and a good Catholic; he behaved in St. Joe very much as if he were at home. His sister was Mother Superior of a convent there, and he went to see her often.

The nuns made much of him, and he enjoyed their admiration and all the ceremony with which they entertained him. When his two daughters were going to the convent school, he used to give theatre parties for them, inviting their friends.

Mr. Trueman's way of amusing himself must have tried his friend's patience—Dillon liked to regulate other people's affairs if they needed it. Mr. Trueman had a lot of poker-playing friends among the commission men in St. Joe, and he sometimes dropped a good deal of money. He was supposed to have rather questionable women friends there, too. The grasshopper men of our town used to say that Trueman was financial adviser to a woman who ran a celebrated sporting house. Mary Trent, her name was. She must have been a very unusual woman; she had credit with all the banks, and never got into any sort of trouble. She had formerly been head mistress of a girls' finishing school and knew how to manage young women. It was probably a fact that Trueman knew her and found her interesting, as did many another sound business man of that time. Mr. Dillon must have shut his ears to these rumors,—a measure of the great value he put on Trueman's companionship.

Though they did not see much of each other on these trips, they immensely enjoyed taking them together. They often dined together at the end of the day, and afterwards went to the theatre. They both loved the theatre; not this play or that actor, but the theatre,— whether they saw *Hamlet or Pinafore*. It was an age of good acting, and the drama held a more dignified position in the world than it holds today.

After Dillon and Trueman had come home from the city, they used sometimes to talk over the plays they had seen, recalling the great scenes and fine effects. Occasionally an item in the Kansas City *Star* would turn their talk to the stage.

"J. H., I see by the paper that Edwin Booth is very sick," Mr. Dillon announced one evening as Trueman came up to take the empty chair.

"Yes, I noticed." Trueman sat down and lit his dead cigar. "He's not a young man any more." A long pause. Dillon always seemed to know when the pause would be followed by a remark, and waited for it. "The first time I saw Edwin Booth was in Buffalo. It was in

Richard the Second, and it made a great impression on me at the time." Another pause. "I don't know that I'd care to see him in that play again. I like tragedy, but that play's a little too tragic. Something very black about it. I think I prefer *Hamlet.*"

They had seen Mary Anderson in St. Louis once, and talked of it for years afterwards. Mr. Dillon was very proud of her because she was a Catholic girl, and called her "our Mary." It was curious that a third person, who had never seen these actors or read the plays, could get so much of the essence of both from the comments of two business men who used none of the language in which such things are usually discussed, who merely reminded each other of moments here and there in the action. But they saw the play over again as they talked of it, and perhaps whatever is seen by the narrator as he speaks is sensed by the listener, quite irrespective of words. This transference of experience went further: in some way the lives of those two men came across to me as they talked, the strong, bracing reality of successful, large-minded men who had made their way in the world when business was still a personal adventure.

II

Mr. Dillon went to Chicago once a year to buy goods for his store. Trueman would usually accompany him as far as St. Joe, but no farther. He dismissed Chicago as "too big." He didn't like to be one of the crowd, didn't feel at home in a city where he wasn't recognized as J. H. Trueman.

It was one of these trips to Chicago that brought about the end— for me and for them; a stupid, senseless, commonplace end.

Being a Democrat, already somewhat "tainted" by the free-silver agitation, one spring Dillon delayed his visit to Chicago in order to be there for the Democratic Convention—it was the Convention that first nominated Bryan.

On the night after his return from Chicago, Mr. Dillon was seated in his chair on the sidewalk, surrounded by a group of men who wanted to hear all about the nomination of a man from a neighbour State. Mr. Trueman came across the street in his leisurely way, greeted

Dillon, and asked him how he had found Chicago,—whether he had had a good trip.

Mr. Dillon must have been annoyed because Trueman didn't mention the Convention. He threw back his head rather haughtily. "Well, J. H., since I saw you last, we've found a great leader in this country, and a great orator." There was a frosty sparkle in his voice that presupposed opposition,—like the feint of a boxer getting ready.

"Great windbag!" muttered Trueman. He sat down in his chair, but I noticed that he did not settle himself and cross his legs as usual.

Mr. Dillon gave an artificial laugh. "It's nothing against a man to be a fine orator. All the great leaders have been eloquent. This Convention was a memorable occasion; it gave the Democratic party a rebirth."

"Gave it a black eye, and a blind spot, I'd say!" commented Trueman. He didn't raise his voice, but he spoke with more heat than I had ever heard from him. After a moment he added: "I guess Grover Cleveland must be a sick man; must feel like he'd taken a lot of trouble for nothing."

Mr. Dillon ignored these thrusts and went on telling the group around him about the Convention, but there was a special nimbleness and exactness in his tongue, a chill politeness in his voice that meant anger. Presently he turned again to Mr. Trueman, as if he could now trust himself:

"It was one of the great speeches of history, J. H.; our grandchildren will have to study it in school, as we did Patrick Henry's."

"Glad I haven't got any grandchildren, if they'd be brought up on that sort of tall talk," said Mr. Trueman. "Sounds like a schoolboy had written it. Absolutely nothing back of it but an unsound theory."

Mr. Dillon's laugh made me shiver; it was like a thin glitter of danger. He arched his curly eyebrows provokingly.

"We'll have four years of currency reform, anyhow. By the end of that time, you old dyed-in-the-wool Republicans will be thinking differently. The under dog is going to have a chance."

Mr. Trueman shifted in his chair. "That's no way for a banker to talk." He spoke very low. "The Democrats will have a long time to be sorry they ever turned Pops. No use talking to you while your Irish is up. I'll wait till you cool off." He rose and walked away, less deliberately than usual, and Mr. Dillon, watching his retreating figure, laughed haughtily and disagreeably. He asked the grain-elevator man to take the vacated chair. The group about him grew, and he sat expounding the reforms proposed by the Democratic candidate until a late hour.

For the first time in my life I listened with breathless interest to a political discussion. Whoever Mr. Dillon failed to convince, he convinced me. I grasped it at once: that gold had been responsible for most of the miseries and inequalities of the world; that it had always been the club the rich and cunning held over the poor; and that "the free and unlimited coinage of silver" would remedy all this. Dillon declared that young Mr. Bryan had looked like the patriots of old when he faced and challenged high finance with: "You shall not press this crown of thorns upon the brow of labour; you shall not crucify mankind upon a cross of gold." I thought that magnificent; I thought the cornfields would show them a thing or two, back there!

R. E. Dillon had never taken an aggressive part in politics. But from that night on, the Democratic candidate and the free-silver plank were the subject of his talks with his customers and depositors. He drove about the country convincing the farmers, went to the neighbouring towns to use his influence with the merchants, organized the Bryan Club and the Bryan Ladies' Quartette in our county, contributed largely to the campaign fund. This was all a new line of conduct for Mr. Dillon, and it sat unsteadily on him. Even his voice became unnatural; there was a sting of come-back in it. His new character made him more like other people and took away from his special personal quality. I wonder whether it was not Trueman, more than Bryan, who put such an edge on him.

While all these things were going on, Trueman kept to his own office. He came to Dillon's bank on business, but he did not "come back to the sidewalk," as I put it to myself. He waited and said nothing, but he looked grim. After a month or so, when he saw that this thing was not going to blow over, when he heard how Dillon had been talking to representative men all over the county, and saw the figure he had put down for the campaign fund, then Trueman remarked to some of his friends that a banker had no business to commit himself to a scatter-brained financial policy which would destroy credit.

The next morning Mr. Trueman went to the bank across the street, the rival of Dillon's, and wrote a cheque on Dillon's bank "for the amount of my balance." He wasn't the sort of man who would ever know what his balance was, he merely kept it big enough to cover emergencies. That afternoon the Merchants' National took the check over to Dillon on its collecting rounds, and by night the word was all over town that Trueman had changed his bank. After this there would be no going back, people said. To change your bank was one of the most final things you could do. The little, unsuccessful men were pleased, as they always are at the destruction of anything strong and fine.

All through the summer and the autumn of that campaign Mr. Dillon was away a great deal. When he was at home, he took his evening airing on the sidewalk, and there was always a group of men about him, talking of the coming election; that was the most exciting presidential campaign people could remember. I often passed this group on my way to the post-office, but there was no temptation to linger now. Mr. Dillon seemed like another man, and my zeal to free humanity from the cross of gold had cooled. Mr. Trueman I seldom saw. When he passed me on the street, he nodded kindly.

The election and Bryan's defeat did nothing to soften Dillon. He had been sure of a Democratic victory. I believe he felt almost as if Trueman were responsible for the triumph of Hanna and McKinley. At least he knew that Trueman was exceedingly well satisfied, and that was bitter to him. He seemed to me sarcastic and sharp all the time now.

I don't believe self-interest would ever have made a breach between Dillon and Trueman. Neither would have taken advantage of the other. If a combination of circumstances had made it necessary that one or the other should take a loss in money or prestige, I think Trueman would have pocketed the loss. That was his way. It was his code, moreover. A gentleman pocketed his gains mechanically, in the day's routine; but he pocketed losses punctiliously, with a sharp, if bitter, relish. I believe now, as I believed then, that this was a quarrel of "principle." Trueman looked down on anyone who could take the reasoning of the Populist party seriously. He was a perfectly direct man, and he showed his contempt. That was enough. It lost me my special pleasure of summer nights: the old stories of the early West that sometimes came to the surface; the minute biographies of the farming people; the clear, detailed, illuminating accounts of all that went on in the great crop-growing, cattle-feeding world; and the silence,—the strong, rich, out-flowing silence between two friends, that was as full and satisfying as the moonlight. I was never to know its like again.

After that rupture nothing went well with either of my two great men. Things were out of true, the equilibrium was gone. Formerly, when they used to sit in their old places on the sidewalk, two black figures with patches of shadow below, they seemed like two bodies held steady by some law of balance, an unconscious relation like that between the earth and the moon. It was this mathematical harmony which gave a third person pleasure.

Before the next presidential campaign came round, Mr. Dillon died (a young man still) very suddenly, of pneumonia. We didn't know that he was seriously ill until one of his clerks came running to our house to tell us he was dead. The same clerk, half out of his wits— it looked like the end of the world to him—ran on to tell Mr. Trueman.

Mr. Trueman thanked him. He called his confidential man, and told him to order flowers from Kansas City. Then he went to his house, informed his housekeeper that he was going away on business, and packed his bag. That same night he boarded the Santa Fé Limited and didn't stop until he was in San Francisco. He was gone all spring. His confidential clerk wrote him letters every week about the business and the new calves, and got telegrams in reply. Trueman never wrote letters.

When Mr. Trueman at last came home, he stayed only a few months. He sold out everything he owned to a stranger from Kansas City; his feeding ranch, his barns and sheds, his house and town lots. It was a terrible blow to me; now only the common, everyday people would be left. I used to walk mournfully up and down before his office while all these deeds were being signed,—there were usually lawyers and notaries inside. But once, when he happened to be alone, he called me in, asked me how old I was now, and how far along I had got in school. His face and voice were more than kind, but he seemed absent-minded, as if he were trying to recall something. Presently he took from his watch-chain a red seal I had always admired, reached for my hand, and dropped the piece of carnelian into my palm.

"For a keepsake," he said evasively.

When the transfer of his property was completed, Mr. Trueman left us for good. He spent the rest of his life among the golden hills of San Francisco. He moved into the Saint Francis Hotel when it was first built, and had an office in a high building at the top of what is now Powell Street. There he read his letters in the morning and played poker at night. I've heard a man whose offices were next his tell how Trueman used to sit tilted back in his desk chair, a half-consumed cigar in his mouth, morning after morning, apparently doing nothing, watching the Bay and the ferry-boats, across a line of wind-racked eucalyptus trees. He died at the Saint Francis about nine years after he left our part of the world.

The breaking-up of that friendship between two men who scarcely noticed my existence was a real loss to me, and has ever since been a regret. More than once, in Southern countries where there is a smell of dust and dryness in the air and the nights are intense, I have come upon a stretch of dusty white road drinking up the moonlight beside a blind wall, and have felt a sudden sadness. Perhaps it was not until the next morning that I knew why,—and then only because I had dreamed of Mr. Dillon or Mr. Trueman in my sleep. When that old scar is occasionally touched by chance, it rouses the old uneasiness; the feeling of something broken that could so easily have been mended; of something delightful that was senselessly wasted, of a truth that was accidentally distorted—one of the truths we want to keep.

The Old Beauty and Others

The Old Beauty

One brilliant September morning in 1922 a slender, fair-skinned man with white moustaches, waxed and turned up at the ends, stepped hurriedly out of the Hôtel Splendide at Aix-lex-Bains and stood uncertainly at the edge of the driveway. He stood there for some moments, holding, or rather clutching, his gloves in one hand, a light cane in the other. The pavement was wet, glassy with water. The boys were still sprinkling the walk farther down the hill, and the fuchsias and dahlias in the beds sparkled with water drops. The clear air had the freshness of early morning and the smell of autumn foliage.

Two closed litters, carried by porters, came out of a side door and went joggling down the hill toward the baths. The gentleman standing on the kerb followed these eagerly with his eyes, as if about to dash after them; indeed, his mind seemed to accompany them to the turn in the walk where they disappeared, then to come back to him where he stood and at once to dart off in still another direction.

The gentleman was Mr. Henry Seabury, aged fifty-five, American-born, educated in England, and lately returned from a long business career in China. His evident nervousness was due to a shock: an old acquaintance, who had been one of the brilliant figures in the world of the 1890's, had died a few hours ago in this hotel.

As he stood there he was thinking that he ought to send tele-grams . . . but to whom? The lady had no immediate family, and the distinguished men of her time who had cherished the slightest at-tention from her were all dead. No, there was one (perhaps the most variously gifted of that group) who was still living: living in seclusion down on the Riviera, in a great white mansion set in miles of park and garden. A cloud had come over this man in the midst of a triumphant public life. His opponents had ruined his career by a whispering campaign. They had set going a rumour which would have killed any public man in England at that time. Mr. Seabury began composing his telegram to Lord H——. Lord H—— would recognize that this death was more than the death of an individual. To him her name would recall a society whose manners, dress, conventions, loyalties, codes of honour, were different from anything existing in the world today.

And there were certainly old acquaintances like himself, men not of her intimate circle, scattered about over the world; in the States, in China, India. But how to reach them?

Three young men came up the hill to resolve his perplexity; three newspaper correspondents, English, French, American. The American spoke to his companions. "There's the man I've seen about with her so much. He's the one we want."

The three approached Mr. Seabury, and the American addressed him. "Mr. Seabury, I believe? Excuse my stopping you, but we have just learned through the British Consulate that the former Lady Longstreet died in this hotel last night. We are newspaper men, and must send dispatches to our papers." He paused to introduce his companions by their names and the names of their journals. "We thought you might be good enough to tell us something about Lady Longstreet, Madame de Couçy, as she was known here."

"Nothing but what all the world knows." This intrusion had steadied Mr. Seabury, brought his scattered faculties to a focus.

"But we must jog the world's memory a little. A great many things have happened since Lady Longstreet was known everywhere."

"Certainly. You have only to cable your papers that Madame de Couçy, formerly Lady Longstreet, died here last night. They have in their files more than I could tell you if I stood here all morning."

"But the circumstances of her death?"

"You can get that from the management. Her life was interesting, but she died like anyone else—just as you will, some day."

"Her old friends, everywhere, would of course like to learn something about her life here this summer. No one knew her except as Madame de Couçy, so no one observed her very closely. You were with her a great deal, and the simple story of her life here would be——"

"I understand, but it is quite impossible. Good morning, gentlemen." Mr. Seabury went to his room to write his telegram to Lord H——.

II

Two months ago Henry Seabury had come here almost directly from China. His hurried trip across America and his few weeks in London scarcely counted. He was hunting for something, some spot that was still more or less as it used to be. Here, at Aix-lex-Bains, he found the place unchanged,—and in the hotels many people very like those who used to come there.

The first night after he had settled himself at the Splendide he became interested in two old English ladies who dined at a table not far from his own. They had been coming here for many years, he felt sure. They had the old manner. They were at ease and reserved. Their dress was conservative. They were neither painted nor plucked, their nails were neither red nor green. One was plump, distinctly plump, indeed, but as she entered the dining-room he had noticed that she was quick in her movements and light on her feet. She was radiantly cheerful and talkative. But it was the other lady who interested him. She had an air of distinction, that unmistakable thing, which told him she had been a personage. She was tall, had a fine figure and carriage, but either she was much older than her friend, or life had used her more harshly. Something about her eyes and brow teased his memory. Had he once known her, or did she merely recall a type of woman he used to know? No, he felt that he must have met her, at least, long ago, when she was not a stern, gaunt-cheeked old woman with a yellowing complexion. The hotel management informed him that the lady was Madame de Couçy. He had never known anyone of that name.

The next afternoon when he was sitting under the plane trees in the *Place,* he saw the two ladies coming down the hill; the tall one moving with a peculiar drifting ease, looking into the distance as if the unlevel walk beneath her would naturally accommodate itself to her footing. She kept a white fur well up about her cheeks, though the day was hot. The short one tripped along beside her. They crossed the Square, sat down under the trees, and had tea brought out from the confectioner's. Then the muffled lady let her fur fall back a little and glanced about her. He was careful not to stare, but once, when he suddenly lifted his eyes, she was looking directly at him. He thought he saw a spark of curiosity, perhaps recognition.

The two ladies had tea in the *Place* every afternoon unless it rained; when they did not come Seabury felt disappointed. Sometimes the taller one would pause before she sat down and suggest going farther, to the Casino. Once he was near enough to hear the rosy one exclaiming: "Oh, no! It's much nicer here, really. You are always dissatisfied when we go to the Casino. There are more of the kind you hate there."

The older one with a shrug and a mournful smile sat down resignedly in front of the pastry shop. When she had finished her tea she drew her wrap up about her chin as if about to leave, but her companion began to coax: "Let us wait for the newspaper woman. It's almost time for her, and I do like to get the home papers."

The other reminded her that there would be plenty of papers at the hotel.

"Yes, yes, I know. But I like to get them from her. I'm sure she's glad of our pennies."

When they left their table they usually walked about the Square for a time, keeping to the less frequented end toward the Park. They bought roses at the flower booths, and cyclamen from an old country woman who tramped about with a basketful of them. Then they went slowly up the hill toward the hotel.

III

Seabury's first enlightenment about these solitary women came from a most unlikely source.

Going up to the summit of Mont Revard in the little railway train one morning, he made the acquaintance of an English family (father, mother, and two grown daughters) whom he liked very much. He spent the day on the mountain in their company, and after that he saw a great deal of them. They were from Devonshire, home-staying people, not tourists. (The daughters had never been on the Continent before.) They had come over to visit the son's grave in one of the war cemeteries in the north of France. The father brought them down to Aix to cheer them up a little. (He and his wife had come there on their honeymoon, long ago.) As the Thompsons were stopping at a cramped, rather mean little hotel down in the town, they spent most of the day out of doors. Usually the mother and one of the daughters sat the whole morning in the *Place*, while the other girl went off tramping with the father. The mother knitted, and the girl read aloud to her. Whichever daughter it happened to be kept a watchful eye on Mrs. Thompson. If her face grew too pensive, the girl would close the book and say:

"Now, Mother, do let us have some chocolate and croissants. The breakfast at that hotel is horrid, and I'm famished."

Mr. Seabury often joined them in the morning. He found it very pleasant to be near that kind of family feeling. They felt his friendliness, the mother especially, and were pleased to have him join them at their chocolate, or to go with him to afternoon concerts at the Grand-Cercle.

One afternoon when the mother and both daughters were having tea with him near the Roman Arch, the two English ladies from his hotel crossed the Square and sat down at a table not far away. He noticed that Mrs. Thompson glanced often in their direction. Seabury kept his guests a long while at tea,—the afternoon was hot, and he knew their hotel was stuffy. He was telling the girls something about China, when the two unknown English ladies left their table and got into a taxi. Mrs. Thompson turned to Seabury and said in a low, agitated voice:

"Do you know, I believe the tall one of those two was Lady Longstreet."

Mr. Seabury started. "Oh, no! Could it be possible?"

"I am afraid it is. Yes, she is greatly changed. It's very sad. Six years ago she stayed at a country place near us, in Devonshire, and I used often to see her out on her horse. She still rode then. I don't think I can be mistaken."

In a flash everything came back to Seabury. "You're right, I'm sure of it, Mrs. Thompson. The lady lives at my hotel, and I've been puzzling about her. I knew Lady Longstreet slightly many years ago.

Now that you tell me, I can see it. But . . . as you say, she is greatly changed. At the hotel she is known as Madame de Couçy."

"Yes, she married during the war; a Frenchman. But it must have been after she had lost her beauty. I had never heard of the marriage until he was killed,—in '17, I think. Then some of the English papers mentioned that he was the husband of Gabrielle Longstreet. It's very sad when those beautiful ones have to grow old, isn't it? We never have too many of them, at best."

The younger daughter threw her arms about Mrs. Thompson. "Oh, Mother, I wish you hadn't told us! I'm afraid Mr. Seabury does, too. It's such a shock."

He protested. "Yes, it is a shock, certainly. But I'm grateful to Mrs. Thompson. I must be very stupid not to have seen it. I'm glad to know. The two ladies seem very much alone, and the older one looks ill. I might be of some service, if she remembers me. It's all very strange: but one might be useful, perhaps, Mrs. Thompson?"

"That's the way to look at it, Mr. Seabury." Mrs. Thompson spoke gently. "I think she does remember you. When you were talking to Dorothy, turned away from them, she glanced at you often. The lady with her is a friend, don't you think, not a paid companion?"

He said he was sure of it, and she gave him a warm, grateful glance as if he and she could understand how much that meant, then turned to her daughters: "Why, there is Father, come to look for us!" She made a little signal to the stout, flushed man who was tramping across the Square in climbing boots.

IV

Mr. Seabury did not go back to his hotel for dinner. He dined at a little place with tables in the garden, and returned late to the Splendide. He felt rather knocked up by what Mrs. Thompson had told him,—felt that in this world people have to pay an extortionate price for any exceptional gift whatever. Once in his own room, he lay for a long while in a chaise longue before an open window, watching the stars and the fireflies, recalling the whole romantic story,—all he had ever known of Lady Longstreet. And in this hotel, full of people, she was unknown—she!

Gabrielle Longstreet was a name known all over the globe,—even in China, when he went there twenty-seven years ago. Yet she was not an actress or an adventuress. She had come into the European world in a perfectly regular, if somewhat unusual, way.

Sir Wilfred Longstreet, a lover of yachting and adventure on the high seas, had been driven into Martinique by a tropical hurricane. Strolling about the harbour town, he saw a young girl coming out of a church with her mother; the girl was nineteen, the mother perhaps forty. They were the two most beautiful women he had ever seen. The hurricane passed and was forgotten, but Sir Wilfred Longstreet's yacht still lay in the harbour of Fort de France. He sought out the girl's father, an English colonial from Barbados, who was easily convinced. The mother not so easily: she was a person of character as well as severe beauty. Longstreet had sworn that he would never take his yacht out to sea unless he carried Gabrielle aboard her. The *Sea Nymph* might lie and rot there.

In time the mother was reassured by letters and documents from England. She wished to do well for her daughter, and what very brilliant opportunities were there in Martinique? As for the girl, she wanted to see the world; she had never been off the island. Longstreet made a settlement upon Madame the mother, and submitted to the two services, civil and religious. He took his bride directly back to England. He had not advised his friends of his marriage; he was a young man who kept his affairs to himself.

He kept his wife in the country for some months. When he opened his town house and took her to London, things went as he could not possibly have foreseen. In six weeks she was the fashion of the town; the object of admiration among his friends, and his father's friends. Gabrielle was not socially ambitious, made no effort to please. She was not witty or especially clever,—had no accomplishments beyond speaking French as naturally as English. She said nothing memorable in either language. She was beautiful, that was all. And she was fresh. She came into that society of old London like a quiet country dawn.

She showed no great zest for this life so different from anything she had ever known; a quiet wonderment rather, faintly tinged with pleasure. There was no glitter about her, no sparkle. She never dressed in the mode: refused to wear crinoline in a world that billowed and swelled with it. Into drawing-rooms full of ladies enriched by marvels of hairdressing (switches, ringlets, puffs, pompadours, waves starred with gems), she came with her brown hair parted in the middle and coiled in a small knot at the back of her head. Hairdressers protested, as one client after another adopted the "mode Gabrielle." (The knot at the nape of the neck! Charwomen had always worn it; it was as old as mops and pails.)

The English liked high colour, but Lady Longstreet had no red roses in her cheeks. Her skin had the soft glow of orient pearls,— the jewel to which she was most often compared. She was not spirited, she was not witty, but no one ever heard her say a stupid thing. She was often called cold. She seemed unawakened, as if she were still an island girl with reserved island good manners. No woman had been so much discussed and argued about for a long stretch of years. It was to the older men that she was (unconsciously, as it seemed) more gracious. She liked them to tell her about events and personages already in the past; things she had come too late to see.

Longstreet, her husband, was none too pleased by the flutter she caused. It was no great credit to him to have discovered a rare creature; since everyone else discovered her the moment they had a glimpse of her. Men much his superiors in rank and importance looked over his head at his wife, passed him with a nod on their way to her. He began to feel annoyance, and waited for this flurry to pass over. But pass it did not. With her second and third seasons in town her circle grew. Statesmen and officers twenty years Longstreet's senior seemed to find in Gabrielle an escape from long boredom. He was jealous without having the common pretexts for jealousy. He began to spend more and more time on his yacht in distant waters. He left his wife in his town house with his spinster cousin as chaperone. Gabrielle's mother came on from Martinique for a season, and was almost as much admired as her daughter. Sir Wilfred found that the Martiniquaises had considerably overshadowed him. He was no longer the interesting "original" he had once been. His unexpected appearances and disappearances were mere incidents in the house and the life which his wife and his cousin had so well organized. He bore this for six years and then, unexpectedly, demanded divorce. He established the statutory grounds, she petitioning for the decree. He made her a generous settlement.

This brought about a great change in Gabrielle Longstreet's life. She remained in London, and bought a small house near St. James's Park. Longstreet's old cousin, to his great annoyance, stayed on with Gabrielle,—the only one of his family who had not treated her like a poor relation. The loyalty of this spinster, a woman of spirit, Scotch on the father's side, did a good deal to ease Gabrielle's fall in the world. For fall it was, of course. She had her circle, but it was smaller and more intimate. Fewer women invited her now, fewer of the women she used to know. She did not go afield for those who affected art and advanced ideas; they would gladly have championed her cause. She replied to their overtures that she no longer went into society. Her men friends never flinched in their loyalty. Those unembarrassed by wives, the bachelors and widowers, were more assiduous than ever. At that dinner table where Gabrielle and "the Honourable MacPhairson," as the old cousin was called, were sometimes the only women, one met promising young men, not yet settled in their careers, and much older men, so solidly and successfully settled that their presence in a company established its propriety.

Nobody could ever say exactly why Gabrielle's house was so attractive. The men who had the entrée there were not skilful at defining such a thing as "charm" in words: that was not at all their line. And they would have been reluctant to admit that a negligible thing like temperature had anything to do with the pleasant relaxation they enjoyed there. The chill of London houses had been one of the cruellest trials the young Martiniquaise had to bear. When she took a house of her own, she (secretly, as if it were a disgraceful thing to do) had a hot-air furnace put in her cellar, and she kept coal fires burning in the grates at either end of the drawing-room. In colour, however, the rooms were not warm, but rather cool and spring-like. Always flowers, and not too many. There was something more flower-like than the flowers,—something in Gabrielle herself (now more herself than ever she had been as Lady Longstreet); the soft pleasure that came into her face when she put out her hand to greet a hero of perhaps seventy years, the look of admiration in her calm grey eyes.

A century earlier her French grandmothers may have greeted the dignitaries of the Church with such a look,—deep feeling, without eagerness of any kind. To a badgered Minister, who came in out of committee meetings and dirty weather, the warm house, the charming companionship which had no request lurking behind it, must have been grateful. The lingering touch of a white hand on his black sleeve can do a great deal for an elderly man who has left a busy and fruitless day behind him and who is worn down by the unreasonable demands of his own party. Nothing said in that room got out into the world. Gabrielle never repeated one man to another,—and as for the Honourable MacPhairson, she never gave anything away, not even a good story!

In time there came about a succession of Great Protectors, and Gabrielle Longstreet was more talked about than in the days of her sensational debut. Whether any of them were ever her lovers, no one could say. They were all men much older than she, and only one of them was known for light behaviour with women. Young men were sometimes asked to her house, but they were made to feel it was by special kindness. Henry Seabury himself had been taken there by young Hardwick, when he was still an undergraduate. Seabury had not known her well, however, until she leased a house in New York and spent two winters there. A jealous woman, and a very clever one, had made things unpleasant for her in London, and Gabrielle had quitted England for a time.

Sitting alone that night, recalling all he had heard of Lady Longstreet, Seabury tried to remember her face just as it was in the days when he used to know her; the beautiful contour of the cheeks, the low, straight brow, the lovely line from the chin to the base of the throat. Perhaps it was her eyes he remembered best; no glint in them, no sparkle, no drive. When she was moved by admiration, they did not glow, but became more soft, more grave; a kind of twilight shadow deepened in them. That look, with her calm white shoulders, her unconsciousness of her body and whatever clothed it, gave her the air of having come from afar off.

And now it was all gone. There was something tense, a little defiant in the shoulders now. The hands that used to lie on her dress forgotten, as a bunch of white violets might lie there . . . Well, it was all gone.

Plain women, he reflected, when they grow old are—simply plain women. Often they improve. But a beautiful woman may become a ruin. The more delicate her beauty, the more it owes to some exquisite harmony in modelling and line, the more completely it is destroyed. Gabrielle Longstreet's face was now unrecognizable. She gave it no assistance, certainly. She was the only woman in the dining-room who used no make-up. She met the winter barefaced. Cheap counterfeits meant nothing to a woman who had had the real thing for so long. She must have been close upon forty when he knew her in New York,—and where was there such a creature in the world today? Certainly in his hurried trip across America and England he had not been gladdened by the sight of one. He had seen only cinema stars, and women curled and plucked and painted to look like them. Perhaps the few very beautiful women he remembered in the past had been illusions, had benefited by a romantic tradition which played upon them like a kindly light . . . and by an attitude in men which no longer existed.

V

When Mr. Seabury awoke the next day it was clear to him that any approach to Madame de Couçy must be made through the amiable-seeming friend, Madame Allison as she was called at the hotel, who always accompanied her. He had noticed that this lady usually went down into the town alone in the morning. After breakfasting he walked down the hill and loitered about the little streets. Presently he saw Madame Allison come out of the English bank, with several small parcels tucked under her arm. He stepped beside her.

"Pardon me, Madame, but I am stopping at your hotel, and I have noticed that you are a friend of Madame de Couçy, whom I think I used to know as Gabrielle Longstreet. It was many years ago, and naturally she does not recognize me. Would it displease her if I sent up my name, do you think?"

Mrs. Allison answered brightly. "Oh, she did recognize you, if you are Mr. Seabury. Shall we sit down in the shade for a moment? I find it very warm here, even for August."

When they were seated under the plane trees she turned to him with a friendly smile and frank curiosity. "She is here for a complete rest and isn't seeing people, but I think she would be glad to see an old friend. She remembers you very well. At first she was not sure about your name, but I asked the porter. She recalled it at once and said she met you with Hardwick, General Hardwick, who was killed in the war. Yes, I'm sure she would be glad to see an old friend."

He explained that he was scarcely an old friend, merely one of many admirers; but he used to go to her house when she lived in New York.

"She said you did. She thought you did not recognize her. But we have all changed, haven't we?"

"And have you and I met before, Madame Allison?"

"Oh, drop the Madame, please! We both speak English, and I am Mrs. Allison. No, we never met. You may have seen me, if you went to the Alhambra. I was Cherry Beamish in those days."

"Then I last saw you in an Eton jacket, with your hair cropped. I never had the pleasure of seeing you out of your character parts, which accounts for my not recognizing——"

She cut him short with a jolly laugh. "Oh, thirty years and two stone would account, would account perfectly! I always did boy parts, you remember. They wouldn't have me in skirts. So I had to keep my weight down. Such a comfort not to fuss about it now. One has a right to a little of one's life, don't you think?"

He agreed. "But I saw you in America also. You had great success there."

She nodded. "Yes, three seasons, grand engagements. I laid by a pretty penny. I was married over there, and divorced over there, quite in the American style! He was a Scotch boy, stranded in Philadelphia. We parted with no hard feelings, but he was too expensive to keep." Seeing the hotel bus, Mrs. Allison hailed it. "I *shall* be glad if Gabrielle feels up to seeing you. She is frightfully dull here and not very well."

VI

The following evening, as Seabury went into the dining-room and bowed to Mrs. Allison, she beckoned him to Madame de Couçy's table. That lady put out her jewelled hand and spoke abruptly.

"Chetty tells me we are old acquaintances, Mr. Seabury. Will you come up to us for coffee after dinner? This is the number of our apartment." As she gave him her card he saw that her hand trembled slightly. Her voice was much deeper than it used to be, and cold. It had always been cool, but soft, like a cool fragrance,—like her eyes and her white arms.

When he rang at Madame de Couçy's suite an hour later, her maid admitted him. The two ladies were seated before an open window, the coffee table near them and the percolator bubbling. Mrs. Allison was the first to greet him. In a moment she retired, leaving him alone with Madame de Couçy.

"It is very pleasant to meet you again, after so many years, Seabury. How did you happen to come?"

Because he had liked the place long ago, he told her.

"And I, for the same reason. I live in Paris now. Mrs. Allison tells me you have been out in China all this while. And how are things there?"

"Not so good now, Lady Longstreet, may I still call you? China is rather falling to pieces."

"Just as here, eh? No, call me as I am known in this hotel, please. When we are alone, you may use my first name; that has survived time and change. As to change, we have got used to it. But you, coming back upon it, this Europe, suddenly . . . it must give you rather a shock."

It was she herself who had given him the greatest shock of all, and in one quick, penetrating glance she seemed to read that fact. She shrugged: there was nothing to be done about it. "Chetty, where are you?" she called.

Mrs. Allison came quickly from another room and poured the coffee. Her presence warmed the atmosphere considerably. She seemed unperturbed by the grimness of her friend's manner; and she herself was a most comfortable little person. Even her too evident plumpness was comfortable, since she didn't seem to mind it. She didn't like living in Paris very well, she said; something rather stiff and chilly about it. But she often ran away and went home to see her nieces and nephews, and they were a jolly lot. Yes, she found it very pleasant here at Aix. And now that an old friend of Gabrielle's had obligingly turned up, they would have someone to talk to, and that would be a blessing.

Madame de Couçy gave a low, mirthless laugh. "She seems to take a good deal for granted, doesn't she?"

"Not where I am concerned, if you mean that. I should be deeply grateful for someone to talk to. Between the three of us we may find a great deal."

"Be sure we shall," said Mrs. Allison. "We have the past, and the present—which is really very interesting, if only you will let yourself think so. Some of the people here are very novel and amusing, and others are quite like people we used to know. Don't you find it so, Mr. Seabury?"

He agreed with her and turned to Madame de Couçy. "May I smoke?"

"What a question to ask in these days! Yes, you and Chetty may smoke. I will take a liqueur."

Mrs. Allison rose. "Gabrielle has a cognac so old and precious that we keep it locked in a cabinet behind the piano." In opening the cabinet she overturned a framed photograph which fell to the floor. "There goes the General again! No, he didn't break, dear. We carry so many photographs about with us, Mr. Seabury."

Madame de Couçy turned to Seabury. "Do you recognize some of my old friends? There are some of yours, too, perhaps. I think I was never sentimental when I was young, but now I travel with my photographs. My friends mean more to me now than when they were alive. I was too ignorant then to realize what remarkable men they were. I supposed the world was always full of great men."

She left her chair and walked with him about the salon and the long entrance hall, stopping before one and another; uniforms, military and naval, caps and gowns; photographs, drawings, engravings. As she spoke of them the character of her voice changed altogether,— became, indeed, the voice Seabury remembered. The hard, dry tone was a form of disguise, he conjectured; a protection behind which she addressed people from whom she expected neither recognition nor consideration.

"What an astonishing lot they are, seeing them together like this," he exclaimed with feeling. "How can a world manage to get on without them?"

"It hasn't managed very well, has it? You may remember that I was a rather ungrateful young woman. I took what came. A great man's time, his consideration, his affection, were mine in the natural course of things, I supposed. But it's not so now. I bow down to them in admiration . . . gratitude. They are dearer to me than when they were my living friends,—because I understand them better."

Seabury remarked that the men whose pictures looked down at them were too wise to expect youth and deep discernment in the same person.

"I'm not speaking of discernment; that I had, in a way. I mean ignorance. I simply didn't know all that lay behind them. I am better informed now. I read everything they wrote, and everything that has been written about them. That is my chief pleasure."

Seabury smiled indulgently and shook his head. "It wasn't for what you knew about them that they loved you."

She put her hand quickly on his arm. "Ah, you said that before you had time to think! You believe, then, that I did mean something to them?" For the first time she fixed on him the low, level, wondering look that he remembered of old: the woman he used to know seemed breathing beside him. When she turned away from him suddenly, he knew it was to hide the tears in her eyes. He had seen her cry once, a long time ago. He had not forgotten.

He took up a photograph and talked, to bridge over a silence in which she could not trust her voice. "What a fine likeness of X—! He was my hero, among the whole group. Perhaps his contradictions fascinated me. I could never see how one side of him managed to live with the other. Yet I know that both sides were perfectly genuine. He was a mystery. And his end was mysterious. No one will ever know where or how. A secret departure on a critical mission, and never an arrival anywhere. It was like him."

Madame de Couçy turned, with a glow in her eyes such as he had never seen there in her youth. "The evening his disappearance was announced . . . Shall I ever forget it! I was in London. The newsboys were crying it in the street. I did not go to bed that night. I sat up in the drawing-room until daylight; hoping, saying the old prayers I used to say with my mother. It was all one could do . . . Young Harney was with him, you remember. I have always been glad of that. Whatever fate was in store for his chief, Harney would have chosen to share it."

Seabury stayed much longer with Madame de Couçy than he had intended. The ice once broken, he felt he might never find her so much herself again. They sat talking about people who were no longer in this world. She knew much more about them than he. Knew so much that her talk brought back not only the men, but their period; its security, the solid exterior, the exotic contradictions behind the screen; the deep, claret-coloured closing years of Victoria's reign. Nobody ever recognizes a period until it has gone by, he reflected: until it lies behind one it is merely everyday life.

VII

The next evening the Thompsons, all four of them, were to dine with Mr. Seabury at the Maison des Fleurs. Their holiday was over, and they would be leaving on the following afternoon. They would stop once more at that spot in the north, to place fresh wreaths, before they took the Channel boat.

When Seabury and his guests were seated and the dinner had been ordered, he was aware that the mother was looking at him rather wistfully. He felt he owed her some confidence, since it was she, really, who had enlightened him. He told her that he had called upon Gabrielle Longstreet last evening.

"And how is she, dear Mr. Seabury? Is she less—less forbidding than when we see her in the Square?"

"She was on her guard at first, but that soon passed. I stayed later than I should have done, but I had a delightful evening. I gather that she is a little antagonistic to the present order—indifferent, at least. But when she talks about her old friends she is quite herself."

Mrs. Thompson listened eagerly. She hesitated and then asked: "Does she find life pleasant at all, do you think?"

Seabury told her how the lady was surrounded by the photographs and memoirs of her old friends; how she never travelled without them. It had struck him that she was living her life over again,—more understandingly than she lived it the first time.

Mrs. Thompson breathed a little sigh. "Then I know that all is well with her. You have done so much to make our stay here pleasant, Mr. Seabury, but your telling us this is the best of all. Even Father will be interested to know that."

The stout man, who wore an ancient tail coat made for him when he was much thinner, came out indignantly. "Even Father! I like that! One of the great beauties of our time, and very popular before the divorce."

His daughter laughed and patted his sleeve. Seabury went on to tell Mrs. Thompson that she had been quite right in surmising the companion to be a friend, not a paid attendant. "And a very charming person, too. She was one of your cleverest music-hall stars. Cherry Beamish."

Here Father dropped his spoon into his soup. "What's that? Cherry Beamish? But we haven't had such another since! Remember her in that coster song, Mother? It went round the world, that did. We were all crazy about her, the boys called her Cherish Beamy. No monkeyshines for her, never got herself mixed up in anything shady."

"Such a womanly woman in private life," Mrs. Thompson murmured. "My Dorothy went to school with two of her nieces. An excellent school, and quite dear. Their Aunt Chetty does everything for them. And now she is with Lady Longstreet! One wouldn't have supposed they'd ever meet, those two. But then things *are* strange now."

There was no lull in conversation at that dinner. After the father had enjoyed several glasses of champagne he delighted his daughters with an account of how Cherry Beamish used to do the tipsy schoolboy coming in at four in the morning and meeting his tutor in the garden.

VIII

Mr. Seabury sat waiting before the hotel in a comfortable car which he now hired by the week. Gabrielle and Chetty drove out with him every day. This afternoon they were to go to Annecy by the wild road along the Echelles. Presently Mrs. Allison came down alone. Gabrille was staying in bed, she said. Last night Seabury had dined with them in their apartment, and Gabrielle had talked too much, she was afraid. "She didn't sleep afterward, but I think she will make it up today if she is quite alone."

Seabury handed her into the car. In a few minutes they were running past the lake of Bourget.

"This gives me an opportunity, Mrs. Allison, to ask you how it came about that you've become Lady Longstreet's protector. It's a beautiful friendship."

She laughed. "And an amazing one? But I think you must call me Chetty, as she does, if we are to be confidential. Yes, I suppose it must seem to you the queerest partnership that war and desolation have made. But you see, she was so strangely left. When I first began to look after her a little, two years ago, she was ill in an hotel in Paris (we have taken a flat since), and there was no one, positively no one but the hotel people, the French doctor, and an English nurse who had chanced to be within call. It was the nurse, really, who gave me my cue. I had sent flowers, with no name, of course. (What would a bygone music-hall name mean to Gabrielle Longstreet?) And I called often to inquire. One morning I met Nurse Ames just as she was going out into the Champs-Élysées for her exercise, and she asked me to accompany her. She was an experienced woman, not young. She remembered when Gabrielle Longstreet's name and photographs were known all over the Continent, and when people at home were keen enough upon meeting her. And here she was, dangerously ill in a foreign hotel, and there was no one, simply no one. To be sure, she was registered under the name of her second husband."

Seabury interrupted. "And who was he, this de Couçy? I have heard nothing about him."

"I know very little myself, I never met him. They had been friends a long while, I believe. He was killed in action—less than a year after they were married. His name was a disguise for her, even then. She came from Martinique, you remember, and she had no relatives in England. Longstreet's people had never liked her. So, you see, she was quite alone."

Seabury took her plump little hand. "And that was where you came in, Chetty?"

She gave his fingers a squeeze. "Thank you! That's nice. It was Nurse Ames who did it. The war made a lot of wise nurses. After Gabrielle was well enough to see people, there was no one for her to see! The same thing that had happened to her friends in England had happened over here. The old men had paid the debt of nature, and the young ones were killed or disabled or had lost touch with her. She once had many friends in Paris. Nurse Ames told me that an old French officer, blinded in the war, sometimes came to see her, guided by his little granddaughter. She said her patient had expressed curiosity about the English woman who had sent so many flowers. I wrote a note, asking whether I could be of any service, and signed my professional name. She might recognize it, she might not. We had been on a committee together during the war. She told the nurse to admit me, and that's how it began."

Seabury took her hand again. "Now I want you to be frank with me. Had she then, or has she now, money worries at all?"

Cherry Beamish chuckled. "Not she, you may believe! But I have had a few for her. On the whole, she's behaved very well. She sold her place in Devonshire to advantage, before the war. Her capital is in British bonds. She seems to you harassed?"

"Sometimes."

Mrs. Allison looked grave and was silent for a little. "Yes," with a sight, "she gets very low at times. She suffers from strange regrets. She broods on the things she might have done for her friends and didn't—thinks she was cold to them. Was she, in those days, so indifferent as she makes herself believe?"

Seabury reflected. "Not exactly indifferent. She wouldn't have been so attractive if she'd been that. She didn't take things very hard, perhaps. She used to strike me as . . . well, we might call it unawakened."

"But wasn't she the most beautiful creature then! I used to see her at the races, and at charity bazaars, in my early professional days. After the war broke out and everybody was all mixed up, I was put on an entertainment committee with her. She wasn't quite the Lady Longstreet of my youth, but she still had that grand style. It was the illness in Paris that broke her. She's changed very fast ever since. You see she thought, once the war was over, the world would be just as it used to be. Of course it isn't."

By this time the car had reached Annecy, and they stopped for tea. The shore of the lake was crowded with young people taking their last dip for the day; sunbrowned backs and shoulders, naked arms and legs. As Mrs. Allison was having her tea on the terrace, she watched the bathers. Presently she twinkled a sly smile at her host. "Do you know, I'm rather glad we didn't bring Gabrielle! It puts her out terribly to see young people bathing naked. She makes comments that are indecent, really! If only she had a swarm of young nieces and nephews, as I have, she'd see things quite differently, and she'd be much happier. Legs were never wicked to us stage people, and now all the young things know they are not wicked."

IX

When Madame de Couçy went out with Seabury alone, he missed the companionship of Cherry Beamish. With Cherry the old beauty always softened a little; seemed amused by the other's interest in whatever the day produced: the countryside, the weather, the number of cakes she permitted herself for tea. The imagination which made this strange friendship possible was certainly on the side of Cherry Beamish. For her, he could see, there was something in it; to be the anchor, the refuge, indeed, of one so out of her natural orbit— selected by her long ago as an object of special admiration.

One afernoon when he called, the maid, answering his ring, said that Madame would not go out this afternoon, but hoped he would stay and have tea with her in her salon. He told the lift boy to dismiss the car and went in to Madame de Couçy. She received him with unusual warmth.

"Chetty is out for the afternoon, with some friends from home. Oh, she still has a great many! She is much younger than I, in every sense. Today I particularly wanted to see you alone. It's curious how the world runs away from one, slips by without one's realizing it."

He reminded her that the circumstances had been unusual. "We have lived through a storm to which the French Revolution, which used to be our standard of horrors, was merely a breeze. A rather gentlemanly affair, as one looks back on it . . . As for me, I am grateful to be alive, sitting here with you in a comfortable hotel (I might be in a prison full of rats), in a France still undestroyed."

The old lady looked into his eyes with the calm, level gaze so rare with her now. "Are you grateful? I am not. I think one should go out with one's time. I particularly wished to see you alone this afternoon. I want to thank you for your tact and gentleness with me one hideous evening long ago; in my house in New York. You were a darling boy to me that night. If you hadn't come along, I don't know how I would have got over it—out of it, even. One can't call the servants."

"But, Gabrielle, why recall a disagreeable incident when you have so many agreeable ones to remember?"

She seemed not to hear him, but went on, speaking deliberately, as if she were reflecting aloud. "It was strange, your coming in just when you did: that night it seemed to me like a miracle. Afterward, I remembered you had been expected at eight. But I had forgotten all that, forgotten everything. Never before or since have I been so frightened. It was something worse than fear."

There was a knock at the door. Madame de Couçy called: *"Entrez!"* without turning round. While the tea was brought she sat looking out of the window, frowning. When the waiter had gone she turned abruptly to Seabury:

"After that night I never saw you again until you walked into the dining-room of this hotel a few weeks ago. I had gone into the country somewhere, hiding with friends, and when I came back to New York, you were already on your way to China. I never had a chance to explain."

"There was certainly no need for that."

"Not for you, perhaps. But for me. You may have thought such scenes were frequent in my life. Hear me out, please," as he protested. "That man had come to my house at seven o'clock that evening and sent up a message begging me to see him about some business matters. (I had been stupid enough to let him make investments for me.) I finished dressing and hurried down to the drawing-room." Here she stopped and slowly drank a cup of tea. "Do you know, after you came in I did not see you at all, not for some time, I think. I was mired down in something . . . *the power of the dog,* the English Prayer Book calls it. But the moment I heard your voice, I knew that I was safe . . . I felt the leech drop off. I have never forgot the sound of your voice that night; so calm, with all a man's strength behind it,— and you were only a boy. You merely asked if you had come too early. I felt the leech drop off. After that I remember nothing. I didn't see you, with my eyes, until you gave me your handkerchief. You stayed with me and looked after me all evening.

"You see, I had let the beast come to my house, oh, a number of times! I had asked his advice and allowed him to make investments for me. I had done the same thing at home with men who knew about such matters; they were men like yourself and Hardwick. In a strange country one goes astray in one's reckonings. I had met that man again and again at the houses of my friends,—your friends! Of course his personality was repulsive to me. One knew at once that under his smoothness he was a vulgar person. I supposed that was not unusual in great bankers in the States."

"You simply chose the wrong banker, Gabrielle. The man's accent must have told you that he belonged to a country you did not admire."

"But I tell you I met him at the houses of decent people."

Seabury shook his head. "Yes, I am afraid you must blame us for that. Americans, even those whom you call the decent ones, do ask people to their houses who shouldn't be there. They are often asked *because* they are outrageous,—and therefore considered amusing. Besides, that fellow had a very clever way of pushing himself. If a man is generous in his contributions to good causes, and is useful on committees and commissions, he is asked to the houses of the people who have these good causes at heart."

"And perhaps I, too, was asked because I was considered notorious? A divorcée, known to have more friends among men than among women at home? I think I see what you mean. There are not many shades in your society. I left the States soon after you sailed for China.

I gave up my New York house at a loss to be rid of it. The instant I recognized you in the dining-room downstairs, that miserable evening came back to me. In so far as our acquaintance was concerned, all that had happened only the night before."

"Then I am reaping a reward I didn't deserve, some thirty years afterward! If I had not happened to call that evening when you were so—so unpleasantly surprised, you would never have remembered me at all! We shouldn't be sitting together at this moment. Now may I ring for some fresh tea, dear? Let us be comfortable. This afternoon had brought us closer together. And this little spot in Savoie is a nice place to renew old friendships, don't you think?"

X

Some hours later, when Mr. Seabury was dressing for dinner, he was thinking of that strange evening in Gabrielle Longstreet's house on Fifty-third Street, New York.

He was then twenty-four years old. She had been very gracious to him all the winter.

On that particular evening he was to take her to dine at Delmonico's. Her cook and butler were excused to attend a wedding. The maid who answered his ring asked him to go up to the drawing-room on the second floor, where Madame was awaiting him. She followed him as far as the turn of the stairway, then, hearing another ring at the door, she excused herself.

He went on alone. As he approached the wide doorway leading into the drawing-room, he was conscious of something unusual; a sound, or perhaps an unnatural stillness. From the doorway he beheld something quite terrible. At the far end of the room Gabrielle Longstreet was seated on a little French sofa—not seated, but silently struggling. Behind the sofa stood a stout, dark man leaning over her. His left arm, about her waist, pinioned her against the flowered silk upholstery. His right hand was thrust deep into the low-cut bodice of her dinner gown. In her struggle she had turned a little on her side; her right arm was in the grip of his left hand, and she was trying to free the other, which was held down by the pressure of his elbow. Neither of those two made a sound. Her face was averted, half hidden against the blue silk back of the sofa. Young Seabury stood still just long enough to see what the situation really was. Then he stepped across the threshold and said with such coolness as he could command: "Am I too early, Madame Longstreet?"

The man behind her started from his crouching position, darted away from the sofa, and disappeared down the stairway. To reach the stairs he passed Seabury, without lifting his eyes, but his face was glistening wet.

The lady lay without stirring, her face now completely hidden. She looked so crushed and helpless, he thought she must be hurt physically. He spoke to her softly: "Madame Longstreet, shall I call—"

"Oh, don't call! Don't call anyone." She began shuddering violently, her face still turned away. "Some brandy, please. Downstairs, in the dining-room."

He ran down the stairs, had to tell the solicitous maid that Madame wished to be alone for the present. When he came back Gabrielle had caught up the shoulder straps of her gown. Her right arm bore red finger marks. She was shivering and sobbing. He slipped his handkerchief into her hand, and she held it over her mouth. She took a little brandy. Then another fit of weeping came on. He begged her to come nearer to the fire. She put her hand on his arm, but seemed unable to rise. He lifted her from that seat of humiliation and took her, wavering between his supporting hands, to a low chair beside the coal grate. She sank into it, and he put a cushion under her feet. He persuaded her to drink the rest of the brandy. She stopped crying and leaned back, her eyes closed, her hands lying nerveless on the arms of the chair. Seabury thought he had never seen her when she was more beautiful . . . probably that was because she was helpless and he was young.

"Perhaps you would like me to go now?" he asked her.

She opened her eyes. "Oh, no! Don't leave me, please. I am so much safer with you here." She put her hand, still cold, on his for a moment, then closed her eyes and went back into that languor of exhaustion.

Perhaps half an hour went by. She did not stir, but he knew she was not asleep: an occasional trembling of the eyelids, tears stealing out from under her black lashes and glistening unregarded on her cheeks; like pearls he thought they were, transparent shimmers on velvet cheeks gone very white.

When suddenly she sat up, she spoke in her natural voice.

"But, my dear boy, you have gone dinnerless all this while! Won't you stay with me and have just a bit of something up here? Do ring for Hopkins, please."

The young man caught at the suggestion. If once he could get her mind on the duties of caring for a guest, that might lead to something. He must try to be very hungry.

The kitchen maid was in and, under Hopkins's direction, got together a creditable supper and brought it up to the drawing-room. Gabrielle took nothing but the hot soup and a little sherry. Young Seabury, once he tasted food, found he had no difficulty in doing away with cold pheasant and salad.

Gabrielle had quite recovered her self-control. She talked very little, but that was not unusual with her. He told her about Hardwick's approaching marriage. For him, the evening went by very pleasantly. He felt with her a closer intimacy than ever before.

When at midnight he rose to take his leave, she detained him beside her chair, holding his hand. "At some other time I shall explain what you saw here tonight. How could such a thing happen in one's own house, in an English-speaking city . . . ?"

"But that was not an English-speaking man who went out from here. He is an immigrant who has made a lot of money. He does not belong."

"Yes, that is true. I wish you weren't going out to China. Not for long, I hope. It's a bad thing to be away from one's own people." Her voice broke, and tears came again. He kissed her hand softly, devotedly, and went downstairs.

He had not seen her again until his arrival at this hotel some weeks ago, when he did not recognize her.

XI

One evening when Mrs. Allison and Madame de Couçy had been dining with Seabury at the Maison des Fleurs, they went into the tea room to have their coffee and watch the dancing. It was now September, and almost everyone would be leaving next week. The floor was full of young people, English, American, French, moving monotonously to monotonous rhythms,—some of them scarcely moving at all. Gabrielle watched them through her lorgnette, with a look of resigned boredom.

Mrs. Allison frowned at her playfully. "Of course it's all very different," she observed, "but then, so is everything." She turned to Seabury: "You know we used to have to put so much drive into a dance act, or it didn't go at all. Lottie Collins was the only lazy dancer who could get anything over. But the truth was, the dear thing couldn't dance at all; got on by swinging her foot! There must be something in all this new manner, if only one could get it. That couple down by the bar now, the girl with the *very* low back: they are doing it beautifully; she dips and rises like a bird in the air . . . a tired bird, though. That's the disconcerting thing. It all seems so tired."

Seabury agreed with her cheerfully that it was charming, though tired. He felt a gathering chill in the lady on his right. Presently she said impatiently: "Haven't you had enough of this, Chetty?"

Mrs. Allison sighed. "You never see anything in it, do you, dear?"

"I see wriggling. They look to me like lizards dancing—or reptiles coupling."

"Oh, no, dear! No! They are such sweet young things. But they are dancing in a dream. I want to go and wake them up. They are missing so much fun. Dancing ought to be open and free, with the lungs full; not mysterious and breathless. I wish I could see a spirited waltz again."

Gabrielle shrugged and gave a dry laugh. "I wish I could dance one! I think I should try, if by any chance I should ever hear a waltz played again."

Seabury rose from his chair. "May I take you up on that? Will you?"

She seemed amused and incredulous, but nodded.

"Excuse me for a moment." He strolled toward the orchestra. When the tango was over he spoke to the conductor, handing him something from his vest pocket. The conductor smiled and bowed, then spoke to his men, who smiled in turn. The saxophone put down his instrument and grinned. The strings sat up in their chairs, pulled themselves up, as it were, tuned for a moment, and sat at attention. At the lift of the leader's hand they began the "Blue Danube."

Gabrielle took Mr. Seabury's arm. They passed a dozen couples who were making a sleepy effort and swung into the open square where the line of tables stopped. Seabury had never danced with Gabrielle Longstreet, and he was astonished. She had attack and style, the grand style, slightly military, quite right for her tall, straight figure. He held her hand very high, accordingly. The conductor caught the idea; smartened the tempo slightly, made the accents sharper. One by one the young couples dropped out and sat down to smoke. The two old waltzers were left alone on the floor. There was a stir of curiosity about the room; who were those two, and why were they doing it? Cherry Beamish heard remarks from the adjoining tables.

"She's rather stunning, the old dear!"

"Aren't they funny?"

"It's so quaint and theatrical. Quite effective in its way."

Seabury had not danced for some time. He thought the musicians drew the middle part out interminably; rather suspected they were playing a joke on him. But his partner lost none of her brilliance and nerve. He tried to live up to her. He was grateful when those fiddlers snapped out the last phrase. As he took Gabrielle to her seat, a little breeze of applause broke out from the girls about the room.

"Dear young things!" murmured Chetty, who was flushed with pleasure and excitement. A group of older men who had come in from the dining-room were applauding.

"Let us go now, Seabury. I am afraid we have been making rather an exhibition," murmured Madame de Couçy. As they got into the car awaiting them outside, she laughed good-humouredly. "Do you know, Chetty, I quite enjoyed it!'

XII

The next morning Mrs. Allison telephoned Seabury that Gabrielle had slept well after an amusing evening: felt so fit that she thought they might seize upon this glorious morning for a drive to the Grande-Chartreuse. The drive, by the route they preferred, was a long one, and hitherto she had not felt quite equal to it. Accordingly, the three left the hotel at eleven o'clock with Seabury's trusty young Savoyard driver, and were soon in the mountains.

It was one of those high-heavenly days that often come among the mountains of Savoie in autumn. In the valleys the hillsides were pink with autumn crocuses thrusting up out of the short sunburned grass. The beech trees still held their satiny green. As the road wound higher and higher toward the heights, Seabury and his companions grew more and more silent. The lightness and purity of the air gave one a sense of detachment from everything one had left behind "down there, back yonder." Mere breathing was a delicate physical pleasure. One had the feeling that life would go on thus forever in high places, among naked peaks cut sharp against a stainless sky.

Ever afterward Seabury remembered that drive as strangely impersonal. He and the two ladies were each lost in a companionship much closer than any they could share with one another. The clean-cut mountain boy who drove them seemed lost in thoughts of his own. His eyes were on the road: he never spoke. Once, when the gold tones of an alpine horn floated down from some hidden pasture far overhead, he stopped the car of his own accord and shut off the engine. He threw a smiling glance back at Seabury and then sat still, while the simple, melancholy song floated down through the blue air. When it ceased, he waited a little, looking up. As the horn did not sing again, he drove on without comment.

At last, beyond a sharp turn in the road, the monastery came into view; acres of slate roof, of many heights and pitches, turrets and steep slopes. The terrifying white mountain crags overhung it from behind, and the green beech wood lay all about its walls. The sunlight blazing down upon that mothering roof showed ruined patches: the Government could not afford to keep such a wilderness of leading in repair.

The monastery, superb and solitary among the lonely mountains, was after all a destination: brought Seabury's party down into man's world again, though it was the world of the past. They began to chatter foolishly, after hours of silent reflection. Mrs. Allison wished to see the kitchen of the Carthusians, and the chapel, but she thought Gabrielle should stay in the car. Madame de Couçy insisted that she was not tired: she would walk about the stone courtyard while the other two went into the monastery.

Except for a one-armed guard in uniform, the great court was empty. Herbs and little creeping plants grew between the cobblestones. The three walked toward the great open well and leaned against the stone wall that encircled it, looking down into its wide mouth. The hewn blocks of the coping were moss-grown, and there was water at the bottom. Madame de Couçy slipped a little mirror from her handbag and threw a sunbeam down into the stone-lined well. That yellow ray seemed to waken the black water at the bottom: little ripples stirred over the surface. She said nothing, but she smiled as she threw the gold plaque over the water and the wet moss of the lower coping. Chetty and Seabury left her there. When he glanced back, just before they disappeared into the labyrinth of buildings, she was still looking down into the well and playing with her little reflector, a faintly contemptuous smile on her lips.

After nearly two hours at the monastery the party started homeward. Seabury told the driver to regulate his speed so that they would see the last light on the mountains before they reached the hotel.

The return trip was ill-starred: they narrowly escaped a serious accident. As they rounded one of those sharp curves, with a steep wall on their right and an open gulf on the left, the chauffeur was confronted by a small car with two women, crossing the road just in front of him. To avoid throwing them over the precipice he ran sharply to the right, grazing the rock wall until he could bring his car to a stop. His passengers were thrown violently forward over the driver's seat. The light car had been on the wrong side of the road, and had attempted to cross on hearing the Savoyard's horn. His nerve and quickness had brought every one off alive, at least.

Immediately the two women from the other car sprang out and ran up to Seabury with shrill protestations; they were very careful drivers, had run this car twelve thousand miles and never had an accident, etc. They were Americans; bobbed, hatless, clad in dirty white knickers and sweaters. They addressed each other as "Marge" and "Jim." Seabury's forehead was bleeding: they repeatedly offered to plaster it up for him.

The Savoyard was in the road, working with his mudguard and

his front wheel. Madame de Couçy was lying back in her seat, pale, her eyes closed, something very wrong with her breathing. Mrs. Allison was fanning her with Seabury's hat. The two girls who had caused all the trouble had lit cigarettes and were swaggering about with their hands in their trousers pockets, giving advice to the driver about his wheel. The Savoyard never lifted his eyes. He had not spoken since he ran his car into the wall. The sharp voices, knowingly ordering him to *"regardez, attendez,"* did not pierce his silence or his contempt. Seabury paid no attention to them because he was alarmed about Madame de Couçy, who looked desperately ill. She ought to lie down, he felt sure, but there was no place to put her—the road was cut along the face of a cliff for a long way back. Chetty had aromatic ammonia in her handbag; she persuaded Gabrielle to take it from the bottle, as they had no cup. While Seabury was leaning over her she opened her eyes and said distinctly:

"I think I am not hurt . . . faintness, a little palpitation. If you could get those creatures away . . ."

He sprang off the running-board and drew the two intruders aside. He addressed them; first politely, then forcibly. Their reply was impertinent, but they got into their dirty little car and went. The Savoyard was left in peace; the situation was simplified. Three elderly people had been badly shaken up and bruised, but the brief submersion in frightfulness was over. At last the driver said he could get his car home safely.

During the rest of the drive Madame de Couçy seemed quite restored. Her colour was not good, but her self-control was admirable.

"You must let me give that boy something on my own account, Seabury. Oh, I know you will be generous with him! But I feel a personal interest. He took a risk, and he took the right one. He couldn't run the chance of knocking two women over a precipice. They happened to be worth nobody's consideration, but that doesn't alter the code."

"Such an afternoon to put you through!" Seabury groaned.

"It was natural, wasn't it, after such a morning? After one has been *exaltée,* there usually comes a shock. Oh, I don't mean the bruises we got! I mean the white breeches." Gabrielle laughed, her good laugh, with no malice in it. She put her hand on his shoulder. "How ever did you manage to dispose of them so quickly?"

When the car stopped before the hotel, Madame de Couçy put a tiny card case into the driver's hand with a smile and a word. But when she tried to rise from the seat, she sank back. Seabury and the Savoyard lifted her out, carried her into the hotel and up the lift, into her own chamber. As they placed her on the bed, Seabury said he would call a doctor. Madame de Couçy opened her eyes and spoke firmly:

"That is not necessary. Chetty knows what to do for me. I shall be myself tomorrow. Thank you both, thank you."

Outside the chamber door Seabury asked Mrs. Allison whether he should telephone for Doctor Françon.

"I think not. A new person would only disturb her. I have all the remedies her own doctor gave me for these attacks. Quiet is the most important thing, really."

The next morning Seabury was awakened very early, something before six o'clock, by the buzz of his telephone. Mrs. Allison spoke, asking in a low voice if he would come to their apartment as soon as possible. He dressed rapidly. The lift was not yet running, so he went up two flights of stairs and rang at their door. Cherry Beamish, in her dressing-gown, admitted him. From her face he knew, at once,—though her smile was almost radiant as she took his hand.

"Yes, it is over for her, poor dear," she said softly. "It must have happened in her sleep. I was with her until after midnight. When I went in again, a little after five, I found her just as I want you to see her now; before her maid comes, before anyone has been informed."

She led him on tiptoe into Gabrielle's chamber. The first shafts of the morning sunlight slanted through the Venetian blinds. A blue dressing-gown hung on a tall chair beside the bed, blue slippers beneath it. Gabrielle lay on her back, her eyes closed. The face that had outfaced so many changes of fortune had no longer need to muffle itself in furs, to shrink away from curious eyes, or harden itself into scorn. It lay on the pillow regal, calm, victorious,—like an open confession.

Seabury stood for a moment looking down at her. Then he went to the window and peered out through the open slats at the sun, come at last over the mountains into a sky that had long been blue: the same mountains they were driving among yesterday.

Presently Cherry Beamish spoke to him. She pointed to the hand that lay on the turned-back sheet. "See how changed her hands are; like those of a young woman. She forgot to take off her rings last night, or she was too tired. Yes, dear, you needed a long rest. And now you are with your own kind."

"I feel that, too, Chetty. She is with them. All is well. Thank you for letting me come." He stooped for a moment over the hand that had been gracious to his youth. They went out into the salon, carefully closing the door behind them.

"Now, my dear, stay here, with her. I will go to the management, and I will arrange all that must be done."

Some hours later, after he had gone through the formalities required by French law, Seabury encountered the three journalists in front of the hotel.

Next morning the great man from the Riviera to whom Seabury had telegraphed came in person, his car laden with flowers from his conservatories. He stood on the platform at the railway station, his white head uncovered, all the while that the box containing Gabrielle Longstreet's coffin was being carried across and put on the express. Then he shook Seabury's hand in farewell, and bent gallantly over Chetty's. Seabury and Chetty were going to Paris on that same express.

After her illness two years ago Gabrielle de Couçy had bought a lot *à perpétuité* in Père-Lachaise. That was rather a fashion then: Adelina Patti, Sarah Bernhardt, and other ladies who had once held a place in the world made the same choice.

The Best Years

I

On a bright September morning in the year 1899 Miss Evangeline Knightly was driving through the beautiful Nebraska land which lies between the Platte River and the Kansas line. She drove slowly, for she loved the country, and she held the reins loosely in her gloved hand. She drove about a great deal and always wore leather gauntlets. Her hands were small, well shaped and very white, but they freckled in hot sunlight.

Miss Knightly was a charming person to meet—and an unusual type in a new country: oval face, small head delicately set (the oval chin tilting inward instead of the square chin thrust out), hazel eyes, a little blue, a little green, tiny dots of brown. . . . Somehow these splashes of colour made light—and warmth. When she laughed, her eyes positively glowed with humour, and in each oval cheek a roguish dimple came magically to the surface. Her laugh was delightful because it was intelligent, discriminating, not the physical spasm which seizes children when they are tickled, and growing boys and girls when they are embarrassed. When Miss Knightly laughed, it was apt to be because of some happy coincidence or droll mistake. The farmers along the road always felt flattered if they could make Miss Knightly laugh. Her voice had as many colours as her eyes—nearly always on the bright side, though it had a beautiful gravity for people who were in trouble.

It is only fair to say that in the community where she lived Miss Knightly was considered an intelligent young woman, but plain—distinctly plain. The standard of female beauty seems to be the same in all newly settled countries: Australia, New Zealand, the farming country along the Platte. It is, and was, the glowing, smiling calendar girl sent out to advertise agricultural implements. Colour was everything, modelling was nothing. A nose was a nose—any shape would do; a forehead was the place where the hair stopped, chin utterly negligible unless it happened to be more than two inches long.

Miss Knightly's old mare, Molly, took her time along the dusty, sunflower-bordered roads that morning, occasionally pausing long enough to snatch off a juicy, leafy sunflower top in her yellow teeth. This she munched as she ambled along. Although Molly had almost the slowest trot in the world, she really preferred walking. Sometimes she fell into a doze and stumbled. Miss Knightly also, when she was abroad on these long drives, preferred the leisurely pace. She loved the beautiful autumn country; loved to look at it, to breathe it. She was not a "dreamy" person, but she was thoughtful and very observing. She relished the morning; the great blue of the sky, smiling, cloudless,—and the land that lay level as far as the eye could see. The horizon was like a perfect circle, a great embrace, and within it lay the cornfields, still green, and the yellow wheat stubble, miles and miles of it, and the pasture lands where the white-faced cattle led lives of utter content. All their movements were deliberate and dignified. They grazed through all the morning; approached their metal water tank and drank. If the windmill had run too long and the tank had overflowed, the cattle trampled the overflow into deep mud and cooled their feet. Then they drifted off to graze again. Grazing was not merely eating, it was also a pastime, a form of reflection, perhaps meditation.

Miss Knightly was thinking, as Molly jogged along, that the barbed-wire fences, though ugly in themselves, had their advantages. They did not cut the country up into patterns as did the rail fences and stone walls of her native New England. They were, broadly regarded, invisible—did not impose themselves upon the eye. She seemed to be driving through a fineless land. On her left the Hereford cattle apparently wandered at will: the tall sunflowers hid the wire that kept them off the road. Far away, on the horizon line, a troop of colts were galloping, all in the same direction—purely for exercise, one would say. Between her and the horizon the white wheels of windmills told her where the farmhouses sat.

Miss Knightly was abroad this morning with a special purpose— to visit country schools. She was the County Superintendent of Public Instruction. A grim title, that, to put upon a charming young woman. . . . Fortunately it was seldom used except on reports which she signed, and there it was usually printed. She was not even called "the Superintendent." A country schoolteacher said to her pupils: "I think Miss Knightly will come to see us this week. She was at Walnut Creek yesterday."

After she had driven westward through the pasture lands for an hour or so, Miss Knightly turned her mare north and very soon came into a rich farming district, where the fields were too valuable to be used for much grazing. Big red barns, rows of yellow straw stacks, green orchards, trim white farmhouses, fenced gardens.

Looking at her watch, Miss Knightly found that it was already after eleven o'clock. She touched Molly delicately with the whip and roused her to a jog trot. Presently they stopped before a little one-storey schoolhouse. All the windows were open. At the hitch-bar in the yard five horses were tethered—their saddles and bridles piled in an empty buckboard. There was a yard, but no fence—though on one side of the playground was a woven-wire fence covered with the vines of study rambler roses—very pretty in the spring. It enclosed a cemetery—very few graves, very much sun and waving yellow grass, open to the singing from the schoolroom and the shouts of the boys playing ball at noon. The cemetery never depressed the children, and surely the school cast no gloom over the cemetery.

When Miss Knightly stopped before the door, a boy ran out to hand her from the buggy and to take care of Molly. The little teacher stood on the doorstep, her face lost, as it were, in a wide smile of tremulous gladness.

Miss Knightly took her hand, held it for a moment and looked down into the child's face—she was scarcely more—and said in the very gentlest shade of her many-shaded voice, "Everything going well, Lesley?"

The teacher replied in happy little gasps, "Oh yes, Miss Knightly! It's all so much easier than it was last year. I have some such lovely children—and they're all *good*!"

Miss Knightly took her arm, and they went into the schoolroom. The pupils grinned a welcome to the visitor. The teacher asked the conventional question: What recitation would she like to hear?

Whatever came next in the usual order, Miss Knightly said.

The class in geography came next. The children were "bounding" the States. When the North Atlantic States had been disposed of with more or less accuracy, the little teacher said they would now jump to the Middle West, to bring the lesson nearer home.

"Suppose we begin with Illinois. That is your State, Edward, so I will call on you."

A pale boy rose and came front of the class; a little fellow aged ten, maybe, who was plainly a newcomer—wore knee pants and stockings, instead of long trousers or blue overalls like the other boys. His hands were clenched at his sides, and he was evidently much frightened. Looking appealingly at the teacher, he began in a high treble: "The State of Illinois is bounded on the north by Lake Michigan, on the east by Lake Michigan . . ." He felt he had gone astray, and language utterly failed. A quick shudder ran over him from head to foot, and an accident happened. His dark blue stockings grew darker still, and his knickerbockers very dark. He stood there as if nailed to the floor. The teacher went up to him and took his hand and led him to his desk.

"You're too tired, Edward," she said. "We're all tired, and it's almost noon. So you can all run out and play, while I talk to Miss Knightly and tell her how naughty you all are."

The children laughed (all but poor Edward), laughed heartily, as if they were suddenly relieved from some strain. Still laughing and punching each other they ran out into the sunshine.

Miss Knightly and the teacher (her name, by the way, was Lesley Ferguesson) sat down on a bench in the corner.

"I'm so sorry that happened, Miss Knightly. I oughtn't to have called on him. He's so new here, and he's a nervous little boy. I thought he'd like to speak up for his State. He seems homesick."

"My dear, I'm glad you did call on him, and I'm glad the poor little fellow had an accident,—if he doesn't get too much misery out of it. The way those children behaved astonished me. Not a wink, or grin, or even a look. Not a wink from the Haymaker boy. I watched him. His mother has no such delicacy. They have just the best kind of good manners. How do you do it, Lesley?"

Lesley gave a happy giggle and flushed as red as a poppy. "Oh, I don't do anything! You see they really *are* nice children. You remember last year I did have a little trouble—till they got used to me."

"But they all passed their finals, and one girl, who was older than her teacher, got a school."

"Hush, hush, ma'am! I'm afraid for the walls to hear it! Nobody knows our secret but my mother."

"I'm very well satisfied with the results of our crime, Lesley."

The girl blushed again. She loved to hear Miss Knightly speak her name, because she always sounded the *s* like a *z,* which made it seem gentler and more intimate. Nearly everyone else, even her mother, hissed the *s* as if it were spelled "Lessley." It was embarrassing to have such a queer name, but she respected it because her father had chosen it for her.

"Where are you going to stay all night, Miss Knightly?" she asked rather timidly.

"I think Mrs. Ericson expects me to stay with her."

"Mrs. Hunt, where I stay, would be awful glad to have you, but I know you'll be more comfortable at Mrs. Ericson's. She's a lovely housekeeper." Lesley resigned the faint hope that Miss Knightly would stay where she herself boarded, and broke out eagerly:

"Oh, Miss Knightly, have you seen any of our boys lately? Mother's too busy to write to me often."

"Hector looked in at my office last week. He came to the Court House with a telegram for the sheriff. He seemed well and happy."

"Did he? But Miss Knightly, I wish he hadn't taken that messenger job. I hate so for him to quit school."

"Now, I wouldn't worry about that, my dear. School isn't everything. He'll be getting good experience every day at the depot."

"Do you think so? I haven't seen him since he went to work."

"Why, how long has it been since you were home?"

"It's over a month now. Not since my school started. Father has been working all our horses on the farm. Maybe you can share my lunch with me?"

"I brought a lunch for the two of us, my dear. Call your favourite boy to go to my buggy and get my basket for us. After lunch I would like to hear the advanced arithmetic class."

* *

While the pupils were doing their sums at the blackboard, Miss Knightly herself was doing a little figuring. This was Thursday. Tomorrow she would visit two schools, and she had planned to spend Friday night with a pleasant family on Farmers' Creek. But she could change her schedule and give this homesick child a visit with her family in the county seat. It would inconvenience her very little.

When the class in advanced arithmetic was dismissed, Miss Knightly made a joking little talk to the children and told them about a very bright little girl in Scotland who knew nearly a whole play of Shakespeare's by heart, but who wrote in her diary: "Nine times nine is the Devil"; which proved, she said, that there are two kinds of memory, and God is very good to anyone to whom he gives both kinds. Then she asked if the pupils might have a special recess of half an hour, as a present from her. They gave her a cheer and out they trooped, the boys to the ball ground, and the girls to the cemetery, to sit neatly on the headstones and discuss Miss Knightly.

During their recess the Superintendent disclosed her plan. "I've been wondering, Lesley, whether you wouldn't like to go back to town with me after school tomorrow. We could get into MacAlpin by seven o'clock, and you could have all of Saturday and Sunday at home. Then we would make an early start Monday morning, and I would drop you here at the schoolhouse at nine o'clock."

The little teacher caught her breath—she became quite pale for a moment.

"Oh Miss Knightly, could you? Could you?"

"Of course I can. I'll stop for you here at four o'clock tomorrow afternoon."

II

The dark secret between Lesley and Miss Knightly was that only this September had the girl reached the legal age for teachers, yet she had been teaching all last year when she was still under age!

Last summer, when the applicants for teachers' certificates took written examinations in the County Superintendent's offices at the Court House in MacAlpin, Lesley Ferguesson had appeared with some twenty-six girls and nine boys. She wrote all morning and all afternoon for two days. Miss Knightly found her paper one of the best in the lot. A week later, when all the papers were filed, Miss Knightly told Lesley she could certainly give her a school. The morning after she had thus notified Lesley, she found the girl herself waiting on the sidewalk in front of the house where Miss Knightly boarded.

"Could I walk over to the Court House with you, Miss Knightly? I ought to tell you something," she blurted out at once. "On that paper I didn't put down my real age. I put down sixteen, and I won't be fifteen until this September."

"But I checked you with the high-school records, Lesley."

"I know. I put it down wrong there, too. I didn't want to be the class baby, and I hoped I could get a school soon, to help out at home."

The County Superintendent thought she would long remember that walk to the Court House. She could see that the child had spent a bad night; and she had walked up from her home down by the depot, quite a mile away, probably without breakfast.

"If your age is wrong on both records, why do you tell me about it now?"

"Oh, Miss Knightly, I got to thinking about it last night, how if you did give me a school it might all come out, and mean people would say you knew about it and broke the law."

Miss Knightly was thoughtless enough to chuckle. "But, my dear, don't you see that if I didn't know about it until this moment, I am completely innocent?"

The child who was walking beside her stopped short and burst into sobs. Miss Knightly put her arm around those thin, eager, forward-reaching shoulders.

"Don't cry, dear. I was only joking. There's nothing very dreadful about it. You didn't give your age under oath, you know." The sobs didn't stop. "Listen, let me tell you something. That big Hatch boy put his age down as nineteen, and I know he was teaching down in Nemaha County four years ago. I can't always be sure about the age applicants put down. I have to use my judgment."

The girl lifted her pale, troubled face and murmured, "Judgment?"

"Yes. Some girls are older at thirteen than others are at eighteen.

Your paper was one of the best handed in this year, and I am going to give you a school. Not a big one, but a nice one, in a nice part of the county. Now let's go into Ernie's coffee shop and have some more breakfast. You have a long walk home."

Of course, fourteen was rather young for a teacher in an ungraded school, where she was likely to have pupils of sixteen and eighteen in her classes. But Miss Knightly's "judgment" was justified by the fact that in June the school directors of the Wild Rose district asked to have "Miss Ferguesson" back for the following year.

III

At four o'clock on Friday afternoon Miss Knightly stopped at the Wild Rose schoolhouse to find the teacher waiting by the roadside, and the pupils already scattering across the fields, their tin lunch pails flashing back the sun. Lesley was standing almost in the road itself, her grey "telescope" bag at her feet. The moment old Molly stopped, she stowed her bag in the back of the buggy and climbed in beside Miss Knightly. Her smile was so eager and happy that her friend chuckled softly. "You still get a little homesick, don't you, Lesley?"

She didn't deny it. She gave a guilty laugh and murmured, "I do miss the boys."

The afternoon sun was behind them, throwing over the pastures and the harvested, resting fields that wonderful light, so yellow that it is actually orange. The three hours and the fourteen miles seemed not overlong. As the buggy neared the town of MacAlpin, Miss Knightly thought she could feel Lesley's heart beat. The girl had been silent a long while when she exclaimed:

"Look, there's the standpipe!"

The object of this emotion was a red sheet-iron tube which thrust its naked ugliness some eighty feet into the air and held the water supply for the town of MacAlpin. As it stood on a hill, it was the first thing one saw on approaching the town from the west. Old Molly, too, seemed to have spied this heartening landmark, for she quickened her trot without encouragement from the whip. From that point on, Lesley said not a word. There were two more low hills (very low), and then Miss Knightly turned off the main road and drove by a short cut through the baseball ground, to the south appendix of the town proper, the "depot settlement" where the Ferguessons lived.

Their house stood on a steep hillside—a storey-and-a-half frame house with a basement on the downhill side, faced with brick up to the first-floor level. When the buggy stopped before the yard gate, two little boys came running out of the front door. Miss Knightly's passenger vanished from her side—she didn't know just when Lesley alighted. Her attention was distracted by the appearance of the mother, with a third boy, still in kilts, trotting behind her.

Mrs. Ferguesson was not a person who could be overlooked. All the merchants in MacAlpin admitted that she was a fine figure of a woman. As she came down the little yard and out of the gate, the evening breeze ruffled her wavy auburn hair. Her quick step and alert, upright carriage gave one the impression that she got things done. Coming up to the buggy, she took Miss Knightly's hand.

"Why, it's Miss Knightly! And she's brought our girl along to visit us. That was mighty clever of you, Miss, and these boys will surely be a happy family. They do miss their sister." She spoke clearly, distinctly, but with a slight Missouri turn of speech.

By this time Lesley and her brothers had become telepathically one. Miss Knightly couldn't tell what the boys said to her, or whether they said anything, but they had her old canvas bag out of the buggy and up on the porch in no time at all. Lesley ran toward the front door, hurried back to thank Miss Knightly, and then disappeared holding fast to the little chap in skirts. She had forgotten to ask at what time Miss Knightly would call for her on Monday, but her mother attended to that. When Mrs. Ferguesson followed the children through the hall and the little back parlour into the dining-room, Lesley turned to her and asked breathlessly, almost sharply:

"Where's Hector?"

"He's often late on Friday night, dear. He telephoned me from the depot and said not to wait supper for him—he'd get a sandwich at the lunch counter. Now how *are* you, my girl?" Mrs. Ferguesson put her hands on Lesley's shoulders and looked into her glowing eyes.

"Just fine, Mother. I like my school so much! And the scholars are nicer even than they were last year. I just love some of them."

At this the little boy in kilts (the fashion of the times, though he was four years old) caught his sister's skirt in his two hands and jerked it to get her attention. "No, no!" he said mournfully, "you don't love anybody but us!"

His mother laughed, and Lesley stooped and gave him the tight hug he wanted.

The family supper was over. Mrs Ferguesson put on her apron. "Sit right down, Lesley, and talk to the children. No, I won't let you help me. You'll help me most by keeping them out of my way. I'll scramble you an egg and fry you some ham, so sit right down in your own place. I have some stewed plums for your dessert, and a beautiful angel cake I bought at the Methodist bake sale. Your father's gone to some political meeting, so we had supper early. You'll be a nice surprise for him when he gets home. He hadn't been gone half an hour when Miss Knightly drove up. Sit still, dear, it only bothers me if anybody tries to help me. I'll let you wash the dishes afterward, like we always do."

Lesley sat down at the half-cleared table; an oval-shaped table which could be extended by the insertion of "leaves" when Mrs. Ferguesson had company. The room was already dusky (twilights are short in a flat country), and one of the boys switched on the light which hung by a cord high above the table. A shallow china shade over the bulb threw a glaring white light down on the sister and the boys who stood about her chair. Lesley wrinkled up her brow, but it didn't occur to her that the light was too strong. She gave herself up to the feeling of being at home. It went all through her, that feeling, like getting into a warm bath when one is tired. She was safe from everything, was where she wanted to be, where she ought to be. A plant that has been washed out by a rain storm feels like that, when a kind gardener puts it gently back into its own earth with its own group.

The two older boys, Homer and Vincent, kept interrupting each other, trying to tell her things, but she didn't really listen to what they said. The little fellow stood close beside her chair, holding on to her skirt, fingering the glass buttons on her jacket. He was named Bryan, for his father's hero, but he didn't fit the name very well. He was a rather wistful and timid child.

Mrs. Ferguesson brought the ham and eggs and the warmed-up coffee. Then she sat down opposite her daughter to watch her enjoy her supper. "Now don't talk to her, boys. Let her eat in peace."

Vincent spoke up. "Can't I just tell her what happend to my lame pigeon?"

Mrs Ferguesson merely shook her head. She had control in that household, sure enough!

Before Lesley had quite finished her supper she heard the front door open and shut. The boys started up, but the mother raised a warning finger. They understood; a surprise. They were still as mice, and listened: A pause in the hall . . . he was hanging up his cap. Then he came in—the flower of the family.

For a moment he stood speechless in the doorway, the "incandescent" glaring full on his curly yellow hair and his amazed blue eyes. He was surprised indeed!

"Lesley!" he breathed, as if he were talking in his sleep.

She couldn't sit still. Without knowing that she got up and took a step, she had her arms around her brother. "It's me, Hector! Ain't I lucky? Miss Knightly brought me in."

"What time did you get here! You might have telephoned me, Mother."

"Dear, she ain't been here much more than half an hour."

"And Miss Knightly brought you in with old Molly, did she?" Oh, the lovely voice he had, that Hector—warm, deliberate . . . it made the most commonplace remark full of meaning. He had to say merely that—and it told his appreciation of Miss Knightly's kindness, even a playful gratitude to Molly, her clumsy, fat, road-pounding old mare. He was tall for his age, was Hector, and he had the fair pink-cheeked complexion which Lesley should have had and didn't.

Mrs. Ferguesson rose. "Now let's all go into the parlour and talk. We'll come back and clear up afterward." With this she opened the folding doors, and they followed her and found comfortable chairs—there was even a home-made hassock for Bryan. There were real books in the sectional bookcases (old Ferg's fault), and there was a real Brussels carpet in soft colours on the floor. That was Lesley's fault. Most of her savings from her first year's teaching had gone into that carpet. She had chosen it herself from the samples which Marshall

Field's travelling man brought to MacAlpin. There were comfortable old-fashioned pictures on the walls—"Venice by Moonlight" and such. Lesley and Hector thought it a beautiful room.

Of course the room was pleasant because of the feeling the children had for one another, and because in Mrs. Ferguesson there was authority and organization. Here the family sat and talked until Father came home. He was always treated a little like company. His wife and his children had a deep respect for him and for experimental farming, and profound veneration for William Jennings Bryan. Even little Bryan knew he was named for a great man, and must some day stop being afraid of the dark.

James Grahame Ferguesson was a farmer. He spent most of his time on what he called an "experimental farm." (The neighbours had other names for it—some of them amusing.) He was a loosely built man; had drooping shoulders carried with a forward thrust. He was a ready speaker, and usually made the Fourth of July speech in MacAlpin— spoke from a platform in the Court House grove, and even the farmers who joked about Ferguesson came to hear him. Alf Delaney declared: "I like to see anything done well—even talking. If old Ferg could shuck corn as fast as he can rustle the dictionary, I'd hire him, even if he is a Pop."

Old Ferg was not at all old—just turned forty—but he was fussy about the spelling of his name. He wrote it James Ferguesson. The merchants, even the local newspaper, simply would not spell it that way. They left letters out, or they put letters in. He complained about this repeatedly, and the result was that he was simply called "Ferg" to his face, and "old Ferg" to his back. His neighbours, both in town and in the country where he farmed, liked him because he gave them so much to talk about. He couldn't keep a hired man long at any wages. His habits were too unconventional. He rose early, saw to the chores like any other man, and went into the field for the morning. His lunch was a cold spread from his wife's kitchen, reinforced by hot tea. (The hired man was expected to bring his own lunch— outrageous!) After lunch Mr. Ferguesson took off his boots and lay down on the blue gingham sheets of a wide bed, and remained there until what he called "the cool of the afternoon." When that refreshing season arrived, he fed and watered his work horses, put the young gelding to his buckboard, and drove four miles to MacAlpin for his wife's hot supper. Mrs. Ferguesson, though not at all a meek woman or a stupid one, unquestioningly believed him when he told her that he did his best thinking in the afternoon. He hinted to her that he was working out in his head something that would benefit the farmers of the county more than all the corn and wheat they could raise even in a good year.

Sometimes Ferguesson did things she regretted—not because they were wrong, but because other people had mean tongues. When a fashion came in for giving names to farms which had hitherto been designated by figures (range, section, quarter, etc.), and his neighbours came out with "Lone Tree Farm," "Cold Spring Farm," etc., Ferguesson tacked on a cottonwood tree by his gate a neatly painted board inscribed: WIDE AWAKE FARM.

His neighbours, who could never get used to his afternoon siesta, were not long in converting this prophetic christening into "Hush-a-bye Farm." Mrs. Ferguesson overheard some of this joking on a Saturday night (she was marketing late after a lodge meeting on top of a busy day), and she didn't like it. On Sunday morning when he was dressing for church, she asked her husband why he ever gave the farm such a foolish name. He explained to her that the important crop on that farm was an idea. His farm was like an observatory where one watched the signs of the times and saw the great change that was coming for the benefit of all mankind. He even quoted Tennyson about looking into the future "far as human eye could see." It had been a long time since he had quoted any poetry to her. She sighed and dropped the matter.

On the whole, Ferg did himself a good turn when he put up that piece of nomenclature. People drove out of their way for miles to see it. They felt more kindly toward old Ferg because he wrote himself down such an ass. In a hard-working farming community a good joke is worth something. Ferguesson himself felt a gradual warming toward him among his neighbours. He ascribed it to the power of his oratory. It was really because he had made himself so absurd, but this he never guessed. Idealists are seldom afraid of ridicule—if they recognize it.

The Ferguesson children believed that their father was misunderstood by people of inferior intelligence, and that conviction gave them a "cause" which bound them together. They must do better than other children; better in school, and better on the playground. They must turn in a quarter of a dollar to help their mother out whenever they could. Experimental farming wasn't immediately remunerative.

Fortunately there was never any rent to pay. They owned their house down by the depot. When Mrs. Ferguesson's father died down in Missouri, she bought that place with what he left her. She knew that was the safe thing to do, her husband being a thinker. Her children were bound to her, and to that house, by the deepest, the most solemn loyalty. They never spoke of that covenant to each other, never even formulated it in their own minds—never. It was a consciousness they shared, and it gave them a family complexion.

On this Saturday of Lesley's surprise visit home, Father was with the family for breakfast. That was always a pleasant way to begin the day—especially on Saturday, when no one was in a hurry. He had grave good manners toward his wife and children. He talked to them as if they were grown-up, reasonable beings—talked a trifle as if from a rostrum, perhaps,—and he never indulged in small-town gossip. He was much more likely to tell them what he had read in the *Omaha World-Herald* yesterday; news of the State capital and the national capital. Sometimes he told them what a grasping, selfish country England was. Very often he explained to them how the gold standard had kept the poor man down. The family seldom bothered him about petty matters—such as that Homer needed new shoes, or that the iceman's bill for the whole summer had come in for the third time. Mother would take care of that.

On this particular Saturday morning Ferguesson gave especial attention to Lesley. He asked her about her school, and had her name her pupils. "I think you are fortunate to have the Wild Rose school, Lesley," he said as he rose from the table. "The farmers up there are open-minded and prosperous. I have sometimes wished that I had settled up there, though there are certain advantages in living at the county seat. The educational opportunities are better. Your friendship with Miss Knightly has been a broadening influence."

He went out to hitch up the buckboard to drive to the farm, while his wife put up the lunch he was to take along with him, and Lesley went upstairs to make the beds.

"Upstairs" was a story in itself, a secret romance. No caller or neighbour had ever been allowed to go up there. All the children loved it—it was their very own world where there were no older people poking about to spoil things. And it was unique—not at all like other people's upstairs chambers. In her stuffy little bedroom out in the country Lesley had more than once cried for it.

Lesley and the boys liked space, not tight cubbyholes. Their upstairs was a long attic which ran the whole length of the house, from the front door downstairs to the kitchen at the back. Its great charm was that it was unlined. No plaster, no beaver-board lining; just the roof shingles, supported by long, unplaned, splintery rafters that sloped from the sharp roof-peak down to the floor of the attic. Bracing these long roof rafters were cross rafters on which one could hang things—a little personal washing, a curtain for tableaux, a rope swing for Bryan.

In this spacious, undivided loft were two brick chimneys, going up in neat little stair-steps from the plank floor to the shingle roof—and out of it to the stars! The chimneys were of red, unglazed brick, with lines of white mortar to hold them together.

Last year, after Lesley first got her school, Mrs. Ferguesson exerted her authority and partitioned off a little room over the kitchen end of the "upstairs" for her daughter. Before that, all the children slept in this delightful attic. The three older boys occupied two wide beds, their sister her little single bed. Bryan, subject to croup, still slumbered downstairs near his mother, but he looked forward to his ascension as to a state of pure beatitude.

There was certainly room enough up there for widely scattered quarters, but the three beds stood in a row, as in a hospital ward. The children liked to be close enough together to share experiences.

Experiences were many. Perhaps the most exciting was when the driving, sleety snowstorms came on winter nights. The roof shingles were old and had curled under hot summer suns. In a driving snow-storm the frozen flakes sifted in through all those little cracks, sprinkled the beds and the children, melted on their faces, in their hair! That was delightful. The rest of you was snug and warm under blankets and comforters, with a hot brick at one's feet. The wind howled outside; sometimes the white light from the snow and the half-strangled moon came in through the single end window. Each child had his own dream-adventure. They did not exchange confidences; every "fellow" had a right to his own. They never told their love.

If they turned in early, they had a good while to enjoy the outside weather; they never went to sleep until after ten o'clock, for then came the sweetest morsel of the night. At that hour Number Seventeen, the westbound passenger, whistled in. The station and the engine house were perhaps an eighth of a mile down the hill, and from far away across the meadows the children could hear that whistle. Then came the heavy pants of the locomotive in the frosty air. Then a hissing—then silence: she was taking water.

On Saturdays the children were allowed to go down to the depot to see Seventeen come in. It was a fine sight on winter nights. Sometimes the great locomotive used to sweep in armoured in ice and snow, breathing fire like a dragon, its great red eye shooting a blinding beam along the white roadbed and shining wet rails. When it stopped, it panted like a great beast. After it was watered by the big hose from the overhead tank, it seemed to draw long deep breaths, ready to charge afresh over the great Western land.

Yes, they were grand old warriors, those towering locomotives of other days. They seemed to mean power, conquest, triumph—Jim Hill's dream. They set children's hearts beating from Chicago to Los Angeles. They were the awakener of many a dream.

As she made the boy's beds that Saturday morning and put on clean sheets, Lesley was thinking she would give a great deal to sleep out here as she used to. But when she got her school last year, her mother had said she must have a room of her own. So a carpenter brought sheathing and "lined" the end of the long loft—the end over the kitchen; and Mrs. Ferguesson bought a little yellow washstand and a bowl and pitcher, and said with satisfaction: "Now you see, Lesley, if you were sick, we would have some place to take the doctor." To be sure, the doctor would have to be admitted through the kitchen, and then come up a dark winding stairway with two turns. (Mr. Ferguesson termed it "the turnpike." His old Scotch grandmother, he said, had always thus called a winding stairway.) And Lesley's room, when you got there, was very like a snug wooden box. It was possible, of course, to leave her door open into the long loft, where the wood was brown and the chimneys red and the weather always so close to one. Out there things were still wild and rough—it wasn't a bedroom or a chamber—it was a hall, in the old baronial sense, and it reminded her of the lines in their *Grimm's Fairy Tales* book:

> Return, return, thou youthful bride,
> This is a robbers' hall inside.

IV

When her daughter had put the attic to rights, Mrs. Ferguesson went uptown to do her Saturday marketing. Lesley slipped out through the kitchen door and sat down on the back porch. The front porch was kept neat and fit to receive callers, but the back porch was given over to the boys. It was a messy-looking place, to be sure. From the wooden ceiling hung two trapezes. At one corner four boxing gloves were piled in a broken chair. In the trampled, grassless back yard, two-by-fours, planted upright, supported a length of lead pipe on which Homer practised bar exercises. Lesley sat down on the porch floor, her feet on the ground, and sank into idleness and safety and perfect love.

The boys were much the dearest things in the world to her. To love them so much was just . . . happiness. To think about them was the most perfect form of happiness. Had they been actually present, swinging on the two trapezes, turning on the bar, she would have been too much excited, too actively happy to be perfectly happy. But sitting in the warm sun, with her feet on the good ground, even her mother away, she almost ceased to exist. The feeling of being at home was complete, absolute: it made her sleepy. And that feeling was not so much the sense of being protected by her father and mother as of being with, and being one with, her brothers. It was the clan feeling, which meant life or death for the blood, not for the individual. For some reason, or for no reason, back in the beginning, creatures wanted the blood to continue.

*   *

After the noonday dinner Mrs. Ferguesson thoughtfully confided to her daughter while they were washing the dishes:

"Lesley, I'm divided in my mind. I would so appreciate a quiet afternoon with you, but I've a sort of engagement with the P.E.O. A lady from Canada is to be there to talk to us, and I've promised to introduce her. And just when I want to have a quiet time with you."

Lesley gave a sigh of relief and thought how fortunate it is that circumstances do sometimes make up our mind for us. In that battered canvas bag upstairs there was a roll of arithmetic papers and "essays" which hung over her like a threat. Now she would have a still hour in their beautiful parlour to correct them; the shades drawn down, just enough light to read by, her father's unabridged at hand, and the boys playing bat and pitch in the back yard.

Lesley and her brothers were proud of their mother's good looks, and that she never allowed herself to become a household drudge, as so many of her neighbours did. She "managed," and the boys helped her to manage. For one thing, there were never any dreary tubs full of washing standing about, and there was no ironing day to make a hole in the week. They sent all the washing, even the sheets, to the town steam laundry. Hector, with his weekly wages as messenger boy, and Homer and Vincent with their stable jobs, paid for it. That simple expedient did away with the worst blight of the working man's home.

Mrs. Ferguesson was "public-spirited," and she was the friend of all good causes. The business men of the town agreed that she had a great deal of influence, and that her name added strength to any committee. She was generally spoken of as a very *practical* woman, with an emphasis which implied several things. She was a "joiner," too! She was a Royal Neighbor, and a Neighborly Neighbor, and a P.E.O., and an Eastern Star. She had even joined the Methodist Win-a-Couple, though she warned them that she could not attend their meetings, as she liked to spend some of her evenings at home.

Promptly at six thirty Monday morning Miss Knightly's old mare stopped in front of the Ferguessons' house. The four boys were all on the front porch. James himself carried Lesley's bag down and put it into the buggy. He thanked the Superintendent very courteously for her kindness and kissed his daughter good-bye.

It had been at no trifling sacrifice that Miss Knightly was able to call for Lesley at six thirty. Customarily she started on her long drives at nine o'clock. This morning she had to give an extra half-dollar to the man who came to curry and harness her mare. She herself got no proper breakfast, but a cold sandwich and a cup of coffee at the station lunch counter—the only eating-place open at six o'clock. Most serious of all, she must push Molly a little on the road, to land her passenger at the Wild Rose schoolhouse at nine o'clock. Such small inconveniences do not sum up to an imposing total, but we assume them only for persons we really care for.

V

It was Christmas Eve. The town was busy with Christmas "exercises," and all the churches were lit up. Hector Ferguesson was going slowly up the hill which separated the depot settlement from the town proper. He walked at no messenger-boy pace tonight, crunching under his feet the snow which had fallen three days ago, melted, and then frozen hard. His hands were in the pockets of his new overcoat, which was so long that it almost touched the ground when he toiled up the steepest part of the hill. It was very heavy and not very warm. In those days there was a theory that in topcoats very little wool was necessary if they were woven tight enough and hard enough to "keep out the cold." A barricade was the idea. Hector carried the weight and clumsiness bravely, proudly. His new overcoat was a Christmas present from his sister. She had gone to the big town in the next county to shop for it, and bought it with her own money. He was thinking how kind Lesley was, and how hard she had worked for that money, and how much she had to put up with in the rough farmhouse where she boarded, out in the country. It was usually a poor housekeeper who was willing to keep a teacher, since they paid so little. Probably the amount Lesley spent for that coat would have kept her at a comfortable house all winter. When he grew up, and made lots of money (a brakeman—maybe an engineer), he would certainly be good to his sister.

Hector was a strange boy; a blend of the soft and the hard. In action he was practical, executive, like his mother. But in his mind, in his thoughts and plans, he was extravagant, often absurd. His mother suspected that he was "dreamy." Tonight, as he trailed up the frozen wooden sidewalk toward the town, he kept looking up at the stars, which were unusually bright, as they always seem over a stretch of snow. He was wondering if there were angels up there, watching the world on Christmas Eve. They came before, on the first Christmas Eve, he knew. Perhaps they kept the Anniversary. He thought about a beautiful coloured picture tacked up in Lesley's bedroom; two angels with white robes and long white wings, flying toward a low hill in the early dawn before sunrise, and on that distant hill, against the soft daybreak light, were three tiny crosses. He never doubted angels looked like that. He was credulous and truthful by nature. There was that look in his blue eyes. He would get it knocked out of him, his mother knew. But she believed he would always keep some of it—enough to make him open-handed and open-hearted.

Tonight Hector had his leather satchel full of Christmas telegrams. After he had delivered them all, he would buy his presents for his mother and the children. The stores sold off their special Christmas things at a discount after eleven o'clock on Christmas Eve.

VI

Miss Knightly was in Lincoln, attending a convention of Superintendents of Public Instruction, when the long-to-be-remembered blizzard swept down over the prairie State. Travel and telephone service were discontinued. A Chicago passenger train was stalled for three days in a deep cut west of W——. There she lay, and the dining-car had much ado to feed the passengers.

Miss Knightly was snowbound in Lincoln. She tarried there after the convention was dismissed and her fellow superintendents had gone home to their respective counties. She was caught by the storm because she had stayed over to see Julia Marlowe (then young and so fair!) in *The Love Chase*. She was not inconsolable to be delayed for some days. Why worry? She was staying at a small but very pleasant hotel, where the food was good and the beds were comfortable. She was New England born and bred, too conscientious to stay over in the city from mere self-indulgence, but quite willing to be lost to MacAlpin and X— County by the intervention of fate. She stayed, in fact, a week, greatly enjoying such luxuries as plenty of running water, hot baths, and steam heat. At that date MacAlpin houses, and even her office in the Court House, were heated by hard-coal stoves.

At last she was jogging home on a passenger train which left Lincoln at a convenient hour (it was two hours late, travel was still disorganized), when she was pleased to see Mr. Redman in conductor's uniform come into the car. Two of his boys had been her pupils when she taught in high school, before she was elected to a county office. Mr. Redman also seemed pleased, and after he had been through the train to punch tickets, he came back and sat down in the green plush seat opposite Miss Knightly and began to "tease."

"I hear there was a story going up at the Court House that you'd eloped. I was hoping you hadn't made a mistake."

"No. I thought it over and avoided the mistake. But what about you, Mr. Redman? You belong on the run west out of MacAlpin, don't you?"

"I don't know where I belong, Ma'm, and nobody else does. This is Jack Kelly's run, but he got his leg broke trying to help the train crew shovel the sleeping-car loose in that deep cut out of W—. The passengers were just freezing. This blizzard has upset everything. There's got to be better organization from higher up. This has taught us we just can't handle an emergency. Hard on stock, hard on people. A little neighbour of ours—why, you must know her, she was one of your teachers—Jim Ferguesson's little girl. She got pneumonia out there in the country and died out there."

Miss Knightly went so white that Redman without a word hurried to the end of the car and brought back a glass of water. He kept muttering that he was sorry . . . that he "always put his foot in it."

She did not disappoint him. She came back quickly. "That's all right, Mr. Redman. I'd rather hear it before I get home. Did she get lost in the storm? I don't understand."

Mr. Redman sat down and did the best he could to repair damages.

"No, Ma'm, little Lesley acted very sensible, didn't lose her head. You see, the storm struck us about three o'clock in the afternoon. The whole day it had been mild and soft, like spring. Then it came down instanter, like a thousand tons of snow dumped out of the sky. My wife was out in the back yard taking in some clothes she'd hung to dry. She hadn't even a shawl over her head. The suddenness of it confused her so (she couldn't see three feet before her), she wandered around in our back yard, couldn't find her way back to the house. Pretty soon our old dog—he's part shepherd—came yappin' and whinin'. She dropped the clothes and held onto his hair, and he got her to the back porch. That's how bad it was in MacAlpin."

"And Lesley?" Miss Knightly murmured.

"Yes, Ma'm! I'm coming to that. Her scholars tell about how the schoolroom got a little dark, and they all looked out, and there was no graveyard, and no horses that some of them had rode to school on. The boys jumped up to run out and see after the horses, but Lesley stood with her back against the door and wouldn't let 'em go out. Told 'em it would be over in a few minutes. Well, you see it wasn't. Over four feet of snow fell in less'n an hour. About six o'clock some of the fathers of the children that lived aways off started out on horseback, but the horses waded belly-deep, and a wind come up and it turned cold.

"Ford Robertson is the nearest neighbour, you know,—scarcely more than across the road—eighth of a mile, maybe. As soon as he come in from his corral—the Herefords had all bunched up together, over a hundred of 'em, under the lee of a big haystack, and he knew they wouldn't freeze. As soon as he got in, the missus made him go over to the schoolhouse an' take a rope along an' herd 'em all over to her house, teacher an' all, with the boys leading their horses. That night Mrs. Robertson cooked nearly everything in the house for their supper, and she sent Ford upstairs to help Lesley make shakedown beds on the floor. Mrs. Robertson remembers when the big supper was ready and the children ate like wolves, Lesley didn't eat much—said she had a little headache. Next morning she was pretty sick. That day all the fathers came on horseback for the children. Robertson got one of them to go for old Doctor Small, and he came down on his horse. Doctor said it was pneumonia, and there wasn't much he could do. She didn't seem to have strength to rally. She was out of her head when he got there. She was mostly unconscious for three days, and just slipped out. The funeral is tomorrow. The roads are open now. They were to bring her home today."

The train stopped at a station, and Mr. Redman went to attend to his duties. When he next came through the car Miss Knightly spoke to him. She had recovered herself. Her voice was steady, though very low and very soft when she asked him:

"Were any of her family out there with her when she was ill?"

"Why, yes, Mrs. Ferguesson was out there. That boy Hector got his mother through, before the roads were open. He'd stop at a farmhouse and explain the situation and borrow a team and get the farmer or one of his hands to give them a lift to the next farm, and there they'd get a lift a little further. Everybody knew about the school and the teacher by that time, and wanted to help, no matter how bad the roads were. You see, Miss Knightly, everything would have gone better if it hadn't come on so freezing cold, and if the snow hadn't been so darn soft when it first fell. That family are terrible broke up. We all are, down at the depot. She didn't recognize them when they got there, I heard."

VII

Twenty years after that historic blizzard Evangeline Knightly—now Mrs. Ralph Thorndike—alighted from the fast eastbound passenger at the MacAlpin station. No one at the station knew who she was except the station master, and he was not quite sure. She looked older, but she also looked more prosperous, more worldly. When she approached him at his office door and asked, "Isn't this Mr. Beardsley?" he recognized her voice and speech.

"That's who. And it's my guess this is, or used to be, Miss Knightly. I've been here almost forever. No ambition. But you left us a long time ago. You're looking fine, ma'm, if I may say so."

She thanked him and asked him to recommend a hotel where she could stay for a day or two.

He scratched his head. "Well, the Plummer House ain't no

Waldorf-Astoria, but the travelling men give a good report of it. The Bishop always stays there when he comes to town. You like me to telephone for an otto [automobile] to take you up? Lord, when you left here there wasn't an otto in the town!"

Mrs. Thorndike smiled. "Not many in the world, I think. And can you tell me, Mr. Beardsley, where the Ferguessons live?"

"The depot Ferguessons? Oh, they live uptown now. Ferg built right west of the Court House, right next to where the Donaldsons used to live. You'll find lots of changes. Some's come up, and some's come down. We used to laugh at Ferg and tell him politics didn't bring in the bacon. But he's got it on us now. The Democrats are sure grand job-givers. Throw 'em round for value received. I still vote the Republican ticket. Too old to change. Anyhow, all those new jobs don't affect the railroads much. They can't put a college professor on to run trains. Now I'll telephone for an otto for you."

Miss Knightly, after going to Denver, had married a very successful young architect, from New England, like herself, and now she was on her way back to Brunswick, Maine, to revisit the scenes of her childhood. Although she had never been in MacAlpin since she left it fifteen years ago, she faithfully read the MacAlpin *Messenger* and knew the important changes in the town.

After she had settled her room at the hotel, and unpacked her toilet articles, she took a cardboard box she had brought with her in the sleeping-car, and went out on a personal errand. She came back to the hotel late for lunch—had a tray sent up to her room, and at four o'clock went to the office in the Court House which used to be her office. This was the autumn of the year, and she had a great desire to drive out among the country schools and see how much fifteen years had changed the land, the pupils, the teachers.

When she introduced herself to the present incumbent, she was cordially received. The young Superintendent seemed a wide-awake, breezy girl, with bobbed blond hair and crimson lips. Her name was Wanda Bliss.

Mrs. Thorndike explained that her stay would not be long enough to let her visit all the country schools, but she would like Miss Bliss's advice as to which were the most interesting.

"Oh, I can run you around to nearly all of them in a day, in my car!"

Mrs. Thorndike thanked her warmly. She liked young people who were not in the least afraid of life or luck or responsibility. In her own youth there were very few like that. The teachers, and many of the pupils out in the country schools, were eager—but anxious. She laughed and told Miss Bliss that she meant to hire a buggy, if there was such a thing left in MacAlpin, and drive out into the country alone.

"I get you. You want to put on an old-home act. You might phone around to any farmers you used to know. Some of them still keep horses for haying."

Mrs. Thorndike got a list of the country teachers and the districts in which they taught. A few of them had been pupils in the schools she used to visit. Those she was determined to see.

The following morning she made the call she had stopped off at MacAlpin to make. She rang the doorbell at the house pointed out to her, and through the open window heard a voice call: "Come in, come in, please. I can't answer the bell."

Mrs. Thorndike opened the door into a shining oak hall with a shining oak stairway.

"Come right through, please. I'm in the back parlour. I sprained my ankle and can't walk yet."

The visitor followed the voice and found Mrs. Ferguesson sitting in a spring rocker, her bandaged right foot resting on a low stool.

"Come in, Ma'm. I have a bad sprain, and the little girl who does for me is downtown marketing. Maybe you came to see Mr. Ferguesson, but his office is—" here she broke off and looked up sharply—intently—at her guest. When the guest smiled, she broke out: "Miss Knightly! Are you Miss Knightly? Can it be?"

"They call me Mrs. Thorndike now, but I'm Evangeline Knightly just the same." She put out her hand, and Mrs. Ferguesson seized it with both her own.

"It's too good to be true!" she gasped with tears in her voice, "just too good to be true. The things we dream about that way don't happen." She held fast to Mrs. Thorndike's hand as if she were afraid she might vanish. "When did you come to town, and why didn't they let me know!"

"I came only yesterday, Mrs. Ferguesson, and I wanted to slip in on you just like this, with no one else around."

"Mr. Ferguesson must have known. But his mind is always off on some trail, and he never brings me any news when I'm laid up like this. Dear me! It's a long time." She pressed the visitor's hand again before she released it. "Get yourself a comfortable chair, dear, and sit down by me. I do hate to be helpless like this. It wouldn't have happened but for those slippery front stairs. Mr. Ferguesson just wouldn't put a carpet on them, because he says folks don't carpet hardwood stairs, and I tried to answer the doorbell in a hurry, and this is what come of it. I'm not naturally a clumsy woman on my feet."

Mrs. Thorndike noticed an aggrieved tone in her talk which had never been there in the old days when she had so much to be aggrieved about. She brought a chair and sat down close to Mrs. Ferguesson, facing her. The good woman had not changed much, she thought. There was a little grey in her crinkly auburn hair, and there were lines about her mouth which used not to be there, but her eyes had all the old fire.

"How comfortably you are fixed here, Mrs. Ferguesson! I'm so glad to find you like this."

"Yes, we're comfortable—now that they're all gone! It's mostly his taste. He took great interest." She spoke rather absently, and kept looking out through the polished hall toward the front door, as if she were expecting someone. It seemed a shame that anyone naturally so energetic should be enduring this foolish antiquated method of treating a sprain. The chief change in her, Mrs. Thorndike thought, was that she had grown softer. She reached for the visitor's hand again and held it fast. Tears came to her eyes.

Mrs. Thorndike ventured that she had found the town much changed for the better.

Yes, Mrs. Ferguesson supposed it was.

Then Mrs. Thorndike began in earnest. "How wonderful it is that all your sons have turned out so well! I take the MacAlpin paper chiefly to keep track of the Ferguesson boys. You and Mr. Ferguesson must be very proud."

"Yes'm, we are. We are thankful."

"Even the Denver papers have long articles about Hector and Homer and their great sheep ranches in Wyoming. And Vincent has become such a celebrated chemist, and is helping to destroy all the irreducible elements that I learned when I went to school. And Bryan is with Marshall Field!"

Mrs. Ferguesson nodded and pressed her hand, but she still kept looking down the hall toward the front door. Suddenly she turned with all herself to Mrs. Thorndike and with a storm of tears cried out from her heart: "Oh, Miss Knightly, talk to me about my Lesley! Seems so many have forgot her, but I know you haven't."

"No, Mrs. Ferguesson, I never forget her. Yesterday morning I took a box of roses that I brought with me from my own garden down to where she sleeps. I was glad to find a little seat there, so that I could stay for a long while and think about her."

"Oh, I wish I could have gone with you, Miss Knightly! (I can't call you anything else.) I wish we could have gone together. I can't help feeling she knows. *Anyhow,* we know! And there's nothing in all my life so precious to me to remember and think about as my Lesley. I'm no soft woman, either. The boys will tell you that. They'll tell you they got on because I always had a firm hand over them. They're all true to Lesley, my boys. Every time they come home they go down there. They feel it like I do, as if it had happened yesterday. Their father feels it, too, when he's not taken up with his abstractions. Anyhow, I don't think men feel things like women and boys. My boys have stayed boys. I do believe they feel as bad as I do about moving up here. We have four nice bedrooms upstairs to make them comfortable, should they all come home at once, and they're polite about us and tell us how well fixed we are. But Miss Knightly, I know at the bottom of their hearts they wish they was back in the old house down by the depot, sleeping in the attic."

Mrs. Thorndike stroked her hand. "I looked for the old house as I was coming up from the station. I made the driver stop."

"Ain't it dreadful, what's been done to it? If I'd foreseen, I'd never have let Mr. Ferguesson sell it. It was in my name. I'd have kept it to go back to and remember sometimes. Folks in middle age make a mistake when they think they can better themselves. They can't, not if they have any heart. And the other kind don't matter—they aren't real people—just poor put-ons, that try to be like the advertisements. Father even took me to California one winter. I was miserable all the time. And there were plenty more like me—miserable underneath. The women lined up in cafeterias, carrying their little trays—like convicts, seemed to me—and running to beauty shops to get their poor old hands manicured. And the old men, Miss Knightly, I pitied them most of all! Old bent-backed farmers, standing round in their shirt-sleeves, in plazas and alleyways, pitching horseshoes like they used to do at home. I tell you, people are happiest where they've had their children and struggled along and been real folks, and not tourists. What do you think about all this running around, Miss Knightly? You're an educated woman, I never had much schooling."

"I don't think schooling gives people any wisdom, Mrs. Ferguesson. I guess only life does that."

"Well, this I know: our best years are when we're working hardest and going right ahead when we can hardly see our way out. Times I was a good deal perplexed. But I always had one comfort. I did own our own house. I never had to worry about the rent. Don't it seem strange to you, though, that all our boys are so practical, and their father such a dreamer?"

Mrs. Thorndike murmured that some people think boys are most likely to take after their mother.

Mrs. Ferguesson smiled absently and shook her head. Presently she came out with: "It's a comfort to me up here, on a still night I can still hear the trains whistle in. Sometimes, when I can't sleep, I lie and listen for them. And I can almost think I am down there, with my children up in the loft. We were very happy." She looked up at her guest and smiled bravely. "I suppose you go away tonight?"

Mrs. Thorndike explained her plan to spend a day in the country.

"You're going out to visit the little schools? Why, God bless you, dear! You're still our Miss Knightly! But you'd better take a car, so you can get up to the Wild Rose school and back in one day. Do go there! The teacher is Mandy Perkins—she was one of her little scholars. You'll like Mandy, an' she loved Lesley. You must get Bud Sullivan to drive you. Engage him right now—the telephone's there in the hall, and the garage is 306. He'll creep along for you, if you tell him. He does for me. I often go out to the Wild Rose school, and over to see dear Mrs. Robertson, who ain't so young as she was then. I can't go with Mr. Ferguesson. He drives so fast it's no satisfaction. And then he's not always mindful. He's had some accidents. When he gets to thinking, he's just as likely to run down a cow as not. He's had to pay for one. You know cows will cross the road right in front of a car. Maybe their grandchildren calves will be more modern-minded."

Mrs. Thorndike did not see her old friend again, but she wrote her a long letter from Wiscasset, Maine, which Mrs. Ferguesson sent to her son Hector, marked, "To be returned, but first pass on to your brothers."

Before Breakfast

Henry Grenfell, of Grenfell & Saunders, got resentfully out of bed after a bad night. The first sleepless night he had ever spent in his own cabin, on his own island, where nobody knew that he was senior partner of Grenfell & Saunders, and where the business correspondence was never forwarded to him. He slipped on a blanket dressing-gown over his pyjamas (island mornings in the North Atlantic are chill before dawn), went to the front windows of his bedroom, and ran up the heavy blue shades which shut out the shameless blaze of the sunrise if one wanted to sleep late—and he usually did on the first morning after arriving. (The trip up from Boston was long and hard, by trains made up of the cast-off coaches of liquidated railroads, and then by the two worst boats in the world.) The cabin modestly squatted on a tiny clearing between a tall spruce wood and the sea,—sat about fifty yards back from the edge of the red sandstone cliff which dropped some two hundred feet to a narrow beach—so narrow that it was covered at high tide. The cliffs rose sheer on this side of the island, were undercut in places, and faced the east.

The east was already lightening; a deep red streak burnt over the sky-line water, and the water itself was thick and dark, indigo blue—occasionally a silver streak, where the tide was going out very quietly. While Grenfell stood at his window, a big snowshoe hare ran downhill from the spruce wood, bounded into the grass plot at the front door, and began nervously nibbling the clover. He was puzzled and furtive; his jaws quivered, and his protruding eyes kept watch behind him as well as before. Grenfell was sure it was the hare that used to come every morning two summers ago and had become quite friendly. But now he seemed ill at ease; presently he started, sat still for an instant, then scampered up the grassy hillside and disappeared into the dark spruce wood. Silly thing! Still, it was a kind of greeting.

Grenfell left the window and went to his walnut washstand (no plumbing) and mechanically prepared to take a shower in the shed room behind his sleeping-chamber. He began his morning routine, still thinking about the hare.

First came the eye-drops. Tilting his head back, thus staring into the eastern horizon, he raised the glass dropper, but he didn't press the bulb. He saw something up there. While he was watching the rabbit the sky had changed. Above the red streak on the water line the sky had lightened to faint blue, and across the horizon a drift of fleecy rose cloud was floating. And through it a white-bright, gold-bright planet was shining. The morning star, of course. At this hour, and so near the sun, it would be Venus.

Behind her rose-coloured veils, quite alone in the sky already blue, she seemed to wait. She had come in on her beat, taken her place in the figure. Serene, impersonal splendour. Merciless perfection, ageless sovereignty. The poor hare and his clover, poor Grenfell and his eye-drops!

He braced himself against his washstand and still stared up at her. Something roused his temper so hot that he began to mutter aloud: "And what's a hundred and thirty-six million years to you, Madam? That Professor needn't blow. You were winking and blinking up there maybe a hundred and thirty-six million times before that date they are so proud of. The rocks can't tell any tales on you. You were doing your stunt up there long before there was anything down here but—God knows what! Let's leave that to the professors, Madam, you and me!"

This childish bitterness toward "millions" and professors was the result of several things. Two of Grenfell's sons were "professors"; Harrison a distinguished physicist at thirty. This morning, however, Harrison had not popped up in his father's mind. Grenfell was still thinking of a pleasant and courtly scientist whom he had met on the boat yesterday—a delightful man who had, temporarily at least, wrecked Grenfell's life with civilities and information.

It was natural, indeed inevitable, that two clean, close-shaven gentlemen in tailored woods clothes, passengers on the worst tub owned by the Canadian Steamships Company and both bound for a little island off the Nova Scotia coast, should get into conversation. It was all the more natural since the scientist was accompanied by a lovely girl—his daughter.

It was a pleasure to look at her, just as it is a pleasure to look at any comely creature who shows breeding, delicate preferences. She had lovely eyes, lovely skin, lovely manners. She listened closely when Grenfell and her father talked, but she didn't bark up with her opinions. When he asked her about their life on the island last summer, he liked everything she said about the place and the people. She answered him lightly, as if her impressions could matter only to herself, but, having an opinion, it was only good manners to admit it. "Sweet, but decided," was his rough estimate.

Since they were both going to an island which wasn't even on the map, supposed to be known only to the motor launches that called after a catch of herring, it was natural that the two gentlemen should talk about that bit of wooded rock in the sea. Grenfell always liked to talk about it to the right person. At first he thought Professor Fairweather was a right person. He had felt alarm when Fairweather mentioned that last summer he had put up a portable house on the shore about two miles from Grenfell's cabin. But he added that it would soon vanish as quietly as it had come. His geological work would be over this autumn, and his portable house would be taken to pieces and shipped to an island in the South Pacific. Having thus reassured him, Fairweather carelessly, in quite the tone of weather-comment small talk, proceeded to wreck one of Grenfell's happiest illusions; the escape-avenue he kept in the back of his mind when he was at his desk at Grenfell & Saunders, Bonds. The Professor certainly meant no harm. He was a man of the world, urbane, not self-important. He merely remarked that the island was interesting geologically because the two ends of the island belonged to different periods, yet the ice seemed to have brought them both down together.

"And about how old would our end be, Professor?" Grenfell meant simply to express polite interest, but he gave himself away, parted with his only defence—indifference.

"We call it a hundred and thirty-six million years," was the answer he got.

"Really? That's getting it down pretty fine, isn't it? I'm just a blank where science is concerned. I went to work when I was thirteen—didn't have any education. Of course some business men read up on science. But I have to struggle with reports and figures a good deal.

When I do read I like something human—the old fellows: Scott and Dickens and Fielding. I get a great kick out of them."

The Professor was a perfect gentleman, but he couldn't resist the appeal of ignorance. He had sensed in half an hour that this man loved the island. (His daughter had sensed it a year ago, as soon as she arrived there with her father. Something about his cabin, the little patch of lawn in front, and the hedge of wild roses that fenced it in, told her that.) In their talk Professor Fairweather had come to realize that this man had quite an unusual feeling for the island, therefore he would certainly like to know more about it—all he could tell him!

The sun leaped out of the sea—the planet vanished. Grenfell rejected his eye-drops. Why patch up? What was the use . . . of anything? Why tear a man loose from his little rock and shoot him out into the eternities? All that stuff was inhuman. A man had his little hour, with heat and cold and a time-sense suited to his endurance. If you took that away from him you left him spineless, accidental, unrelated to anything. He himself was, he realized, sitting in his bathrobe by his washstand, limp! No wonder: what a night! What a dreadful night! The speeds which machinists had worked up in the last fifty years were mere baby-talk to what can go through a man's head between dusk and daybreak. In the last ten hours poor Grenfell had travelled over seas and continents, gone through boyhood and youth, founded a business, made a great deal of money, and brought up an expensive family. (There were three sons, to whom he had given every advantage and who had turned out well, two of them brilliantly.) And all this meant nothing to him except negatively—"to avoid worse rape," he quoted Milton to himself.

Last night had been one of those nights of revelation, revaluation, when everything seems to come clear . . . only to fade out again in the morning. In a low cabin on a high red cliff overhanging the sea, everything that was shut up in him, under lock and bolt and pressure, simply broke jail, spread out into the spaciousness of the night, undraped, unashamed.

❧

When his father died, Henry had got a job as messenger boy with the Western Union. He always remembered those years with a certain pride. His mother took in sewing. There were two little girls, younger than he. When he looked back on that time, there was nothing in it to be ashamed of. Those are the years, he often told the reformers, that make character, make proficiency. A business man should have early training, like a pianist, *at the instrument*. The sense of responsibility makes a little boy a citizen: for him there is no "dangerous age." From his first winter with the telegraph company he knew he could get on if he tried hard, since most lads emphatically did not try hard. He read law at night, and when he was twenty was confidential clerk with one of the most conservative legal firms in Colorado.

Everything went well until he took his first long vacaton—bicycling in the mountains above Colorado Springs. One morning he was pedalling hard uphill when another bicycle came round a curve and collided with him; a girl coasting. Both riders were thrown. She got her foot caught in her wheel; sprain and lacerations. Henry ran two miles down to her hotel and her family. New York people; the father's name was a legend in Henry's credulous Western world. And they liked him, Henry, these cultivated, clever, experienced people! The mother was the ruling power—remarkable woman. What she planned, she put through—relentless determination. He ought to know, for he married that only daughter one year after she coasted into him. A warning unheeded, that first meeting. It was his own intoxicated vanity that sealed his fate. He had never been "made much over" before.

It had worked out as well as most marriages, he supposed. Better than many. The intelligent girl had been no discredit to him, certainly. She had given him two remarkable sons, any man would be proud of them. . . .

Here Grenfell had flopped over in bed and suddenly sat up, muttering aloud. "But God, they're as cold as ice! I can't see through it. They've never lived at all, those two fellows. They've never run after the ball—they're so damned clever they don't *have* to. They just reach out and *take* the ball. Yes, fine hands, like their grandmother's;

long . . . white . . . beautiful nails. The way Harrison picked up that book! I'm glad my paws are red and stubby."

For a moment he recalled sharply a little scene. Three days ago he was packing for his escape to this island. Harrison, the eldest son, the physicist, after knocking, had entered to his father's "Come in!" He came to ask who should take care of his personal mail (that which came to the house) if Miss O'Doyle should go on her vacation before he returned. He put the question rather grimly. The family seemed to resent the fact that, though he worked like a steam shovel while he was in town, when he went on a vacation he never told them how long he would be away or where he was going.

"Oh, I meant to tell you, Harrison, before I leave. But it was nice of you to think of it. Miss O'Doyle has decided to put off her vacation until the middle of October, and then she'll take a long one." He was sure he spoke amiably as he stood looking at his son. He was always proud of Harrison's fine presence, his poise and easy reserve. The little travelling bag (made to his order) which on a journey he always carried himself, never trusted to a porter, lay open on his writing table. On top of his pyjamas and razor case lay two little books bound in red leather. Harrison picked up one and glanced at the lettering on the back. *King Henry IV, Part I.*

"Light reading?" he remarked. Grenfell was stung by such impertinence. He resented any intrusion on his private, personal, non-family life.

"Light or heavy," he remarked dryly, "they're good company. And they're mighty human."

"They have that reputation," his son admitted.

A spark flashed into Grenfell's eye. Was the fellow sarcastic, or merely patronizing?

"Reputation, hell!" he broke out. "I don't carry books around with my toothbrushes and razors on account of their reputation."

"No, I wouldn't accuse you of that." The young man spoke quietly, not warmly, but as if he meant it. He hesitated and left the room.

Sitting up in his bed in the small hours of the morning, Grenfell wondered if he hadn't flared up too soon. Maybe the fellow hadn't meant to be sarcastic. All the same he had no business to touch anything in his father's bag. That bag was like his coat pocket. Grenfell never bothered his family with his personal diversions, and he never intruded upon theirs. Harrison and his mother were a team—a close corporation! Grenfell respected it absolutely. No questions, no explanations demanded by him. The bills came in; Miss O'Doyle wrote the checks and he signed them. He hadn't the curiosity, the vulgarity to look at them.

Of course, he admitted, there were times when he got back at the corporation just a little. That usually occurred when his dyspepsia had kept him on very light food all day and, the dinner at home happening to be "rich," he confined himself to graham crackers and milk. He remembered such a little dinner scene last month. Harrison and his mother came downstairs dressed to go out for the evening. Soon after the soup was served, Harrison wondered whether Koussevitzky would take the slow movement in the Brahms Second as he did last winter. His mother said she still remembered Muck's reading, and preferred it.

The theoretical head of the house spoke up. "I take it that this is Symphony night, and that my family are going. You have ordered the car? Well, I am going to hear John McCormack sing *Kathleen Mavourneen.*"

His wife rescued him as she often did (in an innocent, well-bred way) by refusing to recognize his rudeness. "Dear me! I haven't heard McCormack since he first came out in Italy years and years ago. His success was sensational. He was singing Mozart then."

Yes, when he was irritable and the domestic line-up got the better of him, Margaret, by being faultlessly polite, often saved the situation.

When he thought everything over, here in this great quiet, in this great darkness, he admitted that his shipwreck had not been on the family rock. The bitter truth was that his worst enemy was closer even than the wife of his bosom—was his bosom itself!

Grenfell had what he called a hair-trigger stomach. When he was in his New York office he worked like a whirlwind; and to do it he had to live on a diet that would have tried the leanest anchorite. The doctors said he did everything too hard. He knew that—he always had done things hard, from the day he first went to work for the Western Union. Mother and two little sisters, no schooling—the only capital he had was the ginger to care hard and work hard. Apparently it was not the brain that desired and achieved. At least, the expense account came out of a very other part of one. Perhaps he was a throw-back to the Year One, when in the stomach was the only constant, never sleeping, never quite satisfied desire.

The humiliation of being "delicate" was worse than the actual hardship. He had found the one way in which he could make it up to himself, could feel like a whole man, not like a miserable dyspeptic. That way was by living rough, not by living soft. There wasn't a big-game country in North America where he hadn't hunted; mountain sheep in the wild Rockies, moose in darkest Canada, caribou in Newfoundland. Long before he could really afford it, he took four months out of every year to go shooting. His greatest triumph was a white bear in Labrador. His guide and pack-men and canoe men never guessed that he was a frail man. Out there, up there, he wasn't! Out there he was just a "city man" who paid well; eccentric, but a fairly good shot. That was what he had got out of hard work and very good luck. He had got ahead wonderfully . . . but, somehow, ahead on the wrong road.

≥●

At this point in his audit Grenfell had felt his knees getting cold, so he got out of bed, opened a clothes closet, and found his eiderdown bathrobe hanging on the hook where he had left it two summers ago. That was a satisfaction. (He liked to be orderly, and it made this cabin seem more his own to find things, year after year, just as he had left them.) Feeling comfortably warm, he ran up the dark window blinds which last night he had pulled down to shut out the disturbing sight of the stars. He bethought him of his eye-drops, tilted back his head, and there was that planet, serene, terrible and splendid, looking in at him . . . immortal beauty . . . yes, but only when somebody *saw* it, he fiercely answered back!

He thought about it until his head went round. He would get out of this room and get out quick. He began to dress—wool stockings, moccasins, flannel shirt, leather coat. He would get out and find his island. After all, it still existed. The Professor hadn't put it in his pocket, he guessed! He scrawled a line for William, his man Friday: "BREAKFAST WHEN I RETURN," and stuck it on a hook in his dining-car kitchen. William was "boarded out" in a fisherman's family. (Grenfell wouldn't stand anyone in the cabin with him. He wanted all this glorious loneliness for himself. He had paid dearly for it.)

He hurried out of the kitchen door and up the grassy hillside to the spruce wood. The spruces stood tall and still as ever in the morning air; the same dazzling spears of sunlight shot through their darkness. The path underneath had the dampness, the magical softness which his feet remembered. On either side of the trail yellow toadstools and white mushrooms lifted the heavy thatch of brown spruce needles and made little damp tents. Everything was still in the wood. There was not a breath of wind; deep shadow and new-born light, yellow as gold, a little unsteady like other new-born things. It was blinking, too, as if its own reflection on the dewdrops was too bright. Or maybe the light had been asleep down under the sea and was just waking up.

"Hello, Grandfather!" Grenfell cried as he turned a curve in the path. The grandfather was a giant spruce tree that had been struck by lightning (must have been about a hundred years ago, the islanders said). It still lay on a slant along a steep hillside, its shallow roots in the air, all its great branches bleached greyish white, like an animal skeleton long exposed to the weather. Grenfell put out his hand to twitch off a twig as he passed, but it snapped back at him like a metal spring. He stopped in astonishment, his hand smarted, actually.

"Well, Grandfather! Lasting pretty well, I should say. Compliments! You get good drainage on this hillside, don't you?"

Ten minutes more on the winding uphill path brought him to the edge of the spruce wood and out on a bald headland that topped a cliff two hundred feet above the sea. He sat down on a rock and grinned. Like Christian of old, he thought, he had left his burden at the bottom of the hill. Now why had he let Doctor Fairweather's perfectly unessential information give him a miserable night? He had always known this island existed long before he discovered it, and that it must once have been a naked rock. The soil-surface was very thin. Almost anywhere on the open downs you could cut with a spade through the dry turf and roll it back from the rock as you roll a rug back from the floor. One knew that the rock itself, since it rested on the bottom of the ocean, must be very ancient.

But that fact had nothing to do with the green surface where men lived and trees lived and blue flags and buttercups and daisies and meadowsweet and steeplebush and goldenrod crowded one another in all the clearings. Grenfell shook himself and hurried along up the cliff trail. He crossed the first brook on stepping-stones. Must have been recent rain, for the water was rushing down the deep-cut channel with sound and fury till it leaped hundreds of feet over the face of the cliff and fell into the sea: a white waterfall that never rested.

The trail led on through a long jungle of black alder . . . then through a lazy, rooty, brown swamp . . . and then out on another breezy, grassy headland which jutted far out into the air in a horse-shoe curve. There one could stand beside a bushy rowan tree and see four waterfalls, white as silver, pouring down the perpendicular cliff walls.

Nothing had changed. Everything was the same, and he, Henry Grenfell, was the same: the relationship was unchanged. Not even a tree blown down; the stunted beeches (precious because so few) were still holding out against a climate unkind to them. The old white birches that grew on the edge of the cliff had been so long beaten and tormented by east wind and north wind that they grew more down than up, and hugged the earth that was kinder than the stormy air. Their growth was all one-sided, away from the sea, and their land-side branches actually lay along the ground and crept up the hillside through the underbrush, persistent, nearly naked, like great creeping vines, and at last, when they got into the sunshine, burst into tender leafage.

This knob of grassy headland with the bushy rowan tree had been his vague objective when he left the cabin. From this elbow he could look back on the cliff wall, both north and south, and see the four silver waterfalls in the morning light. A splendid sight, Grenfell was thinking, and all his own. Not even a gull—they had gone screaming down the coast toward the herring weirs when he first left his cabin. Not a living creature—but wait a minute: there was something moving down there, on the shingle by the water's edge. A human figure, in a long white bathrobe—and a rubber cap! Then it must be a woman? Queer. No island woman would go bathing at this hour, not even in the warm inland ponds. Yes, it was a woman! A girl, and he knew *what* girl! In the miseries of the night he had forgotten her. The geologist's daughter.

How had she got down there without breaking her neck? She picked her way along the rough shingle; presently stopped and seemed to be meditating, seemed to be looking out at an old sliver of rock that was almost submerged at high tide. She opened her robe, a grey thing lined with white. Her bathing-suit was pink. If a clam stood upright and graciously opened its shell, it would look like that. After a moment she drew her shell together again—felt the chill of the morning air, probably. People are really themselves only when they believe they are absolutely alone and unobserved, he was thinking. With a quick motion she shed her robe, kicked off her sandals, and took to the water.

At the same moment Grenfell kicked off his moccasins. "Crazy kid! What does she think she's doing? This is the North Atlantic, girl, you can't treat it like that!" As he muttered, he was getting off his fox-lined jacket and loosening his braces. Just how he would get down to the shingle he didn't know, but he guessed he'd have to. He was getting ready while, so far, she was doing nicely. Nothing is more embarrassing than to rescue people who don't want to be rescued. The tide was out, slack—she evidently knew its schedule.

She reached the rock, put up her arms and rested for a moment, then began to weave her way back. The distance wasn't much, but Lord! the cold,—in the early morning! When he saw her come out dripping and get into her shell, he began to shuffle on his fur jacket and his moccasins. He kept on scolding. "Silly creature! Why couldn't she wait till afternoon, when the death-chill is off the water?"

He scolded her ghost all the way home, but he thought he knew just how she felt. Probably she used to take her swim at that hour last summer, and she had forgot how cold the water was. When she first opened her long coat the nip of the air had startled her a little. There was no one watching her, she didn't have to keep face—except to herself. That she had to do and no fuss about it. She hadn't dodged. She had gone out, and she had come back. She would have a happy day. He knew just how she felt. She surely did look like a little pink clam in her white shell!

He was walking fast down the winding trails. Everything since he left the cabin had been reassuring, delightful—everything was the same, and so was he! The air, or the smell of fir trees—something had sharpened his appetite. He was hungry. As he passed the grandfather tree he waved his hand, but didn't stop. Plucky youth is more bracing than enduring age. He crossed the sharp line from the deep shade to the sunny hillside behind his cabin and saw the wood smoke rising from the chimney. The door of the dining-car kitchen stood open, and the smell of coffee drowned the spruce smell and sea smell. William hadn't waited; he was wisely breakfasting.

As he came down the hill Grenfell was chuckling to himself: "Anyhow, when that first amphibious frog-toad found his water-hole dried up behind him, and jumped out to hop along till he could find another—well, he started on a long hop."

Five Stories

The Enchanted Bluff

We had our swim before sundown, and while we were cooking our supper the oblique rays of light made a dazzling glare on the white sand about us. The translucent red ball itself sank behind the brown stretches of corn field as we sat down to eat, and the warm layer of air that had rested over the water and our clean sand-bar grew fresher and smelled of the rank ironweed and sunflowers growing on the flatter shore. The river was brown and sluggish, like any other of the half-dozen streams that water the Nebraska corn lands. On one shore was an irregular line of bald clay bluffs where a few scrub-oaks with thick trunks and flat, twisted tops threw light shadows on the long grass. The western shore was low and level, with corn fields that stretched to the sky-line, and all along the water's edge were little sandy coves and beaches where slim cottonwoods and willow saplings flickered.

The turbulence of the river in springtime discouraged milling, and, beyond keeping the old red bridge in repair, the busy farmers did not concern themselves with the stream; so the Sandtown boys were left in undisputed possession. In the autumn we hunted quail through the miles of stubble and fodder land along the flat shore, and, after the winter skating season was over and the ice had gone out, the spring freshets and flooded bottoms gave us our great excitement of the year. The channel was never the same for two successive seasons. Every spring the swollen stream undermined a bluff to the east, or bit out a few acres of corn field to the west and whirled the soil away to deposit it in spumy mud banks somewhere else. When the water fell low in midsummer, new sand-bars were thus exposed to dry and whiten in the August sun. Sometimes these were banked so firmly that the fury of the next freshet failed to unseat them; the little willow seedlings emerged triumphantly from the yellow froth, broke into spring leaf, shot up into summer growth, and with their mesh of roots bound together the moist sand beneath them against the batterings of another April. Here and there a cottonwood soon glittered among them, quivering in the low current of air that, even on breathless days when the dust hung like smoke above the wagon road, trembled along the face of the water.

It was on such an island, in the third summer of its yellow green, that we built our watch-fire; not in the thicket of dancing willow wands, but on the level terrace of fine sand which had been added that spring; a little new bit of world, beautifully ridged with ripple marks, and strewn with the tiny skeletons of turtles and fish, all as white and dry as if they had been expertly cured. We had been careful not to mar the freshness of the place, although we often swam to it on summer evenings and lay on the sand to rest.

This was our last watch-fire of the year, and there were reasons why I should remember it better than any of the others. Next week the other boys were to file back to their old places in the Sandtown High School, but I was to go up to the Divide to teach my first country school in the Norwegian district. I was already homesick at the thought of quitting the boys with whom I had always played; of leaving the river, and going up into a windy plain that was all windmills and corn fields and big pastures; where there was nothing wilful or unmanageable in the landscape, no new islands, and no chance of unfamiliar birds—such as often followed the watercourses.

Other boys came and went and used the river for fishing or skating, but we six were sworn to the spirit of the stream, and we were friends mainly because of the river. There were the two Hassler boys, Fritz and Otto, sons of the little German tailor. They were the youngest of us; ragged boys of ten and twelve, with sunburned hair, weather-stained faces, and pale blue eyes. Otto, the elder, was the best mathematician in school, and clever at his books, but he always dropped out in the spring term as if the river could not get on without him. He and Fritz caught the fat, horned catfish and sold them about the town, and they lived so much in the water that they were as brown and sandy as the river itself.

There was Percy Pound, a fat, freckled boy with chubby cheeks, who took half a dozen boys' story-papers and was always being kept in for reading detective stories behind his desk. There was Tip Smith, destined by his freckles and red hair to be the buffoon in all our games, though he walked like a timid little old man and had a funny, cracked laugh. Tip worked hard in his father's grocery store every afternoon, and swept it out before school in the morning. Even his recreations were laborious. He collected cigarette cards and tin to-bacco-tags indefatigably, and would sit for hours humped up over a snarling little scroll-saw which he kept in his attic. His dearest pos-sessions were some little pill-bottles that purported to contain grains of wheat from the Holy Land, water from the Jordan and the Dead Sea, and earth from the Mount of Olives. His father had bought these dull things from a Baptist missionary who peddled them, and Tip seemed to derive great satisfaction from their remote origin.

The tall boy was Arthur Adams. He had fine hazel eyes that were almost too reflective and sympathetic for a boy, and such a pleasant voice that we all loved to hear him read aloud. Even when he had to read poetry aloud at school, no one ever thought of laughing. To be sure, he was not at school very much of the time. He was seventeen and should have finished the High School the year before, but he was always off somewhere with his gun. Arthur's mother was dead, and his father, who was feverishly absorbed in promoting schemes, wanted to send the boy away to school and get him off his hands; but Arthur always begged off for another year and promised to study. I remember him as a tall, brown boy with an intelligent face, always lounging among a lot of us little fellows, laughing at us oftener than with us, but such a soft, satisfied laugh that we felt rather flattered when we provoked it. In after-years people said that Arthur had been given to evil ways even as a lad, and it is true that we often saw him with the gambler's sons and with old Spanish Fanny's boy, but if he learned anything ugly in their company he never betrayed it to us. We would have followed Arthur anywhere, and I am bound to say that he led us into no worse places than the cat-tail marshes and the stubble fields. These, then, were the boys who camped with me that summer night upon the sand-bar.

After we finished our supper we beat the willow thicket for drift-wood. By the time we had collected enough, night had fallen, and the pungent, weedy smell from the shore increased with the coolness. We threw ourselves down about the fire and made another futile effort to show Percy Pound the Little Dipper. We had tried it often before, but he could never be got past the big one.

"You see those three big stars just below the handle, with the bright one in the middle?" said Otto Hassler; "that's Orion's belt, and the bright one is the clasp." I crawled behind Otto's shoulder and sighted up his arm to the star that seemed perched upon the tip of his steady forefinger. The Hassler boys did seine-fishing at night, and they knew a good many stars.

Percy gave up the Little Dipper and lay back on the sand, his hands clasped under his head. "I can see the North Star," he announced, contentedly, pointing toward it with his big toe. "Anyone might get lost and need to know that."

We all looked up at it.

"How do you suppose Columbus felt when his compass didn't point north any more?" Tip asked.

Otto shook his head. "My father says that there was another North Star once, and that maybe this one won't last always. I wonder what would happen to us down here if anything went wrong with it?"

Arthur chuckled. "I wouldn't worry, Ott. Nothing's apt to happen to it in your time. Look at the Milky Way! There must be lots of good dead Indians."

We lay back and looked, meditating, at the dark cover of the world. The gurgle of the water had become heavier. We had often noticed a mutinous, complaining note in it at night, quite different from its cheerful daytime chuckle, and seeming like the voice of a much deeper and more powerful stream. Our water had always these two moods: the one of sunny complaisance, the other of inconsolable, passionate regret.

"Queer how the stars are all in sort of diagrams," remarked Otto. "You could do most any proposition in geometry with 'em. They always look as if they meant something. Some folks say everybody's fortune is all written out in the stars, don't they?"

"They believe so in the old country," Fritz affirmed.

But Arthur only laughed at him. "You're thinking of Napoleon, Fritzey. He had a star that went out when he began to lose battles. I guess the stars don't keep any close tally on Sandtown folks."

We were speculating on how many times we could count a hundred before the evening star went down behind the corn fields, when someone cried, "There comes the moon, and it's as big as a cart wheel!"

We all jumped up to greet it as it swam over the bluffs behind us. It came up like a galleon in full sail; an enormous, barbaric thing, red as an angry heathen god.

"When the moon came up red like that, the Aztecs used to sacrifice their prisoners on the temple top," Percy announced.

"Go on, Perce. You got that out of *Golden Days*. Do you believe that, Arthur?" I appealed.

Arthur answered, quite seriously: "Like as not. The moon was one of their gods. When my father was in Mexico City he saw the stone where they used to sacrifice their prisoners."

As we dropped down by the fire again some one asked whether the Mound-Builders were older than the Aztecs. When we once got upon the Mound-Builders we never willingly got away from them, and we were still conjecturing when we heard a loud splash in the water.

"Must have been a big cat jumping," said Fritz. "They do sometimes. They must see bugs in the dark. Look what a track the moon makes!"

There was a long, silvery streak on the water, and where the current fretted over a big log it boiled up like gold pieces.

"Suppose there ever *was* any gold hid away in this old river?" Fritz asked. He lay like a little brown Indian, close to the fire, his chin on his hand and his bare feet in the air. His brother laughed at him, but Arthur took his suggestion seriously.

"Some of the Spaniards thought there was gold up here somewhere. Seven cities chuck full of gold, they had it, and Coronado and his men came up to hunt it. The Spaniards were all over this country once."

Percy looked interested. "Was that before the Mormons went through?"

We all laughed at this.

"Long enough before. Before the Pilgrim Fathers, Perce. Maybe they came along this very river. They always followed the watercourses."

"I wonder where this river really does begin?" Tip mused. That was an old and a favorite mystery which the map did not clearly explain. On the map the little black line stopped somewhere in western Kansas; but since rivers generally rose in mountains, it was only reasonable to suppose that ours came from the Rockies. Its destination, we knew, was the Missouri, and the Hassler boys always maintained that we could embark at Sandtown in floodtime, follow our noses, and eventually arrive at New Orleans. Now they took up their old argument. "If us boys had grit enough to try it, it wouldn't take no time to get to Kansas City and St. Joe."

We began to talk about the places we wanted to go to. The Hassler boys wanted to see the stock-yards in Kansas City, and Percy wanted to see a big store in Chicago. Arthur was interlocutor and did not betray himself.

"Now it's your turn, Tip."

Tip rolled over on his elbow and poked the fire, and his eyes looked shyly out of his queer, tight little face. "My place is awful far away. My Uncle Bill told me about it."

Tip's Uncle Bill was a wanderer, bitten with mining fever, who had drifted into Sandtown with a broken arm, and when it was well had drifted out again.

"Where is it?"

"Aw, it's down in New Mexico somewheres. There aren't no railroads or anything. You have to go on mules, and you run out of water before you get there and have to drink canned tomatoes."

"Well, go on, kid. What's it like when you do get there?"

Tip sat up and excitedly began his story.

"There's a big red rock there that goes right up out of the sand for about nine hundred feet. The country's flat all around it, and this here rock goes up all by itself, like a monument. They call it the Enchanted Bluff down there, because no white man has ever been on top of it. The sides are smooth rock, and straight up, like a wall. The Indians say that hundreds of years ago, before the Spaniards came, there was a village away up there in the air. The tribe that lived there had some sort of steps, made out of wood and bark, hung down over the face of the bluff, and the braves went down to hunt and carried water up in big jars swung on their backs. They kept a big supply of water and dried meat up there, and never went down except to hunt. They were a peaceful tribe that made cloth and pottery, and they went up there to get out of the wars. You see, they could pick off any war party that tried to get up their little steps. The Indians say they were a handsome people, and they had some sort of queer religion. Uncle Bill thinks they were Cliff-Dwellers who had got into trouble and left home. They weren't fighters, anyhow.

"One time the braves were down hunting and an awful storm came up—a kind of waterspout—and when they got back to their rock they found their little staircase had been all broken to pieces, and only a few steps were left hanging away up in the air. While they were camped at the foot of the rock, wondering what to do, a war party from the north came along and massacred 'em to a man, with all the old folks and women looking on from the rock. Then the war party went on south and left the village to get down the best way they could. Of course they never got down. They starved to death up there, and when the war party came back on their way north, they could hear the children crying from the edge of the bluff where they had crawled out, but they didn't see a sign of a grown Indian, and nobody has ever been up there since."

We exclaimed at this dolorous legend and sat up.

"There couldn't have been many people up there," Percy demurred. "How big is the top, Tip?"

"Oh, pretty big. Big enough so that the rock doesn't look nearly as tall as it is. The top's bigger than the base. The bluff is sort of worn away for several hundred feet up. That's one reason it's so hard to climb."

I asked how the Indians got up, in the first place.

"Nobody knows how they got up or when. A hunting party came along once and saw that there was a town up there, and that was all."

Otto rubbed his chin and looked thoughtful. "Of course there must be some way to get up there. Couldn't people get a rope over someway and pull a ladder up?"

Tip's little eyes were shining with excitement. "I know a way. Me and Uncle Bill talked it all over. There's a kind of rocket that would take a rope over—life-savers use 'em—and then you could hoist a rope-ladder and peg it down at the bottom and make it tight with guy-ropes on the other side. I'm going to climb that there bluff, and I've got it all planned out."

Fritz asked what he expected to find when he got up there.

"Bones, maybe, or the ruins of their town, or pottery, or some of their idols. There might be 'most anything up there. Anyhow, I want to see."

"Sure nobody else has been up there, Tip?" Arthur asked.

"Dead sure. Hardly anybody ever goes down there. Some hunters tried to cut steps in the rock once, but they didn't get higher than a man can reach. The Bluff's all red granite, and Uncle Bill thinks it's a boulder the glaciers left. It's a queer place, anyhow. Nothing but cactus and desert for hundreds of miles, and yet right under the Bluff there's good water and plenty of grass. That's why the bison used to go down there."

Suddenly we heard a scream above our fire, and jumped up to see a dark, slim bird floating southward far above us—a whooping-crane, we knew by her cry and her long neck. We ran to the edge of the island, hoping we might see her alight, but she wavered southward along the rivercourse until we lost her. The Hassler boys declared that by the look of the heavens it must be after midnight, so we threw more wood on our fire, put on our jackets, and curled down in the warm sand. Several of us pretended to doze, but I fancy we were really thinking about Tip's Bluff and the extinct people. Over in the wood the ring-doves were calling mournfully to one another, and once we heard a dog bark, far away. "Somebody getting into old Tommy's melon patch," Fritz murmured sleepily, but nobody answered him. By and by Percy spoke out of the shadows.

"Say, Tip, when you go down there will you take me with you?"

"Maybe."

"Suppose one of us beats you down there, Tip?"

"Whoever gets to the Bluff first has got to promise to tell the rest of us exactly what he finds," remarked one of the Hassler boys, and to this we all readily assented.

Somewhat reassured, I dropped off to sleep. I must have dreamed about a race for the Bluff, for I awoke in a kind of fear that other people were getting ahead of me and that I was losing my chance. I sat up in my damp clothes and looked at the other boys, who lay tumbled in uneasy attitudes about the dead fire. It was still dark, but the sky was blue with the last wonderful azure of night. The stars glistened like crystal globes, and trembled as if they shone through a depth of clear water. Even as I watched, they began to pale and the sky brightened. Day came suddenly, almost instantaneously. I turned for another look at the blue night, and it was gone. Everywhere the birds began to call, and all manner of little insects began to chirp and hop about in the willows. A breeze sprang up from the west and brought the heavy smell of ripened corn. The boys rolled over and shook themselves. We stripped and plunged into the river just as the sun came up over the windy bluffs.

When I came home to Sandtown at Christmas time, we skated out to our island and talked over the whole project of the Enchanted Bluff, renewing our resolution to find it.

Although that was twenty years ago, none of us have ever climbed the Enchanted Bluff. Percy Pound is a stockbroker in Kansas City and will go nowhere that his red touring-car cannot carry him. Otto Hassler went on the railroad and lost his foot braking; after which he and Fritz succeeded their father as the town tailors.

Arthur sat about the sleepy little town all his life—he died before he was twenty-five. The last time I saw him, when I was home on one of my college vacations, he was sitting in a steamer-chair under a cottonwood tree in the little yard behind one of the two Sandtown saloons. He was very untidy and his hand was not steady, but when he rose, unabashed, to greet me, his eyes were as clear and warm as ever. When I had talked with him for an hour and heard him laugh again, I wondered how it was that when Nature had taken such pains with a man, from his hands to the arch of his long foot, she had ever lost him in Sandtown. He joked about Tip Smith's Bluff, and declared he was going down there just as soon as the weather got cooler; he thought the Grand Canyon might be worth while, too.

I was perfectly sure when I left him that he would never get beyond the high plank fence and the comfortable shade of the cottonwood. And, indeed, it was under that very tree that he died one summer morning.

Tip Smith still talks about going to New Mexico. He married a slatternly, unthrifty country girl, has been much tied to a perambulator, and has grown stooped and gray from irregular meals and broken sleep. But the worst of his difficulties are now over, and he has, as he says, come into easy water. When I was last in Sandtown I walked home with him late one moonlight night, after he had balanced his cash and shut up his store. We took the long way around and sat down on the schoolhouse steps, and between us we quite revived the romance of the lone red rock and the extinct people. Tip insists that he still means to go down there, but he thinks now he will wait until his boy Bert is old enough to go with him. Bert has been let into the story, and thinks of nothing but the Enchanted Bluff.

Tom Outland's Story

I

The thing that side-tracked me and made me so late coming to college was a somewhat unusual accident, or string of accidents. It began with a poker game, when I was a call boy in Pardee, New Mexico.

One cold, clear night in the fall I started out to hunt up a freight crew that was to go out soon after midnight. It was just after pay day, and one of the fellows had tipped me off that there would be a poker game going on in the card-room behind the Ruby Light saloon. I knew most of my crew would be there, except Conductor Willis, who had a sick baby at home. The front windows were dark, of course. I went up the back alley, through a tumble-down ice house and a court, into a 'dobe room that didn't open into the saloon proper at all. It was crowded, and hot and stuffy enough. There were six or seven in the game, and a crowd of fellows were standing about the walls, rubbing the white-wash off on to their coat shoulders. There was a bird-cage hanging in one window, covered with an old flannel shirt, but the canary had wakened up and was singing away for dear life. He was a beautiful singer—an old Mexican had trained him—and he was one of the attractions of the place.

I happened along when a jack-pot was running. Two of the fellows I'd come for were in it, and they naturally wanted to finish the hand. I stood by the door with my watch, keeping time for them. Among the players I saw two sheep men who always liked a lively game, and one of the bystanders told me you had to buy a hundred dollars' worth of chips to get in that night. The crowd was fussing about one fellow, Rodney Blake, who had come in from his engine without cleaning up. That wasn't customary; the minute a man got in from his run, he took a bath, put on citizen's clothes, and went to a barber. This Blake was a new fireman on our division. He'd come up town in his greasy overalls and sweaty blue shirt, with his face streaked up with smoke. He'd been drinking; he smelled of it, and his eyes were out of focus. All the other men were clean and freshly shaved, and they were sore at Blake—said his hands were so greasy they marked the cards. Some of them wanted to put him out of the game, but he was a big, heavy-built fellow, and nobody wanted to be the man to do it. It didn't please them any better when he took the jack-pot.

I got my two men and hurried them out, and two others from the row along the wall took their places. One of the chaps who left with me asked me to go up to his house and get his grip with his work clothes. He'd lost every cent of his pay cheque and didn't want to face his wife. I asked him who was winning.

"Blake. The dirty boomer's been taking everything. But the fellows will clean him out before morning."

About two o'clock, when my work for the night was over and I was going home to sleep, I just dropped in at the card-room to see how things had come out. The game was breaking up. Since I left them at midnight, they had changed to stud poker, and Blake, the fireman, had cleaned everybody out. He was cashing in his chips when I came in. The bank was a little short, but Blake made no fuss about it. He had something over sixteen hundred dollars lying on the table before him in banknotes and gold. Some of the crowd were insulting him, trying to get him into a fight and loot him. He paid no attention and began to put the money away, not looking at anybody. The bills he folded and put inside the band of his hat. He filled his overalls pockets with the gold, and swept the rest of it into his big red neckerchief.

I'd been interested in this fellow ever since he came on our division; he was close-mouthed and unfriendly. He was one of those fellows with a settled, mature body and a young face, such as you often see among working-men. There was something calm, and sarcastic, and mocking about his expression—that, too, you often see among working-men. When he had put all his money away, he got up and walked toward the door without a word, without saying good-night to any-body.

"Manners of a hog, and a dirty hog!" little Barney Shea yelled after him. Blake's back was just in the doorway; he hitched up one shoulder, but didn't turn or make a sound.

I slipped out after him and followed him down the street. His walk was unsteady, and the gold in his baggy overalls pockets clinked with every step he took. I ran a little way and caught up with him. "What are you going to do with all that money, Blake?" I asked him.

"Lose it, to-morrow night. I'm no hog for money. Damned barber-pole dudes!"

I thought I'd better follow him home. I knew he lodged with an old Mexican woman, in the yellow quarter, behind the round-house. His room opened on to the street, by a sky-blue door. He went in, didn't strike a light or make a stab at undressing, but threw himself just as he was on the bed and went to sleep. His hat stuck between the iron rods of the bed-head, the gold ran out of his pockets and rolled over the bare floor in the dark.

I struck a match and lit a candle. The bed took up half the room; on the dresser was a grip with his clean clothes in it, just as he'd brought it in from his run. I took out the clothes and began picking up the money; got the bills out of his hat, emptied his pockets, and collected the coins that lay in the hollow of the bed about his hips, and put it all into the grip. Then I blew out the light and sat down to listen. I trusted all the boys who were at the Ruby Light that night, except Barney Shea. He might try to pull something off on a stranger, down in Mexican town. We had a quiet night, however, and a cold one. I found Blake's winter overcoat hanging on the wall and wrapped up in it. I wasn't a bit sorry when the roosters began to crow and the dogs began barking all over Mexican town. At last the sun came up and turned the desert and the 'dobe town red in a minute. I began to shake the man on the bed. Waking men who didn't want to get up was part of my job, and I didn't let up on him until I had him on his feet.

"Hello, kid, come to call me?"

I told him I'd come to call him to a Harvey House breakfast. "You owe me a good one. I brought you home last night."

"Sure, I'm glad to have company. Wait till I wash up a bit." He took his soap and towel and comb and went out into the patio, a neat little sanded square with flowers and vines all around, and washed at the trough under the pump. Then he called me to come and pump water on his head. After he'd stood the gush of cold water for a few seconds, he straightened up with his teeth chattering.

"That ought to get the whisky out of a fellow's head, oughtn't it? Felt good, Tom." Presently he began feeling his side pockets. "Was I dreaming something, or did I take a string of jack-pots last night?"

"The money's in your grip," I told him. "You don't deserve it, for you were too drunk to take care of it. I had to come after you and pick it up out of the mud."

"All right. I'll go halvers. Easy come, easy go."

I told him I didn't want anything off him but breakfast, and I wanted that pretty soon.

"Go easy, son. I've got to change my shirt. This one's wet."

"It's worse than wet. You oughtn't to go up town without changing. You're a stranger here, and it makes a bad impression."

He shrugged his shoulders and looked superior. He had a square-built, honest face and steady eyes that didn't carry a cynical expression very well. I knew he was a decent chap, though he'd been drinking and acting ugly ever since he'd been on our division.

After breakfast we went out and sat in the sun at a place where the wooden sidewalk ran over a sand gully and made a sort of bridge. I had a long talk with him. I was carrying the grip with his winnings in it, and I finally persuaded him to go with me to the bank. We put every cent of it into a savings account that he couldn't touch for a year.

From that night Blake and I were fast friends. He was the sort of fellow who can do anything for somebody else, and nothing for himself. There are lots like that among working-men. They aren't trained by success to a sort of systematic selfishness. Rodney had been unlucky in personal relations. He'd run away from home when he was a kid because his mother married again—a man who had been paying attention to her while his father was still alive. He got engaged to a girl down on the Southern Pacific, and she double-crossed him, as he said. He went to Old Mexico and let his friends put all his savings into an oil well, and they skinned him. What he needed was a pal, a straight fellow to give an account to. I was ten years younger, and that was an advantage. He liked to be an older brother. I suppose the fact that I was a kind of stray and had no family made it easier for him to unbend to me. He surely got to think a lot of me, and I did of him. It was that winter I had pneumonia.

Mrs. O'Brien couldn't do much for me; she was overworked, poor woman, with a houseful of children. Blake took me down to his room, and he and the old Mexican woman nursed me. He ought to have had boys of his own to look after. Nature's full of such substitutions, but they always seem to me sad, even in botany.

I wasn't able to be about until spring, and then the doctor and Father Duchene said I must give up night work and live in the open all summer. Before I knew anything about it, Blake had thrown up his job on the Santa Fé, and got a berth for him and me with the Sitwell Cattle Company. Jonas Sitwell was one of the biggest cattle men in our part of New Mexico. Roddy and I were to ride the range with a bunch of grass cattle all summer, then take them down to a winter camp on the Cruzados river and keep them on pasture until spring.

We went out about the first of May, and joined our cattle twenty miles south of Pardee, down toward the Blue Mesa. The Blue Mesa was one of the landmarks we always saw from Pardee—landmarks mean so much in a flat country. To the northwest, over toward Utah, we had the Mormon Buttes, three sharp blue peaks that always sat there. The Blue Mesa was south of us, and was much stronger in colour, almost purple. People said the rock itself had a deep purplish cast. It looked, from our town, like a naked blue rock set down alone in the plain, almost square, except that the top was higher at one end. The old settlers said nobody had ever climbed it, because the sides were so steep and the Cruzados river wound round it at one end and under-cut it.

Blake and I knew that the Sitwell winter camp was down on the Cruzados river, directly under the mesa, and all summer long, while we drifted about with our cattle from one water-hole to another, we planned how we were going to climb the mesa and be the first men up there. After supper, when we lit our pipes and watched the sunset, climbing the mesa was our staple topic of conversation. Our job was a cinch; the actual work wouldn't have kept one man busy. The Sitwell people were good to their hands. John Rapp, the foreman, came along once a month in his spring-wagon, to see how the cattle were doing and to bring us supplies and bundles of old newspapers. Blake was a conscientious reader of newspapers. He always wanted to know what was going on in the world, though most of it displeased him. He brooded on the great injustices of his time; the hanging of the Anarchists in Chicago, which he could just remember, and the Dreyfus case. We had long arguments about what we read in the papers, but we never quarrelled. The only trouble I had with Blake was in getting to do my share of the work. He made my health a pretext for taking all the heavy chores, long after I was as well as he was. I'd brought my Caesar along, and had promised Father Duchene to read a hundred lines a day. Blake saw that I did it—made me translate the dull stuff aloud to him. He said if I once knew Latin, I wouldn't have to work with my back all my life like a burro. He had great respect for education, but he believed it was some kind of hocus-pocus that enabled a man to live without work. We had *Robinson Crusoe* with us, and Roddy's favourite book, *Gulliver's Travels,* which he never tired of.

Late in October, Rapp, the foreman, came along to accompany us down to the winter camp. Blake stayed with the cattle about fifteen miles to the east, where the grass was still good, and Rapp and I went down to air out the cabin and stow away our winter supplies.

II

The cabin stood in a little grove of piñons, about thirty yards back from the Cruzados river, facing south and sheltered on the north by a low hill. The grama grass grew right up to the door-step, and the rabbits were running about and the grasshoppers hitting the door when we pulled up and looked at the place. There was no litter around, it was as clean as a prairie-dog's house. No out-buildings, except a shed for our horses. The hill-side behind was sandy and covered with tall clumps of deer-horn cactus, but there was nothing but grass to the south, with streaks of bright yellow rabbit-brush. Along the river the cottonwoods and quaking asps had already turned gold. Just across from us, overhanging us, indeed, stood the mesa, a pile of purple rock, all broken out with red sumach and yellow aspens up in the high crevices of the cliffs. From the cabin, night and day, you could hear the river, where it made a bend round the foot of the mesa and churned over the rocks. It was the sort of place a man would like to stay in forever.

I helped Rapp open the wooden shutters and sweep out the cabin. We put clean blankets on the bunks, and stowed away bacon and coffee and canned stuff on the shelves behind the cook-stove. I confess I looked forward to cooking on an iron stove with four holes. Rapp explained to me that Blake and I wouldn't be able to enjoy all this luxury together for a time. He wanted the herd kept some distance to the north as long as the grass held out up there, and Roddy and I could take turn about, one camping near the cattle and one sleeping in a bed.

"There's not pasture enough down here to take them through a long winter," he said, "and it's safest to keep them grazing up north while you can. Besides, if you bring them down here while the weather's so warm, they get skittish, and that mesa over there makes trouble. They swim the river and bolt into the mesa, and that's the last you ever see of them. We've lost a lot of critters that way. The mesa has been populated by run-aways from our herd, till now there's a fine bunch of wild cattle up there. When the wind's right, our cows over here get the scent of them and make a break for the river. You'll have to watch 'em close when you bring 'em down."

I asked him whether nobody had ever gone over to get the lost cattle out.

Rapp glared at me. "Out of that mesa? Nobody has ever got into it yet. The cliffs are like the base of a monument, all the way round. The only way into it is through that deep canyon that opens on the water level, just where the river makes the bend. You can't get in by that, because the river's too deep to ford and too swift to swim. Oh, I suppose a horse could swim it, if cattle can, but I don't want to be the man to try."

I remarked that I had had my eye on the mesa all summer and meant to climb it.

"Not while you're working for the Sitwell Company, you don't! If you boys try any nonsense of that sort, I'll fire you quick. You'd break your bones and lose the herd for us. You have to watch them close to keep them from going over, I tell you. If it wasn't for that mesa, this would be the best winter range in all New Mexico."

After the foreman left us, we settled down to easy living and fine weather; blue and gold days, and clear, frosty nights. We kept the cattle off to the north and east and alternated in taking charge of them. One man was with the herd while the other got his sleep and did the cooking at the cabin. The mesa was our only neighbour, and the closer we got to it, the more tantalizing it was. It was no longer a blue, featureless lump, as it had been from a distance. Its sky-line was like the profile of a big beast lying down; the head to the north, higher than the flanks around which the river curved. The north end we could easily believe impassable—sheer cliffs that fell from the summit to the plain, more than a thousand feet. But the south flank, just across the river from us, looked accessible by way of the deep canyon that split the bulk in two, from the top rim to the river, then wound back into the solid cube so that it was invisible at a distance, like a mouse track winding into a big cheese. This canyon didn't break the solid outline of the mesa, and you had to be close to see that it was there at all. We faced the mesa on its shortest side; it was only about three miles long from north to south, but east and west it measured nearly twice that distance. Whether the top was wooded we couldn't see—it was too high above us; but the cliffs and canyon on the river side were fringed with beautiful growth, groves of quaking asps and piñons and a few dark cedars, perched up in the air like the hanging gardens of Babylon. At certain hours of the day, those cedars, growing so far up on the rocks, took on the bluish tint of the cliffs themselves.

It was light up there long before it was with us. When I got up at daybreak and went down to the river to get water, our camp would be cold and grey, but the mesa top would be red with sunrise, and all the slim cedars along the rocks would be gold—metallic, like tarnished gold-foil. Some mornings it would loom up above the dark river like a blazing volcanic mountain. It shortened our days, too, considerably. The sun got behind it early in the afternoon, and then our camp would lie in its shadow. After a while the sunset colour would begin to stream up from behind it. Then the mesa was like one great ink-black rock against a sky on fire.

No wonder the thing bothered us and tempted us; it was always before us, and was always changing. Black thunder-storms used to roll up from behind it and pounce on us like a panther without warning. The lightning would play round it and jab into it so that we were always expecting it would fire the brush. I've never heard thunder so loud as it was there. The cliffs threw it back at us, and we thought the mesa itself, though it seemed so solid, must be full of deep canyons and caverns, to account for the prolonged growl and rumble that followed every crash of thunder. After the burst in the sky was over, the mesa went on sounding like a drum, and seemed itself to be muttering and making noises.

One afternoon I was out hunting turkeys. Just as the sun was getting low, I came through a sea of rabbit-brush, still yellow, and the horizontal rays of light, playing into it, brought out the contour of the ground with great distinctness. I noticed a number of straight mounds, like plough furrows, running from the river inland. It was too late to examine them. I cut a scrub willow and stuck a stake into one of the ridges, to mark it. The next day I took a spade down to the plantation of rabbit-brush and dug around in the sandy soil. I came upon an old irrigation main, unmistakable, lined with hard smooth cobbles and 'dobe cement, with sluices where the water had been let out into trenches. Along these ditches I turned up some pieces of pottery, all of it broken, and arrowheads, and a very neat, well-finished stone pick-ax.

That night I didn't go back to the cabin, but took my specimens out to Blake, who was still north with the cattle. Of course, we both knew there had been Indians all over this country, but we felt sure that Indians hadn't used stone tools for a long while back. There must have been a colony of pueblo Indians here in ancient times: fixed residents, like the Taos Indians and the Hopis, not wanderers like the Navajos.

To people off alone, as we were, there is something stirring about finding evidences of human labour and care in the soil of an empty country. It comes to you as a sort of message, makes you feel differently about the ground you walk over every day. I liked the winter range better than any place I'd ever been in. I never came out of the cabin door in the morning to go after water that I didn't feel fresh delight in our snug quarters and the river and the old mesa up there, with its top burning like a bonfire. I wanted to see what it was like on the other side, and very soon I took a day off and forded the river where it was wide and shallow, north of our camp. I rode clear around the mesa, until I met the river again where it flowed under the south flank.

On that ride I got a better idea of its actual structure. All the way round were the same precipitous cliffs of hard blue rock, but in places it was mixed with a much softer stone. In these soft streaks there were deep dry watercourses which could certainly be climbed as far as they went, but nowhere did they reach to the top of the mesa. The top seemed to be one great slab of very hard rock, lying on the mixed mass of the base like the top of an old-fashioned marble table. The channels worn out by water ran for hundreds of feet up the cliffs, but always stopped under this great rimrock, which projected out over the erosions like a granite shelf. Evidently, it was because of this unbroken top layer that the butte was inaccessible. I rode back to camp that night, convinced that if we ever climbed it, we must take the route the cattle took, through the river and up the one canyon that broke down to water-level.

III

We brought the bunch of cattle down to the winter range in the latter part of November. Early in December the foreman came along with generous provisions for Christmas. This time he brought with him a super-cargo, a pitiful wreck of an old man he had picked up at Tarpin, the railroad town thirty miles northeast of us, where the Sitwells bought their supplies. This old man was a castaway Englishman, Henry Atkins by name. He had been a valet, and a hospital orderly, and a cook, and for many years was a table steward on the Anchor Line. Lately he had been cooking for a sheep outfit that were grazing in the cattle country, where they weren't wanted. They had done something shady and had to get out in a hurry. They dropped old Henry at Tarpin, where he soon drank up all his wages. When Rapp picked him up there, he was living on hand-outs.

"I've told him we can't pay him anything," Rapp explained. "But if he wants to stay here and cook for you boys till I make my next trip, he'll have plenty to eat and a roof over him. He was sleeping in the livery stable in Tarpin. He says he's a good cook, and I thought he might liven things up for you at Christmas time. He won't bother you, he's not got any of the mean ways of a bum—I know a bum when I see one. Next time I come down I'll bring him some old clothes from the ranch, and you can fire him if you want to. All his baggage is that newspaper bundle, and there's nothing in it but shoes—a pair of patent leathers and a pair of sneakers. The important thing is, never, on any account, go off skylarking, you two, and leave him with the cattle. Not for an hour, mind you. He ain't strong enough, and he's got no head."

Life was a holiday for Blake and me after we got old Henry. He was a wonderful cook and a good housekeeper. He kept that cabin shining like a playhouse; used to dress it all out with piñon boughs, and trimmed the kitchen shelves with newspapers cut in fancy patterns. He had learned to make up cots when he was a hospital orderly, and he made our bunks feel like a Harvey House bed. To this day that's the best I can say for any bed. And he was such a polite, mannerly old boy; simple and kind as a child. I used to wonder how anybody so innocent and defenceless had managed to get along at all, to keep alive for nearly seventy years in as hard a world as this. Anybody could take advantage of him. He held no grudge against any of the people who had misused him. He loved to tell about the celebrated people he'd been steward to, and the liberal tips they had given him. There with us, where he couldn't get a whisky, he was a model of good behaviour. "Drink is me weakness, you might say," he occasionally remarked apologetically. He shaved every morning and was as clean as a pin. We got to be downright fond of him, and the three of us made a happy family.

Ever since we'd brought our herd down to the winter camp, the wild cattle on the mesa were more in evidence. They came down to the river to drink oftener, and loitered about, grazing in that low canyon so much that we began to call it Cow Canyon. They were fine-looking beasts, too. One could see they had good pasture up there. Henry had a theory that we ought to be able to entice them over to our side with salt. He wanted to kill one for beef-steaks. Soon after he joined us we lost two cows. Without warning they bolted into the mesa, as the foreman had said. After that we watched the herd closer; but a few days before Christmas, when Blake was off hunting and I was on duty, four fine young steers sneaked down to the water's edge through the brush, and before I knew it they were swimming the river—seemed to do it with no trouble at all. They frisked out on the other side, ambled up the canyon, and disappeared. I was furious to have them steal a march on me, and I swore to myself I'd follow them over and drive them back.

The next morning we took the herd a few miles east, to keep them out of mischief. I made some excuse to Blake, cut back to the cabin, and asked Henry to put me up a lunch. I told him my plan, but warned him not to bear tales. If I wasn't home when Blake came in at night, then he could tell him where I'd gone.

Henry went down to the river with me to watch me across. It had grown colder since morning, and looked like snow. The old man was afraid of a storm; said I might get snowed in. But I'd got my nerve up, and I didn't want to put off making a try at it. I strapped my blanket and my lunch on my shoulders, hung my boots around my neck to keep them dry, stuffed my socks inside my hat, and we waded in. My horse took the water without any fuss, though he shivered a good deal. He stepped out very carefully, and when it got too deep for him, he swam without panic. We were carried downstream a little by the current, but I didn't have to slide off his back. He found bottom after a while, and we easily made a landing. I waved good-bye to Henry on the other side and started up the canyon, running beside my horse to get warm.

The canyon was wide at the water's edge, and though it corkscrewed back into the mesa by abrupt turns, it preserved this open, roomy character. It was, indeed, a very deep valley with gently sloping sides, rugged and rocky, but well grassed. There was a clear trail. Horses have no sense about making a trail, but you can trust cattle to find the easiest possible path and to take the lowest grades. The bluish rock and the sun-tanned grass, under the unusual purple-grey of the sky, gave the whole valley a very soft colour, lavender and pale gold, so that the occasional cedars growing beside the boulders looked black that morning. It may have been the hint of snow in the air, but it seemed to me that I had never breathed in anything that tasted so pure as the air in that valley. It made my mouth and nostrils

smart like charged water, seemed to go to my head a little and produce
a kind of exaltation. I kept telling myself that it was very different
from the air on the other side of the river, though that was pure and
uncontaminated enough.

When I had gone up this canyon for a mile or so, I came upon
another, opening out to the north—a box canyon, very different in
character. No gentle slope there. The walls were perpendicular, where
they weren't actually overhanging, and they were anywhere from
eight hundred to a thousand feet high, as we afterward found by
measurement. The floor of it was a mass of huge boulders, great
pieces of rock that had fallen from above ages back, and had been
worn round and smooth as pebbles by the long action of water. Many
of them were as big as haystacks, yet they lay piled on one another
like a load of gravel. There was no footing for my horse among those
smooth stones, so I hobbled him and went on alone a little way, just
to see what it was like. My eyes were steadily on the ground—a slip
of the foot there might cripple one.

It was such rough scrambling that I was soon in a warm sweat
under my damp clothes. In stopping to take breath, I happened to
glance up at the canyon wall. I wish I could tell you what I saw there,
just *as* I saw it, on that first morning, through a veil of lightly falling
snow. Far up above me, a thousand feet or so, set in a great cavern
in the face of the cliff, I saw a little city of stone, asleep. It was as
still as sculpture—and something like that. It all hung together,
seemed to have a kind of composition: pale little houses of stone
nestling close to one another, perched on top of each other, with flat
roofs, narrow windows, straight walls, and in the middle of the group,
a round tower.

It was beautifully proportioned, that tower, swelling out to a larger
girth a little above the base, then growing slender again. There was
something symmetrical and powerful about the swell of the masonry.
The tower was the fine thing that held all the jumble of houses
together and made them mean something. It was red in colour, even
on that grey day. In sunlight it was the colour of winter oak-leaves.
A fringe of cedars grew along the edge of the cavern, like a garden.
They were the only living things. Such silence and stillness and repose—immortal repose. That village sat looking down into the canyon

with the calmness of eternity. The falling snow-flakes, sprinkling the piñons, gave it a special kind of solemnity. I can't describe it. It was more like sculpture than anything else. I knew at once that I had come upon the city of some extinct civilization, hidden away in this inaccessible mesa for centuries, preserved in the dry air and almost perpetual sunlight like a fly in amber, guarded by the cliffs and the river and the desert.

As I stood looking up at it, I wondered whether I ought to tell even Blake about it; whether I ought not to go back across the river and keep that secret as the mesa had kept it. When I at last turned away, I saw still another canyon branching out of this one, and in its wall still another arch, with another group of buildings. The notion struck me like a rifle ball that this mesa had once been like a bee-hive; it was full of little cliff-hung villages, it had been the home of a powerful tribe, a particular civilization.

That night when I got home Blake was on the river-bank waiting for me. I told him I'd rather not talk about my trip until after supper,—that I was beat out. I think he'd meant to upbraid me for sneaking off, but he didn't. He seemed to realize from the first that this was a serious matter to me, and he accepted it in that way.

After supper, when we had lit our pipes, I told Blake and Henry as clearly as I could what it was like over there, and we talked it over. The town in the cliffs explained the irrigation ditches. Like all pueblo Indians, these people had had their farms away from their dwellings. For a stronghold they needed rock, and for farming, soft earth and a water main.

"And this proves," said Roddy, "that there must have been a trail into the mesa at the north end, and that they carried their harvest over by the ford. If this Cow Canyon was the only entrance, they could never have farmed down here." We agreed that he should go over on the first warm day, and try to find a trail up to the Cliff City, as we already called it.

We talked and speculated until after midnight. It was Christmas eve, and Henry said it was but right we should do something out of the ordinary. But after we went to bed, tired as I was, I was unable to sleep. I got up and dressed and put on my overcoat and slipped outside to get sight of the mesa. The wind had come up and was blowing the squall clouds across the sky. The moon was almost full, hanging directly over the mesa, which had never looked so solemn and silent to me before. I wondered how many Christmases had come and gone since that round tower was built. I had been to Acoma and the Hopi villages, but I'd never seen a tower like that one. It seemed to me to mark a difference. I felt that only a strong and aspiring people would have built it, and a people with a feeling for design. That cluster of buildings, in its arch, with the dizzy drop into empty air from its doorways and the wall of cliff above, was as clear in my mind as a picture. By closing my eyes I could see it against the dark, like a magic-lantern slide.

Blake got over the river before New Year's day, but he didn't find any way of getting from the bottom of the box canyon up into the Cliff City. He felt sure that the inhabitants of that sky village had reached it by a trail from the top of the mesa down, not from the bottom of the canyon up. He explored the branch canyons a little, and found four other villages, smaller than the first, placed in similar arches.

These arches we had often seen in other canyons. You can find them in the Grand Canyon, and all along the Rio Grande. Whenever the surface rock is much harder than the rock beneath it, the softer stone begins to crack and crumble with weather just at the line where it meets the hard rim rock. It goes on crumbling and falling away, and in time this wash-out grows to be a spacious cavern. The Cliff City sat in an unusually large cavern. We afterward found that it was three hundred and sixty feet long, and seventy feet high in the centre. The red tower was fifty feet in height.

Blake and I began to make plans. Our engagement with the Sitwell Company terminated in May. When we turned our cattle over to the foreman, we would go into the mesa with what food and tools we could carry, and try to find a trail down the north end, where we were sure there must once have been one. If we could find an easier way to get in and out of the mesa, we would devote the summer, and our winter's wages, to exploring it. From Tarpin, the nearest railroad, we could get supplies and tools, and help if we needed it. We thought we could manage to do the work ourselves if old Henry would stay with us. We didn't want to make our discovery any more public than necessary. We were reluctant to expose those silent and beautiful places to vulgar curiosity. Finally we outlined our plan to Henry, telling him we couldn't promise him regular wages.

"We won't mention it," he said, waving his hand. "I'd ask nothing better than to share your fortunes. In me youth it was me ambition to go to Egypt and see the tombs of the Pharoahs."

"You may get a bad cold going over the river, Henry," Blake warned him. "It's bad crossing—makes you dizzy when you take to swimming. You have to keep your head."

"I was never seasick in me life," he declared, "and at that, I've helped in the cooks' galley on the Anchor Line when she was fair standing on her head. You'll find me strong and active when I'm once broke into the work. I come of an enduring family, though, to be sure, I've abused me constitution somewhat."

Henry liked to talk about his family, and the work they'd done, and the great age to which they lived, and the brandy puddings his mother made. "Eighteen we was in all, when we sat down at table," he would often say with his thin, apologetic smile. "Mother and father, and ten living, and four dead, and two still-born." Roddy and I used to strain our imagination trying to visualize such a family dinner party.

Everything worked out well for us. The foreman showed so much interest in our plans that we told him everything. He insisted that we should stay on at the winter camp as long as we needed a home base, and use up whatever supplies were left. When he paid us off, he sold us our two horses at a very reasonable figure.

IV

Blake and I got over to the mesa together for the first time early in May. We carried with us all the food we could, and an ax and spade. It took us several days to find a trail leading from the bottom of the box canyon up to the Cliff City. There were gaps in it; it was broken by ledges too steep for a man to climb. Lying beside one of these, we found an old dried cedar trunk, with toe-notches cut in it. That was a plain suggestion. We felled some trees and threw them up over the gaps in the path. Toward the end of the week, when our provisions were getting low, we made the last lap in our climb, and stepped upon the ledge that was the floor of the Cliff City.

In front of the cluster of buildings, there was an open space, like a court-yard. Along the outer edge of this yard ran a low stone wall. In some places the wall had fallen away from the weather, but the buildings themselves sat so far back under the rim rock that the rain had never beat on them. In thunder-storms I've seen the water come down in sheets over the face of that cavern without a drop touching the village.

The court-yard was not choked by vegetation, for there was no soil. It was bare rock, with a few old, flat-topped cedars growing out of the cracks, and a little pale grass. But everything seemed open and clean, and the stones, I remember, were warm to the touch, smooth and pleasant to feel.

The outer walls of the houses were intact, except where sometimes an outjutting corner had crumbled. They were made of dressed stones, plastered inside and out with 'dobe, and were tinted in light colours, pink and pale yellow and tan. Here and there a cedar log in the ceiling had given way and let the second-story chamber down into the first; except for that, there was little rubbish or disorder. As Blake remarked, wind and sun are good housekeepers.

This village had never been sacked by an enemy, certainly. Inside the little rooms water jars and bowls stood about unbroken, and yucca-fibre mats were on the floors.

We could give only a hurried look over the place, as our food was exhausted, and we had to get back over the river before dark. We went about softly, tried not to disturb anything—even the silence. Besides the tower, there seemed to be about thirty little separate dwellings. Behind the cluster of houses was a kind of back court-yard, running from end to end of the cavern; a long, low, twilit space that got gradually lower toward the back until the rim rock met the floor of the cavern, exactly like the sloping roof of an attic. There was perpetual twilight back there, cool, shadowy, very grateful after the blazing sun in the front court-yard. When we entered it we heard a soft trickling sound, and we came upon a spring that welled out of the rock into a stone basin and then ran off through a cobble-lined gutter and dripped down the cliffs. I've never anywhere tasted water like it; as cold as ice, and so pure. Long afterward Father Duchene came out to spend a week with us on the mesa; he always carried a small drinking-glass with him, and he used to fill it at the spring and take it out into the sunlight. The water looked like liquid crystal, absolutely colourless, without the slight brownish or greenish tint that water nearly always has. It threw off the sunlight like a diamond.

Beside this spring stood some of the most beautifully shaped water jars we ever found—I gave Mrs. St. Peter one of them—standing there just as if they'd been left yesterday. In the back court we found a great many things besides jars and bowls: a row of grinding-stones, and several clay ovens, very much like those the Mexicans use to-day. There were charred bones and charcoal, and the roof was thick with soot all the way along. It was evidently a kind of common kitchen, where they roasted and baked and probably gossiped. There were corncobs everywhere, and ears of corn with the kernels still on them—little, like popcorn. We found dried beans, too, and strings of pumpkin seeds, and plum seeds, and a cupboard full of little implements made of turkey bones.

Late that afternoon Roddy and I crossed the river and got back to our cabin to rest for a few days.

The second time we went over, we found a long winding trail leading from the Cliff City up to the top of the mesa—a narrow path worn deep into the stone ledges that overhung the village, then running back into the wood of stunted piñons on the summit. Following this to the north end of the mesa, we found what was left of an old road down to the plain. But making this road passable was a matter of weeks, and we had to get workmen and tools from Tarpin. It was a narrow foot-path, barely wide enough for a sure-footed mule, and it wound down through Black Canyon, dropping in loops along the face of terrifying cliffs. About a hundred feet above the river, it ended—broke right off into the air. A wall of rock had fallen away there, probably from a landslide. That last piece of road cost us three weeks' hard work, and most of our winter's wages. We kept the workmen on long enough to build us a tight log cabin on the mesa top, a little way back from the ledge that hung over the Cliff City.

While we were engaged in road-building, we made a short cut

from our cabin down to the Cliff City and Cow Canyon. Just over the Cliff City, there was a crack in the ledge, a sort of manhole, and in this we hung a ladder of pine-trunks spliced together with light chains, leaving the branch forks for footholds. By climbing down this ladder we saved about two miles of winding trail, and dropped almost directly into Cow Canyon, where we meant always to leave one of the horses grazing. Taking this route, we could at any time make a quick exit from the mesa—we were used to swimming the river now, and in summer our wet clothes dried very quickly.

Bill Hook, the liveryman at Tarpin, who'd sheltered old Henry when he was down and out, proved a good friend to us. He got our workmen back and forth for us, brought our supplies up on to the mesa on his pack-mules, and when one of us had to stay in town overnight he let us sleep in his hay barn to save a hotel bill. He knew our expenses were heavy, and did everything for us at a bottom price.

By the first of July our money was nearly gone, but we had our road made, and our cabin built on top of the mesa. We brought old Henry up by the new horse-trail and began housekeeping. We were now ready for what we called excavating. We built wide shelves all around our sleeping-room, and there we put the smaller articles we found in the Cliff City. We numbered each specimen, and in my day-book I wrote down just where and in what condition we had found it, and what we thought it had been used for. I'd got a merchant's ledger in Tarpin, and every night after supper, while Roddy read the newspapers, I sat down at the kitchen table and wrote up an account of the day's work.

Henry, besides doing the housekeeping, was very eager to help us in the "rew-ins," as he called them. He was more patient than we, and would dig with his fingers half a day to get a pot out of a rubbish pile without breaking it. After all, the old man had a wider knowledge of the world than either of us, and it often came in handy. When we were working in a pale pink house, with two stories, and a sort of balcony before the upper windows, we came on a closet in the wall of the upstairs room; in this were a number of curious things, among them a deerskin bag full of little tools. Henry said at once they were surgical instruments; a stone lancet, a bunch of fine bone needles, wooden forceps, and a catheter.

One thing we knew about these people; they hadn't built their town in a hurry. Everything proved their patience and deliberation. The cedar joists had been felled with stone axes and rubbed smooth with sand. The little poles that lay across them and held up the clay floor of the chamber above, were smoothly polished. The door lintels were carefully fitted (the doors were stone slabs held in place by wooden bars fitted into hasps). The clay dressing that covered the stone walls was tinted, and some of the chambers were frescoed in geometrical patterns, one colour laid on another. In one room was a painted border, little tents, like Indian tepees, in brilliant red.

But the really splendid thing about our city, the thing that made it delightful to work there, and must have made it delightful to live there, was the setting. The town hung like a bird's nest in the cliff, looking off into the box canyon below, and beyond into the wide valley we called Cow Canyon, facing an ocean of clear air. A people who had the hardihood to build there, and who lived day after day looking down upon such grandeur, who came and went by those hazardous trails, must have been, as we often told each other, a fine people. But what had become of them? What catastrophe had overwhelmed them?

They hadn't moved away, for they had taken none of their belongings, not even their clothes. Oh, yes, we found clothes; yucca moccasins, and what seemed like cotton cloth, woven in black and white. Never any wool, but sheepskins tanned with the fleece on them. They may have been mountain sheep; the mesa was full of them. We talked of shooting one for meat, but we never did. When a mountain sheep comes out on a ledge hundreds of feet above you, with his trumpet horns, there's something noble about him—he looks like a priest. We didn't want to shoot at them and make them shy. We liked to see them. We shot a wild cow when we wanted fresh meat.

At last we came upon one of the original inhabitants—not a skeleton, but a dried human body, a woman. She was not in the Cliff City; we found her in a little group of houses stuck up in a high arch we called the Eagle's Nest. She was lying on a yucca mat, partly covered with rags, and she had dried into a mummy in that water-drinking air. We thought she had been murdered; there was a great wound in her side, the ribs stuck out through the dried flesh. Her mouth was open as if she were screaming, and her face, through all those years, had kept a look of terrible agony. Part of the nose was gone, but she had plenty of teeth, not one missing, and a great deal of coarse black hair. Her teeth were even and white, and so little worn that we thought she must have been a young woman. Henry named her Mother Eve, and we called her that. We put her in a blanket and let her down with great care, and kept her in a chamber in the Cliff City.

Yes, we found three other bodies, but afterward. One day, working in the Cliff City, we came upon a stone slab at one end of the cavern, that seemed to lead straight into the rock. It was set in cement, and when we loosened it we found it opened into a small, dark chamber. In this there had been a platform, of fine cedar poles laid side by side, but it had crumbled. In the wreckage were three bodies, one man and two women, wrapped in yucca-fibre, all in the same posture and apparently prepared for burial. They were the bodies of old people. We believed they were among the aged who were left behind when the tribe went down to live on their farms in the summer season; that they had died in the absence of the villagers, and were put into this mortuary chamber to await the return of the tribe, when they would have their funeral rites. Probably these people burned their dead. Of course an archæologist could have told a great deal about that civilization from those bodies. But they never got to an archæologist—at least, not on this side of the world.

V

The first of August came, and everything was going well with us. We hadn't met with any bad luck, and though we had very little money left, there was Blake's untouched savings account in the bank at Pardee, and we had plenty of credit in Tarpin. The merchants there took an interest and were friendly. But the little new moon, that looked so innocent, brought us trouble. We lost old Henry, and in a terrible way. From the first we'd been a little bothered by rattle-snakes—you generally find them about old stone quarries and old masonry. We had got them pretty well cleared out of the Cliff City, hadn't seen one there for weeks. But one Sunday we took Henry and went on an exploring expedition at the north end of the mesa, along Black Canyon. We caught sight of a little bunch of ruins we'd never noticed before, and made a foolhardy scramble to get up to them. We almost made it, and then there was a stretch of rock wall so smooth we couldn't climb it without a ladder. I was the tallest of the three, and Henry was the lightest; he thought he could get up there if he stood on my shoulders. He was standing on my back, his head just above the floor of the cavern, groping for something to hoist himself by, when a snake struck him from the ledge—struck him square in the forehead. It happened in a flash. He came down and brought the snake with him. By the time we picked him up and turned him over, his face had begun to swell. In ten minutes it was purple, and he was so crazy it took the two of us to hold him and keep him from jumping down the chasm. He was struck so near the brain that there was nothing to do. It lasted nearly two hours. Then we carried him home. Roddy dropped down the ladder into Cow Canyon, caught his horse, and rode into Tarpin for the coroner. Father Duchene was preaching there at the mission church that Sunday, and came back with him.

We buried Henry on the mesa. Father Duchene stayed on with us a week to keep us company. We were so cut up that we were almost ready to quit. But he had been planning to come out to see our find for a long while, and he got our minds off our trouble. He worked hard every day. He went over everything we'd done, and examined everything minutely: the pottery, cloth, stone implements, and the remains of food. He measured the heads of the mummies and declared they had good skulls. He cut down one of the old cedars that grew exactly in the middle of the deep trail worn in the stone, and counted the rings under his pocket microscope. You couldn't count them with the unassisted eye, for growing out of a tiny crevice in the rock as that tree did, the increase of each year was so scant that the rings were invisible except with a glass. The tree he cut down registered three hundred and thirty-six years' growth, and it could have begun to grow in that well-worn path only after human feet had ceased to come and go there.

Why had they ceased? That question puzzled him, too. Smallpox, any epidemic, would have left unburied bodies. Father Duchene suggested what Dr. Ripley, in Washington, afterward surmised: that the tribe had been exterminated, not here in their stronghold, but in their summer camp, down among the farms across the river. Father Duchene had been among the Indians nearly twenty years then, he had seventeen Indian pueblos in his parish, and he spoke several Indian dialects. He was able to explain the use of many of the implements we found, especially those used in religious ceremonies. The night before he left us, he summed up the results of his week's study, something like this:

"The two square towers on the mesa top, to which you have given little attention, were unquestionably granaries. Under the stones and earth fallen from the walls, there is a quantity of dried corn on the ear. Not a great harvest, for life must have come to an end here in the summer, when the new crop was not yet garnered and the last year's grain was getting low. The semicircular ridge on the mesa top, which you can see distinctly among the piñons when the sun is low and brings it into high relief, is the buried wall of an amphitheatre, where probably religious exercises and games took place. I advise you not to dig into it. It is probably the most important thing here, and should be left for scholars to excavate.

"The tower you so much admire in the cliff village may have been a watch tower, as you think, but from the curious placing of those narrow slits, like windows, I believe it was used for astronomical observations. I am inclined to think that your tribe were a superior people. Perhaps they were not so when they first came upon this mesa, but in an orderly and secure life they developed considerably the arts of peace. There is evidence on every hand that they lived for something more than food and shelter. They had an appreciation of comfort, and went even further than that. Their life, compared to that of our roving Navajos, must have been quite complex. There is unquestionably a distinct feeling for design in what you call the Cliff City. Buildings are not grouped like that by pure accident, though convenience probably had much to do with it. Convenience often dictates very sound design.

"The workmanship on both the wood and stone of the dwellings is good. The shapes and decoration of the water jars and food bowls is better than in any of the existing pueblos I know, better even than the pottery made at Acoma. I have seen a collection of early pottery from the island of Crete. Many of the geometrical decorations on these jars are not only similar, but, if my memory is trustworthy, identical.

"I see your tribe as a provident, rather thoughtful people, who made their livelihood secure by raising crops and fowl—the great number of turkey bones and feathers are evidence that they had domesticated the wild turkey. With grain in their store-rooms, and mountain sheep and deer for their quarry, they rose gradually from the condition of savagery. With the proper variation of meat and vegetable diet, they developed physically and improved in the primitive arts. They had looms and mills, and experimented with dyes. At the same time, they possibly declined in the arts of war, in brute strength and ferocity.

"I see them here, isolated, cut off from other tribes, working out their destiny, making their mesa more and more worthy to be a home for man, purifying life by religious ceremonies and observances, caring respectfully for their dead, protecting the children, doubtless entertaining some feelings of affection and sentiment for this stronghold where they were at once so safe and so comfortable, where they had practically overcome the worst hardships that primitive man had to fear. They were, perhaps, too far advanced for their time and environment.

"They were probably wiped out, utterly exterminated, by some roving Indian tribe without culture or domestic virtues, some horde that fell upon them in their summer camp and destroyed them for their hides and clothing and weapons, or from mere love of slaughter. I feel sure that these brutal invaders never even learned of the existence of this mesa, honeycombed with habitations. If they had come here, they would have destroyed. They killed and went their way.

"What I cannot understand is why you have not found more human remains. The three bodies you found in the mortuary chamber were prepared for burial by the old people who were left behind. But what of the last survivors? It is possible that when autumn wore on, and no one returned from the farms, the aged banded together, went in search of their people, and perished in the plain.

"Like you, I feel a reverence for this place. Wherever humanity has made that hardest of all starts and lifted itself out of mere brutality, is a sacred spot. Your people were cut off here without the influence of example or emulation, with no incentive but some natural yearning for order and security. They built themselves into this mesa and humanized it."

Father Duchene warmly agreed with Blake that I ought to go to Washington and make some report to the Government, so that the proper specialists would be sent out to study the remains we had found.

"You must go to the Director of the Smithsonian Institution," he said. "He will send up an archæologist who will interpret all that is obscure to us. He will revive this civilization in a scholarly work. It may be that you will have thrown light on some important points in the history of your country."

After he left us, Blake and I began to make definite plans for my trip to Washington. Blake was to work on the railroad that winter and save as much money as possible. The expense of my journey would be paid out of what we called the jack-pot account, in the bank at Pardee. All our further expenses on the mesa would be paid by the Government. Roddy often hinted that we would get a substantial reward of some kind. When we broke or lost anything at our work, he used to smile and say: "Never mind. I guess our Uncle Sam will make that good to us."

We had a beautiful autumn that year, soft, sunny, like a dream. Even up there in the air we had so little wind that the gold hung on the poplars and quaking aspens late in November. We stayed out on the mesa until after Christmas. We wanted our archæologist, when he came, to find everything in good order. We cleared up any litter we'd made in digging things out, stored all the specimens, even the mummies, in our cabin, and padlocked the doors and windows before we left it. I had written up my day-book carefully to the very end, had even written out some of Father Duchene's deductions. This book I left in concealment on the mesa. I climbed up to the Eagle's Nest in which we had found the mummy of the murdered woman we called Mother Eve, where I had noticed a particularly neat little cupboard in the wall. I put my book in this niche and sealed it up with cement. Mother Eve had greatly interested Father Duchene, by the way. He laughed and said she was well named. He didn't believe her death could throw any light on the destruction of her people. "I seem to smell," he said slyly, "a personal tragedy. Perhaps when the tribe went down to the summer camp, our lady was sick and would not go. Perhaps her husband thought it worth while to return un-announced from the farms some night, and found her in improper company. The young man may have escaped. In primitive society the husband is allowed to punish an unfaithful wife with death."

When the first snow began to fly, we said good-bye to our mesa and rode into Tarpin. It took several days to outfit me for my journey to Washington. We bought a trunk (I'd never owned one in my life), and a supply of white shirts, an overcoat that was as heavy as lead and just about as cold, and two suits of clothes. That conscienceless trader worked off on me a clawhammer coat he must have had in stock for twenty years. He easily persuaded Roddy that it was the proper thing for dress occasions. I think Roddy expected that I would be received by ambassadors—perhaps I did.

Roddy drew six hundred dollars out of the bank to stake me, and bought my ticket and Pullman through to Washington. He went to the station with me the morning I left, and a hard handshake was good-bye.

For a long while after my train pulled out, I could see our mesa bulking up blue on the sky-line. I hated to leave it, but I reflected that it had taken care of itself without me for a good many hundred years. When I saw it again, I told myself, I would have done my duty by it; I would bring back with me men who would understand it, who would appreciate it and dig out all its secrets.

VI

I got off the train, just behind the Capitol building, one cold bright January morning. I stood for a long while watching the white dome against a flashing blue sky, with a very religious feeling. After I had walked about a little and seen the parks, so green though it was winter, and the Treasury building, and the War and Navy, I decided to put off my business for a little and give myself a week to enjoy the city. That was the most sensible thing I did while I was there. For that week I was wonderfully happy.

My sightseeing over, I got to work. First I went to see the Representative from our district, to ask for letters of introduction. He was cordial enough, but he gave me bad advice. He was very positive that I ought to report to the Indian Commission, and gave me a letter to the Commissioner. The Commissioner was out of town, and I wasted three days waiting about his office, being questioned by clerks and secretaries. They were not very busy, and seemed to find me entertaining. I thought they were interested in my mission, and interest was what I wanted to arouse. I didn't know how influential these people might be—they talked as if they had great authority. I had brought along in my telescope bag some good pieces of pottery— not the best, I was afraid of accident, but some that were representative—and all the photographs Blake and I had taken. We had only a small kodak, and these pictures didn't make much show,— looked, indeed, like grubby little 'dobe ruins such as one can find almost anywhere. They gave no idea of the beauty and vastness of the setting. The clerks at the Indian Commission seemed very curious about everything and made me talk a lot. I was green and didn't know any better. But when one of the fellows there tried to get me to give him my best bowl for his cigarette ashes, I began to suspect the nature of their interest.

At last the Commissioner returned, but he had pressing engagements, and I hung around several days more before he would see me. After questioning me for about half an hour, he told me that his business was with living Indians, not dead ones, and that his office should have informed me of that in the beginning. He advised me to go back to our Congressman and get a letter to the Smithsonian Institution. I packed up my pottery and got out of the place, feeling pretty sore. The head clerk followed me down the corridor and asked me what I'd take for that little bowl he'd taken a fancy to. He said it had no market value, I'd find Washington full of such things; there were cases of them in the cellar at the Smithsonian that they'd never taken the trouble to unpack, hadn't any place to put them.

I went back to my Congressman. This time he wasn't so friendly as before, but he gave me a letter to the Smithsonian. There I went through the same experience. The Director couldn't be seen except by appointment, and his secretary had to be convinced that your business was important before he would give you an appointment with his chief. After the first morning I found it difficult to see even the secretary. He was always engaged. I was told to take a seat and wait, but when he was disengaged he was hurrying off to luncheon. I would sit there all morning with a group of unfortunate people: girls who wanted to get typewriting to do, nice polite old men who wanted to be taken out on surveys and expeditions next summer. The secretary would at last come out with his overcoat on, and would hurry through the waiting-room reading a letter or a report, without looking up.

The office assistants cheered me along, and I kept this up for some days, sitting all morning in that room, studying the patterns of the rugs, and the shoes of the patient waiters who came as regularly as I. One day after the secretary had gone out, his stenographer, a nice little Virginia girl, came and sat down in an empty chair next to mine and began talking to me. She wasn't pretty, but her kind eyes and soft Southern voice took hold of me at once. She wanted to know what I had in my telescope, and why I was there, and where I came from, and all about it. Nearly everyone else had gone out to lunch— that seemed to be the one thing they did regularly in Washington— and we had the waiting-room to ourselves. I talked to her a good deal. Her name was Virginia Ward. She was a tiny little thing, but she had lovely eyes and such gentle ways. She seemed indignant that I had been put off so long after having come so far.

"Now you just let me fix it up for you," she said at last. "Mr. Wagner is bothered by a great many foolish people who waste his time, and he is suspicious. The best way will be for you to invite him to lunch with you. I'll arrange it. I keep a list of his appointments, and I know he is not engaged for luncheon to-morrow. I'll tell him that he is to lunch with a nice boy who has come all the way from New Mexico to inform the Department about an important discovery. I'll tell him to meet you at the Shoreham, at one. That's expensive, but it would do no good to invite him to a cheap place. And, remember, you must ask him to order the luncheon. It will maybe cost you ten dollars, but it will get you somewhere."

I felt grateful to the nice little thing,—she wasn't older than I. I begged her wouldn't she please come to lunch with me herself to-day, and talk to me.

"Oh, no!" she said, blushing red as a poppy. "Why, I'm afraid you think—"

I told her I didn't think anything but how nice she was to me, and how lonesome I was. She went with me, but she wouldn't go to any swell place. She told me a great many useful things.

"If you want to get attention from anybody in Washin'ton," she said, "ask them to lunch. People here will do almost anything for a good lunch."

"But the Director of the Smithsonian, for instance," I said, "surely you don't mean that the high-up ones like that—? Why would he want to bother with a cow-puncher from New Mexico, when he can lunch with scientists and ambassadors?"

She had a pretty little fluttery Southern laugh. "You just name a hotel like the Shoreham to the Director, and try it! There has to be somebody to pay for a lunch, and the scientists and ambassadors don't do that when they can avoid it. He'd accept your invitation, and the next time he went to dine with the Secretary of State he'd make a nice little story of it, and paint you up so pretty you'd hardly know yourself."

When I asked her whether I'd better take my pottery—it was there under the table between us—to the Shoreham to show Mr. Wagner, she tittered again. "I wouldn't bother. If you show him enough of the Shoreham pottery, that will be more effective."

The next morning, when the secretary arrived at his office, he stopped by my chair and said he understood he had an engagement with me for one o'clock. That was a good idea, he added: his mind was freer when he was away from office routine.

I had been in Washington twenty-two days when I took the secretary out to lunch. It was an excellent lunch. We had a bottle of Château d'Yquem. I'd never heard of such a wine before, but I remember it because it cost five dollars. I drank only one glass, and that pleased him too, for he drank the rest. Though he was friendly and talked a great deal, my heart sank lower, for he wouldn't let me explain my mission to him at all. He kept telling me that he knew all about the Southwest. He had been sent by the Smithsonian to conduct parties of European archæologists through all the show places, Frijoles and Canyon de Chelly, and Taos and the Hopi pueblos. When some Austrian Archduke had gone to hunt in the Pecos range, he had been sent by his chief and the German ambassador to manage the tour, and he had done it with such success that both he and the Director were given decorations from the Austrian Crown, in recognition of his services. Then I had to listen to a long story about how well he was treated by the Archduke when he went to Vienna with his chief the following summer. I had to hear about balls and receptions, and the names and titles of all the people he had met at the Duke's country estate. I was amazed and ashamed that a man of fifty, a man of the world, a scholar with ever so many degrees, should find it worth his while to show off before a boy, and a boy of such humble pretensions, who didn't know how to eat the *hors d'oeuvres* any more than if an assortment of cocoanuts had been set before him with no hammer.

Imagine my astonishment when, as he was drinking his liqueur, he said carelessly: "By the way, I was successful in arranging an interview with the Director for you. He will see you at four o'clock on Monday."

That was Thursday. I spent the time between then and Monday trying to find out something more about the kind of people I had come among. I persuaded Virginia Ward to go to the theatre with me, and she told me that it always took a long while to get anything through with the Director, that I mustn't lose heart, and she would always be glad to cheer me up. She lived with her mother, a widow lady, and they had me come to dinner and were very nice to me.

All this time I was living with a young married couple who interested me very much, for they were unlike any people I had ever known. The husband was "in office," as they say there, he had some position in the War Department. How it did use to depress me to see all the hundreds of clerks come pouring out of that building at sunset! Their lives seemed to me so petty, so slavish. The couple I lived with gave me a prejudice against that kind of life. I couldn't help knowing a good deal about their affairs. They had only a small flat, and rented me one room of it, so I was very much in their confidence and couldn't help overhearing. They asked me not to mention the fact that I paid rent, as they had told their friends I was making them a visit. It was like that in everything; they spent their lives trying to keep up appearances, and to make his salary do more than it could. When they weren't discussing where she should go in the summer, they talked about the promotions in his department; how much the other clerks got and how they spent it, how many new dresses their wives had. And there was always a struggle going on for an invitation to a dinner or a reception, or even a tea-party. When once they got the invitation they had been scheming for, then came the terrible question of what Mrs. Bixby should wear.

The Secretary of War gave a reception; there was to be dancing and a great showing of foreign uniforms. The Bixbys were in painful suspense until they got a card. Then for a week they talked about nothing but what Mrs. Bixby was going to wear. They decided that for such an occasion she must have a new dress. Bixby borrowed twenty-five dollars from me, and took his lunch hour to go shopping with his wife and choose the satin. That seemed to me very strange. In New Mexico the Indian boys sometimes went to a trader's with their wives and bought shawls or calico, and we thought it rather contemptible. On the night of the reception the Bixbys set off gaily in a cab; the dress they considered a great success. But they had bad luck. Somebody spilt claret-cup on Mrs. Bixby's skirt before the evening was half over, and when they got home that night I heard her weeping and reproaching him for having been so upset about it, and looking at nothing but her ruined dress all evening. She said he cried out when it happened. I don't doubt it.

Every cab, every party, was more than they could afford. If he lost an umbrella, it was a real misfortune. He wasn't lazy, he wasn't a fool, and he meant to be honest; but he was intimidated by that miserable sort of departmental life. He didn't know anything else. He thought working in a store or a bank not respectable. Living with the Bixbys gave me a kind of low-spiritedness I had never known before. During my days of waiting for appointments, I used to walk for hours around the fence that shuts in the White House grounds, and watch the Washington monument colour with those beautiful sunsets, until the time when all the clerks streamed out of the Treasury building and the War and Navy. Thousands of them, all more or less like the couple I lived with. They seemed to me like people in slavery, who ought to be free. I remember the city chiefly by those beautiful, hazy, sad sunsets, white columns and green shrubbery, and the monument shaft still pink while the stars were coming out.

I got my interview with the Director of the Smithsonian at last. He gave me his attention, he was interested. He told me to come again in three days and meet Dr. Ripley, who was the authority on prehistoric Indian remains and had excavated a lot of them. Then came an exciting and rather encouraging time for me. Dr. Ripley asked the right sort of questions, and evidently knew his business. He said he'd like to take the first train down to my mesa. But it required money to excavate, and he had none. There was a bill up before Congress for an appropriation. We'd have to wait. I must use my influence with my Representative. He took my pottery to study it. (I never got it back, by the way.) There was a Dr. Fox, connected with the Smithsonian, who was also interested. They told me a good many things I wanted to know, and kept me dangling about the office. Of course they were very kind to take so much trouble with a green boy. But I soon found that the Director and all his staff had one interest which dwarfed every other. There was to be an International Exposition of some sort in Europe the following summer, and they were all pulling strings to get appointed on juries or sent to international congresses—appointments that would pay their expenses abroad, and give them a salary in addition. There was, indeed, a bill before Congress for appropriations for the Smithsonian; but there was also a bill for Exposition appropriations, and that was the one they were really pushing. They kept me hanging on through March and April, but in the end it came to nothing. Dr. Ripley told me he was sorry, but the sum Congress had allowed the Smithsonian wouldn't cover an expedition to the Southwest.

Virginia Ward, who had been so kind to me, went out to lunch with me that day, and admitted I had been let down. She was almost as much disappointed as I. She said the only thing Dr. Ripley really cared about was getting a free trip to Europe and acting on a jury, and maybe getting a decoration. "And that's what the Director wants, too," she said. "They don't care much about dead and gone Indians.

What they do care about is going to Paris, and getting another ribbon on their coats."

The only other person besides Virginia who was genuinely concerned about my affair was a young Frenchman, a lieutenant attached to the French Embassy, who came to the Smithsonian often on business connected with this same International Exposition. He was nice and polite to Virginia, and she introduced him to me. We used to walk down along the Potomac together. He studied my photographs and asked me such intelligent questions about everything that it was a pleasure to talk to him. He had a fine attitude about it all; he was thoughtful, critical, and respectful. I feel sure he'd have gone back to New Mexico with me if he'd had the money. He was even poorer than I.

I was utterly ashamed to go home to Roddy, dead broke after all the money I'd spent, and without a thing to show for it. I hung on in Washington through May, trying to get a job of some sort, to at least earn my fare home. My letters to Blake had been pretty blue for some time back. If I'd been sensible, I'd have kept my troubles to myself. He was easily discouraged, and I knew that. At last I had to write him for money to go home. It was slow in coming, and I began to telegraph. I left Washington at last, wiser than I came. I had no plans, I wanted nothing but to get back to the mesa and live a free life and breathe free air, and never, never again to see hundreds of little black-coated men pouring out of white buildings. Queer, how much more depressing they are than workmen coming out of a factory.

I was terribly disappointed when I got off the train at Tarpin and Roddy wasn't at the station to meet me. It was late in the afternoon, almost dark, and I went straight to the livery stable to ask Bill Hook for news of Blake. Hook, you remember, had done all our hauling for us, and had been a good friend. He gave me a glad hand and said Blake was out on the mesa.

"I expect maybe he's had his feelings hurt here. He's been shy of this town lately. You see, Tom, folks weren't bothered none about that mesa so long as you fellows were playing Robinson Crusoe out there, digging up curios. But when it leaked out that Blake had got a lot of money for your stuff, then they begun to feel jealous—said them ruins didn't belong to Blake any more than to anybody else.

It'll blow over in time; people are always like that when money changes hands. But right now there's a good deal of bad feeling."

I told him I didn't know what he was talking about.

"You mean you ain't heard about the German, Fechtig? Well, Rodney's got some surprise waiting for you! Why, he's had the damnedest luck! He's cleaned up a neat little pile on your stuff."

I begged him to tell me what stuff he meant.

"Why, your curios. This German, Fechtig, come along; he'd been buying up a lot of Indian things out here, and he bought your whole outfit and paid four thousand dollars down for it. The transaction made quite a stir here in Tarpin. I'm not kicking. I made a good thing out of it. My mules were busy three weeks packing the stuff out of there on their backs, and I held the Dutchman up for a fancy price. He had packing cases made at the wagon shop and took 'em up to the mesa full of straw and sawdust, and packed the curios out there. I lost one of my mules, too. You remember Jenny? Well, they were leading her down with a big box on her, and right there where the trail runs so narrow around a bump in the cliff above Black Canyon, she lost her balance and fell clean to the bottom, her load on her. Pretty near a thousand feet, I guess. We never went down to hold a post-mortem, but Fechtig paid for her like a gentleman."

I remember I sat down on the sofa in Hook's office because I couldn't stand up any longer, and the smell of the horse blankets began to make me deathly sick. In a minute I went over, like a girl in a novel. Hook pulled me out on the sidewalk and gave me some whisky out of his pocket flask.

When I felt better I asked him how long this German had been gone, and what he had done with the things.

"Oh, he cleared out three weeks ago. He didn't waste no time. He treated everybody well, though; nobody's sore at him. It's your partner they're turned against. Fechtig took the stuff right along with him, chartered a freight car, and travelled in the car with it. I reckon it's on the water by now. He took it straight through into Old Mexico, and was to load it on a French boat. Seems he was afraid of having trouble getting curiosities out of the United States ports. You know you can take anything out of the City of Mexico."

I had heard all I wanted to hear. I went to the hotel, got a room, and lay down without undressing to wait for daylight. Hook was to drive me and my trunk out to the mesa early the next morning. All I'd been through in Washington was nothing to what I went through that night. I thought Blake must have lost his mind. I didn't for a minute believe he'd meant to sell me out, but I cursed his stupidity and presumption. I had never told him just how I felt about those things we'd dug out together, it was the kind of thing one doesn't talk about directly. But he must have known; he couldn't have lived with me all summer and fall without knowing. And yet, until that night, I had never known myself that I cared more about them than about anything else in the world.

At the first blink of daylight I jumped up from my damnable bed and went round to the stable to rout Hook out of his bunk. We had breakfast and got out of town with his best team. On the way to the mesa we had a break-down, one of the old dry wheels smashed to splinters. Hook had to unhitch and ride back to Tarpin and get another. Everything took an unreasonably long time, and the afternoon was half gone when he put me and my trunk down at the foot of the Black Canyon trail. Every inch of that trail was dear to me, every delicate curve about the old piñon roots, every chancy track along the face of the cliffs, and the deep windings back into shrubbery and safety. The wild-currant bushes were in bloom, and where the path climbed the side of a narrow ravine, the scent of them in the sun was so heavy that it made me soft, made me want to lie down and sleep. I wanted to see and touch everything, like home-sick children when they come home.

When I pulled out on top of the mesa, the rays of sunlight fell slantingly through the little twisted piñons,—the light was all in between them, as red as a daylight fire, they fairly swam in it. Once again I had that glorious feeling that I've never had anywhere else, the feeling of being *on the mesa,* in a world above the world. And the air, my God, what air!—Soft, tingling, gold, hot with an edge of chill on it, full of the smell of piñons—it was like breathing the sun, breathing the colour of the sky. Down there behind me was the plain, already streaked with shadow, violet and purple and burnt orange until it met the horizon. Before me was the flat mesa top, thinly sprinkled with old cedars that were not much taller than I, though their twisted trunks were almost as thick as my body. I struck off across it, my long black shadow going ahead.

I made straight for the cabin, it was about three miles from the spot where the trail emerged at the top. I saw smoke rising before I could see the hut itself. Blake was in the doorway when I got there. I didn't look at his face, but I could feel that he looked at mine.

"Don't say anything, Tom. Don't rip me up until you hear all about it," he said as I came toward him.

"I've heard enough to about do for me," I blurted out. "What made you do it, Blake? What made you do it?"

"It was a chance in a million, boy. There wasn't any time to consult you. There's only one man in thousands that wants to buy relics and pay real money for them. I could see how your Washington campaign was coming out. I know you'd thought about big figures, so had I. But that was all a pipe dream. Four thousand's not so bad, you don't pick it up every day. And he bore all the expenses. Why, it was a terrible expensive job, getting all that frail stuff out of here. Who else would have bought it, I want to know? We'd have had to pack it around at Harvey Houses, selling it at a dollar a bowl, like the poor Indians do. I took the best chance going, for both of us, Tom."

I didn't say anything, because there was too much to say. I stood outside the cabin until the gold light went blue and a few stars came out, hardly brighter than the bright sky they twinkled in, and the swallows came flying over us, on their way to their nests in the cliffs. It was the time of day when everything goes home. From habit and from weariness I went in through the door. The kitchen table was spread for supper, I could smell a rabbit stew cooking on the stove. Blake lit the lantern and begged me to eat my supper. I didn't go into the bunk-room, for I knew the shelves in there were empty. I heard Blake talking to me as you hear people talking when you are asleep.

"Who else would have bought them?" he kept saying. "Folks make a lot of fuss over such things, but they don't want to pay good money for them."

When I at last told him that such a thing as selling them had never entered my head, I'm sure he thought I was lying. He reminded me about how we used to talk of getting big money from the Government.

I admitted I'd hoped we'd be paid for our work, and maybe get a bonus of some kind, for our discovery. "But I never thought of selling them, because they weren't mine to sell—nor yours! They belonged to this country, to the State, and to all the people. They belonged to boys like you and me, that have no other ancestors to inherit from. You've gone and sold them to a country that's got plenty of relics of its own. You've gone and sold your country's secrets, like Dreyfus."

"That man was innocent. It was a frame-up," Blake murmured. It was a point he would never pass up.

"Whether he's guilty or not, you are! If there was only anybody in Washington I could telegraph to, and have that German held up at the port!"

"That's just it. If there was anybody in Washington that cared a damn, I wouldn't have sold 'em. But you pretty well found out there ain't."

"We could have kept them, then," I told him. "I've got a strong back. I'm not so poor that I have to sell the pots and pans that belonged to my poor grandmothers a thousand years ago. I made all my plans on the train, coming back." (It was a lie, I hadn't.) "I meant to get a job on the railroad and keep our find right here, and come back to it when I had a lay-off. I think a lot more of it now than before I went to Washington. And after a while, when that Exposition is over and the Smithsonian people get home, they would come out here all right. I've learned enough from them so that I could go on with it myself."

Blake reminded me that I had my way to make in the world, and that I wanted to go to school. "That money's in the bank this minute, in your name, and you're going to college on it. You're not going to be a day-labourer like me. After you've got your sheepskin, then you can divide with me."

"You think I'd touch that money?" I looked squarely at him for the first time. "No more than if you'd stolen it. You made the sale. Get what you can out of it. I want to ask you one question: did you ever think I was digging those things up for what I could sell the for?"

Rodney explained that he knew I cared about the things, an

proud of them, but he'd always supposed I meant to "realize" on them, just as he did, and that it would come to money in the end. "Everything does," he added.

"If that nice young Frenchman I met had come down here with me, and offered me four million instead of four thousand, I'd have refused him. There never was any question of money with me, where this mesa and its people were concerned. They were something that had been preserved through the ages by a miracle, and handed on to you and me, two poor cow-punchers, rough and ignorant, but I thought we were men enough to keep a trust. I'd as soon have sold my own grandmother as Mother Eve—I'd have sold any living woman first."

"Save your tears," said Roddy grimly. "She refused to leave us. She went to the bottom of Black Canyon and carried Hook's best mule along with her. They had to make her box extra wide, and she crowded Jenny out an inch or so too far from the canyon wall."

This painful interview went on for hours. I walked up and down the kitchen trying to make Blake understand the kind of value those objects had had for me. Unfortunately, I succeeded. He sat slumping on the bench, his elbows on the table, shading his eyes from the lantern with his hands.

"There's no need to keep this up," he said at last. "You're away out of my depth, but I think I get you. You might have given me some of this Fourth of July talk a little earlier in the game. I didn't know you valued that stuff any different than anything else a fellow might run on to: a gold mine or a pocket of turquoise."

"I suppose you gave him my diary along with the rest?"

"No," said Blake, his voice growing gloomier and darker, "that's in the Eagle's Nest, where you hid it. That's your private property. I supposed I had some share in the relics we dug up—you always spoke of it that way. But I see now I was working for you like a hired man, and while you were away I sold your property."

I said again it wasn't mine or his. He took something out of the pocket of his flannel shirt and laid it on the table. I saw it was a bank passbook, with my name on the yellow cover.

"You may as well keep it," I said. "I'll never touch it. You had no right to deposit it in my name. The townspeople are sore about the money, and they'll hold it against me."

"No they won't. Can't you trust me to fix that?"

"I don't know what I can trust you with, Blake. I don't know where I'm at with you," I said.

He got up and began putting on his coat. "Motives don't count, eh?" he said, his face turned away, as he put his arm into the sleeve.

"They would in anything of our own, between you and me," I told him. "If it was my money you'd lost gambling, or my girl you'd made free with, we could fight it out, and maybe be friends again. But this is different."

"I see. You make it clear." He was quietly stirring around as he spoke. He got his old knapsack off its nail on the wall, opened his trunk and took out some underwear and socks and a couple of shirts. After he had put these into the bag, he slung it over one shoulder, and his canvas water-bag over the other. I let these preparations go on without a word. He went to the cupboard over the stove and put some sticks of chocolate into his pocket, then his pipe and a bag of tobacco. Presently I said he'd break his neck if he tried riding down the trail in the dark.

"I'm not riding the trail," he replied curtly. "I'm going down the quick way. My horse is grazing in Cow Canyon."

"I noticed the river's high. It's dangerous crossing," I remarked.

"I got over that way a few days ago. I'm surprised at you, using such common expressions!" he said sarcastically. *"Dangerous crossing;* it's painted on signboards all over the world!" He walked out of the cabin without looking back. I followed him to the V-shaped break in the rim rock, hardly larger than a man's body, where the spliced tree-trunks made a swinging ladder down the face of the cliff. I wanted to protest, but only succeeded in finding fault.

"You'll catch your knapsack on those forks and come to grief."

"That's my look-out."

By this time my eyes had grown accustomed to the darkness, and I could see Blake quite clearly—the stubborn, crouching set of his shoulders that I used to notice when he first came to Pardee and w~ drinking all the time. There was an ache in my arms to reach and detain him, but there was something else that made me absolutely powerless to do so. He stepped down and settled his foot into the first fork. Then he stopped a moment and straightened his pack, buttoned his coat up to the chin, and pulled his hat on tighter. There was always a night draught in the canyon. He gripped the trunk with his hands. "Well," he said with grim cheerfulness, "here's luck! And I'm glad it's you that's doing this to me, Tom; not me that's doing it to you."

His head disappeared below the rim. I could hear the trees creak under his heavy body, and the chains rattle a little at the splicings. I lay down on the ledge and listened. I could hear him for a long way down, and the sounds were comforting to me, though I didn't realize it. Then the silence closed in. I went to sleep that night hoping I would never waken.

VII

The next morning the whinnying of my saddle-horse in the shed roused me. I took him down to the foot of the trail where I'd left my trunk, and packed my things up to the cabin on his back. I sat up late that night, waiting for Blake, though I knew he wouldn't come. A few days later I rode into Tarpin for news of him. Bill Hook showed me Roddy's horse. He had sold him to the barn for sixty dollars. The station-master told me Blake had bought a ticket to Winslow, Arizona. I wired the station-master and the dispatcher at Winslow, but they could give me no information. Father Duchene came along, on his rounds, and I told him the whole story.

He thought Blake would come back sometime, that I'd only miss him if I went out to look for him. He advised me to stay on the mesa that summer and get ahead with my studies, work up my Spanish grammar and my Latin. He had friends all along the Santa Fé, and he was sure we could catch Blake by advertising in the local papers along the road; Albuquerque, Winslow, Flagstaff, Williams, Los Angeles. After a few days with him, I went back to the mesa to wait.

I'll never forget the night I got back. I crossed the river an hour fore sunset and hobbled my horse in the wide bottom of Cow yon. The moon was up, though the sun hadn't set, and it had that glittering silveriness the early stars have in high altitudes. The heavenly bodies look so much more remote from the bottom of a deep canyon than they do from the level. The climb of the walls helps out the eye, somehow. I lay down on a solitary rock that was like an island in the bottom of the valley, and looked up. The grey sage-brush and the blue-grey rock around me were already in shadow, but high above me the canyon walls were dyed flame-colour with the sunset, and the Cliff City lay in a gold haze against its dark cavern. In a few minutes it, too, was grey, and only the rim rock at the top held the red light. When that was gone, I could still see the copper glow in the piñons along the edge of the top ledges. The arc of sky over the canyon was silvery blue, with its pale yellow moon, and presently stars shivered into it, like crystals dropped into perfectly clear water.

I remember these things, because, in a sense, that was the first night I was ever really on the mesa at all—the first night that all of me was there. This was the first time I ever saw it as a whole. It all came together in my understanding, as a series of experiments do when you begin to see where they are leading. Something had happened in me that made it possible for me to co-ordinate and simplify, and that process, going on in my mind, brought with it great happiness. It was possession. The excitement of my first discovery was a very pale feeling compared to this one. For me the mesa was no longer an adventure, but a religious emotion. I had read of filial piety in the Latin poets, and I knew that was what I felt for this place. It had formerly been mixed up with other motives; but now that they were gone, I had my happiness unalloyed.

What that night began lasted all summer. I stayed on the mesa until November. It was the first time I'd ever studied methodically, or intelligently. I got the better of the Spanish grammar and read the twelve books of the *Æneid*. I studied in the morning, and in the afternoon I worked at clearing away the mess the German had made in packing—tidying up the ruins to wait another hundred years, maybe, for the right explorer. I can scarcely hope that life will give me another summer like that one. It was my high tide. Every morning, when the sun's rays first hit the mesa top, while the rest of the world was in shadow, I wakened with the feeling that I had found everything instead of having lost everything. Nothing tired me. Up there alone, a close neighbour to the sun, I seemed to get the solar energy in some direct way. And at night, when I watched it drop down behind the edge of the plain below me, I used to feel that I couldn't have borne another hour of that consuming light, that I was full to the brim, and needed dark and sleep.

All that summer, I never went up to the Eagle's Nest to get my diary—indeed, it's probably there yet. I didn't feel the need of that record. It would have been going backward. I didn't want to go back and unravel things step by step. Perhaps I was afraid that I would lose the whole in the parts. At any rate, I didn't go for my record.

During those months I didn't worry much about poor Roddy. I told myself the advertisements would surely get him—I knew his habit of reading newspapers. There are times when one's vitality is too high to be clouded, too elastic to stay down. Hurrying from my cabin in the morning to the spot in the Cliff City where I studied under a cedar, I used to be frightened at my own heartlessness. But the feel of the narrow moccasin-worn trail in the flat rock made my feet glad, like a good taste in the mouth, and I'd forget all about Blake without knowing it. I found I was reading too fast; so I began to commit long passages of Virgil to memory—if it hadn't been for that, I might have forgotten how to use my voice, or gone to talking to myself. When I look into the *Æneid* now, I can always see two pictures: the one on the page, and another behind that: blue and purple rocks and yellow-green piñons with flat tops, little clustered houses clinging together for protection, a rude tower rising in their midst, rising strong, with calmness and courage—behind it a dark grotto, in its depths a crystal spring.

Happiness is something one can't explain. You must take my word for it. Troubles enough came afterward, but there was that summer, high and blue, a life in itself.

Next winter I went back to Pardee and stayed with the O'Briens again, working on the section and studying with Father Duchene and trying to get some word of Blake. Now that I was back on the railroad, I thought I couldn't fail to find him. I went out to Winslow and to Williams, and I questioned the railroad men. We advertised for him in every possible way, had all the Santa Fé operatives and the police and the Catholic missionaries on the watch for him, offered a thousand dollars reward for whoever found him. But it came to nothing. Father Duchene and our friends down there are still looking. But the older I grow, the more I understand what it was I did that night on the mesa. Anyone who requites faith and friendship as I did, will have to pay for it. I'm not very sanguine about good fortune for myself. I'll be called to account when I least expect it.

In the spring, just a year after I quarrelled with Roddy, I landed here and walked into your garden, and the rest you know.

Willa Cather's Unfinished Avignon Story
an article by George N. Kates

Not yet enough noticed in the career of a "classic" writer like Willa Cather, whose reputation rests—with justice—on her discovery for American letters of regions like Nebraska, is the increasing and finally dominant pull that Europe exerted upon her. It can be traced from the very beginning of her long career; it impregnates the whole body of her work. When for her, about 1922, in a period of internal strain "the world broke in two," there is no doubt upon which half she took her stand. One of the most interesting results of this development, moreover, came in the very last years of her life, a project never completed: to place the setting of a story straight across the world, quite far into the past—leaving America entirely—in the setting of medieval Avignon.

Very little comment has been made in print about the significance of this radical departure. In her old age had Willa Cather played out her interest in the field where she had conquered her fame? Was she moving, very late, even farther into one to which even in the beginning she had given her loyalty? Many problems are involved, and the situation is complex.

The chief mention of the little that has been published is on page 190 of her friend Edith Lewis's *Willa Cather Living,* a most sensitive book, which happily makes good some of our lacks because of the adamant fate that Willa Cather reserved for those of her letters and papers she did not herself destroy. Miss Lewis has chronicled the chief facts with care:

> She had wanted for years to write an Avignon story. On her many journeys to the south of France, it was Avignon that left the deepest impression with her. The Papal Palace at Avignon—seen first when she was a girl—stirred her as no building in the world had ever done. In 1935 we were there together. One day, as we wandered through the great chambers of white, almost translucent stone, alone except

for a guide, this young fellow suddenly stopped still in one of the rooms and began to sing, with a beautiful voice. It echoed down the corridors and under the arched ceilings like a great bell sounding— but sounding from some remote past; its vibrations seemed laden, weighted down with the passions of another age—cruelties, splendours, lost and unimaginable to us in our time.

I have sometimes thought that Willa Cather wished to make her story like this song.

She had brought with her [on a journey in June 1941, six years before her death] to San Francisco Okey's little history of Avignon; and she often spent her mornings on the open roof garden of the Fairmont, walking to and fro, and reading in this book. It was probably then that she planned the general outline of the Avignon story.

The manuscript, by Willa Cather's direction, was destroyed after her death; and it is a heavy loss. It had been in her mind to succeed *Sapphira and the Slave Girl,* of 1940 (her last published work, except for the stories gathered together under the heading of *The Old Beauty,* which were issued posthumously in 1948); and although these last years became a period of illness and non-productivity, the story's place at the terminus of the great swing of her development is critical. Did we not know of it by hearsay, the subject matter might never have been anticipated.

The dial needle, though, starts moving in this general direction from the earliest time. There had always been a great curiosity and interest about Europe, every part of it, even when Willa Cather had been merely an unusually active child, growing up freely on the Divide. Passage after passage in the Nebraska novels, taken autobiographically, makes this clear. Her first journey to the Old World, nevertheless, had come only in her twenty-ninth year, when she went abroad from Pittsburgh with her friend Isabelle McClung, in the summer of 1902.

In his *Willa Cather, a Critical Biography,* E. K. Brown has summarized its Provençal days most sympathetically (pages 103–4):

In September they journeyed to the south, into the warm land of Alphonse Daudet, where the mistral blew "more terrible than any wind that ever came up from Kansas." Willa Cather drank in the warmth and color of the land and rejoiced in its people. The impressions of Provence garnered now were ineffaceable to the last. She rejoiced in the landscape, the history, the architecture, the food, the wine; she stayed at the hotel in the ancient Papal city of Avignon, which Henry James had affectionately praised in his travel writings. Willa Cather and Isabelle McClung were the only English-speaking people in the town; there seemed to be no other tourists and Willa Cather enjoyed saturating herself with the life and aspect of the place. Here on the bank of the Rhône the young woman from the Divide had found something that touched her more deeply than the metropolitan density of London or the luminous quality of Paris; a life rooted in the centuries—what she later had in mind when she spoke of the things that lie deep behind French history and French art. That art extended to the sense of well-being that comes from sun and light and artfully cooked food; it is reflected in Bishop Latour's remark when he tastes the soup cooked by Father Vaillant: ". . . a soup like this is not the work of one man. It is the result of a constantly refined tradition. There are nearly a thousand years of history in this soup."

Later he tells us (page 269): "The story she was writing in the last years of her life was to express what Avignon, the Avignon of the popes, had meant to her over a period of forty years." Its roots therefore grew deep; and rich living was to nourish them.

A decade later—but Willa Cather developed late, and slowly—presumably after the publication in 1912 of her first full-length, Jamesian tale, *Alexander's Bridge,* and while *O Pioneers!,* her first novel of the soil, was still in manuscript, she even assured her friend Elizabeth Shepley Sergeant, as we are told in the latter's *Willa Cather, a Memoir* (page 97), that "Some time . . . there would be a story with sharp clear definite lines like the country in which I then was [the South of France]." So we have an expressed intention, even at the beginning of a long and fertile career, which first would take her to very different regions. To use the classic expression of Sarah Orne Jewett, some story about Avignon had begun to tease her a full generation before she took it up in sober earnest.

To understand the powerful symbol for her work which Avignon became, with its overtone of religion and, above all, its particular expression of what to Willa Cather was true beauty, one must slowly follow the thread of her whole career. Patiently wound up, this will lead us through the labyrinth.

At the very beginning there is a major vacillation, which it took her a long while to work through. This came in the difficult Pittsburgh years (1896–1906), which Edith Lewis has judged, and no doubt rightly, to have been for a number of reasons among the hardest in her life. Too little considered had been her first book of short stories—in their original version—*The Troll Garden,* of 1905, which came exactly at the end of this period, and was its summation. A symmetrical pattern of alternation is so clear that, of the seven stories composing it, the first three odd-numbered are distinctly Jamesian, both in setting and delineation of character, while the three even ones were drawn with considerable courage and skill from her own bare world of the West. The seventh and concluding one, "Paul's Case," forms a separate and hybrid Pittsburgh epilogue. One could not ask for a better graphic representation of her differing experiments in the attempt to find her proper field.

The contents of the Jamesian first, third, and fifth stories of this book—"Flavia and Her Artists," "The Garden Lodge," and "The Marriage of Phaedra"—show that while she still was teaching high school in Pittsburgh, writing from Judge McClung's house where she was a guest, she must have imagined it almost obligatory for herself to attempt tales of worldly people of high fashion whom she could not possibly have known at this time, people of established place and assured means, preoccupied almost wholly in a dissection of their own emotions. These were the chic puppets of the hour; but were everywhere taken quite seriously.

In the first story, she writes of a large house party in Tarrytown, high life in an eleborate setting, maids and valets, a conservatory, a smoking-room with Turkish hangings and "curious weapons on the wall." The action of the second tale unrolls in "a place on the Sound," with "a glorious garden." It belongs to a man who when he married the heroine "had been for ten years a power in Wall Street." There a new summer house seems planned chiefly for another house par

In "The Marriage of Phaedra," set in London, we find people of title who come and go, casual mentions of Paris and Nice. Willa Cather seems determined to qualify as a sophisticate, although she has as yet come no farther from Red Cloud than Pittsburgh. Still, this was the fashion of the time; and as she devised them, these settings seemed proper even for popular consumption. "Society" in America was still enthroned by popular consent, nourished by general interest. We are in the period before it gave way to the romances of film stars; and its sins were told in every Sunday supplement.

Parenthetically, what is even more of a pure pastiche of Henry James exists. This is a story titled "Eleanor's House," published in *McClure's* for 1907 (Vol. XXIX), soon after Willa Cather had joined that magazine in New York. Here her protagonists have such complete leisure and are depicted as so removed from the hard facts of life in "their own place on the Oise" that, although one man is actually mentioned as "at work in the library," it is almost impossible to imagine what occupies him there. Such expatriate wraiths may want to "finish the summer in Switzerland" or even as a final touch be "very keen about going to America"—this from Willa Cather!—yet their behavior is altogether shadowy. Every description of the feel of a place, a stream, or a rampart brings her back to us; almost nothing else in this short story does.

In sharpest planned alternation with the tales, in *The Troll Garden,* of a life that even in the future never was to become her own, is the stark, tragic trilogy of the stories with a Western background. "A Wagner Matinée," "The Sculptor's Funeral," and "A Death in the Desert" all three represent already the Willa Cather of the Nebraska Divide and the Southwest whom we familiarly know, looking the grim fates boldly in the eye, competently grasping with both hands the tragedies of human destiny. "Paul's Case," the last in the book, in which she is so sensitively aware of dim hungers, takes her hero from a Pittsburgh variant of this drab world into that other, into the muffled luxury of the hotels, the perfume of hothouse flowers, the music, of snow-covered, wintry New York. Yet Paul must pay for this so brief pleasure by taking his own life. The alternation of a pair powerfully beaten and contrasting rhythms with a final coda is ̓ect.

* *

Quite curiously, at her next stage of development the whole search for a proper field has to be gone through once again—this time in full scale. There is exactly the same contrast, both in setting and subject matter, between the worldly *Alexander's Bridge,* of 1912, and the rustic *O Pioneers!,* of the following year. How Willa Cather judged that these together also made a single unit, and how she had labored in giving them birth, she makes clear in a pregnant little essay of self-revelation contributed as late as 1931 to *Colophon Part 6.* It was titled "My First Novels (There Were Two)."

Setting, however, as well as scale and depth, has now expanded. *Alexander's Bridge* gives us clear and capable pictures of the Back Bay in Boston, which, through her friendship with Mrs. James T. Fields, of unsurpassable literary memories, she now knew at first hand. Indeed, in it we almost enter Mrs. Fields's house, at the beginning of the book. There are also London scenes, no longer divined through others' eyes, but become much less mysterious to her through her work and travel there for *McClure's. O Pioneers!,* which is really a story of a Scandinavian farmer's daughter's love for Willa Cather's own wild land, definitely wins the upper hand, of course. Thus her career is finally launched, to rise to glorious heights. Willa Cather was now forty years old; at last free to fulfill her destiny and consume herself in her work, as once she had dreamed.

This is not the place to explore in detail the development of her internal feeling for the Nebraskan or the Virginian scene, the two that by inheritance she could fairly call her own. Here also there was much fluctuation: young fear and repulsion only very gradually transformed by a prolonged metamorphosis into their opposites. Against the materialism of the aftercomers alone, the second generation, that lesser breed after the pioneers, was she to remain adamant in lifelong hostility. Here were enemies she moved to slay whenever she rediscovered them. So we can at this place, without losing the clue, pass beyond *The Song of the Lark,* of 1915, and *My Ántonia,* published three years later.

There followed *Youth and the Bright Medusa,* in 1920, a book of collected short stories, in which she turned for new material to four pieces (three already published in magazines) about artists and their struggles—thus often speaking for herself—while at the same time reissuing the three earlier Western stories, somewhat revised, and also adding "Paul's Case," from *The Troll Garden*. This last book had long been out of print, and was now fifteen years behind her. "The Diamond Mine," "A Gold Slipper," and "Scandal" all concern the stage and have American settings; "Coming, Aphrodite," new—and thus used to begin the book—represents her first days in Greenwich Village. We have in all of them the American scene of their decade, with steamships and motor cars to match; and there are only as many fleeting references to Europe as needed.

The contemporary world is now hers in this neat packet, with all the variants that she felt had permanent interest for her. Jamesian or Whartonian subjects, it is to be noted, in which she had earlier tried to qualify, are now sternly omitted; and one field she never entered: the chronicling of society for itself. Indeed, the only part of the Metropolitan Opera House she will apparently never touch, in spite of her long preoccupation with singers and their lives, is its Diamond Horseshoe.

From this satisfactory time, recapitulation achieved, a further—and for our present purposes most interesting—development begins. She embarks on a war story, *One of Ours,* which will take both us and herself from the later Nebraska, where the best seems already departed, over to France. On this novel of transition she worked for no less than four years. As for her hero, so for herself it was "The Voyage of the Anchises" (the title of one of its books), which bore her away from a familiar land to another where the adventure of life was to begin afresh, more glorious and with other vicissitudes. *One of Ours* was also published in what we shall see became a critical year of her life, 1922.

The story of the novel progresses from the shallowness of a mechanized Nebraska, deeply ugly and frustrating to a sensitive and inarticulate boy, pathetic in his stubborn loyalty to ideals that he cannot even define, across the seas to France, where he finds the fullness of his life in wonder, only a little before the war ends it. Here Willa

Cather shows rare skill. The evocation of the church of Saint Ouen, in Rouen, for example, the crimson and purple colors of its rose window, its grave and deep-toned bell—we are simply taken there; we see and hear as through the just-awakened senses of diffident—oh, so diffident—youth. And the nearest approach to a true love affair in the book, Claude's meeting with Mademoiselle de Courcy—who represents so well the fineness of a tradition that even in Europe was to pass—how effectively this comes after the horror and trap of a completely loveless marriage, to a frigid and unseeing neighbor, back in Nebraska! There is a sureness amounting to divination as to what mattered, in the mature European point of view, and what did not. I do not believe that this sensitive juxtaposition of the American West with France, so fleeting and fragile, so quietly evocative of the highest loyalties of each, has yet been noticed for what it is.

The novel ends far away from where it began: with a grave in France for Claude, who "died believing his own country better than it is, and France better than any country can ever be." Here Willa Cather is also surely speaking for herself.

A few sentences later, at the book's close, she is impelled to the heights. "Perhaps it was as well to see that vision, and then to see no more." Suddenly the mood becomes absolutely black: "One by one the heroes of that war, the men of dazzling soldiership, leave prematurely the world they have come back to. Airmen whose deeds were tales of wonder, officers whose names made the blood of youth beat faster, survivors of incredible dangers—one by one they quietly die by their own hand. Some do it in obscure lodging houses, some in their office, where they seem to be carrying on their business like other men. Some slip over a vessel's side and disappear into the sea." . . . "And they found," she concludes, "they had hoped and believed too much." The end of the war only clamped tighter upon American life the shackles of materialism which were for her a profanation and a torment. Her world had been so very near to a splendid liberation; and now it could lapse, slip back, into this!

Such feelings, I believe, help to explain a cryptic and critical sentence, as self-revelatory as any she ever wrote—Willa Cather was not given to enlargement of her personal feelings—that we find, fourteen years later (1936), in the Prefatory Note to *Not Under Forty,* a book of essays published in that year.

Here it is with its preceding context:

> The title of this book is meant to be "arresting" only in the literal sense, like the signs put up for motorists: "ROAD UNDER REPAIR" etc. It means that the book will have little interest for people under forty years of age. The world broke in two in 1922 or thereabouts, and the persons and prejudices recalled in these sketches slid back into yesterday's seven thousand years. . . ."

The painful disillusion, after what she had hoped would come from the war, had taken the usual eternity (to borrow the phrase she got from Stephen Crane) "to filter through the blood." Now, fourteen years later, she could submerge her personal disappointment within larger issues; she could take her stand, refusing to be budged from tested excellencies, refusing to yield to what she considered ignoble and inferior. She had been of her place and of her time, she would remain so; and if this meant lack of comprehension by the younger generation—in part, perhaps, matching hers also of them—well, they were warned, and could keep away. There is ferocity and bitterness here; but rather than march in the festal train of the Bitch Goddess of worldly success, she will pay any price, even that of alternating between public scorn and private silence. The world has caged her; but beware of her paws! There is to be no silliness about the matter.

Yet she was not permanently caged. A restless, splendid character such as hers would be bound, in the end, to escape—and did. From now on she begins ranging farther and farther afield. "Away, away in time and space" seems to be her mood. After another book published in 1923, a penultimate glance at the Nebraska of her youth, four great novels succeed one another within the space of a single decade. The book of that year is familiar to many: *A Lost Lady,* a story of decline and fall, of elegiac reminiscence and of tender regret for vanished frailty. The "Lady" is also lost, one must observe, in the snows of yesteryear.

Then we come to the wayfarer's high plateau, where it is already afternoon with lengthening shadows, and a constant preoccupation over the meaning of life—and also with death at the end much nearer. The titles themselves are highly evocative. Here is the succession:

The Professor's House	(1925)
My Mortal Enemy	(1926)
Death Comes for the Archbishop	(1927)
Shadows on the Rock	(1931)

Note the allegory and symbolism in their wording. The Professor's true house, as his story makes abundantly clear, is his own grave; this is *his* long home. The enmity of Myra Henshawe for her husband, in the next novel, is maintained, indeed grows and battens, under miserably straitened and constricting circumstances that finally allow her only the manner of choosing her death. Then great Death itself— like a Holbein series, the grim procession continues—comes for the Archbishop in his cell near the desert; while in another austere region, rock-bound Quebec, we can watch shadows fall on further lives. There is no escape from pessimism, or at least from the firmest grasp on the realities of time and human destiny. As in the legend, in this last book, of the Canadian heiress who longed to become a recluse and then—ardors over —lapsed into terrible and prolonged aridity, every device that can be used presses the one inescapable conclusion: we are mortal, we must die.

The Professor's House, of 1925, as E. K. Brown has pointed out, is an allegory contrived with extraordinary skill, especially the mechanism of inserting a long *nouvelle* into the center of it, to give an effect of distant clarity and lyric beauty, of sunlit aerial color, seen beyond a dull, conventional foreground. Dead Tom Outland looms, sweet in the purity of young strength, towering beyond the pettiness of the life of a small academic community, where vulgar Louie Marsell and his shallow wife revel in his succession. The Professor him passes in the course of the story from later middle age, success achieved but becoming meaningless, into the much colder and passive region of his last years; and Willa Cather has fashioned him of exactly the same age as herself.

Nowhere is she cleverer than in the symbolism of the various houses that are so important to this story. There is the Professor's old house, where we see him first, the one he is so reluctant to leave, from the very beginning casting a lingering look behind—jerry-built and uncomfortable, but a place where there had been deep and joyful living. There is the new house that can never have true life infused into it; he has even lost his love for the woman who will be its mistress. We are given glimpses also of the elaborate monstrosity of the Marsellus ménage, tricked out with money inherited from the dead Tom Outland, and even named—a profanation—with his last name, used as a wretched pun. Tom's own group of cliff dwellers' houses, the houses that he has discovered, simple and intrinsically beautiful, thus makes the clearest contrast between spurious values and those high and ancient ones that can outlast calamity. Finally the Professor's house-to-be, his grave, completes the grim symbolism.

Willa Cather can be very direct in such matters. After a close call from accidental death through sheer and symptomatic lethargy, she makes the Professor reflect that his sagging old couch is already his coffin, with poor sham upholstery: "Just the equivocal American way of dealing with serious facts," she says. "Why pretend that it is possible to soften that last hard bed?" No palliative, no trickery or ornamentation will blind her to the essential hardness, to the punishments of life. She will have none of the cheap standards, the petty consolations, about her.

In terminating his own discussion of the book (on page 246), E. K. Brown makes a significant remark: "Not by any answers it proposes, but by the problems it elaborates, and by the atmosphere in which they are enveloped, *The Professor's House* is a religious novel." So we have come out onto the last great plateau of Willa Cather's own journey. She is now much nearer to a finish with the local scene and its rather minuscule passions, which she has definitely appraised.

* *

The development continues inevitably, inexorably. One of the hardest, most obstinate stories of her whole work is the relatively short, but strangely intense, novel published in 1926 (only one year later, and in her own fifty-third), *My Mortal Enemy*. It remains a mysterious work. E. K. Brown, who must long have pondered its cryptic subject matter, does suggest a clue. In the end, he says (page 250): "... it becomes plain to us that this worldly woman has passed out of worldliness into preoccupation with primary realities." This is the place to which Willa Cather wanted to bring her heroine, after headstrong youth and an ill-considered elopement with a much weaker man, whose character could never match her own. Finally Myra goes straight to religion, which here is not treated by implication, as in *The Professor's House,* or even as an anodyne, consoling the end to the unhappy life of a once worldly woman, of fierce will power, *détraquée.* Here it becomes a principal part of the story. The way now opens for the next two, perhaps the greatest pair of Willa Cather's novels.

A light ever seems to radiate from broad sun-swept stretches in the Southwestern desert landscape of *Death Comes for the Archbishop* (1927). There is also a marvelous unity to the book, made up in large part of deceptively simple passages; here a local story retold, there a pious legend remembered. To this corresponds the harmonious and expanded character of Father Latour himself. In part he may be taken to represent Willa Cather's own late summer hours—or at least her aspiration for them—in the country she had discovered far beyond her old West, in one of the great adventures of her intellectual life.

What is significant in the new direction of her journey—which through much reminiscence of Auvergne, the province from which both priests in the book had started, becomes also a pilgrimage in the direction of Avignon—is that she now is a declared seeker for a faith that will console her, nostalgic as she always has been, for the perishability of life. Indeed, that life of "The Best Years"—the title of a very touching later tale—had passed first, as Virgil had phrased it in words that she long held in memory. For her, also, "*Optima dies ... prima fugit. . . .*" It is significant also that in the year 1922, when the geological break in the continuity of her life had occurred, in that year she herself entered the Episcopal church, being confirmed at the same time as her parents. As is Episcopal to Baptist, it would seem, so is the great beauty of what once was and now is gone to the more prosaic world of the present. Yet her treatment of Catholics in this book, as well as later in *Shadows on the Rock,* became so sympathetic as she went along that many readers quite unconsciously must have thought her speaking for her own faith—which in a sense she was. She had indeed already moved her setting far away from her own youth and early novels.

Death Comes for the Archbishop also constantly takes one backward and forward, on missions of religion, between the Old World and the New; it is as if Willa Cather were intent upon weaving a cable of many strands between them. She seems to delight in flashing before us the scenery of Rome or Clermont, intermittently, to contrast them with Santa Fé or Taos; demonstrating that the greatest discrepancies vanish, and only harmonies remain, for those who are dedicated to a great ideal and thus in part transcend their surroundings. Here, on such firm heights, the unhappy and restive self perishes, to give way at the last to harmony and tranquillity. Vicariously this was her coming to terms with her own destiny. It further explains her intention behind the disarming and lovable simplicity of the small events in the foreground of the novel, symbols that with the economy of a great artist she has used for great purposes.

Colder, later in personal time, and more remote also by more than a century—for the action is set in the time of Louis XIV—is the next story, the serious, not to say somber, *Shadows on the Rock,* of 1931. Willa Cather is now in her fifty-eighth year. Her heroine is a young, motherless girl whose somewhat frail life revolves almost wholly about her touching effort to achieve a woman's warmth and service for the household of an aging father. The characters of Count Frontenac and Monseigneur Laval are drawn as those of already old men.

The bastion of the great rock on which Quebec has been founded, the climate, the cold winters, somehow all seem of an unvarying gray after the smiling warmth of the open Southwest. Here and there a sheen as of unexpected late sunset wonderfully suffuses her mood; although Willa Cather herself seems to have moved still farther away, both in time and space. Religion also is very near the heart of this book. The characters are American in the sense that they come to live permanently in the New World—although even Cécile, her young heroine, is represented as born in Paris—but their pathos is in their continuing attempt, destined for never more than partial success, to transplant and keep alive, under hard and adverse conditions, the standards of the full civilization of France, their distant and revered "*mère des arts et des lettres*." This must be accomplished in a world where even the flora and fauna are as on another planet, often menacing as in a nightmare.

Willa Cather makes much of Old World cooking, of cleaning and polishing, of the amenity of a sensitive and quiet bourgeois "*foyer*." By the night fireside in the little house on the crooked street the old values still have force and power. The latent threat comes from the genius of the new land itself; and the ships that sail slowly across the stormy seas, and whose arrival becomes as vital to the reader as it is for the inhabitants of Quebec itself, these ships bear the very life-blood that must continually be transfused if what was admirable and remembered can continue under such difficulties.

Subtly Willa Cather's sympathies seem to have changed; or is it such a change, after all, because from the earliest time her German musicians, her young men from Prague—or Bergen or Upsala—even arriving as poor immigrants, these had brought to the outlying farms about Red Cloud values that the young girl who was also Willa Cather sensed by every worthy measurement as far transcending what they found in possession about them. Excellence does not change, whatever the circumstances, the fluctuations in its appreciation.

As so often after a major advance Willa Cather now seems to need rest on her flinty journey. There comes about a time of retrospect; first with the three stories collected in the volume titled *Obscure Destinies* (1932), and in the sensitive portrayal of touching *Lucy Gayheart* (1935), a last full-length evocation of the world of her morning years. Then, going back even earlier, she turns to the dim days of her earliest childhood in Virginia, this last a theme scarcely touched before—indeed, except as a background it had not determined her life. As is to be expected, the development proceeds step by step with a decline in her own vitality.

She had early rebelled against her destiny, born on the fringe of things; she had defied, she had never surrendered. Now she seems to wish passionately to submit. The violins tune to some of the most beautiful melodies of all: in "Old Mrs. Harris," a tale in *Obscure Destinies,* she can touch sublimity—can create it out of almost nothing. The same is just as true of another touching and so delicate short story, already mentioned, "The Best Years," published posthumously in *The Old Beauty.* It is also about the earliest Western time, but now seen as far behind and long ago vanished. The journey may be wilder, the hour late, and there is no "going home" now except to death; yet courage and love have not failed her.

The place of *Sapphira and the Slave Girl,* begun in 1937 and published only in 1941, four years later and in her own sixty-seventh, is curious. It is a cold, slow-paced book, the chief character a willful and repellent invalid. One receives the impression that the material was never turned to in affection—at least, with the old spontaneous and warm affection that Willa Cather could give to the destiny of Ántonia, who had been such a match for her fate—but rather in an attempt, a decision, to cultivate one more area that she knew well but never had used. The action occurs near Winchester, Virginia, and the uneventful year is 1856.

This novel, as E. K. Brown comments (page 317), is not about "heroic moments in American life—the moment when the French made a civilization in the Canadian wilderness, the moment when the Southwest was at it apex, the moment when the wild land of Nebraska took the first impress of the pioneer. Now it was enough to evoke quite ordinary moments from the past; and these too had vanished, taking with them the burden of beauty for which there was nothing to compensate."

It almost seems as if Willa Cather had come to a dead end; and indeed this may have been so, for in illness and fatigue she published nothing else during the seven years remaining before her death in April 1947, in her seventy-fourth year.

At this point the story about Avignon consequently takes on added interest. For Willa Cather apparently attempted her most difficult task, the summoning of reality from a remotely distant time and place, which in any event she never could have known personally—as in some measure she did know something about all that had gone before—when life had most worn and tired her. So the circumstances surrounding the work were somber and not very favorable. Personally, she was facing the adamant combination of old age, illness, and the slow approach of death—that ultimate engagement in which triumph was impossible. Perhaps also she reached the field of the tale in a historical setting just too late: energies never sufficed, we must remember, over seven years, to bring it to completion. And this may have been one of the reasons—which we must respect—why at the end she ordered its destruction.

Even if she surmised that her powers were failing, she may still have wanted the companionship and solace of a piece of work in the making, as it always had been for her in the richer years of her own life. To work, also, was to pray. This may explain what was going on in her mind when we see her as Edith Lewis describes her, pacing the "open roof garden of the Fairmont, walking to and fro, and reading. . . ." Okey's little guide-book become a breviary.

It is easy to see why a French palace like that at Avignon rather than the one at Versailles should have seized on Willa Cather's imagination. Her firmly expressed distastes would normally find the latter artificial and flimsy, just where the noble pile beside the Rhône was the reverse. The surprise and splendor of the conception, the wonderful spareness of the lofty architecture, these broad halls set high above rich farming-land, this capital of popes in exile, across the mountains and beside a broad, rushing Provençal river: all would have spoken clarion words.

Constant similarities between the rural life of Provence and regions she had known all her life in the West must also have been in mind. Farming is farming: to plow and to sow, to harvest and to garner, require the same labor, take their toll with the same fatigue no matter by whom performed, where—or when. Yet there were also the particular vigor and sap of this people. From her own twenty-ninth year, now long in the past, she had been consciously drawn to their special character, which apparently never ceased to delight her.

Once the definite conception had taken shape, she did, for a while, proceed. As Edith Lewis tells us (pages 195–6):

> She worked fitfully at the Avignon story in the next two years [i.e., 1944 and 1945]; but her right hand was so troublesome [with a long disability that set in], became instantly so painful when she tried to write, that she was unable to make much headway. It was a story of large design, and needed concentrated vigour and power. Her knowledge of this often led her to put it aside entirely and try to forget about it until better times should come.

Alas, they did not; and now even this incomplete manuscript is destroyed.

Why, we must ask, did she at the last thus turn so completely away from America? The fact that the world had broken apart for her personally in 1922 has become clear enough. That in *One of Ours* she turned savagely against the American present is attested by the dark flow at the end of the book. She also reverts to this same theme in the story about "The Old Beauty," which, although written earlier, was only published posthumously, in 1948. Here she sets her story wholly in Aix-les-Bains—how unthinkable this would have been earlier in her career!—which her middle-aged American finds, to his satisfaction, "unchanged" in a world already transformed; and this story is also set in the fateful year of 1922.

She is no longer at any pains to conceal her disillusion and aversion to most of the life about her. For a writer as classic both in feeling and style as Willa Cather, this judgment was natural enough. Indeed, in her private life she took no trouble to conform to newer interests about her, in literature, or art, or music. To preserve her entity, in a time of too facile communication, she became almost a recluse, certainly not "keeping up" with contemporary movements. Her defense was dogged and complete. She does, in the essay titled "A Chance Meeting," in *Not Under Forty,* qualify Marcel Proust as "the greatest French writer of his time"; but otherwise one hears of no later enthusiasms whatsoever. She will not go beyond Thomas Mann and Katherine Mansfield. Indeed, in the last months of her life she turned away from everything of the present, back even to Shakespeare and to Chaucer. Here was her grandeur and her consolation.

A soliloquy in the critical *One of Ours* should at this point be recalled. Of her hero, Claude, she says (page 406):

> He had begun to believe that the Americans were a people of shallow emotions. That was the way [his friend] Gerhardt had put it once; and if it was true, there was no cure for it. Life was so short that it meant nothing at all unless it were continually reinforced by something that endured; unless the shadows of individual existence came and went against a background that held together.

Thus France could give one meaning to life which it was impossible to find in America.

It could not have been easy, nevertheless, for her to turn to Europe, to expatriate herself—even if only spiritually—as had Henry James and Edith Wharton (although for very different reasons) before her. Even for them, as we know, the task was of immense magnitude and yielded dubious results; and they were wealthy patricians who without great effort could remove themselves from any place to any other. Willa Cather, embedded as she had been in Nebraska, and with a much harder destiny in many ways than those of such comparative darlings of fortune, took much longer; but in the end and by gradual steps she did very nearly the same thing. Like many people of plain origins, her first great need had been to be reassured, to still the youthful panic of seeming to possess only an inferior brand of everything that her more fortunate brothers and sisters took as naturally theirs. This was a prime need; but she had conquered it in her own way, which was the way of genius.

Furthermore, Edith Wharton and Henry James lived much the same cosmopolitan life wherever they happened to be, following—

even when they were railing at—contemporary fashion. Willa Cather reached first for the stars over the pure air of Nebraska, and then, when their light became obscured, would accept nothing less beautiful in their place simply because it was American. Her position was grander; the evolution of vastly more moment. Her stubborn loyalty to excellence, and the tenderness of her love, refused to alter because they had come upon alteration. Thus the Avignon story, incomplete and vanished as it is, remains the last great testimony of what she believed in, and of what she had lived for.

We should have to conclude on this lofty but rather barren note were it not for a piece of singular good fortune, a circumstance that is the origin of this essay. Miss Lewis does remember quite a little of the manuscript that no longer exists; and she has been kind enough to give the following account of it, thus adding a precious last chapter to the history of Willa Cather's writing:

> The title of Willa Cather's unfinished and unpublished Avignon story was *Hard Punishments*.
>
> The setting was Avignon of the 14th century (1340), at the time of the papal residence of Benedict XII.
>
> The central characters were two youths—whom she tentatively called Pierre and Andŕe; and the story was of their friendship.
>
> It opened with a scene on the height above the Papal Palace, overlooking the Rhône. This place is now a park; but in the 14th century it was a sort of ash-heap, where refuse from the Palace was thrown over the cliff. Pierre, a peasant boy from a farm beyond the river, has climbed up there in order to sit and look across toward his former home. He is a criminal, according to the law of the time. A simple, childlike, rather stupid boy—he had traded off his father's cart and donkey, and a load of pottery he was carrying to market, for a wonderful monkey belonging to a sailor who was passing through the town. His father had denounced him for theft to the authorities, and as punishment he was strung up for several hours by his thumbs. His hands are now useless, and he is an outcast—homeless, in constant pain, and unable to work. A woman in the town who keeps a brothel has taken him in and given him a corner in which to sleep. He sits on the height above the Palace, crying from homesickness and misery.

It is the day on which Benedict XII, on his great stallion, surrounded by a magnificent train, has gone down to meet Alfonso of Castile and his embassy, who have ridden from Spain to seek an indulgence from the Pope. The Palace is half empty, for many of its occupants, and most of the townspeople of Avignon, have flocked to see the splendid meeting.

While the peasant boy sits crying on his ash-heap, he hears a noise of breaking branches in the hedge that divides this spot from the Papal gardens; and there emerges the other youth in the story— André.

This boy is handsome, spirited, intelligent, well-born—his uncle holds an important post among the servitors in the Palace. But he cannot speak. His tongue has been torn out as a punishment for blasphemy.

Willa Cather was greatly interested in the subject of blasphemy, as it was regarded in the 14th century. It was not only a sin, but a crime, and was punished by the civil law. According to the records, it was a rather frequent transgression, in spite of the terrible punishment for it. Why was it held in such special reprobation? And why, in spite of the risk, did people so often succumb to the temptation to blaspheme?

Some time before the meeting of the two boys, there had been a great banquet in the Papal Palace. André had certain special duties to perform; but when they were over, he slipped away and joined a group of wild companions in the town, with whom he had lately become involved—in a sense a revolutionary group, who met in a low dive to air subversive theories against the Church and State. Excited by the daring of their reckless talk, André tries to out-do the others. The dive was that night spied on by the police, and André and his companions were reported and punished. Tearing out the tongue with red-hot pincers was the usual punishment for blasphemy.

A scene is given in which an old blind priest, who had been André's friend and confessor since the boy's childhood, comes to him after his ordeal, where he lies tossing on his cot in his cubicle in the Palace, talks to the frantic boy, comforts him, fortifies him, and absolves him. This was perhaps the central scene in the story.

My own understanding of it (I never discussed it with Miss Cather) was that she meant the deep root of the boy's despair to be, not the disgrace, nor even the mutilation, but his sense of a sort of personal dishonor—of having irretrievably betrayed something sacred in himself, thereby making the future impossible. The priest's compassionate reassurance enables him to take up his life again. And when he does so, it is on a new plane. His disability becomes for him a challenge— to his courage and resourcefulness, to his pride. After his encounter with Pierre, the poor peasant boy becomes a part of this challenge. He sets out to succor, perhaps to rescue, one even more unfortunate than himself.

The latter part of the story was told only in notes, and was not completed.

It is with hesitation that I have given even this brief account— for it is like the story of an opera without the music. How much would a short summary of *My Ántonia* or *Old Mrs. Harris* mean to one who could never by any possibility read them? Whatever elements of beauty and power the unfinished Avignon story may have pos- sessed—they are lost to us now. But to the student of Willa Cather's work these notes may be of interest in indicating the tenor of her thoughts and the direction her genius took in the last years.

With the help of this precious information we at least now possess an outline of the unfinished story. There is a further treasure that Miss Lewis with great kindness has also made available to the author, Willa Cather's own much-marked copy of "Okey's little history": *The Story of Avignon,* by Thomas Okey [Mediaeval Towns Series], London, J. M. Dent and Sons, Ltd., 1926.

Here we come wonderfully close to the creative process; for not only is this book much marked with single and even double lines in the margins, and further with checks and crosses; but on the last flyleaf and the inside of the back cover, in Willa Cather's own hand we have half a dozen—seven, to be exact—notations of what became of special importance for her in planning this tale. A study of these brings illumination. We come very close to the times in which she placed her story, to its setting, and no little detail of its circumstances.

First of all, there is the problem of the years in which it occurred. Inside the back cover she has noted "Benedict XII" by name and also written out the years of his reign: "1334 to 1342." She has also placed opposite this two references to the text, one to page 93, where one of his biographers describes him—he had been born Jacques Fournier, in the County of Foix, and first became a Cistercian monk—

as "hard, obstinate, avaricious; he loved the good overmuch and hated the bad; he was remiss in granting favours, and negligent in providing for the services of the Church; more addicted to unseemly jests than to honest conversation; he was a mighty toper and 'Bibamus papaliter—let us drink like a pope'—became a proverb in his day."

On page 88, which she has further noted and even circled, we find this description: "Pope Benedict . . . was a big man and *molto corpulento*. He was a most holy man who never would give dispensation for marriage between kinsfolk, and was careful and diligent in searching the moral characters of all candidates for benefices, and many he examined himself. *Non bolea ideote*—he would have no illiterates— he went about seeking good and efficient clerics, and honoured them much because he found so few." How clear it is that a man of this stamp would have drawn her interest!

Benedict XII, though, is not the only pope mentioned inside the back cover. Willa Cather there has also written down the year "1305"—merely the four ciphers; but she gives a reference for this date to page 44 of the text, where she has marked a sentence reading: "On June 5, 1305, after eleven months of obscure intrigue and patent discord, Raymond of Goth, Archbishop of Bordeaux, was elected to the papal chair, and assumed the title of Clement V." We now know that she definitely placed her story within the first half of the fourteenth century and in the reign of Benedict XII, but perhaps at one stage it was to have at least a start in this earlier time.

"Law" and "Prisons" are words that she has also noted in this place, both of them referring to the same page, 242. Here a corner is turned down, and on this and the pages following there are marks showing concentrated attention. On page 243 she notices and marks, among a list of punishments inflicted in 1328 and 1329—only a few years previous to the accession of Benedict XII—not one but two mentions of the tearing out of tongues, the first with red-hot pincers, the second for the crime of "swearing against the Virgin Mary."

On the page following, 244, there are not less than two lines and two checks marked opposite part of the text giving the detail of crimes publicly denounced: "Promulgated by a papal government, they naturally begin with penalties against the denial of God, or of the Virgin Mary, or blaspheming against these or God's saints, or

profane swearing at play or in taverns or the public streets. . . ." Willa
Cather has documented herself securely on the "hard punishments"
of the time.

Next we come to the setting; and for this there is a whole series of
markings, too detailed to be transcribed—but showing how she had
made herself familiar with the whole complex fabric of the papal
palace and the various stages of its building. She notices on page 20,
with a double line, "the great stone conduit which drained the kitchen
into the Sorgue. . . ." On page 223 she has put a check opposite a
mention recording payment "for carving four apes of stone in human
form to be placed . . . over the portal of the palace," which we learn
served as gargoyles. The creative process is feeling its way. Indeed,
the whole of Okey's Chapter XV, part of which was titled "Life in
a Mediaeval City," has been carefully worked over: it is much marked.
One can see clearly how from a few suggestive sentences she brooded
deep into her story.

The famous bridge across the Rhône apparently fascinated her. She
first notices, with a checking on page 25, the community of Friars
Hospitallers, founded "to establish ferriers, build bridges, and give
hospitality to travellers along the rivers of Provence." She checks
heavily on this same page a sentence reading: "Now, since the Pont
St. Benezet was the only stone bridge between Lyons and the sea,
until the building of the Pont St. Esprit in 1309, the importance it
conferred on Avignon may easily be conceived."

The whole medieval town had become familiar. On page 305 she
has especially marked the following description:

> . . . a scene of incomparable beauty awaits us at the end of the shady
> walk that rises from the platform to the modern Promenade du Rocher
> des Doms. This, once the barren, wind-swept acropolis of Avignon
> which was crowned in papal times with the windmills and the
> forts, . . . and which in floodtime served as a cemetery, has been
> transformed into a delightful garden. . . . The view from the Belvedere
> over the Rhone and four departments of France is remarkable both
> for range and beauty. At our feet sweeps the broad majestic Rhone,
> hastening seaward *per aver pace co' seguaci sui,* and embracing in

its course the great island of la Barthélasse with the remaining arches of the bridge, and the chapel of St. Nicholas; opposite are the hills and mountains of Languedoc, their nearer slopes, above poor dilapidated Villeneuve, fallen from her ancient splendour. . . . far in the background stands the square tower of Chateauneuf des Papes.

So this was the setting, familiar to her over many years, in which Willa Cather planned the encounter of her two boys: here there were space and breadth, distances of her own kind.

How she would have set about to make the region vivid, with all the charm of its trees and flowers—details in which she always took so much interest—is also certain. Earlier in the book, on page 5, a double line scores these sentences:

At Valence the dark cypress and her spire—that sentinel of the south—comes into view; the mulberry, the olive, the almond, the chestnut, the oleander, the myrtle, the ilex and the stone-pine, tell of sunnier skies. Even the common flowers of the north are transfigured under the magic of the bright, translucent sky. . . .

There is a very urgent marking on page 229—two lines with a check between—of the whole of the following paragraph:

Among the amenities of the old palace were the spacious and lovely gardens on the east, with their clipped hedges, avenues of trees, flower-beds and covered and frescoed walls, all kept fresh and green by channels of water. John XXII maintained a menagerie of lions and other wild and strange beasts; stately peacocks swept proudly along the green swards, for the inventory of 1369 specifies seventeen peacocks, some old and some young, whereof six are white.

In one monastery garden, page 348, a "tall hedge of laurel 'high as a pine tree' " is further noted. The pencil mark is proof of her admiration.

That events could be made gorgeous in a setting such as this is in no doubt; and there was apparently also no little meditation on medieval feasting and carousal. Much marked and checked is a long passage, pages 237–8, abbreviated below:

> . . . The most striking example of lavish splendour is afforded by the State banquet given to Clement V by the Cardinals Arnaud de Palegrue and Pierre Taillefer in May 1308: Clement, as he descended from his litter, was received by his hosts and twenty chaplains, who conducted him to a chamber hung with richest tapestries from floor to ceiling; he trod on velvet carpet of triple pile; his state bed was draped with fine crimson velvet, lined with white ermine; the sheets of silk were embroidered with silver and gold. The table was served by four papal knights and twelve squires [this last word circled by Willa Cather in the text—could it have been a possible role for André?], who each received silver girdles and purses filled with gold from the hosts: fifty cardinals' squires assisted them in serving the banquet, which consisted of nine courses of three plates each—twenty-seven dishes in all. The meats were built up in fantastic forms: castles, gigantic stags, boars, horses, etc. . . . Then followed a concert of sweetest music, and dessert was furnished by two trees—one of silver, bearing rare fruits of all kinds, and the other loaded with sugared fruit of many colours. Various wines were then served, whereupon the master cooks, with thirty assistants, executed dances before the guests. . . .

A triumphal entry in 1340, a solemn embassy from Alphonso the Brave, King of Portugal, and his ally Alphonso of Castile, is also given special notice. This date is repeated in Miss Cather's hand on the margin of the passage, checked and scored, on page 89; and now we know that it was, effectively, the one determined upon for her story. "As the glittering pageant approached Avignon," we read in Okey, "red-robed cardinals went forth to meet it; a solemn pontifical mass was celebrated by Benedict himself, who preached a fine sermon. . . ."

Thus the material accumulated and took shape in her mind, to furnish a rich backdrop for the simple tale Willa Cather obviously wished—perhaps even in very strong contrast—to place against this splendor. On page 236 there are marked sentences mentioning ermine and beaver, payments to Tuscany for silk, for brocade to Venice: "The richness of the papal utensils beggars description: jewelled cups, flagons of gold, knife handles of jasper and ivory, forks of mother-of-pearl and gold. . . ." There was plenty to choose from. She marks a passage on page 221 mentioning "chests and cupboards for the silver vessels and scarlet of our lord the pope." A bell, also on this page, seems to have been of special interest, the "pontifical bell, which from its silvery tone was known as the *cloche d'argent.*" One recalls those in *One of Ours* and in *Death Comes for the Archbishop.* By her nature Willa Cather is conditioned to notice once more—here in medieval France—the objects that always had evoked most meaning.

She was not drawn, however, merely by descriptions of richness. On page 71 she has checked and underlined a mention of the no less than 65,000 letters relating to the reign of John XXII on the Vatican registers. The same underlining is found a little earlier, page 66, to notice the Pope's marshall, "one Walsingham, an Englishman." Thrice marked is this passage on page 239: ". . . amid all this luxury, strange defects of comfort appear to the modern sense. Windows, as we have seen [and Willa Cather has also put a mark opposite the previous mention earlier in the book, on page 218], were generally covered with waxed cloth or linen; carpets were rare, and rushes were strewn on the floors of most of the rooms."

A last item, which nonetheless heads the seven tabulated inside the back cover, must not go unmentioned. It is cryptic, reading only "Toulouse 170." If we turn to this page, which is also turned down at the corner, we find that it refers to the later reign of Pope Urban V (1362–70). The single sentence mentioning Toulouse states that this pope "loved learning, founded colleges and bursaries for poor students; he cared for the amenity of the services of the papal chapel, and sent a music master and seven boys to study music and singing at Toulouse."

Might it just possibly be that this was one way in which Willa Cather could have made the unfinished story develop, later sending her younger boy away to another city—even helped by the mute—thus to fulfill himself in song? We have far too little evidence to present this as more than a mere possibility; but the fact that the name of this other city, across France, heads the list of her seven mentions may be significant.

A strong caution is needed at this point. Miss Lewis has written to the author mentioning "how *little* of the historical material [above] Miss Cather actually introduced in the story ... few of her stories have been so completely démeublé. There was almost no description; two or three paragraphs about the Palace itself—as she felt it rather than as it appeared; half a dozen words about Benedict XII, as he rode down to meet Alfonso. . . . The only room she described at all was the roasting kitchen in the Palace. No costumes, no functions. And yet, she managed to give the feeling of the place and time—I suppose because she herself felt it all so strongly."

So the technique of making the reader sense very much more than he is actually told—chiefly because it has been passed through the alembic of a powerful imagination, and there has been reduced to quintessence—this technique, one surmises, here was used by Willa Cather in the completest control of her great powers. To have taken everything possible in; but then calmly to cut most of it out: this is a procedure she had pressed to extremest use, as she herself has told us, even with the actual pounds of manuscript that she discarded from *Sapphira and the Slave Girl*. Here her subject was incomparably richer; and her scale was planned—as Miss Lewis recalls—to be merely that of a long *nouvelle*.

We have come a long distance indeed from the Willa Cather of her earlier years, from imitative experiment in the long ago—as in "Eleanor's House"—and from the first attempts to find herself; to find, above all, in Dostoevsky's phrase, who she was; and then to learn the secrets of her own art, her own creation.

At first one may see in this Avignon story many differences from the bulk of that earlier work. Certainly we are far from the windswept stretches of the Nebraska Divide, from nineteenth-century pioneers, the struggling farmers, the immigrant "hired girls." No one here is caught in the ugliness and problems of the present; we are under other skies and in quite another place. Yet if one dwells with the subject for even a little while, one becomes aware that in this Avignon story there must have been far less difference from Willa Cather's earlier work than might at first appear. The setting exists for an almost familiar group of circumstances. Far from entering a past where the ills of life have been mitigated and struggle washed away, pressures have only become more literal, the pains and penalties of living more direct. Religion, in this papal setting, seems also neither more nor less present than it has been for some time.

The title alone, *Hard Punishments*, affects a wonderful affiliation with past work. All of Willa Cather's characters know suffering, know handicap, know the hardness of life. It was the only fundamental circumstance, apparently, that interested her and seemed real to her; and this may be one of the reasons why she never—without exception—in her mature work, dealt with those born rich and privileged, who in so many ways therefore had nothing to struggle for; or at least whose private goals, in a totally different living habit, were to her unknown territory.

If one goes back in retrospect, even Alexander, the bridge-builder of the first novel, is observed and selected by her because of the fatal punishment that was to overtake him. In that early time her philosophy was already direct enough: "Some get a bad hurt early and lose their courage; and some never get a fair wind," says his old teacher, of the failures of life. It is all there thus at the beginning, even to the classical concision of her summary.

Ántonia's lot was hard. So was that of Thea; so was Lucy Gayheart's. Myra Henshawe's fate was adamant. In their destinies Claude and the Professor finally move into the region of death, where Tom Outland has gone before them. The ancient people of the Southwest, ages before, had only known the lesson perhaps better. In *The Song of the Lark,* the brewer's son discusses this with Thea: ". . . You mean the idea of standing up under things, don't you, meeting catastrophe? No fussiness." Willa Cather indeed knows what she herself means. In the Avignon story she in no way changed her course; indeed, she only reaffirmed it by giving to pain and suffering a simpler physical expression. Life without them would be impossible. "Old Mrs. Harris" states this definitively: "Everything that's alive has got to suffer." The law is as true in one time as in another.

So it seems as if, rather than shift from the only material she felt important, rather than move into the diminished lives of a younger—and, to her, petty—generation at home, Willa Cather remained true to her principles simply by abandoning America, the later America that she so castigated, as a setting. It was to bypass the morass of shallowness, to avoid a sense of decline, a pervading feeling of insignificance and triviality, that she moved her scene away; now we know with how little essential shift of interest. To capitalize on old success, to be static, or continue a familiar pattern, these were for her the fundamental impossibilities.

There is one change, however, that should be noted. Miss Lewis has thought that the action of the Avignon story might only have been meant to last for less than a year; and that its length was to be somewhat like that of *My Mortal Enemy*. In this setting of an expanded *nouvelle*, Willa Cather apparently wanted to deal with youth once more. We seem to have come through a tunnel, with the longer novels dealing with the end of life, with old age, its gloom and its decline. These, in retrospect, seem behind. It may be that here also, to quote a sentence in "Before Breakfast," the short story written after 1942 and published after her death in *The Old Beauty*, she feels that "Plucky youth is more bracing than enduring age." Certainly it is youth that Willa Cather is again considering; and almost certainly, in the end, youth triumphant. We thus come to our close on a fine, clear note, securely—though with transcendent compassion; even if the actual termination, as in Schubert's "Unfinished Symphony," was destined never to be written.

This incomplete story, then, does show a progression beyond the last point reached in Willa Cather's published work, beyond not only *Sapphira and the Slave Girl,* but also the two stories in the volume of *The Old Beauty* that stress the penalties of old age. As in the central story of that book, she has gone back to "The Best Years" once more. Enormous and mature power now long had been hers; there was indeed more to say, even in this setting, unthinkable at the beginning of her career. Life was being divined, strong situations created, even across the centuries. Essentially, however, the material has not changed. The problems were still those that had absorbed even her earliest characters; and these new ones set about to solve theirs in ways with which she now has made us familiar. Far from proving a refuge from the ills of the present, her new field reveals penalties only more intense than in the past, with greater challenge—but with response still adequate. From their own "hard punishments" her shadowy lads would undoubtedly have wrested the inner strength, one feels, that would have made them matches for their destiny. At the end, therefore, even in this unfinished story set in medieval Avignon, Willa Cather simply remains herself.

___ **The Romance of Tristan and Iseult** by Joseph Bedier $9.00   0-679-75016-9

___ **A Lost Lady** by Willa Cather $9.00   0-679-72887-2

___ **Collected Stories** by Willa Cather $14.00   0-679-73648-4

___ **Death Comes for the Archbishop** by Willa Cather $9.00   0-679-72889-9

___ **My Ántonia** by Willa Cather $8.00   0-679-74187-9

___ **My Mortal Enemy** by Willa Cather $8.95   0-679-73179-2

___ **O Pioneers!** by Willa Cather $9.00   0-679-74362-6

___ **One of Ours** by Willa Cather $12.00   0-679-73744-8

___ **The Professor's House** by Willa Cather $10.00   0-679-73180-6

___ **Forty Stories** by Anton Chekhov, $12.00   0-679-73375-2
translated by Robert Payne

___ **A Tale of Two Cities** by Charles Dickens, $7.95   0-679-72965-8
with an introduction by Simon Schama

___ **The Brothers Karamazov** by Fyodor Dostoevsky, $16.00   0-679-72925-9
translated by Richard Pevear and
Larissa Volokhonsky

___ **Crime and Punishment** by Fyodor Dostoevsky, $14.00   0-679-73450-3
translated by Richard Pevear and
Larissa Volokhonsky

___ **The Aeneid**, translated by Robert Fitzgerald $8.00   0-679-72952-6

___ **The Odyssey**, translated by Robert Fitzgerald $8.00   0-679-72813-9

___ **Madame Bovary** by Gustave Flaubert, $11.00   0-679-73636-0
translated by Francis Steegmuller

___ **Three Classic African-American Novels**, $15.00   0-679-72742-6
edited and with an introduction by
Henry Louis Gates, Jr.
Clotel by William Wells Brown,
Iola Leroy by Frances E.W. Harper,
The Marrow of Tradition by Charles W. Chesnutt

___ **The Sorrows of Young Werther** $10.00   0-679-72951-8
by Johann Wolfgang von Goethe,
translated by Elizabeth Mayer and Louise Bogan,
with a foreword by W. H. Auden

___ **The Ink Dark Moon: Love Poems** $10.00   0-679-72958-5
    by Ono No Komachi and Izumi Shikibu,
    Women of the Ancient Court of Japan,
      translated by Jane Hirshfield with Mariko Aratani

___ **The Panther and the Lash** by Langston Hughes $10.00   0-679-73659-X

___ **Selected Poems of Langston Hughes** $10.00   0-679-72818-X
    by Langston Hughes

___ **The Ways of White Folks** by Langston Hughes $9.00   0-679-72817-1

___ **Stories** by Katherine Mansfield, $12.00   0-679-73374-4
    with an introduction by Jeffrey Meyers

___ **The Republic of Plato**, translated by B. Jowett $9.00   0-679-73387-6

___ **Cyrano de Bergerac** by Edmond Rostand, $9.95   0-679-73413-9
    translated by Anthony Burgess

___ **The Tale of Genji** by Murasaki Shikibu, $11.00   0-679-72953-4
    translated and abridged by Edward Seidensticker

___ **Dr. Jekyll and Mr. Hyde** by Robert Louis Stevenson, $7.00   0-679-73476-7
    with an introduction by Joyce Carol Oates

___ **Democracy in America: Volume I** $12.00   0-679-72825-2
    by Alexis de Tocqueville,
    translated by Phillips Bradley,
    with an introduction by Daniel J. Boorstin

___ **Democracy in America: Volume II** $12.00   0-679-72826-0
    by Alexis de Tocqueville,
    translated by Phillips Bradley

___ **Narrative of Sojourner Truth** $9.00   0-679-74035-X
    by Sojourner Truth,
    edited and with an introduction by
    Margaret Washington

___ **Germinal** by Émile Zola $8.00   0-679-75430-X

Available at your bookstore or call toll-free to order: 1-800-793-2665.
Credit cards only. Prices subject to change.

VINTAGE BOOKS / THE LIBRARY OF AMERICA

___ *The Education of Henry Adams* $14.50   0-679-73232-2
    by Henry Adams
    Introduction by Leon Wieseltier

___ *The Red Badge of Courage* by Stephen Crane $8.50   0-679-73223-3
    Introduction by Robert Stone

___ *The Souls of Black Folk* by W.E.B. DuBois $9.50   0-679-72519-9
    Introduction by John Edgar Wideman

___ *Essays: First and Second Series* $11.50   0-679-72612-8
    by Ralph Waldo Emerson
    Introduction by Douglas Crase

___ *The Autobiography* by Benjamin Franklin $8.50   0-679-72613-6
    Introduction by Daniel Aaron

___ *The Scarlet Letter* by Nathaniel Hawthorne $7.50   0-679-72526-1
    Introduction by Harold Bloom

___ *Indian Summer* by William Dean Howells $9.50   0-679-72614-4
    Introduction by John Updike

___ *The Rise of Silas Lapham* $10.50   0-679-72517-2
    by William Dean Howells
    Introduction by Evan Connell

___ *The Bostonians* by Henry James $10.50   0-679-73381-7
    Introduction by Alison Lurie

___ *Washington Square* by Henry James $8.50   0-679-73229-2
    Introduction by Elizabeth Hardwick

___ *The Varieties of Religious Experience* $14.50   0-679-72491-5
    by William James
    Introduction by Jaroslav Pelikan

___ *Public and Private Papers* by Thomas Jefferson $12.50   0-679-72536-9
    Introduction by Tom Wicker

___ *Selected Speeches and Writings* $11.50   0-679-73731-6
    by Abraham Lincoln
    Introduction by Gore Vidal

VINTAGE BOOKS / THE LIBRARY OF AMERICA

___ *The Call of the Wild* by Jack London $8.50   0-679-72535-0
     Introduction by E.L. Doctorow

___ *Moby-Dick* by Herman Melville $12.50   0-679-72525-3
     Introduction by Edward Said

___ *McTeague* by Frank Norris $10.50   0-679-73273-X
     Introduction by Alfred Kazin

___ *Selected Tales* by Edgar Allan Poe $9.50   0-679-72524-5
     Introduction by Diane Johnson

___ *Uncle Tom's Cabin* by Harriet Beecher Stowe $11.50   0-679-72537-7
     Introduction by James M. McPherson

___ *Walden* by Henry David Thoreau $9.50   0-679-73574-7
     Introduction by Edward Hoagland

___ *The Adventures of Tom Sawyer* by Mark Twain $8.50   0-679-73501-1
     Introduction by Russell Baker

___ *Life on the Mississippi* by Mark Twain $10.50   0-679-72527-X
     Introduction by Jonathan Raban

___ *The House of Mirth* by Edith Wharton $9.50   0-679-72539-3
     Introduction by Mary Gordon

Available at your bookstore or call toll-free to order: 1-800-733-3000.
Credit cards only. Prices subject to change.